DARK DEMON

DARK DEMON

THE ABI ACARDI SERIES

E.A.Stark

DARK DEMON

THE ABI ACARDI SERIES

Taken

Amidst the chaos, the girls clung to a fragile sense of safety inside the bunker. To them, the room felt small. Suffocatingly so. Lit by a single flickering fluorescent bulb, it cast eerie shadows on the cold, concrete walls. Every faint scream that pierced the barrier separating them from the commotion outside only intensified their fears.

Remnants of the explosion flashed through Abi's mind frame by frame, almost reverberating, each tremor a cruel reminder of what they just survived. Sitting on the sterile floor, her hands trembling, she looked up at Jade, whose frustration and anxiety worsened while she paced back and forth, unable to sit still. Her impatience grew with each passing second. Suddenly, the girl's eyes darted toward the heavy steel door.

"I can't take this anymore," Jade muttered, her voice a mix of terror and anger.

Sensing her friend's desperation, Abi tried to sound optimistic. "The guys will be back soon," she said, her voice wavering.

"I need to know what's happening." Biting her nails, about to explode, Jade lunged for the latch and unlocked it. "I'm leaving."

When the door opened, Abi stood back. Her breath caught in her throat. Overwhelmed by the mayhem, she gasped. "Maybe you should just wait."

"Sorry, Abs, but I need to find Reg." Ready to walk out, Jade turned. "Are you with me?"

Afraid to be alone, she reluctantly nodded. "I'm coming."

Upon hearing that, the girl suddenly ran and disappeared into the shadows, leaving Abi behind.

Trying to be brave, she inched forward, but every step weighed her down. The air was thick with dread. *How could this happen?* she thought, panic clawing at her insides.

Throughout the estate, countless frightened bodies huddled together, comforting one another. The pungent smell of smoke lingered in the air, a grim reminder that made Abi raise her sleeve to cover her mouth. Eyes burning, coughing profusely, she surveyed those walking around, dazed and confused, some coherent enough to record the madness on their phones.

Scanning every face, searching for Shane and Reg, she spotted Jade through the haze. The girl was scaling the hillside. Prepared to head in the same direction, Abi hoped she'd found the guys. Gathering the courage, she stepped out onto the grass just as a band of security guards passed. She assumed they were there to save their boss's kid as they systematically fanned out across the gardens. When she was about to run, one of them eerily turned and zeroed in on her. The rest followed suit. Swiftly converging, Abi took off, but soon, they caught up.

"You need to come with us," a deep voice said, his words sending an alarming jolt through her.

"What? No!" Bolting, trying to get away, Abi felt him grab her arm and pull her back. Another did the same. Restrained, she yelled, "No! What are you doing? Let me go!"

Fighting with everything she had, they forced her toward the front gates. Not seeing a familiar face, she frantically begged for help, but most looked at her blankly and did nothing. Heart pounding, unable to break free or loosen their grip, she scoured the yard for Shane. Locating Jade, she saw her talking with him.

The football player immediately looked around and yelled, "Abi!"

With every ounce of her being, she cried, "Shane! Help!" then pleaded with the men, "Please! Let me go!"

Watching him glance left, then right, she figured he was trying to pinpoint the sound of her voice amidst the crowd. "Abi? Abi!"

"Shane!"

Urgently inspecting multiple darkened faces, he shouted, "Abi! Where are you?"

When their eyes finally met, he found the men dragging her along against her will as she screamed, "Help me!"

Bolting in her direction, she saw him dodging people in his path.

"Move! Move!" he shouted, shoving them out of the way.

Forced into an SUV, the door shut. Abi heard the interior locks click. Desperate to escape, she pulled on the handle, but it wouldn't open. Repeatedly yanking on it and pressing the unlock button to no avail, the truck started moving when Shane got to her.

"Abi!" he shouted, trying to open the door. Pounding his fists on the glass, their hands mere millimeters apart, he tried everything to get her out. "Hold on! Hold on!"

"Help!" she cried in absolute terror as the truck broke free of the masses gathered on the street.

"No!" he said, sprinting alongside it, hearing her muffled cries pleading with the driver.

"No! Please! Stop!"

Soon, Shane fell further and further behind, and instantly, she knew that was it.

An ominous voice cut through the silence. "Drive," it said.

Startled, she snapped to her left as the air expelled from her lungs.

A figure, blending with the black leather seats, emerged from the darkness like a demon in the night.

Hit by a stroke of terror, Abi felt the SUV accelerate. Turning, she saw Shane stopped in the middle of the road, helplessly watching them fly down Mountain Drive. Defensively crossing her arms, she inched closer to her door to distance herself from the man. Body vibrating, on the verge of tears, she tried to be brave.

"Let me go," she said with a hint of false confidence.

Nobody spoke a word.

"I said, let me go!" she demanded.

Keeping his back to her, he glanced over. His face remained concealed.

"What do you want from me?"

He held out his hand between them. "Give me your phone."

The beastly sound of his voice seemed familiar.

"What? No!" Abi refused.

Impatient, he said sternly with his hand waiting in mid-air, "Now!"

Taken off guard by his threatening tone, Abi tossed the device onto the seat between them. She watched him pick it up and turn it off before slipping it into a padded silver envelope and sealing it.

About to demand it back, Abi noticed the driver's sights divert to the rearview mirror.

"Sir?" he said, gripping his hands on the steering wheel at ten and two. "We've got company."

With little emotion, the shadow instructed, "Lose 'em."

The driver smirked and said, "Yes, Sir," before accelerating.

Weaving in and out of traffic on Sunset, Abi spotted a white Porsche challenging them. Neck and neck, she kept sliding from side to side in her seat.

Without warning, the black figure abruptly turned. His face still hidden from sight, he grabbed her seat belt and yanked on it. Only seeing a hint of his eyes as they caught the street lights, she felt the belt slide across her chest and heard the latch click before he turned his back to her again.

The car's horn honked repeatedly. Suddenly, the passenger-side window rolled down.

Abi quickly rose from her seat to get a better look at the driver. Her heart dropped. "Shane?" she whispered.

Intent on running the Porsche off the road, the man behind the wheel sharply veered left.

Abi shouted. "No!"

The driver kept his eyes on the sports car as it threaded between oncoming vehicles.

Thankfully gaining control, the football player remained glued to them at high speed.

When the car thrust forward, the man braced for impact and said in a monotone voice, "He's gonna cut us off."

"Please don't hurt him!" Abi pleaded. I'll do whatever you want. Just don't..." Not getting a response, she tried to distract them. "I know who you are!" she said, turning to the dark shadow. "You're Black Lyon." Out of options, she reached for his hood. Before she could grab it, the security guard in the front seat launched at her and grabbed her wrist.

Staring her down, he said sternly, "Don't."

Waved off, the guy obeyed and let her go.

The shadow didn't move.

"I know you won't hurt me," Abi said.

Silent, the hood shifted her way slightly and pointed right. In an instant, the driver moved in that direction.

Abi watched the Porsche fly past them. "Shane!" she shouted.

In disbelief, a flood of brake lights illuminated the intersection. Smoke emanated from the wheels while the car wildly spun out of control and disappeared when they rounded the corner inside the East Gates of Bel Air. Everyone in the SUV fell silent as they slipped into the night.

Darkness closed in around her, crushing her hopes of being rescued. Trapped, now at the mercy of the ominous shadow with unknown intentions, she realized her worst nightmare was coming true.

2

Unfazed

Sitting stoically, unable to distinguish their direction, Abi looked to her left. Black Lyon seemed unfazed by what had happened as he sat there motionless. Hands shaking, her breathing erratic, she concentrated on getting her bearings while the driver slickly maneuvered each corner. Focused on the street signs, she squinted but couldn't read any of them since it was so dark.

Still, nobody spoke.

Panic set in. Heart beating out of her chest, she finally gained the courage to whisper, "Why are you doing this? What have I done?"

About to glimpse her way, believing she would see his face, the famous DJ hesitated and stared out the window. "You've done nothing wrong," he mumbled with a slight hint of sincerity.

After making a sharp turn, they approached a gatehouse in front of a large home. Granted access, they passed the security checkpoint and drove up the steep incline. That is when Abi recognized the place.

It's the mansion across the canyon, she thought. *What am I doing here?*

They stopped outside a dark glass garage door, waiting for it to open. On the way inside, the sound of the engine echoed off the walls of the large space.

The driver shifted the gear in park.

Abi felt like she was on a ride at the fair as they rotated around on a turntable, the floor sparkling beneath them. It was an onyx diamond mix.

Silent, Black Lyon grabbed the envelope with her phone and jumped out. Slamming the door, he disappeared.

Abi didn't have time to say anything.

Now facing forward, the man turned off the ignition. "Everyone out," he said.

A security guard opened her side. "This way, Miss."

Guided into the house toward an elevator, the guy pressed the button and waited. When the doors parted, they stepped inside and ascended to the second floor.

As they moved upward, fear settled in deeply. Her mouth went bone dry. About to step out when the doors opened, Abi found a familiar face standing before her.

"Martin?" she said, so happy to see him.

"Hello, Miss," he greeted, his hands positioned regally behind his back. "Come with me, please. We need to chat."

Aftermath

Timidly following the older gentleman into the kitchen, she looked around the beautiful, modern home. It looked much larger than what she thought it would.

Before he could address her further, Abi asked, "What is going on? Tell me the truth, please."

Standing tall behind the island, he motioned with his hand for her to have a seat. "Master B thought it would be safer to keep you here until…"

"Until what?"

"We receive further details on Eastwood Korolev's release from police custody. Over the past few hours, we've received countless threats. I have it on good authority that some include you."

Hearing this frightened her to the core.

"By bringing you here, we are mitigating that situation. So please be patient."

"What do you mean, mitigating?"

"We have taken you out of the equation, Miss."

"Because?" She had no clue what his cryptic message meant.

"I'm sorry. That is all I can divulge for now. Master B will speak to you shortly and share what he knows. For the time being, make yourself at home. Can I get you something to eat? Maybe some water, perhaps?"

"Water would be great. Thank you." Abi quietly sat on the stool across from him. He took a bottle from the beverage fridge and placed it before her. "When can I have my phone back? I need to see if my Dad texted."

"Sorry, Miss. We need to take precautions."

"Martin, I'm serious. I need my location services working at all times. Otherwise, he will call the police if he can't contact me or see where I am. Please, I beg you. I've caused him so much pain recently."

Understanding her dilemma, he nodded and said, "Kindly give me a moment. I will check on the status of your device."

The butler disappeared into a back room and closed the door. Left behind, with two guards, she noticed the beautiful artwork hanging on the walls. It was hard not to.

In seconds, Martin returned with the envelope in hand. "You have five minutes to send a message to your Father. Be a dear and tell him you are staying at a girlfriend's house tonight and will talk to him tomorrow."

Abi removed the phone from the pouch and looked at the screen while the man watched her like a hawk. Initially typing the word *HELP!*, ready to drop a pin on her location, Abi stopped as her finger hovered over the send button. Thinking about what had happened and why Black Lyon rescued her again, she backspaced and erased each letter before doing what Martin asked. While waiting, she saw her Father's thinking bubbles activate. His message then popped up.

Okay, Sweetheart. Have fun. I will talk to you tomorrow.

Abi typed, *Sounds good. Night, Dad. Love you.*

Love you, too, Sweetheart. He replied.

When their conversation ended, Martin held out his hand. Taking hold of the phone, he did something before giving it back to her.

Looking down, she noticed the signal had terminated.

Giving her the silver padded envelope, he said, "Please slip your device inside and leave it there for safekeeping. We must be diligent until we discover who is tracking you."

"Tracking me?" Hearing that caught her off guard. Abi's sights dropped to the floor, lost for words.

A security guard appeared and spoke to the butler.

Whispering in his ear, Martin nodded and said, "He will see you now."

Scared to know what the famous DJ would divulge, she nervously followed the men to the elevator and got in.

Arriving on the roof, Martin held the doors for Abi and had her exit first. He was close behind.

She spotted a silhouette along the glass railing, admiring the view blanketed by city lights. It was the black hooded figure. Seeing her home lit up across the canyon, she recalled the lonely man standing solo every night around this time.

All along, it was him? She thought in disbelief.

Holding a glass of champagne, he did not turn around as they approached. Seeing the lights on her pergola go off, Black Lyon raised a glass and took a drink.

"Sir? Miss Abi for you."

"Thank you, Martin. That will be all for now," he said firmly.

The butler stepped back and stood with the security guards, keeping watch.

"So, Abi Acardi. Do you know why you're here?"

"No, I, umm... don't..." Stumbling on her words, she caught his slight accent.

He didn't turn around. "We suspect the Korolev family has their sights on you."

She stayed silent.

"The explosion at the party was no accident. You were the intended target."

In shock, she said, "But why? I'm a nobody." Tilting her head slightly, she hoped to glimpse at his hidden face.

"Since last Saturday, you've become a pawn in a rather dangerous game, and it's my move now."

"What does that mean?"

Ignoring her, he said, "I've arranged for you to stay with a friend tonight. He will keep you safe."

"No, I'm not going anywhere with anyone."

He slipped his hands in his pockets. "You have no choice if you want to live."

Abi went out on a limb. "Who are you?"

He stayed silent.

"What is your real name?"

Suddenly, the elevator chimed. Abi turned around. There, standing, talking to Martin and Black Lyon's security, was another familiar face.

"What on earth?" Abi whispered. "What is he doing here?"

Her friend approached and rubbed his hand along her arm before continuing past her.

Black Lyon turned to greet him. His face remained hidden in the shadows. "Thanks for comin'," he said, reaching out to the guy.

"Hey, man." Burton shook his hand. "Sorry, I got here as soon as I could."

"I've got a job for you."

"Sure. What do you need?" he agreed without hesitation.

Abi watched Burton look directly at the mysterious DJ. Standing mere feet from him, the two spoke civilly.

"No problem," her friend replied. "Will do."

"Do what?" Abi asked, wanting to be involved in the conversation.

Burton glanced over briefly, raised a hand to silence her, and then brought his attention back to the guy to receive further instructions since they hadn't finished talking.

Angry, knowing her life was hanging in the balance, she tried to decipher the mumbling but barely caught a word here and there.

Soon, the men shook hands a second time.

"Don't worry. I'll handle it," Burton confirmed.

"Good," is all the celebrity said before he slowly walked away and disappeared.

Turning around, Burton went to Abi. She looked like she'd seen a ghost.

"You knew him all this time and didn't tell me. Why? Why did you lie?"

"I didn't lie. You never asked, so I never said. Besides, I couldn't anyway. I signed an NDA."

"NDA?"

"You know, a non-disclosure agreement." He got closer and rested both hands on her upper arms. "Are you okay?"

She couldn't answer.

His phone rang. Seeing Shane's name appear on the screen, he said, "Excuse me for a moment. I have to take this. Hold that thought." A safe distance away from her, he answered, "Hello?"

"Hey, man."

"Hey. What's wrong?" he said under his breath.

Shane didn't know where to start.

Not getting a response, Burton played him and sternly asked, "Why are you calling? Did something happen?"

"We were at Reggie's afterparty tonight, and there was an explosion."

"Is Abi okay?" he whispered.

Wanting to select his words carefully, Shane paused.

"Well?"

"Amidst the panic and chaos, these guys... They took her."

"When?"

"Forty-five minutes ago."

"You should have called me sooner."

Shane knew he was right. "They were in a Bentley Bentayga. Apparently, Jade knows it belongs to Black Lyon. Not sure how."

"Is she certain?"

"Yeah."

"I'll call you back." Burton hung up on him and returned to Abi.

Hearing his tone, she asked, "What was that about?"

"Just business. Nothing major."

Abi seemed shell-shocked. He knew he needed to get her out of there.

Martin looked on as Burton hugged her. Clearing his throat, the butler prompted, "I believe you should get moving, Sir."

Letting go of Abi, he replied, "Yes. We're going."

"Where exactly?" she questioned.

"I've been instructed to take you to my place for a couple of days until this blows over."

"Until what blows over?"

"Can't say. Just know I'll keep you safe in the meantime." Burton hovered his hand along her lower back. "Come on. My vehicle is out front."

"What am I going to tell my Dad? Won't he see my location in a different place when I turn my phone on?"

His eyebrows raised. "Don't worry. I'll fix that."

"How?"

"You'll see."

Escorting them to the front door, Martin had a McLaren and six other vehicles waiting in line.

Assuming the exotic car was his, she walked in that direction.

Burton stopped her. "Umm, Abs. No. This one," he said, opening the passenger side of the black G-Wagen.

Hesitating, she joined him and got in.

When he closed her door, she watched Burton speak to Martin and bid him goodbye before rounding the back of the vehicle and slipping into the driver's seat.

"Ready?" he asked.

"Guess so."

"Pass me your phone."

"Why?"

Hand waiting, he tilted his head. "Abi? Phone."

Reaching behind him, he grabbed his laptop from his bag while she handed over the padded envelope with the device inside. Leaving it in the sleeve, he connected it to a chord attached to his computer and did a few things. Unhooking it, he sealed the end and handed it back to her. "Your location will remain at this house until I change it."

"How did you do that?"

Putting the laptop away, he said, "Magic."

Upon shifting gears, they moved down the laneway.

"Shouldn't we go by my place to get some clothes?"

"Aren't you supposed to be sleeping over at a friend's place? Why would you go home? Besides, I've got that covered."

She didn't like this snarky version of Burton.

"What the hell is going on, and how are you involved?"

Cautiously pulling onto the road, placing an earbud in his ear, he said, "I know you have a lot of questions. I will answer them once we get through phase two."

"Phase two?" Abi had no idea what that meant.

The caravan of vehicles left simultaneously. Along Bellagio Road, Burton stayed quiet and paid close attention to their movements. When they reached Sunset, one SUV turned left while the others followed them. Approaching the 405, two merged north, and the McLaren continued straight while they headed south onto the highway with two SUVs on their tail.

Staying aware of where they were going, she asked, "How do you know him?"

Careful about how to respond, Burton answered, "I work on his tech systems."

"Tech?"

"I'm the guy who built the rave apps."

"And during our conversations, you neglected to tell me that because?"

He turned to her and shot a look, knowing they'd already covered this.

"NDA?" she conveyed.

"Yes." He kept his eye on the road and glanced in the mirrors periodically.

Her mind was reeling. "Do you know his identity?"

"In a round-about way."

"So you know what he looks like?"

He laughed. "Can't say."

"That's a page from Martin's playbook."

"Possibly," he chuckled, knowing the butler said it often.

Noticing the black SUVs following them in her rearview mirror, she asked, "Is that them?"

"Who?"

"The guys who have been watching over me at night?"

Burton paused and said, "They're the night staff."

Driving along, his Mercedes merged onto the PCH with one vehicle and headed west while the other SUV continued south and left them.

"You said before that you live along the highway? Is it far?"

"No. It's just past Geoffrey's."

"Does anybody else know where you live?"

"Only a couple of people. I rarely have company."

"Not even the girl you were with in Cabo?" she said snarkily.

He glanced at her. "No comment."

"Hmm," is all that escaped Abi's mouth.

Silence washed over them while driving through the darkness of Malibu.

"Can you tell me what I've gotten mixed up in?"

"Not yet. When things simmer down, I'll share what I can. Until then, you've gotta trust me."

She didn't know what to think.

Not hearing her confirm either way, he asked, "You still trust me, right?"

Hesitating, Abi said, "Suppose so."

"Good. Because things are about to get dicey."

In an instant, hearing that sent a sudden jolt of fear. Not having seen Burton for years, she wondered what he was hiding. Had his newfound wealth connected him to some questionable people? Was he in over his head? Was she really safe? Abi didn't know. All she could do was wait and see what would happen next.

4

Hidden

Paddleshifting gears, Burton slowed down before turning right and accelerating up the steep incline, the headlights illuminating a sign that read *Carbon Beach Terrace*. Winding around tight corners, they passed an impressive home lit beautifully, then plunged back into darkness. Black Lyon's men followed close behind. Over the hill, she spotted another mansion shining brightly atop the canyon. Upon approaching the gate, security was everywhere.

Runway lights embedded in the driveway stones guided them to the four-car garage as they entered the estate. Abi marveled at the turquoise and white lighting accenting the modern structure. Inside, she saw the two-story glass staircase with strings of bubbled lights dangling from the ceiling.

Burton pulled in after remote-opening the frosted garage door. By the time he turned off the engine, it had closed behind them.

"Home sweet home," he said as his phone rang. Seeing Shane's name on the screen, he muted the device and slipped it into his pocket as she joined him. "This way," he said, his hand hovering along the small of her back.

Passing his matte black McLaren, he opened a steel door that led into a mud room. They stopped there for him to secure the lock behind them. Emerging on the staircase landing, he casually descended the steps into the kitchen below.

"Are you hungry? Thirsty?" he asked while threading between the three islands. "What can I get you?"

She looked outside at the pool with purplish blue lights. "Water would be good. Thanks."

Walking around the sitting room, she scanned the beautiful built-ins showcasing various art sculptures before standing along the floor-to-ceiling wall of glass. The moon cast an eerie hue over the vast ocean below.

He set his sights on the sleeved phone she was carrying in her hand. Unsure how to ask, Burton just came out with it and said, "Abs, I'm going to need your phone again."

"Why?"

"I need to do some diagnostics. We believe it may be compromised. If it is, it's a security issue. The wrong people could discover where you are. We can't have that."

Understanding the seriousness of it, she had no issue giving it up.

Taking it from her, he set it on the counter and slid the Fleetwood door open without saying a word. Abi walked outside. He followed. With arms wrapped around herself, she stood there timidly, unsure what to feel.

Concerned by the expression on her face, he said, "What are you thinking?"

Eyes affixed to the moon lofting high on the horizon; it took a minute for her to answer. "My life has taken a crazy turn. Somehow, it got out of control, and I don't know how to stop it."

"Don't worry." He stepped forward and stood beside her. "I've got your back."

Reality set in. "Martin and Black Lyon believe I was the intended target tonight. How do they know that?"

"I'm sorry, Abs. I'm not privy to the full story."

"So you can't tell me anything?"

"No."

"I feel you've lied to me since day one," she stated accusingly. "Was this all planned? Like, the day we met at the coffee shop? Was that really a coincidence?"

"What? You think I orchestrated this?"

She stopped. "You let me go on and on about Black Lyon this whole time. Is that why you warned me?"

"Abs, I knew what goes on at those raves but had no idea what Eastwood would do. I just wanted to protect you. That's all. I couldn't share the rest. I signed a contract."

"I get it. But I thought I was your friend. Doesn't that trump any outside agreement?"

Approaching with caution, he knew a hug would settle her nerves.

Instantly, her hands went up between them when she stepped back.

"Abi, I promise you're safe here." He could see she wasn't convinced. Intent on giving her a moment to process everything, Burton figured he'd return Shane's call. "You'll have to excuse me for a second. I'll be right back."

Leaving her with four security guards, Burton walked inside and grabbed her phone on the way to his office at the far end of the house. Sliding the pocket doors shut, he sat in his chair behind the desk. Quickly pulling out the top drawer, he flipped open the lid of a steel box and slipped the device inside before closing it again. Removing his phone from his pocket and attaching a cable, he plugged it into his computer. With lines of code entered on a black screen, he changed their location in case the call got traced and double-checked everything before dialing. Selecting Shane's number from his contact list, Burton heard it ring. The reroute on his location went to Salt Lake City, Utah.

"Hey, man."

Shane got straight to the point. "Did you find out anything?"

"Don't worry. I got her. She's okay."

"What? Really? How?" He sighed with relief. "Where are you? I'll come and get her."

"No, she needs to stay with me for forty-eight hours."

"What? Why?"

"I can't get into the details. A lot is going on. You gotta trust me. The bottom line is, she's safe."

"She's not answering her phone. Let me talk to her."

"We've shut it down. It's compromised."

"How?"

Burton exhaled. "Look, I'll explain more in a couple of days. This is for the best. I'll call you when I know more."

"Wait! Burton!"

Ignoring him, he said, "Sorry, I've gotta go."

"Burton!" Shane pleaded angrily. "Just let me speak to..."

Abruptly ending the call, he disconnected his device and turned it off. "Sorry, man." Leaving it in the steel box alongside Abi's, he returned to the kitchen. Going out the door, he found her still lying on a chaise chair.

Looking up at him, she said, "Everything okay?"

He smiled and said, "Yes. All good."

5 |

Harbored

The breeze coming off the ocean was cooler than usual. The gusts created calming sounds, like that of white noise. Millions of stars sparkled in the sky as the odd plane passed beneath them.

Sitting down beside Abi, Burton re-sparked their conversation. "It's peaceful. Isn't it? I love it when the nights are clear like this."

"Me, too." Chilled, she zipped her jacket closed.

Reaching up, he covered her head with the hood. "It's late. Maybe we should call it a night? You need to rest since you've barely slept this week."

Abi nodded. "Yeah. Maybe I should."

Burton stood and offered his hand to help her up. Walking inside, his security team followed them through the kitchen and locked the house down.

"The guest room is upstairs," he said.

While Abi climbed the modern floating steps, he was close behind.

Upon reaching the top, Burton directed, "Turn left. It's the last one on your right."

Walking down the dimly lit hallway, she pointed at a door.

He nodded. "Yes. That one."

Slowly inching into the room, she scanned the floor-to-ceiling windows facing the ocean, showcasing the same moonlit view she'd admired moments ago.

"You'll find everything you need in the bathroom." Thinking a second, he said, "One minute. I'll be back."

Leaving her alone, she looked about the space. Complete with a king-sized bed, desk, television, and a shared balcony, she discovered a full private ensuite lined with Carrera marble.

Her handsome friend soon reappeared with a pajama shirt in hand. "Here. You can wear this if you want. It's big enough to act as a nightgown. Hope that's okay. I don't have anything else."

Taking it from him, she said, "That'll work. Thank you."

"My room is at the far end of the hall if you need me."

When he said that, she started feeling a little scared and uncertain.

An awkwardness set in. "Well, goodnight, then. I'll see you in the morning."

"Goodnight," she whispered.

He walked out the door and closed it behind him. Sitting on the end of the bed, she felt displaced and out of sorts. Going into the bathroom, Abi examined the vast array of spa-worthy toiletries. Unboxing a new toothbrush, she brushed her teeth and washed her face with an aromatic cleanser. Running the comb through her long hair, she pulled it back and secured it with a hair tie from her wrist. Thinking of Shane, certain he'd be worried, she wondered how she could call him to say she was okay. In search of a landline, she found nothing. Even if there was a phone, she realized she didn't know Shane's cell number by heart, so it was pointless.

Exhausted, she pulled back the covers and slipped between the soft sheets, turning off the light. The house was so quiet. Unable to stop the day's events from overwhelming her, Abi fixated on the explosion and everything that happened afterward. Needing to think on her feet, she got up again and paced the floor.

"What if we were in the Jeep when that happened? We'd be gone right now," she said, thinking of her Dad. "He could have lost his daughter and soon his wife all in one fell swoop." The seriousness of it caused an extreme level of anxiety-so much so she could hardly breathe.

Utterly performing a post-mortem, she said, "The bottom line is, whoever planted that bomb wanted me dead." That fact hit her hard.

Gazing out the side window, she counted fifteen security guards wandering about the property. Somehow, seeing that gave little comfort. The place was like Fort Knox.

"Why so many?" she mumbled, believing it must be for good reason. Several negative scenarios clouded her thoughts. "Stop thinking. You're going to make yourself sick."

Convincing herself to slip under the covers again, she tried to get comfortable but tossed and turned. Terrified, her mind veered down some pretty dark paths. Contemplating going to find Burton, she got up and sat on the edge of the bed.

"He's probably sleeping already," she said, afraid to disturb him. Standing up and opening the door, Abi peered down the hall. At the end, she could see a light. Wrapped in a white robe, she quietly walked along on her tiptoes. Slowly approaching his room, she peeked around the corner. The large frosted glass pivot door was open. Abi knew he was working after hearing him flipping pages and his fingers typing on the keys. Unsure whether to bother him, the sick feeling in her stomach gave her no choice.

"Excuse me, Miss?" A deep voice cut through the silence. "Can I help you?"

Startled, her feet jumping off the floor, she turned and found two men standing on the lower landing.

"Umm, I...umm..." she stammered.

Burton emerged. "Abs? Is everything okay?"

Seeing him bare-chested, wearing only shorts, she quickly looked away. "Sorry..."

"It's okay, guys. You can go." He walked back into the room as the men dispersed. "Come in if you want," he said to her.

Abi followed.

"Can't sleep?"

She shook her head and looked around. Trying not to stare at his body, she surveyed the style of the room.

Realizing she was uncomfortable, he said, "Give me one second."

He disappeared around the corner and returned wearing a black T-shirt.

Abi stood just inside the entrance, fidgeting with the belt on her robe.

"What is it? What's wrong?" He approached and rested his hands on her arms.

"I can't stop thinking about Shane. I keep recalling the car chase. He kept up with us until the driver diverted off Sunset and through the gates. That's the last I saw him." She quickly shook her head. "Umm, is there any way I could call him? Make sure he's okay and let him know I'm safe?"

Burton was not surprised to hear this. "I'm sorry. We can't risk it."

Trusting him, she conceded, "I understand."

"Maybe we can try tomorrow."

Hands trembling, thinking things through, she whispered, "Can I ask you something?"

"Sure."

"Will they try again?"

"Try what?"

"To kill me?" In disbelief, the words rolled off her tongue and made her gasp.

Seeing how scared she was, he replied, "They will prevent that from happening."

"Who are *they*?"

Burton knew he couldn't reveal that. "I'm sorry, Abs. I can't say."

"Why not?" she pleaded loudly. "Shouldn't I know what is happening to me?"

"Nobody is going to hurt you. I promise. I will protect you." Hoping to diffuse her fears, he took a blanket from the chair and handed it to her, keeping a safe distance.

Taking it, she grabbed hold like her life depended on it.

"I am just finishing some work. You're welcome to stay. Maybe it's best if you aren't alone right now."

She paused and looked to the floor before nodding her head. "If that's all right," she replied.

"Absolutely."

Leading her around the modern, king-sized bed, he removed the decorative pillows and opened the covers on that side. Sitting her down, he helped Abi slip in before covering her up. Cuddled with the blanket he gave her, she turned on her side.

"How is that? Good?" he asked.

She silently nodded.

"All right. You get some sleep. I'll be right over there."

"Thank you."

"No problem."

Burton went to the sofa on the opposite side of the room and dimmed the light. He continued to work a while longer, but soon, his eyes got heavy. Closing his laptop quietly, he set it on the side table. Not hearing a sound, he assumed she'd fallen asleep. Lying on the sofa with one hand on his chest and the other behind his head, he turned and took one last glimpse at her before closing his eyes.

"Goodnight, Burton," she whispered, dosing lightly, thankful she wasn't locked up in a room at Black Lyon's house.

"Night, Abs."

Silent for a moment, she suddenly said, "Burton?"

He looked over. "Yeah?"

She immediately began to sob. "Thank you for coming to get me."

His heart sank. "Of course, I would." He walked to the bed and sat down.

Abi turned to face him.

Feeling the need to comfort her, he slid a little closer. "Everything will be okay."

"Why is this happening?" she asked fearfully. "What did I do?"

"Nothing," he replied. Reaching his arm behind her, Abi cuddled alongside him with her hands tucked under her chin. Holding her tightly, he said, "You were in the wrong place at the wrong time. That's all. It'll be okay. I'll make sure of it."

Hearing him say that caused a surge of feelings to surface. "You promise?" Her chest heaved intermittently as his body warmed her.

"I promise," he said, resting his cheek atop her head. "Now, get some sleep."

While lying there, Abi didn't move. She felt safe and protected – something she could not ignore. Burton was strong, brave, and never afraid. He wore his heart on his sleeve most days and had a way of effortlessly making her feel better. Aware of his feelings for her, she hoped he wouldn't get the wrong idea. Shane came to mind as a level of guilt swept over her. It wasn't hard to see she loved them both since each gave her something the other didn't have. Inhaling deeply, she closed her eyes and tried to relax.

Minutes had passed. Hearing her breathing rhythmically, Burton peered down at his best friend. Her face was now angelic and peaceful, devoid of fear. Staring at the ceiling, he hated that all of this was his fault.

You should have been more careful, he thought. *This is why you keep a low profile. This is why you have people at arm's length.*

As a few strands of hair fell across her face, he gingerly moved them to the side. Looking to the future, he thought, *This is something I could get used to.*

Thinking of Shane, he realized the guy had done some heroic things that night to try and save Abi.

I can't fault him for loving her, he thought. *I would have done the same.*

6 |

Peaceful

The morning light spread across the room. When Abi woke, she rubbed her eyes and rolled over, but Burton was not there. Sitting up, she looked around to get her bearings, remembering what had happened the night before. Yet another nightmare had become a reality.

Straightening her robe and tying the belt around her waist, she noticed Burton must have moved back to the couch since a pillow and blanket lay across it. Walking to the window to gaze at the ocean, amidst her thoughts, she caught movement in the pool below. Carefully sliding the Fleetwood door open, she stepped out onto the balcony and found him doing laps - his body moving through the water effortlessly with brute strength and precision. She stayed quiet and took in the view, not wanting to disturb him.

Soon, he stopped at the far end and ran his hand along his face to remove the water droplets. In the process, he saw her.

"Good morning."

"Morning," she replied.

Getting out, he grabbed a towel and walked toward the balcony. Looking up, he asked, "Did you sleep well?"

"Yes, I did."

"That's good to hear."

Captivated by her beauty, he watched her suddenly reach up and release her hair from the tie, causing her long, dark locks to cascade freely over her shoulders.

Burton tried to refrain from staring. "Are you hungry?"

She nodded. "A little."

"Okay. I'm on my way up."

Disappearing below, she could hear him ascending the stairs.

When he entered the room, he saw Abi peacefully sitting on the lounge chair.

Feeling his presence, she turned around. "Hey."

He smiled and moved closer. Taking a seat across from her, Burton thought her face looked more relaxed than the night before. "How are you feeling?"

Abi's sights remained locked on the horizon. "Despite everything, I'm okay, I guess."

"Good."

Fidgeting with the belt on her robe, she said awkwardly, "Thank you for...well, you know...last night and all..."

He knew she was referring to him consoling her. "Yeah. No problem."

"I hope I didn't keep you up."

"No, I fell asleep not long after you."

She nodded. "Sorry, you had to move to the couch. I'm sure it wasn't comfortable."

"It was fine." Realizing he was again without a shirt, he said, "I'm just gonna go and shower."

"Okay. I should do the same."

"Maybe we can meet at the staircase in, say, fifteen minutes?"

"Sure."

"No rush, though. If you want to sit here a little longer, feel free. I don't mind."

Loving the view, she replied, "Maybe a few more minutes."

He tapped her shoulder and said, "Okay."

When he got up, he walked into his ensuite and turned on the shower.

Abi could hear the water splashing against the tile. Unsure what the day would hold, she figured her Dad would be home at some point to change and grab fresh clothes. The thought put her on edge.

Walking inside, afraid to pass by and catch Burton naked, she waited a moment and heard the water trickling over his body before heading back to her room. Catching a glimpse of his silhouette behind the frosted glass shower, she quickly looked away, intent on giving him privacy, and strolled down the hall to the guest room to do the same.

7 |

Unsettled

After washing away her worries that morning, she emerged from the bathroom, unable to find her clothes. With her hair gathered in a towel, she put on the robe and walked down the hall as Burton emerged from his room.

"Silly question, but do you know what happened to my clothes?" she said.

He suspected who had them. "One minute. Let me check on that. Rosa must have put them in the wash."

"Who's Rosa?"

"My housekeeper."

Following him down one flight of stairs, she watched him turn the corner into the mud room. Abi stayed on the landing and peered inside, trying to get a glimpse of the tiny woman standing behind Burton.

"Good morning, deary." Abi heard her say to him. Unable to make out much more of their conversation, Burton returned and said, "Your clothes will be dry in about thirty minutes."

"Okay." She peeked inside the laundry room and said, "Thank you," as the woman turned and acknowledged her with a smile before continuing to fold the sheets.

"Would you like breakfast now?" he asked her on the way down the stairs.

"Sure. Umm, can I just go and brush my hair? It won't take long. I'll be there in a second."

Burton smiled. "Absolutely. Take your time."

Returning upstairs, Abi quickly blow-dried her hair. Thinking of her parents, she knew her Father would expect to see her at home. With that, her Mother came to mind.

"Guess I can't see her today?" Given the situation, she wondered if it was even safe.

Descending the stairs and walking into the kitchen with her hair tied in a messy bun, she saw Burton sipping a coffee, speaking with a man expertly making breakfast in hammered copper pans.

The guy turned upon seeing Burton deviate from him.

"Morning, Miss," he greeted in a thick Italian accent.

"Morning," she replied nervously.

"Abi, meet Anton, my personal chef."

"Nice to meet you, Anton."

"Likewise, Miss."

"Would you like some coffee?" Burton got a mug from the cupboard.

She nodded. "That would be great." Joining him on the far side of the kitchen, she sat on a bar stool. "Thank you."

"You're welcome." Prepping the Miele machine, assuming what she preferred, he confirmed, "Iced coffee with a double shot of espresso?"

Impressed that he knew her so well, she said, "Yes. That's perfect."

In minutes, he placed a tall, square tumbler in front of her with ice and cream swirling amidst the freshly brewed blend.

As she took a sip from the straw, he waited. "Good?"

"Excellent."

He was happy to hear it. "So, Anton's making me a keto breakfast. Is that okay for you?" he asked. "If not, he can make you whatever you'd like."

"That works for me. I'm not fussy."

Burton nodded to the chef.

The man plated the food he'd prepared. Presenting them with scrambled eggs, sliced avocado, tomatoes, grilled asparagus, slices of bacon, and a bowl of chai pudding with mixed berries on the side, he happily said, "Buon appetito."

Abi unrolled her cutlery tucked inside the napkin. "This looks wonderful. Grazie."

Anton's face brightened upon hearing that. "Prego," he said while bowing to acknowledge her Italian before tidying up the space.

About to take their first bite, the short little woman, barely five feet tall, appeared from around the corner. Making eye contact with Burton, she raised Abi's folded clothes and smiled.

He acknowledged her with a thumbs up. "Thank you, Rosa. Appreciate that."

"I will place them in her room," she said before disappearing.

Caught off guard, Abi felt bad for not saying a word to her. *You will have to make up for that later,* she thought.

"When I moved to California, she was the first person I hired. She reminds me of my Mother."

"Yes, your Mom is tiny, too."

"Tiny but mighty," he chuckled, then lowered his head, recalling memories of her.

Abi picked up on the change in his manner. "What is it?"

Shaking his head, he said, "Nothing. Just miss them, that's all."

"When was the last time you saw your parents?"

"It's been two years now."

"Do you have any plans to visit them? Could they come here?" Abi asked, sipping her coffee.

"No. It's complicated."

Anton returned the kitchen to its original state. Leaving, he gave them some privacy.

Nothing was said between them until Abi broke their silence. "Before I forget, my Father might be home later this afternoon to change clothes and shower before returning to the hospital. If I'm not there, he will get concerned. What do I do?"

"I'm sorry. You can't be seen anywhere near there today, maybe after forty-eight hours. We'll have to see."

Abi analyzed what he said. "If it's not safe for me to go home, won't it be the same for him?"

"They have security surrounding the place. We also have guys embedded at the hospital watching your Mom."

"What does this mean?"

Burton exhaled. "Look, Abi. I don't want you to worry. Your parents are safe. They are on top of it."

"Again with the *they*. Who are *they*?"

He looked away.

"I know... You can't say." She got extremely frustrated. "So, what are we going to do today, then?"

"Sadly, we need to keep a low profile until I get confirmation that it's safe to take you home."

"Is that still in the realm of possibilities?"

"Of course. It's the end game. You can't stay here forever." Saying that made him realize he wouldn't mind if she did. "After today, this also means you will have security assigned twenty-four-seven. Sorry, but if anyone asks, you blame that on me, okay?"

"So men will be hovering around me like poor Taizo?"

"The actor?"

"Yeah. The guy arrives at school via helicopter, surrounded by goons. He never looks happy."

"Helicopter, huh?" Burton had an idea. "Give me a few minutes. I'll be back."

When he left, Abi got up and washed off her plate. Placing it in the dishwasher, she climbed the stairs to go and get dressed. Rounding the corner to her room, she found Rosa tidying her bathroom.

"Hello. Rosa, is it?"

"Yes, Miss."

Abi reached out her hand to her. "So nice to meet you. I'm Abi."

She shook her hand, not surprised by this. "We have heard so much about you, Miss Abi. Mr. Burton has said many nice things."

"He has?"

"Yes, he always speaks very highly of his neighbor from Boston."

"Well, we've known each other for a long time." Wondering whether Rosa would spill some information, she asked, "So, Rosa. How long have you worked here?"

"It's been just over two years now. The boy needed lots of help when he moved into this house," she giggled.

"Is that right?"

"Mr. Burton is very busy. He works so much."

"Being a student at UCLA is a full-time job."

"Student?" Rosa questioned just as Burton appeared from around the corner.

Giving Rosa the eye, she looked at her watch and graciously said, "Oh! Look at the time. I must go to the store with Anton. I'm sure I will see you later on, Miss Abi."

"Yes. I guess I'm stuck here until tomorrow."

Rosa waved to her and walked past Burton.

Abi stared at him. "She is under the impression..."

He quickly interrupted, "Look, I have not told them my situation. They don't know what I do when I leave here each day. All they know is I depart in the morning and return at night—nothing more. I keep everyone at arm's length."

"Why?"

"It's safer that way."

That comment confused her. "Does this have anything to do with the death threats you've mentioned?"

"Somewhat."

"So why allow me into your life?"

"Because I trust you."

"And you don't trust them? They work in your house." Abi couldn't understand the rationale.

"I tell them what they need to know."

She thought about what he said.

"It keeps the line drawn in the sand where our professional relationship is not blurred."

"Fair enough. I get that. But isn't it a lonely existence? You not confiding in them?"

"No," he replied, leaving it at that.

His thought process was strange to her. Thinking of Gerald and how she let him into her life during their first meeting, Abi couldn't think of treating anyone like that.

Maybe it is easier for a man. Women are more sympathetic, she rationalized.

Burton announced, ready to change the subject: "I have arranged for us to go out."

"Out? Where?"

"That, my dearest Abi, is a surprise," he smiled. "Just figured you wouldn't want to be stuck inside four walls all day."

She squinted one eye and tilted her head. "You know I don't like surprises, right?"

"Well, I think you'll make an exception here. How about you get dressed and come downstairs? In about thirty minutes, I'll tell you more."

"Umm, Burton? What do I do about my Dad?" Hesitant, she hoped he'd help her. "He will be angry if he gets my voicemail. I don't want that."

He heard what she said. "If you called your dad and said I picked you up from your friend's place so we could spend the afternoon together, would it help ease his mind and yours?"

"Perhaps. But so that you know, I feel you're no longer in his good books."

"Oh? How's that?"

"He suspects something is going on between us."

Burton smiled mischievously. "He does, does he?"

Abi's face went stoic. "Well, if it's any consolation, he doesn't like Shane, either."

"I'm not surprised."

Having beaten around the bush, Abi needed an answer. "So, what do I do?"

"Join me downstairs when you're ready. I have a few things to do beforehand, and then we can address your Dad situation. Deal?"

"Deal."

"Good. I will see you shortly."

8

It's a Surprise

Quickly getting dressed, thankful to put on clean clothes, she couldn't believe Rosa got the dirt and grass stains out. Running the brush through her hair again, Abi pulled it back in a ponytail and secured it with two hair ties. That is when she realized a major part of her morning routine was missing.

"No make-up..." she said, looking at her pale face in the mirror. "Great..."

Not having a choice but to go without it today, she descended the stairs and searched for Burton.

"Hello?" she said, hearing voices coming from somewhere.

Rosa appeared from the kitchen. "Mr. Burton is in his study. Come with me. I'll show you the way."

The housekeeper led her past the dining room, foyer, and living room to an alcove on the left. When they arrived, the glass pocket doors were closed. There, they discovered Burton in a meeting with three men.

Seeing them, he quickly stood up and walked around the desk to slide one panel open.

"Give me a moment, gentlemen," he said, closing it again before addressing his housekeeper. "Thank you, Rosa."

She nodded and left to go about her duties.

"So, this is your office?" Abi peered through the glass at the men gathered around. "Who are they?"

"That is your new security team."

Taken off guard, she said, "Pardon?"

Wanting her to meet them, he offered his hand and said, "Come with me. I'll introduce you."

Nervous, she held onto him and walked into the room.

"Gentlemen? This is Abi Acardi."

Each stood tall, hands fastened behind their backs militarily. One by one, they smiled and acknowledged Burton as he introduced them. "This is Andrew, Ted, and Matt.

"Nice to meet all of you."

"Good to meet you, too, Miss," Andrew said, stepping forward on behalf of the team. "Don't worry. We are here now to ensure your protection."

"Appreciate that."

"These guys will be on duty at eight in the morning to drive you to school and will stick with you the whole day until six in the evening before changing shifts with Black Lyon's team."

"So, they will be with me in school – following me from class to class like Taizo's guys do?"

"Don't worry, Miss," Andrew interrupted. "We'll wait in the hall-way."

Ted piped up. "You won't even know we're there after a while."

Able to see Abi was questioning things, Burton abruptly said, "Alright. Meeting adjourned. You guys can head out. We'll see you there."

"Will do," Matt confirmed first.

"Safe travels, Sir," Ted said before bidding goodbye to Abi. "We will see you soon, Miss."

Confused, she watched the men leave. "What do they mean by safe travels? Are we going somewhere?"

"Like I said. It's a surprise." Burton sat in his chair behind the desk and typed on his computer. "Give me a few more minutes, and we'll get moving."

Curious to see what was on the three massive monitors, she swung around to take a peek. With a landing page with a password prompt on two of them and a black coding screen on the one in the middle, the text he entered meant nothing to her.

"Is this where you study most often?"

"Among other things." He thought he'd give her a sliver of information. "I run my Father's mining operation from here."

"I guess that's a huge responsibility."

"It has many working parts. I have over three hundred people employed in the north. My firm stationed here helps with payroll and legal matters."

"Where is that?"

"What? Do you mean the office?"

"Yes." Abi slowly walked around the modern space, examining the sculptures on the shelves and his collection of books.

He analyzed her every move. "Just off the 110 at West 5th Street."

She had no clue where that was but made a mental note of it.

Exiting his computer, leaving it on the encrypted lock screen, he stood up and clapped his hands, startling her.

She jumped.

"Sorry. Didn't mean to scare you? Ready to go?" Burton chuckled.

"Sure." Afraid to ask, she said, "Can I have my phone?"

His face went blank. "I'm sorry, Abs. I can't do that." He sat back in his chair again and said, "Here. Look at this." Pulling up a dark screen with a chart and a few graphs, he explained, "This is a list of your mobile phone breaches from an unknown IP address." He scrolled down the list. It was about two hundred lines long. "This chart shows the frequency of the breaches. I wouldn't mind sitting with you at some point to see where you were when these things occurred. It would be helpful."

The data scared her.

"I've ordered you a new phone. One that has encryption and is unhackable."

Dazed, she mumbled, "Thank you. I guess."

"No worries." He realized hearing this was worrisome. "Are you good?"

Shaken from the news, she replied, "Suppose so."

Exiting again to the lock screen, he stood up. "Ready for your surprise?"

Less enthusiastic, she said, "Sure."

"Got your hoodie?"

"Yes. It's on the chair in the living room. But what about my Dad?"

He'd hoped she had forgotten about that. Turning around, he returned to his computer a third time. When he entered his password, he clicked on a file from the main desktop labeled Abi's Phone.

"Hey?" she pointed. "Is that what I think it is?"

"Hear me out." He swiveled the chair to face her. "I backed up your phone on my computer. That way, when I receive the new one, it is easy to restore its contents. I've already swept it through my software and removed some malicious material."

She didn't know what to think of that.

"Look, I'll erase this file once I restore the phone. I promise. I have no intention of invading your privacy if that's what you're afraid of."

The tone of his voice eased her mind. "Fine."

He found her Father's cell number and wrote it down on a Post-it note. Unlocking the screen of his fancy device, he brought up the phone mode.

"Dial your Dad's number and tell him your phone died because you forgot your charger at home. Your friend has a different device, and the cords are different."

She hated the thought of lying to him yet again. At this point, it seemed she needed to atone for a string of things. Not wanting him to worry, she felt she had no choice.

Dialing, her Father soon answered on the second ring.

"Hello. This is Dr. Acardi."

"Hi, Dad. It's me."

"Abi? Is everything alright?"

Remembering what Burton said, she told him, "My phone just died. I forgot my cord when I packed a bag yesterday." Disappointed in herself, she rolled her eyes. "Burton texted me early this morning and asked if I wanted to spend the day with him. I just wanted to let you know where I was in case you got worried."

"Well, thank you for that."

"We just got to his place in Malibu. It's so beautiful, Dad. The view is amazing."

There was silence on the other end.

"Hello? Dad?'

"Abi, is there something going on between you two?"

"No, of course not. He knows I've been having a difficult week and wanted to hang out while he was free between assignments. You know, cheer me up a bit."

Hearing her say that so casually helped ease his concerns. "I'm trusting you, Abi."

"I know." Changing the subject quickly, she asked, "How's Mom?"

"Same. No change."

"If you need me today, call Burton's number."

"Okay, Sweetheart. I will."

"Okay, then. I'll talk to you later."

"Bye, Sweetie. Love you."

"Love you too." When Abi ended the call, she turned to her friend. Deep in thought, she added, "He sounded sad. When I hear his voice, it hurts. I'm a terrible daughter. Again, this is why they created Hell. It's for people like me."

"You're not a bad person, Abs. But you do have a lot of bad things happening to you. There's a difference."

"I know. But it's how I feel." The moment she said it, a loud sound rumbled over the house. "What is that?"

"I think it's our cue. Time to go."

"Go where?"

With a smirk, he replied, "You'll see."

Fumbling with his laptop bag, about to put his wallet in his pocket, he dropped it at Abi's feet. She quickly bent down, picked it up, and saw his driver's license inside, noticing the name was different, but the photo was his. Not letting on anything, she handed it to him.

"Thanks," he said while slipping it into his pocket, not saying a word.

"Okay." She grabbed her hoodie from the chair and tried to surpass the awkwardness. "Where are we going?"

Burton led her to the front door. "Follow me," he said, ushering her outside.

Abi looked left. Then right. There was nothing there. The driveway was empty.

"We have to walk a little farther," he smiled before ascending the stairs.

Once at the top, Abi looked to the road. There, at the end of the driveway, was a white helicopter. She immediately stopped in her tracks. "Is that for us?"

He offered her his arm. "Ready for a little adventure today?"

"I don't know, Burton."

"Why? What's the matter?"

"I've never flown in a helicopter before."

"It'll be fine. Since we can't drive anywhere, this was the only other mode of transportation I could arrange."

"Are you sure it's safe?"

"Trust me. I'll be by your side the entire time."

"Promise?" She grabbed hold of his arm.

He reached over to rest his opposite hand on hers. "I promise."

Greeted by the pilot as they got closer, the man shook Burton's hand in the most gentlemanly way. "Hello, Sir. My name is Mac. I will be your pilot today."

"Nice to meet you, Mac. This lovely lady is Abi, and I'm Burton."

She graciously waved hello.

"Welcome aboard," he said, sliding the side door open. "Ladies, first."

Burton took her hand and helped her.

While she settled in, he whispered something to the guy and got in on her left. "What did you tell him?" she asked.

"Hmm," he replied mischievously. "I can't seem to remember."

She tilted her head, knowing he was up to something.

He assisted her with the seat belts and grabbed hold of her headset. Slipping it on her head, Burton carefully covered her ears and did the same as the pilot fired up the engine. Blades swirling overhead, Abi nervously clung to Burton's arm. He could tell she was terrified.

Wanting to test the headphones, he adjusted his mouthpiece. "Hey, Abs? Can you hear me?"

She positioned the mic closer to her mouth as he did. "Yes."

Mac glanced back at the two of them. "Ready, Sir?"

He gave him a thumbs up and said, "We're good to go."

Soon, they lifted off the ground and briefly hovered before he turned on a dime and flew over the top of the house. With the nose slightly lower, they were cutting through the air at an angle.

Tightly hanging on, Abi said, "Oh my..." as her stomach did a few flips.

"You doing okay?"

Seeing him sitting there so calmly, she said, "Truthfully? I'm freaking out."

"Can you level out, Mac?"

"Will do, Sir."

Now flying more horizontally, Burton lifted his arm and put it around her. She moved in as close as she could while the ocean came into full view. Abi was in awe when they passed over the PCH. Above the water, the sun's rays sparkled. In the distance, they could see an island chain.

He pointed at it. "We are headed to Santa Cruz."

"Really?"

"I was told the cliff views from the air are unreal."

Anticipating their arrival, Abi focused on the scenery as they approached. The waves were high, crashing against the mountainous rocky cliffs, creating swirls of churning whitewater. Soaring above the island's southern shores, they moved west to Santa Rosa.

Upon approach, Burton pointed and said, "We are coming up on Water Canyon Beach."

Abi loved the blue water and the white sand. Picture-perfect, like a postcard, she spotted a vessel floating in a cove and realized it was a large boat. "Wow, look at that."

He turned to her and smiled proudly.

Suspicious, she asked, "What? What is it?"

"Well, that is part two of your surprise."

"I don't understand?"

"We are going to land on that boat and have some lunch. What do you think?"

Lost for words, she replied, "Are you joking?"

"No. Not in the slightest."

"That's more than just a boat. It's a yacht."

Excited to share his elite world, he said, "Yes, it is. But you will never hear old money call it that. So, like them, it's simply a boat to me. Nothing more."

When he said that, Abi could feel the helicopter descending. Scared and thrilled at the same time, she clung to his arm again. "Whatever you call it, I've never been on one before."

"There's a first time for everything."

Wavering in the crosswinds, Abi held her breath until they touched down on the vessel's stern.

"We couldn't risk going anywhere populated today. Luckily, being here makes us hard to track."

Taking a breath, she said, "I bet."

Burton removed his headphones when the engine turned off.

She did the same. "Do you own it?"

"No. It belongs to a friend of mine. We are just using it for the day. He owed me a favor."

"What kind of favor?"

He snickered. "The kind I can't share."

When Abi heard that, her guard went up.

Mac slid the door open for them.

Stepping onto the deck, Burton slung his laptop bag on his shoulder and offered Abi his hand. Taking hold, she stepped down and saw the crew awaiting their arrival.

A woman walked over happily. "Hello! Welcome aboard, Altessa. My name is Leslie. I'm the Chief Stew. Should we take a little tour?"

"Sure. Lead the way." Burton got Abi to proceed as they followed Leslie to the upper deck.

The one-hundred-and-eighty-degree view was spectacular.

The woman stopped at a table set for two - a white banquette accented with charcoal-black cushions. "Please take a seat. We will be serving lunch shortly." Noticing Abi fawning over the exquisite silver chairs nearby, she smiled. "They're Gucci."

"Pardon me?" Abi thought she heard her wrong.

"The chairs." Smiling, she could tell Abi was surprised by that.

"Wow. I guess I won't be sitting there then." Walking over, she slid in behind the table.

Burton set his messenger bag down before finding a spot beside her, facing the desert-like scenery.

Hearing the crew's voices, Abi felt the vessel move.

"We are going to circle the islands. It's the best way to take in the sights."

Leslie returned with two other crew members, carrying small platters.

"Here we are. We've prepared a light menu of Burrata with heirloom tomatoes, Beef Carpaccio, Ahi tuna salad, and a Charcuterie board with a selection of meats, cheeses, figs, olives, and grapes. And as requested, Kobe Beef Sliders," she ended enthusiastically.

"Awesome. Thank you so much." Unrolling his napkin, Burton draped it across his lap.

Following his lead, Abi did the same. "This looks amazing." When the women departed, Abi leaned over and brushed his shoulder. "This is a lot of food for only two of us."

"I agree. Martin might not have been clear. I ordered small plates for two. We can't change it now. So, enjoy."

It was hard for Abi to do that. The sheer luxury of it was difficult to swallow. Never in her wildest dreams would she have thought she'd be eating lunch while drifting through the ocean along a channel of islands. It was surreal, but somehow, she felt she didn't fit in. Burton, on the other hand, seemed used to it. At every turn, he looked pretty comfortable.

While traversing the coastline, Abi took a few bites and sipped her sparkling water with lemon. Thoughts of the explosion, being taken by Black Lyon, and arriving at Burton's Malibu mansion somehow felt like it happened days ago, not just yesterday. All of it had magically whisked away when she entered this strange world where money was no object. Thinking of Shane, she missed him. Given everything she'd learned, Abi hoped and prayed he would remain safe.

"Penny for your thoughts?"

Abi broke from her blank stare. "Sorry, what?"

"Abs? Is everything alright?"

Just as he said it, his phone rang. Glancing at the screen, he picked it up and placed his napkin on the table. "Sorry. I need to take this. Excuse me a moment."

Abi tried to listen to his conversation as he moved to the opposite side of the deck. Unable to hear him, knowing he was using a low tone for a reason, all she could decipher was, *No problem. I'll handle it. Thanks for the heads up.*

Returning to the table, he said, "Sorry about that."

"Do you have any updates?" She hoped he would tell her the truth, not keep her in the dark.

The second he sat back down, Burton placed his napkin across his lap again. Before saying a word, he took a drink of water. "That was Black Lyon's team."

"When can I go home?"

Not looking her in the eye, he said, "There's been a change of plans. After lunch, we will be leaving the yacht. They suggested we move on."

"Why?"

"They located Alexi Korolev and his son. They believe it is in your best interest not to be in LA."

Panicked, Abi said, "But what about my parents? Shane? My friends? Are they in danger?"

Burton rested his hand on hers. "Abs? Listen to me."

Her eyes filled with uncertainty and fear.

"Everyone is safe. But our main priority is you."

She stared at the horizon. "I don't understand. How did I get mixed up in this nightmare? The guy saved me from Eastwood. So he retaliated against him? Is that it?"

As the tears fell, Burton took his napkin and blotted her face. "Unfortunately, you are an innocent bystander. Look, we need to get through another twenty-four hours. Can you do that?"

Hesitant and afraid, she silently nodded.

"Good. I will be with you the whole time. You have nothing to worry about." He reached over with open arms.

She immediately fell into them.

He held her tightly. His strength and protective nature made Abi's heart flutter. With a tearful gaze, she said, "Thank you."

"You're welcome." He pulled her in a little closer.

With her head tucked under his chin, he peered out over the ocean, knowing he'd have to tell her the truth - the entire story from beginning to end. The thought of letting anyone into his life was unnerving, but with what they'd been through, he trusted her above all others. Amidst the intimate moment, his phone chimed. Glancing at the screen, he knew they had to go.

9

The Transfer

The yacht slowly came to a stop as the crew barked orders back and forth at each other to drop anchor.

Still sitting peacefully, embraced in each other's arms, their pilot rounded the corner.

Believing he'd interrupted something, Mac backed off and said, "Sorry, Sir."

Burton turned to him. "It's fine."

Careful how much he'd reveal, Mac said, "We just got word…"

"I'm aware," Burton confirmed. "Proceed. We will join you in a moment."

"Yes, Sir."

Waiting for the man to depart, Abi sat up. "What's the matter?"

"We need to leave. Sorry, we can't stay longer. But I promise I'll take you to where it's safe."

Fearful, she nodded. "Okay. I trust you."

He got up from the table and held out his hand to help her. Grabbing his computer bag, they walked together to the staircase.

Abi hesitated. The blades were already moving fast as the deck vibrated under their feet.

"It's okay!" Burton shouted over the loud sound of the machine.

Continuing to the level below, a security guard offered assistance as they ducked their heads upon approach and got in.

Buckled and secured, Burton helped Abi. "All good?" he asked, giving her a thumbs-up.

She offered the same gesture and leaned to rest her head upon his shoulder, not knowing what would happen next.

Her stomach did a few flips when the helicopter lofted high into the air before Mac leveled out.

Flying across the water, they watched land come into view in the distance. Bypassing mountainous terrain, desolate desert sand, and the farmland patchwork of green squares and circles, they soon began their descent.

"We will be landing momentarily. Your jet is waiting, Sir," Mac informed through their comms.

"Roger that," Burton acknowledged. Looking down at Abi, he found her eyes affixed to the scenery on her side. Checking his phone, having received updates along the way, he reviewed over twenty text messages from Shane Coppersmith, each pleading to speak to Abi. Stressed, knowing he'd have to connect the two at some point, he watched as they landed at the private FBO. Not moving a muscle when the helicopter skids touched down, Abi stirred upon feeling the slight bump.

Jolting up, she turned to Burton. "Where are we?"

"We're in Bakersfield."

Not knowing where that was geographically, hearing it meant nothing. "Why are we here?"

"Changing locations."

Hearing this, she looked around. "What do you mean? Where are we going?"

"North," he answered. "Sorry, Abs. We have no choice."

Abi zeroed in on his solemn tone. "Are we in danger?"

Unable to tell her the truth, he answered, "No."

Not convinced, a fear spread through her. "Okay..."

"Don't worry. I promise we're good."

When Mac opened the side door, Abi and Burton transferred to a golf cart and got whisked to the jet.

"We're flying?"

"I'm taking you to my place in Tahoe," he divulged casually, ensuring the driver did not hear as he stopped the cart beside the plane. The pilot had already fired up the engines. Burton knew they were minutes away from departure.

"But I don't have my passport."

Approached by one of his security guards, he handed Burton an envelope. Holding it up, he said, "You do now."

Abi was baffled. "How did you..."

"Connections," he stated firmly.

Climbing the steps into the aircraft's cabin, Abi admired the quilted grey leather chairs before taking a seat. Across from her, she saw Burton set his laptop bag on the floor.

"Whose plane is this?" she asked, impressed by how beautiful it was.

Without hesitation, he replied, "Mine."

"It is?"

"Yes."

Somehow, in an instant, her thoughts on Burton changed. He went from being a rich student struggling at UCLA to suddenly becoming a businessman acquainted with a highly affluent lifestyle. He seemed much older now, and by association, so did she.

The pilot announced their impending destination, Truckee Airport, and the flight time of thirty-one minutes while Abi buckled her seat belt.

The attendants secured the door and ran through their pre-flight checks before the plane left the hangar.

Wheels leaving the ground, they lifted off again and smoothly rose into the cloudy sky. The air around them was thick, and Burton knew it. Contemplating how to explain himself, he made a mental checklist of what needed to happen upon arrival.

10

The Truth Be Told

Barely in the air for ten minutes, Burton pulled his laptop from his bag. Watching him working, Abi suddenly missed her cell phone and wished she could scroll mindlessly through YouTube or TikTok to pass the time.

"You never mentioned that you had a place up north."

He glanced up from his screen. "Guess it never came up. That said, I'm not one to brag. You know that."

Understanding it to be true, she looked out the window. "Is it nice?"

"From what I've seen in the pictures, I believe so."

"I don't understand."

"The deal went through a couple of weeks ago. My real estate advisor thought it would be a sound investment."

"So, this is your first trip there?"

He chuckled. "Yeah."

"That's gutsy to buy something sight unseen."

"Well, that's not entirely true. I walked through virtually."

Hearing this, she conceded and did not argue as his fingers hit the keys. "What are you working on?"

"Just some new coding." For the first time, her presence made him nervous. There was so much he wanted to say. "It's pretty complicated."

Focused on the mountainous terrain and secluded lakes and rivers below them, Abi left him be despite feeling out of control. Anxiety surfaced. Something she hadn't dealt with in months. Fidgeting with the zipper on her hoodie, she tried to calm the heaviness on her chest.

Burton caught her breathing heavily. "What is it?"

She initially replied, "Nothing. Why?"

He tilted his head, not believing her.

"I'm sorry. I'm scared," she hesitated. "Can you blame me?"

Wanting to calm her nerves, he said, "Once we get to the house, you and I will sit and talk. Sorry, I just need to finish some work before we land."

She timidly acknowledged him. "Alright..."

Staring out the window, she tried her best to keep it together. Desperate to make sense of the past twenty-four hours, Black Lyon came to mind. Having been so close to the guy, she couldn't believe she still had no idea who he was. But one thing was certain: he was more than just a DJ. She figured he was harboring an even darker secret.

Not long after, while flying over the deep blue lake, circling it from east to west, the wheels firmly touched the ground at Truckee Airport. Taxiing to an empty hangar, Abi noticed three Chevy SUVs parked in a line, with Andrew, Ted, and Matt waiting for them.

"Ready?" Burton asked, quickly packing his laptop.

"I guess."

Once stopped, the attendants opened the cabin door. Abi got up and followed him down the stairs as Andrew opened the passenger side of the middle vehicle.

"Welcome to Tahoe, Miss."

"Hi." A bit stunned to see them, she climbed in and slid across to the opposite side.

Commanding their transition, Burton got in on her right.

About to depart, Ted turned around and handed him a rectangular black box.

"Thanks, man," he said casually.

"Sure thing, Sir."

Quickly discarding the cellophane wrap and separating the lid from its base, Abi watched her friend remove a device from its holder as the caravan departed swiftly in unison.

"This is your new phone," Burton said while installing the SIM card and booting up his laptop. Locating the cord, he connected the USB to his computer. "I'll get your backup loaded. You can call Shane and your Dad once we get to the house."

"Really?" She was relieved to hear that.

Slightly disappointed by her reaction, he replied, "Of course. I know you need to stay connected with them."

"Thank you."

"No problem."

"Is it an iPhone?"

"No, it's not."

"It looks expensive?"

He turned to her. "Don't worry about that. It's the same as mine. A Bittium. It's more secure than all the others."

"Never heard of it."

"Only certain people know of this brand," he smirked. "It has an Android OS, so you must get used to that. Otherwise, it's pretty straightforward."

Driving through the desolate, flat, monochrome terrain toward the vibrant mountains in the distance, Abi asked, "How long until we get there?"

The sun was starting to descend in the west.

"Not long. Fifteen minutes max."

She watched as his fingers passed over the keys. The black screen filled with code meant nothing to her, but to him, it was a technological conversation that would secure Abi's safety.

With evergreen trees now on either side, Burton disconnected the device and handed it to her.

"The outside isn't fancy, but it has encrypted end-to-end communications and multi-faceted features that will protect your data. The US military uses this device in the field. That's how trusted it is."

She held it in her hands and looked at the screen. "What's the PIN?"

"I used your house number and my birthday. 833120. Hopefully, it will be easy to remember then."

Punching in the numbers, she saw the home screen pop up. Burton leaned over and showed her a USB-looking key chain. Holding it to the back of the phone, it automatically unlocked the device, and Abi's apps appeared. Holding up the key chain, he said, "Do not lose this. It is the only way to open it securely. Mine is attached to my wallet. That way, I can hover the phone over the key at any time. All of your data is there. It's just presented differently than what you're used to."

"Are you sure this is necessary? It seems a little extreme."

"Do you know multiple entities accessed your phone hundreds of times since you moved to California?"

"Entities? Like who?"

"I would have to dig deeper to divulge that," he said, not wanting to reveal the results of his recent analysis. It would scare her to know the truth. "The main thing is all your data is now safe - even your conversations. Nobody can hack this phone. Check it out. See what you think."

Not having a choice, she said, "Fine."

He closed his laptop and slipped it back into his bag just as the lake came into view. Stopping at the three-way intersection, the driver signaled left before proceeding through the green light.

Captivated by the mountains and the pretty water, Abi peered past Burton and suddenly felt far from home. Driving through a small community with restaurants, motels, and shopping, the driver maneuvered the roundabout and headed toward the state line.

Spotting a coffee shop, craving caffeine, she asked, "Can we stop for a..."

The driver glimpsed in the rearview mirror. "Sorry, Miss. Our orders are to transport you directly to the house. No detours."

Displeased, she turned to Burton.

"Yeah, what he said."

"You're serious?"

"Sorry, Abs," Burton confirmed before returning to what he was reading on his phone. "Don't worry. My kitchen has a kick-ass machine. Well, apparently."

Turning off the main highway, they traversed the cliffside on a one-way street. Bypassing many large cottages one by one, the driver made a sharp left and rounded the corner. Now closer to the lake, with the dimness of late afternoon fast approaching, the SUVs stopped in front of a black-clad garage.

Seemingly in the middle of nowhere, she recalled the name in Burton's wallet. The secluded location made her second-guess her decision to listen to him. Instantly, fear and doubt spread through her like wildfire. Why did he change his name? Who was the wealthy yacht owner who owed Burton a favor? Especially the kind that could not be shared or talked about. How did Andrew, Ted, and Matt get there so fast if there was an unexpected change of plans? Suddenly, she had a million questions that needed answers. Feeling naïve, she knew she'd made a big mistake.

When Burton got out, he slipped his messenger bag on his shoulder and waited for Abi to slide over to him. Given his hand, she apprehensively followed. Walking toward the front door of the small building, they went inside. Directly ahead was a staircase showcasing an eighteen-foot cathedral window. To her surprise, there were more buildings beyond the tiny house they were currently in.

Taking off his shoes, Burton said, "This way."

She carried hers while descending the maple wood staircase to the lower level. At the bottom, on either side, were walls of glass and a fully enclosed tunnel connected to the main house. Burton stopped partway down the corridor and hung a left. Entering the large bedroom, he put his shoes next to the bed and grabbed slippers.

"Would you like a pair?"

Abi figured anything he would give her would be way too big. "It's fine. I'm sure you don't have my size."

"We can check the guest closet and see if there's something suitable."

Leading her down the hall, adjacent to four large boulders sitting outside, they soon entered a great room. The space was light and airy. Elevated high above the water, filled with natural tones, nothing compared to the backdrop. From left to right was the most incredible water vista.

"This is beautiful." In awe, she walked past the living areas to the sliding glass wall. Arms crossed in front of her, Abi knew what she needed to do. Turning around, staying focused, she said, "Burton..."

"Yeah," he said while searching through the closet. Not hearing a response, he looked at her.

"What are Andrew, Ted, and Matt doing here?"

Concerned by her tone, he stopped. "Change of plans, remember?"

"Did they know we'd be here when I met them this morning?"

Dreading this conversation for almost a month, he answered, "Truth?"

She held her ground and waited.

"I arranged for the guys to fly here in case we needed more security. I also wanted you to get acquainted. As discussed this morning, they will spend most of your day with you."

"So this whole time, you knew this and didn't think to share it with me?"

He could understand why she was upset. "Abs, it's complicated," he mumbled.

"What? Do you think I'm not smart enough to keep up?"

"That's not what I meant."

"Well, I suggest you uncomplicate it. And, fast." She zeroed in on him. "Who are you?"

"What do you mean?" He moved closer and flashed a look of confidence despite being challenged.

Not backing down, she said, "I saw the name on your driver's license. Who is Burton Baxter?"

"Abi, I think you should have a seat."

"No, I prefer to stand, thanks."

"Suit yourself." Burton leaned against the island in the kitchen. His hands grasped the edge of the counter as they heard someone walking up the stairs.

Seeing who emerged from the lower level, Abi greeted the familiar face. "Martin? What are you doing here?"

Put on the spot, the now casually dressed butler gave Burton the eye.

He, in turn, prompted the older gentleman to answer. "Yes, Martin. Please, tell us why you're here."

Perplexed by what was happening, he straightened up and latched his hands behind his back. Chin up, he said formally, "I came to help Master B."

"What? Black Lyon is here?" She quickly walked to the railing and peered down into the lower level.

"Yes, he is," the man confirmed.

"Where?" Abi wondered if he would finally reveal himself.

Nobody said a word until she heard a male voice say - "I'm here."

Shifting directions, she was speechless.

Having stepped forward, he said, "It's me."

"Wait? You're..." In shock, she backed up, her arms defensively extended outward as Burton got closer.

Moving her sights past him to Martin, now standing nearby, she asked, "Is this true?"

"Yes, Miss. He is Master B."

Eyes on her childhood friend, a cascade of questions and unspoken sentiments churned like a turbulent storm. Memories of that dreadful night haunted her still. Unable to see the identity of her rescuer clearly, she looked at him in disbelief and said, "It was you? You saved me?"

Without question, he nodded hesitantly.

She doubted it for a split second. "But how? This can't be..."

He cautiously reached for her and said, "Abi, listen to me. We watched Eastwood on the cameras and saw him and his goons follow you into that room. I was in the security office, three doors down. Usually, I send my team to handle such things, but when I saw it was you, I went myself. When we busted through the door, you were fearfully cowering in the corner. Your hands were covering your head, and you were beyond terrified. I scooped you up, carried you out of the room, and brought you into the office, where I got you a bottle of water and a blanket while my guys took care of the situation. Not long after, I asked Martin to drive you home."

Reliving it while he described what happened to a tee, she knew he was telling the truth. He couldn't have known the intricate details if he wasn't there.

"And, Eastwood?"

"Once you left, I saw red. Knowing he intended to hurt you, of all people, I wanted to kill him. Instead, we roughed him and his goons up before stranding them in the middle of the desert. He got off easy, considering. Doing this added to the whole retaliatory mess."

Listening to what he'd done, her legs weakened. Indebted and thankful, she uncontrollably lunged forward and wrapped her arms around his neck. Clinging tightly, feeling his encircle her waist, she came to terms with the news as the tears flowed. "Thank you..." she said, her body trembling. Hit by this newfound verity, Abi loosened her grip and let her hands fall, tracing Burton's shoulders and arms. Lifting her hand to cover his nose and mouth, she discovered the eyes she'd seen that night. "You're him."

"Yes," he replied quietly. "I told you I'd always be there to protect you."

A sudden surge made Abi's heart leap. Irresistibly drawn to her hero, every beat seemed to echo the intensity of his words. Overwhelmed by a whirlwind of emotion, her chest tightened, and her breath quickened.

In that moment, nothing else mattered. Movements, graceful and deliberate, she lifted onto her tiptoes and impulsively pressed her lips to his seamlessly as the world faded into oblivion. Aware of what she'd done, she gradually regained her senses and pulled away, allowing her lips to linger a little longer. The two hovered inches apart, their eyes still closed. Amidst the stillness, she took a sip of air and exhaled delicately.

A charged silence filled the room. Heavy with undeclared feelings, Burton looked into her eyes, the intensity of their connection still strong. Caught in the aftermath, he knew their relationship had shifted. For him, it triggered something deep inside - a love that was always there.

Nervousness set in, making Abi instantly recoil, believing he'd consider her advances childlike, similar to that of a naïve little girl. "Oh, my goodness...umm..." she stammered, "I... aah...I don't know why I..."

Burton surveilled her while she paced the floor, somewhat frantic. Going against his better judgment, he reached out and took hold of her hand. The feel of it stopped Abi in her tracks and calmed the raging storm. Successfully getting her attention, he stepped forward, reducing the space between them, pondering his next move with a hesitant heart.

Embarrassed, her sights slid away from his.

Standing confidently, he assumed the universe had conspired to bring them together. Wanting to give her the world, he lovingly lifted her chin with his finger, coaxing her gaze upward. Abi's beauty captivated him as his thumb caressed the curve of her lips, tracing each contour with admiration, his sights reading her every move. Unable to resist her effect on him, Burton surrendered to the invisible force, drawing them closer as her eyes drifted shut trustingly.

A gentle collision, tender and sweet, each brush of his lips sparked an intoxicating warmth. Like the flicker of a gentle flame, his touch ignited a fire within her that burned brighter with each passing moment, unexpectedly setting her soul ablaze with a passion she had never known before.

11

The Reveal

Hearts pounding in sync, both left breathless, their intense connection transformed a lifetime of friendship into something more meaningful.

A smile tugged at the corners of Abi's lips as Burton peered down at her. Awstruck, her eyes had yet to open. When they did, she found him desperately analyzing her response, trying to draw a positive or negative conclusion. Hands encircling his waist, Abi rested her head upon his chest, causing him to pull her in lovingly. Melting into him, she didn't want to let go. Focused on his heart thumping violently and his breathing uneven, she immediately wondered what he was thinking. Indebted to him for rescuing her, reminded of Shane, a torrent of guilt hit like a freight train.

Inhaling deeply, he held it in and said, "Abs?"

Hesitant, she whispered, "Yes?"

Never having to second-guess his actions, he entered unfamiliar territory. "Say something?" he asked while awaiting the verdict.

Caught up in the day's events, pulled in two directions, she suddenly felt love for two people. "I, umm...I..." she stuttered.

Based on her hesitation, he got his answer. "You don't have to say it. I know you're with Shane."

"Why didn't you tell me sooner?" she said softly.

"I couldn't. It was..."

"Complicated?" she interrupted, anticipating what he'd say.

"Yeah." Stepping back, he turned and noticed they'd unintentionally cleared the room. "I'm sorry. I crossed the line. I had no right to...."

"Don't be sorry. Besides, I kissed you first. It's my fault."

He stared at her intensely.

Gaining the courage, seeing hints of the famous DJ standing before her, she added, "I still can't believe it's you. But somehow, I feel I knew all along."

Martin reappeared. Clearing his throat, he strongly interrupted, "Excuse me, Master B?"

Unable to veer from her, wishing she'd finished her sentence, Burton blindly replied, "Yeah, Martin? What is it?"

"Urgent call for you, Sir," he paused. "The one you were expecting."

Running his hand across his forehead, reluctantly breaking their connection, Burton knew what it was regarding and said, "Excuse me for a moment. I'll be back. Hold that thought."

"Alright," she replied.

"Stay with her, Martin."

"Will do, Sir."

They watched Burton head downstairs as Abi moved to the sofa in the living room.

The butler sat in an adjacent chair.

Dazed by what just happened, things began to make sense as she tied certain events together.

"So, the security team outside my house all those nights was technically there because of him?"

"Yes, Miss. I believe he will explain more as the evening progresses. Please be patient."

With her mind a chaos, she silently acknowledged that.

"This secret has been weighing on Master B for quite some time. It will be good for him to share and open up to someone. I've known him for a little over two years. I am acutely aware that the boy does not easily let people in."

"But what about at the house on Friday night? You said you were taking me to talk to Black Lyon. He wasn't the man standing along the railing. Burton came out of nowhere and spoke to that guy."

"Master B was in the Bentley that removed you from the scene. When you arrived at the house, he disappeared to swap clothes with Matteo, one of our security guards. That man assumed the role of Black Lyon in his place so Burton could keep up appearances. Think of it as an act of smoke and mirrors."

Angered by the craziness, she recalled the fear she felt. Assessing his actions, she couldn't help but point out the obvious. "So, he kidnapped me and deliberately put Shane in danger? Why? If he'd asked, I would have gotten into the vehicle without question." Thinking of everything they'd experienced, she added, "Why all the drama? Why did he make me suffer through that?"

The sound of a door shutting and echoing down the long corridor distracted them. Soon, Anton appeared with grocery sacks filled with fresh food.

"Hello, Miss," he greeted while placing the heavy bags on the counter.

"Hey, Anton."

The chef could tell by the look on her face something had happened. Needing to know the details, he asked inquisitively, "So, what did I miss?"

"Does he know, too?" she questioned.

Playing along, not wanting to let the cat out of the bag, Anton answered, "Know what?"

Abi tilted her head at the guy.

The butler looked over at him. "It's okay, Anton. Master B cleared the air."

Stopping everything, he rested his hands on the counter, lowered his head, and smiled. With eyebrows raised, he turned to Martin. "Everything, huh?"

"Well, not everything, but enough. She knows who you work for."

"Thanks, God!" he said dramatically in a thick Italian accent. "I hate secrets, you know. So, so stressful." Carrying on, unpacking, and filling the fridge, he seemed more light-hearted.

Burton climbed the stairs and returned to the main level. With everyone's eyes on him, he could tell a conversation had occurred in his absence.

Abi did not say a word.

Needing a break from the staff, he asked, "Abs? Can we go somewhere and talk?"

"Sure." Leaving the sofa, she followed him down the stairs.

Uncomfortable, Burton strangely avoided eye contact. Opting for general conversation, he figured he'd show her around to buffer the awkwardness. "There are two guest rooms down here and a bunk room around the corner if I remember correctly." Walking through the family room, he added, "This seating area leads outside to the courtyard and the water access. Want to see?"

Scanning the contemporary décor, feeling stressed, she answered, "Okay."

When they stepped onto the deck, they found the hot tub, outdoor living room, and fire pit. Guiding her down the steps toward the water and reaching the dock below, they walked to the end as small ripples rhythmically hit the shoreline. Despite being in the freshest air imaginable, a thickness returned.

He slipped his hands in his pockets and glanced at the house high above them. "So, do you like it?"

"It's amazing."

He could tell she wanted an explanation. Seeing Martin and his security guards watching, he turned and sat on the end of the dock.

Abi joined him. "I need to know everything," she stated firmly.

"Yeah. I just don't know where to start," he said, shimmying around. "Maybe it's better if you pose the questions, and I answer them."

"Okay," she thought a moment. "Let's begin with your name. Why Burton Baxter and not Lancaster?"

He smirked and shook his head.

She rested her hand on his forearm.

Drawn to it and feeling its warmth, her touch became his only weakness as he gathered his thoughts.

"It's okay. You can tell me," she prompted.

The breeze whispered through the towering evergreens, carrying the faint scent of pine. Burton looked towards the mountain range and said, "Since day one, Lancaster Diamonds always seemed riddled with controversy. When I moved to LA, I had to separate myself from it, mostly for safety reasons."

"Why?"

"Remember when you asked me how my parents were? I said they were good."

"Yes."

He rubbed his palms together. "Well, truth is, they're not."

"Oh..." She waited for him to elaborate.

Flashing a sorrowful look, he mumbled, "They're dead, Abi."

"What?" A chill rolled through her, like ghosts making their presence known.

"And their death is my fault."

She straightened up fearfully. "What do you mean, your fault?"

"They are dead because of something I did." He turned to her. "I arrogantly challenged the Korolev family and lost the two most important people in my life as a result."

"Oh, my god, Burton..." She reached over to rest her hand on his back.

"Korolev owned a mine nearby. Knowing he was corrupt and had illegally taken possession of the property, I convinced my Father to buy up the land around it to landlock him. That is when we discovered the true owner of his mine had died suspiciously. Wanting justice, I gave the RCMP an anonymous tip, and they investigated Korolev's operation. From that moment onward, my Father received threats and didn't tell me. One night, out of the blue, my parents sat me down to discuss college options. I believed they thought I'd suffered in the North long enough. Little did I know, this was for good reason. Both of them agreed it was time for me to move on with my life. Things moved quickly. Within days of issuing the school a substantial donation, I left the Territories and moved to LA. Given unlimited funds, I bought the Malibu house. Days later, I got word my parents were dead, and suddenly, I was the sole heir to their enormous estate. Not only did I inherit millions, but also a long list of enemies. I'd disturbed a hornet's nest, and these were the consequences." He shifted himself from left to right. Still rubbing his palms together, he said, "At that point, I hit rock bottom. Thankfully, I had hired Rosa and Martin. Despite what I said about them earlier this morning, I do consider them my family and trust them wholeheartedly."

Turning to her, he waited to hear the next question.

"Why music and the rave scene?"

"One Friday, I went out with friends to take my mind off things. Running in elite circles, we crashed an upscale rave with a secret location and unlimited perks. What I discovered that night was unreal. The rave was a front for a series of underground networks. Midway through the evening, most of the young elites attending got wasted. Some ran their mouths off and carelessly revealed family secrets. The wealth, power, and resources at their disposal were mindblowing. Many business dealings in this setting involved private, untraceable crypto exchanges. Some legitimate and some not. Gathering info from so many conversations got me thinking." About to divulge his biggest secret, he suddenly stopped and analyzed the repercussions of her knowing about this part of his life. "What I am about to tell you, I am not proud of, but I'm immersed in this now. What truly intended to be a legitimate venture morphed into something I can no longer escape."

A look of concern splashed across her face.

"While phishing data at these events, I found a common thread. Alexei Korolev. Eastwood's Father. Determined to get revenge for what he did to my parents and others, I started gathering intel on him. While sifting through more and more information to uncover his business dealings, I stumbled upon proof that Korolev was a middle-man for a crypto operation. Wanting to sweep his business out from underneath him and steal his clients, I designed a decentralized app that grants access to a vault gateway to facilitate these blockchain exchanges in the shadows and keep them ultra-secure. To my knowledge, it's the most advanced system in the world. I started my raves to lure these people in by offering my hidden service for a fee, and not long after, word spread through those elite social circles. Clients can only access my vault under the guise of my events - no other time. So, they need to keep returning. It creates a steady income stream that has become extremely lucrative."

Abi looked away and tried to process what he'd said.

"To safeguard my systems, I installed a fingerprint verification system for tickets and not names to help keep identities secure for innocent rave guests, but for my clients, no tickets exist. They present their specific QR codes at the entrance to activate their Nightfall account. After that, they can make upwards of twenty transactions per visit without gas fees."

"What are gas fees?"

"Transaction costs for crypto exchanges. I've included it in the annual membership they pay me."

Not knowing anything about cryptocurrency or the clandestine underworld networks using it, Abi did not comment.

"But two months ago, the FBI learned what I was doing and brought me in for questioning."

"You were arrested?"

"Not quite. They were interested in the intel I was collecting and asked me to work with them. Really, I didn't have much of a choice. It was either that or jail."

"So, you work for the FBI?"

"In a roundabout way, I'm an informant, but mostly for selfish reasons because, in return for passing along info, they occasionally open doors for me. It's a win-win. Thus, your emergency passport."

"That's how you got it so fast."

"Just FYI, your old one is no longer valid," he divulged with a hint of humor.

"Alright."

"To them, I'm now considered a Red Hat."

"What is that?"

"Someone working outside the arms of the law using tech skills to infiltrate organizations running illegal operations."

Abi was stunned by this. "Wait? So you work both sides of the fence?"

"To a degree."

She nodded, "Wow..."

"When they issued the warrant for Black Lyon's arrest for kidnapping Eastwood and his guys, it was a cover. They never intended to arrest me. It was a narrative that had to come out in the press to make it look like they were doing something about it. I needed to be showcased as the bad guy to keep up appearances. They knew where I had dropped them off and asked me to confiscate their phones. I, in turn, passed the devices along to the bureau for analysis. That was the largest collection of intel they'd gotten on the Oligarchs in years."

"Burton, this is dangerous..."

"Yes - deadly, really. But it does not only affect me. It affects those around me. This is where you come in..."

"Me? How?"

"While sifting through data from the latest rave, I came across a flagged text message that read – We know who you are, and then outlined a list of activities Black Lyon needed to turn a blind eye to at his events. If I didn't, they said there would be dire consequences, and attached was a photo of you and me from Zuma Beach."

Abi's heart sank.

"The person who sent the message intended to target you. It took days to decipher the IP linked to the text, but I finally cracked it and discovered the source. Eastwood Korolev."

The guy's name sent a stroke of fear through her every time.

"Despite the most advanced encryption on all my networks and my name change from Lancaster to Baxter, he still made the connection. But I haven't figured out what connection it is. Does he know I'm Black Lyon and Dark Demon? Or just the systems mastermind behind the guy's Nightfall crypto vault? Maybe he discovered I'm the only living heir of Lancaster Diamonds Corp. I'm still not certain either way. Somehow, I believe he stumbled on things by accident." Burton turned to her. "Regardless, I've been watching over you ever since."

Abi felt a weight on her chest. Unable to collect sufficient air, she inhaled deeply. "So it wasn't a coincidence that you bought a house across the canyon?"

"Don't hate me, but when I met some friends for lunch in late August, I saw a man who looked much like your Dad. After hearing the waiter confirm his name, I sat nearby, listened to his conversation, and learned you were moving to LA. I might have snuck a peek into his phone. There, I discovered an email thread from his realtor."

"Is that so..." She wasn't sure if she should be mad or not.

He heard the disappointment in her voice. "After everything I've told you, do you hate me? Because if you do, you have every right."

She paused and considered her answer. "No, I don't hate you, but I wish you would've told me the truth."

"I couldn't. There is a protocol for this. It's imperative I stay quiet for obvious reasons."

"Why tell me now?"

"Because I trust you. On top of that, we need to be on the same page. You need to know these precautions are necessary and for good reason. This is a game most don't win, Abs. When it comes to you, I need to defeat the odds. I must be smarter and faster and always on guard."

"Is that why you have so much security?"

"Yes."

"And you bought the house across the canyon to..."

"Spy on you and keep you safe," he said without hesitation.

Remembering Martin had confirmed this, she had to hear him say it. "And Black Lyon's night security outside my house?"

"Mine."

"You drove the Bentley past my place that morning?"

He lowered his head. "Yes."

"You know you scared the crap out of me?"

"That wasn't my intention. It was bad timing. I never thought you'd follow me all over Bel Air," he unnervingly chuckled. "You looked pretty determined."

"I wanted to talk to him – well, you. I felt so bad that I didn't thank you for saving me before I left the rave that night."

"Don't worry. I knew. You didn't have to say it."

"So on our drive up the PCH that Sunday after the rave, I shared everything that happened…"

"And I listened because I wanted to hear your side of the story."

"What about the letter in the black envelope delivered to me at school?"

Burton shook his head and pointed straight at her. "No, that wasn't me. I was surprised you thought it was, though."

"Then who sent it?"

"We believe it was the Korolev family trying to spook you. These people make a living inflicting prolonged psychological damage on top of destroying property, stalking, manipulating, and harming friends and family to get what they want. Typical psychopathic behavior."

"Why did you kidnap me and put Shane in danger? I would have gone with you, no questions asked. You didn't need to do it that way. Shane could have gotten injured or killed."

He wasn't proud of what happened. "In hindsight, I suppose I should have done things differently. But the explosion was unexpected. It threw me off. We assumed it was a warning shot. These people are notorious for that. Usually, death occurs shortly after. All I wanted was to get you to safety as fast as possible. He just got caught in the crossfire. That's it. I would have never intentionally hurt him."

"Then explain why you hate him so much?"

"I'm just not a fan. That said, I don't think I'd like anyone you date." He straightened his posture.

"Why?"

"Because it's not me," he said in a deep voice, staring straight ahead confidently, wondering how she'd respond.

Taken by surprise, Abi whispered, "Burton..."

"I know what you're gonna say. The age gap isn't ideal. Hell, I'm sure it's not even legal."

"I have to say, I liked it better when you were just a UCLA student. As it stands, you are running multi-million-dollar companies, and I'm a senior in high school." She tilted her head, analyzing the complexities of that.

"When you put it that way, it paints me as a bad guy, preying on you or something."

"But you're not."

He was glad to hear that. "I could never hurt you. Ever."

She believed him wholeheartedly. He'd proven that time and time again. "So, what happens now?"

Knowing they needed to change the subject, he said, "As we speak, there's a sting op going down to incarcerate Korolev and his son. When they found Eastwood wandering back to LA from where I dropped them in the desert, the guy stayed in custody for questioning after his friends were released. Interrogating him before letting him go days later, the bureau hoped he'd screw up and lead them right to his Father, which it seems he did. We are just waiting to hear the outcome. They have people watching your parents. Shane, Reg, and Jade, also. I just pray everyone comes out of this unscathed. I brought you here because they needed us out of the equation. We couldn't be in LA."

Everything now made sense to her. "Still, you should've told me..."

Burton interrupted. "I know, I know, but as I said, it was..."

"Complicated. I get it."

Hesitant, unable to change things now, she reached out to him and grabbed his hand. He looked at it before she offered open arms. Turning, he embraced her, too. Respectfully kissing her forehead, it took every ounce of his being to keep it at that.

Abi's feelings intensified with the warmth of his lips against her skin. Maybe it was their longstanding history or perhaps the situation they found themselves in. She didn't know. But her heart now felt deeply connected to his.

She gently snuggled into the curve of his neck. "So, I guess we need to get through this together."

"Yeah, we do," Burton said quietly. Resting his chin atop her head, he sadly opted to keep one last secret from her. Deciding not to share the details of his phone call that afternoon, he added, "Don't worry. I will never let anything happen to you."

Hearing those words made her heart spiral out of control. Unsettled, needing to address what happened between them, she repeated a phrase he often used to buffer her next statement. "Please don't hate me..."

"Oh, no. Why would I hate you?" he replied, bracing for what Abi would say.

"I don't want you to think I don't care about you because I do."

Burton waited for the ball to drop.

"But, given what happened, the truth is..."

"You're with Shane," he said point blank.

"Yes, and I feel I've betrayed him to the utmost degree."

Believing he should do the right thing, Burton conceded, "I get it. You love him."

"But, I love you too, you know."

"I know." He lightly patted her back before parting ways.

Amidst the silence and the water rippling, a cool breeze whistled through the trees, making Abi tighten her hoodie around her body.

"Excuse me, Sir!" Martin bellowed from the upper deck. "Dinner is served!"

"We're coming!" Getting up from the dock, he effortlessly helped Abi to her feet. "Shall we?" he asked in a gentlemanly voice.

"Yes," she smiled.

Walking hand in hand up the path, Burton opened the back door for Abi and followed her inside. To his surprise, another security team had arrived.

"What is going on?" a voice said wearily.

Shocked, Burton's sights bounced between the people gathered around and landed on one in particular. "Sara? What are you doing here?"

The young woman stared Abi down with icy eyes and said, "Who's she?"

12

Sara

Martin rolled his eyes, clearly unimpressed with the theatrics, as the girl glanced around the room, embarrassed, feeling like the odd one out.

Abi recognized her immediately. She knew she was the woman on Burton's arm at Blu Brennan's extravagant party in Cabo. The memory flashed vividly in her mind: the salty air, the vibrant music, and the woman's radiant presence, capturing the attention of everyone around them. Seeing her, Abi felt a mix of curiosity and unease.

"What are you doing here?" Burton questioned, refusing to check Abi's reaction.

"With everything going down, I thought you needed company." Her glare moved from him to the hand he was holding. "Obviously, I was wrong."

"By coming here, you risked compromising her and me," he said, standing tall.

Confused by their conversation, Abi didn't understand what was happening.

The girl lightened up. "Calm down." Giving Burton the eye, Sara suggested, "Shouldn't this be a conversation you and I have - alone?"

"It's fine. She knows."

"About what?" she asked, dumbfounded.

"Everything except you."

"Yeah, of course," she hurtfully replied, adding a devious snicker. "I guess HR will have a heyday with this one."

"This is none of their concern." He stood firm in his statement. "Look, I need you to go."

The woman did not move a muscle. "See, this is the thing. I can't. Cap sent me. He wanted more eyes on you. There are five others with me. They stationed us in the vacation house next door."

"Well, then, you need to stay there." Frustrated, Burton tried to bring it back to a civilized conversation. "We're just about to sit down for dinner."

It was hard for Sara to see she wasn't welcome. "Fine," she said. Leaving the great room, she walked up the corridor and disappeared. The door echoed as it slammed shut behind her.

"Well, that was heated," Andrew muttered under his breath while dishing out his plate before starting his night watch.

Ted and Matt knew of the girl's involvement with their boss. They were surprised by what happened.

Burton turned and said, "Abi?" and signaled for her to follow him.

Agreeing, she went.

Closing his bedroom door, he faced her and said, "Sorry about that."

Arms crossed, she replied, "It seems I'm not the only one with someone else."

"For the record, the whole Cabo thing was fake. We were there for a specific purpose. Nothing else."

"You don't have to explain."

"Yes. I do." He ran his hand through his hair. "Please don't get the wrong idea."

Abi suddenly put two and two together. "Wait? Is she an undercover agent?"

Not elaborating, he said, "Something like that."

"She looked pretty hurt, Burton."

He didn't answer.

"What happened between you two?"

Uneasy about divulging the truth, he leaned against the wall and buried his hands deep in his pockets. "I apologize for how I acted that day."

"When?"

"In Cabo."

"Oh..." She looked down, recalling the makings of it. "I can't lie. What you did hurt."

"I wasn't expecting you to be there." He glanced at the ceiling. "Everything that happened was an act – all of it."

"For whatever reason, seeing you with her was hard."

Immediately, his eyes glued to hers. "Watching you make out with Shane was harder."

"You saw?"

He didn't answer. Pausing, not proud of what he was about to say, he looked away. "Afterwards, I had a moment of...weakness, nothing more."

Assuming what he meant, she quickly pounced on that statement. "From what I just witnessed, I think it meant more to her."

"Apparently so." He hated the way this came across. "Abs, I promise you, I'm not that guy. I don't let people in, I don't use people, and I don't attach to anyone."

"Not even me?"

He froze. "You are the only exception to that rule. Just say the word, and I'm yours."

Her heart was tearing in two as she recalled Shane desperately trying to rescue her. "I'm sorry. I can't give you that right now. I love Shane, but please know..." she paused.

"You love me, too."

"Yes," she admitted. "I also feel indebted to you for saving me. If you weren't there that night, I shudder to think of what could have happened."

"I'm just glad I was."

She didn't like the reminder of that fateful night.

He pointed out, "So, the way I see it, we seem to be in a predicament."

"Suppose so."

Burton didn't want to fight or say something they would regret. "Let's just get through the next twelve hours. Once the smoke clears, maybe things will look different."

"I agree."

He opened the bedroom door. "We should grab some food. Anton doesn't like when stuff gets cold."

"Alright."

Letting Abi lead the way back to the kitchen, all eyes were on them as they grabbed their plates. Helping to dish her food out, he grabbed Abi sparkling water from the bar fridge while she sat at the table.

"Go ahead and eat," he said before making himself a plate.

A million thoughts rolled through Abi's head. Immersed in an adult world, she strangely missed the high school drama. Thinking of her Mom, Dad, and Shane, she said, "Will my Dad track my location from the new phone?"

He sat down beside her and set his food down. "No. You might have to take one for the team on this."

She hated sports analogies. "What do you mean?"

"Your location services are off, and the phone is not accepting incoming calls."

"What? Please tell me you're joking." Abi's anxiety surfaced again.

"I suggest you call or text him tonight and tell him the truth."

"And what is that?"

"You are with me. We flew to Tahoe to look at a lake house for sale, and I bought it."

Distraught, knowing lying to her Dad had become a terrible and unforgivable habit, she moved the potatoes around the plate with her fork, wondering what she'd say.

"If you want, you can put it on speaker, and I can be with you to smooth any ruffled feathers."

"I think you might regret that."

Cutting his chicken and taking a bite, he said, "Knowing your Dad, I probably will."

13

The Call

While finishing her dinner and fretting over the call she needed to make, Abi asked Burton to help her rehearse what to say. Disappearing, the two went to his room.

As she dialed the number on her new phone and it rang on the other end, she heard him answer formally, "This is Dr. Acardi."

"Hi, Dad. It's me."

"Abi? I've been trying to call Burton's phone, but there's no answer. I tried yours, and it says it's no longer in service. Why?"

He checked his phone on the nightstand and realized her Dad had called countless times while they were on the dock, talking.

"Burton said the battery in my phone is fried. It won't hold a charge anymore, so he got me a new one today."

"Well, that was generous of him."

"Yeah, it was. The number I'm calling you from is my new number. You can reach me here."

"Are you at home?"

"Umm, no." Abi took a deep breath. "Please don't be mad, but I'm in Lake Tahoe."

"What? Abi!"

"I know. Burton wanted me to see this amazing lake house he bought just over the border on the Nevada side. It is so beautiful."

"Abi, what are you doing? Just because I am preoccupied with your Mother doesn't give you carte blanche to do whatever you please."

"Dad, no... It's not like that."

"I know you are young, and your Mother's situation is hard, but you will have to face it bravely at some point. Right now, it seems you want to sweep her under the rug. I'm pretty disappointed in your behavior these days - have to say."

Abi started to cry. "I'm sorry..."

"These apologies seem to be a growing trend," he paused. "I need to go. Tomorrow, we need to sit down and talk."

"Okay..."

"Goodnight..."

"Goodnight, Dad..."

He ended the call abruptly without saying he loved her.

"Damn it!" she shouted, punching the bed with her fist.

Burton tried his best to comfort her. "It's okay. It's not your fault."

"He doesn't know that."

Hugging her tightly, he let her sob. "I'm sorry. I promise I'll fix this."

14

Saturday Night

As the heaviness of the call passed, with very little emotion left to expel, Abi flopped backward onto the bed. Staring at the ceiling, she asked, "Can you show me which room is mine? I need a moment and wouldn't mind having a shower." She let out an exhausted sigh. "Also, is it possible to rewash my clothes?"

"The guys, Anton and Martin, are all in the spare rooms. So, you can have this one. I'll take the sofa."

She tilted her head slightly. "No, Burton, you don't have to sleep there. It's not like we haven't shared a bed in the past. Remember all the campouts in the tent in the backyard? Or the time your parents had that fight, and you slept at my house to escape all the yelling?"

In hindsight, he chuckled. "Yeah, I barely got any sleep that night."

"Why?"

"Because I slept on that trundle. You know, the one tucked under your bed. Man, that mattress was firm. It was like sleeping on a board."

She laughed. "Really? I didn't know that. I'm so sorry."

"It's true," he chuckled fondly.

"Well, for me, that night, I felt safe."

"Is that right?" he replied in a low tone.

"You were between me and the monsters in my closet," she laughed, bumping her shoulder with his. "Even then, you were my protector."

"I guess so." Staring at her, he knew the makings of today had changed things between them. "Are you sure you're okay with me staying in here?"

"Yes, of course. I trust you." She casually reached over and rested her hand on his arm. "Now. As for the laundry?"

"Sorry, I forgot," he said. "The machines are on the lower level. There is a white robe in the closet you can use."

"Perfect. Thank you."

"With that said, I'll leave you to it. The bathroom is in there. Help yourself to anything."

"Thanks a bunch."

Burton walked out of the room. For the first time all day, he separated from Abi. Having taken his laptop with him, he decided to check for updates and do some work for the upcoming Nightfall events. Sitting at the kitchen island while Anton tidied up, Martin came and sat beside him.

"How is it going?" he chuckled in a fatherly tone.

"What do you mean?" Burton sat stoically, hoping he wouldn't taunt him too much.

With his thick English accent, he said, "It's been a rather eventful day, wouldn't you say?"

"It certainly has." Logging into his computer, he hoped the man got the hint.

Picking up on it, Martin pulled out his iPad. "We have many things to discuss." Scrolling through emails, he rattled them off one by one despite his boss not being in the mood to work.

"The Ibiza and Miami properties are about to go into escrow. I have arranged for you to meet with the Florida designers on Monday afternoon to review the concepts for the place. The special effects and electrical guys will be there, too. They need to get it wired ASAP. Given the square footage, it will probably take three weeks."

Burton nodded his head and accepted the meeting requests he'd sent. Not liking that he would be out of town for a few days, he knew he had no choice. "What else?"

"You haven't narrowed down your top three guest appearances in December for Japan. We must finalize that soon. Also, the agent from Monaco sent a list of properties for you to see. Based on my findings, I will send you my top two links. Let me know your thoughts."

"Right... Got it."

"When we return to LA, Lancaster Corp has payroll ready for signatures."

Opening Microsoft Project and Lists on his laptop, he added to his ever-expanding responsibilities and incorporated what they'd discussed. "Anything else?"

"The Chicago location is at eighty percent completion."

"So, we'll have to make a trip there soon?"

"Perhaps in two weeks." Zipping down the list, Martin said, "Lastly, you haven't finalized your tracks for the Vegas launch. Are you reusing something or creating something new? We have four hundred and sixty-nine attending from LA, so you might want to switch it up."

"I'm workin' on new material."

"Excellent, Sir. On that note, I will leave you."

"Thanks, Martin. Appreciate your help."

"That is why I'm here." The man smiled and got up from the chair. Patting Burton on the back, knowing he was troubled, he said, "Good-night. I am off to bed. I left your duffle bag in your closet."

He gave the man a thumbs up. "Goodnight."

Far more than a butler, Burton thought of him as his right-hand man and Father figure with an air of secrecy. For an old guy, he was more organized and on the ball than he was half the time.

Anton folded his apron and placed it on the counter. "Good night, Sir. I'm going to do the same. I'll see you bright and early, I'm sure."

"But not too early, I hope," he replied as the chef disappeared downstairs.

Updating his tracklist, he powered through the emails for the next hour that needed his immediate attention.

Looking up the hallway, he saw that Abi hadn't surfaced. He became concerned and went to check on her. Knocking on the room door, he opened it a crack. "Abs? You okay?"

"I'm fine. This bathtub was too tempting to pass up. Your spa products are heavenly."

Standing outside the bathroom, he replied, "Glad you're enjoying them. Just wanted to make sure you were good." His voice sounded tired.

"What's wrong?"

He knew she could read him like a book, even behind a closed door.

Not getting a response, she said, "You can sit and talk to me if you want. Sorry, I'm taking so long. When I have a lot on my mind, it helps to soak and destress."

Burton figured he should try that sometime. Sitting on the floor outside the bathroom, he leaned against the wall and rested his arms on his knees. "Still thinking about your Dad?"

"Among other things."

"Shane, I'm sure."

"Yes, him, Jade, and Reggie. The rest of my friends and my Mom, of course. What my Dad said hit pretty hard." She inhaled and tried to proactively stop herself from bursting into tears again.

"I hear you."

"Hey, what happened to being a buffer during that call."

"Apologize, but your conversation went off the rails, so I chose to stay quiet. I wasn't anticipating it going that way. Besides, if I had intervened, the situation might have escalated. I didn't want that."

"You're probably right."

Offering something positive, he said, "But you told him the truth. Well, mostly."

"And tomorrow, I'll face the music and atone for it all over again."

"Can I offer some advice?"

"Sure."

"This situation aside, from here on out, be as honest as possible and do what you can to help the guy. We know he's under a tremendous amount of pressure. He needs to know you are safe while he's dealing with your Mother. Give him that peace of mind. I promise I won't add to the problem anymore."

Abi took what he said into consideration.

"This week, you should focus on school and your Mom—nothing else. Just so you know, I'll be away on business for two or three days. That way, I won't be around to distract you."

Disappointed to hear that, realizing he didn't elaborate on the details of this business trip, she said, "Oh... Alright."

He rested his head against the wall and looked up. "Will you be okay while I'm gone?"

"Hopefully. I'll try my best."

"The guys will be with you twenty-four-seven, so you don't have to worry."

"Okay..." Abi sounded uncertain.

"Can't believe I'm sayin' this, but maybe you should have Shane around. That's if you want him to be." He waited for her response.

"I'll see."

An awkward silence came upon them.

"Have you spoken to Sara?" Abi blurted out of nowhere.

"Sara?" His eyebrows furrowed. "Why?"

"Because you two need to talk. Honestly, she's noticeably hurt, Burton. If anything, maybe she needs closure. If you don't care for her like that, tell her. Take your own advice. Be as honest as possible."

To a degree, he knew he should clear the air.

"Text her and meet in the courtyard or something. You know, neutral territory."

Taking his phone from his pocket, he pulled up her contact info. It was late, and he wasn't in the best mood, but he needed to address this before tomorrow. "I'll talk to her."

"Good. I am quite shriveled and should get out of the bath anyway. Can you shut the door, please?"

"Will do. I'll be back."

Abi heard him leave. Getting out of the stand-alone soaker tub, she popped the drain and wrapped herself in a towel. Wiping the steam from the mirror, she brushed and dried her hair. Switching to a white robe, Abi peeked out of the bedroom into the glass corridor. Across from her, behind the giant boulders, she could see Sara and Burton sitting around the firepit with flames flickering upon their faces.

"At least they're having a civilized conversation. Or so it seems," she whispered. Recalling the girl walking alongside Burton arm-in-arm in Cabo, that feeling of jealousy returned. Then, a humorous thought hit her. "Am I spying on the spies?" she giggled.

Suddenly, they stood up. Burton offered Sara a hug. Abi was happy to see them leave on good terms. Closing the door, she saw the pretty young woman walk back toward the other house while Burton came inside and locked up.

Returning to the bathroom, unwrapping another guest's toothbrush from the cabinet, she heard a knock at the door.

"Come in," she mumbled. Hearing it close, she asked, "So, how did it go?"

He replied, "You were right. We needed to talk."

"And?"

"And, nothing. I told her my thoughts. She shared hers. That's all."

Understanding that Burton's moment of weakness meant he'd slept with her, she tried to erase that from memory. When she emerged from the bathroom, she gathered her clothes and hinted, "Laundry?"

"Almost forgot. This way. I'll help you."

She quietly followed Burton to the lower level since the men were sleeping. When he flipped on the light, Martin appeared behind them, scaring Abi to bits, making her jump and grab her heart.

"Sorry to interrupt, Sir. Can I have a word?"

Stuffing Abi's clothes in the washer, he replied, "Sure." Pulling a thin, environmentally-friendly soap sheet from the package on the shelf, he closed the machine and turned it on.

"It'll take about twenty minutes," he said to her.

Abi smiled. "Perfect."

"Give me a second, okay?"

"Of course. Take your time."

Burton left the room while Abi climbed the stairs to the main floor.

Joining Martin, Burton asked, "What's up?"

His right-hand man showed him the screen of his iPad. It was a breaking news report. The headline read *Russian Oligarch Alexei Korolev gunned down in drive-by attack.*

"Sounds like the sting went sideways." When he handed him back the device, his gut feeling told him something else. "It was a hit, wasn't it?"

"That's the word on the wire, Sir."

"So, the guy is dead. Is it over?"

"Perhaps. Or is it just beginning?"

Burton crossed his arms in front of his chest.

Martin stood firmly. "This powerful man got gunned down. Those in the family will be out for revenge. I believe they will hunt for the one responsible."

That thought had crossed his mind seconds earlier. "Guess we'll have to see how this plays out. Did we get clearance to head back tomorrow?"

"No. Not yet."

"Let me know when we do."

"I will, Sir." Martin could see how tired Burton was. "If I may. I think you should get some rest, my boy."

"I'm going."

Abi could hear the two men talking in the hallway below. Their low-toned voices made it hard to hear anything concrete. When Burton ascended the stairs, she took a deep breath, wondering if he had bad news.

He scanned the room and found her sitting on the floor, staring at her phone.

"Have you contacted Shane yet?"

"No."

"Why?"

Exhaling, she said, "I don't know. I was thinking about everything that's happened today."

He sat beside her. "And?" he prompted, caring beyond measure. Looking at her sitting there, she briefly resembled the little girl from next door. It made his protective instincts kick in, as they usually do.

"I can't call him now. Don't know what to say."

That moment of clarity made him realize she was still seventeen despite being far more mature than her age. Maybe her Father was right to be concerned, he thought before offering some advice. "Perhaps you should wait until tomorrow. Just sleep on it and see where things stand in the morning."

"I think that's a good idea. I'm exhausted."

"Rightfully so." He folded his arms and said, "I need to tell you something."

"Oh, no... What is it?" Her eyes glued to his. She looked fearful.

"Alexei Korolev died in the sting tonight. The mainstream media is painting a very different picture to keep the bureau out of it."

"Forgive me for saying, but isn't this good news? Now, he won't hurt anyone anymore."

"Yes, but there is talk of family taking revenge on those responsible."

Abi nodded. "Like Eastwood."

"Perhaps."

"So, that means I'm not safe?"

"Security will be with you steady from here on out. These people are ruthless, but my guys are highly trained. I'd trust them with my life."

She silently agreed.

Toying with the idea, he suddenly divulged, "Abs. There's one more thing I think you should know."

"Okay…"

"I debated whether I should say anything, but no more secrets."

"What is it?" She listened intently.

"Remember that important phone call I took today?"

Hesitant, she said, "Yes."

"It was to negotiate a ransom agreement."

"Ransom? For whom?" she questioned.

"You."

It was hard to process what he'd said. She was stunned. Overwhelmed by so many questions, one stood front and center. "Who is doing this?"

"Can't say."

"Can't or won't?" She got a little mad.

"Both." He looked down at the floor. "We issued specific terms to keep you from harm."

"What terms?"

Clarifying that, he said, "I paid for your protection."

"Isn't that extortion?"

"On this playing field, there are no rules. That said, I'd pay any price to keep you safe."

"Burton…"

"It's true."

"How much?" she asked.

He didn't want to tell her.

"Burton? How much?"

"They wanted an installment of two million."

"Installment?"

"Apparently, to keep you alive, there is a payment schedule I must adhere to until the bureau can mitigate things."

"So, the two million is just the start?"

"The guy is doing this to offset what I've taken from him."

Hearing that, she figured it out. "Taken from him? You mean Eastwood?"

He nodded.

"I don't know what to say. Once again, I owe you my life. I don't know how I could repay you."

"Abs, this is my fault. I am to blame. You are in danger because of me. Don't worry. I'll fix it. In the meantime, I thought you should know. As long as they get their money, you will be all right. But that doesn't mean you can take chances. You hear me?"

"Yes," she answered softly.

He watched her thoughts selfishly steal her away. "It's late. Let's get some sleep. Tomorrow will be a long one."

She silently nodded.

"I thought we could go straight to the hospital after we land in LA."

Thankful to hear that, she said, "Are you sure it's safe?"

"Absolutely." He got up off the floor and helped her on her feet. Walking to his room, he felt a weird feeling in the pit of his stomach and couldn't shake it. To give him a second, he said, "I'm going to check on your laundry. I think the washer should have finished its cycle by now."

"Don't worry. I'll do that."

He stopped her. "No, I've got it. You go ahead to bed."

"Can you just hang them up to dry? I'll fluff them in the morning."

"Sure thing."

Abi continued to his room while Burton went downstairs, feeling conflicted. Pulling her clothes from the washer, he hung them on hangers as she asked. They were so small. Thinking of the little girl next door, in an instant, he felt like a monster for loving her.

Slowly climbing the stairs, he returned to the room and found her on the far side of the bed with her back to him. Ducking into the closet quietly, he got the duffle bag Martin had left. Inside was a set of pajamas and a change of clothes.

"Abs?" he said quietly.

She rolled over.

"Do you want my nightshirt?"

Not asleep, she flung off the covers. Still in the robe, she replied, "Sure, if you don't mind."

He handed it to her. "I'm just gonna shower."

"Okay."

Not knowing where her head was, he locked the bathroom door.

Abi heard the water running and got changed. Spreading the robe over her feet at the end of the bed to keep them warm, she cuddled up under the covers again. The stars shining brightly in the night sky captivated her. Thinking about everything that transpired with Burton that day, she wondered what she would say to Shane tomorrow. Given his Dad's track record of cheating on his Mom, he'd made it very clear from the beginning that he wouldn't tolerate it. Based on that, she knew she'd screwed up majorly. Mind reeling, she tried to figure out whether she should tell him the truth, understanding how betrayed he'd feel if she did. To him, out of all the ways she could hurt him, this was the worst in his eyes, and she knew it.

Amidst her thoughts, Burton rounded the corner and turned out the bathroom light. Approaching his side of the bed, he checked the closet and grabbed an extra blanket. Not opening the covers, he laid down and spread it over top of him. With one hand positioned behind his head and the other on his chest, he stayed silent, believing Abi was asleep.

Out of the blue, she whispered, "Goodnight, Burton."

"Night, Abs," he said, keeping things short and sweet, knowing it was better that way.

Rise and Shine

A ribbon of morning light poured into the room as the clouds broke over the mountains. Waking with the sun on her face, Abi rolled over, but Burton wasn't there. She sat up in bed, assuming he'd slept on the couch. It didn't take long for her to gravitate to the view. The water looked like glass. It was so calm. Far from shore, the only ripples in sight were from someone paddleboarding peacefully in the middle of the lake.

With her feet firmly on the floor, she walked to the window and shielded her eyes. Given the silhouette, she figured it was him as he glided toward the house. Their kiss replayed more than once in her mind, but soon after, slivers of guilt followed. Flip-flopping, she knew she felt more like herself in his adult world versus being the teenage girl within the walls of Gilderson. Somehow, Shane seemed like a little boy compared to Burton now - a thought that was hard to shake. After being with him for the past few days, she didn't know how to return to everyday life. Afraid to face the truth, she realized her feelings for her best friend were strong, and he felt the same, but they had so many things stacked against them.

She watched him approach the dock. Two of his security guards were awaiting him. Stepping off the board, he pulled it out of the water. Effortlessly hoisting it on his shoulder, paddle in hand, he carried it up the steps. Partway, he caught sight of her and smiled.

It prompted Abi to wave and smile back.

Disappearing inside the boat house, she waited. Minutes later, he was knocking on the bedroom door.

"Come in," she said.

His face looked refreshed and energized as he rounded the corner. "Good morning."

"Morning. That is certainly a nice way to start the day."

"Yes, the lake is so peaceful. I love it."

"For a guy who thrives on loud music, it's odd to hear you say that."

"Guess so," he smirked. "But, you know that guy doesn't exist, right? He's just a figment of everyone's imagination. This is the real me." He hoped she liked him more than his alter ego.

"Burton, who you are on stage will never overshadow the fact that you are my best friend."

Hearing the word friend, again was like a stab to the chest. It confirmed that Abi had every intention of returning to Shane today. Aware of what needed to be said, he took a breath. "I don't think you should tell Shane about what happened between us."

Abi's mind raced.

"Nothing good will come from it. Trust me." Hands in his hoodie pockets, Burton waited to hear her thoughts.

"So, then, where do we go from here?"

Having to do the right thing, he said, "We continue like nothing happened."

"But it doesn't change the past twenty-four hours. And no matter what you say, I feel forever indebted. You're paying millions of dollars to keep me safe. How can I forget about that?"

He glanced over. "Abs, you're in this mess because of me. I told you. You owe me nothing."

The sun came out from behind the clouds and brightened the room along with Abi's face. Her blue eyes were barely there. He thought she looked so beautiful.

"You okay?" she asked.

Breaking from his stare, he replied, "Yeah, why?"

With such an intense adoration, she inched towards him. "Just wondering." Arms open, she hoped for a hug.

Giving her what she was looking for, he changed the subject: "We should get moving. Gotta leave in a few hours."

"Any chance we can come back sometime?"

"You're welcome here whenever you want. Just say the word."

"It feels like we're in another world. It's just so tranquil."

"I know what you mean." Turning around, he said, "I'm just gonna grab a shower. I'll make it quick."

Abi nodded. "Sure. Take your time."

Walking into the bathroom and closing the door behind him, he stood in front of the mirror. He couldn't stop replaying their conversation as he gazed at his reflection. Despite his strong exterior, his heart hurt. He loved her but knew the timing wasn't right.

Alone, Abi sat on the edge of the bed and watched the sun dip in and out from behind the clouds, dimming and brightening the room. Wanting to get dressed, she went out the door and headed to the laundry room to put her clothes in the dryer. At the end of the hall, she entered the great room and found Anton preparing breakfast and Martin seated on the sofa, sipping a cup of tea, focused on his iPad.

Hearing her, he lowered his head and peered over the top of his reading glasses. "Good morning, Miss Abi."

The chef waved to her. "Good morning, Miss."

"Morning, gentlemen," she replied while heading downstairs.

Anton subtly glanced at Martin. His eyebrows raised noseily.

Martin did the same.

Finding her clothes hanging up, she tossed them in the machine, thankful they weren't damp. While waiting, she thought about what Burton said.

"Maybe he's right. Nothing good could come from telling Shane the truth," she mumbled, "It would hurt him to the core and cause the tension between them to escalate even more." Unable to deal with that, she whispered, "This feud needs to end."

The machine beeped and automatically shut off. Taking everything out, Abi folded each piece neatly before making her way back upstairs.

At the same time, Burton left the bedroom.

When Abi emerged from the lower level, Martin and Anton looked at their boss strangely. The two stood mere feet apart—her drowning in his pajama top and him wearing matching bottoms.

Sara happened to slip in the side door. Shocked to see them, she straightened her posture and quickly delivered the message. "We received clearance to return to LA."

Burton acknowledged her with a nod. Nothing else.

Embarrassed, Abi walked past him sheepishly, clothes in hand.

Unable to contain her emotions, Sara exclaimed, "The jet leaves at thirteen hundred," and promptly exited, having said her piece.

Martin caught Anton's attention while their famous boss seemed unfazed.

With his back to them, making himself a coffee, he could sense something was brewing. "Is there a problem, gentlemen?" he asked, not making eye contact.

"Did you have a good night, Sir?" Anton asked while cooking.

Assuming what the chef was implying, he quickly put the rumors to rest. "For the record, I don't need to explain myself." He paused. "The girl is my best friend. Nothing more."

His butler was happy to hear that. "I trusted you'd do the right thing, Sir."

He turned to him. "Just because I'm Dark Demon doesn't mean I am one. What do you take me for?"

Cutting some avocado, Anton muttered under his breath, "A man in love?"

Burton shot the guy a look.

"I'm sorry, Sir," he said in his thick Italian accent. "It's written all over your face."

Peering down the corridor, he made sure Abi wasn't there. "Well, I can't do anything about that, now can I?"

"Maybe one day, an opportunity will present itself," Martin chimed in wisely, taking a sip of tea. "One must be patient."

He heard a door open and close. Running his pointer finger across his throat, Burton warned them. "Not another word."

Martin earnestly acknowledged him, as did Anton, before flipping an omelet in the pan.

"Would you like your eggs now, B?" the chef asked.

"Yes. Thanks."

Abi joined them while Burton grabbed a mug.

"Can I make you a coffee?"

"Please," she said, sitting on a stool along the island.

"What can I get you this morning, Miss?" Anton asked while plating Burton's food.

Seeing his plate, she said, "That looks good."

"Give her mine. I'll wait," he said, setting the cup in front of her with the cream and sugar.

Anton presented Abi with breakfast and slid her the cutlery hidden inside a rolled napkin.

"I can't take your food," she said.

"It's fine. Don't worry. He'll make me another one."

Exchanging glances with Martin across the room, believing chivalry was not dead, Anton started making another omelet.

Their boss quickly noticed what the two were doing. He clenched his fists just as the security teams made a shift change.

"Good morning, gentlemen. We are departing the house promptly at noon," Martin informed while they gathered around the kitchen.

Smelling the frittata coming out of the oven with hashbrowns and bacon on the side, Anton set up a buffet for the men as they grabbed their plates. Each acknowledged Martin's instructions with a thumbs up.

"I guess this has been a boring trip for all of you?" she speculated while Burton found a seat beside her.

"Usually, when I make rave appearances, they are put through the wringer, so a little downtime is good once in a while, right guys?"

"I'll second that," Ted interjected. "We never know what will come our way most nights. This was a nice break."

The comment made Abi curious as to Burton's secret life. Having seen him on stage only once before, recalling the music and the addictive trance-like sounds he produced, she asked, "So, when will I get a backstage pass to see what goes on behind the scenes?"

"Never," Burton answered concretely.

She was confused. "What? Why not?"

"Abs, you can't ever be seen with me in that capacity."

She was saddened to hear it but knew he was right.

"I'm okay if you're in the crowd, but you'll need the guys with you."

"Why? It's not like Eastwood will be there at any point," she mentioned jokingly.

A serious expression flashed across his face.

"Wait?" Abi tried to read his mind. "What are you saying?"

Andrew chimed in. "We need Eastwood to surface so they can arrest him. He was nowhere to be seen during the sting. They believe he went back into hiding. Word on the street is business operations are resuming, and Eastwood is at the helm in his Father's place."

The thought of him being free sent shivers through her.

Burton looked Abi square in the eye. "This means you stay vigilant until he's behind bars."

Hearing that frightened her.

"With me being out of town on and off for the next while, at least it will take the heat off you."

"So, that means you will be the target, not me?"

"Pretty much."

Processing what he said, her heart sank. It was hard to hear he was putting himself in harm's way. Whispering, she said, "Can we talk? In private."

"Sure." Concerned, he followed Abi to his room.

Once inside, he closed the door behind them. "What's up, Abs?"

Distraught, she tried to stay strong.

Seeing this, he approached and rested his hands on her arms. "Hey... What is it?"

His sympathetic tone and the tilt of his head set her off immediately. "Is there something you're not telling me?" she whimpered. "Could something happen to you?"

"Come here." The tears drifted across her cheeks as he pulled her close. "Nothing is going to happen to me. I promise."

She couldn't respond.

"Besides, I've got all those guys watching my back, remember? Even some you can't see. I'll be fine. Don't worry."

Nodding, she wiped the tears with her sleeve and muttered, "Okay. If you're sure," hoping he was telling the whole truth.

Burton smiled. "I love the way you always think of others before yourself."

Without hesitation, she hugged him tightly. "I love the way you always think of me."

Happy to hear that, he respectfully kissed her forehead and closed his eyes, allowing his lips to rest a second longer before parting. It was the last time he would be able to do that. A battle raging inside, he said, "When we return to LA, you must fix things with Shane."

Right then, she dreaded the thought.

"He's a good guy, Abs. What he did to try and save you on Friday night was heroic."

"I know..."

"He loves you, and you feel the same. So, you gotta see where it goes." Surveying the expression on her face, he knew she felt torn. "We should finish breakfast. Maybe take a short walk and get some air afterward?"

She wholeheartedly agreed.

Slipping his arm around her shoulder, they went out the door and saw Sara making the rounds outside the glass corridor. As she watched them intensely, Abi realized the girl looked like a million daggers had punctured her heart.

"On second thought, maybe you should take Sara for the walk instead?"

"I don't think that's a good idea."

Abi lovingly tapped him on the shoulder. "Why not? She cares about you."

Despite everything that transpired between them, he noticed how their relationship suddenly returned to its usual friendly banter.

Aware of Sara's feelings, he said, "Regardless of what happened, she and I need to keep things professional."

Vowing never to cross that line again, unbeknownst to Abi, Burton knew the plan was for Sara to act as his love interest while they were away on business. He feared this arrangement might ultimately make things far more complicated. With no choice in the matter, the bureau suspected that by doing this, Korolev's people would get distracted, and it would shield Abi from harm. A secret he intended to keep as long as he could.

16 ▌

Friend or Foe

The sun was high in the southern blue sky, but its warmth had faded slightly since yesterday. A few trees on the property showed signs of fall, with hints of red, orange, and yellow leaves amongst the tall evergreens.

By eleven o'clock, the guys and Martin started shutting down the lake house.

Standing beside the bed, Burton looked out the window, praying he'd be able to return to his new vacation home sooner than later. Thoughts of living out the rest of his days there didn't seem like such a bad idea. Soaking up the view and as much peacefulness as possible, he put on his new branded hoodie and instantly transformed into the infamous celebrity before grabbing his duffle bag.

Not looking forward to returning to Bel Air, he joined Abi in the corridor. "Ready?" he asked with a hint of sadness.

"Ready."

Walking up the stairs, he flipped his hood over his head. Not skipping a beat, Burton reached up and gently did the same to Abi, intent on hiding her identity, too.

"Cover your face until we get into the truck, okay?" he said solemnly.

"Alright," she whispered.

About to depart, Martin met with the house management team brought in to monitor and maintain the property in their absence. Having had the staff sign NDAs before arriving that day, he was confident things were under control when the cleaning crew arrived as their group was about to depart.

Security had taken their positions.

"Abi, you go first," Andrew said, with his hand on the door handle. "Sir, you follow."

Burton nodded as the big guy opened the door. Escorting Abi to the SUV, she kept her head down. Quickly transferring, his face hidden from sight, the people stared at Burton on his way past, each notably curious about the new owner's identity. Andrew held the door for him and shut it the second they settled in the back seat. When he got in the front, he found the two seemed quiet as they drove down the lane.

Sad to leave, Abi turned around and took one last look. "Thank you for sharing this place with me," she whispered appreciatively.

"Sorry, it wasn't under better circumstances."

"It would have been nice to stay longer."

Wishing that, too, he thought about what awaited her back in LA. Going home meant he'd have to share her with him. "Anytime you and Shane want to get away, let me know. I'll arrange it," he said, trying to be the friend she needed.

"Appreciate that, but we... Umm, we aren't there yet."

Reading a lot into that simple statement, Burton was secretly happy to hear it. Not wanting to embarrass her, he changed the course of the conversation. "I guess football will rule his life for a while?"

"Perhaps, a lifetime."

He reached for her hand. "Anytime you need to talk, I'm here, day or night. Doesn't matter what it is, okay?"

She took hold and gave it a gentle squeeze. "I will."

It wasn't long before they maneuvered the traffic circle in Crystal Bay. Being off-season, only the locals were on the roads, and the town was fairly quiet.

He handed Abi her passport.

"Ah, yes. Thank you. Still can't believe you were able to get this so quickly."

He shrugged his shoulders. "Remember, the bureau has its perks?"

"Duly noted."

Driving through the northern reaches of Lake Tahoe, they arrived at Truckee airport and pulled up alongside Burton's plane. The team stopped the vehicles and got out to check everything before transferring.

Given the all-clear, Andrew opened Burton's door while Abi slid to his side and got out. Both ascended the stairs and found their seats.

"It feels like we've been gone for a week – not two days," she said, sitting across from him.

Burton saw Martin glance his way and then grab a spot near the front. "Yes, you're right," he said. "But I could've used a few extra days."

"I'm sure you'll return soon enough. How could you not?"

He smiled. "Hope you're right."

Clutching his treasured knife roll, Anton handed them over to the attendant for safekeeping and sat behind them-more than ready to take a break.

One by one, Andrew, Matt, Ted, and Sara were the last on board. The guys stayed near the front with Martin, leaving Sara no choice but to sit adjacent to Burton. Glancing over at Abi, the girl eyed her up and down.

Uncomfortable, Abi figured Sara hated her. Believing her opinion of her was wrong, she wanted to set the record straight as the plane taxied away from the hangar.

Listening to the pilot conversing with air traffic control, everyone could hear a pin drop. When they reached the end of the runway, the plane turned and stopped. Engines ramping up, Burton looked out the window when they jetted down the straight stretch at high speed. Slowly lifting off the ground, the plane soared upwards towards the clouds.

Lake Tahoe was a deep blue as the sun's rays sparkled on the water. Making a loop, they leveled out and headed south.

Burton slipped his laptop from his messenger bag and set up his workstation.

The second the seat belt sign went off, Martin asked, "Master B? A word, please."

"Sure," he said to his advisor. Looking at Abi, he respectfully noted, "Excuse me a second."

She watched him walk towards the front of the plane, leaving her alone with Sara.

Once he was deep in conversation, the girl turned to her. "I remember you from Cabo."

"Yes," Abi answered. "I remember you too."

"Small world."

"Suppose so." She wondered what angle the woman would take.

"Are you still with that guy? You know, the tall, handsome one who ran after you?"

Shooting her a look, Abi assumed she was fishing for information. "Possibly."

Not in the mood for games, Sara rolled her eyes.

It seemed the rudeness she remembered surfaced finally. "What's your problem?" Abi asked bluntly.

The girl straightened in her chair. "Look..." her facial expression softened. "I care about him and don't want to see him get hurt. That's all."

Surprised by her sincerity, Abi took it down a notch. "I don't want to see him hurt either. He's my best friend."

"Friend?" Sara was confused. "But you were sharing pajamas this morning and holding his hand yesterday when you walked into the house."

"He and I have been friends since grade school. We were neighbors in Boston."

The relief on her face brought about a look of embarrassment. "Oh," she said.

"You thought he and I were..." Abi left the girl to fill in the blanks.

"So, you're not..."

"No."

"Sorry, I didn't realize."

"It's fine." Abi wondered why she wasn't more informed as to her situation and why they'd gone to Tahoe in the first place.

Returning to his seat, Burton could tell the girls had conversed. Not wanting to cause a problem, he opened Word on his laptop and typed on the blank page.

Is everything okay? Noticed you talking to S.

Swiveling the laptop around, he showed her.

Abi played along and read what he wrote before typing her answer.

There was a slight miscommunication, but we're good now.

She flipped it back, feeling like she was in grade school.

Finding out that things between them were cop esthetic, Burton relaxed a bit.

For the rest of the trip, he focused on creating new music tracks for his Vegas set. Out of the blue, he handed Abi his headset. "What do you think of this?" he asked, wanting her opinion.

Abi slipped the headphones over her ears.

He clicked the play button and watched her reaction to the track he'd created. Seeing her fingers tapping to the beat and her head bobbing rhythmically, Burton figured she liked it. A smile appeared on her face partway through when she hit the buildup and drop. He took a mental picture of her as she swayed to the beat.

"This is so good," she complimented enthusiastically. When the song finished, Abi removed the headphones. "Thank you for entrusting me with this part of your life. I'm just amazed by it all."

"Thanks. I'm glad you know. No more secrets," he said.

"No secrets," she repeated.

Catching Sara raising an eyebrow at the comment, Abi sat back in her chair and wondered if she was now a friend or foe.

Supported

Descending through the thick, cotton-like clouds, Abi watched the droplets pelt the windows, creating a mesmerizing pattern of streaks and splashes. The turbulence made the aircraft shudder slightly, but she found the rhythmic sound of the rain somewhat calming.

As they circled Van Nuys, she could see the sprawling cityscape below, a patchwork of buildings and streets blurred by the downpour. The familiar hum of the engines accompanied the landing gear, retracting, signaling their final approach. Moments later, the wheels touched down with a gentle thud, and the plane slowed to taxi to the FBO.

"It's not a very nice day," Abi said disappointingly, watching sheets of rain flowing down the glass. There were large puddles everywhere.

Burton looked across at her. "Ready to visit your Mom?"

"Yes and no. Seeing her also means seeing my Dad. Not looking forward to that."

"Don't worry. I'll be there."

She pointed at him and said, "You didn't help me yesterday."

"I promise. We will deal with him together."

"I'll hold you to it."

When the plane came to a stop, Abi noticed a line of three Escalades waiting. The second the attendant opened the door, the guys got out to secure the area.

The wind blowing sideways, Martin and Anton ran to the third truck, trying not to get wet despite those holding umbrellas over them. Sadly, the protection didn't help much.

Sara went next and got in the passenger side of the first truck.

Pouring buckets now, Burton assessed their chances of getting soaked. Flipping their hoods over their heads, he said enthusiastically, "Keep your head down. We go on three," and offered her his hand.

"Okay," she giggled, spotting Sara's dismay.

"Ready. Three!" he shouted as they ran down the steps toward the middle vehicle.

Stopping, allowing Abi to get in first, he jumped in behind her and set his bag on the floor by his feet. "Not bad, Acardi," he said, flipping his hood back.

She did the same and laughed. "Got a little wet. But that's okay."

The wind and rain increased as they passed through the airfield gates.

"Hey, Andrew. We are heading to UCLA Med before taking Abs home."

"Will do, Sir."

Unsure of his plans, she asked, "So, are you staying in Malibu tonight?"

"No, I thought I'd stay across the canyon."

She smiled, thankful he'd be watching her from afar. "So, I've been meaning to ask about your telescope?"

"What about it?"

"Well, is it the same as mine?"

"Maybe."

"Ha! I knew it!" She confirmed her suspicions.

"What?"

"You bought the same one, didn't you?" she pointed accusingly. "It's not a coincidence."

"This is true," he laughed sheepishly.

"So, have you been spying on me?"

Looking away, he replied, "No," before his eyes veered forward. "Well, that's not entirely accurate. I should've said occasionally. When I can't sleep, I check to see if your light is on."

"Interesting..."

"Just wanted to make sure you're safe. Nothing more."

She rested her head against the window.

"Tired?" he asked, offering her his shoulder, which she graciously accepted.

"Yeah, a little."

"You'll have to catch up on sleep this week and not stay out too late."

"Don't worry. I don't think I'll be out anywhere with everything going on."

"When I return on Wednesday, I'll be at the Bel Air house. Stop by any time. Just make sure you're alone. My secret stays between us."

"You can trust me."

"I know."

Pulling into UCLA Med, the team entered through the service bay. Andrew arranged for clearance. His brother-in-law worked logistics there, which helped. When they arrived on the sixth floor, Abi noticed three men sitting in chairs scattered around the halls adjacent to her Mother's room, each reading a newspaper. The second they walked by, one by one, the men left their posts and got in the elevator as if someone remotely told them to take a break.

As she approached the room, Abi noticed her Mom was in the same position, like she was a statue fastened to the bed. Scanning the area for her Father, not seeing him, she let out a sigh of relief. So did Burton.

"You go ahead in. I'll wait out here and keep watch."

"Okay," she nodded.

Sliding open the glass door and closing it behind her, she inched forward amidst the hum of a dozen machines.

"Hi, Mom," she whispered. "Sorry, I haven't visited the past couple of days." She rubbed her arm and took hold of her hand. "There are so many things going on. I wish you were here so I could share it with you and make sense of it all." Thinking of her Father, she felt increasingly guilty. "I haven't been very nice to Dad. He's mad at me. Apparently, he says, *it's a growing trend these days*. But I'm going to change all that. I'm going to be more present and supportive. This week, I will be here every day after school. I promise."

Burton kept a close eye as she talked to her Mother. Unable to hear her, he could see the sincerity on her face.

"Burton Lancaster?" A voice cut through the silence.

Recognizing it, Burton stood tall with his hands in his pockets. "Hello, Sir."

Not facing him, Dr. Acardi made his presence known and said accusingly, "So, you took my seventeen-year-old daughter to Lake Tahoe without parental consent?"

"Apologize, Sir. It was last minute." He turned to the man who had yet to make eye contact.

"My daughter tells me you were on the Nevada side?"

"That's right."

"So, you also took her out of state?"

"Sir, I..." About to tell him about the property, hoping to buffer their conversation, Burton stopped, knowing the man wouldn't be impressed.

Dr. Acardi turned to him. "You...?" he said, waiting for him to finish his sentence.

"Nothing. It won't happen again, Sir."

"Your damn right it won't." Staring at Abi, he added, "You will distance yourself from her. Do you understand?"

He replied, "I understand." Little did the man know Burton had no intention of abiding by that.

"Good."

Leaving him standing there, Dr. Acardi walked into his wife's room.

Burton watched Abi cower to her Father's stern demeanor as he lit into her. It didn't take much for his protective instincts to surface. Remembering his promise to her, he stepped through the door.

Dr. Acardi sternly pointed at him and said, "Get out."

"I'm sorry. I can't do that. I promised." Standing firm to Abi's left, he did not move.

Having him there felt like he'd tossed her a lifeline.

"She did nothing wrong, Sir. It was my fault. I take full responsibility."

Her face went pale. Witnessing Burton's strength, she said, "Dad, I love you, and yes, I've disappointed you too many times to count, but I promise as if today, things will be different."

"Why? Why should I believe you this time? Do you know how much stress I've been under, and on top of that, I don't know where my daughter is or who she's with?" He stared Burton down.

"I know. I know," she sobbed.

Willing to put himself in harm's way, Burton stepped forward and stood between Abi and him.

Upon seeing this, the man got even more angry.

"Once more, I will ask. Do you have something to tell me, Mr. Lancaster? What are your intentions with my daughter?"

Standing firm, he replied, "Abi and I are friends. Nothing more. I will always protect her and be there for her, no matter what. I've been through a rough time recently. She's supported me without question, and I'm thankful for that."

She looked up at him and smiled.

"I would never hurt her or..." Burton hesitated, "Disrespect her in any way, Sir. You have my word."

The certainty and concern in his voice diffused the man's anger slightly.

"I appreciate that." His sights moved from Burton to Abi. "But this behavior still has to stop."

"I know," she said.

Her Father's phone rang. He glanced at the screen. "They need me in emerg. I have to go." Not hugging Abi, he walked out the doors without saying goodbye.

Once he was out of sight, Abi turned to Burton. His arms were waiting. Falling into them, he held her tightly.

"Thank you for that."

"I promised I would."

"When he's stressed, he becomes someone else, and things can get heated."

"Don't worry, I understand. It's fine."

"I think I am ready to go home now."

"Alright." Burton signaled to Andrew that they were on the move.

The guy radioed the security team, and before they left, the men with the newspapers returned to their posts.

She kissed her Mother and rubbed her arm. "Bye. I love you, Mom."

Escorting Abi out of the room to the elevator, they proceeded to the service entrance again. Within seconds, the SUVs pulled up in unison. Loading up, they drove off.

Burton directed, "We're heading to Stradella now."

Thinking of Shane, Abi took out her new phone, pulled up his number, and texted him as Burton looked on.

I'm back safe and sound. Home in twenty minutes. Do you have time to talk?

Barely having pressed send, she got his response.

I'll be there.

The Confrontation

Disoriented, it felt like an eternity since she'd been in LA. Climbing the hills of Bel Air, maneuvering the narrow streets and tight corners, they soon arrived at the cliffside home.

Unable to open the gate remotely, Abi exited the vehicle when she realized she didn't have her old phone. Walking along the road past the gate, Burton got out and followed her.

"What are you doing?" he said.

"Using the utility door." She pointed at it, hoping to solve the problem. Punching the number pegs on the access panel allowed her to proceed to the side entrance. Upon doing the same thing, that door opened, making her quickly run inside to turn off the security alarm as the warning chimes sounded. Entering the password on the touchpad, she deactivated it and calmly moved toward the foyer to press the remote and open the gate.

The men drove into the courtyard and gathered around. Burton joined them to give further instructions. While standing there, a strange vehicle drove in aggressively and stopped, spraying some gravel in its wake.

Going into action, the men assembled in formation as Abi caught a glimpse of the driver.

"It's okay!" she shouted at them. "It's Shane."

The football player got out of the Jeep. With fists clenched at his sides, he was steaming at the sight of Burton. Beelining for him, Abi could see the anger in Shane's eyes.

Andrew, Ted, and Matt were ready to fight, creating a barrier between him and their boss.

"What the hell, man!" Shane shouted, trying to break the line of defense to get his hands on the guy, but security forcefully held their ground. "Why didn't you let me talk to her!"

Burton stared him down and didn't respond.

"What is he talking about?" Abi's voice cut through the confrontation.

"Did you tell her I called and texted countless times?"

Blindsided, she turned to Burton and asked, "Is that true?"

Not making a big deal of it, he responded, "Yes."

"With everything that happened Friday night, you knew he wanted to talk to me, and you never said? Why? Why would you do that?"

"When we got to Malibu, I called him to say you were safe – that I had you. That's all he needed to know," he stated calmly, without anger or ill intent. "When we got to Tahoe, I limited communications."

Shane turned to Abi. "Tahoe? What the hell were you doing there?"

"It's a long story," she replied.

The intensity flaming in Burton's eyes made her believe he did that for a good reason, but she couldn't help but feel deceived.

Still restrained by the guys, Shane struggled.

Burton commanded, "Let him go."

The football player fixed his hoodie when they released him from their grip.

"I'm gonna head out. Three's a crowd, so..." Burton gave Abi the eye as he approached. "I'm sure you two need to get reacquainted." Hugging her, staring at Shane as he did, he whispered in her ear. "Remember, I am always here day or night. Don't hesitate to call if you need me." While walking to the SUV, about to get in, at the last second, he turned to the quarterback. "Word to the wise, dude. Ditch your phone. It's compromised, and for the record, it wasn't me."

Slipping into the back seat, his big security guard closed the door.

Andrew, Ted, and Matt stayed to remain on duty.

Shane saw the expression on her face as Burton left through the gates. "Are you okay?" he asked, cautiously moving closer. "He didn't hurt you, did he?"

Disgusted by the comment, she fired back, "What? No! He would never hurt me. How could you say that? He saved me, remember?" The second the words escaped her mouth, she regretted it. Abi knew the comment hit Shane hard.

Silently nodding and lowering his head, he muttered, "Right..."

Frustrated, she took a moment to regroup. "I'm sorry. I didn't mean that."

Happy she was safe, he said, "Can we go inside and talk?"

She agreed and quietly led the way. Remembering Shane put himself in danger that night and did everything humanly possible to rescue her, she tried to be sympathetic, but the vibe between them was different, and she knew why.

Strangers

Afraid of the drastic change in her behavior, Shane got concerned and figured something was very wrong. About to close the front door behind them, Andrew stepped forward.

"Excuse me, Miss?" he said.

"Yes," Abi addressed as Shane looked on.

"We need to tour the house and the grounds to get the lay of the land."

"Sure. Make yourselves at home. Help yourself to coffee, water, or soft drinks from the kitchen – whatever you need."

Stunned by this, Shane asked, "They're staying?"

She shot him a stern look. "They're my security detail from now on."

A strange confidence emerged on Abi's face. He didn't know what to make of it. "Abs? What aren't you telling me?"

Exhausted, she stared at him angrily. "I've been through a lot. Can you just give me a minute?" Closing the door, she walked into the kitchen. Opening the fridge, she wasn't surprised to find it empty. "I might order pizza. You hungry?"

Walking on eggshells, he said, "Yeah, sure."

When Abi sat on the sofa, she pulled her new phone from her pocket and asked, "So, why are you driving that Jeep? Where's yours?"

He didn't know where to start. "I guess you didn't hear."

"Hear what?"

Wondering how he should break the news, he said, "My Jeep was a casualty of war."

Emotionless, she looked up from her screen. "What do you mean?"

A safe distance from her, he sat down and said, "After hours of searching Bel Air for you, I returned to Reggie's. In speaking with him and the fire chief, I discovered my Jeep was ground zero for the explosion."

Unable to look him in the eye, she remained cold and distant. "It was?" she said, not letting on that she knew that piece of information.

"Yeah...."

"I'm sorry to hear that."

Shane felt he could cut the air with a knife. The awkwardness between them was almost unbearable. It was like they were strangers.

"How bad was the damage to Reggie's house?" she questioned while having difficulty navigating her new phone. With a limited number of apps and some passwords missing, she fumbled with the key fob and had no choice but to open a new account to order pizza. He could see she was reaching a boiling point.

When he didn't respond to her immediately, she glanced up and found him staring straight ahead. "What?" she questioned rudely.

"You tell me."

Abi shook her head.

He cautiously moved closer. "Why did Black Lyon take you?"

"It's a long story."

A horrible thought crossed his mind. "Did he...hurt you?"

She was quick to answer. "No."

"I find it odd that Burton found you so fast."

Unable to divulge any of that, she replied, "Just luck, I guess."

"Come on, Abs. That wasn't luck, and you know it. What aren't you telling me? I'm sorry, but when it comes down to it, I don't trust your friend."

Casting doubt, what he said angered her. "Well, I trust Burton with my life."

"But not me because I didn't save you, right?"

Hating his attitude, she knew she'd sparked that behavior. The silence that ensued made her feel uncomfortable.

Worried, desperate to read her thoughts, he calmed down and stated, "When they forced you into that SUV, I felt this fit of rage. That's when I stole that guy's Porsche and went after you, not thinking of the consequences. At that point, I was willing to do anything. No matter the cost." His protectiveness shining through, he added, "I planned to cut the driver off to get you back. Trying to avoid a collision, I spun out when he swerved at me. Then, in seconds, you were gone. By the time I drove through the East Gates, you were nowhere in sight. I've never felt so helpless in my entire life. I failed you…"

It wasn't hard to see this event shook him, too. "You didn't fail me," she whispered. "I don't blame you, and I'm not angry." She stopped and looked at him sitting there, recalling the makings of that night. "Shane, you risked your life for me, and I haven't thanked you." She regrouped and made a valid attempt to reconnect. Seeing how much he cared melted her heart. "That night is a blur now," she said. "But I think we turned left at that intersection."

"We? What do you mean, we?"

Abi looked away. "Black Lyon was in the truck."

"That was the figure I saw behind the driver?"

"Yes," she nodded and lowered her head.

"You're sure he didn't hurt you?" he reiterated, his instincts heightened again.

"No. He didn't."

A lull returned.

"After I'd searched half of Bel Air, I swallowed my pride and called Burton."

"You did?"

"Yeah. I was desperate."

"What did he say?"

"He told me to hang tight - that he'd be in touch - and then hung up. Next thing I knew, he was calling me hours later saying that he'd found you and you were safe. When I asked to talk to you, he outright refused."

"I wasn't in a good place mentally. That's probably why."

"All I wanted was to hear your voice and know you were okay, and he wouldn't even give me that."

Hearing his sincerity helped ease the tension. "I'm sorry. I didn't know."

"Yeah, so you've said."

"Burton should have told me you called."

Wondering why she seemed so different, he asked, "Abs?" Hesitating, knowing she'd get mad, he said, "There is something I need to know."

"Like what?"

"Did something happen between you two?"

"Who? Burton?"

"No. You and the Black Lyon, Dark Demon, whatever he calls himself now? I know you felt indebted to him for saving you. Jade said he drove by your house, and you followed him. Then, went to find the rave house after school that day."

She was put off by what he said. "Nothing is going on between him and me or anyone else. When I went to his house, I said my piece to the cameras and left. All I wanted was to thank him for rescuing me. Afterward, there was a sense of closure. That's all I wanted."

"Yeah, but a day later, there's a huge explosion, and he happened to be in the area and forcefully took you. It's a little fishy, don't you think?"

Frustrated, she raised her voice. "He did it to protect me!"

"From what?" he prompted, hoping she was about to reveal more.

Abi didn't answer.

His mind reeled, wanting to understand the events that brought them here. "Burton called me back two hours later. So you went from Black Lyon's possession to his. How?"

"What are you saying?"

"Just tell me the truth."

Overwhelmed, tired, and taxed from the weekend, emotionally drained from her confrontation with her Father, she broke down in tears.

Seeing this, he backed off and slid in beside her, hating himself for what he had said. "Don't cry, Abs. I'm sorry."

She buried her head under his chin as he wrapped his arms around her. Comforted, she released two days' worth of emotion.

Amidst it all, he felt they needed to forget everything and start fresh.

Parting, she dried her tears with her sleeve. Unable to focus on placing the pizza order, frustrated with her phone, she tossed it aside and held her head in her hands.

"Don't worry. I've got it," Shane said, quickly pulling his device from his pocket. He placed the order and confirmed, "House number 833, right?"

"Umm, yeah."

Concentrating, he suddenly set his phone down. "There. Done."

"Thank you." She leaned back and rested her head against the sofa.

A glimmer of the old Abi shined through.

Hoping to divert the conversation from her experience, she said, "So, tell me. How are Reg and Jade? Our friends? Please tell me nobody got hurt."

"Allie got a few cuts, and so did Ming. But all in all, nobody was severely injured. There was only one casualty."

Abi turned in horror. "Who?"

"My Jeep, remember?"

"Right..."

"I'm driving a rental. I gotta buy a new ride."

She could see that saddened him.

Noticing, he elaborated, "You know, it took me almost five months to find that Jeep. It was a total custom job. Just the way I wanted it."

"Really?"

He leaned back and laughed. "Guess that sounds like a one percent problem."

"Kind of. I loved that truck, too."

Thinking more about that night, he added, "I think the worst of this is how it's affected Reggie."

"Oh no."

"His Father heard what happened from the property manager. From what I gather, he blamed Jade for the incident and forbade Reg from seeing her anymore. That's as of yesterday."

"What? She'd be crushed."

"It gets worse."

"Really?"

"He told Reg he's not attending Gilderson either. As of Monday, he's working for the company and will train under a senior advisor. Which means..."

Abi put two and two together. "No football."

"Exactly."

Thinking of her best friend, she asked, "Have you checked on Jade?"

"I haven't gotten a chance yet."

"I figured she'd call you."

Abi grabbed her device off the cushion. "I'm still figuring out how to use this stupid phone."

Shane put out his hand. "Here. Let me see it."

She handed it over.

Inspecting it, he said, "Where did you get this?"

"Burton bought it for me. It has special security features and is, apparently, encrypted. Whatever that means..."

"This is expensive. It probably ran him two or three grand."

Abi's face went blank. "You're joking?"

"No." Shane pulled out his device and looked up the brand. Showing her, he said, "See?"

"I had no idea."

"Why did he buy you one, anyway?"

"Because he analyzed mine and found it was compromised hundreds of times by an unknown IP. I'd listen to him if he says yours is compromised, too."

He sheepishly looked at his phone. "I'm sure it's fine."

She giggled. "Don't be so sure."

Looking through her device, Shane found Jade's texts and voicemails and handed it back.

Abi read and listened to each. Her friend sounded distraught and sad. Knowing how worried she'd been, she responded and said she got home safe. Hoping to hear from her, Abi waited and waited, but nothing came through.

"What's wrong?"

She turned to Shane and said, "She usually responds in record time but hasn't. I hope she knows I didn't have access until now."

"Maybe she's still upset about everything?"

Checking the time, seeing it was late, Abi knew she couldn't go and visit her. Tired, she wasn't too keen on venturing out anyway.

With eyes glued to his device, Shane said, "Did you see this?"

The headline read *Oligarch Alexei Korolev killed in a drive-by incident.*

"Yes, I heard." Thinking of what Burton said – about keeping Shane intentionally in the dark, she mumbled, "Don't believe everything you read."

"What do you mean?"

Shaking her head, she said, "Umm, nothing. Never mind." Still thinking of her friend, she stated, "I hope she talks to me tomorrow."

"Who?"

"Jade."

"Speaking of school, I have to say, it's gonna be weird."

"Why?"

"Well, like I said, Reg won't be there. Neither will Alan. Allie will probably feel lost without him. Shawn has a court hearing. We're hoping he doesn't get put in jail."

"Laney would be devastated since he was doing it to protect her."

"Exactly." He paused. "Just a very different vibe. I hear some new players are coming on board. Should be interesting."

"After Cabo, I felt all of us had gotten so close. Now, here we are, a little over a week later, and life seems to have fallen apart."

Staring her way, he said, "Guess you haven't changed after all."

"How so?"

"'Cause you're thinking of everyone else but yourself." Hearing him make the same observation Burton did, she saw him offer his hand and smile. "I missed you, you know."

"Missed you, too," she replied, trying not to think of him as a boy versus the man Burton was in comparison.

The gate notification rang through on the house line.

"That's probably the pizza," she said, picking up the receiver to talk to the delivery guy. Ted walked past the back window as she opened the gate.

About to get up and get the door, Shane held out his hand to stop her. "Don't worry. I got it."

"Thank you."

"Sure."

Reminded to install the gate app on the new device, Abi found it in-store and downloaded it. Needing the password, she went into the kitchen to grab her Father's notebook from the drawer. Entering the code, she successfully paired the gate remote with the phone.

"That looks like it worked," she whispered as all the security cameras loaded in sequence afterward. Seeing the night shift driving up, Andrew walked inside the house with Shane.

She went to the foyer. "You guys switching?" she asked the muscular guard with a six-foot-four frame.

"Yes, Miss. We will return at seven-thirty to start the day."

"Goodnight, then. I'll see you tomorrow."

"Before you go, do you want to meet them?" he asked as the other men walked over. Andrew introduced those who'd watched her from the shadows. "This is Lorenzo, Bray, Rob, and Ethan."

Abi waved timidly to them. "Nice to meet you."

Lorenzo spoke for the group. "Good to meet you after all this time."

"It feels like I've had guardian angels," she said.

Rob smiled. "Happy to help, Miss."

"It's our job to keep you safe," Ethan commented.

"Regardless, I appreciate it very much."

"That's always nice to hear," Lorenzo said humbly.

Getting down to business, Bray looked at Andrew. "We haven't been on this side of the fence, so give us the tour, gentlemen."

Before answering him, Andrew asked Abi, "If they need to get inside the house, what is the door code?"

She hesitated.

Andrew further justified his request. "If anything were to happen and we must get you out, we need access."

Seeing her concern, he offered, "If you want to speak to the boss, please do. He will confirm this for you."

Hearing that, she said, "Don't laugh, okay?"

Not understanding, Bray replied, "Sorry?"

"The code is 90210." She released a subtle giggle. "My Father was a fan of the show ages ago."

"Well, that will be easy to remember, but I suggest you change it to something less familiar."

"Alright. I'll tell him."

"Do you have any questions before we leave you?" Andrew reassured her, "Don't worry, you're in good hands."

She couldn't think of anything off the top of her head. "No. I think I'm good."

"The guys will be outside for the most part. They will make the rounds and won't enter the house at night unless there's a problem."

Unnervingly, Abi nodded as Shane looked on, holding the pizza.

Rob picked up on her change in demeanor. "Don't worry, Miss. Everything will be fine."

"I hope so," she said.

"We will see you in the morning." Andrew bid her goodnight with a raised, steady hand.

"Okay. Goodnight."

Shane put his arm around her and led Abi inside. Closing the door, they walked into the kitchen. He set the pizza on the counter.

"Are you okay?"

The guy's conversation had taken her off guard. "I suppose so."

Watching her gather plates, napkins, and drinks, he had several questions. "So, those guys will be with you twenty-four, seven?"

"Trust me – it's for good reason."

Hesitant, he said, "Will you ever tell me the truth? Because I feel there's more to it."

Recalling Burton's advice, she said word for word, "I think you should know as little as possible."

"Why?"

"Because it is more complicated than you could ever imagine."

20

Reacquainted

With a slice of pizza on her plate, Abi collapsed on the sofa. Her thoughts stole her away for the next few minutes. Thinking about what Martin said, knowing she had somehow gotten entangled in a ruthless battle that had nothing to do with her, the fear returned, making her wish Burton was there. Just as Shane was about to sit beside her, her phone rang. Looking at the screen, she saw it was her Dad. Walking out of the room to answer it, Shane waited.

"Hello?" she said wearingly.

Her Father immediately flew off the handle about Shane being at the house along with countless strange men walking the property.

"Dad! Wait!" she said, barely able to get a word in edgewise.

Twisting the cap to open his sparkling water, Shane took a sip and listened, attempting to make sense of their conversation.

Bray walked past the sliding door and peeked inside.

Abi waved to him.

"Dad, listen... Burton hired them to watch over me while you're not here." Thinking of an excuse for why, she said, "Umm, he heard there's been quite a few break-ins recently. He just wanted to make sure I was safe. It's fine." Abi raised her hand and rested it on her forehead, noticeably distraught.

Shane caught sight of her stressed expression as she listened to her Father on the other end.

"How's Mom?" The girl bit her lip and looked at the ceiling. "But, is she okay?" Shaking her head from side to side, she replied, "No, you stay with her. It's fine. Don't worry. I'll be alright." Shifting her attention to Shane, she answered, "Yes, he and I ordered pizza."

He took a bite of his while she stood in the doorway between the kitchen and living room before walking over to the sofa again.

"No, he won't be staying the night. Yes, I know the rules. Are we done here?" She rolled her eyes. "Our food is getting cold." Wishing their conversation was over, she said, "Yeah. I'll see you tomorrow. Night, Dad." Frustrated, Abi ended the call and tossed the device to her left.

"Everything alright?"

"My Mom's condition has worsened, but he says they're on top of it. Being machine-assisted comes with added challenges."

"I'm sure it does."

The reality of it hit her. Her mother's health was failing. Unable to contain her emotions, the tears flowed again, making her bury her face in her hands. It was all too much.

Shane wished he could take the pain away. "I assume he called to say he wasn't coming home tonight?"

"Umm, yeah," she replied, blotting her face with a napkin.

"Do you need me to stay?"

Hardly able to fashion a sentence, feeling a disconnect between them, she could see Shane was desperately trying to rekindle the closeness they once shared before this happened. Knowing what her Father would say, she turned to Shane and went against his wishes. "Would you?"

"Absolutely." The sincerity in his voice sounded like Burton.

Intent on keeping his distance until she let him in, they ate their pizza and turned on the television to offer a distraction. The news appeared on the screen.

Investigators are still trying to determine whether the death of known Oligarch Alexei Korolev was a random act or part of an assault planned by rivals of the powerful family, the news anchor announced.

Quickly turning the channel, Shane could see Abi was bothered by it. Not about to tackle that topic, he changed the subject. "I think we need to watch a comedy or something."

"That would help."

While he surfed through Netflix, Abi tried to restore her feelings for him, not knowing how they'd gotten sidetracked after only two days apart. She could see he cared for her. That hadn't changed. But had she?

"I'm sorry he treated you like that," she blurted.

"Who? Burton?"

"Yeah."

"I kinda expect it now."

Hearing him say that made her feel bad.

"You know, I thought he and I were on the same team. Didn't think he'd work against me. Now, I know."

While sitting there, thoughts swirled as she felt Burton did what he had to at the time. Not wanting to fuel the fire, she didn't elaborate further.

"Look, tomorrow is a new day. Maybe it will be good for you to get back to normal. I know this was traumatic."

Strangely, Abi thought the opposite but would never say it.

Watching an episode of Friends, they sat quietly.

When they'd finished dinner, he got up from the sofa and took their plates into the kitchen to load them in the dishwasher.

Amidst the silence, she watched him put away the leftovers in the fridge. About to address what was happening between them, Shane suddenly beat her to it.

"Hey, umm," he paused and glanced across the room. "Are we okay? I'm really trying here, Abs, but I feel like something's still off."

She turned to him. "I'm sorry. I'm out of sorts. It's strange to be home."

He returned to his spot on the sectional. "I get it."

"Just be patient. I need to get my bearings."

"Okay." Waiting a second, he added, "I'm not here to make things worse. I'm here to help."

She looked at him and placed her hand on his arm. "I know."

Offering a smile, he took the remote. "Want to watch a movie?"

"Sure."

He sifted through their options. Landing on a Young Adult book adaptation of a Spanish romantic drama with an English voiceover, he clicked on the trailer. "What about this?"

Halfway through the teaser, she said, "Yeah, I think I'd be up for that."

Shane pressed play as the opening credits moved across the screen, and the first scene appeared. Gathering the story's premise, he laughed, "It seems pretty close to our world."

Cuddled in beside him, she grabbed the throw blanket draped over the back of the sofa. "Yes, you might be right."

21

Tremors

Sitting in the darkness, the light from the television illuminated the room in a soft glow as Shane and Abi gravitated to the young forbidden love portrayed on the screen. An enemies-to-lovers narrative immersed in affluent circles, she thought it resembled their lives in a way.

For Abi, the four-year age gap between the characters added to the turbulent tale filled with suppressed feelings, a haunting past, and secret lives. As the story progressed, the male character's protective instincts surfaced. Both Burton and Shane had this rare trait engrained in them. Feeling safe and secure tonight, she nuzzled beside Shane, prompting him to lift his arm above her head and slip it cozily across her shoulders.

Thankful to return to where they'd left off before their horrific weekend, he pulled her close and presented his hand as she willingly took hold. His thumb caressed it as they watched the movie play out. He couldn't help but think of what Abi had endured the past forty-eight hours. Tormented, he silently vowed to be there for her no matter the cost.

Midway through the movie, the stakes increased.

Abi nervously watched as the tension between the characters suddenly escalated. As the couple professed their love, they didn't care about anyone apart from each other. Their words and actions were captivating. Never having witnessed anything so climactic, Abi's innocence and naivety appeared. Stunned by the graphic content ensuing, she looked away periodically, but her curiosity kept bringing her attention back to the screen.

Shane could tell she was flustered. It caused a surge of excitement to also course through him. Shifting slightly, clearing his throat, he kept himself in check. Able to steal a few unsuspecting glimpses without her seeing, he smiled as her cheeks turned the softest hint of pink.

As bodies collided on a beach, of all places, Abi felt there was a beauty to it—this connection where their souls melded together in the purest form. Refusing to look at Shane throughout the heart-pounding scene, she trembled so much that he could feel it.

Unknowingly running her fingers back and forth across his knee as the characters reveled in the blissful aftermath, Abi wasn't aware her touch was having such a profound effect on him.

Finding it hard to contain himself, he leaned over and cautiously brushed his cheek against hers.

With no choice but to look his way, she found the boy she loved as their eyes met in the most intense stare.

"Do you still love me?" he asked.

Unable to deny her feelings, she said, "Of course I do."

Happy to hear her say it, his sights bounced between her pretty gaze and her lips. Anticipation building, mere millimeters away, he hovered. Heart beating only for her, hoping she'd accept his advances, their lips barely touched before she suddenly turned and rested her hand against his chest.

"No, we can't...umm..."

Confused, he watched as she looked to the corner of the room – almost scared.

Realizing her Father could have eyes on them, he veered off and said, "Sorry. I forgot."

She shuffled around and moved back from him slightly.

Shane focused on the final action scene and tried his best to stay neutral after their emotional stir. But it wasn't easy. His heart pounded so hard it almost drowned out the surround sound. Longing for Abi, he knew he had to suppress those feelings, at least for now - something easier said than done.

Living through the suspenseful car chase and the couple's relationship surprisingly being exposed by their parents, Shane and Abi watched the credits roll past.

"That was good," she said. "What's your take?"

"I could watch it again," he grinned.

To their surprise, the television went black before the story continued.

"Oooh. A teaser." Abi was intrigued.

Her heightened reaction amused Shane as she sat on the edge of her seat.

Discovering the short bit left them on a cliffhanger, she exhaled. "Of course, it lures you in for part two," she said enthusiastically, finding his eyes affixed to hers.

"Yeah," he chuckled. "We should keep tabs on the sequel's release date."

"Makes me wonder what will happen next?"

Based on her body language and playful tone, Shane figured she wasn't talking about the movie anymore.

"Well, it's late. We should get some sleep," he said casually, mindful of the cameras. "We gotta leave for school a little earlier so I can swing by my place and change into uniform."

"Alright. No problem. I'll be ready." She stood up. About to fold the blanket herself, he approached and helped her. Bringing the ends together, their hands touching, bodies close, Abi took hold of it and neatly draped it across the back of the sofa.

"Feel free to use the guest room," she said.

"Thanks. Same one as before?"

"Yes."

Turning off the lights in the kitchen and checking all the windows and doors, they climbed the stairs past the wise old tree outside the window. Abi felt like it was somehow judging them.

When they arrived outside her room, she turned and calmly reached for his hands. Fingers intertwined, he scanned the hallway from left to right.

Knowing what he was searching for, she whispered, "There are only cameras on the main floor."

Hearing this snapped his attention back to her. Hesitant, he slowly took steps to lessen the distance between them. A foot inside the doorway, hands attached at waist level, he inched her toward the wall ever so slowly. Towering above her tiny frame, now dangerously close, his gaze locked onto hers, trying to read her mind. The air between them crackled.

Face to face, gradually leaning in, he paused just before their lips met, giving her a moment to escape if she wished. But she didn't. Instead, Shane saw her eyes shut and her head tilt. He took a shallow breath. His lips softly touched hers like a faint breeze, believing she might shatter like glass if he weren't careful. Not rushing, taking his time, they parted briefly. His eyes sought hers again, mindful of her limits. A faint smile played on her lips. It was subtle, barely lifting the corners of her mouth. She exhaled lightly as her cheeks turned rosy. Anxious, he relied on instinct, his heart hammering. Captivated by the intensity in her eyes, he watched Abi nervously bite her lip, a simple gesture that ignited a fire within him. Releasing her hands, he gently traced his fingertips along her neckline, finding the perfect spot behind her ears. Fingers tangled in her long locks, his thumb tenderly swept across her flawless face. Unable to contain himself any longer, firm kisses sent them swirling as the heat between them escalated. Muscles flexed, hands running down her back, his arms encircled her waist. Swiftly lifting her to his level, supporting her weight, her legs encompassed his torso, increasing their intimate embrace.

Wild tremors hit in waves, making her knot her fist in his shirt. Tugging and clinging to him, she got lost in the overwhelming euphoria. Not knowing she was capable of such a fiery response, shivers rolled down her spine. She knew flashes from the movie had stirred this fairytale moment. But, soon, reality set in. Aware of things spiraling out of control, Abi flinched.

Feeling it, Shane halted, his voice barely above a whisper. "I'm sorry..." he muttered, his expression reflecting regret as she buried her face in the hollow of his neck. "I shouldn't have..." He lowered her feet to the floor.

Flushed, she stood there, knowing they'd gotten carried away.

Angry at himself, he turned.

Abi reached up and gently placed both hands on either side of his face to bring him back to her. "I'm not sorry," she said, looking deep into his eyes. "I just don't want to move too fast. Are you mad?"

"Mad?" He shook his head. "No. I could never be mad at you for that." Giving her space, bringing things down a notch, he stole a few extra kisses and said, "I'm just gonna go and..." Mesmerized by her, unable to finish his sentence, he silently pointed to the guest room down the hall.

"I'm gonna grab a shower too."

"Right," he said, slowly recovering, knowing she understood.

Hugging Abi tight, Shane soon let go and disappeared around the corner.

Barely able to stand, she dramatically collapsed as her legs buckled. Her chest pulsating and limbs weak, she ran her fingertips across her lips. Left with her heart bursting at the seams, she couldn't help but smile as she slowly stood and walked into the bathroom. Closing the door, she switched on the faucet to warm the shower.

While staring at her reflection, thoughts of the past forty-eight hours remained fresh. Emotions running high, Abi knew her heart was in two places. What she felt for Shane strongly differed from her feelings for Burton. It seemed each had taken a piece of her. Not knowing what to do, inexperienced and confused, she acknowledged the obvious.

"You can't love them both," she muttered. "You have to choose."

22

Heavy Heart

Following her shower, she gathered yoga pants and a baggy sweatshirt from her closet. Not hearing anything from the guest room, she walked down the hall and found it empty. Only a wet towel remained draped over the bathroom door.

"Shane?" she said while peering over the railing.

"I'm down here."

Skipping down the stairs, she went to say goodnight. Upon rounding the corner into the kitchen, she saw him sitting on the sofa, scrolling through his phone. His hair was still slightly damp.

The air in the room felt heavy.

Mindful of the cameras and mic possibly surveilling them, he let his device fall to his chest and intertwined his fingers, resting his hands over it. "Hey, umm... Are you okay?" he asked uncomfortably.

"I'm fine. Why wouldn't I be?"

Unable to leave things as they did, he said, "I'm sorry about that. I don't want you to think..."

Rescuing him from having to ramble on, she interrupted. "Shane, it's okay. I promise."

"It's just..." Frustrated, he leaned forward and ran his hand through his hair, trying to find the words.

Abi remained silent as she sat beside him.

Elbows resting on his knees, he said, "Remember, on the flight from Cabo, you asked if I was attracted to you in that way."

She blushed and lowered her head. "Yes, I remember."

"Well, that will always stand true for me."

Embarrassed, she replied, "Really?"

He nodded, needing reassurance. "And you? Do you feel the same?"

"Yes," she whispered concretely. Her eyes locked on his. "More than you know."

The relief on his face was evident. It gave way to a more confident-looking Shane Coppersmith.

He hugged her, mindful of the camera invading their privacy. "So..."

"So?" she giggled.

"I think it's best if I sleep down here." He cleared his throat. "That way, I won't be..." Wondering how to describe it, he blurted out with a tilt of his head, "Tempted..."

She smirked, feeling that all too familiar flutter return.

"I also don't want to give your Dad a reason to hate me."

"I think that's wise."

"Don't worry. Everything will be fine tonight," he said as the men crisscrossed the backyard under the floodlights.

"I know."

Getting up from the sofa, he joined her and offered one last embrace before kissing her forehead. "Night, Abs. I love you."

"I love you too. Night." On her way out of the kitchen, she turned. "Shane?"

"Yeah?" he replied.

"Thank you for staying."

"No problem. I'll see you in the morning."

"Okay."

Abi ascended the stairs and walked into her room. Pulling back the covers, she turned out the lights before slipping between the sheets. About to close her eyes, she checked her phone. Seeing a text from Burton asking if she was okay, she replied *Yes, All good,* then set her alarm. When his thinking bubbles activated, another message popped up. *Good night, Abs,* it read. Seeing he hadn't asked for any details, she figured he was fishing to see if she was still angry with him. Keeping it short, she texted back, *Night, Burton.*

When she rolled over, she recalled what happened with Shane, and those feelings returned just as strongly. Erasing the pause between them, allowing things to progress naturally, she fantasized a little, drawing assumptions from what she'd seen in the movie. Unafraid, feeling safe in his arms, she wondered if they'd taken another step forward despite the weekend's setback. Reveling in the butterflies and flutters in her heart, it all seemed quite familiar. Having had the same experience the day before with Burton, she felt conflicted. Both men fit into her life in different ways, making it hard to imagine a future without either of them present. Needing her Mother to help make sense of it, she muttered, "I'll talk to her about it tomorrow." Not knowing if she would hear her at all, Abi stayed positive and believed she could.

23

Thankfully

Waking to a sunny day, Abi looked around. Disoriented, she discovered she was at home and remembered Shane was still there. Anxious to see him, she got dressed and ready for school. Walking out of her room, she found him sitting on the stairs, devouring a protein bar as the ancient tree swayed in the breeze.

Hearing her, he looked up and smiled brightly. "Hey, you. Good morning. How'd you sleep?"

"Good. How about you?"

He chuckled and lowered his head. "It was a lonely night."

"I'm sorry for that," she giggled.

"It's perfectly fine," he said, climbing the stairs and meeting her partway. I have to say, I couldn't stop thinking about you and what happened right...about..." He backed her up slightly. "Here..."

"Really?" The mischievousness in her voice caught him off guard. Suddenly, grabbing his shirt, she steadied herself and kissed his lips. Careful not to fully rekindle their moment, she said, "Guess we should go, or we're gonna be late."

"Suppose so," he said disappointingly, wishing they had more time.

Not having a choice, he followed as Abi lightly floated down the stairs and headed toward the front door. Outside, she found Andrew and the guys waiting for them.

"Good morning, Miss," they each said.

"Morning, gentlemen."

Her upbeat mood made Andrew curious. Just then, Shane walked out and closed the door behind him.

Ignoring Andrew's disapproving look, she asked, "So, how will this work? What's the plan? Do I go with you? Can I drive with Shane?"

Hearing this, the football player interrupted. "You're driving with me."

Ted looked at Andrew and waited. Technically, it was his call, not Shane's.

"That's fine, Miss. We will follow." Giving the football player the eye, Andrew instructed, "No more than a car-length buffer between us."

"Agreed," Shane said while opening the passenger side for Abi. "FYI. We are swinging by my house first."

Andrew acknowledged the request and left it at that while Abi climbed into the Jeep and got settled.

Shane swung around to the other side. Getting in behind the wheel, he started the engine. It didn't growl like his other one did.

"Do you miss it?" she asked.

"Miss what?"

"Your Jeep."

"Yeah, it's gonna be tough to replace it. I could buy a stock version and trip it out, but that would take a lot of time, not to mention cash. I've been checking around to see if something similar exists. It wouldn't be so bad if I had to make minor changes."

Leaving the house and closing the gate as the guys followed, Shane drove down Stradella before traversing Bel Air to Beverly Park Circle, adhering to the car's length between them.

His eyes ventured into the rearview mirror. "Are they going to be hovering all day?"

"Yes."

"Even in school?"

"Just call me Taizo," she laughed and rolled her eyes but knew they were there for good reason. Abi would never say it, but she was thankful

Burton had hired them. Hoping nothing would happen in the coming days, she prayed they'd come out unscathed.

Moving along Summitridge Drive, the vehicles rounded the corner and approached the south gate. Shane slowed and rolled down his window. Seeing Dan on duty this morning, he greeted, "Hey, man. Morning!"

"Morning, Shane." Spying Abi in the passenger seat beside him, he smiled.

"Just FYI, the guys behind me are security. Let them through. They're with me."

"No problem. Go ahead."

Shane waved their SUV onward as they continued into the gated community. Not long after, turning right, he maneuvered the picture-perfect enclave, reached the large wrought iron gate, and waited for it to open. Driving in, the guys followed and turned the SUV around as Shane parked close to the front door.

"Do you want to come in or stay here?"

"I can come in if you want."

"Alright. Better clear that with your goons."

"Don't worry. They'll be fine."

Shane got out. About to go to her side, Abi met him at the tailgate.

"We will only be a few minutes. He needs to change, then we'll be heading to Gilderson," Abi told Matt and Andrew.

He gave her a thumbs-up as she walked to the entrance.

When Shane opened the door, his Dad was on the way out with his briefcase on his shoulder, phone in one hand, and a coffee in the other. Well-dressed in a designer suit, he was surprised to see his son.

"Hey, Dad."

"Morning," his Father said, giving Abi the eye. "Who's this?"

"I'd like you to meet Abi Acardi - my girlfriend."

"What happened to Emile?" he so rudely replied.

Taken off guard, Shane didn't know how to respond. "Umm, yeah. Emile and I broke up a while ago."

"That's too bad," he said, ignoring the introductions. "Anyway, I spoke to your agent this morning. Just paid the guy another ten grand, by the way. After watching a few practices, he and I agree you should look for a new team."

"What? Why?"

"Well, you can't secure a D-I scholarship from a top school if you spend your senior year losing every game. From what he says, unloading you elsewhere won't be hard. Most schools are looking to stack their lineup. Lucky for you, you're in high demand."

"But, Dad..."

"Don't worry. We will handle everything. All you have to do is show up."

Before Shane could say anything, his Father's phone rang.

"Yeah, Coppersmith, here." On the way out the door, phone to his ear, he left with an evil arrogance that could light anything on fire.

As the door slammed behind him, Abi turned to Shane.

Shell-shocked, he hadn't been aware of any of this until now. Leaning forward, he gripped the banister railing, angrily shaking it back and forth like he wanted to break the bolts from the floor. After that conversation, Shane knew his decisions were no longer his own. Everything moved along faster than he could blink whenever his Father got involved.

Dumbfounded, he turned to her. "I'm so sorry about that."

"Don't apologize for his actions. It's not your fault."

"I'm glad you think so." Shane exhaled.

The day had not started on the best foot.

"Are you okay?" Abi asked, witnessing his agony.

Standing tall, his fists at his sides, he replied, "Yeah. I need to find a way to stay at Gilderson."

Thinking logically, she said, "Don't hate me, but maybe he's got a point?"

He flashed a confused look. "You can't possibly be taking his side?"

The hurt in his eyes took Abi by surprise. "The team has been play-ing well up until now. But from what you said, Alan is gone, and so is Reggie. And let's not mention Shawn's fate hanging in the balance too loud since that might disrupt the universe and send it spiraling." She paused. "How can the team win and stay on top without – the team."

"Rumor has it that Coach is bringing on some new players. Maybe we'll be okay."

Abi hoped he was right. "Shane, you should do whatever advances your career, even if that means transferring schools. Don't worry about me." She walked up to him. "I can always transfer too, you know." Looking at her phone, seeing the time, she tapped him on the shoulder. "It's getting late. You gotta get changed."

He broke from his daze. "Yeah..."

They ascended the marble stone staircase and walked down the empty corridor to his room. Seeing him enter his closet, he took off his sweatshirt and pants. Hearing clothes flinging off hangers and drawers slamming systematically, he soon walked out dressed in uniform before dipping into the bathroom to brush his teeth with his tie draped around his neck. Abi could see his reflection in the mirror as he ran his hand through his hair before rushing across the room to grab his gym bag. Unplugging his laptop, he stashed it in his backpack and zippered it shut.

"Okay. Let's go," he said.

Descending the staircase and heading outside, Shane was quiet.

Abi gave Andrew a thumbs up, which he acknowledged.

Settled in their seats, Shane started the engine. Deep in thought, he grasped her hand as they drove out the gates and headed north.

"I'm sorry he treated you like that." He pulled her hand close to his heart and held it there.

"It's fine. He doesn't know me – nor does he care to, it seems. But I'm not here for him. I am here for you."

Recalling the embarrassing moment, he said, "He blindsided me. I didn't even stand up for you. Don't know what to say."

"He's the adult. You shouldn't apologize for him. It's not your fault that he's the way he is."

"I know...but..."

"No buts. From what I see, no offense, but your Dad isn't even half the man you are."

Hearing this, Shane leaned over. Waiting for her to kiss him as he kept his eye on the road, she soon granted it.

"How did I get so lucky?" he asked.

"I don't know. I think your luck changed when you decided to walk up the beach with this girl nicknamed New England."

"It certainly did," he smiled. "Thankfully."

24

Back to Reality

Fighting traffic, moving slowly across Mulholland Drive, they soon skirted down north Sepulveda. Whipping south, Abi's security tight behind, they ducked under the 405 overpass to enter the school's gate. A straight shot from there, the SUVs climbed the hill and arrived at the main building.

The closer they got to the parking attendant booth, Abi kept an eye out for Gerald. Sadly, upon rounding the corner, she saw another strange man had taken his place.

"I need to find out what happened to him. I'm worried. Something's wrong."

"Maybe we should drop by the office and ask." Seeing the time on the dash, he said, "But that might have to wait until lunch."

"Yeah, we're cutting it close today."

Shane slowed down and pulled into the garage. Abi looked in the rearview mirror, believing the guys might have trouble getting through. Seeing Andrew flash a pass to the man at the gatehouse, he quickly waved them in.

"They've thought of everything," she whispered.

"What's that?" Shane hadn't fully heard her.

"Oh, nothing."

He backed into his parking spot while her security found the guest aisle.

Gathering their things, they got out and met at the front of the Jeep.

Matt stayed behind after dropping off the two men. Both acted quickly, scouring their surroundings and taking their positions before Abi and Shane started moving.

Walking to the elevator, keeping a ten-foot buffer with their client, Shane glanced over his shoulder and then at Abi. "This is going to take some getting used to."

"I think so, too."

The ride to the top floor was a quiet one. No one said a word.

As the doors parted, Shane had Abi exit first. He followed along with their shadows.

Anxiety building, unsure what their friends would say about her strange disappearance, she bit her lip and clenched Shane's hand tighter than usual.

He could tell she was nervous. "Everyone will be glad to see you."

She lowered her head. "I know," despite having doubts.

Laney and Allie were the first to rush in her direction. Their hasty presence sparked Andrew and Ted to go on high alert. Swiftly creating a wall around their client, they stopped the girls from making contact.

Shane stepped in to ward them off. "Whoa! Whoa!" he said, arms out to buffer the situation as Andrew and Ted stood there awaiting instructions.

Shocked, Laney rested her hands on her hips. With an immense attitude, she said, "What the hell? Since when do you have hardware?"

"Hardware?" Abi questioned before realizing what she meant. Putting up her hand to stop the men, she said, "It's okay. They're my friends."

The two girls eyed the dudes up and down disapprovingly.

"So, these goons really belong to you?" Allie wanted clarification.

"Yes," she said, introducing them. "Meet Andrew and Ted."

"Hey." Allie flirtatiously flipped her hair. "Nice to meet you."

Andrew answered in a deep voice, "Likewise."

Hesitantly hugging Abi, not wanting to get jumped, Allie clung to her neck. "I'm so happy you're alright. We were so worried. All we heard was Black Lyon kidnapped you. Then, nothing. Not one update. Right, Laney?"

"Yeah. Crickets."

"Look, it's a long story. Everything is okay now. I just want to move on."

"So, how much did your Dad pay?" Allie asked, ignoring her, overly curious about the outcome.

"Pay? For what?"

"The ransom, of course?" Laney intervened.

Abi laughed. "There was no ransom. Black Lyon was protecting me. He brought me back once the danger passed." She wasn't about to explain the exorbitant fee Burton had to fork out to guarantee her life.

Upon hearing this, Shane felt slighted. *Hadn't I tried to do the same?* He thought.

Seeing his dismay, she signaled to Allie, giving her the eye. "I'd rather not talk about it anymore."

The girl followed Abi's line of sight. Glimpsing at Shane, catching her drift, she replied, "No problem. We understand." Elbowing the blonde bombshell to her left, Laney, too, got the hint.

Wanting to sway away from anything Black Lyon-related, Abi changed the subject, knowing the two were without their boyfriends that day. "I heard about Shawn and Alan."

Laney addressed it first: "Yeah, you're not the only one who's suffered through a tough weekend."

"You're not kidding." Allie sadly agreed.

With a sympathetic tone, Abi replied, "I know. I'm sorry."

Trying to put on a brave face, hoping to survive Shawn's legal issues, she replied, "Yeah, thanks. We will see what happens."

"Have either of you seen Jade this morning?"

The girls looked at each other.

It made Abi concerned.

Allie reacted and said, "About that..."

"Did you not hear?" Laney's face went stoic.

"Hear what?" Abi questioned, bracing for bad news.

"Oh, Abs... Jade got dumped," the girl said as her long blonde hair blew in the breeze.

Stunned by this, Abi found Shane on his phone, not paying attention to their conversation. "Is this true?"

The football player didn't know what to say.

"Poor Jade has been at home wallowing. Didn't she call you? I thought you'd be the first to know," Allie assumed.

"Umm, no. I lost my phone. Just got a new one yesterday." Abi's heart ached for her friend.

Curious, Allie got a weird vibe and wanted to put a rumor to rest before the day started. "So...umm. Is it true?" she whispered, "Did you spend the night at Black Lyon's house?"

Angered by this, Shane interrupted, "Come on, Abs. We need to get to class." He'd heard enough.

Moving along, the girls walked ahead of them to the main building - her shadows close behind.

Realizing Abi had not told her friends the entire story, mainly the part about Burton's involvement, Shane hesitated.

"I know what you are gonna say. Please don't. I didn't want to share anything more and have to explain further..."

"Fair enough."

25

Challenged

Reaching the staircase, Allie and Laney noticed a commotion up ahead. Girls were ooohing and awwing over a group of unfamiliar faces standing together, each relatively easy on the eyes. Tall, handsome, and well-built, they were very accepting of all the attention and seemed to expect it. One, in particular, gravitated to Abi on her way by. Shane noticed right away. Shutting it down, he let go of her hand and wrapped his arm tightly around her instead to signify she was his.

The dreamy athlete with dark hair smirked, arrogantly willing to challenge Shane if that was how it needed to be.

Amidst it all, both Laney and Allie appeared on the new boys' radar.

Knowing Abi was off limits, the guy refocused on the pretty blonde and shot her a suggestive smile.

Flattered, accustomed to having that effect, she confidently strutted past with her head held high before saying under her breath, "My gut says he's a conceited jerk."

Allie giggled because she thought the same.

Watching the new students decipher that their small group was where they needed to be, like a crowd of sheep, they followed them down the hallway, clambering for a spot in the school's hierarchy. But Andrew and Ted had other plans. The men kept a buffer between them and Abi. By association, her friends enjoyed the same perk.

"Having your security around might not be so bad," Shane whispered to her.

Suddenly, the tall, confident new football player out-maneuvered security and got ahead of their group. Turning and walking backward, he asked, "Hey? Aren't you Shane Coppersmith?"

Not stopping, Shane replied, "Maybe. Why?"

He stuck out his hand to introduce himself. "Nice to meet ya. I'm Owen Karp, the new QB."

"Is that right?" Shane wasn't impressed by the bold move.

Not getting the reaction he wanted, Owen taunted, "Yeah, I guess they needed someone fresh to carry the team this season."

Shane laughed. "Dude, at this point, with that attitude, the only thing you'll be carrying is the legacy I'll be leavin' behind when I graduate. Nothing more."

Owen stopped.

As they walked by, he looked stunned by the cleverly crafted comeback.

Amidst it all, he noticed everyone watching, knowing they'd heard what the legendary team captain said. To save face, he shouted down the hall, "Well, we'll see about that!"

Immediately, Shane swung around. Facing the guy, he noticed everyone fell silent instantly, expecting a fight to break out.

Abi pulled on his arm, not sure what was happening.

"Alright, hot shot. If you think you can lead this team, tell me your strategy for defeating Palisades this week?"

Put on the spot, not having reviewed the playbook given to him, the guy stuttered and stammered. "Umm, I, aahhh..."

"How about Chaffey? Campbell Hall? Oak Park?"

The young football player stayed silent.

"Anything? We're waiting to hear your words of wisdom."

Unable to give up a single answer, Owen seemingly conceded.

Arms crossed over his chest, with muscles bulging, Shane challenged, "Winning requires discipline and skill. It changes with every opponent we face. We need to know what every player is doing, and our passes and handoffs must be timed and accurate. There's little room for error. We touch the ball on every play. We move based on split-second decisions. That's our responsibility. Our job is to understand the strengths and weaknesses of each opposing player on the line and lead our team into battle and win. Are you prepared to do that?" Shane stood his ground. Giving the guy ample time to respond, not hearing a rebuttal, he said, "I didn't think so."

Leaving it at that, they kept walking.

Abi was proud of how Shane constructively handled the situation. He could have acted in the same immature way, but he didn't. He rose above it.

Continuing to class, Abi looked up at him and smiled.

"What?" he grinned.

"Nothing. Just proud of you."

He leaned over and whispered in her ear, "And I love you for that." His arm tightened, almost squishing her, making Abi giggle as they playfully walked down the hall.

Thinking about the confrontation, he said, "Gotta say, having confidence is one thing, but that guy is kind of an arrogant prick. Practice this afternoon will be interesting," he sighed.

Overhearing, Laney elbowed Allie. They'd called that way beforehand.

Used to giving people the benefit of the doubt and not judging them too harshly right out of the gate, Abi said, "He's just testing the waters to find his place—but before you say anything, there is a right way and a wrong way. Sadly, he chose the latter."

Shane agreed. "Exactly."

26

The Disruptor

Their group arrived outside the classroom at the same time as Professor Walker. Shane stopped at the door and prompted Abi to enter first, followed by their teacher.

"Thank you, Mr. Coppersmith," the gentleman greeted.

"No problem, Sir," the QB said as another new student waltzed in behind them, followed by a huge, wide-shouldered dude. Based on the guy's size, Shane hoped he was his new offensive guard or tackle.

Witnessing the stir caused by the new students, Professor Walker tried to calm the class. "Alright, everyone, take your seats before announcements." He plopped a textbook on the one guy's desk and said, "Welcome to grade twelve Finance and Business Analytics. We are a couple of weeks into the semester. I'm available during study hall if you need help grasping the concepts. Otherwise, you can visit the guidance area and arrange a tutor."

The vain teen sat there and replied smugly, "No, I'm good."

Professor Walker was surprised. It didn't take long to understand what was happening. "Good to know, Mr..."

"Cafaro."

Referring to the revised class list, he read the boy's full name. "Oh yes, here you are. Marco Anthony Enzo Cafaro, I expect you will be ready for Thursday's quiz on Unit Two."

Marco disrespectfully scoffed.

The teacher stared him down. "Do we have a problem, young man?"

"No, Sir."

"Good." About to walk away, he assumed the boy did something to garner attention as a hum spread across the room.

Not turning around on his way to the front, the Professor tactfully said, "And, oh, by the way, no matter how much money your family has, your spot on Varsity depends on an average of seventy-five percent or greater. Dip below that expectation, and I'll make sure you warm the bench all season."

The class immediately erupted, sparking Marco to concoct another jab.

Handing the big guy a textbook, referring to the class list again, their Professor addressed, "Welcome, Mr. MacMillan, I presume."

"Yes, Sir."

"Appreciate the manners." Overhearing some snide comments from the peanut gallery, the Professor clarified, "Contrary to your statement, Mr. Cafaro, I don't accept bribes. So good luck to you."

Clearly winning this round, the lesson got underway. They reviewed the concepts inside the unit two study guide for the next hour. Abi paid close attention, knowing Shane seemed lost on a few things. She figured she'd spend most of study hall helping him prepare for the test.

When the bell sounded, a few girls in the class flirtatiously jockeyed for position, hoping to walk alongside Gilderson's newest grade twelves.

Abi watched as the beyond disrespectful Marco seemed used to having groupies hanging off him since he looked too comfortable, while Ben, on the other hand, was a quiet, gentle giant.

Adjacent to the science wing, the hallways were abuzz with playful whispers as the new jocks moved through rotation, causing a wave of disruption in the social order. With Andrew leading and Ted following close behind, they did not deter Marco from attempting to get to the team Captain more than once.

Shane leaned over and quietly said to Abi, "Gotta hand it to the guy. If nothing else, he's persistent."

"I think you're right."

Marco suddenly cut through Abi's security. "Hey, man," he said from inside their inner circle before Ted and Andrew ousted him again.

Not impressed by the guy's behavior in class, Shane kept walking after witnessing how rudely he addressed their Professor.

Catching up, Marco shouted with an enormous attitude, "Hey! I'm talking to you!"

The comment ticked Shane off. Immediately, needing to address it, he asked, "What's your name again?"

"Cafaro."

"Word to the wise, never talk to me like that again. Stop acting like an idiot. Respect the teachers, the students, and your teammates. No exceptions."

"Why?"

Shane walked over and stared him down. "Because I'll make sure you don't touch a football all season. The scouts won't have anything to see if you aimlessly run down the field for a pass that never comes." Without a hint of emotion, Shane returned to Abi and left him standing there. "What is wrong with these guys? Where did Coach get them from?"

Reaching the science lab, they took their seats while Abi's security proceeded to the back of the room. Following protocol, they opted not to wait in the hallway because the class had two emergency exit doors that could compromise their client.

Ben arrived at the same time as Laney and Allie and gave them the right-of-way. Appreciative of the gentlemanly gesture, seeing the guy was a little overwhelmed, Allie turned and pointed at the seating chart attached to the wall.

Boasting an intimidating presence, he kindly said, "Thanks."

On the other hand, Marco blatantly passed by and purposefully brushed his shoulder against Laney, causing her to fall off balance.

"Watch it," she said, knowing he could care less.

Abi saw him sit at the desk behind them before her friends arrived.

"Oh, this isn't gonna be good," she whispered.

Raising his feet up and lackadaisically reclining in the chair, Laney approached with her hand melded to her hip. "That's our desk," she stated quite concretely. "You need to check the seating chart."

Sleezily scanning her body from top to bottom, he said, "Well, well, well... Hello, ladies."

Hit by tremendous fear, Abi's heart dropped, and her guard went up upon hearing those words and the tone used. Panning the room, she checked for Eastwood. Proving he wasn't there didn't stop her heart from racing and causing a fight-or-flight response.

"What is it, Abs? Are you okay?" Shane noticed her hands trembling.

Discovering where the voice originated, she replied, "Nothing. I'm good," while trying to calm her nerves.

Not in the mood for drama, Laney crossed her arms, ready to shut the delinquent student down. "Move!" she shouted.

Shane overheard. Wanting to stay out of it, he soon started boiling inside.

"Why? I have lots of room here. You can both sit on my lap. I don't mind."

Allie exploded. "Knock it off! You're such an ass!"

"Maybe so, but yours is pretty fine," he said suggestively, making Allie cringe as he tried to get a better angle.

Shane slapped his hand loudly on the desk. He'd heard enough. "That's it!" Turning around, standing tall, he said, "Apologize to her!"

Marco was surprised by the QB's reaction. "Wow, the famous Shane Coppersmith is speaking to me! I've heard a lot of stories about you, man."

Anger in his eyes, he said sternly, "I said apologize!"

Abi held her breath and joined Allie as she slowly backed away.

"Get up!" Shane firmly said as Laney stood there waiting.

Spitefully grabbing her by the waist, Marco pulled the girl closer. "No, I'm good right here."

Shane saw red while the girl tried to escape the unwanted advances. In a blink, he grabbed the guy by the scruff of his neck and swung his fist. The smack and thud were instantaneous as he quickly leveled Marco to the floor, making the class erupt.

"And MacGregor has him on the mat, ladies and gents!" a boy commentated humorously.

The class applauded.

Abi's goons approached, ready to intervene if things got out of hand. But they could see Shane had it under control.

"Are you okay?" Shane asked Laney.

Shaken, still in shock, never mistreated like that before, she said, "Yeah, umm, suppose so. Thank you."

"No problem."

"Mr. Coppersmith! What is the meaning of this!" Professor Grady shouted upon arrival, seeing Shane hovering over Marco, stunned by the blow to the head. Dropping his satchel on the desk loudly, he trudged down the aisle.

Prepared to deal with the repercussions, Shane turned to their teacher.

Laney immediately stepped between them and diverted the man's attention. "Don't be mad at Shane, Sir. He was defending me." Pointing to Marco, she added, "This guy touched me inappropriately. Shane rescued me."

The man was stunned. Turning to the QB, he asked, "Is this true?"
Shane nodded. "Yes, Sir."

"Very well. Have a seat!" Focusing his attention on Marco Cafaro as the boy picked himself up off the floor, he said, "It seems your reputation precedes our introductions, young man!"

Holding his head, he said, "Oh, yeah? How's that?"

Professor Grady projected his voice as he usually did. "It's only mid-morning, and I've already received two reports of your unruly presence in our school! Word to the wise, Mr. Cafaro! My level of sarcasm strictly depends on your level of stupidity!"

"Ooh, burn," someone whispered under their breath as the class burst into laughter after the Professor's unforgiving response.

"Why is the guy yelling so loud?" Marco mumbled to himself.

Without missing a beat, their Professor returned to the front. Not finished with the new student, he turned to him and said, "Now, since it is obvious you will need extra help in my class, given your grade eleven science average, I'm placing you right under my nose!" Pointing to the lab desk closest to the whiteboard, the man in the lab coat and glasses stared him down. "Now! Sit!"

Marco sheepishly did what he said.

Grabbing a textbook, he walked over to Ben, sitting in his assigned seat conveniently beside Ming. She had transferred into the class after discovering she needed it to graduate.

Giving Ben the book, he greeted the young man, "Welcome to Environmental Systems and Societal Management, Mr. MacMillan!"

"Thank you, Sir," Ben replied as Ming looked on pleasantly.

"Happy to see you haven't picked up Mr. Cafaro's bad habits!"

"No, I haven't, Sir," he smiled, knowing the wide receiver's actions made him look like an angel.

27

Bad News

Despite the explosive start to the class, the rest was fairly uneventful. When the bell sounded, Shane got up and ushered Abi into the hallway as her shadows took their positions. He could see word had gotten around quickly. The constant banter echoing through the halls centered around Shane and Marco's altercation. Notably, their Captain's triumph.

Adrian turned the corner about a foot apart from Mei and stopped Shane.

"So, rumor has it you laid a haymaker on the new guy? Sorry, I missed it," he chuckled to his friend.

"Yeah, don't remind me."

With impeccable timing, Marco walked by with a two-inch goose protruding from his temple and cheek.

"Sadly, some learn the easy way, and some, well..." Adrian grinned.

Continuing down the corridor, Shane said, "Man, we are in trouble if these new players don't get with the program."

"Yeah, you're not kidding."

At the art studio, Shane took Abi aside. "I'll see you at lunch. Sure you'll be okay?"

She put on a brave face. "Don't worry. I'll be fine. The guys are never far."

"Alright." Kissing her, he hung onto her hand until he had to let go at the last second.

Watching him walk away, she waved while he stopped to wait for Adrian, who seemingly had his hands full with Mei. Something was definitely wrong. There was trouble in paradise.

When Abi walked inside, she found a seat. Allie and Laney were already there, and both looked pretty down.

"Hey, girls," she greeted, keeping it light.

Each offered a subtle wave when they looked up from their screens.

A tear drifted down Allie's face.

"What's wrong?" Abi asked.

She swept it away with her fingertips and looked up to stop more from falling. "I just got a text from Alan. He's miserable at the new school. They are treating him like an outsider. Oh my gosh..." Her heart ached.

"Be strong for him. He needs that right now."

"Yeah," she nodded. "I'll try. But that won't be easy."

"I know," Abi sympathized while opening her laptop.

Without warning, Mei stomped into the studio ahead of Ming. The girls were both pouting.

"What on earth?" she said aloud, wondering what was wrong.

Each took a seat opposite the other. Nobody said a word.

Amidst it all, Abi happened to catch Emile Raven's name mentioned at the table behind them. That was one face she hadn't seen that morning.

Shiresse sounded concerned.

Caught between two conversations, Abi turned slightly to hear Shiri talk to Mandy about a message she'd received.

"I knew she was depressed - I mean, we all are at some point, right?" the girl divulged.

"Yeah, but this?" Mandy whispered to Shiri.

"We should've picked up on it," Shiresse said solemnly. "I feel awful. Luckily, the maid found her."

Hearing this, Abi whipped her head around. All three sets of eyes gravitated to her. Each glared, making her quickly face forward again just as Summer entered the room, talking with Ms. Ochefsky. The art teacher looked stressed.

"Okay, everyone. Settle down, please. Take your seats." Her voice was shaking.

You could hear a pin drop as the class went silent.

"I wanted to take a minute to address the topic of mental health. As you know, our policy here at Gilderson is to check in with everyone and remind you that we offer a safe space if you need to vent. We understand as grade twelves, you are under incredible pressure this year. Some of you are preparing for post-secondary school education, but most will move on to mentorships within your parents' companies. It's a lot of responsibility for an eighteen-year-old. That said, I want to reiterate no matter what you are going through, it is best to talk about it. Then, somehow, it doesn't seem so bad. As teachers, we will do our very best to be supportive, but that first step begins with you," she paused briefly.

Abi looked to Shiresse, Shiri, and Mandy. The girls were holding in sobs. It gave her a bad feeling.

Lowering her head, Ms. Ochefsky said, "Earlier this morning, we got word that a student tried to take their life last night. Thankfully, that student was not successful."

A hum erupted as the shock spread across the class.

"In light of this, please don't spread rumors or post on social media. From what I understand, word is getting around. This person needs our love and support more than ever right now."

Many students silently agreed with a nod of their heads.

"On that note, there will be no lesson today. Instead, this will be an independent work period. Should anyone wish to speak to me privately for any reason, I am here. Just pull me aside."

The air around the table was thick.

Then, most unexpectedly, Mei quietly mumbled under her breath, "Ming hit on Adrian."

"I did not," her sister fired back, trying to muffle her voice as everyone looked at them.

"Yes, you did. Admit it," Mei whispered, ready to explode.

Abi put her hands up between the siblings. "Whoa...Whoa." About to lash out again, Abi stopped Ming. "Wait. You need to talk this through civilly." Looking over her shoulder, she hoped the teacher wouldn't hear, or it would blow up into a kumbaya moment. Thankfully, Emile's posse had gathered around the teacher in the far corner of the room, and she was too busy comforting the girls.

While the twins whispered insults at each other, Abi tilted her head. "Come on. I'm sure you can work this out. Maybe it's just a misunderstanding?"

Mei rattled off a list of hurtful comments under her breath.

Ming began to sob. "Whatever, Mei..."

"Okay, both of you. That's enough," Abi spouted abruptly.

Her tone caught them off guard.

Laney slid her chair over to Ming to comfort her.

"So, what? You're on her side now," Mei accused. "It happens every time, you know. She cries at the drop of a hat to gain sympathy, and everyone gathers around her. Even Mom and Dad. They always take her side."

"Whatever, Mei," her twin sister rebutted, sniffling.

"Tell everyone the truth, Ming. Go ahead. Tell them you kissed Adrian."

Surprised, Laney, Allie, and Summer simultaneously turned to the girl.

"What?" Allie said, zeroing in.

The sister didn't deny it.

"Oh my gosh, Ming. What were you thinking?" Allie spouted.

"Wait! Wait. Hear me out. The two of them fought all day Saturday. She was mad because he shielded both of us from the explosion."

"What's wrong with that?" Laney asked. "It's commendable."

"Mei didn't like that he had his arm around us both. He could see I was shaken and needed support, too." Her twin didn't flinch while Ming explained more. "When he came to talk to her, she wouldn't even allow him through the gates. I watched through the cameras and saw Adrian sitting on the curb alone. I just couldn't leave him there on the street, so I went out to see if he was okay."

"Yeah, well, I was watching him on the cameras, too," Mei argued snarkily.

Not looking at her, she said, "Can I finish?"

The girls looked on.

"What could you possibly have to say?" Mei's voice got louder.

"Shhh!" Allie interrupted. "Let her speak."

Feeling like she had the floor, Ming said, "The guy didn't know what he'd done wrong. In his mind, he simply saved his girlfriend and her sister from the explosion. It was a chaotic situation, and tensions were high. He said he just did what he had to and had no intention of hurting her or implying anything. I told him he was a good person, and I respected him for that – especially because he treats Mei like gold, regardless of whether she forgets to appreciate it occasionally."

Upon hearing this, Mei looked away.

"When he agreed, I said one day I hoped I'd be lucky enough to find someone half as good as he is."

Each girl sighed whimsically. It was as if they were watching a romantic movie.

Scanning the table, Mei looked at every eye gravitating to Ming's storytelling. "Girls? Hello? She kissed my boyfriend, remember?"

"I told Adrian I was tired of being the third wheel and confided in the guy, asking when was it my turn to find happiness. Being supportive, he told me I was smart, pretty, and nice to talk to and that the right guy would come along and feel lucky to have me. But he said I needed to be patient and not rush into anything because when it is meant to be - it will be. He hoped it would happen fast and compared it to when he met Mei. He said he didn't even know what hit him. He just loved her from the moment he saw her. I said that she felt the same about him. He smiled. I told him I hoped our talk helped. He nodded and referred to me as the sister he never had. I said, good, because he was the brother I always wanted. That is when I kissed his CHEEK," Ming emphasized the word, adding, "Then, I got up and said I would go inside and see if I could convince Mei to come out and talk to him."

Her sister didn't say a word.

"Oh, but wait! That's when I saw her twin bounding down the driveway, yelling at Adrian, calling him a cheater, saying she hated us both."

Speechless, the girls turned to Mei, who sat there blankly.

Being the self-proclaimed mediator, Abi whispered, "Umm, Mei? Don't you have something to say?"

There was silence.

"It seems this was a misunderstanding."

Ming interjected sarcastically. "You think?"

Abi shot the girl a disapproving look.

Hating that her sister refused to acknowledge her, she said, "Mei, unbeknownst to you, I would never come between you and Adrian. Ever. I hope you believe that."

Mei slowly nodded her head. "Maybe I overreacted."

Smiling, Abi said, "Finally. Progress. And..?"

With a roll of her eyes, Mei said, "And I'm sorry for accusing you of that."

"Finally." Ming was so relieved. "Can we get back to normal now?"

She cracked a smile, "Yeah."

The two girls got up from their chairs and hugged it out just as Ms. Ochefsky glanced over.

"Is everyone okay here?" the woman asked, believing she needed to swoop in and save the day.

Abi said, trying to ward her off, "All good here, Miss. Don't worry."

Ming whispered in Mei's ear. "Please promise that you will talk to Adrian at lunch and apologize. The poor guy has been beating himself up for three days."

"Don't worry. I will."

The girls sat around the table and refocused on their growing suspicion that Emile Raven was the girl who tried to end her life.

Somber in the thought, Abi said, "Someone once told me you never know what is happening behind closed doors."

No stranger to that, Laney agreed. "That is so true. Especially here. Everyone sees the money, fame, cars, and our place in high society families and thinks we are happy as punch. Little do they know, most of us are completely miserable."

"Should we do something to help her?" Ming suggested. "I mean..."

"Help, Emile Raven?" Mei whispered super quietly. "Have you forgotten everything she's said and done?"

"I get that," Abi replied, "But she wanted to end it. That is a desperate plea for help."

"Agreed," Laney said.

Summer thought for a second. "So, what do we do? It's not like she'll welcome us with open arms if we went to see her in the hospital."

"Exactly," Mei said.

"I think it's best not to bombard her right away. But as young women, I think we need to support each other. Perhaps let her know we are here for her and leave the ball in her court. See what happens?"

They looked at each other's reaction to Abi's suggestion.

Responding positively, she said, "I will go and see her first."

"Why?" Mei questioned. "I would think you are the last person she'd want to see right now. No offense."

"I suppose," Abi said. "But it wouldn't hurt to try."

Allie flashed a concerned expression. "I think you need to proceed with caution, Abi."

Emile's posse returned to their seats.

Eavesdropping, the girls heard them say Emile was at UCLA Med. Same as Abi's Mom.

Maybe I'll see her later today, she thought. Keeping it to herself, she purposefully didn't tell the others in case they tried to convince her otherwise.

28

The Burden

When the bell sounded, the girls left the studio and headed toward the Bistro. All the way there, Abi wondered how she would tell Shane about Emile if he hadn't heard the news already.

"Tough class, huh?" Laney said, knowing Abi was deep in thought.

"Yeah. You could say that."

Believing her to be shell-shocked still from her traumatic experience, she asked, "What's got your brain smoldering?"

"I was thinking of telling Shane about Emile, but I hope he's already heard."

"So, do you think he'll care?" Laney asked as Allie looked on.

"I assume so. He dated the girl for eighteen months. I would expect him to feel something."

The group walked into the restaurant. Shane was already there laughing and talking with Adrian.

"What's with the morbid flowers?" Laney stated, not a fan of the black-themed arrangements on every table.

Abi agreed. "Yes, not the best choice, given the Emile news today."

"You're not kidding." About to walk away, the blonde said, "I'm just gonna grab food. You coming?"

Eyes on Shane, she said, "Yeah, in a minute."

Understanding, Laney gave a thumbs up and left.

On her way over to him, Abi contemplated how she would approach the subject while she sat down. "Hey. What's got you so focused?"

He looked at her. "Just checking for updates on the showcase this weekend."

Not wanting Adrian to listen in on their conversation, like pulling off a bandaid, she said, "Umm, can we go somewhere and talk for a second?"

The expression on his face turned serious. "Sure. What's up?"

Adrian shot him a look.

Shane shrugged his shoulders, not knowing what it was about.

Signaling for him to follow, Abi stood and headed toward the gardens. Her shadows hovered nearby. Turning to them, she requested, "Andrew, I need a moment alone, please."

Both men acknowledged and gave her a little leeway.

This worried Shane.

"Come on," she prompted him.

He was right behind her. "What is it? You're kinda freakin' me out."

Amidst the winds blowing through the trees, she sat on the concrete bench.

He did the same. Leaning forward, resting his elbows on his knees, he waited to hear what she had to say.

"We got some disturbing news in art class. It has to do with Emile."

"Oh." The burden lightened. "What did she do this time?"

His reaction answered her question. "Shane, umm, Emile tried to end her life last night."

In disbelief, he didn't respond at first. Then said, "I hadn't heard."

"Ms. Ochefsky didn't fully reveal the person's identity, but Emile's friends were visibly upset as they talked about her."

"Honestly, I'm not surprised. It isn't the first time."

"It's not?" Abi was surprised by that.

"No. She's tried a few times before."

"How much is a few?"

"Three times. I was around for the last one."

Taken off guard, Abi said, "Why didn't her friends see it? Her parents? How is it that the maid found her on the floor and nobody else?"

Point blank, he replied, "She has nobody, Abs."

Her heart went out to the girl despite all the negativity between them. "Shouldn't we go visit her and offer support?"

"Are we talkin' about the same person? The one who brutally bullies and abuses people?"

"I know, but what if she acted out like that because of what's happening behind the scenes?"

Shane shook his head. "How can you help a person who isn't willing to help themself."

"She's obviously hurting. This was a cry for help. I just can't sit on the sidelines and do nothing."

"In this case, Abs, given our relationship and my history with her, I think it's best to leave it be. It could backfire otherwise and cause more harm than good, don't you agree?"

She considered what he said. "Perhaps you're right. I feel bad, though."

He was thankful for the girl she was. "Thanks for telling me. I know that must have been hard."

She sighed. "It was the right thing to do."

"Appreciate it."

Abi tapped her hand on his leg.

When Shane got up, he said, "Come on. We should get some lunch before we run out of time."

"Alright."

Rejoining their group, Abi went to grab a salad while Shane visited the pasta station. Waiting in line, he met Adrian.

"What was that about? Everything good?" his friend asked as they placed their orders.

"Abi told me about Emile. Did you hear?"

"Sorry, man. Mei just said."

"Anyway, her attempt failed. It worries me that one day she might succeed."

The guy put his hand on the QB's shoulder. "Dude, the last time, you did so much to help her, then she stabbed you in the back and blamed you for all her troubles instead of facing the truth. It wasn't right."

"I know."

The chef passed along their fresh pasta while Shane and Adrian watched the new players loudly laugh, joke, and fool around.

Adrian slid his tray along the counter. "Despite the new blood coming in, we are still the seniors on this team."

When his friend said it, Shane needed to share what his Dad said that morning. "About that. I have something to tell you."

The big guy stopped in his tracks.

"Oh, no. What?" Adrian asked.

"My Dad and Agent are peddling me to other schools."

Frustrated, Adrian knew full well what that meant. "They're looking to transfer you out?"

"They said it's in my best interest if I want to get a high-level D-1 scholarship. Can't do that without winning a championship."

Immediately, he felt responsible for Gilderson's demise. "We should have never gotten mixed up in that fight. None of this would've happened then."

"You guys were defending Laney and Shawn. You couldn't have known this would happen. Besides, we'd still be short, Reggie, regardless," Shane stated. "Look, I didn't bring it up to blame anyone. Just wanted you to hear it from me in case I get scouted elsewhere."

"Man..." Adrian was noticeably disappointed. "I was hopin' we'd finish Senior Year together."

"I know. I hope nothing materializes, but most teams are in the market for players to boost their roster."

"And you're number one."

"Yeah, unfortunately."

Prying Eyes

While waiting for Shane to return, Abi found a seat and started people-watching. Taking notice of the single black roses on every table, she thought the flowers seemed out of place compared to the seasonal fall mums featured the week before.

"What an odd choice," she mumbled before removing the lid from her salad.

Seeing the new football players gathered around with girls fawning over them, Abi made sure not to make eye contact with Marco. In the process, she spotted Ben sitting calmly amongst all the action – his focus drawn to something on the far side of the bistro. Following his line of sight, she found Ming alone at a table while her sister, Mei, anxiously awaited her boyfriend. When she saw him, Mei waved Adrian over with a pleasant smile, ready to apologize to the boy for her actions.

"Well, hopefully, they clear the air and get back on track," Abi mumbled as Shane set a full plate of pasta with grilled chicken on the table.

"What's caught your attention?" he asked curiously, sitting beside her.

Excited to share, she leaned against his shoulder and pointed, "Okay, don't make it too obvious, but I think the new guy, Ben, may like Ming."

Pretending to look around aimlessly, he noticed the guy's sights on her friend. "Yeah, I think you're right," he chuckled. "Lucky for her, that guy might be the only decent one in the whole group."

Abi watched the gentle giant hesitate twice before getting up and moving in Ming's direction. "Oh, boy! Here we go…"

With anticipation building, she revealed the play-by-play. "He's going in, ladies and gentlemen. Will he succeed, or will he be shot down in flames?"

Ben stopped in front of the pretty girl.

Abi held her breath. Assuming he'd asked permission to have a seat, she saw Ming's face brighten before the girl nodded and said, "Yes."

Straddling the bench opposite her, it was the first time they'd seen a smile on the big guy's face all morning. Until now, he seemed like the more strong, silent type.

"Good for her. After all the drama this morning, this is good."

"What drama?" Shane asked.

Right then, Abi caught Marco staring. Eyes affixed to her body, not veering away, he scanned her from top to bottom intrusively, leaving her feeling violated. Fidgeting uncomfortably, she changed positions.

Noticing this, Shane scoured the restaurant and found the guy smirking at him, knowing he'd sparked a reaction. Getting up, he planned to confront him for the second time today.

Abi quickly grabbed his forearm. "No, don't start a fight. Please. It's fine."

"It's not fine, Abs."

"Please sit. Don't cause a scene," she pleaded.

He thought for a second. "Come on. We're leaving." Putting her food on his tray, he picked up her backpack and slung it on his shoulder with his. Tray in one hand, he offered her the other.

Grabbing hold, she asked, "Where are we going?"

"The roof."

Abi walked alongside him, thankful he was so protective. The guys followed at a safe distance.

When they reached the rooftop, he set their tray on the stone table with their backpacks on a nearby bench.

Offering open arms, he asked, "You okay?"

Safe from Cafaro's prying eyes, she nodded.

He held her tightly. Waving Andrew over, the big security guard approached.

Not saying a word, he stood there waiting for Shane to say something.

"Did you catch the guy staring at Abs?"

Andrew replied, "We had sights on him the whole time."

"That's Marco Cafaro. I'm not sure what his deal is. Can you keep an eye on him?"

Ted got closer as Andrew said, "Will do."

"Thanks."

"No problem." The muscular man stepped a few yards away to give them privacy. Ted followed suit.

Shane offered Abi a seat. "With that said, let's finish lunch."

30

Real-Time

The sun was shining upon them brightly when they left the rooftop. Walking through the bistro with the tray in hand, Shane returned it to the stack, glad the team had cleared out.

With perfect timing, the chimes echoed through the buildings.

"We'd better get moving," she said to him. "We don't want to be late."

As she climbed the stone staircase toward the library's main entrance, Abi saw Shane scan their surroundings. It put her on edge, but she knew the guys were there if problems arose. Recalling Marco's words and tone, similar to Eastwood's, a shiver rolled down her spine. It made her cling tightly to Shane, reaching to wrap both arms around his waist. She was glad things between them were back to normal.

In line to enter the library doors, Abi overheard a few girls talking nearby. Each was checking their phones with urgency. The name Dark Demon surfaced out of the blue. It caught her attention. Looking at Shane, she wondered if he'd heard them. Reading the girl's facial expressions, feeling their level of alarm, Abi took a deep breath as her heart sank. Had something happened to Burton? She was desperate to know. Mindful of Shane's proximity, she thought up a plan.

Her body vibrated with nervous energy as she swiped her card through the turnstile reader before they headed upstairs to their quiet cubicle on the third floor.

Without a soul around, Shane pulled out her chair.

"Thank you," she said, placing her backpack on it. Discreetly stuffing her phone in her jacket pocket, she added, "I'll be right back."

"Sure. No problem."

While she moved across the library, she noticed Andrew and Ted were on her tail.

I won't have much time, she thought to herself. *If I take too long, they'll probably come in after me.*

Ducking into the washroom, she quickly found an empty stall and pulled her phone from her pocket. Abi typed the words Dark Demon into the social media search bar and found multiple posts from tabloid news outlets. At the top of the feed were pictures of Burton disembarking from his private jet at Opa Locka Executive Airport in Miami. But he wasn't alone. Relieved to see he was safe, she clicked on a video and turned down the volume to one dot. As she watched him walk to the SUVs waiting, she tried to magnify the pretty blonde woman on his arm.

"Who is that?" she whispered. "Is it Sara?"

With dark sunglasses shielding her face, the tall, slender woman with sleek, long hair dressed in designer clothes and red-soled heels looked very high-class.

"It can't be her. She's way too thin," Abi figured, recalling Sara's athletic build.

Surprised by the number of pictures and posts, she was totally unaware of Burton's popularity and the fan's obsession since the rebranding announcement on Friday. Below in the comments, many praised and complimented him on his music, while others remained immersed in a war of words, upset to see him with someone in that capacity.

While flipping through several posts, searching for updates, she saw one picture of the two getting into the SUV parked beside the jet. Burton held the woman's hand in a gentlemanly way while she got into her seat.

"Huh? I guess he does that for every girl. Just not me."

One news outlet used that picture to hype the upcoming Nightfall Club opening on Ocean Drive. Other tabloids speculated on the scenes unfolding in real time. Only minutes old, his juicy, detailed arrival had sparked over fifty thousand views thus far.

Checking the time, realizing she'd been gone too long, Abi refreshed the page again but saw nothing new. Assuming additional pics would surface as the day went on, she turned her phone off and slipped it into her pocket to wash her hands. When she glanced up at her reflection in the mirror, for some reason, her heart hurt, and she wanted to cry.

"What are you doing?" she muttered faintly, "Stop this. You're with Shane. Burton can do what he pleases. It's not your business." Abi took a deep breath, huffed, and composed herself. "Okay," she said sternly upon exhaling. "That's enough. Let's go."

Exiting, she found Andrew waiting a few feet away. He acknowledged her but said nothing.

Ted had eagle eyes on her as she walked back to Shane.

About to have a seat, she moved her backpack and took out her laptop.

Shane immediately glanced over. "Everything okay?" he asked.

"Yeah. I'm good."

Not wanting to embarrass her, he nodded and returned to his homework.

While booting her computer and settling in, she started on their math. Concentrating on the questions was difficult, with visions of that woman flashing through her mind. Sneakily peering to her left, she found Shane entirely focused on his work as her intense curiosity prompted her to open a web browsing window. Minimizing it, she dragged the box to the top left-hand side of the screen. Pretending to be answering questions, she continuously refreshed the small window, compelled to find any information about Burton and the mystery girl. But after ten minutes, there was still nothing new. The suspense of it all was killing her. That is when she spotted Andrew and Ted's reflection on her screen. Standing behind her, she knew they saw what she was doing.

Shane happened to turn her way. "Abs?"

Startled, she replied, "Yes."

"What did you get for number seven?"

Just as Abi minimized the browser to return to her homework page, Shane leaned back in his chair. It was a close call.

"Let me see what you got, and we'll work through it together," she suggested.

Doing that, Shane watched his girlfriend handily solve the equation and confirm her answer. In the process, he discovered two small mistakes he'd made in his calculations. Handing him what she'd scribbled on the paper, Abi waited until he looked away before opening the window.

Shane leaned back again.

Thankfully, her cursor was hovering over the X. Sneakily closing it this time, Abi stared at the blank math sheet before her.

He could see she hadn't answered a single question. "Okay. Spill. What's up?"

Quickly formulating an excuse, she said, "Umm, yeah. I'm just not feeling great today. I'm pretty tired."

"Given everything that's happened, I don't doubt it." He reached over and grasped hold of her hand.

Realizing what she was doing, a flood of guilt washed over her. "I'll be okay," she said sorrowfully.

"I know. I'm here if you need me."

The sincere look on his face made her feel worse. "Thank you for that."

"Absolutely."

Knowing he deserved better, she thought, *You need to stop this before he gets hurt.* But that was easier said than done. Not looking on social for updates had suddenly become an addiction she needed to control. For some reason, it was consuming her every thought.

To offer a distraction, she asked, "So? Do you have any questions you want to review?"

"Give me a few more minutes," he chuckled. "I'm a bit slower than you."

"Alright," she said before answering the first ten questions in record time, not visiting the social media pages once. That is when it hit her. Here she was, stuck in high school, finishing homework, and Burton was traveling the world, living an adult life. For a split second, she felt like the little girl next door. Trying her best to block that out, Abi decided to refocus on Shane and not think of Burton. As the hour went by, somehow, the anxiety she felt slowly lifted, but her heart still ached.

31

The Forty-Yard Line

Thankful that the end of the day had finally arrived with the sound of the chimes, Abi was exhausted. While packing her bag, she recalled how Marco repeated Eastwood's haunting words to a tee. Paranoia set in. What were the chances that the guy sounded just like him? She believed it wasn't a coincidence. Not having thought of her terrifying ordeal with the Oligarch's son in a while, memories of their run-in caused anxiety and fear to seep through her veins. Checking Andrew and Ted's proximity, she felt secure and safe, knowing they were on point. More than ready to leave, Abi took a deep breath.

"Are you good to go?" Shane asked, offering his hand to her.

She put on a brave face. "Yep."

On their way downstairs, her shadows mirroring them, Shane asked, "Want to come to practice today? It's open to spectators. It should be interesting with the new players on the field. Maybe you can give me your thoughts? I'm sure you'll be able to see if we gel or not."

"Sure, I can do that." Abi realized how challenging the next two hours would be for him. "No offense, but your work is cut out for you this afternoon. As the Captain, you've got to blend this team sooner rather than later."

He chuckled nervously. "Yeah, I know. No pressure."

She clung to his arm. "I'm sorry."

"No, you're right," he exhaled.

"Hopefully, today will be uneventful, and everyone will get along."

"I wouldn't count on it."

As they made their way to the parking garage, Shane pressed the elevator button. When the doors opened, the guys joined them.

Abi spoke up. "I'm driving with Shane to the Wasserman Center at UCLA. He's got practice."

"Very well, Miss. We'll follow you."

She nodded. "Okay."

Matt was waiting for them below when the doors parted. The two big guys secured the scene as Abi settled in the Jeep. Not observing anything threatening or unusual with her safely tucked away, Andrew and Ted joined Matt and prepared to depart.

Slipping behind the wheel, Shane asked, "Are you sure you need these goons with you twenty-four-seven?"

"Better safe than sorry, I think," she replied as he pulled out of the garage with the SUV close behind. "I can't take the chance right now."

Her comment confirmed she knew more than what she was letting on.

Intent on changing the subject, she said, "So, how are you going to deal with the team?"

He turned left on Sunset. "Not sure. Gotta think about it."

In steller Abi fashion, she offered some encouraging words. "Take the good with the bad."

Recognizing Tom Brady's quote, he smiled. "This is true."

"QBs never get a day off." She patted the top of his hand humorously.

"No," he said. "No, they don't."

"Focus on pulling the team together and merging the old with the new."

"I'll do my best," he said while passing through the UCLA gates.

"I believe in you."

Those words worked like magic. "Thanks. That means a lot."

Enjoying the sunshine, they soon entered the darkness of the parking garage before emerging on the top level. Shane found a spot near the pedestrian bridge. As the two got out, Matt stopped behind them to drop Andrew and Ted off before going to his emergency rendezvous location closer to the Wasserman entrance.

Shane locked up and slugged his bag and Abi's on his left shoulder.

"I can carry mine," she said.

"I'm sure you can," he chuckled. "But I've got it."

About to walk down the ramp, the loud sound of an exotic engine filled the air. Shane peeked over the wall, wondering if, by some miracle, Reggie had arrived. Instead, he found Marco in a red Ferrari Roma. Staring at him, the guy happened to look up before he turned into the garage. After their confrontation today, Shane was certain he'd be out for revenge and assumed the last thing Marco would ever do was fall in line.

Abi could see him thinking as they walked. "Keep your guard up, and don't back down."

"I won't. Believe me."

He opened the door for her. When They entered the lobby, they found Ben and Adrian signing in.

Meeting up with the Captain, Adrian bumped his fist. "Hey, man. How's it going?"

"So far, so good. Should be an interesting practice today. Ready?" Shane said.

"For sure. Bring it on."

Shane turned to the big guy.

"Hi, Cap," the new player said respectfully.

"You're Ben, right?"

"Yeah."

"Are you my guard or left tackle?" Shane questioned.

In a deep voice, he said, "I'm you're LT."

"Happy to hear that. Welcome to the team." He shook Ben's hand.

"Thanks," he said, shaking his. "This season, I got your back."

"Awesome. Counting on you."

Ben gave him a thumbs up.

Adrian offered to show the new guy around. Soon, the two disappeared through the glass doors.

"So, I'll see you in a bit?" Shane hugged Abi tightly and casually kissed her.

Soaking it all in, she smiled when he pulled back. "I'll be watching."

"Positive vibes," he said, letting go and walking towards the locker room door.

"Always." Waving to him as he left, Abi went on her way upstairs with Ted and Andrew. Now, technically alone, she couldn't help but think of Burton and what was happening in Miami. Taking out her phone, she refreshed her social media page and caught up on the latest.

By the time she approached the viewing deck entrance, many pictures had surfaced. Not paying attention, she didn't see Andrew suddenly reach to open the door.

"Let me get that for you, Miss."

Startled, she hid her screen but knew he must have seen it. "Umm, thank you," she said before going outside.

"No problem."

The only spectator there, Abi noticed the guys take their positions to guard the door. Free to relax and scroll through her phone, she found dozens of posts. From what she could gather, Burton and the girl had arrived at a hotel named Setai. Welcomed by management, there was a pic of him shaking the hand of a man dressed in a designer suit. Another pic showed Burton kindly introducing the girl to that man. A bit of jealousy surfaced. It was hard to see someone clinging to Burton's elbow as he rested his hand flat on his chest to escort her properly.

"What does he see in her?" she quietly mumbled.

With a seriousness on her face, Andrew took notice. So did Ted.

Slowly approaching, the second in command asked, "Anything the matter, Miss?"

Startled, she said, "Umm, no. Nothing. Everything's fine."

Given their keen interest, she figured she'd have to be more mindful not to spark anything negative. The guys were very in tune, and she was sure they wouldn't miss a beat. No matter what happened, Abi was aware they were reporting everything back to Burton.

Ted returned to his position by the door adjacent to Andrew. Eyebrows raised, both men knew something was up.

Refreshing the page again, she watched a video of Burton leaving the fancy hotel with his security team, but otherwise, he was alone. All dressed in black, his signature hood over his head to hide his face, he got in the SUV before they closed the door.

"Huh? She's not going with him? Weird."

In minutes, another post showed the ominous figure exiting that SUV along a busy street and sliding into a building seemingly under renovation.

"That must be the new club," she muttered.

At the top of the tabloid feed, read the headline – *Dark Demon steps out in Miami with a Mystery Woman.*

Determined to read further, she clicked on the link that featured several pictures of the woman and identified her as Zoe Sky, a famous social media influencer and model.

Abi pulled her up on TikTok. "Let's see what kind of person you are."

While sifting through her recent videos, she found most showcased makeup tips, designer trends, and luxury vacation spots. Zoe seemed confident but utterly self-absorbed.

"What on earth?" she muttered, perplexed by the uncharacteristic matchup.

Venturing to her Instagram page, Abi subscribed to her posts since Burton showed up on her feed multiple times that day. One picture, taken a few hours ago, showed Burton sitting by the window on his plane with his head and face covered. The caption read – *Miami Bound with My Demon.*

"Huh?" Abi took offense. "He's not your Demon." Thinking more about it, she said, "Or is he?"

She let the phone fall onto her lap. Looking out on the field, she recalled their kiss in Tahoe.

"How can you go from that to this in a matter of days?" The pain and rejection in her heart returned. Beating herself up, she whispered, "You're the one who gave him up, remember?"

Not wanting to see the girl's face anymore, she went back to search for news on Burton. At the same time, the football players flooded out onto the field for the warmup. Finding pictures of her dark hooded hero, looking past the screen to the guy she loved below, she once again felt torn.

"Why do you do this to yourself?"

Turning off the phone, she put it away. Lonely and missing Jade, she watched the guys set up for the practice before deciding to text her friend. While typing her message, she thought there was so much to say. It caused her to stop and dial her number instead. When it rang through to voicemail, she waited for the beep.

"Hey, Jade. It's me, Abi. Missed you at school today," she paused. "So much has happened since Friday. I wanted to reach out. Anyway, this is my new cell number. Lost my phone. Had to get a new one. Call me back, okay?"

Ending things, she recalled their many conversations from that very spot. Somehow, it seemed like a lifetime ago now.

Amidst her thoughts, her phone rang. Seeing the name of the caller illuminated, she smiled. "Hello?"

"Well, it's about time you called me. I was beginning to think you were dead." Jade chuckled.

"No. Not dead yet," Abi answered while Shane and the team stretched with their trainer.

"Oooh... That's not funny."

"Hey, I heard about you and..."

Jade quickly interrupted her. "Yeah, don't say his name," she whimpered. "What a mess, huh?"

"Oh, Jade. I'm sorry. What can I do?"

"Nothing. He made his choice, and it's not me."

"Well, from what I hear, it wasn't his choice at all."

"No, see. That's just it. He chose his family, money, and power."

Trying to defend Reggie, Abi said, "From what Shane says, his Dad has a strong hold on him because he's the only heir."

"Yeah, whatever...I don't care anymore." She noticeably got frustrated. "What happened to you, anyway? You're back without a scratch? How much did your Father pay?"

"Again with the ransom. Is this really a thing?"

"Of course it is. Just because nobody broadcasts it doesn't mean it doesn't exist."

"There was no ransom paid, just FYI."

Knowing her friend sounded hollow, not bright, happy, and full of energy, Abi asked, "Hey, umm, want me to drop by tonight? I can bring pasta and cannolis." She knew they were her favorite.

"No food... I've gained two pounds this weekend, and I'm devastated," Jade whined.

"Okay." Abi thought for a second. "Not even ice cream?" With complete silence on the other end, she figured they'd gotten disconnected. "Hello? Jade?"

"Well, if you want to bring ice cream, I wouldn't object."

"Done! After practice, I'm going to visit my Mom. I'll text you when I'm on my way. We will have lots of time to catch up then. Sound good?"

"Yeah. I'm looking forward to it."

"Me too. Text me your address."

"Abs?" Jade asked.

"Yes?"

"Thank you."

Abi could hear the sincerity in her voice. "You're welcome. Ciao, my friend."

"Ciao," Jade said before Abi ended the call.

Watching the new players mingling on the field, the team gathered to listen to their Coach's instructions. Aside from Ben and Marco, Shane and Adrian were the only remaining grade twelves. Seeing the guys gearing up, she watched the meddlesome Cafaro chirp at her boyfriend and glance at her on the balcony.

Out of nowhere, Shane aggressively launched at him. Boiling with adrenaline, he grabbed Marco's shirt with one hand and clenched the other into a fist. Knuckles white, he coiled back, ready to strike. His muscles rippled as the two faced off. "Watch it, man! Or I swear I'll kill you!" Shane yelled.

The stadium went silent.

Adrian went into action to try and break it up.

"Back off," Shane said to his friend, staring him down, not wanting Adrian to get unduly implicated and deal with repercussions.

Marco stood there smugly, taunting him just by sneering with contempt. Raising his hands in the air, conceding, he waited for Shane to punch him, knowing it would be grounds for suspension.

"No. Don't do it," Abi muttered, hoping he'd restrain himself.

The Coach quickly blew the whistle to gain control of the situation.

Turning away, Shane quickly let go and went to cool off.

Wondering what Marco said, Abi witnessed the Coach yank the players to the sidelines. Both withstood his wrath as he sentenced them to run laps for the next half hour.

Shane accepted the punishment willingly and turned to jog the field's perimeter. On the other hand, Cafaro complained and started storming away in defiance. Unable to dodge the Captain, the two had words.

Abi leaned forward in her chair, trying to hear their conversation at the forty-yard line. Hand gestures flying, they seemed to be having a rational discussion without combativeness. Sternly making his point, out of nowhere, Shane offered his hand to Marco respectfully as their coach looked on. With some hesitation, the disgruntled player looked at it but didn't accept the olive branch.

Believing he'd leave, Abi watched and waited. To her surprise, Marco followed Shane to talk to their coach, and they said something to the man before he acknowledged the two encouragingly.

Running the lines to serve the punishment together, a few players on the team chuckled under their breath.

When the two rounded the far corner, Abi made eye contact with Shane and subtly blew a kiss.

Bashfully lowering his head, he gave a subtle thumbs up.

"Crisis averted," she said happily before sitting back and relaxing again in the chair.

32

Stressed

When the practice ended, Abi saw a well-dressed man in a suit constantly pacing the sidelines and talking on his phone before waving Shane over.

Adrian stayed behind and waited for his friend.

Speaking to the man, it wasn't hard to see Shane looked concerned. His sights kept veering off in disgust during their conversation.

"What is going on?" she whispered. "What is he saying to him?"

As the team cleared the field, Marco looked up at Abi and smirked. She knew whatever truce they'd made earlier was obviously short-lived. To him, the game was back on.

Not falling into his trap, Abi ignored it and stood up to slip her backpack on her shoulder. Leaving the balcony, her guys tight to her, she walked down the hallway wondering what Shane would say about the practice, thinking he would ask her what she noticed from her vantage point.

When she reached the lobby, she sat on the sofa to wait for Shane. Andrew and Ted hovered on either side to cover a three-hundred-and-sixty-degree radius. There were a lot of athletes coming and going. It was a busy time of day.

Desperately trying to avoid pulling out her phone and checking Burton's whereabouts, curiosity got the best of her, and she could not resist taking a peek.

Refreshing the page on X, she found a picture of Burton with his head down, walking with a smartly dressed businessman. Inside the restaurant, Zoe Sky was waiting for them. In the video posted, the girl approached with open arms and hugged Burton before kissing him on the cheek.

"What?" she said, unaware of how loud she'd said it. Lowering her voice, she questioned, "How is that possible?"

Having seen enough, Abi put her phone away but suddenly felt it vibrate. A familiar face appeared on the screen. She answered the call and said, "Hello?"

"Hey. How's the day going so far?"

Caught off guard, she didn't know what to say. "I'm trying to return to the land of the living."

"Security working out, alright?" Burton asked.

"Yeah. I hardly notice 'em."

"That's the point. But if you need help, they're there."

"For sure." She wanted to ask him about Zoe Sky so badly, but she knew she'd look like a stalker, so she waited, hoping he'd say something instead.

"Where are you now?"

"At the Wasserman Center. Shane's practice just ended. I'm heading to the hospital shortly to visit Mom and then have to drop by Jade's before heading home."

"Busy day then?"

"Kind of. How about you?" she fished, wondering what he'd say.

"I'm in Miami. I stopped by the new club. It looks great, and the renos are on schedule."

"Club?"

"It's one of many new permanent locations opening this year, compared to the pop-up raves we've been doing. I'll send you pics later."

"That's exciting."

"Yeah. But I can't think of this project too much yet. We're launching in Vegas this weekend. I'm leaving Miami in two hours to go there and check up on things."

"Is Martin with you?"

"Yes."

"Anyone else?"

Burton paused. "Just the guys."

Abi couldn't believe he lied to her. "Hey, umm, I've gotta go." She could hear people talking to him in the background.

"Me too. You're doing okay, though?" he asked sincerely, picking up a strange vibe.

"It's been a tough day, but I'll survive."

"Glad to hear it. I will check in with you later tonight."

Hesitantly, Abi replied, "Sure. Sounds good. You go. I know you're busy. We'll chat later."

"Bye, Abs."

"Bye."

She heard voices echoing from the locker room hallway when she ended the call. Wondering if Shane was coming, she gathered her wits about her and sat up straight. Disappointed to see Marco Cafaro and Owen Karp emerge, she looked away, but they made eye contact.

Marco mischievously tapped Owen's chest with the back of his hand. "Watch this," he said, his swagger showcasing his arrogance.

Not paying them any mind, Abi hoped the two would pass her by. Instead, the troublemaker got as close as he could before Andrew and Ted stepped between them.

Staring at her, guarded by the wall of muscle, he said, "I have it on good authority that you're Coppersmith's new tart - the one Eastwood's obsessed with."

"Pardon me?" she glared. "I think you're mistaken."

"You're Acardi, right?" he clarified.

The fact he knew her last name sent her mind reeling.

"Back off!" Andrew said sternly, creating a buffer.

Marco raised his hands in the air. Seemingly, this was one of his recurring traits. "Whoa! Whoa!" he said defensively before stepping back a few feet and zeroing in on her. "Word to the wise, chickita. He won't rest until he finishes what you started."

Hearing that sent a chill down her spine, and he knew it.

Forcefully shutting him down, Ted and Andrew went on the offensive.

With a condescending eye on both bodyguards, Marco said, "You'd better keep a close eye on this one. She's marked. Just sayin'."

The men puffed their chests and made the grade twelve look small in comparison.

Owen spotted Shane walking down the hall. Hitting Marco's arm to get his attention, he said, "Hey, man. We gotta roll."

The demon spawn walked out the main doors, not saying another word.

Shane saw them ducking out of the building with the other players. Reading the stress on Abi's face, he asked, "Tell me what they said to you?"

Abi tried to recover from the interaction. "Nothing. It's fine."

Stepping out of turn, Andrew intervened. "Apparently, Eastwood's marked her. Tell me what you know about this guy."

Without hesitation, Shane said, "He and I were competing for the number one NCAA spot. I got it. He obviously didn't. Ever since then, he's had it in for me and Abi by association. He comes from a powerful family."

Acknowledging that, Andrew turned to Ted.

"You can't underestimate him," Shane added. "He's the son of an Oligarch."

Abi felt like she was no longer part of their conversation.

"We will step up security from here on out." Andrew dictated a request on his phone and sent it.

"This development changes things," Ted analyzed.

Hearing them, Shane said, "Yeah, I agree. Threats surfaced on the field today. I wanted to beat the crap out of the guy."

Intervening, Abi turned to Shane. "Maybe he wants you suspended so that Owen can take your place?"

"I'm guessing that too. Eastwood would love nothing more."

Shane took her hand as they walked out together. Turning to the guys, he said, "From now on, Cafaro doesn't get within an eyeshot of her, agreed?"

Although they didn't take orders from him, Ted replied, "I think that would be in her best interest."

"Good." The QB was happy with that.

The two men nodded.

"So, what happened between you and him anyway?" Despite witnessing it, she wanted to know the details.

"They're friends."

"He's friends with Eastwood?" Her face went white. "That explains a lot."

"He told me Korolev's not done with you yet."

"Those were his exact words?" Andrew wanted confirmation of the threat.

"Unfortunately," Shane replied.

A chill gripped Abi's heart. "When he was about to walk off the field, why did you make him stay then? It looked like you made up or something."

"Hell, no. That was just for show. We needed to impress the coach."

"Oh." She couldn't believe she'd gotten it so wrong.

"Initially, he started by threatening you. So I did the same to him. The guy backed off and said he was just the messenger. He knows what Eastwood is capable of and said he wouldn't want to be in my shoes. In a way, I guess that was a warning."

"So, you believe him?"

"To a degree."

Abi's mind swirled with uncertainty.

The guys heard what he said. Andrew stepped away and made a phone call.

Upon seeing this, Shane pulled her aside. "So now they report everything back to Burton? Is that how this works?"

Abi whispered, "It's complicated..."

"Yeah, so you've said. I still can't help but think there is more to this than you're letting on."

They stopped in the middle of the pedestrian bridge.

"You've got enough on your plate, Shane. You don't need to worry about my problems, too."

Hurt by that, he said, "I worry because I care. What are we doing together if you don't trust me."

"It's not like that."

"Then, please explain, 'cause I wanted to kill that guy today to defend you." The desperation on his face was intense.

Inching closer, he wrapped her in his arms. "I love you, but from now on, you can't keep secrets from me anymore."

"I know." She realized he deserved the truth. "Look, I should get to the hospital. Afterward, I want to check in on Jade. I promise we will talk about all of this tonight." Abi hoped it would buy her enough time to sort out her thoughts.

"Fine. I'll hold you to that."

"I promise. No more secrets."

Matt drove up to where Shane was parked. Andrew and Ted stood close with their backs to them.

Not having an ounce of privacy with his girlfriend, Shane felt smothered. Still angry, frustrated, and stressed on many levels, he abruptly raised his voice and rudely said, "Guys? A little space?"

Shocked by his outburst, Abi called him out on it. "Shane?"

"What!" Seeing the shock on her face after he said it, he quickly backtracked. Calming down, he ran his hand through his hair. "Abs, I'm sorry. I...."

She stepped away.

"Today has been a lot," he said, looking at the ground. "But that's no excuse."

At his breaking point, she'd never seen this side of him before.

"My agent paid me a visit."

"The guy in the suit?"

"Yeah. He wanted to talk about my options. Multiple schools are interested. Some are..." he paused, "...out of state. Guess my father has been pressing him for that." He felt his life spiraling out of control.

Inhaling, Abi sighed. "I thought that might happen."

"If I want to stay at Gilderson and play out my senior year here, I need Shawn cleared to play by his doctor, and I've gotta convince Alan's parents to let him return to the team. Then there's Reg..." His friend's name felt weighted as it rolled off his tongue. "Yeah, that's a whole other story."

"What are you going to do?"

Hugging her, he said, "I plan to pay them all a visit. We'll see what happens. Text me when you leave the hospital and go to Jade's house."

"Okay. I'll do that."

Resting his hands on her shoulders, he said sincerely, "I am truly sorry. I shouldn't have snapped."

"It's fine. It's been a rough day all around."

"I'll see you later, then." Leaning in, he respectfully kissed her on the cheek and handed Ted her backpack for him to toss in the truck.

Disappointed with his goodbye, expecting more from him, she said, "Hey? What are you doing? You can't leave me like that." Mischievously grabbing hold of his sweatshirt, she pulled him back.

Her forwardness surprised him. Looking down at Abi, he smiled and gazed into her blue eyes before they drifted shut.

The warmth of his lips against hers sent a tingly wave through her body, and suddenly, every worry she had melted away.

Shane awaited her approval. "Better?" he said in a sexy tone.

"Much."

"Love you."

"Love you too. Bye," she whispered as he opened the SUV door and helped her take a seat.

About to close it, he said to Andrew, "Keep her safe."

"Will do, Sir."

Giving a nod, he shut it and rested his hand on the glass as Abi did the same. Watching them leave, he waited until they rounded the corner before embarking on his list of challenging tasks.

33

Lurking

On the short drive to the hospital, Abi took the time to rest her mind. The SUV was quiet. Nobody said a word.

Needing some music to cut through the silence, she asked, "Hey, Matt?"

"Yes, Miss?"

"Can you turn on the radio? Something current?"

"Sure," he said.

Captivated by the melody drifting through the speakers, each note of the song Greedy cast its spell. Swaying with the beat, she hoped it would take her mind off the past two hours. Caught in the whirlwind of emotions, Abi couldn't shake the images of the two men who held pieces of her heart. One represented comfort and familiarity - this steady presence in her life. Memories of their recent experience tugged at her heartstrings. Yet, there was another, a newcomer, who ignited a spark inside her. His charm and passion drew her in as she discovered feelings she never knew existed. Between the two, she felt torn. Her mind clouded. Each moment spent with one only seemed to deepen her confusion. With a heavy heart, thinking about Shane, she couldn't understand why she was so upset about seeing Burton with Zoe Sky, or Sara. In a moment of clarity, it was apparent. There was only one explanation.

"I'm jealous..." she quietly muttered, surrendering to the realization.

"Pardon, Miss?" Andrew asked, having heard her say something.

Startled, she said, "Umm, nothing. Sorry, just talking to myself."

Watching Matt round the hospital block, they soon arrived at the service entrance. There, they met up with Andrew's brother-in-law, who opened the side door. Slipping by undetected, they made it to the sixth floor.

When the doors parted, they walked down the hall.

Abi found an isolation sign on her Mother's room. Inside was a nurse adjusting a clear tent around her. Unsure what was happening, she waited for the woman to exit.

When she did, Abi asked, "Excuse me?"

"Hello. How can I help you?"

Abi pointed at the sign. "Why is my Mom in isolation?"

The nurse put two and two together. "You're Abi? Dr. Acardi's daughter?"

"That's right."

"One moment, your father wanted me to page him if you arrived."

Leaving her to go and do that, Abi stood along the glass window separating her from her Mom. She looked grey. Her cheeks were color-less, and her eyes seemed a little more sunken. Hearing the nurse page Dr. Acardi to the neuro unit, she noticed the guys standing around, but the other security guards were gone.

"Where are the others, Andrew?" she whispered.

"They've been recalled, Miss."

"Why?"

"I believe that is something you should discuss with Master B."

She pulled out her phone. About to call Burton, she saw her Dad walk off the elevator.

"Abi?"

"Dad? What's happening?"

He saw the desperation on her face. "I know. I'm sorry I didn't call you, Sweetheart. It's been a hectic day here."

"What's wrong with Mom? Can I still go in and sit with her? What does this mean?"

"Calm down. One question at a time." Standing before her, he slipped his hands in his pockets and said, "Mom has an infection. Her immune system is struggling. To help her fight, I've tented her for added protection. We are limiting interaction with anything else that could weaken her further. You can go in with a mask and PPE, but you should refrain from any physical contact."

Not appreciating the cold, clinical explanation, Abi hated that she was lying there in the room alone. "Is she going to be alright?"

"We are doing everything we can. So far, she is stable, and her body is responding well to treatment, so I'm optimistic." He put his arm around her. "It's gonna be okay."

A tear drifted down her face. Wiping it away with her sleeve, she crossed her arms in front of her just as her Father got paged again.

Looking at the speaker in the ceiling, he said, "I'm sorry. I've got to go."

"I understand."

He hugged her. "I'll be here tonight."

Noticing that his bag of clothes inside the room was gone, she said, "Where are you sleeping?"

"Since I can't be in the room any longer, I am sleeping on the couch in my office. That way, if I get paged, I'm not far."

She stayed silent, knowing she would be alone again tonight.

Needing to leave, he said, "I'm sorry, honey..."

"It's fine. Go."

He tapped her shoulder and quickly walked to the elevator to press the button. Seconds later, the doors opened, and he disappeared.

The nurse returned. "Do you want to go in? I can suit you up."

"No, umm..." Abi didn't want to put her at risk. "It's okay. Maybe tomorrow."

"Sure," the pretty blonde nurse smiled. "I'll be here."

Abi nodded. "Alright…" Peering into the room, she prayed, hoping God would hear her. Inhaling, she turned to Andrew and said solemnly, "We can go."

He acknowledged with a nod.

While descending in the elevator, on their way to the main floor, Abi was reminded of something she wanted to do.

"I need to stop by patient services for a second," she told him.

"No problem, Miss."

Landing in the lobby, the men exited first. Abi looked around and found the desk. Walking over, she waited her turn in line.

Stepping forward, the woman asked, "Can I help you?"

"I'm here to see a, umm… A friend." It was odd referring to Emile as that.

"What's the name?"

"Emile Raven."

The woman typed it into the system. "She is on the fourth floor - room 408. But I'm sorry, she is allowed only one visitor daily, and according to our records, that has already happened today. May I suggest you try again tomorrow?"

"I'll do that. Appreciate your help." Abi left and returned to the guys. "We can leave now." Swiftly returning to the logistics area, she was happy to hear Emile had a visitor today, and she wasn't completely alone.

Ted opened the door and found Matt parked nearby, waiting for them. One by one, they got in and pulled away.

About to round the corner at Westwood Plaza, someone caught Abi's eye. Leaning on the building was a dark figure, vaping. She caught a glimpse of his face just before he blew a puff of smoke that quickly shielded him.

Alarmed, her heart dropped. "Oh, my god!

"What is it?" Matt took his foot off the gas.

"I think that was Eastwood!"

The men went on high alert.

"Where?" Andrew asked urgently, scanning their surroundings.

Abi looked back, but the guy was gone. "Umm, he was right there, I swear."

"Are you sure, Miss?" Ted questioned.

She replied, "Yes, I'm pretty sure." Trembling, she wondered if she was seeing things.

Andrew tapped Matt on the shoulder. "Swing back."

He checked his mirror and made an illegal U-turn. Returning to Charles E. Young Drive, Andrew unbuckled his seatbelt and leaned between the seats to get a better view.

"What was he wearing?" Ted asked.

The image of him flashed through her mind. "All black. Jacket, baseball cap, pants, shoes. He was vaping."

Matt drove slowly along the street when they turned left. Each of the men kept their eyes peeled.

She, too, looked from left to right in search of him. But there was nobody on the street that matched that description. It was like she'd seen a ghost.

It made her doubt herself. "I'm not crazy. I saw him. I'm certain of it."

"We believe you, Miss." Ted could tell by Abi's reaction she was telling the truth.

"Let's head out. I'll send an update to the boss."

"You're texting Burton?"

"Yes, Miss. He instructed explicitly to let him know if there's a problem."

She nodded and turned around to peer down the street one last time. But there was nothing. "I swear, he was there," she whispered as Andrew sent the text.

"We will ask our people to call hospital security and check the CCTV cameras. If he was there, they will find him." Andrew received a response. "We've been told to take you home."

"No. Not yet. I need to go to Jade's and see her first."

"Jade, Miss?"

"My friend. She needs me. We are at Defcon One."

Andrew was confused. "Sorry, Miss?"

"It's a girl thing." Checking their location and the nearest ice cream parlor, Abi said, "Can you backtrack to Diddy Riese?"

Ted immediately referred to the GPS and located the store. "Sure. No problem."

It wasn't long before they were in front of the place. Andrew got out and went with Abi while Ted guarded the door ten feet from the truck.

Everyone looked at her oddly, wondering if she was a celebrity needing a sugar fix. Andrew scoured the place on his way in and stood by with his head on a swivel as she waited in line.

Placing her order, she selected four flavors Jade might like and added some brownies and a box of freshly baked cookies. She even got an extra box for the guys to eat on their break. Almost forgetting the hot fudge, she snuck that in at the last second before paying the bill.

With everything packaged, the man behind the counter handed her two red bags with corded white handles—one with the cookies and brownies and the other with the ice cream tubs.

Andrew carried it for her.

"Thank you," Abi said.

He acknowledged her with a smile. "Happy to help."

Ducking out the door, Andrew and Ted shielded Abi's face while getting her back to the vehicle as people tried to take pictures.

Safe in the back seat, Abi pulled up Jade's address before taking the extra cookie box from the bag. "We are heading to Wallingford Drive off Benedict Canyon." She showed Ted the address on her phone and passed along the box. "Oh, and these are for you guys. A little snack for later."

"Thanks, Miss." Ted opened the box, intrigued. "So, what do we have here?"

After checking out the flavors, he took one and held the box for Matt as he maneuvered them north. About to take another, he said to Abi, "Ladies first."

"No, no. These are for you guys to share. I have a sneaky suspicion my dinner this evening will consist of a full-pull dessert, so I'm good."

Andrew took one when Ted passed it back. "This was nice of you."

She smiled, "It's the least I can do." At the same time, her phone rang. Answering it, she saw the name on the screen. "Hey."

"Hi, Abs. How's it going?"

"Good."

He could hear the apprehension in her voice. "So, I briefly heard about what happened at football practice with that Marco kid, and what's this about possibly spotting Eastwood?"

"Burton, don't worry. I'm fine."

"See, that's the thing. I worry about you twenty-four-seven."

She changed the subject. "Where are you now?"

"We are delayed in Miami. Waiting for a storm to pass."

All Abi heard was the word – we.

Met by dead air, he said, "You're sure you're okay?"

"Everything's fine. I'm just heading to Jade's place."

"Thought the guys were taking you home?"

"No. It's important that I see her."

"Do what you must. Just be careful."

"I will. Don't…"

"Worry? Yeah, so you've said." He paused. "I'll call you later."

"Sounds good. Safe travels."

"Thanks."

"Bye," she whispered.

"Bye, Abs."

Ending the call, she missed him but wondered if Zoe was getting on the plane, too. Glancing out the window, staring into oblivion, thoughts of him resurfaced. Unable to stop herself, she opened her phone to check Zoe's Instagram page. Quickly scrolling through the pics, the latest post was of Burton, hooded and hidden, climbing the jet's steps. This time, Sara wasn't far behind. She read Zoe's caption – *Heading to the neon-lit streets of Sin City with Dark Demon lurking.*

34

Eye on the Prize

Snaking their way to the 405 North, Abi watched Matt jump onto the highway to whisk her to Jade's place in Wallingford Estates. He happened to catch her looking at him in the rearview mirror.

Quickly turning away, she'd settled into a somber mood.

Fidgeting with her phone in hand, recalling everything that had happened that day, she tried to breathe, knowing it wasn't over yet. Not only did she have to support her friend through a breakup, but she also had to figure out what information she was willing to share with Shane and what still needed to remain a secret, regardless.

When they merged onto Mulholland Drive, Matt gave her their ETA. "Eleven minutes, Miss."

"Thanks." Texting that to Jade, she gave her a heads up.

Approaching the north gate, Matt slowed and turned into the estate's entrance. Surveying the premises, he stopped at the intercom pillar and rolled down his window. "Does she have a code?"

"Let me ask."

Before she could press send, Jade texted and said she saw them on the cameras. She then gave her the four-digit number to access the street.

She handed Ted her phone. He held it up for Matt, who punched in the code. Soon, the gates moved aside and granted them access.

Meandering down the road, the SUV arrived at a cul-de-sac. Driving up to the gates, it opened on its own.

"She must see we're here."

Threading through the mesh iron gate, they drove between the twelve-foot tall boxwood hedges and pulled into the large courtyard adjacent to a massive white mansion.

They stopped near the front door. Ted got out and opened Abi's side as Andrew rounded the back of the SUV to take up his position.

With two bags in hand, Abi saw Jade standing on the threshold, waiting for her.

"What's with the goons? Since when do you travel with hardware?"

"Not you, too? Is this slang for security guards?"

"What? Hardware?" she giggled.

"Yes. Today was the first time I've heard of it."

"It's common knowledge," Jade said as the men looked on. "Sorry, guys! No offense."

"None taken," Ted said casually, despite Andrew thinking the contrary.

Jade saw her friend toting the red bags and recognized them immediately. "Ooooh! You got the good stuff! Thank you!"

Quickly taking one of them from her, she disappeared inside without so much as a welcoming Hello.

"You're welcome," Abi whispered, pretending she'd been cordial.

Waving to the guys, Abi followed Jade into the grand foyer and closed the door behind her before heading toward the kitchen. By the time she got there, Jade was already unloading the ice cream and placing it on the counter.

"Rocky Road, Vanilla bean, Espresso chip, and pistachio. Great selection."

Abi placed the second bag beside the ice cream.

"Did you get the hot fudge?"

Pulling the tub of liquid chocolate from the cookie bag, she said, "Right here."

"Ooooh. You're the best."

"I know," Abi smirked.

Taking two bowls from the cupboard, she scooped out some vanilla bean and smothered it in hot fudge before topping it with a pistachio almond cookie.

"So, I guess you feel bad for ignoring me all weekend?"

"You're kidding, right? I'm the one who gets kidnapped, and you're mad at me for ignoring you?"

"You don't actually think I'm mad about that?"

"Well, no..." Abi hesitated. "Maybe?"

"Oh my gosh. Come here," the pretty girl said with open arms. "When I heard Burton saved you, I knew you were okay. Just figured you'd answer my texts then. Apparently, I was wrong."

"It's a long story. But no, I didn't have the freedom to do that." Abi wished she could explain.

"Forget it. That's water under the bridge now since you brought ice cream for dinner," she laughed, handing her a bowl and spoon. "Care to join me?"

"Absolutely." Abi loaded hers with a scoop of Rocky Road hot fudge and added a brownie for good measure.

Jade put the tubs in the large freezer. "Come on. Let's go to my room."

It was strange to see her friend alone in such a big house. On their way up the riser-lit stairs, Abi marveled at the artwork on every wall.

Crossing the balcony to the East Wing, Jade walked through a set of double doors just as a maid emerged from another room carrying a stack of fresh towels.

Well, at least there is one other person here, she thought.

Her room was huge, with fifteen-foot ceilings and her mother's art hanging over her bed. Decorated in neutral tones, it was a calming and peaceful space.

Abi turned to her right and walked into the seating area with a sofa, chairs, tables, a stone fireplace, and a mounted big-screen television. The bedroom was through an archway with a king-sized bed.

"Wow, Jade. Your room is incredible."

"It's way too big for one person, but what am I gonna do?" Wanting to ask how the day was, she took a spoonful of ice cream and mumbled, "So, how was school? Rumor has it some new students are roaming the halls. Tell me everything. Are the new guys cute?"

"I suppose so. Didn't notice. Two are kinda rude, though."

"I saw pics of the grade eleven QB. I think his name is Owen."

"That's right."

"He's kinda hot for a junior."

Abi hesitated. "Guess so."

Realizing she was talking about Shane's competition this year, she immediately said, "Sorry…"

"It's fine."

Able to hear a pin drop in the place, concerned about her friend's well-being, Abi wondered if she was left alone for long periods of time. "Where is everybody? Are you mostly here by yourself?"

"Why do you think I spent so much time with Reg? I never wanted to come home. He and I would go for dinner and take walks along the beach. It helped to pass the time. My Mom is in Milan. She returns in ten days. My dad and his girlfriend are on an African safari. So, they won't return for a month."

Abi felt bad, but it wasn't much different from her life. "I'm sorry I wasn't there for you this weekend. A lot happened. Burton discovered my phone was compromised and got me a new one. But I couldn't use it with everything going on. Once I got home, I received your messages. I feel terrible."

She sat there quietly, savoring the decadence in her bowl. "Guess it's been horrid for both of us?"

"I suppose so."

"What happened when they took…" Jade couldn't say it.

"When they took me?"

"I knew immediately the second Shane said they put you in a Bentley Bentayga. Black Lyon had you."

"He was in the back seat beside me."

"Shut up!" Jade inched to the edge of her seat. "OMG! What did he say?"

"That's just it. Nothing. Barely said a word." She recalled snippets of that night. "Shane stole a car and raced down Sunset to get his driver to pull over."

"He said he lost you when the truck diverted into the Bel Air gates."

"That's right. After that, I knew I was on my own."

"Oh, my..." Like watching a horror movie, Jade focused on Abi telling the story.

"When we arrived at the mansion across the canyon..."

"Wait. Wait." She raised her hands to stop her there. "The place you can see from your house? The one you keep talking about all lit up at night – with that creepy guy?"

"That's the one."

"It's his house?"

"Yes." Abi took a spoonful of her ice cream and backtracked, knowing she'd let the cat out of the bag. "Look, swear you won't tell anyone. Please..."

"Mums the word. Don't worry. What happened next?"

"Well, when we drove into the garage, he got out and left me there."

"That's rude."

"Yeah, he just walked into the house and disappeared. His security guards brought me in, and soon, Martin..."

"The Butler?"

"He met with me and explained what was happening." Afraid to say anymore, not sure she should share the rest, Jade looked on, waiting for her to continue. "After about fifteen minutes, Martin said Black Lyon wanted to see me on the roof."

Captivated, the girl ate a spoonful of ice cream and listened intently.

"We went up the elevator, and I walked out. There he was, standing along the glass railing overlooking the city. It was a pretty view. The lights were sparkling like diamonds."

"And?"

"And he said he needed me to go into hiding with his friend for forty-eight hours."

"Why?"

"Because he believed my life was in danger."

She melted in her chair. "Ohh! That's so romantic. So he's still protecting you."

"It's not like that."

"Of course it is. Why else would he have kidnapped you?"

Abi knew she was right, but she didn't dare elaborate.

"So you went with his friend, or did Burton save you?"

"This is the thing... And you can't tell anyone."

Excited to get the inside scoop, Jade put the bowl down. "Oh, no. What?"

"Burton was the friend."

Dropping the spoon, she flung her hands dramatically in the air and fell back onto the sofa. "What!"

"Burton works for him. He created his app and runs his computer systems."

"Holy shit!"

"I know, right."

"A big secret your friend was keepin'." Jade was in shock.

"You're not kidding."

"So what happened next?"

"Burton took me to his place in Malibu, and I stayed there. I was thankful to be with him versus a stranger."

"How was that? You two, all alone?" Her eyebrows raised.

Not prepared to share anymore, Abi stopped there. "It was fine."

Disappointed, Jade grabbed hold of the bowl again and took a bite of the cookie.

"Enough about me. What happened with you and Reg? Shane didn't say much."

After asking that, Abi noticed Jade's mood turn solemn again.

"Reg's house manager called his Father and told him what happened that night. In the process, he said that I threw the party, and my friends destroyed the house."

"No way..."

"For the past while, the house manager and I have butted heads. He didn't like me, and I didn't like him either. We would always avoid each other at all costs. The day of the party, the guy was mad about all the vendors coming in to set up. Reg told him not to say anything and gave him extra money to stay quiet. But when everything went down, Reg and the fire chief discussed what happened. That's when they found remnants of explosives under Shane's charred Jeep. The house manager assumed this was somehow my fault - that I had invited too many people and security couldn't keep up," she huffed. "The man said they couldn't control who was coming and going. He said I compromised the safety of Reg and the house."

"But how could you have known?"

"Looking back at the camera footage, we found a man dressed in black entering the gates and leaving a package under Shane's Jeep."

"That's why Shane believes we were the target?"

"Well, it's kind of obvious. Either that or it was the location of the vehicle that made the guy stick it there. Who knows?"

"So, no ID on this man? Did you see what he looks like?"

"No. Just all black clothing and shoes."

Abi clued into what she said. "Strange, today I was certain I saw Eastwood standing outside the hospital. He looked straight at me, almost as if he wanted me to see him."

"You're kidding?"

"I wish I were. He was dressed fully in black from head to toe, but by the time the guys circled back, he was gone."

Jade shivered. "You gave me chills just now."

"I don't know. Maybe my eyes were playing tricks on me?"

"Or maybe you really did see him."

Abi played with the ice cream in her bowl. "Yeah..."

With all that said, Abi came back to Reggie. "So, I hear the two of you broke up?"

"Can you believe his Father has betrothed him to another girl from overseas? Apparently, marrying her will pave the way for their company to expand into this new innovative technology venture. If he doesn't marry the girl, the deal won't happen. How insane is that?"

"The poor guy doesn't have much choice, then?"

"I guess not. He's the only son. The sole heir."

"That's a lot of pressure."

"Part of me wonders if this whole bomb thing was intentional. It would give them a reason to get me out of his life. I really wouldn't put it past his Father. He does stuff like that, you know– manipulates people for his gain. I'm sure he hates me as much as his property manager does."

"You never know." Abi wished she could tell her the truth. "Has Reggie texted or called?"

"Not a word. According to Shane, Reg's Dad monitors his phone and text conversations. They want to make damn sure we aren't speaking – like at all."

"Do you want to see a picture of the girl his Father picked for him? I found this news article in the Straits Times." Jade scrolled through her phone and got up from the chair to show her.

Seeing the girl with flowing light brown hair and seemingly a chip on her shoulder, Abi said to her friend, "She has nothing on you."

"Thanks, but it says here she is the heiress to the Savoir Royals. I can't compete with that."

Abi scrolled through the pictures of the confident girl in many social situations. It gave her an idea. "So, you know what this girl has that you don't?"

Worried about what Abi would divulge, she braced herself. "No? What?"

"She's clearly independent and driven and is willing to do what is necessary to bring her family into the next century."

"Okay…And that is supposed to make me feel better because?"

"Because you, too, need to show Reggie's Dad that you are worthy of his son. Hiding out in this house and skipping school isn't a good look. You must prove you can take on social pressures and fight for your man. If you love him and he loves you, who knows, maybe Reg will figure out a way for the two of you to be together."

"You think?"

"Yes, but only if you show courage and strength. Can you do that?"

"Yeah. I can." Jade straightened her posture and stopped slouching. Getting up from the sofa, she walked to the window and looked outside. "I live in a castle, too. I'm not below her. My parents are wealthy and show well on the world stage. There is no reason Reggie can't be with me."

"Exactly. When you guys got together, there was this incredible spark. I'm telling you, the guy loves you, and it's just a matter of time before he comes back."

"Maybe by returning to school, I can see if talking to Owen a bit can make Reg jealous."

"Listen, that's a fine line. Talking to him is one thing. Dating him to make Reg jealous is another. That could easily backfire on you. I wouldn't advise it."

"Don't worry. I'll be careful. Just have to keep my eye on the prize."

35

Company

After another hour of deep conversation and two heaping bowls of ice cream, Abi's tummy felt off. Ready to call it a day, she said, "Hey, I should get home. Shane will be waiting for me."

"You're leaving already?" Jade whined, reluctant to part with her best friend.

"Sorry. He's meeting me at my house."

Understanding, thankful for her company the past few hours, she said, "It's fine."

On their way downstairs, she, too, was regretting the second bowl. "Maybe I should have listened to my gut," Jade said with an uncomfortable giggle.

"Yeah, I hear you."

"Thanks for coming over. You're a good friend, Abi." Jade opened her arms. "Most of all, thank you for the pep talk. I needed that. You're right, this isn't over. If I want Reg back, I need to make changes."

Hugging her tightly, she replied, "Happy to hear that."

"I'll see you tomorrow."

Abi pointed her way. "You make sure you're there."

Jade smiled. "I will be. Don't worry."

"Remember what I said."

Jade shot her a thumbs up. "I've got it covered."

"Okay."

Walking out the door, the guys gathered around the SUV and opened Abi's side for her. While waving, she looked at the large home. Every window was dark except for Jade's room on the far side. It was like she was Cinderella.

Matt pulled away and headed toward the south gate, which automatically opened on approach. Exiting the grounds of the lavish estate, they drove down Benedict Canyon Drive to Sunset.

En route, Abi texted Shane to say she'd be at home in twenty minutes.

He quickly responded and said he would meet her there.

On the drive, Abi's thoughts drifted to Burton. Afraid to check social media for updates, she put her phone in her pocket. The music playing faintly on the radio made her tap her hand to the beat as they turned into the gates of Bel Air.

"Sorry, you guys had to work later than usual."

"It's okay, Miss. All part of the job," Andrew confirmed, not phased by the thirteen-hour workday. "The night shift is already at the house, so our transition tonight should be seamless as usual."

"Okay," she said as they rounded the last corner. Spotting Shane's Jeep already there, Abi smiled.

"Home sweet home, Miss," Ted announced on the way through the gates. "Looks like you've got company."

36

The Last Challenge

Abi watched Shane pull in behind them. Heart racing with nerves, she knew she'd promised to tell him the truth. It was her last challenge of the day. But as she tried to gather her thoughts, it felt like she was untangling a messy knot with no clear beginning or end.

Exhausted, she stepped out of the vehicle to greet him. "Hey, looks like I'm on my own tonight yet again."

Shane opened the rear door to grab a duffle bag and his backpack. "No, you're not," he said confidently.

"What do you mean?"

Slinging them on his left shoulder, he said, "I am staying until your Dad can be here to protect you. I don't care what he says."

"In all fairness, he doesn't know what's happening."

"If he did, he'd understand why I'm here."

Thankful, she walked towards the front door. "For the record, I'm not telling him anything. He's under enough stress."

"Fine. So, until then, I'm stepping in." Shane stood there with such conviction.

Andrew smiled. "I'd listen to him, Miss."

The big QB chuckled. "See, he gets it."

Giving Andrew the eye, she drifted back to Shane. "Okay. You know the rules."

"I do, but in exchange, I have one condition."

Eyebrows raised, she asked, "Oh? What's that?"

He walked up to her and slipped his hand around her waist. Leaning in, his lips close to her ear, he whispered so nobody else would hear. "You've gotta tell me everything -the truth, starting with what happened this past weekend because my gut keeps telling me you haven't told me everything."

"I promised I would."

Staring deep into her eyes, he said, "Yes, you did."

Going inside, she removed her shoes, happy to finally be home, and waited for him to join her.

"You go ahead," Shane said, "I'll be there in a second."

"Alright."

Heading upstairs, Abi ducked into her room to change out of her uniform. Slipping on tights and a sweatshirt, she walked into the bathroom to brush her hair and position it in a messy ponytail. Exhaling, looking forward to relaxing before studying and finishing some work, she regretted having so much ice cream.

"You know better than that," she scolded, unable to think of having dinner. "Haven't you learned by now?"

The door closed downstairs. Hearing it, Abi went to see what Shane was up to. Finding him with a bag of Greek takeout in hand, she looked at it on his way to the kitchen.

"I had dinner delivered. Hope you're hungry."

She laughed nervously. "Well, about that..."

He stopped. "What? Don't tell me you hate Greek?"

"No, that's not it," she said. "When I went to Jade's, she only agreed to see me because I said I'd bring ice cream with hot fudge."

His face scrunched up. "Please tell me you didn't."

"Oh, but I did. Two bowls," Abi exhaled uncomfortably. "It's not bad. I just feel really full. I don't know why I do this to myself."

Taking the containers from the bag, he opened his. "How is she anyway?"

"Initially, she was quite sad when I got there."

"Figured as much."

"How is Reg?"

"Same. He misses her a lot."

"Does he want her back?" Abi asked.

Without hesitation, he replied, "It sounds like it."

"She was hoping for that."

"It's not that cut and dry, though."

"What do you mean?"

Shane ate a spoonful of rice. Chewing a bit, he said, "Well, he can't freely get back together with her."

"Why not?"

"Because if he leaves, his Father will send him out the door with nothing, which means he'll have to relinquish his inheritance."

"All of it?"

"Every stitch. In other words, he'll no longer be the heir to the Wilson conglomerate."

Abi sat on the bar stool beside Shane and grabbed her food container. "So, he will have to give up everything to be with her?"

"Pretty much."

"Would he do that?"

"I strongly suspect he might after talking to him today, but his Dad has other ideas. He's hell-bent on that arranged marriage taking place."

"I heard about that. Jade's aware of it. She showed me the girl's picture."

"She knows? I didn't think he told her."

"He didn't. She mentioned an article announcing the merger between the two companies and the excitement of an upcoming engagement." Abi took a bite of her lemon potato.

"Guess that's why time is of the essence to him right now. At least that's the feeling I got from him."

Stabbing a piece of calamari with her fork, she couldn't help but wonder what they could do to help.

Shane glanced over. "I thought you weren't hungry?"

Abi looked down at her food. "I eat when I need to save the world."

"Good to know," he laughed. "How was your visit with Jade otherwise?"

"I got her to return to school tomorrow and make some changes to compete with this girl."

"See, that's the thing. She doesn't need to do that."

Turning to him, she asked, "Why not?"

"Because he loves her. Not the other one. It's not a competition. There's no comparison. Jade wins, hands down. He and I discussed that."

"Oh?"

"I told Reg if he wanted Jade, he would have to change his Dad's mind. A monumental task, no matter how you look at it."

"Absolutely."

"You know, just to see my best friend today, I had to schedule a meeting for coffee and pretend he and I had business to discuss, or his secretary wouldn't have allowed it. His security was not happy to see that I wasn't Mr. Chiang from Singapore. My friend is living in captivity. It's horrible."

"So, they let you speak to him, regardless?"

"Not at first. He had to sternly yell and cause a scene before they granted me fifteen minutes of his time. Sadly, his Father probably got wind of the incident shortly after that. He said there'd be hell to pay."

"The poor guy."

"So, I guess we'll see how this week goes. Maybe he'll figure out how to avoid this disaster." Shane finished the last of his food. "This is changing the subject, but how's your Mom doing?"

"Not good. She's in isolation. Dad says she picked up an infection. Her body is fighting it. I couldn't go into the room. Nurses were in full PPE to do that. Dad says they don't want to overtax her immune system."

Hearing this, he turned to her. "Well, if she is anything like you, strong and resilient, she will get through this."

"I hope so."

Abi closed her takeout container and placed it in the fridge for later while Shane rinsed his out and tossed it in the recycling bin under the sink before pulling a box from his backpack.

"What's that?"

"Breakfast," he said as she collapsed on the sofa.

Joining her, he hinted, "So, maybe you want to watch that movie again from last night?"

She smacked his shoulder, making him wince.

"Hey! Hey! No violence."

Wrestling on the sofa, she suddenly stopped and looked up at the camera in the corner of the room.

He did the same.

Composing themselves, Abi thought a minute. "If you are gone Thursday and Friday, you'll miss the unit test, which means Professor Walker might make you write it Wednesday."

The football player looked to the ceiling, not wanting to study.

"So, that means we should do some review tonight." Getting up, she left the room and disappeared.

"Where are you going?"

Returning with her backpack, she set it on the dining table. "To secure that D-1 scholarship, you need to work on and off the field. Agreed?"

He knew she was right. Moving to sit in a chair beside her, he mischievously said, "I will study for an hour, but if I'm not mistaken, we had a deal."

"What?"

"You don't remember?"

Put on the spot, she chuckled, "Oh, I remember."

"So, are you going to spill or what? I want to know everything."

"What do you mean by everything?" Trying to buy time and determine how she would respond, Abi knew she'd sworn to secrecy, and the whole truth wasn't an option. Moving back to the sectional, she collapsed again.

He joined her. "So? You're stalling, which means there is much to say. My hunch was right."

Abi peered out the window and saw Burton's place illuminated across the canyon. "See that house over there?" she pointed.

"Yeah."

"That is where Black Lyon took me."

"There?"

She cleared her throat and added, "He had it on good authority that my life was in danger."

"How?"

"He never said."

"Okay, then why?"

"The explosion at the party wasn't an accident," she paused. "It was a warning shot."

"A warning? For what?"

"It was not only meant for you but me, too."

"I don't understand."

Having said more than she should have, she immediately regretted it but couldn't turn back now.

"Eastwood was making a point. He showed Black Lyon that he could get close to me despite all the precautions put into place."

Shane leaned back and tried to process what she'd said. "This is not just about the feud between me and him. Is it?"

"No."

"So, how does Burton fit into this?"

Afraid to reveal more, she said, "Look, what I am about to say stays between us. You can't tell anybody, understand?"

"Sure."

"I mean it. Swear."

He raised his right hand. "I swear."

Abi hesitated. "Burton works for the Black Lyon. He is responsible for all his tech systems and he designed the rave apps."

"Wow... Didn't see that coming."

Arms positioned across his chest, he raised his pointer finger to his lips, recalling the events that had occurred. "So, that explains it."

"The DJ knew Burton and I were friends. He called him and asked if he'd take me out of the city. And for good reason. I can't tell you the rest. I promised I wouldn't say anything."

"So, how did you end up in Tahoe?"

"They needed me out of LA." Abi shook her head. "Please don't ask anything else. Just know Black Lyon, Burton, and you are all on the same team. Each of you has my best interest at heart and wants to keep me safe."

"But, this isn't over."

"No." Recalling what happened earlier, she added, "I think I saw him today."

"Who?"

"Eastwood."

Alarmed, he asked, "What? Where?"

"Outside the hospital, about to leave for Jade's, I saw a man out of the corner of my eye. I recognized him immediately as we passed. At least, I think I did. It happened so fast."

"Are you sure?"

"Pretty sure." She rubbed her palms together nervously. "The guys are aware. They have someone checking into the CCTV footage from the hospital cameras. If he was there, they'll find proof."

A million things rolled through Shane's mind.

"Is this connected to Korolev's drive-by shooting?"

Abi turned to him. "Shane, I've already said too much. Now, I need you to stop asking questions and trust me."

"But, Abs. They've pulled you into this mayhem."

"Yes, but Burton is on top of it on his end. So is Black Lyon and the guys. Now that you know in a roundabout way, you can protect me, too."

He understood she was in danger. "As of today, I'm never leaving you alone."

"How can you do that? You've got away games coming up."

"Then, I won't play."

"No, don't even think about sacrificing football for me. You aren't quitting."

Thinking of a solution, he asked, "When is Burton back in town?"

"Wednesday, I think."

"Then, as much as I hate to say it, he'll have to stay with you when I can't be. We have no other choice."

She looked at him, surprised.

"You told me nothing's happening between you - that you're just friends. So, I believe you."

Flashes of Tahoe immediately brought about a sick feeling in her stomach. Burton had told her not to tell Shane the truth – that nothing good would come of him knowing they'd kissed. Part of her wanted to be honest, while the other wanted to forget about it.

Observing her deep in thought, he added, "Besides, the guy already proved he can keep you safe. If you trust him, then I've gotta do the same."

"I don't want the two of you fighting anymore."

He knew that was weighing on her. "I get it. But like I've said before, I don't want to share you, Abs. If I'm with you, then I am *with* you. Nobody else."

She agreed.

"There is something I need to say. Please don't be mad..."

Turning to him, she looked into his eyes. "What is it?"

"Aside from seeing Reg and Alan, I made another stop before that."

"Alright..."

"I went to the hospital to see Emile." He sat there trying to decipher her reaction.

Remembering what the woman behind the patient services desk said, she realized that Shane was the only visitor Emile had that day.

Uncomfortable, he clarified, "I feel partially to blame for her doing what she did. I've added to her stress despite how she's treated us. As I've said, her home life is not what everyone thinks. She has a lot of problems. You think my Dad is bad. Hers didn't even care when she tried to do this the first time."

Abi felt terrible. "When you walked into her room, how did she react?"

"First, she was angry and told me to leave. I explained that I came to check on her and ensure she was getting the help she needed. That pissed her off a bit. Should've known better. She never likes to feel weak or unstable."

"What did you do?"

"About to walk out, she told me I was the only person who'd come to see her since she got admitted."

"Not even her Mom came?"

He exhaled. "Her Mom was too drunk even to know why the ambulance was at the house that night. The maid found Emile on the floor in her room and called 911. Apparently, her Dad is in South America with his secretary. Ecuador, I think she said."

"Does she have any siblings?"

"No. Her Mom got pregnant with her and never legally married her Dad. He comes and goes as he pleases, and the woman is left heartbroken and numb, drowning herself to oblivion every day."

"I guess you never know what is going on in one's life behind closed doors."

"That's so true." He took hold of her. "So, look... I don't want you to worry about this, okay? I only went because I heard her friends abandoned her. Can't imagine what she'd be thinking. She just tried to kill herself, and everybody, including her parents, avoided her like the plague."

"I think what you did was right."

"Thank you for not getting upset. I promise I won't make a habit of it. She needed to know somebody cared. Otherwise, what will give her the willingness to live?"

That comment struck a chord with Abi. Without the support of friends and family, what is left? "That's so sad." Abi stayed silent, processing it.

"I wanted to tell you. No secrets."

Guilt washed over her. "No secrets," she repeated. "Appreciate that."

He nodded, ready to change the subject. "Guess we should call it a day. It's been a busy one."

"Yeah. You're not kidding."

"I might look over a few things in math. If I need help..."

She interrupted, "Yes, just let me know."

"Okay." Shane kissed her on the forehead, mindful of the camera in the far corner of the room. Before heading upstairs, he grabbed his duffle bag and backpack, feeling the news that his visit with Emile had put a slight damper on things between them.

As she climbed the stairs, he did the same.

Peeking in her room, he watched her sit on her bed. Putting his bags down, he stood in the doorway.

She looked up.

"Hey..."

With slight hesitation, she replied, "Yeah?"

"I don't know. You seem down since..."

"Since you mentioned her."

Shane walked over and sat down. Holding her hand, he said, "Abs, I don't love Emile. I never have. With you, it's different. I know, without a doubt, that I want to spend my life with you. That's a tall order at our age, but I can't help what I feel."

She stared at their hands, tightly connected. Hopelessly in love with the boy, his infectious grin lit up the room, a sight that was hard to resist.

Lingering, he leaned forward and waited for her to meet him partway.

It set her soul ablaze with anticipation. Reaching up, she rested her hand along his cheek. Having cast a spell on him, he surrendered.

Drawn to her, each tender kiss that followed made the world slow down and granted them a moment of pure bliss suspended in time. As he crept closer, their bodies pressed together. Falling into the pile of pillows, she savored the familiar tingles spreading from head to toe and the sense of security that only his presence could bring. Yet, amidst the emotional rush, he showed restraint, a subtle reminder of his respect and admiration.

Lightly clearing his throat, he stopped and hugged her. "I, umm, should let you get ready for bed."

Grumbling as he stood up slowly, she asked, "What's wrong?"

"Just a bit sore from practice today. Kinda out of my recovery routine. When I go home, I usually hit the sauna."

She inched to the edge of the bed. "Well, a dry and wet sauna is on the lower level. We have a Japanese soaker tub, too. Want to try that?"

"Sure. If you don't mind."

"No, not at all. Come on, I'll show you."

On the way out of her room, Shane grabbed his duffle bag. "Alright. Lead the way."

Walking through the main floor, past the kitchen, she slid the Fleetwood door aside. "It's this way," she said, descending the hidden outdoor staircase before opening the door at the bottom.

Abi circled to their right.

Shane looked around. "Wow, this is impressive."

"Thanks. I haven't tried it yet, so I can't help you with how each thing works, but I'm sure you can figure it out."

"Yeah, I'll manage."

"Okay, I'll leave you to it."

"Thanks. I'll be up shortly."

"Sure." Leaving the room, she climbed the stairs and missed him already. "Oh, that boy does have my heart," she mumbled while sliding the Fleetwood door shut.

37

Goodnight

Bounding up the stairs, Abi returned to her room. About to slip into the shower, she heard the phone ring. Quickly checking who it was, she put on her white robe and closed the bathroom door. "Hello?"

"Hey, Abs. It's me. Thought I'd call and check in." He didn't waste any time. "Andrew updated me further on the Marco incident and the Eastwood sighting."

"Wow, straight down to business."

"Sorry. I'm just concerned."

"Well, firstly, the fight between Marco and Shane erupted because the guy said Eastwood wouldn't let things with me slide. As for seeing him at the hospital, I don't know. Maybe my eyes were playing tricks on me?"

"I've got people checking the cameras in that area to see if we can ID him. If he was there, they might get a license plate number. When I hear back, I'll let you know."

"Okay."

"How is everything else?"

"Yeah, umm, everything is fine." Immediately, Abi wondered if he heard about Shane's insistence to stay at the house.

"Are things with you and Shane good?"

"I suppose so."

An awkwardness looming, he said, "Glad to hear it. Look, I gotta get moving. We are going for dinner."

"We?"

"Me, Martin, and the guys."

Abi wished he would have told her the truth about Zoe. "Well, enjoy."

"Thanks. I'll call again soon."

"Okay."

"Bye."

"Bye, Burton."

When he ended the call, Abi did too. She sat on the edge of the bathtub, deep in thought.

Her phone rang again. Looking down at the screen, she accepted the call and walked back to her bed to sit down. "Hi, Dad. What's up?"

"I see a lot of activity around the house. What's going on?"

Thinking fast on her feet, she sat up and replied, "Umm, remember I said Burton got wind of a few break-ins on our street?"

"Yes, vaguely."

"He arranged for his security to keep watch, just in case."

"Right, I remember. That explains the men outside, but what about Shane Coppersmith's Jeep in the driveway?"

"I told him about what was happening. He brought dinner and offered to stay for a bit. That way, I'm not alone. He's got two away games this week and will miss the finance test, so I am helping him study for that in case Professor Walker has him write it early."

"Then why is he walking around our house half-naked?"

"What? No, it's not what it looks like, Dad. He had a stressful practice today, so I offered to let him use the saunas. Don't worry, I stayed upstairs."

Somewhat satisfied by how she casually answered, he remained quiet, then said, "Jenna sent me an update on Mom."

"Who's Jenna, again?"

"You're Mom's day nurse."

Recalling the pretty blonde woman making the rounds, she said, "Oh, right."

"Mom is weak, but she's hanging in."

She was about to ask another question when she heard someone urgently speaking to him. At the same time, his phone notifications went off.

"Look, Sweetheart. I have to go. I'm needed downstairs. We will talk tomorrow."

"No problem."

"Have a good night."

"Yeah, you too."

When he abruptly ended the call, she hoped her Mother wasn't the emergency he needed to get to. Resting her hands on her face, she heard Shane's voice cut through the silence. It startled her.

"Was that your Dad?" he said.

Turning to find him standing there in his swimsuit, bare-chested, with a towel wrapped around his waist, she answered, "Umm, yeah."

He asked permission to enter. About to sit down, Abi pushed over. Leaning against the headboard with both arms crossed over his chest, he waited for her to say something.

"I'm just worried about my Mom."

Lifting his arm, Abi snuggled in beside him. "I can't imagine how you are feeling, but I'm here for you whenever you need to talk."

"Thanks."

"You're not alone in this, Abs."

"I know," she paused. "Can we change the subject?"

"Sure."

"We still haven't studied for an hour."

He rolled his eyes. "Oh, man. Anything but that."

Conceding that she did not really want to study either, she asked, "You said you saw Alan today. How did that go?"

"I talked to him about coming back."

"And..."

"I don't know. We'll see. He says his Mom hates what his Dad did. Apparently, he was the one who decided to send him to Westlake."

"Really?"

"I told him to keep pressing her and see if she can convince her husband to let him graduate with his friends versus strangers."

"Oooh, that's a good one. You played on her heartstrings."

"Hopefully, it works. She would do anything for Alan. Doesn't hurt that he is the youngest of six."

"Six kids?" Abi had no idea.

"Crazy, huh?"

"Can't imagine."

"Yeah, me either," he laughed. "Well, I guess I should get showered. Then, we can study. Sound good?"

She nodded. "Okay. I'm going to do the same."

"I'll be quick." Shane jumped off the bed and took his bag to the guest room while Abi walked into her bathroom and closed the door.

Wanting to get a jump on their homework, she decided to leave her shower until morning. Hair and teeth brushed, she stayed in her hoodie and tights. Skipping downstairs to grab her backpack, she returned to her room and settled in bed with her laptop and textbook.

Shane returned to her minutes later with books and his computer in hand. Unsure what he should do, she said, "Come in. I'm too tired to work anywhere else."

He moved closer. Sitting opposite her, he opened his laptop and got reacquainted with the lesson before tackling the test review package.

Helping him through the questions one by one, Abi noticed the hour had passed by in a blink. Eyes fluttering, they got heavier by the minute. It prompted her to put her stuff away.

Shane did the same.

Stretching, she slipped under the covers and rested her head on the pillow with a sigh. "I think we should call it a night," she said. "I need some sleep."

"Alright," he said before sliding over to kiss her. "Sweet dreams, Abs."

"You too."

About to leave and return to the guestroom, he walked around to her side of the bed. Bending down, he kissed her one last time. "Love you."

She looked up at him and smiled. "Love you too."

In an instant, she wanted to ask him to stay. Despite the words ready to roll off the tip of her tongue, with an internal battle raging, she stopped and didn't say another word as he walked out the door and disappeared.

Thankful he was so understanding, she figured most guys wouldn't have been able to handle the slow pace of their relationship. That said, she was now finding it difficult, too.

"I just need a little more time," she muttered softly. Questioning when that might be, she said, "Guess I will know when the moment comes."

38

Tuesday Morning

Greeted by stormy, wet weather the following morning, Abi woke to rain pelting the window before it trickled down the glass. A heavy mist had enveloped the canyon, veiling the landscape in a soft haze. Turning off her alarm, she peered at the trees, each swaying heavily with the weight of the rain. Forcing herself out of bed, she heard the shower on the opposite end of the house. Knowing Shane was already moving motivated her to do the same.

Showered and ready in record time, Abi walked out of her room dressed for school and heard some activity below. She figured Shane had beaten her to it. Descending the stairs, she rounded the corner and discovered a coffee and toast waiting for her on the island.

"Aww… What is this?" she asked happily.

He took a bite of his protein bar. "Just a little breakfast to start the day."

"Well, thank you."

"It's nothing fancy. I don't exactly cook, but I do make a mean scrambled eggs."

Abi giggled. "Good to know."

"Maybe you can give me cooking lessons?" he stated while strolling over to give her a morning hug.

"I'd be up for that."

Mindful of the camera watching them, he kissed her forehead and said, "Hope you don't mind. I threw my uniform in the dryer to freshen it up."

"No. Not at all. That's fine." Abi took a bite of her toast. About to sip the aromatic coffee, a gate notification flagged her phone.

It was Andrew, Matt, and Ted. Allowing them access, the night staff headed out.

Finding Ted making the rounds through the backyard in the rain, Shane turned to Abi and asked, "So, what's the plan for today?"

"Besides school, you mean?"

Taking a seat beside her, he clarified, "Yeah. Are you coming to practice or going to see your Mom after school?"

"Well, based on what happened at football yesterday, I think I should go to that. Then, we can swing by the hospital afterward. Is that okay?"

"Sure. Sounds good."

Finishing her last piece of toast, she added, "I hope Jade will be at school."

"I guess we'll see," he replied. "It's not good for her to wallow in this. I'm glad you changed her perspective. Maybe she'll take your advice."

"Fingers crossed," Abi replied, putting her plate and mug in the dishwasher. "Ready to head out?"

"Yeah. I'll just get dressed."

He disappeared upstairs and returned minutes later, looking sharp in his uniform. Grabbing his backpack and an umbrella from the closet, he walked out the door to bring the Jeep closer and greeted the guys in passing.

Andrew acknowledged by raising his coffee cup to bid him good morning.

Parked a few feet away, Shane got out again and opened the umbrella. Walking around the vehicle, Abi was just about to lock up. Shielding her, he reached to open the passenger side so she could jump in. He ran to his side, quickly folded the umbrella, shook it, and tossed it on the floor behind him. Seated beside her, he'd gotten a little wet.

"Not a nice day," she said, scanning the clouds above.

"Nope. It's gonna be a soaker." He turned on the radio and put the truck in gear. Given the okay from Andrew, they left the house. Abi closed the gate behind them.

Heavy at times, the rain hit the windshield, making it hard to see.

"If this keeps up, there won't be a field practice. Just a gym workout."

"So, I can't watch?"

"Probably not." Maneuvering the road's many twists and turns, he said, "It's unfortunate 'cause we needed all the scrimmage time we could get. As much as I'd like a down day, the team doesn't have the luxury of that right now with these new players and the All-American showcase this weekend."

"Is it a big one?"

"The biggest. The best talent in the country will be there, along with scouts, agents, team reps, and media—everyone in one place."

"Maybe the sky will clear?" Abi checked the forecast on her phone. "See, the rain should stop by three o'clock."

"That's good news. Maybe we'll be okay for the last half."

When they reached Sunset, Shane turned right into the flow of traffic. Inching along at a snail's pace, much slower than usual, Abi texted Jade.

So, are you at school?

Seeing her thinking bubbles rambling, she waited patiently with bated breath. "I just texted Jade to see if she arrived yet."

"This is the moment of truth," he replied while driving over the top of the 405.

When her response came through, Abi read it aloud. "Hey, girl. I'm about five minutes away! Wait for me in the garage."

"You got her out of her slump. Nice work, Acardi."

She gave him the eye.

"What?" Knowing she disapproved of being called by her last name, Shane made light of it and said, "Oh, come on, Abs. Take it as a compliment."

Given the circumstances, she felt quite proud of herself and said, "Fine. I'll let it slide this time."

39

The Introduction

Driving up the hillside to the Gilderson School, Shane moved toward the parking garage. Abi scanned the attendant booth, hoping to see Gerald there, but again, another man had taken his place.

"We need to find out what happened to him."

Not paying attention, he said, "Him, who?"

"Gerald."

Shane turned down the aisle. "Hopefully, nothing bad. He's been gone a while now."

"At lunch, maybe I'll go by the office and see if they can shed some light on that. If he's sick or in hospital, perhaps we can help."

"Sounds like a plan."

While backing into his parking spot, Abi looked at the white Porsche across from them. Inside was her best friend. Getting out at the same time, she rushed over and gave Jade a big hug. "I'm so happy to see you!"

"Why? It's been less than twenty-four hours," the girl giggled.

"You know what I mean."

"Yes, I'm happy to be back, too, girlfriend."

The two girls walked along arm in arm. Strangely, Shane felt like a third wheel. He missed Reg right then.

The courtyard was desolate when they got off the elevator. Steadily raining, Shane hoisted the umbrella above their heads, and they made a run for it. Andrew and Ted did the same.

Opening the door for the girls, they walked in and immediately spotted their friends gathered under the spiral staircase.

Thankful Shawn was back, Shane gave him a manly pat on the back. "Hey, dude. Good to see you."

"Yeah, you too."

"Everything good?"

"Yep. No jail time. Just community service, thank God. My parents did it to scare me straight. They'd had enough of me fightin' and gettin' into hot water."

"You got lucky."

"You're not kiddin'."

A few feet away, Jade and Abi hugged Laney.

Jade announced, "I see you got your man back."

"I sure did. The new and improved version," she giggled.

"What do you mean," Abi asked.

Laney whispered, covering her mouth to keep it on the down-lo. "He left the courtroom and called me to profess his love and promise that his brawling days were over. He said he wants to focus on the future, including making me proud of him."

Abi smiled. "Awww..."

"Yes, eventually, these boys will grow into men. The faster they realize their place in this world, the better," Jade surmised.

Laney nodded. "So happy to see you, Jade."

In an instant, Owen Karp appeared on the scene. Splitting through the crowd like a Hollywood star, the guy almost made time stand still. With a posse of girls nearly fainting in his wake and an entourage of grade elevens wanting to be his best friend, Abi could see Owen believed he was the new Shane Coppersmith.

Jade's sights gravitated his way. It took seconds for the guy to do the same and give her a sexy wink.

Pretending not to be phased by it, Jade confidently stood with her friends. "Hmm...hmm...hmmm. That boy is fine," she said under her breath. "He just made getting out of bed early this morning worth all the trouble."

"He's pretty handsome. Just don't break his heart because the team needs to win this season, and they can't do that if the backup QB gets maimed."

"Don't worry. I'll be gentle," she replied deviously.

"I'm serious, Jade. Shane's agent is peddling him to other schools because ours isn't considered championship-worthy. They need all the help they can get."

"Okay. Okay. I didn't know, Abs." Her friend got defensive.

"Well, now you do. A lot is riding on this season. We need to support Shane so his agent doesn't force a transfer."

"Abs, calm down. He's still the number one pick in the NCAA."

"Nothing is written in stone."

Laney stepped in and rubbed Abi's back. She could tell she was agitated. Witnessing a familiar Jade rising from the ashes, Laney hoped she wouldn't lose sight of herself outside this newfound attention.

As Shawn joined his girlfriend and hugged her tightly, Abi spotted someone else in a different situation. Walking over, she said, "Morning, Allie."

"Oh, hey." The girl flashed a solemn look.

Abi sat beside her. "How are you doing?"

"Good, I guess. Just miss Alan to bits."

"I know. I'm sorry."

"Even though it's nice to see Laney and Shawn together again, it's hard," she sighed. "You know, I haven't seen Alan since Sunday. His Dad has him under lock and key. Poor guy can't leave the house except for attending school and practice."

When she said that, Abi wondered if this house arrest parental tactic was normal in California.

"Hopefully, you will see him on the weekend, or maybe you can meet him at his school after practice and sneak out for food before he heads home."

"Make a grand gesture?"

"Yes. It's worth a try, right?" Abi suggested.

"As much as I'd like to do that, if his Dad ever found out, I'm afraid of what could happen."

"What is with all the fathers being so strict and controlling?" This concept was foreign to her.

"They have a lot riding on their son's toeing the mark. They are the next-gen taking the helm of multi-billion dollar corps. They expect them to be accountable on every level."

"That's sad." Hearing this made sense, but all Abi took from it was these men thought of their kids as business transactions, nothing more. There was very little, if any, human interaction, let alone emotion, in their relationships. It was weird.

The girls watched Owen Karp suddenly break away from the crowd and approach their group with a level of suave not seen before.

"Oh, here we go. That didn't take long," Abi quietly announced.

Standing handsomely before their pretty friend, he said, "You're Jade Webber, right?"

With arms crossed, she replied, "Yes. I am. Who's asking?"

Eyes sparkling, flashing a smile to warm anyone's heart, he put out his hand and said, "Nice to meet you. I'm Owen."

Instantly under his spell, she slipped her hand into his. "Nice to meet you, too."

"Mind if I walk you to class?"

Offering his arm, completely smitten by his gentlemanliness, she accepted. "Sure. I'd like that."

"And off they go," Abi said amongst many whispers flowing like a wave through the student body. Remembering how she and Shane were at that stage a little over three weeks ago, it seemed like forever since they took that walk along Venice Beach.

The chimes echoed through the halls while moving on to their first class. Abi's security wasn't far behind.

Shane took hold of Abi's hand as Allie walked along with them.

Ascending the stairs towards the math hall, they saw Owen talking in close proximity to Jade.

This worried Shane. He knew this guy would move fast. If Reggie didn't do something, he would soon lose the girl he loved.

40

Proposition

The hallways buzzed with the usual chatter as students gathered outside their math class. Passing them by, Shane and Abi found their seats. Backpacks thudded onto the floor, with notebooks and laptops opened. The hum of conversations filled the room as everyone settled in, ready to face another day of equations and formulas.

Jade waltzed in minutes after, seemingly floating on cloud nine.

"Hey?" Abi tried to get her friend's attention.

"Yeah...." she whimsically answered.

"What are you doing?"

Confused, she turned to Abi. "What do you mean?"

"Owen Karp?"

"What? I'm single. Reggie made his choice, and it wasn't me."

"So, what? You're not going to fight for him?"

Jade got put off. "Why? Shouldn't I see where it goes if he isn't pursuing me and Owen is?"

Not responding, knowing, in all honesty, she was right, Abi said, "I get that you're hurt, but Reggie still loves you."

She rolled her eyes. "On Friday, after getting that call from his Dad, he dropped me without giving it a second thought. Do you know how that felt?"

Abi could see how heartbroken she was. "I understand." Believing she should bud out and let the chips fall where they may, she said, "I'm just saying, when you see yourself married in the future, what man is standing beside you?"

At that moment, Jade received a text. Picking up the phone, she stared at it.

Not sure what was wrong, Abi asked, "What is it? Everything okay?"

"Look..." she replied, showing Abi her screen.

Reading the message, she saw it was Reggie. He wanted to talk.

"See. What did I tell you? The guy is in a bit of a pickle. Don't count him out yet."

Professor Walker entered the room and got the class settled down to work. Listening to the lesson review before breaking off into groups to tackle some practice questions, Abi spotted Marco eyeing up Jade across from him.

"Well, well, well," he said, sending a chill down Abi's spine. "Who do we have here? A new student?" The arrogant football player took it upon himself to slide his desk beside Jade's when she joined Abi and Shane.

"No, man. Don't even think about it," the QB defended.

"What? I want to get to know this fine specimen."

The girls cringed.

Jade stood up and leaned forward with her hands flat on the desk. "Did you just say what I think you said?" She was not impressed.

"Nothing wrong with explorin' the waters."

"Just so you know, I'm taken," she stated firmly.

He leaned back in his chair. "That's okay. I don't mind sharin'. You just say the word, honey."

"Honey?" Disgusted by that, Jade put up her hand.

Professor Walker noticed. "Yes, Miss Wilson. Do you have a question?"

"Mr. Walker, this perve just propositioned me!"

Their teacher approached Marco, not surprised. "It's only day two, Mr. Cafaro, and you're already heading to the office for a second time, which means detention after school."

"Wait? What? No way." Hearing that sparked a fire under the guy.

"Eventually, you will discover how things work at Gilderson. How you do that is completely up to you."

Hearing this, Marco looked at Jade and sneered.

"Gather your things, Mr. Cafaro. I'll let Vice Principal DeAngelio know you're on your way."

Angered, he flung his backpack on his shoulder while Jade maliciously waved goodbye.

"Well, that was fun." She felt like she'd done her job by saving the female population from the new Neanderthal football player.

41

A New Couple

The rain started to subside as the teens moved through their morning classes, the steady patter against the windows gradually fading. Slowly, the clouds began to break apart, allowing shafts of sunlight to peek through and cast fleeting glimmers across the damp school grounds. As the bell rang, signaling the end of their science lab, Abi hovered around, her sights on Jade.

The girl had a whimsical bounce in her step and a bright smile as she walked out of class. Heading directly towards Owen Karp, she saw him waiting just down the hall.

Intent on keeping an eye on her friend, she hurried Shane along. "Quick," she said, pulling on his hand. "We've gotta catch up."

He realized his girlfriend was up to something. "Okay, I'm coming."

They followed them to the art wing.

While the two were walking arm and arm, Jade flirtatiously rested her head on Owen's shoulder whenever he made her laugh.

"This isn't good." Abi got concerned.

Shane didn't waste any time. "I agree," he said. Pulling out his phone, he took a picture of Gilderson's latest couple.

"Why did you do that?" Abi asked.

"I'm lighting a fire under someone." When he said it, Shane pressed send.

"You sent it to Reg?"

"Yep. Hopefully, it'll make the guy realize his feelings for her and encourage him to do something about it – and fast."

"I hope you're right."

Shane confided, "If I know Reg, he will be here shortly."

When they reached the studio, Shane and Abi stood in an alcove close by.

Jade and Owen were laughing and smiling at each other. Soon, they were holding hands.

In Shane's arms, Abi remained focused on the two love birds as she eavesdropped on their conversation.

"Will I see you at lunch?" the grade eleven heartthrob asked.

"Sure, I'll meet you there," Jade replied with a sweet tilt of her head.

About to leave for the weight room, Owen reached out and ran his hand along her arm. "Great. See you then," he said in a sexy tone.

Finding Abi's sights affixed to them, Shane tried to get her attention. "Earth to Abs?"

Ignoring him, she concentrated on Owen's actions and watched Jade stare at the new QB, clearly liking the view from that angle as he walked away.

"He asked her to lunch," Abi huffed.

"Don't get involved in this."

She looked up at him. "This coming from the guy who sent that photo to his best friend."

"That's different. I know what I'm doing. It's a bro code. He'll understand. But you getting involved will make Jade angry. She'll turn on you. Trust me."

Abi thought about what Shane said.

"Let me handle it on my end, and we'll see what happens. If Reg truly loves her, he'll come after her. I guarantee it."

"Okay," she grumbled. "We'll do it your way."

Her teacher entered the class.

"I'd better go."

He kissed her and said, "Alright. I'll see you later."

Abi watched Shane disappear into the crowd of students, her thoughts swirling with a mix of hope and doubt. As the bell rang, signaling the start of class, she took a deep breath, ready to face whatever came next, determined to trust his plan—for now.

42

Romantic Gestures

When a sunbeam burst through the skylights, it brought warmth that slowly deteriorated as the dark clouds returned. Abi strolled over to their group. Taking notice of Emile's friends nearby, immersed in a serious conversation, she could tell something was wrong. Having a seat while her guys took their positions on either end of the room, Abi lent a listening ear, hoping to learn more about what had seemingly happened. She assumed they had an update on Emile's condition.

"Have you visited her yet," Mandy questioned the twins.

The two blondes looked at each other regretfully, not knowing who should address her first. "No. We haven't? You?" Shiri asked.

Mandy looked down at the table and silently shook her head. Debating whether she should state why, she took a deep breath. "When my Mom found out what she did, she told me to keep my distance because she needs psychological help."

"That's what our parents said, too," Shiresse revealed somberly.

Abi glimpsed back at them.

Each seemed to feel bad, but it was clear their parents strongly influenced their actions.

"Did you hear Shane went to visit her yesterday?" Mandy whispered, mindful of the QB's girlfriend sitting nearby.

Hearing the girl say her name piqued Abi's interest.

"It was kinda cruel if you ask me," Shiri pounced.

"I don't know. Maybe he was trying to help."

"What has Emile always told us?" Shiri tried to justify things.

Mandy answered, "That she doesn't want our help."

"Exactly. I mean, we all know why she did it. Word's getting around." Her twin sister wanted to give Emile's ex the benefit of the doubt.

Assuming it was because Shane broke up with Emile to be with her, Abi felt partially to blame.

Mandy spit out her thoughts. "Well, no matter what you think, I believe she felt guilty and should. What she did was borderline criminal - the ultimate betrayal. It could have cost her dearly. I really don't know what she was thinking."

"That's just it. She wasn't," Shiresse pointed out. "That was anger and jealousy taking over."

Mandy said unapologetically, "Guess that's what happens when you strike a deal with the devil."

Jade straightened up in her chair upon hearing that. Looking at Abi, she gave her the eye.

Shiri silently agreed. "I don't know about you, but we no longer want to associate with her. This was the last straw."

Hearing bits and pieces of the conversation, Jade and Abi gathered what they could.

Allie whispered covertly, "What are they saying?" covering her mouth in the process.

Not wanting the girls to overhear them, Abi got her Burch book and ripped out a piece of paper to scribble the words - *They know why Emile did it?*

When her friends read the note passed around the table, their eyebrows went up.

"Interesting," Laney muttered.

Allie wrote under Abi's statement. Starting with a series of question marks, she silently shook her head and jotted down her two cents. *They didn't exactly come right out and say it. They just implied they knew the reason.*

Laney read it, slid the paper her way, and wrote, *We need to find out.*

Recalling what Shane said, Abi felt they should not get involved. Coming from a dysfunctional family could very well send anyone spiraling. She knew what she had to write. *It is none of our business, no matter what the reason is.*

One by one, the girls around her table reluctantly agreed.

Crumpling up the note, Abi stuffed it in the bottom of her bag.

Their teacher announced the class would be a work period while playing her favorite music in the background. Focusing, everyone pulled up their masterpieces on their tablets.

To move on from the subject of Emile Raven, Laney smiled at Jade and asked, "So... What's with you and sexy Owen? Care to share?"

Not wanting to make a big deal of it, especially since Abi didn't seem to approve, she replied, "I'm nursing a broken heart. Thought I'd fill the void."

"With a younger man?" Allie pointed out.

"What? They are super attentive. Besides, he's only younger by three months, so that doesn't count."

"If I may, he is a fine-looking boy."

Laughing at Laney's humorous facial expression with pursed lips, Jade said, "Yes, you can." Thinking about Owen, she sincerely added, "He's sweet. That's all."

"Well, if he gets you through a rough patch, so be it," Mei stated.

"It's been a tough few days, but things are looking up now." Jade turned to Abi, hoping she'd support her too.

Taking heed of Shane's second observation, catching on to what she was searching for, Abi replied, "As long as you're happy. That is the main thing."

Her friend smiled. "Thanks, Abs."

"I'm just worried about you."

The pretty girl smiled sincerely and reached out for Abi's hand. Squeezing it, she said, "I appreciate that."

Swaying from Jade, Allie asked curiously, "Talking about budding relationships, how's your gentle giant, Ming?"

Put on the spot, she didn't know what to say.

Allie tilted her head. "Come on, tell us. How is Big Ben? Give us some juicy details."

"I don't think so. A girl never kisses and tells."

Walking right into that one, the girls giggled mischievously.

"So, you've kissed him, then?" Laney speculated.

Ming blushed but did not deny it.

Laney prompted for more. "So, is he a good kisser?" she quietly questioned so only their table would hear.

Suddenly feeling the need to spill, she said, "Ohh, yeah..." Revealing too much, Ming raised her hands and said, "That's all. Don't ask me anything else."

"What's he like?" Allie questioned sincerely. "Is he nice?"

Ming beamed. "Oh, he's so sweet and down to earth." She endearingly sighed. "The strong, silent type." Breaking from her daydream, she added, "He came to Gilderson with his sights set on a football scholarship and hopes to secure a spot on an NCAA team. He wants to pursue a business degree on his terms, free from his parents' control. College for him will be a brief window of freedom and his last chance before his family dictates what comes next."

"Did he ask you to Homecoming?" her sister queried.

Unable to lie, she said, "Yes, he did."

Allie held her hand over her heart. "Awww.... He did? How?"

Initially, not wanting to say, she knew the girls would appreciate the effort he put into it. "Well, you know how much I like art," she giggled, "and my Insta posts, of course. I told him how much I wanted to see Miracle Mile by artist Robert Irwin at LACMA, so he took me last night."

"But, you only met yesterday?" Mei questioned.

"Yeah... So?"

"Wow, he moved fast." Laney knew why. "I bet the guy wanted to make sure nobody else did."

"Maybe," Ming smiled bashfully.

"So, how did he ask you?" Allie wanted all the details.

"Well, after walking around the exhibits, he helped me take the pictures I wanted. We walked through the forest of city street lamps on the way out and were there when they switched on. Admiring them, I turned and found him holding a red rose. That is when he asked if I'd go with him. When I said yes, he kissed me." When she said that, Ming dramatically collapsed at the thought.

"OMG, Ming." Allie had tears in her eyes. "Who knew Big Ben was a hopeless romantic?"

Glad to see her friends so happy for her, she asked, "How about each of you?"

"Shawn asked me, too," Laney replied. "Nothing like that, mind you. He's had a lot on his plate. But we went shopping on Rodeo at my favorite store. Versace, obviously. That is when he proposed on the second-floor balcony. Everyone below cheered when I said yes. It was awesome."

Starting a competition between them, Mei chimed in. "Well, Adrian invited me to visit his family's house on Malibu Crest. Before dinner, he proposed at sunset, overlooking the ocean. I got orchids and my favorite bubble tea."

"How about Shane? Did he ask?" Allie wondered.

After hearing everyone's stories, Abi discovered that while she was gone, everyone seemed to go about their lives, not giving her a second thought.

"Umm, no. He hasn't asked me yet. I was kind of missing up until Sunday..." Not wanting to be the buzz-kill, she asked Allie, "How about Alan?"

Afraid to say where they went on Sunday with everything going on, she paused and said, "Alan remembered my favorite scene in Harry Potter when he asks Cho to the ball. I always wished the girl would have said yes because it was the cutest, most awkward moment. He took me to Universal, and before getting on the Forbidden Journey, we were standing on the steps, and he wished we were up high in the tower. Knowing what he was doing, he quickly asked me to go to the ball with him, just like Harry asked Cho. Lucky for him, I hadn't accepted anyone else's invitation." The thought of it lingered. "I loved that he remembered a small piece of information and used that."

Abi smiled, knowing the exact scene she was describing. "Awww. I loved that part, too. I agree. It would've been much better if Cho'd accepted. You're right."

"Afterward, we yelled and screamed on the ride while he held my hand the whole time." She waited, then reached over to Abi. "I hope you know we thought of you all weekend. You weren't out of sight and out of mind."

Her friends all nodded in agreement.

"When Shane told Shawn that Burton had you, we were thankful you were safe," Laney explained.

"Yeah," Allie said.

Abi smiled. "Appreciate that."

"And don't worry, Abs. I'm sure Shane will ask you soon." Allie turned to Jade. "It's just a matter of time before Owen asks you, too."

The chimes sounded as their conversation dropped off there.

Packing their bags, Shiri, Shiresse, and Mandy walked past.

Abi couldn't help but think of Emile, knowing her friends had abandoned her. Unbeknownst to everyone, this secretly prompted her to make a second attempt to visit the girl, hoping, in the long run, she wouldn't regret the decision.

The Scuffle

Leaving the art studio, the girls animatedly chatted on the way to the Bistro, their laughter echoing down the hallway. Andrew and Ted trailed closely, their conversation more subdued. Although the rain had ceased, lingering dampness hung in the air, making the day seem heavy and dreary. The sun struggled to break through the thick cloud cover, casting a muted, gray light over everything.

As they descended the steps, the group opted to sit inside, wary of the rain's potential return. The atmosphere was warm and inviting - a welcome contrast to the gloomy weather.

Spotting their guys, the girls could see they'd already pulled several tables together, creating a cozy space for them.

Gathered around, grateful for the chance to continue their lively conversation, Abi noticed Shane sitting and waiting for her. The second their eyes met, he smiled brightly and waved.

Standing to greet her with a kiss and a hug, he said, "Hey. How was class?"

Not about to unpack everything they'd discussed, she replied, "Good. Uneventful."

"Hungry? What can I get you?" he asked before joining Adrian and Shawn, already in line.

"Just a beat salad would be great. Thank you."

"You got it."

When Abi took a seat, she watched him walk away. She loved how he moved with such a strong presence, attracting attention as he passed through the crowd. Able to see from the outside in, she found herself amongst the wealthy elite, all beautiful and stylish. Thinking back to her life in Boston, never in her wildest dreams would she have thought this is what her life would be months later.

Hearing a thrilling screech, Abi noticed another homecoming proposal taking place. "Maybe it's not his thing?" she whispered to herself. "But how can you be the football team captain and not attend the dance?" A rash of self-doubt spread over her. Assuming he'd be homecoming King, she couldn't help but question – would she be his worthy Queen?

Amidst her daydreaming, Marco arrived with a major chip on his shoulder. Angry at spending the morning in the principal's office, completing his work outside the confines of the classroom, he walked directly over to Jade, who was sitting beside Laney.

"They told me I need to apologize to you," he said dismissively. "So, yeah. That's it."

Jade locked onto his line of sight with a fire in her eyes and said to Laney, "I did not hear an apology. Did you?"

The blonde leaned forward, elbows on the table, and rested her chin in her hands. "No. No, I don't think I did."

The suave Italian rolled his eyes and looked away.

"So, let's have it." Jade stood and rested her hands on her hips as every student took notice.

Scanning the Bistro area, he looked at his feet before getting closer to her. Assuming he was about to say the words, *I'm sorry*, quietly, Jade leaned in. His lips inches away from her ear, he muttered, "I wouldn't be in this mess if it weren't for you. I'd be careful. It'd be a shame if something happened to that pretty face of yours. For the record, I only give one warning. Consider this it."

Never having been spoken to like that, she stared at him and saw pure evil. It wasn't just a threat. He meant what he said. Jade turned left, then right realizing with the low volume of his voice, nobody seemed to hear him utter what he did. Unafraid, she stood tall and said, "Now, you're threatening me? What is wrong with you?"

"My Father taught me well," he whispered.

Unable to let this slide, Owen walked over to them. "Is that true? Did you threaten her?"

"This is between me and the queen. Back off."

The junior QB knotted his fist in the guy's shirt and pulled back the other, ready to land a punch. "Say it again!" he shouted at his disgruntled teammate.

Before he could do that, Shane intervened. Cuffing Owen's arm, he forcefully separated the two. "Knock it off! Move it! Both of you! Now!" Bluntly pushing the players out of the bistro, Shane kept an eye out for teachers as they rounded the corner.

"What the hell is wrong with you, man?" Owen accused.

Marco smirked at him.

Setting off the young quarterback, he launched again and landed a deep punch to Marco's gut before pinning the guy against the wall, making Shane intervene.

The delinquent player cowered while gasping and groaning to regain the air knocked from his lungs.

"What's your problem, Cafaro!" Shane yelled as the guy slowly stood upright.

Owen pointed at him, his anger boiling. "I swear, if you so much as look at Jade the wrong way, I am gonna beat the shit outta you!"

The Captain pulled his junior replacement aside. "Around here, Cafaro, if you don't fall in line, you either learn the hard way or the hardest way. You pick."

Not another word came from Marco's mouth.

Shane figured he'd gotten through to their teammate. "Look, whether we like it or not, we need you this season. But, so far, your track record means you are more of a liability than an asset. That translates into less time on the field than on it. You're no good to this team on the bench. As of now, you'd better lose this arrogant-ass attitude if you wanna survive here. The rest of the team won't be as forgiving. If you're not willing to do that, I suggest you walk away. Leave. We don't need you. Coach will have someone in your spot by end of day. But if you wanna play football and win a championship, we'll start with a clean slate right here. Your choice. What'll it be? Are you in, or are ya out?"

Marco's sights bounced between the two QBs. He acknowledged them with a nod, nothing more.

"Good. Now, you are going to go over to Jade and apologize. No more disrespecting any of the girls on campus. Do it again. We're done. You hear me?"

Knowing he got his point across, Shane shoved Owen along and prompted Marco to start walking.

Abi saw the three of them emerge from around the corner. Shane pointed in Jade's direction. She looked up at the guy, afraid of what he would say next.

Marco sheepishly said, "I'm sorry. Won't happen again."

About to offer a snide comment, Shane shot her a look and shook his head. "Jade... No."

She turned to Cafaro and said, "Thank you."

The guy painfully rubbed his gut. "Yeah, whatever."

The three joined the rest of the team. With all eyes on Shane, Abi could tell he was giving them a pep talk. When he finished his speech, each reached their fist into the huddle and quietly broke to go about their business. Sitting Marco down with a few players, Shane said, "Keep an eye on him for me."

"No prob, Cap," the big linebacker named Aaron said.

He gave him a thumbs-up.

Before returning to Abi, he grabbed her salad along with his sandwich. Exuding an air of confidence, he crossed the bistro and sat beside her.

"What was that about?" she asked.

Unwrapping his lunch, about to take a bite, he said, "Nothing. All good."

She realized he had rectified the Marco situation but hoped he had dealt with it constructively. Seeing how Marco was acting now, Abi assumed the guys might have forced him to comply.

Intent on avoiding the subject, he asked, "Do you still want to go to the office to ask about Gerald?"

"Yes, if that's okay. Can you go with me?"

"Sure."

Keeping to themselves, they ate quickly. Not having much time, the two finished up. Shane was noticeably annoyed by what happened earlier. She figured he might share the details at one point or another but would never ask.

When he cleaned up their table, he said, "Ready?"

She swung her bag on her shoulder. "Yes."

As they left, everyone watched as they passed by Marco and Owen. It seemed a dark cloud was hovering over Gilderson that day. Hopefully, it wasn't a sign of things to come.

44

Gerald

Breaking away from the crowd, Shane felt like he could breathe again. He hated confrontation but knew there were times when it was necessary.

On the way past the central courtyard, he swung open the door to the administrative building. Inside, they approached the sizeable circular desk with three women working diligently behind it. Waiting for someone to look up and address them, the lady on their left caught sight of Shane Coppersmith. Her face softened the moment he stepped forward.

"Hello, I was wondering if you could help us," he stated calmly.

"Certainly, what can I do for you, young man."

He turned to Abi and spoke on her behalf. "We noticed the parking security guard has not been at work for a few days. Is there a reason why someone is taking his place?"

"I'm sorry, I can not divulge that information," she refused. "It's confidential."

Abi teared up on purpose. "We understand, but I'm worried about him. We just want to make sure he's okay. Are you sure there is nothing you can tell us?"

"Yeah, we'd really appreciate it," Shane urged, leaning on the counter to charm it out of her.

The lady glanced at her busy coworkers. "Well, between you and me, Mr. Thomas has taken a leave of absence. I do not know why. I'm sorry. That's all I know."

Shane grinned and lightly tapped his hand flat on the desk. "Thank you so much."

She smiled, completely awestruck by the heartthrob teen.

Grateful for the information, Abi said, "Yes, I appreciate your help."

By the time they walked through the doors, she'd already pulled her phone from her pocket and was googling something.

"We got his last name. Now all I have to do is search on 411 and see what shows up." Finding only one apartment listing for a Gerald Thomas, she said, "There! Got it."

"What would make him take a leave of absence?"

"Not sure. I hope he's not sick."

Just as they crossed the courtyard to the study hall, the chimes sounded the second they opened the door.

"Perfect timing," Shane chuckled.

Abi and Shane climbed the spiral staircase to the third floor after sliding their cards through a reader at check-in. Below, they could see the new football players hanging around a group of girls vying for their attention. Strangely, two were missing- one big Ben and one arrogant but charming Owen Karp.

While moving to their usual cubicle away from everyone else, unfortunately, they found the missing players huddled with Ming and Jade. The new couples had invaded their territory.

Abi was disappointed to share their quiet space and quickly looked for something quieter with fewer distractions. Shane followed, but in the process, he took another picture with his phone. Typing a message, he hoped a teacher wouldn't spot him doing it.

As he successfully pressed send, Abi asked, "Was that for Reggie?"

"Yep," he said, "The longer he lets this drag on, the worse it'll be."

"You really think he loves her?"

Without a doubt in his mind, he answered, "I'd bet money on it."

"So, then, where is he? Why hasn't he come after her?"

"Knowing him like I do, I assume he's orchestrating something big. Sending him these pics is just giving him an incentive to work faster. That's all."

Hearing Jade giggling, Abi said. "I hope you're right."

45

Motivational

Suffering through two hours of intense study left Shane's brain feeling fried. With a sigh, he closed his books and laptop and carefully slipped them into his backpack, feeling a weight lift slightly. Looking outside, he noticed the sun struggling to break through the persistent cloud cover, casting a dull, diffused light over the campus. Despite the overcast sky, the rain had ceased, leaving the air cool and dry.

"Guess we'll have practice after all." Offering his hand to her, he said, "Ready to head out?"

"Yes. Ready."

Andrew radioed to tell Matt they were on the move as Ted moved across the room to join him. Following the two out the main doors, the men parted the students like Moses and the Red Sea.

"Are you drivin' with me?" Shane asked on their way to the elevator.

"Yes. Of course."

"Abi! Wait!" Jade shouted from twenty feet away.

Stopping, Abi wasn't surprised to see Owen attached to her hip.

"Are you going to practice today?"

"Yes, I'll be there."

"Wait for me in the lobby. We can walk upstairs together."

Flashing a smile, she nodded. "Alright."

"Great. See you soon," she giggled as Owen wrapped his arms around her waist.

When Abi turned, she saw Shane sneak another photo.

"You're gonna drive the guy crazy, you know…"

"That's the idea. Sometimes, it's best to light a fire, then fan the flames."

Descending to the parking garage below, almost at his Jeep, Abi spotted the strange man in the security booth. He was looking at her with eagle eyes. It sparked a weird feeling in the pit of her stomach.

"I really need to find Gerald and figure out why he left."

Worried, Shane said, "Whatever you do, don't go searching for him alone. Understand?"

Chuckling to herself, she turned to Andrew and Ted. "Am I ever?"

Shane opened the tailgate and tossed his bag in along with Abi's. Settled in their seats, he started the engine and sighed.

"Hey?" Abi sensed something was wrong. "What is it?"

"Just stressed. The team's gotta outperform this weekend, or my Father and agent will sign my life away by Saturday night." Leaning his head back, he took a moment to breathe.

She knew by the expression on his face he needed a pep talk.

"I realize how much is riding on this season. But, if you look at it as a whole, you will find it extremely overwhelming."

"Yeah, you're not kidding."

"What I just said didn't exactly sound positive, but this will." She placed her hand upon his cheek and turned his sights to hers. "Don't look too far ahead. Focus on the present – this moment, this practice, nothing else. Today, break it down even further. Get suited, stretch, and warm up. Throw one pass at a time. Zero in on each receiver. Their eyes. Their hands. Their feet. Today, every ball lands in the end zone, one by one, because you will get it there," she smiled. "And if you're in doubt, look at me. I'll remind you."

His eyes brightened. "How do you do that?"

"What?"

"Know what I need to hear."

She placed her hand on her chest. "It comes from my heart."

Reaching out, he wrapped his arms around her. Lips locked to hers, he felt energized and motivated.

"Better?" she said.

"Definitely." Shifting gears, they were soon on their way with Abi's goons following.

Driving along Sunset, she wondered if she should be with him in Vegas this weekend. "Do you want me to go with you?" she asked out of the blue.

"Where?"

"Vegas."

He glanced at her twice, then back to the road again. "You can if you want. I know some of the girls are going."

"I'm sure Jade will be there by the looks of it."

"But shouldn't you stay here to be with your Mom?"

Pulled in two directions, she replied, "If you need me, then I'll go."

"Alright, I'll put your name on the list. But if you change your mind, it's fine. Don't give it a second thought, alright?"

She tapped his hand. "Okay."

46

Practice

Owen and Jade waited by his car as Shane's Jeep drove into the parking garage, its rugged tires echoing against the concrete. He found a spot close to them while the guys stopped to unload. Switching it up, Matt joined Andrew for a change in scenery, leaving Ted with the truck. Each of them stood tall to secure the area. Panning with eagle eyes, they followed Abi and Shane once they were on the move.

Walking slightly ahead, Abi was aware of their protective presence and waved to Owen and Jade.

Abi overheard Owen ask in a low voice, "What's with the muscle?"

Keeping things simple, Jade replied, "She's a valuable asset."

"Guess so," he said.

Aware QB Jr was skillfully trying to elevate his status, Abi smirked, wondering if Jade could see it. She certainly could.

Before walking inside the Wasserman Center, Shane checked his phone. He noticed Reggie had read his messages but had yet to respond. With a smirk, he assumed his plan was working. Opening the door for everyone, Shane wasn't happy to see Marco slip past. "What are you doin' here, man? Don't you have detention?"

He signed in and said, "Coach got me out. We need to practice for the showcase. So, I'm here. Ready to play."

Surprised by his response, he said, "Good. Can I count on you to give a hundred percent today?"

He smirked at the Captain. "No. I'll give you more," he stated, walking away.

Owen shot Shane a look. "He's confident. I'll give him that."

"We'll see. It's time to prove his worth." The Captain turned to him. "And yours."

The guy offered a closed fist. "You got it, Cap." When the Senior reciprocated and hit his fist, the young QB said, "I'll see you inside."

Before leaving, Shane turned to Abi.

"Good luck," she smiled. "Remember what I said."

"I will." With arms wrapped around her waist and lips close to her ear, he whispered, "I love you."

"Love you, too."

Casually kissing her, he held her hand until he had no choice but to let go.

"Watching the two of you could make a girl believe in fairytales," Jade said fancifully.

As they climbed the stairs to the viewing gallery, she replied, "I don't know about that." Abi noticed Jade was acting differently with Owen. "You're moving a bit slow with this one?"

"Just being cautious."

"Afraid to hurt that baby while you're robbing the cradle?" she jabbed.

"Very funny, girlfriend. Laugh, if you will. But he's nice. Guys his age are sweet and attentive. I need that right now." She knew what Abi was thinking. "And don't worry. I won't break his heart."

"I hope not." Hearing her phone ring, she glanced down at the screen. "Umm, I need to take this. Excuse me a second. You go ahead. I'll catch up." When Jade was well ahead of her, Abi accepted the call. "Hey, Burton."

"How's it going, Abs?" Everything okay?"

"Yeah, you?"

"Busy. Had a moment and thought I'd check in."

"I'm doing fine."

There was a pause on Burton's end.

She wondered about Zoe Sky's status. About to ask, he said, "Are you at Wasserman Field?"

"Yes." Looking around, she found Matt and Andrew standing a few feet away and figured he'd just spoken to them.

"Well, I'll let you get back to it. Text me when you're in for the night."

Reading between the lines, she knew he was sincerely keeping tabs on her.

"Sure will. Thank you for thinking of me."

"Always," he answered without a hint of doubt.

Ending the call, each bid the other goodbye.

Moving down the hallway, she felt that every time they talked, their conversations pulled at her heartstrings - like he was doing it purposefully to constantly remind her he was there even though he wasn't.

Before going outside to the viewing deck, she searched for Dark Demon on social. Countless pictures surfaced. Sadly, Abi saw the pretty model was still with him. The sight of her holding his hand sparked another fit of jealousy. Frustrated, she shook her head and mumbled, "Stop it, Abs. You're with Shane."

When she swung open the deckside door, she saw Jade put her phone down.

"Was that Burton?" she asked.

"How'd you know?"

"Word to the wise: Keep your calls out of the shadows. It sparks speculation even when there is nothing to question."

Nodding, Abi thought about what she said. It had merit.

Sitting beside her friend as the team flooded the field for the warmup, Abi noticed Jade's sights remained locked on Owen and barely spoke a word.

"So, is this a serious thing between you two, or is he the rebound guy?"

The girl glimpsed her way, raising praying hands to her lips as Owen took the snap. "Seriously?"

"I'm a bit confused because, after my visit yesterday, I thought you wanted to focus on getting Reg back, not sparking a relationship with someone else."

Jade exhaled. "Abs, I don't want to chase after Reg anymore. I need him to pursue me - to want me."

"Even at the risk of losing him for good?"

"Maybe." She looked out at Owen on the field. Pointing to him, she said, "Now, that guy. He worships me. He wants to be with me. I need that."

"But, do you care for him as much as you care for Reg?"

She closed her eyes. "I will never love anyone like I do him."

"Isn't that enough to fight for?"

The thought of him marrying someone else was too much to bear. "I feel like it's too late." A tear drifted down her cheek. Quickly wiping it away, she said, "I need to accept it. Besides, even if we got back together, we would never live harmoniously with his parents. They would make our lives a living hell."

"But at least you'd be happy. Right?" Abi hoped she'd think about it. "Don't count him out yet."

The girl nodded.

Seeing her friend's mind reeling, Abi figured she'd given her food for thought and left it at that.

Lead by Example

In the thick of it that afternoon, under a layer of low-lying clouds, the atmosphere crackled with energy. Amidst the rhythmic thud of cleats on turf and the occasional whistle blast from the coaches, several voices rose and fell amongst the crunching of bodies colliding. Hearing Shane calling the plays and Adrian keeping the guys on point, both did their best to lead by example.

Shane looked up occasionally, and Abi sent signals to motivate him.

Both girls clapped and whistled to commend every successful pass.

Overhearing the players trading banter, taunts, and encouragement during water breaks, Abi thought the guys' words blended slang and inside jokes that bound them together like a secret language. The players trash-talked a bit, keeping the energy high on the field. It also kept them alert and on their toes. Even through the laughter intermixed with sweat and exertion, the team could feel the level of competition in the air.

Close to five o'clock, the blow of the last whistle called it a day. While the athletes slowly walked off the field, Abi watched Shane perform his usual ritual. Alone, without his best friend now, he stood there and listened to the silence before turning around and walking off. On his way by, he looked up and placed his hand over his heart. Tapping it twice, he smiled and pointed to her.

Blowing him a kiss, she felt like the practice finished on a positive note.

Jade and Abi left the viewing deck and went inside.

While walking down the hall, with Matt leading the way and Andrew following them, Abi asked, "So, are you going to Vegas this weekend to watch Owen play?"

"Yeah, I was planning on it. Ming and Mei are going too. From what I hear, Laney and Shawn are staying in town. He doesn't want to venture across state lines. It's too soon after the court hearing." She turned to her. "Why? Are you thinking of going, too?"

"Perhaps," she said under her breath, shooting her security guard an eye. "I'll have to pass it by Andrew first. It could be a tall order. We'll have to see."

He glanced over. Humorously, one corner of his mouth slightly curled.

Slowly descending the stairs, the girls found empty seats in the lobby and waited for the guys to emerge from the locker room. Soon, one by one, the players started trickling out. Owen was one of the first.

"That was fast," Jade said.

"Yep. Missed you, so I made it snappy."

For whatever reason, Abi thought of him as a little puppy, not a six-foot-four wall of lean muscle.

"Well, guess we're gonna head out. I'll see you tomorrow?" Jade stated.

"For sure. See you then."

Watching the two leave the building, Abi couldn't help but feel Jade was making a mistake regardless of how nice the guy was. Only knowing one man meant for Jade, it wasn't hard to see Owen Karp was not him.

Practically the last to surface, Shane came out looking tired.

"First one on the field and last one to leave. That's a Captain," she complimented. "Great practice."

"Thanks." He reached out to her and wrapped his arms around her shoulders before pulling her in tightly. "Your advice really helped me keep my focus."

"I'm glad."

About to head out the door, he asked, "So, are we heading to the hospital now?"

"I wouldn't mind stopping by. Is that okay?"

"Absolutely." Checking his phone, he added, "Later, would you want to swing by my place for a minute? I'm expecting a delivery."

"What kind of delivery?" Abi was intrigued.

He offered a sexy glance. "You'll see."

48

The Omen

On the short drive to UCLA Med, Abi looked at the ever-thickening clouds hanging low in the September sky. It cast a somber tone as the damp salty air hinted at October's impending rainy season.

Navigating the busy streets, arriving at UCLA, they drove underground into the darkness to find a parking spot. Afraid to see her Mother today, she hoped her condition hadn't worsened. Backing up into an open space, Shane threw the vehicle in park while Matt dropped off Andrew and Ted before moving on to his intended emergency location.

With her security, they maneuvered two sets of elevators. It was a quiet assent as they switched lifts on the lobby level and continued onto the sixth floor. When the doors parted, Abi walked with Shane hand in hand to her Mom's room.

Letting go of him, she stopped in front of the glass as he looked on. He could see sadness flooding her heart when she saw the woman's greyish skin tone and gaunt face.

Desperate to hold her Mother's hand, she knew she couldn't. The isolation sign was still on the door. Staring at her, something inside the tent caught her eye.

"Wait? What is that?" she questioned.

Shane moved beside her. He noticed it, too. "I'm not sure."

Another nurse appeared. Dressed in full PPE from head to toe, Abi stopped her when she was about to enter the room. "Excuse me? What is in my Mother's hands?"

The nurse looked in on her patient. "Oh? I'm not sure, dear. I just started my shift. One minute."

When she went inside, Abi watched her open the tent and reach in to remove the object from her grasp. Bringing it out of the room, she handed it to her.

"It's a flower, Miss."

Examining it, she thought it looked vaguely familiar. Recalling Laney's comment from the day before, she whispered, "Morbid flowers." Her heart began to race as the air escaped her lungs. "It's a black rose."

"Abs? What is it? What's wrong?" Shane questioned, knowing he'd missed something.

She rushed to the nurse's station and interrupted one woman talking with another. "Where did this come from?" she inquired, urgently showing them the flower. "Who left it here?"

"I don't know, Miss. What is your family member's name?"

"Beth Ann Acardi. I'm her daughter."

Hearing that piqued her attention. She checked the marker board on the wall. "The nurse assigned to your Mother is Jenna." She turned around and addressed someone in the back, updating a chart. "Jenna, the daughter of your patient, Beth Ann Acardi, is here."

The pretty woman from yesterday approached. With blonde hair pulled back in a ponytail and striking blue eyes, she smiled. "Hello again. Abi, is it?"

She skipped the pleasantries. "A nurse just pulled this flower from my Mom's hands. Did you see who left it?"

"I'm sorry, Miss. I don't know."

Frustrated and borderline angry, she said bluntly, "Then, how did it get there?"

"I saw it when I started my shift about two hours ago. I assumed family put it there."

"We don't have any family." Abi started to panic.

Witnessing this, Shane said, "We will figure this out, Abs. Stay calm."

She held up the flower as her hands trembled. "Someone went into her room and put it in her hands. She couldn't take hold of it herself. I need to know who was in her room!"

Andrew pulled her aside. "What's happening?"

Panicked, she took a deep breath and fearfully showed him the flower. "Yesterday, Laney noticed these flowers placed on every table in the bistro. She thought it was a weird choice. They are so morbid-looking. How did one make its way here to my Mother's hands? Is that not odd?"

The big man agreed. "Yes, that does seem strange."

"Can you help me?"

He approached the nurse and flashed his badge. "I need your head of security here, now."

The woman immediately got on the phone.

"Don't worry, Miss. We will alert them and look at camera footage." Stepping away with the flower in hand, he snapped a photo of it before making a phone call.

Shane stood alongside her as she tried to listen in. "What are you thinking?" he asked.

"I don't know. With everything going on, maybe I'm just being paranoid."

He gave her a side hug. "They'll find out who did this."

When the security guard returned, he said, "I've called it in. They're on it and will send a team momentarily. In the meantime, I believe it's best if we take you home. It may not be safe."

"But what about my Mom?"

"They are going to station protection detail right outside her room. Nobody will go in or out without passing them by."

Hearing this, she said, "Okay."

Before leaving, Abi asked, "Jenna? Can I go in and see her?"

"Absolutely. Come with me. I will suit you up."

Thankfully granted permission, the woman helped get her dressed in protective gear. Walking in, shortly after, Abi stood at her bedside.

"Don't worry, Mom. They will keep you safe." Wearing gloves, she slipped her hand under the tent and gently rubbed her arm. It felt cold to the touch through the latex, causing her to pull the edge of the blanket and cover her up to her chin.

"I'll be back tomorrow. Hang in there. I love you."

Unable to kiss or hug her, she grasped her hand and gave it a few subtle squeezes. She would give anything to feel something in return.

Reluctantly leaving, Shane helped her carefully peel off the PPE as Andrew and Ted spoke to hospital security. Both were on high alert.

"They've instructed us to get you out of here," Ted announced urgently while still on the phone.

Peering down at his messages, Andrew heard him. "A team just arrived. Let's move."

Assuming Andrew meant the police, they followed him to the elevator as four men stepped off when the doors opened.

The guys gave the team a nod in passing before they took their positions outside of the room.

When they boarded the elevator, Shane stood with Abi as the doors closed.

Reaching the lobby, Andrew corraled them towards the front doors where Matt was waiting. "We will meet you at the house, Shane," he said.

The football player hugged Abi, realizing Andrew was serious. "You go ahead with them. I'll be right behind you."

"I want to wait here until he surfaces?" Abi instructed.

"Very well," Andrew replied.

Believing it to be an honest request given her situation, she asked, "Can Ted go with him?"

Shane tried to save face. "No, it's fine. Abs, I'm good."

"Please. It will give me peace of mind."

"Fine." With some hesitation, Shane said while looking to Andrew for direction, "Whatever you say."

Ted awaited instructions.

The second Andrew said, "Go," they took off.

Safe in the back seat, Abi watched the two jog through the main doors and disappear.

Watching Andrew pacing alongside the curb, talking on the phone, Abi assumed he was speaking with Burton.

It took forever for the Jeep to join them.

When Shane finally pulled up, Andrew jumped in the front seat while Ted stuck with Shane.

Leaving the hospital, not having seen her Dad, she got a sinking feeling.

Are these roses a message? A warning? Or an omen?

49 |

The Delivery

It wasn't long before they climbed the winding hills of Stradella Road, the SUV skillfully navigating the sharp corners and sudden twists of the labyrinth streets.

Approaching her house, Abi tapped her phone to open the gate. It slid aside smoothly, allowing Matt to pull the truck up to the house. Seconds later, Shane and Ted glided in on their right.

Andrew went to help Abi. "Please lock up, Miss. It's just a precaution," he said, his eyes scanning their surroundings with practiced vigilance.

"Alright." Doing what he suggested, the barrier between them and the street shut tightly.

Shane got out to join her.

On her way inside, she noticed him holding back. "Are you coming?" she said.

"You go ahead. I'll be there in a minute."

Initially, not thinking much of it, she replied, "Okay," while turning off the alarm as Ted began his interior rounds. Certain the coast was clear, he disappeared again.

Kicking off her shoes, Abi wanted to change into more comfortable clothes. She trudged up the stairs to reach the top floor. Her gut feeling made her walk through the library and sneak a peek at the courtyard below. There, she found Shane talking with Andrew and Ted while

Matt looked on. Showing them something on his phone, she whispered, "What are you up to?"

When he was on his way inside, she swiftly continued to her room and ducked into the closet. Changing, she felt cozy in black tights and Shane's baggy hoodie. After brushing her teeth, she pulled the elastic from her hair and let it fall over her shoulders. Running her fingers through it, she spread a hint of gloss over her lips.

A knock came to her door.

"Abs? Are you in here?"

She emerged from the bathroom. "What's up?"

"I just wanted to see if you still want to come for a drive with me?" Glancing down at his phone, he said, "I'm expecting that delivery in about forty minutes." Not knowing what she would say, he added, "I already passed it by the guys. They said they'd tag along."

"Is it okay if I wear this?" Abi looked down at her overly casual attire.

"Sure. When I get there, I'll probably do the same."

"Okay. I'll go."

"Great."

The two went back downstairs. Abi grabbed her bag and slipped on her white sneakers. Setting the alarm, they both walked out the door.

Meeting up with Andrew, she said, "Are you sure this is safe?"

"Yes, Miss. We will stay with you. It's fine."

Abi felt reassured.

In his gentlemanly way, Shane opened the passenger side door. Once she settled in, he closed it and waved to the men, ready to head out.

The gate secured the home again, and they were on their way.

Listening to the music playing on the radio, Abi tapped her fingers to the sounds of the band Forester. Their distinct California vibe helped her concentrate on the black rose mystery. From Stradella all the way across Sunset and up Ysidro Drive, Abi stayed quiet. She couldn't stop wondering who'd left it and why.

Her mind noticeably reeling, he squeezed her hand to break her from her daze. "Are you thinking about today?"

"I'm hoping they discover who was in my Mom's room."

While driving north on Summitridge, he said, "I'm sure they will. It didn't get there on its own."

"Exactly."

Approaching the Beverly Park gatehouse, Shane spoke to security and had Abi's team show their credentials as she watched the late afternoon sun begin to burn off the cloud bank. While moving through the large gates, Abi was curious.

"So, what's the big secret?" she asked.

"About what?"

"The delivery."

He smiled. "No secret."

"Then why not come out with it? Just tell me?"

"It's a surprise."

Immediately, she assumed it may have something to do with a homecoming proposal. Disappointed that she wasn't dressed nicer, she got a little excited.

Rounding the corner to his house, they saw a flatbed truck about to unload a brand new matte black, custom Jeep Rubicon.

"Wait?" she said. "Is that yours?"

"Yeah. What do you think?" he said excitedly.

"It's amazing."

"Surprise!" he said.

She loved the Jeep, but sadness washed over her, knowing it wasn't what she thought.

Shane drove toward the house and into the courtyard while the guys circled back and waited for them on the street.

Parking the rental, Shane quickly got out and rushed to meet the man standing at the bottom of the driveway.

Abi followed.

As he spoke to the guy, she watched the man climb aboard the flatbed and start the Jeep before slowly backing it off the truck as it growled. The two did a walkabout and checked the vehicle over before

Shane signed for it and exchanged the paperwork. Installing the new plates, with everything all said and done, he handed Shane the keys.

"Thanks, man. Appreciate it."

The young guy smiled and shook his hand. "Enjoy your new ride."

As he left, Shane admired the Jeep, which looked immaculate. When he got behind the wheel, Abi jumped in on the passenger side. The first thing she noticed was the new car leather smell.

Parking inside the gates, he asked, "Want to go for a drive? Maybe grab something to eat somewhere?"

"We could do that, but then we need to head home to study. You gotta be ready in case you have to write the quiz tomorrow. Deal?"

"I hear you." Shane quickly agreed. "I'll go and change."

"I'll come with you."

Hoping his Father wasn't home, she followed Shane inside and ascended the marble stairs before they drifted down the hallway to his room.

Quickly vanishing into his closet, she sat on the sofa as he rummaged around and flipped clothes off the hangers. Finally, emerging with a duffle bag in one hand and a garment bag in the other, he said, "I'm good. Ready?"

"Yes."

"Let's go."

Returning outside, Abi smiled at how excited he was. Happy for him, she helped move his stuff from the rental to his new beast. It was a little taller than the last one. About to climb in, Shane came up behind her to offer a lift if she needed it.

When he pressed the button to ignite the engine, he put it in gear and said, "It sounds good, don't you think?"

"I suppose."

"Guess that's more of a guy thing?"

She laughed. "I'd say so."

Before taking his foot off the break, he reached for her hand and held it tightly. "Somehow, it feels like the first day you came to football practice with me."

"Except, there are doors and a roof this time."

"That's true," he laughed, recalling how nervous he was to hold her hand that day.

Moving down the driveway, the Jeep drove differently than the old one, and the turning radius wasn't as good with the thick treads.

As they headed north towards Mulholland Drive, Shane got a feel for it. "It rides a bit rougher. Might have to take it to my performance garage to see what they can do. I really like the carbon fiber on the dash." Playing with the LCD screen, he paired his phone while stopped at a red light. Not knowing where to put the device, he handed it to Abi. "I should install a holder," he said while turning onto Coldwater Canyon.

"Where are we going?" she asked, seeing the GPS on his phone mirrored on the screen.

"For a drive. I'm making a loop," Shane said, checking their ETA. "We should be there in forty minutes."

"Where?"

"You'll see. It is well worth the wait. Trust me."

Despite being exhausted, she knew he needed a break from life.

"So, the team was talking about this crazy moon tonight."

"Oh? I hadn't heard. Obviously, a full moon, I assume.?"

"I believe so."

Checking the time, she saw the SUV in the rearview mirror. "Andrew and the guys will need to change shifts shortly."

"It's okay. He's aware, remember. It was Andrew's idea to stick with us for a while. I'm sure he informed the night staff of the change of plans."

"Alright."

"It's all good."

Visibly shaken as they passed the not-so-nice parts of Los Angeles, Abi saw people living in tents beneath the underpasses and freeway ramps, most covered in graffiti. Many buildings and businesses along Franklin Avenue were either abandoned or boarded up compared to when they turned on Los Feliz Boulevard, which had parks, mature trees, and many gated estates. As she rested her head back, it seemed like they were driving forever.

Suddenly, she noticed a street sign. "Hey, we're close to the observatory?"

He glanced at her, hoping she hadn't seen it. "Maybe you want to stop? With the moon being so rare tonight, it would be a good spot to experience it."

She smiled and sat up in her seat. "I've never been to an observatory before."

"That makes two of us."

Climbing the hillside, they rounded the corner and drove into Griffith Park. Able to find a spot in the last row near the back, Shane got out and helped Abi. Paying the fee, he placed the pass on the dash and locked the Jeep.

"I'm excited. This should be fun," he said, offering his hand to her.

She grasped hold. "I think so, too."

Not seeing the guys, she wondered where they'd gone. Having them around twenty-four-seven lately was comforting. When they weren't visible, it felt a bit strange despite being with Shane. But those doubts faded away the second she saw the uplit building. Admiring it, Abi thought it looked magical.

With dusk fast approaching, the two climbed the stairs to the left and found the sky painted orange and red against the darkness creeping in.

Rounding a corner, Shane guided her along the balcony, where they came across a roped-off VIP section with fairy-lit palm trees swaying in the breeze. A red carpet and a table for two with lanterned candlelight looked so romantic.

"Someone must be getting engaged tonight," she said endearingly. Clutching her heart, she exhaled. "Oh, I hope we get to witness it."

The closer they got, Shane said, "Well, they aren't here yet. Maybe we could have a seat." He passed through the barrier and pulled out a chair.

Mortified, Abi quietly panicked. "What are you doing? Get out of there. Someone might see you." Looking left and right, she whispered, "We can't high-jack someone's engagement?"

Shane chuckled at how upset she was. Approaching her, he rested his hands on her arms. "You don't actually believe I'd do something like that, do you?"

"Well, I'd hope not." Confused, she stood there, not moving a muscle. "What is going on?"

Shane looked past her and raised a steady hand. "Hi, Pamela."

When Abi turned, she found a woman grinning from ear to ear.

"It looks great," Shane greeted. "I appreciate your help."

She acknowledged his compliment and said, "So happy you like it."

"Wait..." Abi was in shock.

Extending his hand to her, Shane said, "It's for us. Now, will you join me?"

Her heart started to pump wildly. "What's happening?"

"I brought you here because I have something to ask you."

"You do?" She slowly moved toward him.

Inches apart, he said, "Around this time of year, every guy contemplates this question."

Hanging on his every word, she watched the handsome QB get down on one knee. His eyes glimmered as they caught a hint of light from the candles nestled inside the tall lanterns.

She held her breath as he presented her with a bouquet of roses.

"Abi Acardi, may I have the honor of escorting you to the homecoming dance?"

Exhaling, a smile spread across her face as her eyes welled with tears. Unable to answer him, she nodded happily and whimpered, "Yes."

The crowd clapped when Shane stood to hug her tightly.

"I thought for a second you were going to truly propose," she giggled.

Without skipping a beat, he looked down at her sincerely and said, "Yes, that's next." Drawn in, knowing he was serious, he kissed her. "One step at a time," he said. "This is one of many milestones in our future."

Heart fluttering, she looked over the city. There, cresting along the horizon, was the harvest moon.

"This is the best seat in the house." Standing behind her, he wrapped his arms around her waist.

"I can't believe you planned all of this for me."

"I wanted to make it memorable."

"My first and last homecoming proposal." Cuddling up to him, she felt so loved.

Offered a seat, Abi saw some people look at them enviously. The guys took their places outside the red velvet barriers and kept a six-foot buffer between them and those gathered around. Pamela brought over their dinner and set the table.

Abi was in awe. "Thank you so much."

The woman smiled. "You're very welcome. Enjoy."

"Thanks," Shane replied.

When she left them, the two opened their small sushi platters.

Chopsticks in hand, Shane struck up a normal conversation. "I didn't get to finish telling you about my visit with Alan yesterday."

Eating a roll, she asked, "And? How did that go?"

"Better than expected," he laughed. "His Mom is a bit of a cougar."

Curious to Shane's tone, she said, "Oh, boy... What did you do?"

"Like I said, I played on her weaknesses and made a case for her son – who is her prize possession, by the way."

"You did?"

"I've known her for a few years. She always talked about him and me graduating together, so I focused on that. It caught her attention quickly."

"How did she respond?"

"Long story short, I made her cry," Shane said point-blankly.

"Oh no…"

"See, to me, that's good. Chances are she'll talk to her husband and hopefully tell the man to reinstate Alan at Gilderson before the end of the week."

"You think so?"

He moved his chair right beside hers and wrapped his arm around her. "If not, I guess I'll be playing somewhere else too."

The moon ascended slowly in the sky.

"Don't think twice if you have to do that. Take the offer. We will see each other as often as possible, and I can always tutor you after hours, regardless. It will be fine either way."

"No, it won't. Abs, I don't want us to be separated. I like the way things are."

She tapped his knee with her hand. "I do, too, but like I said, if an opportunity presents itself and it helps you move closer to your dream of playing in the NFL, you need to do whatever it takes. I never want to be the person who stands in the way of that."

He intermittently grasped her hand, amazed by what she said – the selflessness of it all. "You are incredible. Has anyone ever told you that?"

"Well, you thought my football stats analysis was incredible but never really said I was. Only one other person has told me that," she chuckled.

"Who? Burton?" Disappointed, he humorously rolled his eyes.

"Perhaps. But let's leave my *friend* out of this."

The moon was gigantic. It was so bright it drowned out the city lights, allowing a bird's-eye view of the many visible craters.

Resting her head on his shoulder, she said, "Thank you for making this evening so special."

"You're welcome. Excited about the dance?"

"Yes and no."

He sat up and turned to her. "Why?"

Awaiting an answer, she explained, "Well, first, I need to find a dress. Second, I'm kind of nervous. I don't know what to expect. I've never been to anything like this before." She took a deep breath.

"Don't be nervous. I will be by your side the entire time. And no matter what dress you choose, you will look beautiful."

"I suppose I'll have to go shopping with Jade at some point. Based on previous experience, that will be a costly trip."

"Please don't go too crazy."

"Tell her that," she chuckled and focused on the view before them. "You know, I always dreamed of my Mom helping me find the perfect dress. So many times, I envisioned her taking me to get an up-do, fancy nails, and my make-up professionally done. But, that isn't going to happen, so..."

"I'm sorry, Abs. I know it's difficult."

"But, that said, I have to accept my new normal." She paused and looked at him. "Thank you for all the support. It means a lot." Needing to change the subject, she asked, "On a happier note, what's the schedule that weekend?"

"Well, I will be gone for two days beforehand. Away Thursday and Friday. Back in town late Friday night. Our home game is Saturday afternoon, and the dance starts at seven that evening."

"A busy few days for you."

"Yeah, it's hectic."

"Where is the dance being held?"

"I hear it's at the Four Seasons Westlake."

Abi didn't know of the place but assumed it was impressive.

Aware she was dealing with a lot, he said, "Can I just put something out there..."

"What's that?"

"With everything going on, I understand if you don't want to go. No pressure." He rubbed her hand. "I am okay either way. By the time the game ends Saturday, I'm usually exhausted, so if you want to spend a quiet night together, I'm up for that, too."

"But, you're the Captain. You need to be there."

"Not if you don't want to be."

She tried her best to produce a smile. "It'll be fun. If anything, I'll be transported away from my troubles for a little while."

"Are you sure?"

"Absolutely. It's our grade twelve year—our last hoorah. It's hard to believe we will be attending university next fall."

"It feels like it is coming up fast."

"Time waits for no one."

Shane looked at the time. "Guess we should head back now. I know you wanted to get some studying done before bed."

She groaned, not wanting to leave. "Five more minutes? I don't want to go yet. I'm trying to soak it all in."

"Just FYI, I plan to give you a lifetime of surprises such as this. For us, I feel it's only the beginning."

What he said took her breath away.

Moving closer, mere inches apart, he gazed into her eyes and said, "I love you, Abi Acardi."

"I love you too," she whispered before he kissed her gently.

The moon was now majestically above the Griffith Observatory, casting a soft, silvery glow over the iconic structure. High in the clear night sky, its luminous orb dominated the vast expanse, its light reflecting off the domes. The cool, late September winds whispered through the trees as the gentle hum of stargazers and moon enthusiasts gathered around, their eyes turned skyward. The scene was serene yet vibrant, a perfect blend of natural splendor and human curiosity.

Having stayed for ten more minutes, Abi sighed, knowing they had to get home.

He reached out and hugged her. "Shall we go?" he asked.

"Sure."

Shane took her hand.

About to depart, Pamela walked over and asked, "Would you like a picture?"

Abi handed the woman her phone. "Please. That would be wonderful. Thank you."

An expert in her field, unbeknownst to Shane and Abi, she'd already taken several photos since they arrived. Posing for her, Pamela handed Abi her phone back before showing them what she'd sneakily captured on her digital camera.

"I've taken these for you," she said. "I will send them to Shane tomorrow."

They looked through the photos on the small screen. Abi thought they were amazing. Standing behind them, she'd taken shots of their silhouettes with the incredible sunset and a few while Shane proposed on one knee. She even got them sitting in the chairs, holding hands with the moon lofting along the horizon as the city lights sparkled below.

"Oh, thank you so much." Abi was elated.

"I'm so happy you enjoyed your evening."

"You made it so memorable. Absolutely perfect."

"Don't thank me. Thank this guy right here. He planned it all. I just brought his vision to life."

Shane humbly shook his head. "Yeah, but you did all the work." Shaking her hand, he said, "Thanks again. I really appreciate it."

"No problem at all. Have a good night, you two."

Abi and Shane waved to her as the guys keenly followed. Reaching his Jeep, it wasn't long before they pulled away and watched Matt pick up Andrew and Ted on the fly.

Hand in hand, Abi leaned over and rested her head on his shoulder.

"We got lucky weatherwise."

"Thankfully, there were no clouds," she said.

"I've gotta say. When it was raining today, I had doubts this night would even happen how I wanted it to. Sadly, I didn't have a plan B. Thought we'd need to huddle under an umbrella or something," he grinned.

"That wouldn't have been so bad." Abi kissed his cheek.

"Are you tired?"

"A little. The past few days have been a lot."

"I know. I'm sorry. The timing of this is bad, especially given what happened with your Mom today."

"But, it ended on a high note because of you."

"I'm sorry Eastwood's beef with me has pulled you into this feud."

Unable to tell him why things happened the way they did, she wished she could. "I know," she said. "Hopefully, it will come to an end sooner than later."

"I hope so, too."

50

Love and Trust

With music playing softly in the background, the moon now high in the nighttime sky, Abi soaked up the peacefulness. Traversing LA to the confines of Bel Air, returning to familiar territory, Abi didn't want the night to end. Almost home, she received a text. Peering down at the screen, she saw it was from Burton. It prompted her to hide it quickly.

"Is that him?" Shane asked.

"Umm, yeah. He's just checking in."

Shane couldn't help but feel jealous.

"I'll call him back later. I'm not in the mood right now."

Staying quiet the rest of the way, knowing the text put a damper on their evening, Shane pulled up to the gate as Abi opened it remotely. Slowly moving into the courtyard, he parked by the door while the guys greeted the night staff after doing a fair amount of overtime.

Andrew approached. "So, we're heading out, Miss. The night shift is taking over."

While waving to Lorenzo, Ethan, Bray, and Rob, she said, "Okay. Thank you for accompanying us tonight."

"No problem," Andrew replied. "We'll see you in the morning."

"Sounds good. Night."

"Night, Miss."

"Goodnight." Before entering the house, she said to the other team, "Be safe, gentlemen."

Each of them acknowledged with a thumbs up.

Shane grabbed his bag from the Jeep and stopped Andrew before they departed. "Thanks for your help," he said.

"No problem, man." The big guy presented a closed fist, which Shane knocked with his. "See you tomorrow."

"Yeah. For sure."

Andrew watched as the teen walked away. Despite pulling for his boss to be with the girl, he couldn't help but respect the future NCAA QB.

Following Abi, Shane waited as she turned off the alarm and switched on some lights.

"I'm gonna head upstairs," she said.

"I'm right behind you."

Upon reaching her room, she walked in and collapsed on the bed.

Shane peeked inside. "Hey. How are you holding up?"

"I'm fine. Just drained."

"Same," he said while standing in the doorway. "I'm just gonna shower and get changed, alright?"

"Sure, go ahead."

Hearing his feet walking down the hall, she waited for the guest room door to close. When it did, Abi selected Burton's number and called him. She heard his phone ring on the other end before he picked up.

"Hey, Abs."

"Hi," she said with a lack of enthusiasm.

"I hear you had a rough day."

She missed the sincerity in his voice. "You could say that." Pausing a minute, she asked, "Any news on the Eastwood sighting yesterday?"

"Less than an hour ago, we got confirmation. The man you saw outside the hospital was him."

Her heart dropped. "And that's one hundred percent?"

"Unfortunately. But we're still not sure what he was doing there."

"And the black roses?" Abi asked.

"CCTV cameras inside the hallways did not reveal anything concrete. The only thing we do know is that Eastwood was nowhere near your Mother."

Abi breathed a sigh of relief. "Then, how did the flower get there?"

"We aren't sure. They're working on that."

She went quiet. Her mind raced, making it hard to focus. "You do think the rose is odd, right?"

"Absolutely. The fact that the bistro had tables of them makes me wonder if it's connected. We are also investigating where they came from. Getting info out of your school has been difficult. They haven't exactly been forthcoming."

"Hmm."

About to say something, he stopped, then suddenly spit it out. "So, I see you were at the Griffith Observatory tonight."

Surprised to hear that, she replied, "Burton Lancaster. Are you stalking me?"

"No, but given the circumstances, I am watching over you, just in case. There is a difference."

"After the day I've had, I'll let that slide for now."

"So, what was going on at the observatory?"

"Well, if you should know, I saw the harvest moon."

Not missing a beat, he asked, "With Shane?"

"Yes, with Shane. Who else would I be with?"

"I'm just making sure," he hesitated. "Glad the guys were with you. I'm sure it was a busy spot."

Abi could tell he was fishing. Nervous to share the truth, she stuttered a little. "It was, umm, part of a Homecoming proposal."

"Really?" His interest piqued.

"Yes."

"And? How did he ask you?"

Believing it strange to talk to him about this, she tried to be selective with what she divulged. "He had an event planner create a VIP section for us – a front-row seat to watch the moon rise over the city."

"Impressive."

"As much as it made me happy, I also felt sad."

"How so?"

"I told Shane, I used to dream of prom, for instance, and my Mom helping me buy a dress and get my hair and nails done. You know, Mom and daughter stuff. But, it hit me: I won't ever have the experience."

Burton didn't know how to respond, so he kept it simple. "I'm sorry, Abs. I can't imagine."

"I want to be excited about it but feel a little overwhelmed. There's so much to do."

What she said sparked an idea. "It's okay. I'm sure your girlfriend, what's her name again?"

"Jade?"

"Right. Won't she help you?"

Abi thought about her previous shopping experience with her.

Wanting to change her perspective on the milestone event, he said, "One thing I learned during isolation in the north is not to take things like this for granted. I missed every grade twelve milestone. Homecoming, Christmas semi-formal, Prom, and Graduation. All of it."

Abi felt bad to hear this. "I didn't know."

"It's fine. The bottom line is that your Mom would want you to enjoy these experiences, even though she can't share them with you. She would want you to live your life to the fullest regardless of how difficult it's been."

What he said made sense. "You're right."

"And if I can help in any way, just ask."

"Thank you, Burton."

"You're welcome."

Desperate to bring up Zoe Sky, she said, "So, how's Vegas? Everything okay?"

Burton could tell by the upswing of her words that something was troubling her. Wondering if she'd seen the pictures online, he replied,

"All good here. The Club's construction finished on time and passed inspection. We're down to the wire but ready for Saturday."

"I'm glad to hear that."

Enduring an awkward silence, Abi hoped he'd bring up the subject willingly.

"Have you seen any of the Nightfall ads on social?"

"Umm, no," she said, afraid to take the plunge. Deep down, she knew it wasn't any of her business. "Maybe I'll take a peek before bed tonight." Abi let out another yawn, unable to hold it in any longer. Assuming Shane would be out of the shower shortly, she added, "I should get ready for bed. I'm pretty tired."

"Okay, I'll let you go. Call me if you need me, day or night, alright?"

"I will."

"Please don't hesitate," he reassured, hoping when she saw the pictures, she would.

"Night, B."

"Night, Abs. Sweet dreams."

"You too." When they ended the call, she closed her eyes.

A knock came on her door. Turning to find Shane standing there with damp hair, she spotted his textbook and laptop tucked under his arm.

"Can I come in?" he asked.

"Sure." Abi nervously scooched over to the middle of the bed.

Certain of who was on the other line, he wanted confirmation from her as he sat with his back against the tufted headboard. "That was him?"

"Yeah, umm, I thought I'd return his call so he wouldn't worry." She put the phone down. "He said they confirmed Eastwood was at the hospital the day I saw him on the street."

His eyebrows raised. "He was?"

"Unfortunately."

Hearing this changed Shane's perspective on the security team following her around steadily. "How about the black roses?"

"Nothing there yet. They couldn't see anyone entering her room with it."

"Then, how did it get there?"

She rested her hand across her forehead. "They don't seem to know."

"Weird."

"For sure."

Trying to piece things together, he asked, "Why was Eastwood outside the hospital to begin with? Do they know if he was there visiting someone?"

"They're still investigating."

"Good. We need to establish if he was there because of you or to see someone else?"

What he said sent a stroke of fear through her.

"Look, I don't want to scare you, but we've got to be extra vigilant. This guy is dangerous."

She quietly nodded. "Can we, umm, change the subject?"

Seeing her open her computer, he did the same. "Are you up to reviewing a few math concepts?"

"You go ahead and get a headstart. I'm just going to shower first."

"Alright. I'll leave until you finish."

"No, you can stay. I'll make it quick."

"If you're sure..."

"Don't worry. It's fine."

About to walk into the bathroom, her phone rang. It was her father.

"Hey, Dad."

"Hi, Sweetheart. Nurse Jenna said you were here today. What's this about a black rose?"

"I dropped by with Shane this afternoon. When we got there, we found it in her hands."

"She said security was alerted, but they don't know how it got there."

"That's right. I was hoping you might have answers," she replied.

"Sorry, I don't. I saw Mom at around ten thirty this morning. It wasn't there then. Perhaps someone gave it to her in error. Maybe it was meant for another patient. I'm sure there is a rational explanation for it."

"Who is allowed in that room if she's in isolation?"

Her father answered right away. "Nobody. Just the nurses, her doctor, and me."

Abi's mind muddled. Her father didn't think this was an issue, but if he knew what she had been dealing with lately, he wouldn't pass it off so easily.

With a blatant exhale, he said, "I also called to talk to you about Mr. Coppermsith being there."

Abi let out a frustrated sigh. "Shane and I are studying. I told you there's a math quiz this week. I tutor him, Dad. We are going over concepts."

He followed that up. "Since you're not on the main floor, I assume you're upstairs."

"Dad..."

"I expect he's going home afterward, correct?"

The air went dead between them.

"Actually, no..."

"I beg your pardon?" His blood boiled.

"I'm alone in this big house, in the dark, all night. It freaks me out. I asked him to stay in the guest room. That way, at least, I get some sleep knowing someone is with me."

"Well, I'd prefer..."

She pounced, "Yeah, I'd prefer my father at home to watch over me too, but that's not happening, so..."

"Abi, I..."

Realizing why he wasn't there, she backtracked. "Look, I know you're at the hospital for Mom. I get it. But I'm doing my best to deal with it on my end. And it's not easy. So please, give me a little credit. We're not doing anything wrong."

Shane could hear her conversation on the other side of the door.

Understanding what she said, her Dad reminded her, "Fine. You know the rules. Guest room. No exceptions."

"Of course. Where else would he be?"

"I worry about you, that's all." He didn't want to fight.

"Dad, I'm doing okay. He is a big part of that. So please, let it go."

He could tell his daughter had become much more independent in his absence. Her words were strong – they had conviction, and she wasn't afraid to voice her opinion. "Abi?"

"Dad, stop..."

Not given a choice, he sighed. "Okay. I'm trusting you."

"I know. I just hate the thought of being alone with the break-ins and all. That's why Burton has continued supplying security."

Apprehensively giving her the benefit of the doubt, he said, "Okay. Have a good night. Please be good." Saying it, he could imagine the girl rolling her eyes.

"Goodnight, Dad."

"Night, Sweetheart."

Abi ended the call and sat on the edge of the tub. Exhaling, she got up and turned on the shower. Gingerly locking the door, the last thing she wanted was for Shane to hear it and think she didn't trust him. While standing there, she got an uncomfortable vibe. Convinced she was doing something wrong, with him sitting mere feet away, it caused her to shake her head to break from the destructive thoughts despite her conscience eating away at her soul.

"Just have your shower and be done with it."

Undressing and stepping in, she let the water soothingly cascade over her shoulders, hair, and face while the events that day whisked down the drain. The danger of Eastwood lurking, the mysterious black roses, her best friend's one hundred-and-eighty-degree turn, and the overly romantic way Shane asked her to the Homecoming all flashed by in a series of moments. She recalled the expression on his face when he got on one knee. It made her smile. His kisses weren't far behind. Experiencing a rush of emotion, knowing her feelings for him were increasing by the day, she was so thankful that he came into her life when he did.

Wrapped in a towel, she turned off the faucet as the water trickled. Putting on a fluffy white robe, she ran a brush through her tresses before gathering it all in a towel. Carefully twisting it upon her head, she brushed her teeth and realized she'd washed off her makeup. Skin now pale and natural-looking, devoid of any enhancing color, she debated whether to reapply a light layer. Figuring it would look superficial, especially since he'd come from his shower looking fresh with hair still damp, she decided to go without any.

"You just have to walk out there and own it," she whispered. "That's all."

Untying the towel and hanging it up, she brushed her hair a second time before slipping on her night clothes and the robe over the top. With one big breath in, she quietly said, "Okay. Here goes nothing." When the door opened, she took a humorous approach. "Don't laugh, okay?" she said while exiting.

"Why would I laugh?" he asked.

She slowly walked out.

His eyes widened, making him gravitate to her, counting every step.

"Because I'm not wearing makeup and kinda look scary."

He tilted his head. "Well, that's not what I see."

"I told you not to laugh," she repeated timidly, realizing he hadn't.

Shane slowly swallowed. It was hard to formulate a sentence. "You look beautiful, Abs."

"Now, you're just being kind."

"No, it's the truth."

Strangely unable to look her in the eye, Abi noticed. "Is there something wrong?"

Almost afraid to bring it up, he just came out with it. "So, what kind of guy does he think I am?"

"Who? Burton?"

"No, your Dad."

Taken off guard, Abi stumbled a little on her words, knowing he'd heard their conversation. "He, umm, just hasn't gotten to know you well enough to trust you. If he did, he wouldn't be talking like that."

Nodding, Shane looked at his screen. "Guess that's something we need to work on, then."

"Yeah, if he's ever around..." Abi sat on the end of the bed. "So, how did it go?"

"What?"

"The questions, silly." She grabbed her computer and crawled closer. Back supported by the pillows, covering her legs with her robe, she nervously closed the collar around her neck and opened her laptop just as he showed her his screen.

"You tell me. Ten questions in less than fifteen minutes," he revealed. "Not bad, right?"

She leaned over and saw what he'd done.

The spa-like scent of her freshly washed hair was hard for him to ignore as she perused the first equation line for line.

Analyzing his thought process and the answer at the end, she smiled.

Happy to have only made a small error, he watched Abi correct it and heard her explain where he went wrong but could barely focus when she tucked her hair behind one ear.

"Do you see what I did there?" she asked, pointing to the answer on the screen.

His sights locked to hers. "Umm, yeah," he replied, "I see," noting that her eyes seemed more blue than usual. Perhaps it was the lighting or the reflection of the white robe that made them that color. He wasn't sure. But every time she glanced up, they reminded him of the intimate moments shared that week. Torn, he debated what to do. His heart pulled him one way and his conscience another.

She checked the last question and complimented, "All in all, you did really well on these."

Immediately breaking from his thoughts, he cleared his throat. "Thanks. I think I'm finally getting it."

"I'm glad." Intuitively sensing she'd caused some strong feelings to stir, her heart began to race.

"I couldn't have gotten this far without you," he said.

His low, resonant voice caught her attention, sending tingles rippling through her body.

Reaching out, he placed his hand on top of hers. Fingers lovingly linked in a silent display of fondness, he was mindful of the imaginary line drawn between them. Immersed but cautious, he searched Abi's soul, wondering where things stood - a terrifying yet exhilarating feeling like stepping to the edge of a cliff and realizing that the fall might be worth it. Willing to test the waters, he inched closer, his lips hovering before they touched hers ever so softly. A sliver of doubt crept in, making him pull back, his eyes needing a sign, a subtle cue to say she was at ease.

Abi nervously bit her lip again and held her ground amidst his intense stare.

Setting his laptop at his feet, he rolled on his side and propped his head with his hand while the other slipped around her waist. Muscles bulging, he effortlessly slid her body in tight.

Resting his forehead against hers, he said, "Tonight, I told you that the homecoming proposal was a stepping stone toward a future together. I meant what I said."

With every syllable weaving through her senses, her unease faded.

Shifting his weight as their legs intertwined, she rolled onto her back, surrounded by pillows as they collided. Lips barely spending time apart, their hearts beat in perfect harmony. With unbridled affection, each kiss flowed with an innocent charm yet carried an undercurrent of growing intensity. She felt his strength as he gently held her, his hand gliding from her waist to tenderly tuck beneath her shoulder blade. Passion deepening, his body nearly enveloping hers, she became adrift in the sweet blissfulness. More aware, she wrapped her arms around his neck to draw him closer, breaking their rhythm with a content sigh.

Shane got the subtle hint. Parting, giving her space, he pressed his lips firmly against hers, letting them linger, understanding she'd reached her limit, and that was okay. His eyes filled with love, he whispered, "You should get some sleep."

Her heart hurt as he rolled over to sit on the edge of the bed.

"Goodnight, Abs," he said sincerely. Believing what he was doing, was right, he stood and gathered his things.

"Goodnight..."

Bending down, he kissed her one last time. "I'll see you in the morning." About to leave the room, he waved.

Amid the silence, afraid to ask, her thoughts refusing to escape her mouth, she suddenly exclaimed, "Shane?"

He casually swung around. "Yeah?"

Nervous beyond, shrugging her shoulders, she stammered, "Any chance you can...umm...stay? At least until I fall asleep?"

Pausing, he knew he could never refuse. "If you'd like," he said while setting his laptop and textbook on the side table.

She nodded.

Walking around to the opposite side of the bed, he lay beside her above the covers. As she drew closer, nestling her head against him, Shane enveloped her in his arms. Longing for the girl since they met, he tried to appreciate this rare opportunity.

"Thank you," she whispered.

"Absolutely." He tightened their embrace. "Night. I love you."

"Love you too," she said softly. "Night."

Abi did not move. Unable to stay awake any longer, her eyelids soon fluttered shut. Feeling safe and comforted, it wasn't long before she drifted off peacefully.

Absorbed by his thoughts, Shane felt her body relax, her breathing more even. This affirmed the level of trust they'd established. Otherwise, he knew she would've never asked him to stay. A testament to their ever-growing bond, he recognized the significant leap in their relationship. Despite the steady pace they'd been keeping, he figured taking things slow had created a stronger foundation, but he never dreamed it would feel like this. Somehow, the love, intimacy, and commitment were insurmountable and unmatched. Grateful, he reflected on the timing of Abi's arrival, certain she came into his life for a reason. In a short while, she'd become a pillar of strength, a source of motivation, and unwavering support. Watching her sleep, feeling a torrent of emotions, he undoubtedly knew she was the one and couldn't help but envision a future with her at the center of his universe.

51

Torn

Abi awoke with a surge of renewed energy. After a good night's sleep, her eyes opened to the gentle morning light filtering through the blinds. Basking in the sun's warmth with a contented smile that curved her lips, she stretched her arms above her. Both hanging in mid-air, she let them fall before clutching her covers and tucking them under her chin. Taking stock of the week's events thus far, she felt a sense of relief. Jade's return to school lifted a weight from her shoulders, and she was thankful the case was closed on Laney and Shawn's legal troubles. Ming had met the sweetest guy, and then there was the unexpected invitation to Homecoming, which was a highlight that left her excited but nervous. Replaying Shane's proposal, she beamed. About to get up, Abi shifted in bed, then froze. To her surprise, Shane was still lying next to her.

He must have dozed off, she thought, wondering what he would say when he woke up. Watching him sleep, she never realized just how perfect he truly was. From his strong willingness to succeed to his handsome good looks, soft heart, and gentle demeanor that sent her heart into a tizzy, she knew he was tailor-made for her. She sighed. *How did I get so lucky?*

In an instant, his one eye opened. Disoriented, he looked around and jerked himself upward. "Abs? What time is it?"

"Just before seven."

"I'm sorry, I must've fallen asleep." Letting his head fall back on the pillow, he closed his eyes before opening them again and rolling over. Finding her buried under her covers with sights glued to his, he curiously asked, "What are you doing?"

"Watching you."

"Why? Was I snoring?" he chuckled, slightly embarrassed.

"No, not at all," she grinned. "I just feel lucky knowing how much you care about me."

He quickly lifted his head off the pillow and propped it on his hand. "Well, you see. That's where you're mistaken." He ran his fingertips over her hand and up her arm.

Confused, she said, "I don't understand."

"I don't care for you, Abi Acardi."

The negative comment made her frown. "You don't?"

"No, see. Truth be told, it's much more than that."

"It is?" she smiled uncontrollably.

"I'm in love with you. There's a big difference."

Blushing, she didn't know how to respond. It made her bashfully burrow under her pillow and hide.

Laughing at her reaction, he said, "Aren't you gonna say it back?"

Abi reappeared and rested her head on the pillow nearby. "I love you with all of my heart, and I fear I will for a very long time."

Happy to hear it, he inched closer.

Face to face, she stared into his baby blues before hers drifted shut. Soon, she felt the warmth of his touch, but somehow, their kisses had changed. Maybe it was the depth of their conversations or her willingness to open up to him, little by little, every day. Whatever it was, she felt a stronger connection.

Her alarm sounded with perfect timing. Almost in sync, so did Shane's, making both roll away from each other to grab their phones and turn them off.

"Guess that's our cue," he said, tempted by her proximity. "We should get moving."

"I suppose so."

Shane folded the throw blanket and draped it across the footboard as Abi pulled her covers to make the bed. Helping her, he straightened the pillows before walking toward the door. "I'm going for a shower. Meet you downstairs in fifteen?"

"Sounds good."

Abi went into her ensuite and closed the door. Seeing her reflection in the mirror as she brushed her teeth, she stopped as a strange feeling erupted in her chest. She wondered if Shane was under the impression she hadn't woken up beside anyone before. He didn't know Burton was the first ever to do that. "In a non-romantic way," she muttered to herself. A moral debate filled her head as Burton's words resonated.

It's best not to tell Shane about what happened in Tahoe, she recalled. "But is that fair to him?" she whispered, trying to justify her actions. "It's not like it would ever happen again. Those were extenuating circumstances." Still harboring secrets, it weighed on her. "If he knew, it would just hurt him. There's no point," she debated.

On one shoulder was the honest Abi, and on the other was the uncharacteristically deceptive girl who showed up when she moved to the West Coast. "Maybe one day – just not now," she decided while getting dressed. Taking a last look in the mirror, she grabbed her backpack and headed downstairs, certain he'd beaten her to it.

52

Unexpected

Having little time to spare, she met Shane in the foyer. He was patiently waiting by the door.

"Ready?' he said on the way out.

"Yes," she replied while locking up, wondering if her Dad was watching on the cameras. When she turned around, she waved to Andrew, Ted, and Matt, standing beside their vehicle. "Morning, guys."

"Morning," Andrew greeted as the other two men raised their coffee cups to her.

Seeing Shane stop and admire his new ride, she asked, "What are you doing?"

"I love it," is all he said.

"More than the last one?"

He tilted his head. "Quite possibly."

She chuckled at his humorous tone.

Settled in their seats, he started the engine. After Matt gave him the signal, Shane left the courtyard and stopped to allow them to follow before Abi closed the gate.

Driving south on Stradella to Sunset, he focused on the stop-and-go traffic, hoping nobody would hit him.

Able to be with her thoughts, she expected Burton home at some point today. While he was gone, it was nice to focus on Shane and Shane alone. But she remembered the one-on-one time she'd spent with him, too. The thought made her fidget.

Catching it, Shane glanced over but didn't say anything.

When they crossed the bridge over the 405, she asked, "Maybe Gerald will be back?"

"Maybe," he replied. "Now that we Have his name and address, we should pay him a visit next week."

Abi hoped to do that sooner rather than later, but it wasn't possible with him being away for the next four days. Having no choice, she knew she had to wait.

Arriving at school and searching for the man, Abi held her breath as they approached the underground parking booth.

"That's not him," she said disappointingly.

As they passed the strange man, he kept his eyes on them. It gave her a bad feeling.

While Shane parked the new truck, Andrew and Ted checked their surroundings before Abi joined them. On the move, opting to take the stairs since the elevator was in use, they climbed the three flights before emerging in the courtyard above. There, she found their friends gathered around the artisan steps.

Shane noticed how Owen Karp had somehow weaseled his way into their group. Seeing the guy hanging off Jade, he thought of Reggie and hoped his friend would come to his senses before it was too late.

Shawn and Laney were sitting together, talking with Adrian and Mei, but this time, Ming was hand in hand beside Big Ben, who seemed enchanted by the petite girl. Sadly, Allie was the odd one out now. Everyone had paired up but her. Even Summer had met someone. Dating a junior, the guy was an artist protégé - something entirely up her alley since she, too, wanted to pursue art history.

Hearing the warning bell, the group flocked toward the main building.

Taizo had just landed on the helipad and was rounding the corner with four security guards flanking him. Spotting Abi and her guys a few steps behind, he gave a single nod, as did she. It seemed this common thread sparked a certain level of respect. Never having spoken to him, she wondered what the famous teen heartthrob was really like.

Walking through the lobby, avoiding Marco Cafaro at all costs, Owen Karp drifted by them, holding Jade's hand.

"Moving a bit fast there, Karp?" the disgruntled student stated.

Owen smirked. "Are you jealous, Cafaro?"

The jilted Italian said nothing.

Amidst it all, Jade spotted a familiar face emerging from the office. She shouted, "Wait? What? No way!" Letting go of Owen's hand, she physically turned Allie's body. "Hey, girl! Look!"

The girl focused in the direction Jade pointed. Frozen in her tracks, unable to believe her eyes, she started to cry. Hands quickly covering her face, she dropped her backpack. Standing there, in his Gilderson uniform, was Alan.

Shocked to the core, believing she was dreaming, the confident boy with beach blonde hair smiled.

Not wasting time, Allie ran and clung to him tightly. Tears streaming down her face, she said, "Thank God!"

Swinging her in mid-air as she giggled and sobbed simultaneously, he gently set her feet on the ground. "Hey, Sweetness," he said.

Abi moved closer to Shane to watch their reunion. "You did that," she whispered to him.

"Yeah. I guess I did."

Alan looked deeply into Allie's eyes and moved her hair behind her ear before kissing the girl of his dreams.

Their friends looked on fleetingly.

Each girl seemed charmed by the scene unfolding. Some clutched their hands to their chest, while others were just happy for them.

Thankful to have him back, she asked, "Are you..."

"...here to stay?" He finished her sentence. "Yep, thanks to Shane."

Walking over, arm in arm with her, Alan presented his hand to the QB as Shane grabbed hold. Bumping shoulders, he said, "Good to see you, my friend."

"What did he do?" Allie asked.

"Long story. I'll tell you later. We should get to class." Eager to start the day with her, Alan slid his arm along her shoulders while hers circled his waist.

"Now everything is right with the world," Abi surmised as Jade and Owen strolled past, connected at the hip. She looked up at Shane. "Well, maybe not everything."

Suddenly, Jade's expression shifted as if she'd seen a ghost.

Abi chuckled at her friend's reaction before noticing Shane's also turn stoic.

"Umm, Abs..." he said solemnly.

"What? What is it?" She turned to see a man standing outside the office doors. "Dad... Wait. What is he doing here?" His gaze hit her like a freight train, stealing the air from her lungs as her legs weakened.

Dropping her backpack, about to collapse, Shane caught her.

"No..." she mumbled.

His arms enveloped her tightly.

When her Father approached, she defensively raised her hand to stop him. With a whisper, she pleaded, "Please.... don't say it... Please, don't..."

"I know..." he said tearfully. "I'm so sorry, Sweetheart. But, she's gone."

Letting go of Shane, she transferred into her Father's waiting arms. Time stood still as she knotted her fists in his jacket and cried.

Not one person moved an inch. Unable to process what was happening, their friends were in disbelief.

Owen leaned over as Jade tried her best to control her sobs. Whispering in her ear, he asked, "What's happening?"

"Abi's Mom passed away."

Not expecting to hear that, his posture straightened as he comforted Jade.

The once joyful day had now turned somber.

Alan held Allie close as she wiped her tears with her sleeve. Her heart ached for her friend.

Raising praying hands to her trembling lips, Jade didn't know what to do. Urging the girls to go with her, Laney, Mei, Ming, and Allie gathered alongside Abi and her Dad to offer support.

Seeing them, the grieving girl embraced the group. Nothing was said.

Needing to be there for them, the guys encircled the huddle, knowing emotions would run high in the aftermath. Not long after, that was the case.

The vice-principal appeared and quietly instructed the students to return to class.

Reduced to a shell, Abi remained with her Dad while Shane retrieved their backpacks off the floor.

From the far side of the foyer, Andrew and Ted witnessed everything and knew any plans for the day just changed. Pulling his phone from his pocket, he called their boss. Hearing the phone ring, he soon heard him answer.

"Hey, Andrew. What's up? Everything okay?"

With a heavy heart, he replied, "No, Sir."

Burton sat straight in his chair. His expression turned grave. "What happened? Is she alright?"

"It's her Mother, Sir. She passed."

Burton immediately closed his eyes and lowered his head.

Not hearing a response, he said, "Sir? You there?"

"Yeah. I'm coming. We'll leave right now. Stick with her. Make sure she's safe."

"Yes, Sir."

Ending the call, Burton leaned forward, his head in his hands. Turning to Martin, he said, "We gotta get to L.A. ASAP."

Martin's confusion was evident. "Why?"

"Abi's Mother just died."

53

Respectfully

The foyer cleared out quickly. In minutes, you could hear a pin drop. Only Shane, Abi, and her Father remained.

"I'll take it from here, Shane," Dr. Acardi stated while reaching out for Abi's bag.

Unable to let her go through this alone, he courageously said, "With all due respect, Sir, I would like to accompany you both today to offer support."

About to decline the young man, he saw the worry in the athlete's eyes as they remained affixed to his daughter.

"Please, Dad. I need him."

Acknowledging, he said, "Very well."

Shane slung both of their bags on one shoulder.

"We are going to the hospital first."

Shane replied, "I'll follow you."

"Fine."

Before walking back to her office, the Vice Principal approached. "I'm so sorry for your loss, Ms. Acardi."

Unable to speak, she nodded and shook the woman's hand tearfully.

"Abi will not be in class for the rest of the week," her Father instructed.

"Not to worry. I will record the absence."

"Please handle Shane Coppersmith's as well." Dr. Acardi vouched. "He is joining us today."

"Absolutely. Let us know if we can be of assistance. Again, our deepest condolences."

"We appreciate that," the doctor said.

When the woman walked away, Dr. Acardi led Abi out the door and across the courtyard to the VIP parking. Shane, Andrew, and Ted stood by as she got in the car.

Shane placed her bag in the back seat. "I will meet you there," he said as the guys looked on.

Abi could barely respond.

"Where will you be, Sir?"

"Sixth floor. My wife's room."

Placing his hand on Abi's shoulder, Shane gently said, "I'll see you shortly." Closing it, he hurried along. While passing the security team, he stopped to give them instructions. "They are headed to the hospital. Sixth floor."

Andrew gave him a thumbs up.

Unable to think, Shane jogged to his Jeep. Getting in, he started the engine, leaned forward, and rested his forehead against the steering wheel. Flashes of the day his sister died flooded his mind.

"Stay focused," he said quietly before sitting upright again.

Putting the vehicle in gear, he pulled away, intent on catching up to Abi and her Father.

54

Goodbye

It took forever to reach the hospital. The day she'd been dreading was here. Abi stared out the window blankly - the scenery went by in a blur. Still surreal, she looked at the clouds drifting in the blue sky above and wondered if her Mother was watching. Recalling her grandparents' car accident and the aftermath that followed, she got overwhelmed thinking of all the grieving people who would line up to view the casket.

"What happens now? What are we doing?" she asked.

"I asked them to keep Mom in her room to give you a chance to say goodbye."

Used to the quills of death, unable to save a few patients in his day, Abi assumed her Father's straightforwardness resulted from that.

Not hearing a response, he confirmed, "Is that alright?"

"Yes," she said, a bit fearful.

Approaching the hospital, they descended into the underground parking. The light of day disappeared, and the darkness took over.

Dr. Acardi backed into his parking spot as Abi noticed the security team pass by them. Wondering where Shane was, she texted, *Are you here?*

Within seconds, he replied, *Yes.*

Getting out with her Dad, they walked to the elevator and waited for it to open.

On the other side of the hospital, Shane drove into the parking structure and took the first open spot he found. Locking up, he jogged toward the entrance, hoping to catch them on their way to the sixth floor.

Barely present, going through the motions, Abi was quiet while they walked along. When the doors of the first elevator opened, she and her Dad got out and walked hand in hand toward the next set of elevators. There, they found Shane waiting for them, somewhat out of breath. Immediately, she let go of her Father and fell into the QB's arms.

The man observed the undeniable connection between them. Continuing without pause, he pressed the button and waited. As the doors parted, her Father stepped aboard and held them for Shane and his daughter before allowing them to shut. The three stood silently as the elevator ascended, their gaze fixed on the increasing numbers lighting up the panel with each passing floor.

Finally reaching their destination, they got out. Her Father walked ahead of them while Abi suddenly stopped, prompting Shane to do the same.

The nurses on the floor stood idle, knowing what had happened. So many sad faces turned to Abi. Suddenly, her feet felt like they weighed a million tons.

Not saying a word, knowing she was processing things, Shane stayed tight to her left.

"I don't know if I can do this..." she panicked.

"It's okay. Take your time." Wrapping his arms around her, she clung to him as her sights veered to her Dad waiting outside her Mother's room. She knew he was getting impatient. Letting go of Shane and grabbing hold of his hand, he helped her put one foot in front of the other.

When Abi walked in, she first noticed the silence. The rhythmic machines were off. Gently running her hand along her Mother's arm, it felt cold.

Shane watched and waited outside the glass as Abi leaned over and kissed her Mother's temple. Unable to hold it together, a tear drifted down his cheek. With hands folded in front of him, gripping them intermittently to keep his composure in check, he heard the elevator chime. Turning, he found Andrew and Ted. Both stood watch as a nurse walked by and entered the room.

Witnessing the blonde nurse offering condolences, Shane noticed the woman also seemed shaken by the sudden loss.

A porter arrived at the door.

Abi knew it was time to go. Drifting her hand through her Mother's hair, making her look like she was sleeping angelically, she stepped back as her Father pulled the sheet over her face. Inhaling, losing her breath again, she swiftly moved toward Shane, who was waiting with open arms. Muffling her cries with her hand bundled up in her sleeve, he held her head against his chest and stayed in the moment as her body heaved and tried to expel the pain and loss.

Dr. Acardi joined them. "Shane, can you take Abi home? I must make arrangements, and I don't want her to have to wait for me."

"Yes, no problem, Sir."

He rubbed Abi's back and hugged her. "I will see you tonight."

She nodded while her Dad went to the nurse's station.

Meeting up with Andrew and Ted, the guys silently reached out a hand to her and grabbed hold to offer their condolences just as she heard the squeaking sound of the gurney as they wheeled her Mother out of the room and down the hall.

It's over. She's gone, Abi thought. *She's now at peace.*

55

Zuma

Navigating through the corridors and elevators to the parking garage, Shane remained her steadfast rock, supporting her through the heavy burden of grief taking hold. The guys trailed behind, their usual vigilance overshadowed by the solemnity of what just happened. Matt tracked Andrew's location and awaited further instructions as to the plan for the day.

Arriving at the truck, Shane opened the door for Abi as she slowly climbed in. He kept her steady. With her securely seated, he noticed her leaning forward, staring at something. A look of terror followed. Trembling, hands covering her mouth, he urgently opened the door. "What is it? What's wrong?"

All she could do was point at the windshield.

Concerned about what caught her attention, he followed her line of sight and found a black rose tucked under the wiper. Grabbing it, he read the card attached.

"What does it say?" she asked, not looking his way out of fear for the words that might escape his mouth.

Silently reading it, not telling her, his heart dropped. His hand did, too. Anger spread through him as the heat boiled to his neck, making him clench his teeth.

"What? Say it."

"The card reads..." he paused. "Sorry for your loss."

Upon hearing that, Abi couldn't breathe.

Seeing something was wrong, Andrew walked over. "What happened?" he asked.

Not saying a word, Shane handed it to him with the card attached.

Andrew read it. "We'll take care of this. I promise we'll find out who is sending them."

Shane reached for Abi. Immediately, she clung to his neck like she was drowning. Tears flowing and her body heaving, she pleaded, "I want to go home."

He buckled her seat belt and closed the door. "We're going."

"Where are you headed?" Andrew asked from the front seat of the SUV. He was already on the phone.

"Her Dad asked that I take her home."

"Good. We'll be right with you."

Shane got behind the wheel and gave the guys a thumbs-up. Before leaving, he glimpsed over at Abi. It seemed a piece of her had died, too. The second he started the engine, she automatically grabbed his hand and rested her head on his shoulder.

With the parking fee paid, they headed north. The loud sound of his tires running along the pavement drowned out anything else around them.

Abi looked up at the blue sky again. She found solace in the sparsely spaced fluffy clouds, believing her Mom was now watching her from above. It sparked a need to make her proud. Silently promising to be a better person, she knew things would be very different from then on.

"Can we take a drive?" she whispered while Shane headed east on Sunset.

"Where would you like to go?" he asked, glancing down at her before his eyes returned to the road.

"The beach we visited the night of Aramis and Lexi's party. That was a peaceful spot."

"Okay," he said.

Signaling and turning right at the next intersection, he noticed Matt was concerned by the detour. He stopped when the Jeep swung around.

Rolling his window down, Shane did the same. "She wants to go to Zuma Beach."

Andrew didn't hesitate. He gave him an A-OK signal while Matt made the U-turn.

Back on Sunset Boulevard, Shane continued toward the coast. Deciding not to take the highway, they followed the winding road through the Palisades Village and down the hillside before arriving in front of the ocean vista. En route, moving along the PCH, Abi's eyes remained locked on the blue water. With the sun shining brightly, the rays sparkled on the waves rolling in.

The traffic was minimal being a weekday afternoon.

Passing by Geoffrey's, Abi thought of Burton. She assumed Andrew had let him know what had happened. Recalling all the times her neighbor came over to their house years ago, never knowing how difficult his life was behind closed doors, Abi wondered if Burton was hurting as much as she was upon hearing the news.

Seeing their destination coming up, Shane slowed down, signaled, and waited for a chance to proceed when the coast was clear. When he turned, they drove down the side road and maneuvered the bend.

Surprised by how many people were there, Abi was disappointed, but the incredible view changed all that.

Shane pulled over.

Matt did the same.

"I want to get out," she said, taking off her shoes and socks. Opening the door, she peeled off her blazer, as did Shane. The breeze was a bit chilly. Checking his bag for a sweatshirt, he grabbed one for her and helped her slip it on.

Abi walked toward the water.

Taking the beach blanket from the back, Shane locked the Jeep and went to catch up.

She spotted the guys leaving the truck and watched them hover at a distance. Standing along the raised tideline, she gazed at the vast ocean and closed her eyes.

Shane spread the blanket as it fluttered. "Want to sit here?" he asked.

Silently turning to him, she broke from her daze and said, "Sure."

Mindful of her skirt blowing in the breeze, he helped Abi settle before sitting beside her. It wasn't long before she shifted closer. Grasping his arm, she rested her head on his shoulder as the waves rolled in about twenty feet away.

"It's surreal. She was just here yesterday, and now she's gone." The reality of it suddenly hit her hard. "I no longer have a Mom..."

When she said that, the tears cascaded down her cheeks, prompting Shane to hug her tightly. "She will always be watching over you, Abs – no matter what."

Her hands trembled uncontrollably. Agreeing with what he said, she nodded while blotting her tears with her sleeve, understanding Shane was no stranger to grief and loss.

"Do you ever think about her?" she said out of the blue.

Assuming who she meant, he asked, "My sister?"

"Yes."

Unable to answer straight away, he contemplated whether to share his thoughts but figured it might help. "Don't think I'm crazy..."

"I would never. What is it?"

"Sometimes, when I play football, I see her in the stands, especially when we're down. I don't know. Maybe it's not her, but I feel her presence on the field, giving me the strength I need to carry the team forward."

Cuddled against him, she soaked up the sun's warmth on her face. "I'm sure it's her," she said.

"Me too."

Sitting peacefully for the next half hour, Abi heard her phone vibrate on the blanket beside her. Picking it up, she found a text from Burton. His kind, heartfelt condolences made her cry. After all these years, he still had a way with words. Discovering that he'd returned from Vegas, she replied, *I'm at the beach. Needed to clear my head and think. I'll be home in an hour.* Adding a heart, she put down the device.

Shane inquired, "Is that Burton?"

Her guard went up. "Please don't. Not today..." she mumbled, not wanting to deal with their drama. "He flew in from Vegas."

He looked out at the water and didn't say anything more about it.

"I should probably go home. My Dad will wonder where I am."

"I think that's wise." Shane helped Abi to her feet.

Walking back to the Jeep, Abi said, "Thank you for sticking with me today." Her heart sank when she saw the time on her phone. "Shane! You're going to be late for practice."

"It's fine. The guys said they explained what happened to Coach. He understood."

Panicked, she added, "But you have the showcase this weekend."

Trying to calm her down, he said, "Abs?"

Not listening, she rambled on, continuing her train of thought. "I'm sure the guy will be angry that you're not there. I know he can't replace you, but...."

"Abs?"

She paused. "What if Owen gets called up? That can't happen. I don't want to be the reason the team struggles."

"Abi!"

Broken from her worries, she shouted, "What!"

"Everything will be fine. It's only one day." Opening the passenger side, she removed the sand from her feet before setting them on the mat. Remembering her visit to Zuma with Burton, she knew he'd be at her place when they got there.

Slipping on their socks and shoes, Shane started the engine.

Matt pulled up beside them, ready to depart. Given the okay, soon they were back on the road heading toward LA.

56

The Void

Antsy on the way home, Abi wasn't herself for obvious reasons, but Shane knew there was more to it. He could see her mind processing information at lightning speed. Giving her hand a few gentle squeezes, she turned to him.

"What is it?" he asked calmly.

"Are you going to skip the showcase? Because I have a feeling you will."

"Honestly, it hasn't crossed my mind. We have more important things going on right now."

"I want you to go. Don't worry about anything else," she whispered.

He realized what she was saying. "No, Abs. I am not letting you go through this alone."

"But..."

"No buts. I'm not leaving you," he stated firmly.

Climbing the hill towards Stradella, Abi sensed Shane was upset. "I'm just thinking of your future. Nothing else," she said.

"I appreciate that, but sometimes there are more important things than football."

Deep in thought, she didn't know what to say.

"Tomorrow, I want to be the one who stands by you. The one who supports you."

"Versus Burton, you mean."

He quickly turned to her. "This has nothing to do with him."

Not wanting to fight, she let the conversation slide.

When they pulled up to her house, she opened the gate.

Once Matt drove in, Abi got out. "My Dad's not back yet," she said while unlocking the front door. Turning to Andrew, she added, "I think you guys shouldn't be here when he gets home."

"Our orders are to stick with you, Miss."

"I know, but..."

"We will stay on the street, then," Ted suggested.

"Fine. I can't take any conflict today..." she mumbled.

Andrew silently agreed while Shane grabbed his duffle bag from the back of the Jeep.

Abi watched the guys leave the courtyard. With the gate again secured, she sighed and turned on the inside lights. "I'm just going to go and change," she said as he walked in with her.

"I'm gonna do the same."

"Alright."

Heading upstairs, the hallway to her parent's room seemed dark and lifeless. Reality hit her as the absence soon reared its ugliness. Recently, she'd heard people talking about losing loved ones on YouTube. They kept bringing up this emptiness. Many referred to it as a void. Walking to her parent's room, she looked in. Her Father hadn't slept there since they admitted her Mom to the hospital. Rounding the corner, she turned on the light in her Mother's closet. Gently running her hand past her clothes, feeling the fabric touch her fingertips, she spotted her Mom's favorite powder blue hoodie and took it from the hanger. Instinctively burying her face in it, she cried at the faint scent of perfume lingering. Forced to sit with legs buckling, she slipped the hoodie over her head and slowly threaded her arms through the sleeves. Sobbing uncontrollably, trying to muffle the sounds of her chest heaving, she heard Shane.

"Abi? Abi? Where are you?" Following her cries, he found her in the closet. Quickly sitting down beside her, he tightly wrapped her in his arms as she clung to him, expelling the grief and sadness bottled up.

Aware of what she was doing, Abi frantically dried her tears and sat straight. "I'm sorry," she said.

"Don't be. You have every right to cry."

"This hoodie was my Mom's. I can still smell her perfume." About to get off the floor, Shane beat her to it and helped her. Taking hold of his hand, standing there, she wrapped her arms around his waist and rested her head on his chest. "Thank you for being here."

Embracing her, he said, "It might not seem like it now, but it's gonna be okay. I promise. You're not alone. I'm not going anywhere."

She led the way out of the closet.

He followed.

Walking down the hall, they reached her room. Shane stopped at the door while she collapsed in bed and curled up with a pillow.

Seeing him, she asked, "Can you stay with me a while?"

Slowly approaching, he said, "Of course."

Lying beside her, Shane tucked his hand behind his head and wrapped his arm around Abi as she cuddled in.

Resting her hand on his chest, she closed her eyes. Heart hurting, chest heaving as she calmed down in the aftermath of the most emotional afternoon, everything went quiet as the world drifted by.

57

Differences Aside

Hearing footsteps coming up the stairs, Shane turned and found Dr. Acardi staring at him, looking exhausted and stressed. He held his breath, afraid the man would lash out. But strangely, he said nothing. Thankful to see his daughter sleeping soundly, knowing how traumatic the day had been, he stood there momentarily before giving Shane a nod and leaving the two in peace.

As the hours passed, Shane kept answering their friend's texts. Everyone was worried about Abi and felt helpless. Nobody knew what to do.

Finally stirring, Shane watched her wake up, looking confused.

"It wasn't a dream, was it?" she said.

Hating to tell her the truth, he quietly whispered, "No."

She rolled over and stared at the ceiling. Hearing a commotion downstairs, she nervously sat up. "Wait? Is my Father home?"

"Yes, he returned a bit ago."

"We can't have him find you in here."

"Well, about that."

"What?" she said, anxiety surfacing.

"You were sleeping, and…"

Unable to finish his sentence, she interrupted, "He saw us?"

"Yeah…"

"And nothing happened?"

"I think he was relieved to see you calm and not crying."

They inched to the edge of the bed.

"Are you doing okay?"

She nodded. "My head doesn't hurt as much."

Putting his arm around her, he said, "That's good."

They heard the oven door open and close.

"I guess we should go downstairs and see what's happening."

"I think there was a food delivery," Shane said.

Abi walked into her bathroom and fixed her hair. Throwing it into a ponytail, she stared at her swollen face. Taking a deep breath, she rounded the corner.

"Ready?" he asked before escorting her downstairs.

Finding her Father showing the caterers to the front door, Abi and Shane stood in the living room and waited for him. When they'd gone, he closed it.

Abi saw him stop, place his hands on his hips, and tilt his head back. She knew he, too, was exhausted.

A car door shut. It caught his attention. Peeking outside, he reached for the handle and greeted another guest.

Abi wondered who was there. That is when she heard a familiar voice. So did Shane.

"Hello, Sir," Burton said with an outstretched hand. "My sincere condolences."

"Thank you, Burton. I appreciate that. Please, come in."

Peering around the corner, she let go of Shane and rushed to her childhood friend.

Arms open, he hugged her tightly. "I'm so sorry, Abs." He immediately locked eyes with Shane.

When she let go, Burton backed away. He nodded and said to the QB, "Hey, man."

Not responding, Shane replied with silent acknowledgment.

The air thickening, Dr. Acardi said, "Work sent some food. They said to take it out of the oven in ten minutes. I hope you both can join us."

Abi's sights bounced between the two guys.

"Thank you, Sir," Burton replied.

Put off that the guy answered first, Shane quickly chased his response and said, "Yes, Thank you, Sir."

Dr. Acardi went back into the kitchen with Abi.

About to follow them, Burton stopped Shane and whispered, "Let's try and get along – for her. Nothing else."

Agreeing, the two joined them while Dr. Acardi slipped on oven mitts.

About to grab plates, Shane stopped Abi and quickly reached into the cupboard. "Here. Let me get that," he said, towering above her.

"Thank you," she replied as he easily took the stack in hand, turned, and rested them on the counter.

Wanting to be helpful, Burton assisted Dr. Acardi as he moved the food from the oven to the cast iron trivets. Holding each in position as the man set the containers on them, he closed the oven door.

"Well, get a plate, everybody." Dr. Acardi instructed.

The room felt heavy as Abi dished small amounts onto hers.

"You've got to eat more than that, Sweetheart," her Father suggested. "I'm sure you haven't had anything all day."

Not hungry, forcing herself to put another half of a tablespoon of pasta on her plate, she walked to the table by the window and sat on the chair facing the sunset.

Burton and Shane watched her staring out at the canyon. They knew she was not in a good place.

The guys pulled up a chair to her left and right while her Dad sat facing them.

Breaking the silence, Abi asked, "What happens now?"

"The arrangements, you mean?" her Father replied.

"Yes."

Dr. Acardi took a bite of his lasagna. "Weeks ago, your Mom asked to plan everything. She only wanted a service at the cemetery chapel before the burial. No viewing beforehand."

"When is that?" she asked.

"Tomorrow at eleven."

Shocked to hear things were happening so fast, Abi lowered her head and moved the food around the plate with her fork. Her Father could sense she was upset.

"I know it's soon. I'm sorry. But that is what she wanted."

"It's fine." Believing it was for the best, she paused and added, "I'll be right back."

The guys watched her abruptly leave the room.

Her Dad put down his fork. "Excuse me a moment."

Nothing was said between them when he disappeared upstairs until Burton broke the ice. "Were you there when she got the news?"

"Yes. I was."

Glad she wasn't alone, he asked, "How bad?"

Shane shook his head. "Horrible."

Burton wanted to be the bigger man. "She will need our support more than ever – both of us. We have to put our differences aside. For her."

Shane nodded. "Agreed."

"On top of this, we are still dealing with the Eastwood fiasco."

"Yeah, about that..."

"What..." Burton turned to him.

"When we were about to leave the hospital, we found a black rose on my windshield."

Burton's blood boiled.

"There was a card attached," Shane said.

"What did it say?" The DJ looked down at his plate in anger.

"Sorry for your loss."

Assuming Eastwood was playing a game, Burton knew the thrill of it fueled him now. The psycho wouldn't rest until he got his revenge and hurt everyone in his life.

"He's marked her," he said.

Recalling what "Marked? What do you mean?"

"The guy is used to getting what he wants. When he doesn't, he likes the thrill of the chase. He's fixated on her and will continue until he settles the score."

58

Please, Go

Upstairs, Dr. Acardi found Abi frantically floating through her closet in a panic. Taking a deep breath, he found himself in unfamiliar territory.

"What are you doing, Sweetie?" he asked.

Tears streaming down her face, she said, "I only have one black dress, and it's not for a funeral. What am I gonna do?"

Her Dad thought of a solution. "Well, you and your Mom are about the same size. Why don't you look in her closet for something to wear? I know she has a few black dresses. Maybe one of them will work."

She turned to him and nodded.

Darting down the hall, Abi rushed into her mother's closet and turned on the light. Filing through the clothes, she found a few simple scoop-necked sheaths. Holding one in front of her, she looked in the mirror. I think this is nice."

Her father stood back. "But it is missing something." Taking an ivory cardi from its hanger, he placed it over the dress while Abi looked on.

"She used to wear this with that one. Maybe you want to also?"

"It's perfect." Abi managed to smile despite being emotionally drained.

With that settled, she felt a weight lifted. Leaving the room, her Dad stayed a second longer. It was hard to believe his beautiful wife was no longer with them.

Returning downstairs, thankful the guys hadn't killed each other, Abi saw Shane get up and take her plate to the microwave. He placed it inside and waited for it to warm. When it beeped, he took it out and returned to set it on the table.

"That's so sweet. Thank you," she whispered.

Unsure what happened, he asked, "Are you okay?"

"Yeah. I didn't know what to wear tomorrow, but I found one of my Mom's dresses, so I'm good."

Shane rested his hand on top of hers. "Glad that got sorted."

"Me too," she said, notably relieved. Thinking more about the next day, she turned to him and said, "Can we talk for a minute."

"Sure." Having an idea of what she wanted to discuss, he strategized on how to convince her otherwise.

Walking with him, leaving Burton alone at the table, Abi led Shane to the living room.

He sat on the sofa beside her. "Look, I know what you are going to say."

She held his hands in hers. "I want you to go to the showcase tomorrow."

"No, I told you, I'm not going. I'm staying."

As much as she loved to hear him say that, she shook her head. "You have to go. There's so much riding on this. You said it yourself: there will be tons of scouts watching the event. You are the number one pick. You can't miss it."

"This is more important."

"But, Shane..."

Interrupting, he said, "Abi, I'm staying."

"Look, I could not live with myself if you lost out on a great opportunity because of me." Her words were so concrete.

"I won't. Stop worrying about all this right now."

"I need you to go. Please. Do it for me." Peering deep into his eyes, she tried to make it hard for him to say no.

Shane realized Burton would take his place if he did what she asked. "Abs, listen. I won't be able to concentrate anyway because I'll be thinking about you the whole time. If anything, that'll harm my performance."

She ignored that statement. "Tomorrow is going to be very difficult."

"All the more reason for me to be here to support you."

"Will your agent be angry if you aren't there?"

He hesitated, knowing the answer.

"Exactly." About to reason with her, she stopped him. "It's settled."

"Abs, please..."

Tapping his hand with hers, she kissed him on the cheek. "I'm going to say goodnight now. Once you go, don't worry. I am sending Burton home, too. Good luck tomorrow. I'll be thinking of you."

Emotionless, Abi got up off the sofa and waited.

Not given a choice, Shane stood and grabbed his bag off the floor. Walking with her to the door, they went to his Jeep. Outwardly rejected, he felt like a knife just stabbed his chest. Somehow, it felt like a breakup, even though he knew it wasn't. Standing there, he pulled her in close and whispered in her ear, "Please don't ask this of me. I love you, and my place is here with you tomorrow. Not on the field."

She leaned back and found his eyes filled with desperation. "And I love you for saying that. Everything is okay. This is your future, Shane, and I will not stand in the way." Abi stepped back. "Travel safe. I'll talk to you tomorrow, okay?"

Torn and confused, unsure what to do when she opened the driver's side door, he reluctantly got in behind the wheel as she closed it. Not given a choice, he started the engine and left the courtyard as Andrew and the guys looked on.

Abi waved to him as he drove out.

Moving down Stradella, tears drifted down his cheeks. Angrily wiping them away, he nailed the roof with his fist. "Damn it!" he shouted. Drowning in emotion, he straightened up. Reigning in his thoughts, trying to find a solution, he had an idea.

59

Watercolored Sky

When Shane had gone, Abi went back inside to find Burton. Hearing him talking with her Father about the funeral arrangements, Abi sat down to listen.

"I just asked Burton to stay with you while I go and drop off Mom's clothes at the funeral home."

Not expecting that, she replied, "Oh, okay..."

Burton watched him get up from the table and head upstairs. "Where's Shane?" he asked Abi.

"I sent him home."

"What? Why?" He figured the guy wasn't in agreement with that.

She did not answer.

Knowing it wasn't his business, he said, "Guess you have your reasons."

"He has the All-American showcase in Vegas. It starts tomorrow."

Confused, he asked, "So the guy chose football over you?"

"No. Quite the opposite."

"I don't understand."

"He wanted to stay and be with me tomorrow. I told him to go to Vegas. I couldn't let him give up that opportunity."

Burton tilted his head. "Typical, Abi Acardi."

"What does that mean?"

"Here, your life is crumbling, and you're thinking of everyone else but yourself." Reaching for her hand across the table, he took hold. "I'm surprised he agreed to go."

Finishing the last bit of food on her plate, she said, "Oh, he didn't. I made him promise he would."

Putting himself in Shane's shoes, Burton felt bad for the guy. Taking their dishes from the table, he rinsed them off in the sink and placed them in the dishwasher as Abi got up and moved to the sofa. Weighed down, she collapsed into it and exhaled just as her Dad walked down the stairs.

"I'll be back shortly," he said on his way to the door, garment bag in hand.

Hearing him leave, Burton went to sit with Abi.

Deep in thought, she said, "I can't believe this is it."

"I'm sorry. I wish I could say something to take the pain away."

Glimpsing at the sun setting along the canyon, she peeled back the Fleetwood door and walked out.

Burton followed as she climbed the steps to the rooftop patio. With his house visible from across the canyon, he watched Abi stare at it, then divert her attention to the clouds drifting by as the watercolored sky washed in orange, yellow, and darkened tones.

"Do you believe in heaven?" she asked.

"Truth?"

Lying on the chaise, she said, "Always."

"I believe my parents are watching us as we speak and are there when I need to talk to them. They send signs, you know? Signs that they're listening. You just have to ask."

"What do you mean ask?"

"I usually pose a question and wait for them to send me something to show they're there. Afterward, I watch for unexpected rainbows, ladybugs, birds, and butterflies. Once in a while, I spot numbers on a license plate or a clock with 1111s or 3333s, something like that. Once you've verbalized a request, be in tune with what's happening around you, and you'll see or even feel her presence. I promise."

She tearfully nodded. "Maybe I'll try that."

Moving his chaise beside hers, he lifted his arm. Seeing this, she moved closer and cuddled beside him as the wind whistled through the trees amidst the faint sounds of traffic whizzing down the 405.

"Thank you for coming back. I know you're really busy."

"I said I'd stand by you and be here day or night. And I keep my word."

She rested her hand on his chest. He held it tightly as the sun descended on the horizon.

60

Day's End

It was almost dark as the sky dimmed to a dusky hue. With a chill in the air, Abi shivered. Feeling her body trembling, Burton rubbed her arm. He figured her Father would be home shortly.

"We'd better get you inside," he said. "You should get some sleep."

He helped her to her feet. Solemnly walking down the steps and into the house, they noticed headlights out front.

Burton closed the Fleetwood glass behind them and locked up just as her Dad walked through the door. Following Abi into the living room, he knew it was his cue to leave. "I'm going to go now. But I'll see you tomorrow."

"Thank you for staying. Appreciate that," her Father stated.

"No problem, Sir." He shook the man's hand. "I'll see you in the morning. Would you like my guys to drive us to and from the funeral?"

Abi turned to her Father.

Surprised by the offer, he said, "Thank you, we'd appreciate that."

"Alright. I'll be here at nine-thirty, then?"

"Perfect. Goodnight, Burton."

"Night, Sir."

On his way outside, Abi followed. Reaching his car, he lifted the door open.

Empty, she stood there like she were a shell. "Are you gonna be okay?"

Breaking from her daze, she replied, "Yes, eventually..."

With open arms, he brought her in close. Feeling hers slip around his waist, he kissed her forehead. "If you need me, call me. Doesn't matter what time."

"I will."

He squeezed her hand and kissed the back of it before letting go. Sitting behind the wheel, Burton lowered the door and rolled the window down. "Night, Abs."

"Night."

When he started the engine, it growled as he put the car in gear. Raising a steady hand, he slowly drove away.

As the McLaren's sound moved further down Stradella, the silence crept in amidst the winds swirling above. Alone, she thought about what she'd done and said to Shane and felt terrible. Exhausted, she shook her head and went inside.

Her Dad was in the family room, sipping a drink as the ice clinked the crystal. She sat beside him, not saying anything. The house was so quiet.

"I love you, Sweetheart," he said.

"Love you, too, Dad."

"You go upstairs and get some sleep. Tomorrow is going to be a long day."

She nodded. About to leave, she kissed him on the cheek. "Goodnight."

A tear drifted down his face. "Night, dear."

Leaving him, Abi headed upstairs. While passing the wise old tree, she wondered if she should call Shane and apologize for her behavior. Checking the time, she opted against it, believing he'd be packing for the trip. The last thing she wanted was for him to get distracted. He needed to focus.

"Maybe this was for the best," she whispered on her way into her room.

Slipping under the covers, not caring anymore, she turned out the light, thankful the horrible day had finally ended.

61

The Departure

The following day, rising early, realizing she was about to live her worst nightmare, Abi rolled over and tried to gather the courage to face it all. It was hard to get out of bed and put one foot in front of the other, but she somehow managed to get showered.

With her hair pulled back in a sleek bun, she slipped into her Mother's black sheath dress. Taking the cardi from the hanger, she layered it on top and fastened the button. When she stepped back, she looked in the mirror.

"I will always be a part of you," Abi whispered, hoping she would hear her. Surprisingly, not crying a tear, she said, "Guess you've got nothing left to expel."

Finding her black shoes in the closet, she stuffed some makeup and a mound of Kleenex in her bag just as her Dad walked past her room.

Stopping, he looked in with glistening eyes. "You are a spitting image of her, you know."

"Do I look okay?"

"You look perfect, Sweetie."

"Thank you."

Not wanting to upset her, he hugged her tightly and backed away. "We should get going. Are you ready?"

"Yes."

Her Father got a phone notification on their way downstairs. Someone was at the gate. Granting access, he slowly made his way toward the foyer and unlocked the door before opening it.

They watched Burton drive into the courtyard in his G-Wagen, with Andrew, Ted, and Matt following behind in the Cadillac SUV.

"Does he always travel with an entourage?" he asked.

"Most of the time," Abi replied, not about to explain further.

Spotting the two standing somberly in the entryway, Burton approached and kept it simple. "Hi," he said, well-dressed, wearing a black suit and tie.

"Morning, Burton. Please, come in."

Closing the door behind him, Dr. Acardi asked, "Would you like a coffee before we go?"

"No, thank you. I'm good. Had one earlier." Noticing Abi was quiet, he placed his hand on her shoulder. "How are you holding up?" he asked.

"As good as can be expected."

Moving into the kitchen, Abi scoffed down a piece of toast and half of a coffee, knowing she had to have something in her stomach despite the knot that had developed in the center of her chest overnight.

"After the burial, we will invite people back for the luncheon. I've arranged for the caterers to arrive around one o'clock."

"Do you want one of my guys to stay and manage the house while we're gone?" Burton suggested, believing it would lessen his stress.

He pondered his offer, reluctant to accept the help. "If that's not too much trouble," he said.

"No, it's fine. No trouble at all."

"Thank you."

Without an ounce of hesitation, Burton replied, "Absolutely."

Looking at the time, Abi's Dad got them out the door.

Burton messaged Martin and had him send another security team to the house to help Matt as he waved the guy over to issue him instructions.

"Dr. Acardi, meet Matt Gerber. He will keep an eye on things here."

He shook his hand. "Nice to meet you, Sir. My deepest sympathies."

"Thank you, young man. Appreciate your help today."

"Sure thing, Sir."

"Here is the key in case you need it. The gate remote is on the front table in the basket." Dr. Acardi hoped he hadn't forgotten anything.

"Very well, Sir. Don't worry. Everything will be fine."

Dr. Acardi looked at his watch and nodded.

Knowing they were ready to leave, Burton walked over to Andrew seated on the driver's side.

"Where are we headed?" the big guy asked.

"Forest Lawn Cemetery. The one off of Highway 134," his boss instructed.

"Got it. We will follow you."

Tapping the vehicle with his hand, he said, "Okay."

Seeing Abi standing by herself, watching all of them, Burton went to her.

"Hey, Abs. Come with me." Offering his arm, she gripped it tightly while he helped her into his SUV after opening the rear passenger side.

Her Father got in opposite her. He found his daughter sitting quietly, her hands folded on her lap.

When Burton slipped behind the wheel, he glanced back. "Ready?" he asked.

She turned to him and said, "Guess so..." just as her Father silently acknowledged him.

Starting the truck, Burton gave Andrew a wave.

"Do they follow you everywhere?" Dr. Acardi asked curiously.

"Yes, unfortunately. It's better to be safe than sorry."

62

It is Finished

It was a silent ride up the 405. Burton peered into the rearview mirror periodically to check on Abi as she sat sorrowfully, the sun flashing its rays upon her face. The closer they got to the cemetery, he could see her fidgeting while trying to hold back tears.

Merging onto Forest Lane Drive, flower vendors were set up alongside the road, selling bouquets to those visiting their loved ones. Looking away, she focused on the rolling hills to her left with large trees scattered about the fields of green. It framed the picture-perfect piece of heaven.

"Is this it?" she asked.

Her Dad nodded. "Yes."

Burton signaled and stopped before turning in.

With a flowing fountain on one side and a white house on the other, Abi got nervous when they passed through the iron gates. But the serenity of the place soon offered a sense of calm.

"It looks so peaceful here," she whispered.

"That is what Mom thought, too."

"She was here?"

"Yes."

Upset to hear that, she questioned, "And you didn't tell me?"

"That was her decision. I abided by it. After so long, she was just thankful you were finally happy at school, had friends, and got reacquainted with this guy."

Burton smiled.

"She didn't want to ruin that for you."

Many cars were coming and going.

Abi thought about what he'd said. "That's something she'd do. Think of others before herself."

Her Dad's face brightened. "See. You come by it honestly."

"I guess so," she said, knowing he was right.

While Burton followed the winding road, it wasn't easy to see people gathered under collapsable canopies to shelter them from the sun during the burials.

In the distance, she saw a white steeple inset amongst the trees. "Are we going there?"

"That's the chapel."

"It looks like our church back home in Boston."

"That's why she wanted the service here."

They noticed the hearse parked near the space reserved for them.

"Mom is already inside," he said.

Burton shut off the truck and got out.

With a few breaths, Abi felt like a brick was sitting on her chest. It was hard to breathe. Her hands trembled. Her body felt weak. She didn't know if she could do this. So many cars were there. Knowing people had come to pay their respects, her stomach felt sick.

When Burton opened the door for her, her Dad exited on his side, straightened his tie, and buttoned his jacket before closing it. He, too, was nervous.

Offering Abi his hand, Burton said, "I'll be by your side the whole time. I'm not leaving you."

When she heard this, Abi's heart dropped. It was the exact same thing Shane had said. Heart pounding, she got out and held onto Burton's arm as he locked the truck.

Andrew and Ted looked on as they moved across the brick herring-bone path toward the chapel.

About to enter, her Father waited and bowed his head. Burton placed his opposite hand on his shoulder to give him strength.

He took a deep breath and said, "Okay."

As they walked in, sunlight flooded the aisle. The creeky sound of the wooden door echoed inside, causing everyone to turn around. Eyes glued to them, they made their way to the casket surrounded by baskets of flowers. Her Mother's picture graced the screen suspended above.

Abi watched the memories of her fade in and out on the slideshow.

Holding back, Burton let them approach first and have a moment alone. In seconds, Abi reached her quivering hand behind her in search of him. Stepping forward, holding it, he bowed his head as Abi cried and fidgeted with her tissue in hand.

Her Mother looked so beautiful in her white dress. Hands crossed, clutching a single white rose, her face looked angelic despite everything that had happened. No longer was she pale with eyes sunken and dark.

Remembering the kind woman who welcomed him into their home years ago, Burton looked up to keep his emotions in check. Wiping a single tear away with his finger, he spotted something. Immediately, his guard went up. It ignited an internal rage. There, in the back row, was a basket of black roses. Knowing what to do, intent on not making a scene, he waited for an opportunity to discreetly dispose of them without Abi noticing.

The second they crossed themselves, Burton gave Abi to her Dad. Stealthily walking around behind the casket, he removed the large basket of morbid flowers and stashed the card in his pocket. Hiding them from sight, he quickly replaced the void with another bursting with white lilies. Crisis averted, thankful Abi hadn't seen him, he joined her in the first pew.

Leaning over, she whispered tearfully, "Is something wrong?"

Wanting to keep her calm, he said, "No, nothing. Everything is fine."

While sitting, people approached the casket. Burton took out his phone and texted Andrew, revealing that Eastwood had sent his calling card and warned him to be on the lookout. Slipping the device into his interior jacket pocket, he brought his focus back to Abi and turned slightly to his left to get a better view of those in the church.

Finding his men scanning the congregation, now knowing what Eastwood looked like, Burton waited for an update. The moment his phone vibrated, he secretly checked the message. Reading the words – *All clear*, he breathed a sigh of relief.

One by one, Abi and her Dad shook people's hands as they paid their respects. Going through the motions, she suddenly saw familiar faces in the line-up. Solemnly following suit with those in front of them, Jade and Owen stepped forward to shake her Father's hand before Jade hugged her friend tightly. The tears flowed for both girls, making Owen and Burton quickly comfort them. Behind her best friend, she found Adrian and Mei, Shawn and Laney, Alan and Allie, and Ming and Ben.

When Laney hugged her, Abi whispered, "The whole team is here? How?"

Unable to answer her, the pretty blonde veered her sights to the right. There, approaching the casket last, was Shane.

Heartbroken to see him standing alone, Abi got up and went to him. Slipping her hand in his, he hugged her tightly before offering his condolences to her Father as Burton looked on.

Abi ushered Shane to their pew and sat beside Burton. As the line continued, she noticed the day nurse who looked after her Mother. The woman was teary-eyed as she offered her sympathies. The rest were strangers, and she assumed they worked at the hospital.

Once everyone was seated, the Pastor surfaced, and the service began. The choir started singing a few of their family's favorite hymns. Recognizing two from her grandparents' funeral, she couldn't join in. Emotions running high, she felt numb.

Invited by the Pastor to have one last look before he blessed and closed the lid, Abi and her Father walked up.

Touching her hand, he kissed his wife's forehead.

Abi did the same. "Love you, Mom," she said as her legs buckled slightly.

Needing help, Burton stood and held onto her until she settled.

Shane kept his composure but didn't like sitting on the sidelines.

The moment was so raw there wasn't a dry eye in the church.

Amidst the silence, the Pastor climbed the stairs to the raised pulpit, where he took out a piece of paper and read aloud.

"We gather here today to mourn the loss of Beth Ann Acardi. Weeks ago, I had the pleasure of meeting her. Our time together was brief but memorable. She was full of life despite her diagnosis. With bright eyes and a clear vision of what she wanted this day to be, we did our best to fulfill her wishes." Breaking away from the paper, he said, "I don't know if there is a deeper sense of loss than that of a wife and Mother. The woman who you gave your life to and raised a family with. The woman who brought you into this world and taught you right from wrong." Looking down at Abi and Dr. Acardi, he said, "I want to extend my sincere condolences for your loss. I hope these words give you solace in some way," he paused. "From what I am told from Beth Ann herself, she kept her terminal prognosis private. Only Anthony knew the extent of what was to come. She never wanted to burden anyone, especially her daughter Abi. Thankful to see her thriving in her new life on the West Coast, she told me how proud she was of you and that you had recently shared a few memorable moments before her body had other plans."

Hearing this, she thought of the bath and bubbles incident. Recalling the look on her face and the laughter they shared, she knew that was the memory she'd spoken of.

"For those who didn't know Beth Ann, she was an only child. Her parents stood by her side and supported her through her battle with cancer until their untimely passing a month after Beth had gone into remission. The tragic loss of her parents was immense, especially when Beth discovered her cancer returned two years later. Taking inventory of her life, always wanting to live in California and loving the sand and surf, she asked Anthony if he would consider relocating. Realizing she was not fully up to the task, he felt compelled to fulfill this dream. Abi and Beth were still living in Boston when Anthony started his new job at UCLA Med." He looked straight at Abi. "Your Mother told me how mature, courageous, and brave you were at handling many adult tasks when preparing for the move. She said she couldn't have done it without you. Throughout her good and bad days, she described how you would run back and forth from school so you could tend to her needs. It was a lot for a seventeen-year-old to handle, but she said you did it with grace and poise. You never faltered or backed down from the challenge. Her heart warmed when she talked about how happy you were at your new school and shared the details of the friends you'd met. Beth Ann was certain these young people would surround, love, and support you through the horrible aftermath."

Abi cried upon hearing his words, prompting Burton to wrap his arm around her as she leaned into him.

Cast aside, feeling he should be the one comforting her, it wasn't easy to witness this, but in all fairness, Shane knew the guy probably thought of her Mother like his own. Constantly hearing that Burton was more of a brother, Shane willingly took a back seat for now. They were family. He wasn't.

"Beth Ann came into your lives briefly, laughed with you, cried with you, danced, and made you smile. She made you feel special, then left too quickly. I suppose when we look at death, that makes life beautiful. We know our time here is short and must make the most of it - remember what is important. Abi, even though your Mother has passed, a part of her will always live inside you. While your hearts are breaking, know heaven has no pain or suffering. She is at peace with your grandparents in God's kingdom."

The organist played How Great Thou Art as the Pastor descended the stairs. It was her favorite hymn. The funeral director and his associates closed the casket and prepared for the blessing and processional.

Seeing them line up alongside it, Shane stood and walked over to take the place of one man. He didn't want Abi to see strangers carrying her Mom. Soon, following his lead, Burton, Adrian, Alan, Shawn, Ben, and Owen did the same.

Abi collapsed into her Dad's arms. Following them down the aisle, Abi and her Father walked along tearfully. Moving through the doors, the men carried her Mother to the hearse as everyone gathered around.

Waiting for them, Burton stood alongside his vehicle and opened the rear door when Dr. Acardi and Abi approached. Sitting them together in the back, Burton soon got in on the driver's side.

Shane watched them from a distance.

Once everyone was ready to depart, the black car drove to the final resting place. Leaving the church, Burton followed the hearse, feeling Abi's pain through her sobs. Unable to make it go away, a few droplets drifted down his cheeks.

When they stopped along Ascension Road, they could see her plot with a green canopy and seating underneath a shady tree. Shane respectfully walked alongside Dr. Acardi as Burton held onto Abi. Slowly walking across the grass, they prepared for the last piece of their tearful goodbye.

Their friends gathered around quietly.

Escorting Abi with her Dad to the grave, Burton and Shane returned to help as pallbearers. The funeral director spoke to all the football players and gave them instructions. The young men listened intently. Ready to carry Beth Ann, each took hold of the handles and followed the man before placing her gently on the lowering frame.

The next twenty minutes were a blur. Abi was present in body but not in spirit. Overwhelmed by grief, her mind was incapable of processing anything, as the devastating feeling of loss made her feel like she was about to explode.

The guys looked at each other and then back at her.

Staring into oblivion, not focused on anyone or anything, Abi saw the casket lower below ground level.

Her Father suddenly took a few white lilies from a floral basket and placed them on top. He could not bring himself to take a handful of earth.

The Pastor announced that everyone was invited back to the Acardi home for a luncheon in Beth's honor. As people left in silence, a solemness hung over them like a cloud.

"Would you like to place a few flowers?" Burton asked as she looked his way blankly.

Barely registering what he said, she nodded. Offering a few white ones, he helped her. Setting them on top, she rested her hand flat on the cold steel.

After all these years, she thought, *it is finished.*

Her heart ached uncontrollably, knowing they would soon bury her in the ground. "I want to leave," she whispered desperately. "Please…"

Burton helped her walk down the hillside before her Father joined them and took her hand.

To Abi, the people standing around the vehicles parked curbside looked like black shadows. Not one had a face. Getting straight into Burton's SUV when he opened the door, she didn't notice her friends waiting to speak to her. Curled up in the back seat, she only wanted to go home. Nothing else.

In a daze, hearing the sound of engines starting, Burton drove them away. Watching the world go by the window, she did not see Shane standing there, hoping to hug her.

Jade quickly saw the disappointment and helplessness on his face. "Don't take it personally," she said quietly. "She's going through the motions right now and can't think of anything besides her grief."

Figuring as much, he broke from his dull gaze.

"Come on," she coaxed. "Let's head out. It won't be long, and we'll have to hit the road."

Silently acknowledging her with a nod, he knew their day was far from over.

63

Supportive Friends

By the time they arrived at Abi's house along the canyon, the light winds blew through the trees more forcefully, rustling the leaves as they passed. The sun dipped in and out from behind the clouds, making the day seem less dim.

Pulling into the courtyard, passing a line of cars parked along Stradella, she noticed groups of people gathered around. Knowing she would have to engage in conversation, part of her just wanted to escape and hide in her room.

Once they stopped, Burton turned off the ignition and glimpsed at Abi in the rearview. Amidst the stillness, Dr. Acardi took a deep breath and paused before throwing himself into the final phase of the day.

When he left the vehicle, Abi watched him walk over to everyone and invite them inside. Still in the backseat, she saw Burton get out, swing around, and open the door for her.

Eyes swollen, Abi's head hurt tremendously. "No, not yet," she mumbled. "I want to wait until they go in."

He closed it until she was ready.

Shane came through the gates and saw Burton standing idle. Giving him the eye, he pointed. "Is she there?"

Burton replied, "Yes. She needs a minute."

Approaching, he asked, "Can I talk to her – alone?"

Hesitant, identifying the sadness on the guy's face, Burton stepped away and went to join Andrew, Matt, and Ted.

Standing alongside the vehicle, Shane placed his hand flat on the glass, not wanting to spook or stress her out.

Finding his shadow with the sun illuminating him, she reached out and did the same.

He was happy to see this.

Still half-present, Abi stayed this way for a minute before Shane cautiously opened the door. Not saying a word, he leaned in and hugged her. A rag doll at first, she suddenly came alive and clung to him so tightly, remembering what she'd done and said to him, causing a flood of tears to follow.

"It's okay. I'm here," he said comfortingly.

Expelling everything she could for the moment, she wiped her tears with trembling hands. "You're supposed to be in Vegas," she said, chest heaving intermittently, gasping for air.

"I know you asked me to go, but I couldn't. I'm sorry." Drifting his fingertips across her forehead, tucking a few strands of hair behind her ear, he explained, "It's like your mother said—she was thankful you had good friends surrounding you—friends who would love and support you through this. And you know, I love you with all my heart."

Those words brightened the darkness around her. "I love you too," she replied, feeling so lucky to have such a close-knit group to go through life with. Glancing at the house, she saw all of them standing, waiting for her to surface.

"Come on. They're waiting for you," he said. "It's okay. I'm here."

She nodded silently.

Offering her his arm, she got out. Closing the door behind her, he kissed her forehead and said, "We will do this together."

Their friends saw Abi emerge. Each stopped, eyes affixed to her. Sadness was still lingering.

Jade was the first to embrace her tightly. Trying to be strong for her friend, she held back her tears as long as she could before the droplets crept across her face. "Whatever you need.... Just say the word."

Filled with emotion, Abi couldn't respond, but Jade knew she heard her.

Laney was next, followed by Allie, who struggled not to break down. She couldn't say a word through her sobs and immediately found Alan afterward, ready to console her.

The twins gave Abi a double hug.

"No matter what, we are family now," Mei said. "Whether you like it or not."

She wholeheartedly agreed. "Thank you for coming. You don't know what this means to me."

Laney could see the girl needed a lighthearted moment. "Group hug, everyone."

Surrounded, feeling their love and support, Burton watched as Abi almost cracked a smile. Following them inside, Shane walked Abi through the crowd as people stared.

Thankful to find the TV room mostly empty since many had gathered on the patio, Shane sat Abi on the sofa. "Want me to make you a small plate of something?"

Not hungry, knowing she needed to eat, she replied, "Sure."

Jade poured her a cup of tea while Shane gathered a selection of finger sandwiches, cheese, crackers, and veggies with dip to start.

Hovering nearby, seeing her friends cater to her, Burton kept a close eye.

After Shane handed her the plate of food, the girls gathered around. That gave him a chance to talk to Burton. Grabbing a water, he confidently moved in the guy's direction. The two briefly made eye contact before standing along the wall facing forward.

"I saw what happened at the casket." Shane cracked the seal, removed the cap, and took a drink. "We'd just arrived," he said. "The black roses? Did Eastwood send them?"

Burton pulled the card signed with an E from his inside pocket and showed him.

"Does she know?"

"No."

Shane's anger surfaced. His fists clenched. "Why the hell is this guy screwing with her head? We need to deal with him once and for all."

"I'm working on it." Burton paused as his sights drifted to her. "Don't do anything stupid. This guy is dangerous. Unpredictable."

"If anybody knows that, it's me."

Shawn and Alan joined them.

Looking at the time on his phone, Shawn said, "Hey, man. You guys are cutting it kinda close."

"I know - just a few more minutes. Then we'll go," he replied.

"What's going on?" Burton asked, wondering why they were in a hurry.

Shane turned to him. "We need to drive to Vegas for the Showcase. The skills comp is tonight at seven under the lights."

Alan interrupted. "Yeah, and it's a four-hour drive."

"We are gonna change here," Shane said. "Then, we need to hit the road."

Burton thought a minute. "Why don't you fly?"

"This was all kind of last minute. With everything going on, we haven't had a chance to think that far ahead."

"Do you need a plane?"

The guys looked at Shane first. They knew the drive would be daunting and would probably burn them out before the event scheduled a few hours from now.

"You have one?" the QB questioned.

"Yep. I won't need it until early tomorrow afternoon. So, it's yours, if you want. That way, you can spend a little more time here with her."

Gathering the consensus from those around him, Shane said, "Appreciate that. Thanks."

"I'll call my people and make the arrangements. It's parked at Van Nuys."

Appreciative, Shane reached out his hand. "Thanks, man."

Burton shook it. "No problem."

Abi looked across the room. Finding the two men in her life getting along warmed her heart.

Her Dad walked in from the patio outside and joined Abi and her friends. "I wanted to thank each of you for supporting my daughter today. Thank you, boys, for being pallbearers. I'm grateful to see my Abi has such wonderful people to lean on."

Laney smiled. "She's pretty great, too, Sir."

Before making the rounds to speak to his colleagues, he added, "Well, you are all welcome here any time."

64

In Good Hands

Able to spend two more hours together, her friends took turns getting changed while Burton made sure the plane was ready for them on time.

The last to get out of his suit, Shane stood by Abi with his duffle bag on his shoulder.

Approaching their group, Burton went through a checklist. "Everyone can load up their baggage in Matt's SUV. He will make sure everything is on board when you leave. Do you have your passports?"

"We're good. The showcase required two types of ID at check-in," Shane said.

Alan turned to Allie. "Do you have yours?"

She shook her head no.

The other girls said the same.

Hearing this, Burton, being a problem solver by nature, offered a solution. "I am leaving tomorrow at one o'clock for Vegas if any of you want to ride with me. It's probably not safe to drive in the dark tonight."

Their sights bounced back and forth between them.

Jade said, "Okay, if you don't mind. We'll hitch a ride, then." Surprised by the guy's generosity, she smirked. "It seems I was wrong."

Burton curiously asked, "About what?"

"You're not so bad after all."

Initially questioning if she meant it as a compliment or an insult, he opted to take it as a win.

The girls followed their boyfriends to the SUV. Hugging them and saying goodbye, they wished them good luck.

"Mind if I leave my Jeep here?" Shane asked Abi, realizing it was still on the street.

Abi wrapped her arms around Shane's waist. "No problem. That's fine. I'll keep an eye on it for you."

"Thanks. Hold that thought. I'll be right back."

He jogged outside the gate and drove the black beast to the far side of the courtyard beside her Mini Cooper. Getting out, he locked it and walked back to hand her the keys.

"Here you go." Not wanting to leave, he hugged and held on tight.

"Hopefully, I can find the showcase highlights somewhere."

He looked into her eyes. "I'll send you the links. Please call me if you need me. Doesn't matter. Day or night, we can talk." He paused. "Well, unless we have a game."

"Okay."

Soaking it in, she gave him his pep talk. "I want you to leave it all on the field this weekend. No holds barred. You are the number one pick for a reason. I need you to show everyone that."

He stared at the certainty in her eyes. "I will."

"Please don't get distracted. Stay focused. One flawless throw at a time. I want to see touchdowns on those highlight reels."

"Got it."

He looked down at her and gently kissed her forehead. "You gonna be okay?"

"Eventually..."

"I love you," he whispered. Cupping her cheeks, he kissed her lips.

"Love you too."

Before getting in the truck, Shane waved. "Bye," he said softly.

She, in turn, tearfully raised a hand and tried to smile.

Soon, he was gone.

"We are going to let you get some rest," Jade said as the girls hovered behind her. "I'm sure you're exhausted."

"Yeah, kinda."

"We are home tonight if you need us," Allie added.

Laney stepped forward. "Shawn and I are here all weekend. So, call me, too, anytime. I'm free."

"Thank you again for being here."

Jade clung to Abi's hand. "There is no other place we would be."

Waving goodbye as they walked out of the courtyard to drive the guys' vehicles home, Burton approached.

"You have a good group of friends there."

"I know. I feel so lucky. Never had that in Boston." Realizing what she'd said, Abi backtracked. "Except for you, of course."

He rested his hand on her back as people slowly started trickling out of the house. "We should get you inside," he said.

Agreeing, she followed him through the threshold. Desperate for space, she said, "I'm going upstairs. Can you...umm..."

"Sure."

The two climbed the steps to Abi's room.

Burton sat on the bed when she entered her closet and closed the door to change.

Emerging moments later, dressed in her Mom's powder blue hoodie and black tights, she pulled her hair up in a messy bun and fastened it with a scrunchie from her side table. Hands resting on her hips, she stopped. Peering at the floor, she mumbled, "I can't believe she's gone. It's like she just disappeared." Hearing herself state the obvious, she covered her mouth to refrain from sobbing. But it didn't work. She sat beside him on the bed.

Sliding over, he held her tight to comfort her as much as he could.

Back in his arms, she felt different—protected and secure. He knew her better than anyone else did. "Can you stay for a bit longer?"

Willing to do whatever she needed, he replied, "If you want me to."

She mumbled, "Please." Crawling across the covers to the stack of pillows, she curled up with one and closed her eyes.

He removed his shoes, tie, and suit jacket. Unbuttoning the two top buttons on his shirt, he rolled his sleeves to his elbows and sat back down. Stretching his legs out, he leaned against the headboard. Looking at Abi, it didn't take long for her to fall asleep. It was hard to hear her body heave periodically from crying so much. Her face was pale, and her eyes were swollen and red. Taking the throw blanket from the footboard, he covered her with it. She did not move a muscle.

In the silence, he slipped his phone from his pocket to catch up on emails and texts in preparation for the Nightfall launch in Vegas. Despite having a list of tasks, he could not leave her.

Within the hour, Burton heard Dr. Acardi ascend the stairs. While passing by in the hall, he looked in and found Burton there.

"Is she okay?" he asked quietly, not to wake her.

"She's good. Just exhausted."

Wholeheartedly agreeing, he gave Burton a thumbs-up before continuing to his room to change, knowing she was in good hands.

65

Have You Decided?

Hearing only the catering company cleaning up, washing dishes, and storing the leftovers in the fridge, Burton kept checking on Abi as she slept. Thinking about the black roses, he still wondered if Eastwood was there somewhere, lurking in the shadows despite their best efforts. Confident the guy was going for shock and awe on the worst day of her life, his anger worsened exponentially. It brought about a similar theory surrounding his parents' tragic passing. The fact Abi found it in her Mother's hands the day before she died made him wonder if her death was not a natural one. Grasping at straws, Burton didn't know for sure. He needed proof.

Right then, Abi stirred and stretched. When her eyes opened, she found him there.

"Hey, sleepy head," he greeted pleasantly.

"Hi..." Disoriented, she asked, "What time is it?"

"Almost six."

"Have you been here this whole time?"

"Of course."

She inched toward him.

Lifting his arm, she cuddled in close.

"Thank you for staying."

He patted her shoulder. "Nowhere I'd rather be."

"I guess you need to go soon?" Abi dreaded the thought of being alone.

He put his phone down. "Unfortunately, but I'll check on you in the morning before I head to the airport. In the meantime, if you need me, call. I'll be right across there tonight," he pointed to his house.

"Okay." She placed her hand on top of his chest.

Resting his on hers, he grabbed hold and brought it to his lips. Kissing the back, he said, "I should probably give you and your Father some space. I believe you need to reconnect with him."

"You might be right."

He sat up. Hugging her, Burton kissed her forehead. "Okay... I'm off." Slowly sliding to the edge of the bed, he gathered his things and put on his shoes. While tying them, Abi sat there, wishing he could stay a bit longer. But she couldn't be selfish. He had so much on his plate.

"I'll walk you out," she said.

On their way downstairs, they heard her Dad in the kitchen.

"Thank you again," she said softly.

"Your Mother was like a Mom to me, too."

"You're the only one who knew her before all this..."

Reaching out to him, he embraced her one last time.

Her Father rounded the corner just as the two parted ways.

"Thank you for your support today. It meant a lot - to both of us."

"Glad I could help."

When Dr. Acardi shook his hand, he unexpectedly pulled the burly DJ in for a manly pat on the back. Surprised by that, Burton figured things would be different between them from now on.

"On that note, I will be on my way." He looked at Abi. "Call if you need me."

She nodded and crossed her arms in front of her.

Leaving them, he walked outside and got into his SUV as the security team changed shifts. Matt had returned from the airport and was ready to take their team home.

Waving to Burton as he drove away, her Father asked, "So, have you decided yet?"

"Decided what?" Abi asked.

"Who you love more?" he said point blank while closing the door.

Embarrassed, her eyes drifted to a spot on the floor. "Dad, I'm not discussing this with you?"

"Why not?" he said disappointedly, managing a half-smile in the process. "It's something your Mother would ask, isn't it?"

Thinking of her, Abi could see her face as plain as day and hear her giggling during their bubbles incident.

"What does your heart say? Because it's obvious both of them love you. Now, you must choose."

Overwhelmed by the seriousness of his questions, she exhaled. "I can't think of anything else past tomorrow."

"I understand. Neither can I."

Noticeably pulled in two directions, he suggested, "Why don't you sleep on it? I'm sure things will be much clearer in the morning."

"I wish it were that easy..." she mumbled.

"Night, Sweetheart."

"Night."

Worried about her, he inquired as she climbed the stairs, "Are you going to be alright without Mom?"

"Never..." Offering a subtle wave, she continued to her room.

Settling in, she thought, this would be the first of many sleeps without her here. Knowing she was probably watching from heaven, feeling her presence gave Abi a sense of security. "Guess I have a guardian angel now. How many people can say they have one of those?" she whispered, looking at her Mother's picture on her bedside table. "Night, Mom. I love you."

Late Night

Hours later, waking up in the middle of the night, Abi looked around her room. The moon was cascading through the glass and casting a dull light beyond the hills of Bel Air. The world seemed still, and the silence was almost deafening.

"I probably should've passed on the afternoon nap," she said before leaving her bed. Walking to the window, she looked at Burton's house across the canyon. There, she found one room illuminated on the lower level. Moving her telescope from the corner, she lined it up perfectly and peered through the eyepiece. Focused in, she saw Burton sitting in bed, working on his computer.

"Does he ever sleep?" she asked aloud. Contemplating texting him, she grabbed her phone but stopped. "No. I should probably leave him be. I've disturbed him enough today."

About to return to bed, she saw a shadow move through his room and catch his attention.

"Who's that?" Curious, she zeroed in.

Bringing the frame into focus, she soon saw Sara sitting with him. Knowing she was invading her friend's privacy, she tried to look away but couldn't for some reason. Watching them talk, she wondered if he had told her about his day and how difficult it was for both of them.

Believing the girl hated her, she said, "I bet she wouldn't care anyway."

Suddenly, Burton closed his computer, and the room went dark. Unable to see anything, she somehow felt betrayed.

Rationalizing it in her head, she said, "No, Abs... You have no right to be upset. He's not yours." For a split second, a part of her wished he was.

Breaking from her thoughts, she returned the telescope to the corner of the room and got into bed. Tossing and turning, thoughts of him kept her from falling asleep, especially after seeing Sara.

About to give in and call Shane, she stopped again. "He's sleeping and needs to play today. You can't call and wake him."

Needing to keep her heart from hurting, she opened her Fishdom app on her phone, hoping some games would distract her.

Partway through challenging level 3021, she recalled what her dad had said. "So, Abi. How are you gonna choose?"

With the girl there, it seemed Burton had made that decision for her. In all fairness, she had insisted he give Sara a chance. It was now a decision she regretted.

Rolling her eyes, putting down her phone for a split second, she mumbled, "Guess he took my advice."

Reminded of Shane's words and how supportive he'd been, she smiled. Leaving the game mid-stream, she opened her photos and went through them. Finding one of Shane with his back to her and the setting sun illuminating his silhouette, she scrolled on and found a few more. So handsome, with eyes that drew her in, Abi's heart felt full.

"How lucky am I? He's mine."

Focused on their relationship and nothing else, she knew they needed each other.

"I guess whatever is meant to be will be."

Believing that, she rolled over, hoping to see Shane in her dreams.

67

Confessions

Ribbons of morning light delicately moved across Abi's face as she stirred in bed. Afraid for the day to begin, she rolled over. The weight of the past forty-eight hours was still there - a heavy burden made almost unbearable by her Mother's absence. She couldn't shake the ache in her heart. With each passing moment, a shadow spread across the new day dawning outside her window, but the warmth of her covers offered solace amidst her grief. Unsure what to do, she tried to gather the strength to get up and shower. Intent on spending time with her Father, hoping they could get through this together, she mustered the courage to rest her feet on the floor and persevere. This was her worst nightmare despite living in the land of California dreams. Everything had changed in an instant, and there was no going back.

The notification bell on her phone cut through the silence as she shuffled around, trying to find it. Figuring it was probably under her blankets somewhere, it sounded a second time, giving away its hiding spot. Phone in hand, she read the text. It was from Burton.

"How is he up so early after having such a late night?"

She read his message and discovered he was on his way over with breakfast and coffee. Seeing this immediately kicked her into high gear. Moving about her room, she tried to make herself look presentable.

Done in record time, wrapped in her robe, Abi headed down the hall to check on her Dad. Expecting to find him sleeping, she discovered a perfectly made bed and his drapes pulled back neatly. Able to dip into her Mother's closet without worry, she found another one of her sweatshirts and buried her face in the fabric. It, too, had her scent. Heather grey in color with a white speckle, Abi took it back to her room to change out of pajamas and get dressed.

On her way downstairs, she said, "Dad?" Believing she wasn't getting an answer because he was watching television with his headphones on, she said a second time, "Hello?" Rounding the corner into the kitchen, Abi sadly found it empty. "Huh? Where is he?" She spotted a note on the counter. Picking it up, it read, "Gone to work. I want to keep my mind busy. Be back later this afternoon. Love Dad." Disappointed, she looked around the huge house. It felt so empty.

The gate notification sounded. Abi set the piece of paper down and opened the gate for Burton, on the way to the foyer to greet him. As he drove in, so did Andrew, Ted, and Matt.

The butterfly door on the McLaren flipped upward as the guys waved to her.

Doing the same, she could tell they were concerned about how they'd find her this morning.

Burton climbed out of his car, looking sharp in tapered khakis, a fitted navy tee, and white sneakers. She had yet to see the same outfit twice on the guy.

"How many clothes does he own?" she whispered, wondering what his closet must look like.

"Morning. How are we doing?" he asked while grabbing the coffee and breakfast from the passenger side.

"Doing okay, I guess."

Walking over, he handed her one of the white bags with corded handles. "How'd you sleep?"

"Truthfully, I should never have had that nap," she said on the way inside.

Entering the kitchen, he set his sunglasses on the island. "Abs, you needed to rest. You were exhausted yesterday."

"I know. But then it screwed up my night."

Burton looked around. "Hey? Where's your Dad?'

Abi slid the note across the counter.

Reading it, he said, "You're joking... This is the one morning he should be here."

"I know." As sad as it was, Abi sighed. "That's what I thought, too."

"I even brought him breakfast." Burton tilted his head sympathetically. "Sorry, Abs."

"Yeah, well. What am I going to do?"

He thought about that. "Why not grab lunch and take it to his work? Tell him you want to spend some time with him. I'm sure he can spare a half hour."

"Maybe I'll do that."

"The guys can drive you wherever you want to go. Just say the word."

"Thank you for them, by the way. I know they must be costing you a fortune."

He debated telling her about the roses. Wanting to keep her guard up and make sure she didn't become complacent, he said, "I need to tell you something."

"Don't worry, if you need to scale back on them, it's okay."

"No, that's not the case."

"What do you mean?" Abi was confused.

Hesitant, he felt it was best just to come out with it. "Abs, I think I might have to increase your security."

"What? Why?"

"Yesterday at the chapel, when we were standing at the front, I found a basket of black roses beside your Mother's casket."

The blood drained from her face.

"I moved them so you wouldn't notice."

Staring blankly, Burton could tell her mind was reeling. "The guys did a sweep of the grounds and congregation. He wasn't there."

"You're positive?"

He nodded.

"Even on a day like that, he found a way to instill fear and make me feel violated." The thought angered her. "What does he want? Just to torture me? Make me look over my shoulder constantly while he waits in the shadows to attack?"

"Look, I'm not telling you this to scare you. You must remain diligent and always aware of your surroundings. Don't take chances, alright?"

Noticeably shaken, she felt pressure on her chest.

Witnessing this, he wished he hadn't told her. Getting up from the chair, he wrapped his arms around her. "It'll be okay. I promise. We're working on it."

"Again, with the *we*," she said. "Can you just divulge who that is?"

"Nope."

"Fine," she said timidly. "Can you at least share what you've found out so far? I want to know."

Feeling her body trembling, he let go. "It's concerning that your Mother had a flower in her hands the day before she passed. My guys checked the hospital security footage of the hallway outside her room. Only nurses went in and out of there that day. Nobody else. Not one janitor, porter, or visitor. Your Dad, too, of course. But that's it."

"So, we have no idea who did it?"

"At this point, no." Adding to that, he said, "They who shall not be named are wondering if there is a connection between that flower and her passing."

A look of shock spread across her face. "What are you saying?"

"We want to prove her death was a natural one, but your Father opted against an autopsy, so there is no way of confirming that now."

As the gravity of Burton's words settled in, she didn't know what to think. Panicked, needing to put this behind her, she stopped him from sharing anything more. "We need to change the subject."

He realized this news was hard to hear. Silently nodding, he said, "Fair enough."

Hands shaking, she opened the tab on her coffee cup and carefully took a sip.

"Were you up often last night?" he asked, hoping to change the subject of their conversation.

"For a few hours, yes. Mostly between three and five." Curious about his evening, she decided to fish a little. "How about you?"

"Me? I, umm, had work to finish. A lot goin' on today."

Debating whether to dig deeper, she figured he would never reveal what happened between him and Sara last night.

"I saw your light on at 3:10."

"That's about right. Think I went to bed around four." He sipped his coffee and removed the breakfast containers from the bag. "Eggs Benny or Spanish omelet?"

"Definitely, Benny."

He slid the container over and handed her some cutlery from the drawer.

Removing the lid, she said out of the blue, "So, have you spoken to Sara lately?"

Burton took a bite of his eggs and paused. "I talk to her every day. She's part of the team." Analyzing what she said, he immediately assumed the girl had spied on him. Upon taking a second bite to buy some time, he knew whatever he divulged from here on out would not be the truth but an outward lie. The only way out was to come clean. "So, umm, what did you see?" he asked uncomfortably.

Her eyebrows went up. Careful how she phrased her confession, she cleared her throat before taking another sip of her coffee. "Don't be mad."

He shot her a stern eye. "Abs?"

"I saw your light on and used the telescope." She scrunched her face.

He rolled his eyes and muttered, "Oh, my god..."

"You were working on your computer in bed. I was going to call you but thought I'd bothered you enough already."

"Please, don't ever think that."

"I know. But you looked stressed," she paused. "Anyway, I decided not to call and was about to put the telescope away when I saw your attention move from your screen. That's when I saw..."

"Sara."

"I didn't invade your privacy. I swear," Abi quickly confessed, raising her right hand.

He nodded embarrassingly. "Hmm..." Mortified at the possibility.

Wanting to know more, she prompted, "So, things are good with her?"

He took another bite. "I'm not discussing my private life with you."

"Why not? Come on, B. I need a break from all the sadness. Feel like I'm on the verge of crying every second," she whined. "I just want some happy news, that's all."

Unable to defy her charm, he smirked. "How do you do that?"

"Do what?"

"Make me want to tell you everything." Rotating his cup on the counter, he contemplated his answer. "Look, she and I... We are, umm, just seeing where it goes. That's all."

"So, that's good, right?"

"I suppose," Burton replied, having a few questions of his own - things that would determine the status of his place in her life. "How about you and Shane?"

She smiled through glistening eyes. "We are in a good place."

"Well, I'm happy for you both."

"Even though I told him not to be there yesterday, he couldn't stay away. He gave up a lot to support me. All of my friends did."

"I saw that. You're lucky to have such a close-knit group. People like that are hard to come by. Hold onto them." He knew, technically speaking, that all he had was her.

On the subject of truths, she wanted to know one more thing. "Can I ask you a personal question?"

"Oh, no... What?" he chuckled. "More personal than spying on me in my bedroom?"

She shrugged her shoulders. "Maybe."

He sat back in his chair and braced for impact. "Okay, hit me. What is it?"

"Why were you with Zoe Sky in Miami and in Vegas?"

Burton looked away. He figured it was just a matter of time before she discovered the pictures of them.

His silence worried her. Embarrassed, she bailed. "I'm sorry. You know what? It's none of my business. I apologize for being nosey."

He waited until she calmed down. "Abs, listen."

She turned to him.

"Martin hired Zoe to bring attention to Nightfall Inc. She has over a million followers on social. It's her business. She's an influencer. We had her on the trip to drum up interest for the launch. That's all."

"But, she kissed you and saw your face under the hood. Does that mean she knows who you are?"

"In a roundabout way. Not my real name, mind you. She signed our NDA. It has a hefty penalty should she breach that agreement." Addressing the flirtatiousness, he said, "As for the rest, it's just how she is. Being European, she kisses every person on the cheek to greet them. Including Martin," he smirked, knowing the guy felt awkward about it every time. "The media just took something innocent and spun it for clickbait."

To get peace of mind, she blurted, "So, nothing is going on between you?"

"No," he paused. "Since we're trying to make things work, Sara felt she shouldn't be in the public eye in that capacity. That is part of the reason why we added Zoe to the mix."

"What do you mean?"

"We hoped by her acting as my love interest, Eastwood might move from you to her."

"So, you did this to keep me safe?"

"That was the plan." Seeing the look on her face, he decided to turn the tables. "Hey, you're not jealous, are you?"

She shrugged her shoulders again. "Maybe a little."

He was secretly pleased to hear that.

Burton's phone chimed. Looking at the screen, he said, "I should get moving. I have to drop off the car at the house before I head out to meet your girlfriends at Van Nuys. Maybe you want to come?"

She thought for a second, forgetting about the arrangements they'd made. Being there to cheer Shane on was tempting. "No, I think it's best if I stay here. Dad is alone. I don't want him coming back to an empty house tonight."

"You're right."

"I might do what you suggested. You know, take him lunch. I think that would help us reconnect." Abi knew that after everything that's happened, it would be a tall order.

Burton closed his empty food container and put it in the recycle bin. Grabbing his coffee, he placed her Father's breakfast in the fridge for later before heading toward the front door. "Remember, if you need me, day or night, don't hesitate to call. You're never bothering me, okay?"

Abi followed him. "I know. Thank you for that."

Setting everything on the side table, with arms free, he hugged her tightly and kissed her on the forehead.

"Have a safe trip. Good luck with the Nightfall launch," she said as they parted ways.

"Thanks. We've got fifteen hundred registered. Needed to reject upwards of eight thousand ticket requests. Fire regulations."

"That's amazing. Congratulations."

"Appreciate that." Leaving with his coffee in one hand, phone and keys in the other, he added, "I'll see you when I get back."

"Alright." Holding onto the edge of the door, she once again felt alone while waving goodbye as he drove away. Closing it behind her, she looked at the time and felt compelled to take lunch to the hospital. Going back outside, Andrew walked over.

"Morning, Miss. Everything okay?"

"Yes, umm, I was hoping you could drive me to the hospital. I want to have lunch with my Dad."

"Absolutely. No problem," he replied. "Just let us know when."

"Thanks." Abi looked at the time. "Maybe in a half hour?"

"We will be ready."

"Perfect." About to walk away, Andrew suddenly stopped her.

"Miss?"

Abi turned around. "Yeah?"

"The guys and I are sorry about your Mom. We wanted to offer our sympathies properly, but with all the commotion yesterday, we didn't get the opportunity." He sounded so sincere.

"Thank you so much. I will try not to be so sad today, but I can't promise anything."

"We are here for you no matter what, Miss."

Getting a warm feeling in her heart, she went to him with open arms. "That means a lot." Hesitant, she asked, "Can I give you a hug?"

The big man nervously obliged.

His arms open, she slowly moved in and wrapped hers around his waist. "I haven't told you how grateful I am you guys are around. I've felt so safe and protected all this time. So, thank you for that."

Parting ways, he said, "You're welcome."

"On that note, I'll see you shortly. Perhaps twenty minutes?"

"We will be waiting."

When she went inside, Abi headed upstairs to change. It was hard to put one foot in front of the other. She figured it would be easier to collapse in bed and sleep the day away, but she knew her Mother wouldn't want her doing that.

"Come on, Mom," she said. "Help me get ready to go and see Dad."

68

A Brand New Day

While staring at her reflection in her closet mirror, she decided to wear what she had on. It was comfortable, and she didn't need to impress anyone that day. Besides, wearing her Mom's clothes helped her feel closer to her.

Quickly submitting an online order to Wolfglen Restaurant, she grabbed her crossbody bag and keys before heading downstairs again. Since eating there with Jade, she'd been craving their burgers and truffle fries. The thought of sharing them with her Dad today was almost exciting.

About to walk out the door, Abi's phone rang. Checking to see who it was, she was happy to find Shane's face on the screen. Accepting the video call, she sat on the living room sofa and said, "Hey, you."

Surprised to find her dressed, expecting her to still be in bed, Shane said, "Good morning. I'm glad you're up and moving."

"It wasn't easy, but yes. I'm trying."

He noticed her bag over her shoulder. "Going out?"

"I am actually. Believe it or not, my Dad went to work this morning."

This bothered him. "So you woke up to an empty house?"

His sympathetic tone pulled at her heartstrings. About to cry, Abi looked away. "Yeah, umm, I was kind of hoping, of all days, he'd be here."

"I agree. That's pretty messed up."

"He said in his note that he needed a distraction, so I'm heading to the hospital with lunch. Hopefully, he'll have a free half hour."

"Where'd you order from?"

"Wolfglen," she smiled.

"Good choice," Shane chuckled lightly before presenting a straight face. He did not want to be too upbeat, given the circumstances. He could tell Abi felt weighed down.

"Maybe he and I will reconnect today."

"That's not a bad idea."

Seeing Shane resting his back against the headboard in his hotel room, dressed in Gilderson colors, she said, "What's happening there?"

"We have an exhibition game in three hours."

"Nervous?"

"Not really." Knowing she was reading his body language, he paused and said, "Well, maybe a bit. There were so many scouts and TV crews there last night."

"How was the skills thing?"

"Coach was happy with our performance. Apparently, the scouts were talkin' about me. I got a lot of positive feedback."

"Was this the one with three, five, and seven-step drops?" she questioned.

The audio went dead, and Shane seemed to have frozen on screen.

"Hello?" she said. "Hello?"

He suddenly looked away and back at her.

"There you are. Thought I'd lost you."

"The call didn't drop. It wasn't a bad connection," Shane laughed. "Abs, how do you know about the drops?"

"I didn't sleep much last night, so I Googled QB Combine skills competition and drills. I learned the three-step drops focus on under-center. Five-step is on intermediate routes, and seven-step is a deep throw. Footwork is key. Accuracy is a must. Right?"

Speaking his language, he shook his head in amazement. "Unbelievable."

"Think it mentioned you must show you can run on a slant, an out, a throw-in, corner route, and deep route, AKA The Go," she reiterated word for word, her eyes veering upward and to the left as she recalled the sports article she'd read.

"You're insane," he smiled from ear to ear. "And I mean that in the best way possible."

"Hey, I'm just trying to keep my mind occupied. Otherwise, sad thoughts will consume me." Her eyes welled. She looked down. "This is her sweatshirt, by the way."

"It's really nice. I love the color."

"Yeah, me too." Tears streamed across her cheeks. Seeing herself on the screen, disappointed in her appearance, she sat up straight and patted her face with a Kleenex. "I didn't want to do this today, especially when talking to you."

"That's what I'm here for."

"But you need to concentrate and not worry about me. I'll be fine." She tried to exude a brave façade.

"Just in case you call, and I don't answer, please know I'm on the field or doing press stuff. It's not because I don't want to talk to you. Leave me a message or drop a text. I'll call you as soon as I can, okay?"

"Alright."

"Once we get back to LA, I'm all yours."

"Yes, you are," she said with a smitten smile. "Guess you should go."

Checking the time on his phone, he said, "Soon." He stared into her eyes and added, "Are you gonna be okay today?"

Trying her best to be strong, she replied, "Yep. All good."

Based on her tone, he did not believe her. "Remember, Laney stayed in town if you need company."

"I know. She told me to call her." Despite not being up to socializing, Abi figured she might chat with the girl when she got home. Thinking of her other friends, she stated, "I assume the rest of the girls should be landing there around three."

With a hint of jealousy, he said, "Right. Burton's bringing them out on the jet."

"Hey, it was nice of him to help you guys yesterday, too."

He knew she was right. "If we'd driven, I don't think we would've done as well in the skills comp. Guess I owe him one."

"You certainly do. See, B's not so bad."

"I hate to say it, but I might agree with you on that."

Abi was grateful to hear he was coming around and that there was less friction between them.

"So that you know, he's got a girlfriend named Sara."

"Really?" Shane perked up. "Good to hear."

Alan knocked on Shane's door. Peeking his head in the room, he said, "Hey, man. Gotta roll in ten. Is that Abi?"

"Yeah." Turning his screen around, their friend waved.

"Hey, Abs." The handsome blonde-haired boy raised a steady hand and flashed a partial smile.

"Hi, Alan," Abi waved back.

Shane faced the camera again.

"Okay, you go." She knew he had to get on with his day.

"Love you," he said. "We'll talk soon."

"Love you too. Good luck."

"Thanks. Appreciate it. I'll tell you all about it later tonight." Waving to her, he ended the call.

Abi did the same. Suddenly, the house seemed empty again. Holding back tears, she stood up and shook it off. "Okay, Abi Acardi. Let's get moving."

When the guys saw her emerge and lock the door, Matt started the truck while Andrew opened the passenger side. Ted was already seated behind Matt opposite her.

"Where are we off to, Miss?" Andrew asked.

She showed him the restaurant's address. "Wolfglen is on Glendon Avenue."

Andrew took a look and entered it into the GPS.

"After picking up the food, we'll go to the hospital."

Matt nodded. "Sounds good."

Leaving the courtyard, Abi closed the gate on their way out. While driving down Stradella, she searched Twitter, YouTube, and Instagram for anything on the Nightfall launch and the All-American Combine. It was a quiet ride while reading up on both until Matt faintly threw on some eighties music. Recognizing a Simple Minds song, she put down her phone and looked out the window as it played, focusing on a memory she'd almost forgotten.

Ted happened to glance over at her while scanning their surroundings. Seeing a tear drift down Abi's cheek, he quickly tapped Matt's shoulder, making the guy peer into the rearview mirror. Tilting his head, Ted prompted his attention to Abi.

Concerned, Matt turned the radio off.

She looked at him. "It's okay. You can let it play. It just reminded me of how Mom used to dance to this song in the kitchen while baking chocolate chip cookies."

He switched it back on.

Blotting her face with a tissue, she added, "She grew up in the eighties and always said they were the best years of her life." Abi chuckled. "Can you imagine a world without computers, cellphones, or AI? And heaven forbid, don't get me started on the whole Netflix, Prime, or Crave thing."

They smiled at her humor.

"When were you guys born?" Waiting for one of them to answer, not getting any takers, she pried, "Come on, then. Don't be shy."

Ted answered first. "Nineteen ninety-two," he said, followed by Matt, who replied, "Ninety-six."

After doing the math and figuring out their ages, Abi said, "So, thirty-two and twenty-eight, respectively." Pointing to Andrew, she awaited his answer. "So?"

"Eighty-eight," he answered.

"Being born in the eighties doesn't count. Technically, you hit high school in the two-thousands."

Andrew smiled. "Yes, that's right." He was impressed by Abi's level of intellect.

As the song changed to one from Sting, she asked, "Can you turn it up?"

"Sure can," Matt said.

Listening to the words, she hoped this was the start of a brand new day. Sadly, it was the first of many ahead of her without her Mom. She still couldn't believe she was gone. Not going to visit her today felt strange.

You'll just have to create a new normal from here on out, she thought.

As the song joyfully made her tap her feet, she got a break from the grief and sadness gripping her soul.

"You'll be okay," she muttered, looking down at her hoodie. Lifting her eyes to the sky, she took comfort in the thought that heaven had gained an amazing angel.

69

Deceived

When they arrived at the restaurant, Matt was lucky to find an open parking spot across the street. About to get out and grab her order, Andrew stopped her.

"Don't worry, Miss. I've got it," he said, holding her back.

"Oh, are you sure? I don't mind going myself."

"No, it's better if we do."

"Thank you so much," she said, peering between the front seats. "It's under my name. I paid already."

"Very good." The big guy got out and walked inside the place. In less than a minute, he was on his way back with food in hand.

Seeing this, she suddenly felt so bad. "Oh, I'm so sorry, guys. I'm not on the ball today. I should have ordered something for you, too."

Ted turned to her. "No worries, Miss. We will grab something on the fly."

Moving again, it wasn't long before they arrived at the hospital's main entrance.

Unsure where her Father's office was, she thought she'd ask at the patient services desk where she could find him.

Andrew and Ted got out to accompany her.

Waiting in line, the woman cheerfully asked, "And how can I help you?"

"Yes, I am looking for Dr. Anthony Acardi's office."

"Do you have an appointment today?"

"Umm, no. He's my Dad. I brought him lunch. It's a surprise."

Delighted, she said, "Well, in that case, let me write down some directions for you."

Sliding the paper across to her, Abi took it and said, "Thank you so much."

"Sure thing, deary. Enjoy!"

"Thank you."

The guys helped Abi decipher where they were going. Maneuvering the labyrinth of hallways to his secretary's office door, she asked them to wait there.

The two agreed.

When she went in, his assistant wasn't at her desk, but she could hear voices in her Dad's office. Respectfully knocking before peeking inside, her Father stood up from the sofa by the window.

"Dad?"

"Abi?" He quickly let go of someone sitting with him before greeting his daughter. "What are you doing here, Sweetheart?"

Eyes glued on them, she knew she'd interrupted something.

Immediately, the woman looked worried.

"I got your note and, umm, brought lunch, hoping we could eat together," Abi said innocently, quickly putting two and two together, realizing what she'd stumbled upon.

Her Father approached and tried to save face.

"Please. Come in," he said politely before telling the lady, "We'll finish our meeting later."

Abi knew who she was. "You're the day nurse who looked after my Mom. We spoke about the flower."

"Yes, that's right."

He introduced them. "Abi, this is Nurse Jankovich."

"Jenna," she corrected. Putting out her hand, she said, "I'm so sorry for your loss, dear."

"Thank you," Abi replied, leery of her.

"Speak with my secretary to reschedule, Ms. Jankovich."

Nurse Jenna smiled at Dr. Acardi. "Yes, I'll ask her when you're available."

"Sounds good."

The second she left the office and closed the door, Abi shot him a confused look. "What was that?"

Her tone made him respond defensively. "It's not what it looks like."

Hearing this sparked a stroke of anger. "Like hell, it's not!"

"I beg your pardon, young lady. You don't speak to me that way."

"Based on what I just witnessed, you don't deserve respect."

He raised his voice. "That's enough!"

"So, what? All this time, you said you were staying here for Mom, but really, you were spending time with her?" About to explode, she shouted, "Mom's nurse! How could you, Dad?"

Not responding, he stood there, silent.

"How long? Tell me the truth! Don't lie!"

Pushed to the brink, he blurted, "It's not like I planned for this to happen! It just did."

"You were screwing around while she was dying?" Shaking her head, she didn't know what to do. "If the roles ever were reversed, she would've never done that to you," she shuddered through the tears, shaking her pointer finger. "We buried her yesterday, and here you are... Guess you're in the clear now, right."

"You don't know how..."

"How what? How hard it is to be alone? 'Cause I know all too well! For weeks, you've been M.I.A. I've had to fend for myself and live in fear because you weren't home to protect me. Now, on top of burying my Mother, I find out you're having an affair?"

He turned his back on her and faced the window. "As of now, what I do in my personal life is none of your concern."

She nodded tearfully, taken off guard by his stern demeanor, "Right... Then my life is no longer yours either."

"I am your Father whether you like it or not. You will do what I say without question."

Abi smirked. "We will see about that."

Walking out the door, overwhelmed by a mixture of emotions, she passed by Andrew and Ted.

Surprised by the state she was in, they quietly followed. Having heard the yelling inside the office, Andrew knew it wasn't good.

When they reached the lobby, Abi stopped amongst the crowd, coming and going.

The guys stayed by her side.

Trying to decide what to do, she spotted a familiar but unfriendly face.

Emile Raven was walking toward a well-dressed woman who didn't seem very happy to see her. Based on their interaction, Abi figured it must have been her Mother. The girl turned suddenly and locked eyes with Abi. Feeling sorry for her, seeing her wrists bandaged with white ribbons of gauze, Emile sneered before walking out the doors. It fueled Abi's anger even more.

Frustrated, she felt smothered and out of control. "I'm going to need a minute," she told the guys before rushing along in desperation and disappearing inside the women's washroom. Leaning over the sink, about to scream, she spotted a woman exiting a stall with her little girl.

Cute as a button, she couldn't have been more than three years old. With medium-length brown hair in pig-tails, Abi watched the Mother hoist the toddler up on her knee so she could reach the water pouring from the faucet. Reminded of her childhood while they counted to twenty, she watched them celebrate when their hands were clean before the two moved to the wind dryer, where the child giggled with delight to see her Mother's hair swirling around in the breeze.

Guilt washed over Abi. Missing her Mom terribly, she realized how self-centered she'd been the past while. She wished she had spent more time with her in the last days. She thought back to their talks as the

Mother and daughter happily skipped out the door without a care in the world.

The washroom was now empty. Abi looked to the ceiling, still wanting to yell at the top of her lungs. Barely able to catch a breath, gasping here and there, the more she tried to breathe, the more emotions took over. Sobbing uncontrollably, she felt trapped and abandoned. There was nothing she could do about it. Her Father had moved on, and life was about to get overly complicated. In an instant, Burton came to mind.

"Out of everyone, he'd understand," she whispered amidst her tears. "I need to go to Vegas."

Thinking up a plan, she realized she'd have to lose her security detail. Guilt spread over her. "If I don't," she said, "They will stop me from going." To avoid that, she knew she needed help. Recalling everyone but Laney and Shawn were at the showcase, she pulled out her phone and dialed Laney's number.

As it rang once, then twice, the girl suddenly picked up. "Hey, Abi. Everything okay?"

The gentle tone in her voice sparked the tears to flow.

Sounds of her crying on the other end prompted the pretty blonde to respond swiftly. "Oh my gosh, Abs. What's wrong? What is it?"

"Can you pick me up? Please..."

Without hesitation, she replied, "Yes. Absolutely. Where are you?"

"UCLA Med. I'll meet you out front." Abi could hear her grabbing a few things and going out the door.

"Okay. Okay. I'm on my way."

"Thank you."

"I'll call you when I'm close. Probably twenty minutes."

"Alright," Abi sniffled.

Laney backed out of the garage and bolted down the street, wondering what had caused her friend to call, sounding so desperate. Worried, her mind flipped between a few different scenarios. Scared to know the truth, she didn't know what she was driving into.

70

Shattered

Abi huddled in the confines of the washroom. The walls felt too close, suffocating her already strained breaths. Her mind spun chaotically, unable to grasp the enormity of what she'd just learned. The news hit her like a wrecking ball to the chest, shattering the fragile cocoon built around her family. No longer a pillar of strength, her Father's betrayal cast a long, dark shadow over what little was left standing. Heart aching with raw, unimaginable pain, a mixture of rage, disbelief, and the profound sense of loss was overwhelming.

"How could he betray her?" Knowing she had given him everything, even when cancer ravaged her body, the image of her Mother's frail form flashed before her eyes, a painful reminder of the injustice of it all. "Why couldn't it have been him," she mumbled.

But amidst the fury and hurt, something deeper gnawed at her core. Lurking was a sense of abandonment. In one fatal blow, his infidelity shattered the very foundation of trust and security she had taken for granted. Adrift, Abi felt she had no compass to guide her through this storm. Tears welling in her eyes, angry and bitter, she struggled to make sense of the chaos. Wanting to lash out at the world, she found herself paralyzed and unable to move. Desperate to leave, she hoped Laney would be directly out front of the building so she could jump in before the guys could scramble and react.

Tracking her when Laney shared her location a few times, she leaned against the wall, knowing the party girl was no stranger to this type of drama.

"If anyone can get me to Vegas, it's her," she whispered.

Soon, the phone rang. "I am just approaching the hospital now," the girl updated.

"Okay. Text me when you get here. As soon as you see me, get ready to bolt."

"Why?" she questioned, concerned by the sudden urgency.

"I'll explain later."

"I hope so."

Abi ended the call and waited for her text. When Laney's message came through saying she was out front, she took a deep breath and reached for the door handle.

"On three," she said nervously. "One, two, three, go!" Whipping the door open, Abi sprinted as fast as she could toward the exit. Beyond the glass, she could see Laney sitting in her Mercedes parked on the street. Hitting the crash bar with both hands and pushing the door open, she ran and jumped into her convertible without opening the door. Not looking back, she shouted, "Go! Go! Go!" as Andrew and Ted ran towards them.

The blonde bombshell hit the gas and sped off, her hair flowing wildly in the crosswinds as she cut through traffic.

Spotting Andrew in the side mirror, Abi watched him radio Matt through his earpiece. He looked panicked. Immediately, she felt terrible. Guilt settled in deeply.

The guys were only doing their job. None of this was their fault, she thought.

Knowing her world had just been upended, trying to justify her actions, her mind silently debated the repercussions. Beating herself up, reminded of Burton's warning to be diligent and aware of her surroundings, she said aloud, "Damn it! Why are you doing this?"

Frantic, Laney turned to her. "What? What did I do?"

"I'm sorry. It's not you. Urghh! I shouldn't have left them! It's reckless and stupid. I'm not thinking straight!"

Laney could see the girl was almost hyperventilating. She reached over and grabbed her arm. "Abs, I need you to breathe, okay? Whatever it is, I got you. We are going to figure this out. I promise."

Nodding her head, Abi inhaled and exhaled. In shock and disbelief, she cried hysterically as the ongoing nightmare intensified. Now, there was no going back. Reality hit hard.

I no longer have a family, she thought.

Driving along Sunset, Laney asked, "Tell me what's going on?"

Afraid to explain, she replied, "I just caught my Dad with another woman."

Stunned, she turned to her. "What? Who?"

"The nurse who looked after my Mom all this time. How could he do this? To her? To me?"

Venturing into familiar territory, Laney knew she had just veered into the cheating realm, a situation most kids in Bel Air find themselves in at one point or another.

"While my Mom was on her deathbed and I was alone at home night after night, he's been with her!" she shouted at the top of her lungs. "Now it all makes sense. How could I be so stupid?"

The black SUV caught up.

With them on their tail, Laney asked, "Where are we headed?"

"Can we go to your place? It's gated, right?"

"Yeah, it is. Don't worry, you'll be safe there."

"I need time to sort this out and think. Can't do that with them hovering." She crouched in her seat. "Thank you for coming to get me."

"Absolutely. I'm glad you called." She kicked it into high gear to run the yellow light. Glimpsing in her rearview, she saw the black SUV stop for the red.

Flying past Mountian Drive, Laney refrained from signaling. Slowing down, she stopped and waited in the turn lane before zipping north on Sunset Plaza. Keeping an eye on the Escalade still trailing in the distance, she asked, "What are you gonna do about them?"

"I don't know." Abi realized it was no use. They were tracking her phone.

With precision, Laney maneuvered each corner while Abi's body vibrated inside. It was like she was going to explode. Heart palpitating, she gasped for air and started to panic. On the verge of tears repeatedly, feeling betrayed by her Father, she wished she could talk to Shane or Burton, but that was impossible. It was mid-afternoon. Shane was in the middle of a football game, and Abi assumed Burton was busy preparing for the Nightfall launch. The last thing she wanted was them worrying about her.

I just need to get there, she thought. *The faster, the better.*

Approaching a large set of gates at the end of the road, with a tall gatehouse and security watching over the premises, Laney waved to the man in the building before continuing into the courtyard alongside six dark navy garage doors.

"Wow...." Abi looked around. "This is your house?"

"Yep," the pretty girl replied while one of the bays slowly retracted after she pressed the remote.

Abi was in awe. Inching inside, coming to a stop, she looked at the floor sparkling with white diamonds and grey speckles similar to Burtons. The walls were finished nicely in white, with modern moldings and sconces, which seemed far from normal. Adjacent to them, she noticed a Land Rover, Urus, Maybach, and a Rolls Royce convertible as the door closed behind them. Getting out, impressed by the twenty-foot custom-beamed ceiling with hanging light fixtures brightening the place, Abi waited.

"Come on. Follow me," her friend said.

Heading towards the end of the long building, she opened a ten-foot steel entryway door. Inside was a main staircase adorned with a skylight and a decorative chandelier resembling a strand of illuminated pearls. The modern home was minimalistic, with all-white walls and ceilings, grey book-matched marble hall floors, and tall archways, making it look overly grand.

Casually walking down the corridor toward the kitchen, they passed a living room with black-framed glass windows and a dining area boasting seating for twenty. Turning left, Laney disappeared into the hidden pantry. Organized like a grocery store, she grabbed a small wicker basket and selected a few snacks and drinks before leading Abi outside past the outdoor dining and kitchen spaces. Moving to the right of the property, captivated by the view of the canyon, Abi marveled at the hills on either side, which framed the city skyline beautifully.

Setting the basket on a table under a stone pergola, Laney jumped onto the light grey sofa, hugged a cushion, and got cozy. "Now that we're here, you can relax and tell me more about what happened."

Not knowing where to start, Abi divulged, "My Dad left for work this morning. I thought he'd stay home because he hadn't been there since Mom got admitted. All I wanted was to wake up, come downstairs, and see him sitting in front of the television, maybe watching football. But once again, I woke up to an empty house and found a note. When I read that he'd gone to the hospital, I couldn't understand how. Especially after yesterday. We were both so exhausted. Giving him the benefit of the doubt, I figured he needed to do that to deal with the grief. Never did I imagine this..."

Wondering where the cheating part came in, Laney clarified, "So, he went there to see this woman?"

"I took food, hoping we could eat lunch together. She was in his office and sitting pretty close to him when I barged in." Frustrated, Abi ran her hand along her forehead. "I mean, aren't there rules about this in the workplace? They shouldn't be sneaking around. Does he not think his co-workers will figure it out eventually if they haven't already?"

Laney shrugged her shoulders. "That doesn't stop them, unfortunately."

Thoughts rambling on, Abi suddenly broke down. "How could he do that to her? I don't understand." The more the moment replayed, the more it festered. "What kind of man cheats on his dying wife?"

"I hate to say it, but around here, men do stuff like this all the time. It's not surprising."

She stood and started pacing with Laney's eyes glued to her. "When I opened the door, they were laughing and talking. His hand was on her leg." Hitting the support pillar with her flat hand, she shouted, "What the hell!"

Jumping up, Laney hugged her friend. "What can I do? Anything, just name it."

Recalling her original thought, she answered, "I need to get to Las Vegas. Can you help me?"

Laney looked at her and said without hesitation, "Absolutely."

71

Vegas, Baby!

In seconds, Laney pulled out her phone. It didn't take long to put a plan into action.

Sitting on the sofa beside her, Abi grabbed a bottle of water from the wicker basket. "Who are you calling?" she asked.

"Shawn can help us. I'm sure he can cross state lines. I just think he can't get on a plane." The girl was trying to remember the terms of his court order. "Hey, Babe. It's me. When you get this message, call me back ASAP."

"What are you thinking?"

Ending the call, she said, "Well, at this point, my parents took the plane, so we will have to drive, which isn't a bad thing because Shawn can go with us. I wouldn't make that trip in the dark alone. Especially just the two of us. It's not safe."

Laney's phone rang. Answering it, she said, "Hey, what are you doing right now?"

Unable to hear Shawn's answer, she listened in on their conversation.

"You need to come over. Abi's here. Interested in a road trip? Vegas? Up for it?" The girl smiled and gave a thumbs-up.

Realizing they would help her, Abi assumed her friends thought she wanted to see Shane, but truthfully, she needed both him and Burton, and the only way to do that was to go there.

"He'll be here in a half hour," Laney said, getting up from the sofa. "That gives us enough time to pack our bags before heading out."

"Pack?"

"Yeah, you can borrow my clothes and stuff. That way, it saves us time not having to go by your place. We can get on the road faster." Taking the basket in hand, she grabbed Abi's arm. "Come on. Let's go! There's no time to waste."

Dropping off the snacks on the counter in the kitchen, passing a few maids dusting nearby, the girls shuffled along to the staircase. Climbing the marble steps, making a right at the top, they made it to Laney's room.

Taken by the view, Abi stopped in the doorway.

Seeing her, she laughed before ducking into her walk-in closet. "What's wrong?"

With windows and a balcony spanning over twenty feet, Abi approached the glass and looked out at the incredible vista while her friend placed two suitcases on the bed and flipped them open.

"This view is amazing."

"Yes, it is, but can we focus, please? We need to get you to Shane, and we're on a schedule," she giggled before going all business.

Realizing she was right, Abi turned. "Okay. What do I do?"

"Selected three casual outfits from my closet and add a dress or two."

"Dresses? Why?"

"It's Vegas! We are going out to have some fun! I'll show you around. We can shop, eat, and sightsee on top of watching the team play."

Not about to argue, Abi said, "Yeah, sure. That would be great."

"Awesome! It will give your mind a break from things, too."

"Hopefully, so." Wishing she could tell her about Burton, knowing she couldn't, Abi replied, "Thank you for helping me."

"No problem." The girl stopped folding the clothes she'd gathered on the bed. "That's what friends are for?" Sensing the uncertainty in Abi's eyes, she added, "You know it does get better even though it seems like your world is falling apart. Trust me. I know from experience."

Abi nodded.

"While we're on the topic..." Laney continued packing again. "Nobody knows this, but umm, I know how you feel. My parents have an understanding."

Confused, Abi repeated, "Understanding?"

"Yeah, they are married but have other people outside that."

"How?"

Embarrassed to a degree, her pretty friend elaborated. "They don't love one another anymore, or maybe they do but aren't in love with each other. How my Mom described it is complicated, but they decided to still live under one roof, with separate rooms. Each has a significant other whom they spend time with. So, even though I have parents, they are not together in a traditional sense. The only reason they didn't get a divorce was because they couldn't disrupt the success of their company. A split would ultimately play with the bottom line. Long story short, they are together for business purposes only."

Shocked to hear this, Abi sincerely said, "I'm sorry. I didn't know."

"It's okay. That's the way it is." She exhaled. "So, when I say I understand how you're feeling, now you know why."

"Thank you for confiding in me. It means a lot."

"Of course. You're my friend and a pretty good one at that." Smiling, she looked at their half-packed suitcases. "Now, on that note, we gotta hurry. Shawn will be here soon."

Quickly filling the bags and raiding her shoe closet, they added a tote with every stitch of cosmetics and toiletry from her vanity.

"What else do we need?" Laney looked around. She ran the checklist through her head. "Guess that's it." Stopping in the doorway, she shouted, "Oh! Almost forgot!" Running to her dresser, she grabbed a set of keys from the drawer. "We're staying at the Heaven's Edge house in Henderson."

"Where is that?"

"It's a gated burb."

After being in her home here in LA, Abi wondered what awaited them In Vegas as they descended the stairs to the main level.

The bubbly blonde got a notification on her phone. "That's Shawn. Are you ready to go?"

"Yes." Abi gave her a thumbs-up.

The girls met the football player in the courtyard.

Unable to resist, Laney ran to hug and kiss her handsome boyfriend.

Indulging in her affections, he stopped and said, "Umm, Abs. I think we've got a problem."

"What is it?" she asked.

"I assume you don't want any of your hardware following us. Just FYI, there's a black SUV parked out front."

"I know. They tracked me."

Thinking fast on her feet, Laney said, "We could leave your phone behind. Would that work? Maybe we can hide in the back of Shawn's truck when we leave or take the Urus. The windows are pretty dark. They wouldn't know it was us if we didn't show our faces."

"I vote Urus," Shawn raised his hand willingly, always wanting to drive it.

"Okay. It's settled." Asking for her phone, Laney said, "Give it here. I'll put it upstairs in my side table drawer for safe-keeping."

Abi handed it to her, unsure if it was a good idea to leave it behind. "Wait. I need a few numbers from it first. Do you have a piece of paper?"

"Pull them up. I'll take a snap," Laney instructed.

Doing that, Abi hesitated when she showed her Burton's contact info, then Shane's.

Confused, she looked at her strangely. "Why do you need his number?"

"Never know. He's the only family I've got now."

Promptly correcting her, Shawn said, "You mean other than all of us."

"You're right."

With photos of the numbers safely stored on Laney's device, the three headed out to the garage. Handing Shawn the keys to the Urus, she quickly yanked them back. "Promise you will guard this truck with your life. If anything happens to it, my head won't be on a silver platter – it will be on a chopping block."

Wrapping his arm around her waist, he sincerely said, "I give you my word." Kissing her lips, she handed them over before opening the doors.

Abi got in the back seat.

"Maybe we should jump in the rear, just in case the guys stop Shawn on the way out and see us," her friend suggested. "Once we're on the road and they are nowhere in sight, we can climb into the front."

"Alright." Placing their luggage on the floor behind the front seats, Laney activated the garage door at the touch of a button before lifting the cargo hatch and jumping in. Abi climbed in beside her.

"I feel like we are spies or something, and we need to escape the country," the mischievous girl said enthusiastically. "This is awesome!"

"Okay, there, double-O-seven," Shawn chuckled as he closed the hatch and got behind the wheel. Familiarizing himself with the controls, he got hyped. "Oh, man. This is nice."

"Remember what I said!" Laney shouted.

"Don't worry, Babe. I got this!" Starting it up, hearing the engine growl, Shawn waited for the RPMs to lower before backing out. "This is insane." About to leave the grounds, he asked, "Ready?"

His girlfriend yelled, "Hit it!"

When the gates swung open, Shawn tried to act cool and collected while passing the Escalade, still parked in the cul-de-sac. Ignoring the driver, he made certain not to bring attention to them.

Thankfully, not stopped or followed, he drove down the road and around the corner. "Looks like we might be in the clear. Stay there until we hit Sunset."

"Okay," Laney said, all curled up beside Abi. Concerned by the look on her face, she asked, "Hey. Are you doing alright?"

Abi broke from her stoic expression. "Yeah. I'm good."

"You sure?"

"I just never thought in a million years I'd be here, doing something like this," she stated.

"Me either, but just roll with it. This road trip will be fun. I promise."

Before merging onto Sunset Boulevard, Shawn pulled over. "Okay. Better take your seats now."

Shoving the back seat forward, the girls crawled up front. Laney got into the passenger seat beside Shawn while Abi sat behind her and reclined hers a little.

With everyone buckled up, Shawn got them back on the road. "Next stop, Vegas, baby!"

Heaven's Edge

That night, traveling along the Mojave Freeway, Shawn drove below the speed limit to keep a low profile despite being in a Lamborghini. Laney kept the music flowing to lighten the mood. Both knew they had precious cargo on board – a troubled friend who needed their help.

The moon shining brightly in the clear sky, Abi peered through the glass roof at the stars above, wondering if her mother was watching.

I will never see her again. She thought, *Well, perhaps one day.*

Riding a rollercoaster of emotions, the thought of her Mom no longer existing in this life caused her heart to hurt so bad she covered her mouth and gasped. Trying to muffle the sound of her heaving, she watched Laney and Shawn, hoping they hadn't heard her. Desperate to think of anything else, she drifted to Shane and Burton. So much had happened that week. The moments she'd had with them weren't far behind. Veered in two different directions, she didn't know what to do.

Unable to deny her love for one or the other, she looked up.

Help me, Mom? Please send me a sign.

Without warning, her mind replayed the confrontation with her Father. Evidently, he'd already moved on, and she could do nothing about it. Given the timing of the rose, her death, and now this, a morbid thought crossed her mind. The information Burton supplied wasn't far off. Questioning whether her passing wasn't a natural one, she remembered her Dad was one of the people allowed in her room that day. This cheating incident was a strong motive for him to interfere.

But would he be capable of doing that? She silently questioned. *Could he have sped up the process so he could get on with his life?* Hesitating, she said, *No, stop. He couldn't have done it. He loved her.*

As much as she wanted that to be true, this theory wasn't out of the realm of possibilities. Not wanting to go there, she sat up in her seat and shimmied around.

Hearing her, Laney turned. "Hey. You okay?"

"Yeah, all good."

Noticing a billboard announcing the Nightfall Club's grand opening, her friend pointed and said, "Hey, look! It's Dark Demon." Laney watched as the captivating advertisement whisked by. Pulling out her phone, she said, "I almost forgot! I received a VIP invite a few days ago to his pre-launch concert but haven't claimed my tickets. I really wanted to go, but I couldn't leave Shawn at home. Now, this works out!" She turned to Abi in the back seat. "What do you think? Up for it?"

Believing this was possibly the sign she was looking for, Abi perked up, knowing this was her chance to see Burton. "Maybe. But Shawn? Are you sure you don't want to go?"

He shook his head. "No can do. I can't be seen in Vegas, let alone at a big event like that. It's too early. The last thing I need is for someone to take pics of us or worse. I'm already stepping outside the box. I shouldn't be out of state. You two have fun. I'm good."

"See," Laney coaxed. "It's fine."

Now, all Abi could think of was finding her best friend. She knew he'd help make sense of this mess. "Okay, I'll go," she said, praying she could get close to Burton, despite his celebrity status.

Surprised, Laney smiled. "Great!"

Recalling the lulling vibes of Burton's rave, Abi longed for the same mind-freeing feeling again.

"Oooh! I'm so excited!" Quickly opening the VIP invitation on her new Dark Demon app, Laney arranged everything. Within minutes, she turned around. "All done! We can't get into his Omnia appearance 'cause of their strict age policy, but we can catch him on the main stage at Ceasar's Forum before getting escorted to his new Nightfall Club." Barely able to contain herself, she giggled. "Eeee! I can hardly wait!"

"Don't get too excited. I'm not exactly happy about all the guys that will be vying for your attention," Shawn divulged.

"Babe, don't worry. I'm just going for the music and will record some content for social. But I am a little nosey about what the place looks like. Apparently, the reviews say it's like stepping into this alternate universe or fantasy world."

Hearing this, Abi figured she'd try and find Martin standing amidst the crowd. That way, he'd somehow find a way to connect them secretly. She spotted another billboard. Not realizing what a big deal this launch was, she rethought her plan.

What am I thinking? I can't do this to him on his big night? I can't ruin it by unloading my problems on him.

Silently sitting there, she decided to go with Laney to the event but would refrain from talking until they returned home.

The GPS directed Shawn to the St. Rose Parkway exit.

Abi turned to her left when they reached the top of the off-ramp. Emanating in the darkness was the glowing Vegas Strip.

"We aren't far now," Laney advised.

Winding their way through a newly developed corporate park amidst rows and rows of cookie-cutter subdivisions surrounded by nothing but desert sand, palm trees, and low-level bushes, Shawn followed the directions and entered the Ascaya Development. Climbing the hillside, Abi could see they'd entered a very posh area. It was like the Bel Air of Vegas. The spot was stunning, with beautifully manicured curbside grounds and architecturally elaborate homes with loads of security. Abi didn't know where to look first.

As they approached a main gatehouse, Shawn slowed down and stopped.

The guard stepped out.

Greeting him, Laney leaned over and registered her name with the man and supplied the access password while he ran the license plate and verified her identity.

"Thank you, Miss Bass. You may proceed," he said with little emotion.

The arm blocking their path lifted, allowing them to enter the prestigious enclave.

While moving along, the engine rumbled. Maneuvering the roundabout, Laney guided Shawn onto Cloud Chaser Boulevard, where they traversed the hillside before making a right on Heaven's Edge.

Pulling into the beautifully uplit home, Shawn stopped under the covered portico.

"This is it. We're here." Laney got out and walked over to the massive pivot door. Using her key, she unlocked it and swung it open. Immediately stepping to her left, the spacious interior illuminated. Laney left her bag on the side table and returned to help unload the rest.

Rolling her suitcase alongside her, Abi timidly walked in and scanned the modernly furnished living and dining rooms before her sights gravitated to the view. Moving closer to get a better look, she could see the entire city core sparkling like diamonds.

Finding her friend, Laney pressed a button. The Fleetwood glass walls slid across their tracks, removing the obstruction. The pool lights turned on while starting her family's routine of opening the large home. "So? What do you think?" she asked.

"It's incredible."

Smiling, Shawn brought the rest of their things inside. "Do I put the truck in the garage, then?" he shouted across the house to his girlfriend.

"Yes, please!" Laney slipped her hand into a red bowl on the kitchen counter. Grabbing a remote, she said, "Here! Use this. I'll meet you at the service entrance."

"Okay," he said, not having a problem doing that.

"Thanks a bunch, babe."

"No problem."

When he walked out the door, Laney found Abi in a bit of a daze. "Come on," she said, "Let me show you around."

Wheeling their suitcases down the hall, she led Abi into the room on their left. The view of the city and pool filled the window-scape. Exploring, she found a modern bath in black, grey, and white tones.

"Hope this is okay. It's usually my room." Hesitating, she said, "Shawn and I will use my parent's principal suite. It's the next one over."

"It's perfect."

"Do you want to call Shane? Maybe you should talk to him about what happened? You can use my phone."

As tempting as it was, Abi knew he had a lot going on this weekend and didn't want to interfere. "Umm, no. I'm pretty tired. I think I'm just going to head to bed."

"Sure," Laney said, standing in the doorway. "I'm here if you need me, alright?"

"Thanks..."

"Of course." About to move down the hall, she got a fright. "Oh, hell! I forgot to open the service door for Shawn. I'll be right back!"

Hearing her run across the house, Abi turned to the view, knowing Burton and Shane were out there somewhere. It made her feel less alone. Lifting the suitcase onto her bed, she unzipped it and found a nightgown. Everything she needed was in the bathroom, from shampoo to conditioner, skincare products to makeup—even a wrapped tooth-brush and toothpaste.

"This is better than staying in a hotel," she whispered before starting the shower.

The second she stepped under the rainfall, Abi closed her eyes as the tears mingled with the water cascading down her cheeks. Overcome with emotion, she leaned forward and rested her forearms on the wall – her head on top of that. Sobbing, needing a good cry, it seemed she'd lost a lot in the past twenty-four hours. From here on out, life would be very different.

How can I go home and act like nothing happened? She dreaded the thought. Feeling betrayed, she knew it would be hard to look him in the eye after all this.

Things will never be the same.

Washing her hair with the floral-scented shampoo and spreading some body wash on the luffa, the aromatic scents lifted her spirits slightly. Ready for bed, she turned off the water, stepped out, and wrapped herself in a towel. The sound of Laney laughing echoed throughout the home. Based on the direction it was coming from, it sounded like they were watching television. Opening the king-sized bed and peeling back the covers, she debated whether to join them. With lights out, she sat there looking at the city lights, wondering what tomorrow would bring, hoping by some miracle, the sadness in her heart would lessen by morning. Instantly, she believed that wouldn't be the case.

A Guilt-filled Soul

Waking on the outskirts of Sin City, Abi's harsh reality caused emotions to collide. Forcing her eyes open, the unrelenting grief and her Father's betrayal settled upon her chest like a weighted blanket. With a heavy heart, she recalled the previous day's events, each memory cutting through her like a knife. The loss of her Mother was a wound that seemed impossible to heal. Her absence loomed, a silent reminder of all the love and warmth rapidly snatched away.

Miles from her troubles and the danger lurking in LA, part of her could hardly wait to see Burton perform tonight and experience what he created, while the other felt a spark of fear, recalling the last rave she attended. Not having the guys with her added to the anxiety.

"If you don't bring attention to yourself, you'll be fine," she encouraged.

Unsure of what to wear, she opened her suitcase and looked at what Laney had packed just as her friends rambled down the hall quietly.

Moments later, dressed and ready, she rested her hand on the door latch. Afraid to face the day, she smelt the heavenly aroma of coffee and bacon wafting into the room.

"Come on, Abs. You can do this. One hour at a time. That's all you need to do."

Successfully threading through the narrow hall and rounding the corner, she found Laney sitting with Shawn along the breakfast bar, sipping coffee while a strange man dressed in a white coat cooked up a storm on the opposite side of the counter.

"Good morning. You're up." She left her chair to hug her. "How'd you sleep?"

"Good. I needed that."

"Have a seat. This is Georgie. He is our chef." She turned to the man and said, "Georgie, this is my friend Abi."

"Good morning, Miss."

"Morning. Nice to meet you."

"You as well."

Laney intervened. "What would you like? He'll make you anything you want. Just ask."

"We are having omelets and bacon," Shawn said.

"That sounds good."

"Very well, Miss. One omelet and bacon, coming up."

Shawn turned around. "I hope you don't mind, but I was texting with Shane this morning. I told him we were here."

"You did?" A look of surprise spread across Abi's face.

"Is that alright?"

"What did he say? Did you tell him what happened?"

"Umm, I did..." he paused. "Look, I'm sorry. I didn't know you wanted to keep it a secret."

A million thoughts rolled through her head. "It's fine." Assuming Shane probably tried calling her, Abi asked, "Can I borrow your phone, Shawn?"

"Yeah, sure." He unlocked it with facial recognition.

"I'll be back." Leaving them, she returned to her room. Along the way, she texted Shane. *Hi. It's Abi. Can you talk?*

Sitting on the bed, having closed the door, she watched his thinking bubbles go into action and then stop. Seconds later, the phone rang.

"Hello?" she said.

"Hey, Abs. Are you okay? Shawn told me what happened with your Dad. I've been trying to call you."

"Sorry, I left my phone at Laney's house in LA. I didn't want the guys following me. I needed a breather."

"You left the team behind? I don't think that was wise."

"I know. It's just..." Her voice wavered.

Hearing her tone, wanting to be supportive, he asked, "What can I do?"

"Nothing. It is what it is." She went quiet before blurting out, "I think he was seeing that woman this whole time...." About to cry again, she stopped herself. "Who does that?"

"I know. That's a hard one to wrap your head around. The way he went about it wasn't right, but it's done. You've gotta move forward."

"Where do I go from here? How do I look him in the eye?"

"In time, it'll blow over. In my case, I had no choice but to accept it. If not, it would've eaten away at me. You may forgive eventually, but you'll never forget."

"I feel so betrayed. Like, so angry."

"I wish I could do or say something to help you through this."

"Just listening helps."

"Then I'm all ears."

On his end, she heard banter in the background. "What time is the game?"

"Two o'clock today. Why? Are you coming to watch?"

"I'm not sure what the plan is. Haven't spoken to Laney yet. I don't want to distract you today."

He sighed. "I always want you in the stands, Abs."

"Really?"

"Yes, only if you feel up to it. If not, I understand."

Taking a moment to think, she wanted to be forthcoming with the plans scheduled that evening. "Don't be mad, but Laney got tickets for the Dark Demon launch at the Forum."

"Yeah, Shawn said something about that. I, umm, don't know if it's a good idea. The guys aren't there to protect you."

"We're in Vegas. I'll probably blend being surrounded by so many people. I'm sure there is anonymity in mass numbers. I promise we won't stay long."

Hitting a lull in the conversations, he felt compelled to ask. "Abi, does this have anything to do with Burton? Is he working the show or the club? Is that why you're going?"

That hit a nerve. "Shane, we've been over this. I just can't keep going in circles."

"I take that as a yes."

She didn't like his tone. "He's probably going to be too busy to talk to me anyway, so…"

"Yeah, I'm sure." His coach called him over. "Look, I gotta go. There's a team meeting now."

"Okay. If I don't get to see you before the game, good luck this afternoon."

The way she said it, Shane assumed she wouldn't be coming to the field. "Yeah, thanks."

"If you want to get a hold of me, call Laney or Shawn's phone."

"Will do."

"Bye," she whispered.

"Bye."

Ending the call, she fell back into the pillows on her bed. In essence, she was no better than her Father. Torn between him and Burton, she couldn't strike a balance.

Football game or rave? Shane will be angry if I don't go and support him. Burton won't know either way, but Laney will be disappointed if I don't go with her. Nodding her head, she decided on what to do. *Why not both?*

When she returned to the kitchen to eat her food, Chef Georgie saw her coming and removed her plate from the warming drawer before placing it on the placemat in front of her.

"Thank you so much."

"No problem, Miss.

Laney finished her last bite. "So, did you talk to Shane?"

"Yes."

"And?"

"And, if it's not too much trouble, can we attend the game at two o'clock?"

Shawn looked happy with that suggestion, but Laney frowned.

"Umm, is there any chance we can change those plans?" she asked, scrunching.

"Why?" her friend said suspectingly.

"Don't be mad, but I booked us in at the Bellagio Spa for manis, pedis, hair, and make-up before we go to the event tonight. But even before that, we have appointments at Fendi and Louis V." Seeing Abi was about to dispute her upscale agenda, knowing she couldn't afford the lux spree, Laney put up her hands and said, "Wait, before you say anything, it's my treat. You've been through a lot this week, and I want to do this for you. No arguing."

"But..."

"No, buts either," Laney giggled. "Please..." She reached out to her friend and grabbed hold of her hands. Staring into Abi's tear-filled eyes, she added, "It'll be fun. I promise."

Not given a choice, she nodded. "Okay. But I must tell Shane I won't be at the game then."

"Let me do that. He will understand if I say I arranged this surprise for you."

"Fine." Abi figured if Laney explained, it might not seem like she was blowing him off to see Burton since, in hindsight, replaying their conversation in her head, that was the impression she probably gave off. Rolling her eyes, she looked at the ceiling in disgust. The last thing she wanted was to anger Shane in any way. He was under enough stress, and now she'd added even more by being there and inadvertently refusing to go that afternoon. "You're so stupid, Abs," she muttered silently. "Guaranteed, you've broken his heart. This is what you were trying to avoid."

Barely having a second to think, Laney finished saying her piece to the QB and ended the call. "It's settled. All good. You are coming with me! Now, let's get you dressed. We have a full afternoon planned."

Guilt filling her soul, she wanted to tell Laney to cancel it all, but witnessing her excitement, she couldn't, especially when she said, "This is awesome! It's like having a sister to do this stuff with."

Abi conceded. "So, what do I wear on this crazy shopping spree and spa day?"

Trying to contain herself, the blonde girl shrieked, "Oooo! I'll put an outfit together for you." before disappearing around the corner.

She turned to Shawn. "I guess you're stuck with us this afternoon?"

"It's fine. I'll watch over you. Make sure you guys stay safe. Promised Shane I would."

"Is he upset?"

Shawn scrolled through his texts. "More disappointed, I think."

"I hate myself right now. I should be at the game."

"So, tell her that."

Torn again, Abi didn't know what to do. "But, then, she will be disappointed also. I can't win."

"Gotta say, shopping with that girl is a once-in-a-lifetime experience. I'm sure if I tell Shane that, he'll understand. Lane knows all the VIP ins and outs here. She's been exposed to it her whole life. The secrets she is privy to are quite amazing, actually."

Nervous, she didn't know what to think. This was out of her comfort zone. Taking a deep breath, she said, "Guess I should go and see what I'm wearing today."

"Good luck with that. I'll see you girls shortly," Shawn chuckled while scrolling. He knew she was about to become a human Barbie doll.

74

Spoiled

At twelve-thirty, the girls emerged from their rooms dressed in timeless Ralph Lauren. Locking up the house, they found Shawn waiting outside in the Urus. In seconds, the two jumped in.

"Where are we headed first?" Shawn asked with his finger positioned over the LCD screen, prepared to enter the address into the GPS.

"The Bellagio Shops," Laney replied while sneakily texting Shane an idea. Thankfully, he texted back and agreed.

Leaving the confines of the Ascaya gated community, the blonde-haired girl pointed out, "We will be there in twenty-five minutes or so."

Weaving through the residential area, Shawn soon merged onto the interstate highway and headed west. Seeing the mountain range ahead, they got a short glimpse of the Vegas strip and the gold Mandalay Bay hotel gleaming in the mid-day sun.

While passing the Allegiant Stadium, Shawn kept glancing over.

Laney caught on. "You will play there one day," she said with certainty.

He reached across to take her hand and said, "Sure hope so."

Slowly moving in bumper-to-bumper traffic adjacent to the Luxor Pyramid and the Aria concrete jungle, Abi spotted the Bellagio sign towering over the highway on the right.

"Take this exit," Laney instructed. "It's just up here. Not far."

He did as she asked and turned at the lights.

Abi peered overwhelmingly at the Caesar's Palace and Bellagio buildings, not knowing where to look first.

"Turn in here, Babe." She guided Shawn up the cobblestone driveway lined by beautifully manicured gardens. The truck growled as they approached the valet.

A man held out his hand for them to stop. Rolling down his window, Shawn greeted, "Hey, man."

"Good afternoon, Sir." Seeing two women in the vehicle, the guy hastily rounded the truck and opened their doors.

"I need you to keep it close by," Laney stated with little emotion.

"Certainly, Miss. No problem."

She handed him the fob and slipped him two one hundred dollar bills while he exchanged it for the valet ticket.

"We won't be long," she said snappily.

"Very well. Enjoy your visit."

Like a fish out of water, Abi followed their lead. People in the crowd gravitated to Laney immediately. It seemed she turned heads wherever she went. Maybe the air of confidence, her flawless beauty, and her long, flowing blonde hair captured everyone's attention.

Shawn took her hand, proudly escorting her through the doors. The two looked like they belonged in a magazine.

Entering the building, veering left, her friend turned to find Abi lagging. She quickly hooked her arm around hers. "Come on, my friend. We have some shopping to do."

As they moved through the luxurious corridor, lined with marble and glass, almost reaching the end, she said, "Our first appointment of the day is at Fendi. After that, we will visit Louis V before heading to the spa for manis, pedis, blowouts, and full makeup."

Abi's body was shaking on the inside. Right then, she wished she was at the football game instead. Thankful for all the trouble the girl went through to plan the special day for her, she subtly inhaled, letting the air escape faintly so as not to sigh and come across rudely. Spotting the Fendi store sign, her nerves erupted.

Speaking to the security guard at the door, the girl greeted, "Hello. I'm Laney Bass. I have an appointment at 1:30."

The man did not say a word. He looked down at his iPad before unlatching the burgundy velvet rope attached to the stanchion posts. "Right this way."

Entering the shop, Laney smiled at the woman who came to greet her.

"Miss Laney Bass." Air kissing her on one side, then the other, the woman said, "So good to see you, my dear."

"You too, Gilianna. I'd like you to meet Abi Acardi and the love of my life, Shawn O'Donnell."

"It's so nice to meet you both." She returned her sights to her favorite client. "I hear we are looking for three specific pieces today."

Voicing her preferences, Laney replied, "Yes. The orange studded jersey, the light blue animalier, and the blue FF silk."

"I have everything ready for you. Come with me." Walking behind the woman, passing the beautifully displayed bags and accessories on the various shelves and tables, Laney gave Abi a side hug and giggled. "I'm so excited! Aren't you?"

With a forced smile, she nodded. "Yes, very much." But deep down, she was scared beyond words. Experiencing déjà vu from her shopping trip with Jade, a sick feeling churned in her stomach. She'd never stepped foot in any of these stores, let alone bought anything. Not knowing what Laney had chosen for her, she watched the staff offer Shawn a seat as Gilianna reappeared with the items in hand, each dangling above the floor. Preparing their dressing rooms, she asked, "I assume the orange studded is for you, Laney dear?"

She laughed. "Oh! You know me too well."

Hanging the two blue dresses in one room and the orange in another, she said, "Enjoy. I will return in a moment."

They stood outside Abi's changeroom. "I thought these would look great on you," Laney said. "They suit the event tonight. What do you think?"

"Both are beautiful."

"I'll leave you to try them on. Come out and show me. I want to see." She closed the door behind her and left Abi to change.

Staring at the garments hanging before her, she opted to try the navy blue one first. With an interesting asymmetric cross-over with snap buttons, she slipped the silk garment on. It fit nicely, but the midi hem draped a little mid-calf because she was short. Leaving the changeroom, Abi emerged.

"That looks really nice, Abs," Shawn said, treading carefully, knowing she seemed less enthused.

"Thanks. I'm not sure, though." She turned around and looked in the mirror. Noticing a black monogrammed short-sleeved knit dress to her left, she recalled her family's Italian tradition and knew she should wear black since she was supposed to be mourning. Shaking her head, she thought, *Who goes to Vegas while they're grieving? Once again, this is why Hell exists. It's for people who do stupid things like this.* A feeling of dread hovered.

In full fashionista mode, Laney came out in the orange studded dress. Shawn's eyes lit up. "Wow!"

"What do you think?" his girlfriend asked, looking in the mirror. "I love it!" Finding Abi tucking the black knit dress in the dressing room, she said, "So, the navy one is a no-go?"

"I feel the length is not flattering for me," Abi divulged honestly. "But I'd like to try this one if that's okay."

"For sure, Abs. Whatever you'd like."

Happy to hear her say that, she hoped she wasn't offended. Slipping out of the navy silk dress and into the monogram knit, it fit her like a glove. The length hit at just the right place, and she surprisingly felt pretty in it. Stepping out, Laney was still admiring herself.

"Oooh! That fits you so well!"

"If you don't mind, I'd rather this one." About to explain her reasons, she refrained, afraid to put a damper on the experience.

"It looks wonderful on you, Abs. I think you should go with that."

Spotting an iconic blue silk scarf with added ivory, beige, and black undertones, Gilianna approached and tied it stylishly around her neck. "This will finish the look." Turning to face the mirror, she said, "So lovely."

Abi liked the added touch of color. "Yes, it is."

The saleswoman beamed.

Settled on her choice, believing her first luxury retail outing wasn't too bad, Abi ducked back into the room. Curious, she looked for the black and white tags on her dress and the scarf. "Seventeen hundred, ninety? Five hundred and twenty?" The air escaped her lungs as she said it. "How can someone spend that much on two pieces of clothing?" she whispered. Feeling the unsurpassed quality and texture of the fabric, soft and supple, she checked the tags on the other two dresses. "Thirty-one, ninety and...five thousand?" Her eyebrows raised. "I guess mine was the better deal."

Getting dressed, she joined her friends as Gilianna reappeared. "I will just put the other two dresses away and be with you momentarily."

Shawn stood beside Abi. "You okay?" he asked.

"Yeah, why?"

"Look, I know you are probably going through the motions right now. If this is all too much for you, just tell Laney. She'll understand."

Seeing the sincerity on his face, she smiled. "I'll keep that in mind. She's gone through so much trouble to cheer me up. Clothes aside, I'm just grateful to have friends who care." Tears about to flood her cheeks, Abi leaned her head back.

"Well, we're happy to have you, too," he said.

Unable to speak, she choked up.

Offering open arms, he hugged her just as Laney reappeared.

"Hey? What did I miss?"

Abi looked away, hoping she wouldn't see her cry.

"Oh, no... What's wrong?"

The tone in her voice set her off. "Nothing," she whimpered. "I'm okay."

"No, you're not."

Realizing the girl needed space, Shawn distracted his girlfriend. "Lane, she just needs a minute."

Able to step away, Abi checked her face in the mirror.

He whispered in his girlfriend's ear. "She's having a tough time. Maybe we should rethink things?"

Cautiously approaching, Laney asked, "Hey, Abs. I'm sorry. I feel like an idiot…"

"Don't be. I'm the one who should be apologizing to you. You've planned such a nice day for us, and I'm ruining it."

"No, you're not." She rubbed Abi's arm. "I've thrown you into all this without thinking."

"You had nothing but good intentions."

Laney snickered. "My Father knows I shop when I'm sad or lonely. It's my number one vice. I just figured you'd be the same."

Hugging her, Abi mustered a smile and took a deep breath. "I want to enjoy this day and get rid of the sadness."

"Are you sure? We don't have to. I can cancel the appointments. It's no problem."

"No, I'm okay. Just had an emotional moment. All good now."

"Alright. If you're sure."

Abi put on a brave face. "I'm sure."

Walking arm and arm toward the desk, Laney pulled out her Amex Black as Gilianna scanned their items, including an impulse buy of shoes and two small baguettes for each to compliment their dresses. Another woman boxed everything beautifully in the store's signature gold totes.

Not broadcasting how much they owed, it seemed like there was an unspoken rule regarding the total. Laney simply looked at it, handed her the credit card, and the woman proceeded without saying a thing.

Able to see the amount that had popped up on the POS before Laney pressed the OK button, Abi didn't know how she was so calm.

Handed the receipt, the woman said, "Thank you for visiting us, Miss Bass. We hope to see you again soon."

"Absolutely. Thank you for your expertise."

Breaking a smile, Abi added, "Yes. Thank you so much."

"I am so happy to meet you, my dear. Here is my card. When you are back in the city, call me, and we will arrange your next visit."

Abi smiled, knowing the chances were slim.

Gilianna and her junior sales associate handed Abi and Laney their packages. On the way out the door, the two girls were arm and arm as Shawn led the way, bidding the security guard a good afternoon.

"Twenty-one thousand dollars, Lane?" Abi was in shock.

Not batting an eye, she replied, "What? After a while, a thousand dollars seems like a measly hundred." Wanting to change the subject, she asked, "Ready for phase two of the day? Three hours of utter bliss."

Shawn stopped in his tracks. "Wait? Three hours? Tell me you're kidding?"

Realizing the poor guy had been through enough, Lane grabbed his cheeks. Looking deep into his eyes, she said, "Do you want to go and watch the football game?"

He wondered if it was a trick question. Careful with his words, he said, "As much as I would love to stay, I should probably go and support the team."

Perking up, she giggled and said, "Okay! Pick us up later? We will head to Nobu afterward for a bite."

With arms wrapped around his neck, she kissed him lovingly, making Abi look away.

"I'll see you soon," he said before departing with this confident swagger.

Thinking of Shane, Abi shouted, "Hey, Shawn?"

He swung around. "Yeah?"

"Please tell him I'm thinking of him."

"I will."

Parting ways, Laney watched until he disappeared amidst the crowd. Turning, she said, "Onward we go. Get ready to be pampered to high heaven!"

75

Center of Attention

Nearing the end of their luxurious spa appointment two and a half hours later, Abi felt more relaxed. For the first time in days, she could breathe. Listening as the tranquil music immersed her heart and soul, hands and feet now airy, her freshly washed and styled hair cascaded over her shoulders, giving her a slight bounce in her step. The makeup artist had airbrushed the dark circles from her face and gave a hint of pink to her cheeks. Rejuvenated, she hadn't forgotten the week she'd had, but somehow the burden seemed less.

Paying the bill and leaving the ladies a lavish tip, Laney checked her phone and confirmed that Shawn was waiting near the main entrance. Ethrawed by his messages, she didn't notice Abi step away.

Across the hallway, adorned in marble and gold, was the fall-themed Botanical Gardens they'd seen briefly before entering the green doors of the Spa. Abi walked through the arch to take another look at the display as the magical setting drew her in, like Alice in Wonderland.

"Isn't it beautiful," Laney said when she caught up to her.

Having trouble breaking away from the scenery, she turned and said, "It's stunning."

The whimsical music and fall colors felt warm and cozy. In a way, the design reminded her of Burton's Nightfall-themed rave. The creations had a similar vibe, but they were more cheery.

Laney received a text. "Ready to go?" she asked her. "Shawn is here."

Sad to leave, Abi nodded, "Sure."

The two moved through the crowd in the ornate lobby. Abi marveled at the ceiling made of blown glass lily pads in a rainbow of colors. Passing the Hermes store, they exited to find Shawn amongst the chaotic arrival of weekend guests.

Parked mere feet away, the cobalt blue Lambo stood out and wasn't hard to spot. Walking towards it, Abi found someone she didn't expect to see.

"Hey, you," a voice said.

Abi tilted her head slightly, happy to find Shane's smiling face as he appeared from behind a pillar.

"I thought I'd bring him along," Shawn stated, wanting to take full credit for the surprise despite Laney arranging it.

She hugged the tall, handsome guy as he said, "Wow. You look beautiful. Then again, you always do."

"That's so sweet," she replied before he kissed her lips lightly, not wanting to mess up her lipstick. "What are you doing here?"

"Shawn said you were having a rough day."

About to speak, not sure what she could say, he stopped her.

"And justly so. You don't need to explain. You've been through a lot."

"Thank you for understanding."

"Of course," Shane said, casually pulling her close.

Concerned that he'd left the team behind, she asked, "Are you sure you won't get in trouble with Coach?"

"No, I cleared it with him first. Just have to return for the team meeting at eight."

"Okay, you two love birds," Laney taunted. "We need to get to the restaurant."

"We're coming," Shane said. Opening the rear door for her, Abi jumped in before he sat beside her.

As Shawn got behind the wheel, his girlfriend prepared to guide him where they needed to go.

"It's just up the street," she said. "Not far."

Heading north along the palm tree-lined Las Vegas Boulevard, they passed the Flamingo and waited in the left lane to turn into Caesar's Palace.

Amazed by the hotel's grandeur as they drove forward on the advanced green, the first thing that grabbed Abi's attention was the sign for Omnia. Below it was an LCD screen showcasing Dark Demon's appearance that evening and at the Forum in preparation for the grand opening of Nightfall. Breaking away from it, hoping Shane didn't notice, she moved slightly and looked forward instead. The entrance to the place made her feel like she was entering another world. It was indescribable.

Pulling up in the Valet line, a gentleman stopped them.

Shawn and Laney got out while Shane did the same. Holding his hand out to Abi, he said, "My Lady."

"Thank you, kind Sir."

Shawn handed over the fob as his girlfriend slipped the guy a heavy tip and told him to keep it close.

"Will do, Miss," the man replied hastily before passing her the ticket.

Abi saw Laney in a different light. It was strange to see how comfortable she was in this environment. Watching her confidently lead the charge, she went directly to the desk on the left-hand side of the lobby.

"What are you doing?" Shawn asked her.

"I'm getting us a room. We need a place to change for the event tonight. It doesn't make sense to drive to the house and back." As she stepped forward to talk to the man behind the reservations desk, she again handed him the black card.

His eyebrows raised upon seeing it. From then on, it seemed she got whatever she wanted.

Room key in hand, she said, "Okay. All done. Let's go."

On a mission, guiding them through the casino, Shane pointed to the Nobu sign down the hallway. Passing another desk, they finally made it to the entrance with origami cranes hanging from the ceiling. The modern entry was so unique. Abi tried to soak it all in.

Her friend spoke to the young hostess as if she owned the place. "Reservation for Laney Bass."

"Yes, Miss Bass. Right this way."

Without missing a beat, they followed the girl dressed in black to a table tucked inside a large woven basket. Inching around the banquette to have a seat, about to distribute menus, Laney promptly held up her hand. "No need. We will have the Chef's Daily Omakase."

Taken off guard, she replied, "Very well, Miss."

"What did you just order for us?" Shawn questioned.

"Trust me. You'll love it."

"It better not be something crazy," he said.

"No, of course not. It's just the twelve-course Chef's Daily tasting menu. It has fish, steak, shrimp and lobster. My Dad always requests it when we visit here."

"Should be an interesting experience," Shane said, reaching for Abi's hand on the seat between them.

"So, did you win earlier today?" she asked.

Shawn couldn't help but interrupt. "Yeah, they sure did. Fifty-six to ten. A slaughter, really."

Abi smiled. "I'm so proud of you."

"It was a team effort." Eyeing up his teammate, he said, "I wish this guy would get cleared to play soon."

Shawn examined his hand. "Dr said one more week."

"I'll hold you to that, man. We need you."

"I'm workin' on it."

Finding Abi staring at the table, Shane could tell she had less life in her. "Hey?" he whispered. "How are you, really?"

Based on the look he gave, she knew she couldn't fool him. "Truthfully? I'm struggling. But what am I to do?"

"Hang in there. Things will get better."

"Promise?" she said, resting her head upon Shane's shoulder.

He accepted her snuggles. "It will with time." Just then, his phone vibrated in his pocket. Looking at the screen, he smirked. "Do you have any idea why Burton has called and texted me ten times an hour?"

"It might have something to do with leaving my phone in LA."

"I told you that wasn't a good idea."

"I know."

"And ditching the guys? Really?"

She didn't want to hear it. "I hate myself for that. In all fairness, I wasn't thinking clearly at the time."

Burton called again.

He handed her the phone. "Think you should tell him you're okay."

Reluctantly taking it from him, she texted, *Burton, it's Abi. Don't worry. I'm good. Please stop calling Shane.*

Immediately, he sent another message. *Where are you?*

Safe. That is all you need to know. Not seeing another reply, she handed back his device. "He won't bother you anymore."

Their waiter delivered the first of their twelve courses to the table. He described the Yellowtail Jalapeno dish with a light level of culinary expertise.

With napkins spread over their laps and chopsticks in hand, the four indulged in the delicious buttery texture lightly dipped in minced garlic and surrounded by yuzu ponzu sauce.

"Is there anything else happening tonight other than the team meeting?" Abi asked.

"No, but a bunch of us plan to walk the strip. That's pretty much it."

"Is your agent here for the event?"

Shane devoured his fourth piece of tuna. "Yeah."

"And? What did he think?"

"At this point, the prestige of Gilderson and our win today must have convinced him I should stay. He texted me shortly after the game and said they were rethinking that strategy."

Laney heard the news. "That's good, right?"

"For sure. Don't want to go anywhere else." Hearing some people at the next table talking about Dark Demon, Shane felt compelled to ask, "Are you sure you will be okay at the event tonight? I don't like the idea of you two going alone."

Before Abi could reply, Laney intervened. "Why? We are just hitting the Forum, which is outdoors. Lots of people around. Security will be everywhere."

"But not at the Nightfall Club," Shane clarified.

"Honestly, I think we'll just check it out and then head home. Sound good, Abs?" The girl turned to get her thoughts.

Relieved to hear that, Abi said, "Yes, that sounds good to me. I'm pretty tired. Wouldn't mind making it an early night."

Shane's phone rang.

Seeing Burton's name on the screen, he answered, "Hello?"

"Put her on," he demanded.

"She doesn't want to talk to you."

Abi knew right away who it was. She reached for the phone and asked Shane to let her out from the table. When he slid across the banquette and stood up, she left and rounded the corner.

"Burton?"

He interrupted before she could say another word, "You ditched security? Are you crazy?"

"B?"

"Don't even. Where are you?" he asked firmly.

Not given a choice, she replied, "Vegas."

"What? How?"

"Long story."

"Abs, you know it's not safe."

The concern in his voice worried her. "I'll be okay."

"Oh, yeah? What if you're not? This isn't a joke."

She could tell something was going on.

"Where are you staying?" he asked point blank.

She figured she'd ease his mind. "Laney Bass's gated community on the outskirts of the city. I think she said Heaven's Edge."

"So, you're not on the strip?"

Put on the spot, she answered his question. "Not exactly."

Burton could hear she was amongst a crowd. "Stay at your friend's place. Hang out. Nothing more." He knew she wasn't telling him the truth.

Hating to be bossed around, she answered, "Fine," hoping it would ward him off.

"Promise me you'll keep a low profile."

"I'll do my best," she said but didn't promise anything.

Shane came looking for her.

"Burton, I've gotta go."

"Abs?"

"What..."

"I just don't want anything happening to you."

"I know," she paused. "I'll be fine. I'm with Shane."

Those words hit him. "Hope you're right."

"Bye, B."

He wanted to find her but knew he couldn't. "Stay safe."

"I will." An awkward silence looming, she added, "Burton?"

"Yeah?"

"Good luck tonight. Concentrate on that."

"Right..."

Ending their conversation, hanging up as Shane approached, she handed him his phone.

"Everything okay?" he asked.

She didn't elaborate. "Let's get back to the table."

Realizing she didn't want to discuss it, he let it go.

Just as they sat down, the woman returned to remove their dishes and serve a Uni Cucumber shooter, describing it as a blend of sea urchin, scallions, and a quail egg suspended in a ponzu sauce. Unsure of the concoction, they saw Laney suddenly down it in one gulp. Following suit, the guys did the same before taking a drink to help it along. The odd one out, Abi tried very hard to overcome the thought of eating it but ultimately decided to pass.

Laney waved it over, not letting it go to waste. "Give it here. I'll have it."

After passing it to her friend, their waiter returned continuously with various delicacies such as Toro Carpaccio, black cod, Wagyu beef, shrimp, and lobster dishes accented by micro greens. Hidden under a mysterious glass dome filled with a grey haze inside was the seabass. He said they'd find the smokiness would infuse every bite of the fish. And it did.

At the end of their culinary adventure, the group was beyond full but could not resist the Vanilla Miso tart and Japanese Whisky cappuccino presented so beautifully on the platter.

Checking her phone, Laney requested the bill. It was time to head to the room and get changed. Showing her the amount owed, she handed him the black card and completed the transaction, oblivious to the thirteen-hundred dollar total.

"Okay, let's get moving. We need to grab our dresses first."

Allowing his girlfriend to lead, Shane walked with Abi hand and hand. Each thanked the hostess on the way by.

The girls waited in the lobby when the guys went to the truck.

"Wait until you see this room," Laney said enthusiastically. It's amazing." She paused, "Well, I guess it's not as amazing as what I'm used to, but you guys will like it."

"What do you mean? Please tell me you got something basic and nothing fancy."

She looked at her with a questionable expression. "That is not within my DNA, Abs. Over time, you'll get used to it."

"You have almost spent thirty thousand dollars today if I could wager a guess."

"So what? It's been fun, hasn't it?" She waited for the verdict.

Afraid to offend her, she said, "Everything has been awesome."

Getting a positive reaction, she silently clapped her hands together happily. "Good distraction, right?"

"Absolutely."

With gold Fendi bags in hand, the guys returned. Making their way through the Casino, they reached the Julius Tower elevators. Pushing the thirteenth-floor button, they soon ascended to the very top.

The doors parted. Laney stepped across the hall and waved the card over the reader to access the room behind the double doors. Swinging one side open, Shawn held it for her as she went inside, followed by Abi.

Amazed by the vestibule with moldings and marble inlay floor, Laney turned and flung her arms in the air. "Do you like it?"

Abi's sights soared upward to the patterned cathedral ceiling, followed by the wrought iron staircase that led to a second level.

"This is pretty incredible." Shane was impressed.

"I was going to grab the villa my Dad usually has, but it didn't make any sense since we are only using it to change clothes."

"Well, this is beyond beautiful." Abi couldn't believe her eyes.

"You guys can go upstairs and play pool if you'd like," the girl pointed.

Curious, Shawn and Shane checked it out while Laney brought Abi into the large primary suite. Setting their bags on the bed, she signed into her Dark Demon app. "I just got our confirmation for VIP seating at the Forum show. It begins at eight. After that, we take a private car to the Nightfall location. It doesn't say where we meet, though. Perhaps they will send another notification closer to the time."

Nervous about getting through the rest of the evening, Abi changed into her dress and slipped on the shoes. Her hair was still light and wavy as she looked in the mirror and patted some powder on her face. Re-applying her lipstick purchased at the spa that day, she stepped back and looked at her reflection in the mirror.

"Damn!"

Abi flew out of the bathroom. "What? What is it?"

"We didn't buy any jewelry. I really need a chunky necklace or something."

Seeing Laney draped in the bold, high-collar, burnt orange-studded dress, she said, "No, my friend, you don't need a thing. You look stunning."

"Yeah?" she questioned as the compliment calmed her down.

"Absolutely."

Hearing the boys striking the pool balls with their cue, the girls folded and packed their day clothes in the Fendi bags neatly before walking out of the bedroom.

"Excuse me, gentlemen?"

Shawn and Shane looked over the railing above them.

"Wow! My baby looks good." Unable to contain himself, Shawn bounded down the spiral stairs. "I don't know if I want you goin' out looking so pretty without me."

"Why?"

He strolled up to her. "Because you're mine."

Having come a long way from the timid football player she met a few weeks ago, Abi thought Shawn had grown into the kind of guy capable of ushering Laney on his arm. Noticing Shane descending the stairs slowly, his eyes locked to hers, he reached out and took hold of her hands.

"You look gorgeous."

"Thank you."

"I'm siding with Shawn on this one. Are we sure we can't get tickets to the show, too?"

"Sorry, guys. It's just Abs and I tonight. But I'll text you when we're on our way home. Shane, you're welcome to stay over if you'd like?"

He turned to Abi. "Might have to take you up on that."

By seven-thirty, they were leaving the room behind and moving back through the crowded lobby. Shawn handed the valet the ticket, and he, in turn, presented the Lamborghini fob. Carting the Fendi bags in one hand and clutching Laney's in the other, the truck was in the same place they'd left it. Lifting the hatch, he placed everything inside before opening the rear door for the girls.

"Shane, you ride up front with me," Shawn suggested. "We'll drop them off and hopefully make that team meeting."

He gave the guy a thumbs-up. While getting in the front seat, he looked back at Abi and got a sinking feeling. Somehow, he had this urge to go with and protect her.

Leaving Ceasar's Palace, venturing north on Las Vegas Boulevard, Shawn swung around the block where Abi got her first glimpse of the Sphere. Lit up like a planet had fallen from the sky and crashed landed, they continued south toward the Forum. Seeing rotating lights illuminating the cloud cover above, Abi looked to her right and saw a giant Ferris wheel. Lit in red, she wondered if that was in honor of Dark Demon's performance that evening. Turning the corner, waiting in the VIP line, a security guard tapped the window.

Laney rolled it down.

"May I see your ticket?" he said monotonely.

She brought it up on the App and showed him.

He scanned the QR attached to verify their arrival.

"Stay in the queue and move along to the landing area. When you arrive, someone will escort you to your seats."

"Thank you," she said joyfully.

"No problem," he replied and flashed a smitten smile.

Shawn saw this. "See! This is why I should be with you tonight. Every guy is gonna think you're single."

His girlfriend giggled. "Don't tell me you're jelly."

He looked back at her. "Of course I am."

She leaned forward between the seats and kissed him. "Well, you have nothing to worry about. Tonight is all about social and business."

Shane looked at Abi. He could tell she was nervous. "Sure you want to do this?"

His girlfriend nodded hesitantly.

"Well, if you need us, we will pick you up. Just say the word."

"Sounds good. But I think we'll be fine."

It was beyond him how she could have lost her Mother days ago and be here doing this. Somehow, it made him wonder if she was more affected by what happened than she was letting on. It was so uncharacteristic of her. He was certain this behavior was a coping mechanism to deal with the loss. Determined to get her through it, he reached back to hold her hand.

Abi squeezed it lovingly before mustering a bit of a smile.

As they inched forward, Shawn stopped at the landing zone.

A security guard opened the back door. "May I see your ticket?"

Laney showed him their VIP pass.

"You're in box eleven," he said before relaying the information to another man. Offering them his hand in a gentlemanly way, the girls emerged stylishly as the boys looked on.

Photographers on the left side of the aisle snapped pics at an alarming rate. Used to the spotlight, Laney struck a few poses and smiled at those shouting for her to look their way. She live-streamed their red carpet walk as her followers lit up the comments.

Shawn hid underneath his hat, hoping not to be seen while Laney put on a show for the cameras.

Having no choice but to move through the drop-off line, Shane watched Abi as they left. He thought she looked so pretty. But beyond her, his sights moved upward at the screens, where he saw the dark-hooded DJ appear, looking larger than life. *It's okay.* Shane thought. *It's only for a couple of hours.* He wished they could be sitting on the beach in Malibu instead. "How do you do this, man?"

"What?" Shawn questioned.

"Share her with the world."

"In the end, I know she's with me. Nobody else."

Shane nodded. "Yeah. Guess you're right."

"I believe Laney's desire to be known started with her parent's neglect. Some people seek fame for acceptance and love they aren't getting anywhere else. For her, it makes her feel significant. Seen. She needs admiration, and I understand that."

Shane looked back at Abi. She seemed thrust into the chaotic scene when Laney hooked her arm around hers and confidently led her into the venue. Even though he found it hard, he knew he had to trust her.

Maybe that's it. I lack trust. Guess I'm a product of my environ-ment, too.

Forum Launch

Escorted to their VIP box by a hunky, well-built man, Laney could see all eyes on her and Abi as they got closer to the front row.

"Here we are," the man said, stepping aside.

Looking up at him, fluttering her lashes, Laney smiled. "Thank you so much. Appreciate it."

He offered a sexy smirk. "No problem. I'll be standing by if you need anything."

"Okay."

Seeing a connection develop between the two, Abi felt compelled to whisper in the girl's ear when they sat down, "Wow, Laney. Flirt much?"

"Trust me. There's a method in the madness. You never know who you may need help from at these events. The number one rule for girls is to connect with the big guys in charge - someone with a protective instinct, so if something goes wrong, he'll be waiting in the wings. That's all. It's not a marriage proposal."

Despite her initial thoughts, what she said made sense. "That's a good idea."

She giggled arrogantly. "Of course it is."

Sifting through the gift basket on the table between them, Laney asked, "What would you like?"

Abi grabbed bottled water while Laney took the sparkling Badoit. She kept an eye out for Burton and hoped to see him just before his performance. Impressed by the scale of the event, Abi felt like she didn't know her friend fully. To a degree, he continued to keep this extravagant part of his life hidden from her.

Perhaps it's for good reason, she thought.

"Who are you looking for?" The pretty girl paused, tracking her line of sight. "Please don't tell me you still have a thing for the DJ. I thought that was over."

"It is." Unable to tell her the truth, not even a hint of it, she said, "Must say, though. I am curious."

"Abs..." Laney looked back at the crowd. "See all these people?"

"Yes."

"He will not recognize you or me amongst them, I promise you. The only thing he will see is the bright lights. That's it."

Abi looked around. There were so many pretty girls in the other VIP sections, so much so that she wondered if he'd purposefully selected them based on their apparent social media obsession since each was either streaming live content or posting in real-time.

"He's getting maximum coverage," she mumbled. "Genius."

"What's that?" Laney asked, not having heard her.

"Umm, nothing," she replied as the lights dimmed unexpectedly.

Recognizing the lead-up to the first track, the girls stood when the dark hooded figure appeared from under the stage. The crowd went wild and clapped to the beat, raising the sound barrier hundreds of decibels.

Girls screaming, she watched Burton take his place behind the deck, his arms raised as the crowd cheered. Abi's stomach felt sick. But strangely, he came across as cool and collected, concealing his identity while scanning all the faces locked on him.

His fans swayed with the ambient flow before bouncing to the transitioned syncopated rhythmic pattern featuring a Guns N' Roses mashup with female vocals weaved within the bassline frequencies. Energizing the air, bodies moving in unison, each anticipated the upcoming drop before the music climaxed, sparking unbridled pandemonium.

Effortlessly creating a contagious atmosphere to keep people dancing, Burton's hands moved across the table, switching the lighting and visual effects with the beat. Expertly manipulating the music, grabbing samples of popular songs to draw people in and lull them into a transient state, Abi could see the effect he had on the entire venue. It gave her chills and sparked emotions as the chorus settled in, pleading – *How could it end this way? Don't Leave Me...*

The words caught her attention. She wondered if he'd meant those lines for her.

Panning the stage, seeing pictures flashing in and out on the screens, she caught a glimpse of two people sitting on a dock by the water.

Wait. Is that? She thought.

As the pictures cycled through, she noticed a few more taken in Tahoe. Unbeknownst to her, many captured them from a distance. One by one, each pulled at her heartstrings and sparked memories of their experience at the lakeside retreat. Listening more intently as the music pleaded *to love me just a little bit longer*, she wondered if he'd infused a message in the track.

Amidst it all, she caught a man staring her way. Unfortunately, Zoe Sky was beside him. Flanked in the shadows off stage right, Abi raised a steady hand to Martin, who inevitably broke his stoic façade and produced a smile.

The lights dropped and spot-lit the masses. In a split second, Burton looked straight at her and stopped. As the bass reverberated off her body, Abi knew he'd spotted her. Able to see his eyes, he didn't seem surprised. Hoping he wasn't mad as the performance continued, she enjoyed the show and danced with Laney as fans all around them screamed and called his name.

Near the end of his last set, the screens announced his appearance at Omnia afterward to entice concert-goers to continue the party and flood the iconic, multi-level club. The grand opening advertisement for Nightfall followed, featuring a sequence of teaser videos showcasing the mysterious location and unparalleled technology housed inside. Like a wave, suddenly, everyone around them started looking at their phones. Laney included.

The girl pointed at Dark Demon's Nightfall blast on her screen. The timing of it all was unbelievable.

Abi couldn't get over the effort it took to produce an event like this. She felt so proud of Burton as he finished and left the stage while the rhythmic beats cycled repeatedly to end his segment. Disappearing off stage, surrounded by security, she saw Martin pull him aside and say something in his ear. His head turned to her, and he gave a subtle wave before being whisked away.

Hoping Laney hadn't seen it, her friend grabbed her arm. "Did you see that? I think he waved at me!"

Saved by the bell, Laney received another text. Reading it aloud, having to shout above the noise, she said, "Your transportation awaits!" Reading the map, she pointed to the street. "Looks like there are cars for us curbside."

Walking with the other VIPs, their security guard stayed close, keeping an eye out for danger as every elite guest filtered into lines of red Rolls Royce Phantoms.

"This is incredible," Abi muttered, completely amazed.

Her phone recorded their every move as Laney shouted, "DJ DD sure knows how to party! Now this, my friends, is VIP vibin'!"

When it was their turn to leave, the man assigned to them opened the backward-hinged suicide door for the girls to slide in gracefully. Safely in the car, the heiress checked the pics she'd taken. "I'm not a fan of red, but wow, this dress really pops against it."

"Good evening, Ladies," a voice announced from behind the wheel.

"Hello," Laney answered.

"Welcome. I'm your driver, Iman."

"Nice to meet you. I'm Laney, and this is Abi."

"We are heading to Nightfall."

"Sounds good. Let's go!"

While driving away from the venue, another message appeared on the DD App. Pressing play, the girls watched the screen darken and flash pictures from another world.

"Guess that's what awaits us there?" Abi stated.

It was funny to see Laney so captivated by what Burton created. Drawn to him after he'd spotted her in the crowd, Abi felt somewhat starstruck and hoped she'd see him face-to-face that night. It reminded her of a conversation they had almost a week ago when she asked about backstage passes.

"Never..." she mumbled.

"What was that?"

"Nothing."

"Abs, I swear you're hallucinating or something. Why are you talking to yourself so much?"

"I've got a lot on my mind..."

Laney caught herself. "Sorry, with everything going on tonight, I've forgotten about..."

"No, don't say it. Please..."

The pretty blonde nodded and grabbed hold of her friend's hand. "Okay."

When the video ended, the girls looked up. Not knowing where they were, both realized they'd paid attention to the video and not the direction they were going.

Immediately, Abi suspected the timing of it, and the trip was no accident. It was a smoke and mirrors distraction – a look over here while I do something else over there move.

"Where are we, Iman?"

"Can't say, Miss."

His calculated response was even familiar. Those were Martin's words. Abi recognized them right away.

Pulling into a dark corporate warehouse parking lot, the two panicked slightly.

"Is this the place?" Laney asked, not seeing any signage or identifiable markings.

"Yes, Miss."

They approached a single door with two guards out front. Thankfully, another red Rolls Royce had just departed and turned the corner after dropping an older gentleman at the door with the young woman latched to his arm.

Witnessing this calmed Abi's nerves a bit.

"I will wait for you. Afterward, they assigned me to drive you home." He checked his phone. "Heavenly Edge Court, correct?"

"Yes, that's right."

Stopping the vehicle, he reached back and handed Laney a card with a QR code on it. "Scan this when you wish to leave, so I will be ready when you are."

"Sounds good." Laney tucked the card in her bag." Thank you, Iman."

"Enjoy your Nightfall experience."

"We will."

A security guard helped the girls out of the car. Another held open the door and said, "Welcome to Nightfall. Right this way."

Guiding them through the passage, the girls walked into the ominous corridor. Without warning, the walls came to life, then the ceiling. A curvy living lattice of white with a liquid mirror moving beyond it, the girls walked the long hall, spying fluffy angelic clouds in the distance overhead.

When they reached the end and emerged into a large room filled with leafy green trees, foliage, and water trickling over boulders, the place looked almost heavenly. The LCD screens blended seamlessly with the props, making the room look vast. Taken by the tranquil sights and sound of birds, Abi wondered what awaited them next. It wasn't Burton's nature to be bright and airy. Realizing the opposite of heaven was hell, she figured the atmosphere would soon change.

Greeted by a man dressed in black, a stark contrast to their surroundings, he asked, "Code?"

Laney showed him her QR.

"Finger."

She placed her finger on the iPad screen, knowing the drill. The light turned green.

"There are two of you on one ticket. Your friend isn't registered."

"No, I booked the tickets as a gift."

"Finger."

Abi reluctantly set it on the scanner. It immediately turned red.

"I'm sorry, Miss. I need to deny entry."

Shocked, Laney turned to Abi, then the guy. "Come on. Let her pass. I've paid over four grand for these tickets."

"Can't, she's underage. Gotta be twenty-one."

Having dealt with this in the past, Laney reached into her bag and pulled a thousand dollars in hundreds. In conspicuously sliding it under the iPad on the desk, she smiled and said, "I'm sure we can work this out."

The man stared temptingly before making eye contact with another guy guarding the elevator.

He nodded and pressed the button. The bell sounded as the elevator doors opened, subtly signaling that he should accept the bribe.

"Go ahead," the man said, sliding the iPad over and pocketing the cash.

Keeping her cool, she simply replied, "Thanks."

"Sure."

Right on cue, the girls stepped aboard. Reaching inside, he pressed the DD button and left them.

As the doors closed, Laney asked, "When you registered for Black Lyon, what birthdate did you put on file? Please tell me you didn't put your own."

Abi scrunched up her face.

Rolling her eyes, she moaned, "Oh, Abs... No wonder."

The floor illuminated slightly. Abi watched the screen under their feet as the walls suddenly faded along with the ceiling, creating the illusion of a glass box descending from the clouds about a hundred miles in the air.

"Oh, my god!" Laney clung to Abi. "I hate heights!"

"It's not real," she said as it sped up like they were falling.

The girl closed her eyes dramatically. "Tell me when it's over!"

Holding onto her, Abi saw the clouds disperse and the ground come into view. Dark, rocky mountains appeared, devoid of color. Embers floated upwards the closer they got, and a faint smell of smoke hung in the air.

"Can I look yet?"

Alert, Abi said, "We're almost there."

Laney peeked slightly. Bouncing her sights from one side to the other, they slowly landed in the middle of a creepy dark forest with strange creatures walking beyond the tree line. Flames emanating from cracks in the earth, the girls waited for the doors to open as an entity appeared before them.

"Aaahhh!" she screeched. "What the hell is that!"

Scaring Abi to bits, she assured, "It's not real, Lane."

"I know. But it's creeping me out!"

Black, devoid of facial features, it stood there tilting its head curiously before disappearing - a breeze hit their faces when it passed.

"You should've been filming this."

The girl looked at her phone. Reminiscent of other Black Lyon events, cell service remained suspended. Her hands trembling, she said, "I guess I can record and post it later. Just can't live stream."

The doors opened to the pounding pulse of bass inside the confining walls of a cave. Not seeing a single soul, they followed the tunnel left, right, and left again. A mist hovered along the floor. Laney stayed beside Abi while they inched closer to an opening. Only one thing stood between them and what was beyond it. A wall of shimmer blocked their path.

"Is it real or virtual?" Laney reached out. The light gave her fingers a prickly sensation. "We need to step through that?"

"We'll go on three?" Abi grabbed hold of her hand.

"Right, go on three."

"One. Two," Abi prompted.

Laney fearfully closed her eyes. "Three!"

A sensory surge of prickles went through their body from head to toe.

On the other side, each looked up. They'd passed the portal and landed in a humongous domed cavern. Actual trees towering above them twenty feet in the air, amongst otherworldly things, felt like they were on another planet or had shifted into an alternate universe. Beyond the branches, the LED, sixteen-K resolution walls created an immersive depth to the surrounding mountains, stars, and planets. Patrons moved about the space in awe while creatures with the long legs of a mosquito and the body of an elk stalked them on their way to the dance floor. Strangely lurking in the shadows, glowing crimson eyes caused paranoia to surface, making most people glance over their shoulders.

Mingling amongst the crowd to locate their VIP booth, Abi perused the other spaces and noticed many well-dressed people with their faces illuminated by the light from their devices.

"How do their phones work, and I have no signal?" Laney asked, not understanding what was going on. "I'm going to have to complain about that."

Paying close attention, Abi knew the real reason the vast majority were there. Mindlessly oblivious to what was happening behind the scenes, the rest were just looking for a good time.

"Here's booth eleven," Laney pointed, surveying all the perks while venting her opinions inside the small room with a sectional sofa, snack bar, and drinks.

Not paying her any mind, Abi saw the stage. She didn't bother looking for Burton. She assumed it would be at least an hour before he'd finish his appearance at Omnia and make his way there. Deciding to people-watch in the meantime, she marveled at the Club's design, admiring the attention to detail, unaware she had caught someone's eye and they were doing the same to her.

77

Nightfall

The dance floor, bordered by five-dimensional holographic flames, added to the long list of technology that went into this fantasy-infused atmosphere. Abi truly felt like she was no longer on Earth. And just when she got used to the creepy forest scenery, without warning, the Club morphed into an other-planetary beach scene, with glowing white palm trees replacing the creepy tall pines. Beyond the walls were bioluminescent beaches and reams of stars sprinkled around the black-hole sun.

"This is insane!" Laney shouted. "Look at this! Come on! Let's dance!" she screeched, grabbing Abi's hand and dragging her through the crowd.

Mingling amidst the reckless partygoers, she heard a different version of the same song Burton ended the concert with. The repetitive chorus made her replay the words in her head. There was so much she wanted to say to him. Witnessing the event first-hand, she now understood the degree of stress he'd been under the past few weeks. It made her appreciate how he was there for her at the funeral that much more.

Conforming with the dancing mob, bouncing to the beat in unison, two handsome young men joined them. Dressed in designer clothes with expensive watches displayed proudly on their wrists, Laney entertained their interest. Flirting as she normally did, recording various clips for later, both guys tried to get closer to them. Not thinking anything of it, she embraced the one guy's forwardness.

His friend tried to do the same, but Abi kept him at bay. Invading her space, flashbacks of Eastwood sparked fear. She knew both of them assumed they were twenty-one. Backing away, the dark-haired guy tried sliding his arms around her waist, causing an immediate fight-or-flight response. Spiraling, she didn't want to leave Laney and return to their booth alone. The thought of being separated terrified her.

Trapped amidst the strobe lights, creating a slow-motion effect on the crowd, Abi prayed for her Mother to keep her safe from all harm and danger. Staying close to her friend, she scanned the stage periodically, hoping to see Burton. Once again, she felt like she needed saving.

Hot and flustered, Laney silently signaled she needed a break. Heading to the bar, she shouted over the noise to order a drink. "Frozen Mango Bellini, please!" Turning to Abi, she asked, "Want anything?"

"No, I'm good."

Handed the pretty orange frozen concoction with a hint of red swirled through it, Laney liked how the glass illuminated. Returning to their private space, the guys from the dancefloor followed.

"Mind if we join you?" the dreamy one with blue eyes shouted close to her ear.

"Sure!" Laney said.

Glass in hand, he said, "What are your names?"

"I'm Laney. This is Abi."

Grabbing a Badoit, Abi cracked the seal and took a sip. About to take another, two security guards approached.

"Laney Bass?" the big man asked.

"Yes?"

"May we have a word?"

Taking her aside, Abi joined as the handsome boys stood by the door, bouncing their heads to the beat of the music.

"What is the problem, gentlemen?" she bossed with attitude.

Barely finishing her sentence, the man replied, "We need to escort you out."

Laney pounced. "What? Why?"

"We have reason to believe you and your friend are underage. The state of Nevada has a strict policy, Miss."

Abi was secretly happy to hear this. Looking up at the crazy night sky that appeared, she saw a meteor cruise past. That was her sign. Deep down, she knew her Mother was protecting her.

The girl's hands locked to her hips. "This is ridiculous!"

"Laney," Abi tugged on her arm. "It's fine."

"No, it's not."

Hoping to soften the blow to the girl's ego, Abi played on her sympathy. "Look, I didn't want to tell you earlier, but can we leave?" Tears developed in her eyes. "It's a bit much for me right now." As a droplet fell across her cheek, Abi wiped it away.

Immediately melting with abundant sympathy, Laney said, "Oh, Abs... Why didn't you say something sooner?"

"I didn't want to spoil your fun. I'm sorry..."

"OMG! Don't be sorry!"

"It's fine. Can we just leave peacefully and not make a scene?" Abi asked as another tear streamed down her face.

Laney hugged her. "Absolutely." Turning to the gentlemen, she said, "We'll go. Just give us a second."

Not saying a word, the big man just nodded and waited with his hands knotted behind his back.

Bidding the handsome boys goodnight, they exchanged numbers with Laney and left to mingle with the crowd on the dancefloor to hone in on their next target.

With her bag in one hand and sparkling water in the other, applause suddenly filled the air, and shouts emanated from every corner. Abi turned and found Dark Demon stepping on stage as an infinite beat spread through the Club. With his face covered, Burton took his rightful place behind the deck.

Abi noticed him wearing a black hoodie with a gold lion head pin over his heart—the same one he'd worn the night he saved her.

Prompted by security to move along, Abi silently requested a minute. They stayed close, ensuring the two didn't evade their sights.

Burton's eyes shifted about the controls as the beat built up, the pulsating rhythm growing louder and more complex. The bass thumped like a heartbeat, steady and powerful, while layers of synths and percussion wove together in a mesmerizing dance. The melody climbed higher, each note escalating the tension. Lights flashed in sync with the rising tempo, casting a kaleidoscope of colors across the room. Then, in a split second, Burton looked straight at Abi, his eyes locking onto hers as the music peaked and a wave of electrifying energy crashed over the crowd.

She knew then he was the reason they'd gotten removed.

Winking, he gave a subtle raise of his hand.

Laney noticed right away. "Hey, did he just…"

"No, definitely not," Abi said wanting to avoid further comment.

Unfortunately for her, Laney wasn't the only one to notice the DJ's blatant indiscretion. Zoe Sky and Sara were off stage right and saw everything as the beat erupted, sending the floor ballistic.

"That's your cue, ladies," the security guard said.

Forcefully urged to leave, Abi took one last look at him before leaving arm-in-arm with Laney. Surrounded by two security guards in the front and two flanking their back, Abi peeked inside the other VIP booths and spotted a familiar face.

"Is that…" she said aloud as Laney noticed her attention veer.

"Hey, it's Reggie. What's he doing here?" the blonde spouted.

Not knowing the answer, Abi replied, "Good question."

"Should we go and say Hi?"

About to do that, their path got blocked by one of the men. "Sorry, Miss. It's time to go - easy way or hard way?"

Desperate to leave, Abi pulled on the girl's arm.

Escaping through the portal, feeling the prickly sensation course through their veins a second time, a group of well-dressed, university-age students exited the elevator. Wildly flipping upon seeing the special effects, a couple were noticeably half in the bag.

"I guess they aren't here for the vault," Abi mumbled.

Piling into the elevator, the guards flanking either side, Laney prepared for the scary illusion. Hating the thought of making the terrifying journey to the surface, she again held onto Abi and closed her eyes.

"Tell me when it's over!" she whined.

Ascending in the elevator, leaving the haunting darkness, she strangely felt like she'd left Burton a million miles away. Unable to speak to him in person, her heart missed the guy as the dark faded, and the light emerged when they passed through the clouds above.

Soon, the doors opened. Abi guided Laney into the corridor.

The unsettled girl turned on a dime and flashed a look of anger. "You'd better hope the refund for my tickets lands in my account by the time we reach the car."

He didn't miss a beat. "Already done, Miss." Handing her the money slipped to the guards, he added, "Including your generous tip."

Shocked that the men they'd bribed were no longer there, Abi asked, "I guess they were..."

He answered, "Fired? Yes, Miss."

Placing the money in her bag and taking out Iman's card, Laney scanned it with her phone. It sparked a pop-up box that read, *Message sent*. Needing to save face as patrons passed them by, intent on looking important, the bossy blonde demanded, "Surround us on the way to the car."

The guys humored her and obliged.

Iman was already waiting.

As the two exited and walked toward the red Rolls, one of the men hastened to open the suicide door as another group of partygoers were about to walk into the Club. Curious, each smiled excitedly, believing the girls were celebrities given the security presence.

When they took pictures of them leaving, Laney felt special. Not wanting to miss the moment, she recorded all the attention and took a few last pics before the car door shut.

Safe in the vehicle, Iman glimpsed in the rearview mirror. "So, how was it? You ladies enjoy yourselves?"

"Yes, it was amazing, thank you," Abi smiled.

"Heading home early?"

To Laney, those words were the kiss of death. Rolling her eyes, she said, "Yes. When you've seen one Club, you've seen them all."

Abi shot her a look.

Never having seen that expression before, her blonde friend asked, "What?" Clearing the air, she quickly fessed up, "Actually, the truth is my friend lost her Mother this week, and I just selfishly dragged her all over Vegas."

"It wasn't all that bad. She took me to the Spa." Facing Laney, she said, "I just wasn't prepared for all this after what happened at the last rave."

Laney's phone suddenly got service as they left the property. Receiving message notifications from Shawn, she texted him back and said they were on their way home.

Surprised, Shawn wondered why.

Leaving the bright lights of the strip and heading into the dark outskirts of the city, she said Abi wasn't doing well, and they would meet him there.

78

Terror Reigns

After a hectic day, the ride home was peaceful. Laney kept busy creating videos for her social media posts while Abi's eyes grew heavy, almost drifting off. Gazing out the window in a daze, she reminisced about her time with Shane but worried that Burton would be angry at her for not telling him she was attending the event.

Thankfully, amidst it all, Laney got a text.

"Jade wants to know where we are."

Hearing this, Abi perked up.

Seconds later, the phone rang.

Laney answered on speaker. "Hello."

Jade jumped straight to the point. "We're bored. Is it okay if we came over?"

While looking out the window at the city lights, Abi heard her extend the invite to all their friends.

"Sure. Why not."

"Send me the address. We'll leave now."

Doing that, Laney said, "Done. See you soon."

For Abi, even though a part of her wanted to be alone, the other half wouldn't mind seeing Shane, so she didn't debate the plans they'd made.

As they slowly moved down the street toward her parent's desert home, the driver passed through the security gates and climbed the hill.

Pulling in front and getting out, Iman opened the door for the ladies. Each bid him goodnight before Laney slipped him a cash tip.

"Thank you so much, Miss," Iman said gratefully. "Enjoy the remainder of your evening."

"You as well," she replied before unlocking and entering the front door.

Once inside, she walked around, flipping switches before heading toward the kitchen, excited that the evening wasn't over.

"Despite getting kicked out of the Club, I'm happy we're having company." She looked out over the pool. Sliding the wall of glass open a few feet to prep the backyard, she turned on the fire bowls and pool lights. "What the hell is this!" she shouted.

"What? What is it?" Abi went over to where she was standing. Her heart dropped, and the air escaped her lungs at the sight of the infinity-edge oasis. Weighed down, her arms and legs going limp, a level of terror spread through her like wildfire. Paralyzed by the sheer mass of black rose petals floating in the water, she urgently scanned the yard for movement. "Lane..." she whispered, her voice vibrating. "Hurry, get inside and lock the doors." Swiftly shoving her friend along, Abi slid the wall shut and locked the mechanism while looking left and right systematically.

"What's got you spooked?"

Abi realized she didn't know about the flowers. Gasping, she whispered, "It's Eastwood."

The girl's face went white. "What do you mean, Eastwood? Where?"

"The petals. He knows I'm here."

"Oh, my god." Her eyes frantically bounced about the backyard. "Are you sure?"

Abi nodded. "We need to call the police. Where's your phone?"

She pointed to the kitchen counter. "It's over...there." Laney hesitated, "Wait? It's gone."

"Well...well...well. Who do we have here?" a deep voice split through the silence. "It's the two Dark Demon VIP groupies."

The girls clung to each other as three shadows appeared around the corner.

Shielding her friend, Laney shouted, "Get out of my house! I've pressed the silent alarm. The police are on their way." Knowing she hadn't, she hoped it would scare him off.

"This won't take long," he smirked. "Acardi and I have unfinished business."

Eastwood stepped forward, holding a single black rose.

One of his goons had Laney's bag with her phone inside.

"I didn't expect to see you out and about so soon after your Mother's untimely death. Shouldn't you be home grieving or something? Not that I'm complaining, of course. I mean, you've added an element of intrigue to a rather dull evening." Showing her the rose, he smirked sinisterly, "Did you like the flowers I sent this week?"

Fuming with anger, Abi said, "No!"

He smelt its sweet scent. "That's too bad," he said, slithering toward them. "Black roses aren't really black, you know." Examining the petals, he explained, "They're a deep, dark purple. Some say they symbolize hatred and despair. Even misery, mourning, and even death. All of which describes your life in a nutshell, don't you think?"

Hearing this validated her hunch. Toying with the words escaping her mouth, she suddenly blurted out, "You killed her, didn't you?'

"What does it matter? From what my sources tell me, she had one foot in the grave already, right? I just helped her along, maybe sped it up a little. You should be thanking me. At least she's not suffering anymore."

His words inflicted a pain she'd never experienced. Worse than being stabbed a million times and unable to breathe, a wave of fiery anger spread through her body, making her clench her fists as her legs stiffened. Seeing the way he stared at her, she knew he was going to kill her next.

He watched her hands shaking, and it fueled him. The look of disgust on her face also did.

Unable to control herself, filled with rage, Abi launched at the guy. But his goons stopped her and handed her over to him.

Grasping hold of her hands, he whipped her around and stood behind her. Trapped, held against her will, she felt his body tight against hers. His lips close to her ear, he whispered. "Feisty. I love that."

"Don't you dare touch her!" Laney threatened.

He stared the girl down. "Or what? What are you going to do, blondie? If memory serves me correctly, you're the Bass family heiress. Aren't you? Word on the street says your parents are currently in Dubai on business. Funny, your Dad doesn't seem to be with your Mom, or so I've heard. Think of how terrible it would be if they each had an unfortunate accident."

A stroke of terror thrust through her body.

"How is your Ex, David, by the way?"

"What do you mean?" she questioned. "How do you know him?"

"What, he didn't tell you?" Eastwood let out a sinister snicker. "He works for me. Sorry to hear about Shawn. For the record, David took it upon himself to rough up your new beau. Those orders didn't come from me."

In less than a minute, Abi discovered he'd been hiding in the shadows, watching them this entire time. Barely able to speak, she asked, "What do you want? Why are you doing this?"

"Let me see. Where do I start? There are so many reasons why. How can I possibly choose?" he mocked sarcastically. "I suppose instilling fear is the most notable. It's like a drug I need daily. Until now, it's been easy with the help of Emile Raven. She proved to be quite an asset, but sadly, she couldn't face the consequences of her actions. Maybe it's because I led her to believe she was to blame for the death of the great Shane Coppersmith. After that, she didn't care if she lived or died, by the way. Finally, I told her it was a warning shot. I'm not surprised she couldn't handle the heat. Since then, the coward's grown a conscience. I threatened her and said if she breathed a word of it to anyone, things would inevitably end badly. I guess that's why she tried to beat me to it.

Too bad her attempt failed." He paused with the most evil expression on his face. It was like he was the devil himself. "What else can I add to the Acardi hit list?" He thought for a second. "Maybe it's the fact you're dating Coop - the guy who stole my only ticket out of this god-forsaken family. And let's not forget your connection to Burton Lancaster. He assumed he could outsmart one of the most powerful families in the world. That was his first mistake, and he paid a heavy price for it." He smiled deviously. "And we can't forget Black Lyon coming after me for what I did to you and humiliating my family with his little stunt." He stood there, livid. "I will get my revenge. And you, dear Abi, are the common thread to all my troubles. There is nothing I hate more than loose ends. So, this is how I see it..." His personality turned on a dime - his voice now strangely upbeat. "If I hurt you, I kill three birds with one stone," he stated with little emotion. "Or, should I say TWO birds because we all know the DJ and Lancaster are one and the same?" Seeing Abi wasn't surprised, he added, "But you already knew that. Didn't you?"

She stayed tight-lipped.

Stunned, Laney processed what the guy said as her sights bounced between the two.

Abi could see she'd figured it out.

His lips touched her cheek. "Huh. Look at that. Blondie didn't know."

Without warning, the doorbell chimed and echoed through the large home.

Eastwood turned and signaled to his goon, unfazed. "Take her."

The man grabbed Laney by the arm.

"Whoever it is, get rid of them," Eastwood ordered, pulling a gun from his beltline and pointing it at Abi's head. "Make one wrong move, and your pretty friend here will suffer."

Quietly acknowledging, Laney put her hands up. "Okay, okay," she said, walking toward the front door with the man, who had also pulled a gun from his hidden holster.

Tucking out of sight, he prompted her to open it. "Don't do anything stupid," he said, holding her right arm, the barrel of the gun digging into her ribs.

Fearfully nodding, she took a deep breath and unlocked the latch. Pulling the pivot panel open a crack, she found Jade, Allie, Ming, and Mei waiting.

"Good, you're here. Love the house!" Jade said as Laney looked past them and saw the guys laughing and talking in the driveway.

"Thanks," she replied with a lack of enthusiasm.

Allie piped up. "So, where's Abs? We are so surprised she came."

"Umm, yeah. Change of plans. She's exhausted and has gone to bed."

"After what she's been through this week, I can understand that," Jade said, getting a strange vibe. She knew something was wrong.

"What do you mean?" Allie interjected. "We drove all this way, and you're not gonna let us in?"

"It's okay." Jade nudged the girl. "We should go. It's late."

Looking utterly confused, Allie shrugged her shoulders. "Fine. Guess we will see you tomorrow then?"

Before leaving, Jade saw tears welling in Laney's eyes. She stopped. "Hey, Lane? Maybe we can go shopping before we head back to LA?"

"Yeah, umm, that would be great. I'd like that," the pretty girl replied in a monotone voice as she bit her lip.

"I found this cute shop on the strip. Bought a pretty dress there today. Thought you might like one, but I couldn't remember your favorite color. Remind me. What is it, again?"

Knowing what she meant, Laney stated, "It's red, silly," trying her best to stay composed.

"Perfect," Jade replied. "Red it is." She turned to the girls. "Come on, we should let them get some sleep. I'll call you in the morning."

"Okay. Goodnight."

"Night, Laney. Tell Abi we're thinking of her."

"Yeah, I will. Thanks, Jade."

"No problem."

The girls hurried down the walkway.

When they were far enough away, the man said, "Shut it."

Eastwood clapped. "Well done. Hell of a performance."

Dragging Abi to the sectional sofa, he tossed her there and motioned for his goon to do the same with her friend. Huddled together, the girls didn't know what he would do next.

"Leave us," he ordered as his men obediently walked out the back door.

Eastwood sat before them on the coffee table, placing his hand on Abi's knee, stroking her thigh slightly.

She pulled away and slapped his hand.

Leaning closer, he looked into her eyes with the coldest stare. "For generations, my family has marked people who betray them."

Abi was about to say something.

He held up his hand. "No!" he yelled, "Don't talk! Listen!"

The girls cowered.

In a malicious tone, he stated, "I guess the question is, how do I end this? Our unfinished business feels...how should I say–anticlimactic. It's lost its luster. Maybe we should continue this cat-and-mouse game for a while longer. It's more entertaining."

He spotted a commotion outside. Seeing his guys fighting, he stood up and walked towards the window.

Abi grabbed Laney. "Run," she said as they bolted toward the front door.

Almost free, Laney pulled on the lever, hoping to escape.

"Stop!" he yelled. The sound of him racking the slide on a gun followed.

They didn't move.

"Lock it! Now!" he shouted.

Afraid he was about to snap, Laney pretended to do as he asked. Abi noticed the door stayed unlocked while they slowly backed away from it.

He came up behind them and grabbed Abi's arm. Pointing the gun at Laney, he roared, "On the floor! Face down! Now!"

Trembling, she lay flat with her hands over her head, believing that was it.

"Eastwood!" Shane shouted on his way into the back of the house.

The villain used Abi as a shield.

Her eyes locked on Shane's. He could see the absolute terror in them.

"Not another step, Coop! Don't think I won't do it! This is a walk in the park for me now!"

Shane ignored him and bravely inched forward. "You don't have to do this." Trying to calm the guy, he raised his hands peacefully in front of him.

"Don't ever tell me what to do!" Eastwood immediately aimed the gun at Shane's head.

He did not move a muscle.

"Impressive," he snickered, "You didn't even flinch. My father would have liked you. He always enjoyed a good game of roulette – except his version included one bullet in the chamber of a pistol aimed at my head," cagily revealing, "It took me a few years to master that. Think I was five or six. After a while, I learned to live with it. You've gotta be numb to death when you're staring down the barrel."

"Let the girls go. This is between you and me, man."

His psycho mystique broke as Eastwood's personality flipped. Laughing hysterically, he whispered in Abi's ear, "He doesn't know either. Does he?"

"Know what?" the QB questioned.

"That this isn't all about you! I have bigger fish to fry. And that's Lancaster. Or whatever he calls himself now. Black Lyon? Dark Demon? Baxter? Can't keep it all straight."

Shane looked at Abi. "Wait? Is that true?"

She didn't need to answer. He could tell by the look on her face.

"See, despite my hatred for you, he's target number one. But like I told Acardi, she's the common thread - the one thing I could use to hurt you and him. It's too bad this news won't make it past these walls. I'm ending this here!"

Without warning, the front door kicked open violently.

"Get down!" Shane yelled. The world moving in slow motion, he lunged forward, ready to shield Abi as she fell to the floor. Immediately, hearing two shots and a loud thud amidst it all, the sound seemed strangely muffled.

Covering her head, Abi heard the loud bangs as shadows flooded the foyer, clad in black tactical gear. Their movements were precise and purposeful. With weapons raised and adrenaline coursing through their veins, the shadows swept through the house like a force of nature. Thin beams of light searched for targets. Each room was methodically cleared, with occupants swiftly detained.

Soon, the house fell silent with the word, "Clear!"

Abi fearfully raised her head.

"Abs!" a voice cut through it all.

There, she saw Burton - his arms straight, with a gun pointed at the floor as he scanned the premises while rushing to her.

Kneeling, he asked, "Are you hurt?"

Barely able to speak, she took inventory of her body and shook her head no.

Laney screamed. "Oh, my god!"

Burton turned. "We need a medic over here!" he shouted before leaving Abi to assess Shane.

Sitting up, she saw the QB on the floor with blood soaking through the shoulder of his hoodie. He wasn't moving. Abi crawled to him. Cradling his head in her hands, she hunched over and said, "Shane? Shane? Can you hear me?" The tears flowed.

His eyes opened slightly. "Abs?" he muttered, "Are you okay?"

She nodded tearfully, unable to speak.

The first responders gathered around him. She backed off to give them space. His eyes did not leave hers for a second.

As another group of emergency workers brought equipment through the door, Abi saw Eastwood's body in a pool of blood.

The man attending to him said, "We have a pulse! Gotta move!"

The girls watched as they loaded him on a stretcher. Backing away, hugging each other, shell-shocked while leaning against the wall, their attacker got wheeled out the door.

Clinging to her friend, Abi said, "Are you good? Are you okay?"

Laney shook her head as her body trembled.

Their attention veered to Shane. Put on a bed, he, too, was wheeled out.

Burton reached for Abi and helped her up.

Launching into his arms and encircling hers tightly around his waist, he embraced her. "It's over. It's over. You're okay," he repeated.

Offering the same help to Laney, the girl quickly put up her hands, not ready to move just yet.

Shawn saw his girlfriend from outside the taped-off area. Desperate to get to her, he dodged the police officers and ran inside without a second thought. "Lane! Lane!"

"Shawn!" she cried hysterically.

He slid across the floor to grab her and hold her close. "I got you! Are you okay?" Checking her for injuries, he gripped her tightly. "You're safe. You're safe."

Burton moved Abi out the door while the SWAT team loaded Eastwood's handcuffed men into an armored vehicle.

"How did you know?" Abi mumbled, still alarmed.

"We were watching you at the Club and knew he was there. That's why my guys escorted you out, but it was too late. He was onto you."

She half-listened to what he'd said.

He could tell she was vaguely coherent. "You know what? Doesn't matter. We're just happy we got to you in time."

Partway to Shane's ambulance, her friends gathered around her.

Jade was the first to hug her as Burton stayed by Abi's side, his hand resting on the small of her back.

"Thank God you're okay," she said.

Burton checked on the football player and found the guy glaring directly at him. He knew he was angry.

Ming, Mei, and Allie offered a group hug while the rest joined in.

"How did you know we were in trouble?" Abi asked Jade.

"Color warning. It's a signal we created in case of emergency. A secret code, really."

"Oh?"

"Yeah, I asked Laney what her favorite color was. She said red."

"So, that's not her favorite?" Abi didn't follow.

"Hell, no. Laney hates red. It clashes with her hair. Hearing that tipped me off that something was wrong."

"What's your favorite color then?"

"Navy, for obvious reasons."

Not wanting to ask her to clarify why, she said, "I'll remember that for future reference."

"You?" her friend asked. "What's yours?"

"Definitely yellow."

"Okay. Yellow it is."

Burton tapped Abi's arm.

She turned to him while Laney stared at the famous DJ, starstruck.

Burton caught on. "What is it?"

Hoping to clarify, Abi revealed, "Eastwood. He, umm, said..."

"Said what?"

Fidgeting, she pulled him aside. "He knew you're identity and spilled it to them before revealing the connection between you and me."

"So it's out there?"

Abi urgently surveyed their group. "Yes. We should address it before word gets around."

"Now it makes sense."

"What?" she asked.

Burton pointed to Shane. "He looks like he wants to kill me."

"He will have to wait. First things first." Abi returned to Laney. Burton was close behind.

"Excuse me, Laney. Can we have a word?" Burton asked, guiding her away from Shawn and their friends. At a safe distance, with Abi by his side, he added, "It's come to my attention that Eastwood has divulged some private information."

The girl crossed her arms. "So, you're him? What do I call you with the whole name change and all?" she questioned, her eyes whimsically affixed to his.

"That part isn't important." He glanced at Abs before bringing his attention back to the blonde. "This runs far deeper than me being a DJ. It's a matter of security. I'm asking that you keep this quiet. Given the circumstances, if this got out, it would put all of us in danger. Can we trust you?"

Reading the stern expression on his face, somewhat understanding the severity of it, she changed her tune. "Of course, yeah. You have my word. I haven't told anyone. I was just grateful to come out of this alive. I guess that is thanks to you, I take it. Don't worry. Your secret is safe with me."

"Appreciate that." Seeing the EMS guy tending to Shane, he told Abi. "We need to talk to him next."

"Alright," she said while wrapping her arms around Laney. "I'm going to the hospital with Shane. We'll talk later."

"I'll check in on you guys in a few hours." Looking back at her family's house, swarming with police, she said, "Quite the day..."

Seeing the worry on her face, Abi asked Burton, "Can you arrange a hotel for her and Shawn tonight? I don't want them staying here."

Without hesitation, Burton replied, "For sure. No problem."

The shaken girl managed to produce a smile. "Thank you."

"I'll take care of it. Give me one second, okay?" he said, helping Abi walk to the ambulance.

Staring Burton down, Shane shouted, "Lancaster!"

The two guys squared off.

"What, Coppersmith?"

"So, UCLA student by day. Famous DJ by night, huh?" Shane shook his head and smirked. Looking at Abi, he asked, "You knew about this?"

She reluctantly nodded.

"It was you who kidnapped her in the SUV?" He raised his voice. "I was friggin' chasing you down to save her? What the hell is wrong with you?"

"You got it all wrong."

"Really?" Shane smirked. "That's not how I see it."

"Despite what you may think, I'm not the bad guy here."

"So, what? You're a cop?"

Unwilling to further that narrative, he said, "Can't say."

Because he answered the way he did, Shane fished, "So, a three-letter agency, then?"

Abi stepped in and pleaded, "Shane, stop. You can't tell anyone? Please..."

Because she asked, he hesitated and reluctantly said, "Fine. I won't. But I'm doing it for you, not him."

Burton took a breath.

"I guess in the great scheme of things, we owe you. Not sure what would have happened if you hadn't shown up when you did."

"Glad we got here in time." Burton offered his hand to the guy.

He shook it with his left while they attended to his right side.

A person approached, dressed in full tactical gear. Raising the black shield attached to the helmet, Abi saw who it was. "Sara?"

"Hey, Abi. Everybody okay?"

"Yeah," Burton replied.

"Contained?" she asked curiously, giving him the eye.

"Don't worry. We won't talk if that's what you mean," Shane confirmed, aware of what she meant.

Sounding chipper, the girl said, "Good to know."

Abi ignored his comment. "Thank you for saving us."

"Just doin' my job." Hearing someone call her, she said casually, "Look, I've gotta go." Before flipping her shield down, she mischiefly patted Burton on the butt. "I'll see you later?"

Embarrassed, he smiled and said, "Guess so."

When Sara left, Abi taunted with eyebrows raised, "What was that?"

"Nothing," he replied sheepishly despite his strong presence. Quickly changing the subject, he said, "You should focus on your hero here. The guy took a bullet to protect you."

"Yeah, well, I'd do it again if I had to." Shane stared at Abi with love in his eyes.

"Be careful what you wish for, man," Burton snickered as the ambulance attendants prepared to head out. "On that note, you guys go. I'll call you after, Abs." He stopped and raised his pointer finger. "Oh, but wait... I can't. Can I?" Eyes locked to hers, he recalled, "Because someone left their phone in LA." He tilted his head disapprovingly.

She knew he wasn't happy about what she did. "I'm sorry."

"Like I said, don't ever do that again," he warned sincerely.

"I won't." She held Shane's hand and waved to Burton as they closed the doors.

En route, Shane leaned over.

Meeting him halfway, she kissed his cheek, then his lips.

"Not the way I thought this night would end," he said, concerned about her well-being.

"Thanks to you." She gazed into his eyes. "About Burton... I appreciate you keeping his secret."

"All that aside, this thing between him and me isn't over." Shane looked away. "And I don't like that you haven't exactly been honest with me, either."

She slumped in her seat as the ambulance pulled away from the scene.

He interrupted, about to justify her actions. "But I get it. It's complicated. You wanted to protect your friend—but you lied to me."

"I know... I'm sorry."

"We talked about this already. I need us to be honest with one another. Good, bad, it doesn't matter. I'll battle with you in the trenches and celebrate our wins. But no more secrets between us, deal?"

Abi agreed with a smile. "Deal."

79

Sunday

Released from the hospital the following day with a bandaged surface wound from the bullet grazing his upper arm, Shane walked with Abi across the street to where Laney and Shawn had parked.

"At least I don't have to play today," he told her. "I'm looking forward to sleeping on the way home."

Greeting their friends, each reached out to Abi. With hugs all around, Shane offered only a fist pump.

"Did you text coach?" Shawn asked, hoping the guy got cleared to drive home with them.

"Yeah, I told him I was heading back with you and my girlfriend, who had just lost her Mom. The guy didn't question a thing."

"We grabbed your bags from Jade at the hotel," Laney said. "Everyone else is going on the team bus."

He nodded. "Okay. Thanks."

Laney rubbed Abi's arm. "I got our stuff from the house, too."

"How is it? Was it damaged?"

She replied, "Surprisingly, it's like nothing happened. A clean-up crew fixed everything and returned it to normal in less than an hour."

Afraid to bring up the subject, Shawn asked, "So, do we know anything about Eastwood's condition? Did the guy make it?"

"We tried to find out, but they wouldn't tell us his status." Shane turned to Abi. "Maybe Burton knows. The guy seems to have connections."

Disappointed by his comment, she tilted her head.

"Speaking of your old neighbor, what the hell, Abs?" Laney giggled. "Never would have thought – like in a million years."

"Yeah, that's pretty crazy," Shawn replied.

"You told him?" It came as a surprise to Abi, given their conversation the night before.

The girl sheepishly said, "Yeah. He's my boyfriend. It's not like he'll say anything. Right?"

The guy agreed. "Don't worry. I can keep a secret."

"We asked you to keep it to yourself." A bit put off, she stated, "Let's make a pact right here. We don't breathe a word of this to anyone."

Laney and Shawn agreed. Shane stayed silent.

"He deserves that much after what he did for us," Abi justified.

"Fine," the QB said.

She looked up at him, happy to hear he wouldn't harbor ill will towards Burton. "Thank you."

He nodded. "Sure."

Shawn clapped his hands together. "So, are we ready to get this show on the road, or what? We've got a four-and-a-half-hour drive ahead. Should probably get a move on."

"Yeah," Shane replied. "Let's go home."

Abi slipped into the back seat with Shane while their friends got in the front.

The engine growled when Shawn started it. "I love that sound," he said joyfully.

"Don't get too used to it." Laney knew they wouldn't make a habit of borrowing the expensive vehicle. "I'm sure my Dad would have a bird if he knew I took it on a road trip."

Shane received a text from Adrian. Reading it, he said, "Looks like we came second in the showcase out of thirty teams. Not bad, considering the turmoil on the field."

"What turmoil?" Abi questioned.

Shawn explained, "We can sum that up in one word..."

Laughing, Shane blurted the name, "Marco."

"What did he do?" Laney could only imagine.

"The guy's a menace. Happy he was on our side and not against us."

Shawn added, "He stirred up a lot of controversy."

"And made a few enemies," Shane laughed. "But we made it. So, now, after all is said and done, I have to see what my agent says. Hopefully, I can stay at Gilderson."

Abi nuzzled against him. "I hope so, too."

Heading southwest, they merged south onto Interstate 15.

Surrounded by desolate mounds on either side, Abi spotted Dark Demon's Nightfall Club billboard. Despite Shane's heroic actions, she knew if Burton hadn't intervened, their situation might have ended differently. But she would never say that aloud.

As Shane moved gingerly and winced, Abi sat up. "Is it sore?"

He put on a brave face. "No. I'm good."

"But you got shot. It doesn't hurt at all?" she questioned.

"Not shot. Grazed," he clarified.

She tilted her head.

Tapping her leg with his hand, he said, "Besides, I did it to save my girlfriend."

"Yes, you did. My hero."

80

Face the Music

Choosing the quieter, northern route into the city, Shawn drove down the 405 towards Bel Air. Maneuvering their way across Sunset Boulevard a few minutes before five o'clock, he knew Shane wanted Abi safe at home before moving on. Given how she left things with her Dad, there was a chance her return could get heated.

On their way up the street, Abi didn't see any security around. She felt bad for betraying the men who put their lives on the line to protect her and hoped she'd get the opportunity to apologize at some point.

When they pulled up to the gate, Abi said, "Press the button. If my Dad is there, he'll open it for you."

Shawn rolled down the window and did as she asked.

"Yes?" her Father said.

Abi leaned forward and answered, "Dad, it's me. Open the gate, please."

Not hearing a reply, it suddenly slid aside.

Moving forward into the courtyard, Shawn parked by the door.

"Well, I guess I'll go in and face the music."

Shane squeezed her hand. "I'll come with you. Make sure you're okay before I go."

She nodded. "Okay."

They slipped out of the back seat.

Laney exited and hugged her. "Call me later."

"I can't," she laughed. "My phone is at your place."

"Oh, right. Want me to drop it by tonight? I can do that."

"No, it's okay. I'll get it from you at school tomorrow."

"Alright."

Shawn hugged Abi before Shane walked her inside.

The couple then got back in the truck to wait for him.

The second Abi entered the foyer, her Father appeared. He was noticeably angry.

Shane stood there, unafraid after what they'd just gone through. However, judging by the look on the man's face, he could tell that this was about to get ugly.

"Where have you been? I've been worried sick!" her Father yelled with his hands resting along his beltline.

She fired back. "Didn't think you'd notice since you've been so busy with that woman."

"It's not like that."

"Yes, it is."

He was shocked by her quick response. "I went to the hospital on Friday thinking you'd be alone and might like to have dinner together for once. But I found you with her. The day after Mom's funeral. Really?"

"We are just friends."

"Friends don't hold hands. What do you take me for? I'm not stupid, Dad. I know what I saw."

Frustrated that Abi was speaking about this in front of Shane, her Father asked, "Can you give us a moment?"

"No, Dad. He stays," she said, pointing her finger at Shane.

"We need to talk - alone."

"Anything you say to me, you can say to him. He's no stranger to dads who cheat. His Father did, too."

Angry to hear that, he replied, "I never intended for this to happen. Initially, she was just someone to talk to – confide in. She'd lost her husband three years ago to cancer and knew what I was feeling."

"So you neglected me to be with her?"

"There is no excuse for how this all transpired. I'm sorry. I can't change it now." He lowered his head. "I knew your Mother was dying – that she wasn't coming back. The thought of going through life without her scared the hell out of me..."

"Then you went looking for someone to replace her? Is that it?"

Her Father didn't respond.

Hurt by that, she ran upstairs.

"Abi!" her Dad yelled.

Shane looked at Dr. Acardi and put out his hand to stop him from going after her. "Please, Sir. Let me go."

Consenting, the man reluctantly prompted him to follow.

Shane climbed the steps to her room and knocked before going further. He found Abi in her closet with a suitcase open on the bed. She was frantically gathering everything from her room.

"Abs? What are you doing?"

"Packing. I'm not living here anymore."

"Where will you go?"

"I'll move in with you, Jade, or..."

"Burton?" he questioned.

Abi stopped, buried her face in her hands, and sobbed.

He approached cautiously and wrapped her in his arms. "It's okay. I got you. We'll figure this out."

Crying so hard, she could barely breathe, she let go of Shane and paced the floor before turning and yelling at the top of her lungs, "I'm losing everything!"

Her Father heard her from the main level. His heart broke.

Legs weakening, about to collapse, Shane caught her and held her tightly. Effortlessly helping her up, mindful of his arm, he sat her on the bed and cradled her. "It's okay. Don't cry."

Calming down, she looked at him and dried her tears. "Take me away from here. Please. I beg you. Please..." she pleaded.

Against his better judgment, he recalled how he felt in the same situation. "Okay, I'll do whatever you want."

Abi got up and continued packing. Shane carried the one suitcase while Abi took her backpack and five other small totes down the stairs.

"What are you doing?" her Dad asked in desperation. "You're not leaving!"

"Yes, I am!" Abi said tearfully.

"No! I forbid it!"

As the situation escalated, Shane stepped in. "With all due respect, Sir, Abi needs time to process all this. You need to give her a minute."

The football player's sincerity caught him off guard as his daughter walked out the door. Shane followed. Closing it behind them, Shawn and Laney saw them.

"What's happening? Is she leaving?" Laney questioned, getting out to help her with the bags.

"Apparently," Shawn replied. "It must've been bad." He took the suitcase from Shane and lifted it into the back of the SUV while Abi tearfully put the rest beside it.

Slipping into the truck, she saw her Dad in the doorway. He was no longer the Father she loved and respected. That was all gone now. Then again, she thought, was it ever truly real? Immediately looking away when Shawn got in the driver's seat, Abi said, "Quickly. Drive."

He threw it in gear.

Laney turned round. "What are you doing?"

"I'm moving out," she said as they breached the gates and drove down Stradella. "I can't stay here."

Without hesitation, her friend offered, "You can move in with me. I'm in that big house by myself most of the time. It would be nice to have company. That's if you don't mind."

Abi sobbed. "That would be great. Thank you."

She reached back and held Abi's hand. "Absolutely."

Shane wrapped his arm around her and held her tightly. "It's going to be okay. I promise."

81

The House Guest

Lost in her thoughts, unaware of their surroundings, Abi got her bearings as they drove along Sunset Plaza Drive toward Rising Glen. Reaching the secluded court, Shawn pulled into the gated estate. Beautifully up-lit, they approached the white mansion and snuck the Lamborghini back into its empty bay.

Everyone got out to help bring Abi's things inside.

Laney guided the guys upstairs to the guest room down the hall.

As Abi walked around the stately space, reality set in. Soon, she started to panic. "Oh, my god. What have I done?"

Shane watched her pace the floor.

"I have no money? No car? I walked away with nothing," she vented.

"That's not true," he said. "You have all of us. We will support you through this, Abs."

Confused, she nodded hesitantly.

He looked into her eyes. "Despite our parents' mistakes and shortcomings, we will survive – together. Agreed?"

"Agreed."

"Look, I'm gonna head out and let you settle in. Are you going to be okay?" Shane asked, wrapping his arms around her.

Thankfully, close, she said, "I hope so."

"I'll see you in the morning, alright?" Standing in the doorway, he turned to her. "Do you want me to swing by and pick you up?"

"No, it's okay. I'll hitch a ride with Lane. No point in you driving all the way here."

"I guess there's no more security team?"

"With Eastwood out of commission, I assume everything will return to normal. Maybe I won't need them."

"Yeah, hopefully so," he said, rubbing her arm.

Walking down the hall to Laney's room to find Shawn, they found them making out.

Hearing their friends knock to interrupt them, the two stopped and composed themselves.

Embarrassed, Laney rested her hand on Shawn's cheek. "Given what happened, I feel lucky to be here still. It puts things into perspective."

"I know what you mean," Abi sighed.

Wanting to address the concern on Shane's face as all four of them descended the stairs and walked towards the front door, Laney said, "Don't worry. Abs and I will be fine. She's safe here."

The QB nodded while she went outside with Shawn to the SUV. Reaching for his girlfriend, Shane didn't want to leave. With his sights locked on hers, he watched Abi's eyes fall shut.

Feeling their lips touch tenderly, in an instant, the love they shared returned.

"Night, Abs."

"Night," she said on their way out the door.

"Text if you need me. Doesn't matter the time."

"I will."

Letting go, Shane got in the passenger seat beside Shawn after putting his bags in the back. Waving to her as they left the courtyard, Abi blew him a kiss when they drove through the gates.

"Guess it's just you and me now," her friend said, closing the door. "What do you want to do first?"

"Sleep."

"Oh, I was hoping you'd say that. I'm exhausted, too."

On the way back upstairs, Laney was curious. Moving down the hallway, she went into Ab's room and plopped on her stomach across the mattress.

Resting her head on the pillow beside her, Abi closed her eyes.

"So, Burton is Black Lyon," Laney stated bluntly. "Still can't believe that. It's crazy."

"I know, right..." Looking at her, she prompted, "But, remember..."

"I get it. I won't say anything," she paused. "Gotta say, it's kinda strange knowing who the guy is after all this time. It's not a mystery anymore."

"Is that bad?"

She thought about it. "No. But I feel pretty special. It's like knowing Batman or an Avenger."

Abi laughed, "Not quite, but okay."

Wanting to clarify something, the girl decided to go out on a limb. "I need to ask you a question. I solely based it on observation, so don't get mad, alright?"

Abi propped her head on her hand, afraid to hear what she would say.

"I know you're with Shane, and you love him. I'm a huge fan of his, but I gotta ask - do you have feelings for Burton?"

Stunned, she didn't know what to say. "What? No, umm..." she paused. "No, definitely not."

"Now, wait. Hear me out," she tried to calm her down. "I saw the way he looks at you and vice versa. What you have is more than friendship whether you are willing to admit it or not."

Abi stayed quiet and exhaled.

"So?"

"The truth is, when I found out he was the one who saved me from Eastwood the night of the rave, my heart did gravitate to him – but..."

"But what? In a way, that's kinda romantic, Abs."

"Regardless of what I feel, that can't happen. He's my best friend. There's almost three years between us and he's dating Sara. Aside from all that, I love Shane. Case closed."

Laney rolled over on her back and rested her hands on her stomach. "Alright... So maybe the timing is off. The bottom line is you care for him. Maybe even love him?"

Abi looked out at the view. Golden hour had spread across both canyons. "Perhaps." When she said it aloud, her heart sank. "Just hearing myself say those words makes it feel wrong."

"But what if it's not."

Abi recalled what happened in Tahoe.

"You two have a history. Of course, you'd have feelings. There's nothing bad about that."

Opting to never confess to kissing him, Abi promised to take that secret to the grave. "You might have a point," she said casually.

"Without a doubt, Shane's a prize. But, sometimes, the heart wants what it wants, and you can't ignore it."

Intentionally yawning, ready to bypass the topic, Abi was more confused than ever. "I'm pretty tired. Think I'm going to try and get some sleep."

Laney looked at her phone. "Yeah, it's getting late, and tomorrow comes early." On the way out the door, she turned and said, "So, he's dating that pretty SWAT girl?"

"Apparently."

Double-checking, she said, "And nothing's happened between you two?"

Not given a choice, she shook her head. "No."

"That's too bad. He is pretty handsome. Super nice guy, too."

"Laney, he's my best friend. That's all."

"If you say so." She let it go even though she had a hunch otherwise.

About to leave, Abi stopped her. "Lane?"

The pretty blonde swung around. Her hair floated through the air and landed on the opposite shoulder. "Yeah?"

"Thank you for taking me in."

"Happy to help," she smiled. "It's kinda nice having you here. Usually, it's just me and the staff."

"Well, I owe you a lot. So, thanks."

She walked back to her house guest and hugged her. "You owe me nothing. That's what friends are for." Letting go, she said excitedly, "You get some sleep. Six days until Homecoming."

Acknowledging her with a lack of enthusiasm, she said, "Can't wait."

When Laney left the room, Abi whispered, "Homecoming... How am I going to buy a dress? I have no money." Flopping onto the bed, she buried her face in the pillow. Trying to think of solutions to her problem, she rolled over and stared at the ceiling.

"Maybe she has something I can borrow?" Abi took a deep breath and exhaled. "Just deal with one thing at a time," she said, somewhat overwhelmed.

Barely hanging on, she forced herself to shower. Finally ready for bed, Abi looked in the mirror and tried to picture herself with Shane and Burton. At that moment, she could never choose. Frustrated, she turned out the light and walked across the room to slip under the covers. When she checked her phone, there were several texts from her Dad - mostly apologies, wishing she'd return home.

With impeccable timing, Burton sent a message asking to talk.

Dialing his number, it only rang once before he picked up. "Hey, Abs. I'm just checking in. How are things?"

"I've been better..."

"I'm sure." Wanting to know, he asked, "What happened? I see you're not at home."

"Things didn't go well when I got there. Dad and I had a blowout. I left. Well, actually, I moved out."

"Oh, Abs..."

Hearing that made her second guess her decision. "What am I doing? I have no money? No home? No Mom? I've literally lost everything."

He wondered what he could say to help ease her mind. "Abs, if you need a place to stay, you can always live with me. I have six empty guest-rooms." Assuming she was about to bring up her boyfriend, he said, "And, before you say anything, I won't drive a wedge between you and

Shane. You can come and go as you please. He is in on the secret, so that won't be an issue. I can provide a stable environment. You will never have to worry about money. Safety. Nothing. I will take care of it. No questions asked."

"But you've done so much for me already," she sobbed. "I can't ask you for…"

"Abs," he interrupted. "Don't give it a second thought. You know I'd do anything for you."

"Thank you, but…"

"No, buts." Almost forgetting, he said, "Hey, just FYI, the guys just arrived outside."

Despite being happy to hear that, her heart flooded with guilt. "I'm so sorry about what I did to them."

"I'm sure I don't have to tell you that you've got to apologize."

"I will."

"They'll forgive you." Hearing silence on the other line, he said, "But, for now, get some sleep. Tomorrow is another day."

She dried her tears. "Alright."

"Night, Abs. Call me if you need me."

"I will. Night, B."

82

Monday Morning

Waking to her alarm, feeling like she'd only slept an hour or two, Abi opened her eyes and looked about the room. Not realizing where she was, it took a moment for her brain to catch up. Turning off the intrusive sound, she slowly got out of bed, tired and weary. With flashes of the weekend gone wrong, a piece of her missed her life in Boston despite the stresses that came with it. Thinking back, recalling how lonely she was, Abi reevaluated her current circumstances.

"I would never want to be without friends," she muttered.

A knock came on her door. "Morning! Just checking to see if you're up."

"I'm pretty tired but good."

"Me too," she yawned. "Ready to leave in forty-five minutes?"

"Sure. I can do that."

When Laney disappeared, Abi dragged herself to the suitcases and bags occupying a small corner of the room. Without a penny to her name, she had nothing else. A dreadful familiar feeling hit her while sitting on the floor.

"Once again, you're homeless," she whispered, recalling her thoughts on the flight to California a few weeks prior. Straightening her posture, she added, "I guess, at this point, you had no choice..."

Feeling betrayed by her Father, she couldn't understand how he could do it. Anger festering, she got sidetracked and frantically tried to clear her mind and focus on the task at hand. Finding her uniform, she laid it on the bed and walked into the ensuite after grabbing her make-up bag. Hair fastened in a ponytail, she applied some color to her face and sprayed a light dusting of perfume before getting dressed.

Backpack and crossover bag in hand, she saw Laney.

"Ready, Abs? Gotta move!" her friend said on her way down the hall.

"Wait! I'm coming!"

Both descended the marble staircase, flooded with morning light, as the artistic string of pearls light fixture cast a shadow on the wall.

Veering left, Laney hurried to the kitchen. "Morning, Michelle!"

A pretty woman with a short pixie cut did not lose her focus on the texture of the shake in the blender. "Morning, Lane." She took the lid off the container and poured the vanilla smoothy with berries into two to-go cups.

"Michelle, this is Abi. Abi, meet Michelle, my in-house nutritionist and chef."

"Nice to meet you, Abi."

"You as well."

The blonde woman slid drinks across the counter. "As you requested, twin smoothies and Americanos for the road."

"You're the best," the girl complimented.

Shamelessly tooting her own horn, she replied, "Yeah. I know."

Loving the lighthearted and friendly atmosphere, Laney handed two drinks to Abi and took hold of her own. "We've gotta bolt. We're running late."

"Enjoy your day! Make healthy choices for lunch!" Michelle shouted as the words echoed down the marble corridor.

"We will!" the girl yelled back, hastily heading toward the mud room leading to the garage. Stopping in the vestibule, she stared at the board housing a number of car keys. "Bimmer or Lambo?"

"Does it matter?"

Hit by the negative comment, Laney fired back, "It always matters." Hesitating, she unhooked a fob. "Definitely a Lambo sort of day."

Punching the button, bringing the beast of an SUV to life, Laney hit the garage remote labeled "L."

As Abi jumped in, her friend tossed her bag in the back.

Behind the wheel, the Bass family heiress ignited the engine. It growled with a familiar rumble as she waited for the RPMs to level out. Once it purred, Laney reversed slowly and went on their way out the gate.

Immediately noticing Andrew, Ted, and Matt waiting for them in the court, thankful to see them, Abi waved and received the same in return. Pondering how to word her apology, she figured she'd resolve things with them once they got to school.

Petal to the metal, the girls sped down the hillside and around the corners, leaving a gap between them and the SUV following. Hands positioned at ten and two, Lane expertly maneuvered the curves with great precision.

It prompted Abi to ask, "Where did you learn to drive like this?"

"Don't tell Shawn, but I used to date a guy who now drives F1."

Unable to fathom the world she'd grown up in all these years, she hung onto the door handle and leaned into the corners all the way to Sunset Boulevard. As expected, traffic was already bumper to bumper.

Checking the time, Laney noticed Abi's nervousness. "Don't worry. I deal with this every morning. I know the ins and outs."

"Okay," she said, not knowing what she meant.

"It's like a dance, really." Changing lanes on a dime, sneaking between two cars, and waving gratefully in the process, she said, "That was Charlie."

"Charlie? Who's that?"

"Have no idea. I just read the license plates. His plate was CHRLEE."

Abi peered in the side mirror to confirm that. She was right.

"The black Bentley coupe coming up is MR BEEE with three E's." Inching past the car, she said, "He's always slow as molasses, so I have to get ahead of him."

Surprised by her ability to read the road, Abi watched her swiftly and successfully get them to their destination.

As they rounded the corner, the first thing she noticed was yet another strange man occupying the school's security gatehouse.

I really need to know what happened to Gerald, she thought. *It's been far too long.*

83

Apologies

Laney reverse-parked into her assigned spot. Grabbing their things, they got out and hurried along.

Seeing the guys standing by, Abi knew what she had to do.

"Give me a second," she told Laney. "I'll be back." Walking to the SUV, she met Andrew and Ted as they assumed protective positions. Corraling them to Matt's side as he rolled down his window, she said sheepishly, "Morning."

"Morning, Miss." Andrew stood militarily with his hands behind his back while the other two looked on.

"I want to apologize for what I did last week. That wasn't my finest moment. Worst of all, I put you in a difficult position, and I'm sorry."

Each seemed silently disappointed.

"Under the circumstances, you can probably guess I was not in my right mind. I felt trapped. Like I was suffocating and just needed to escape. I know it was stupid. It won't happen again."

"Appreciate the sentiment," Andrew replied. He glanced at his peers and added, "After your run-in with Eastwood, I don't need to remind you that the game isn't over. Not in the slightest. You know that, right?"

The way he stared scared her, making her lower her head. "I do."

"Whatever decisions you make are your choice. We are putting our lives on the line to protect you from some pretty bad people, and we can't stop you if you don't want to accept that protection. A little advice: the latter is not in your best interest."

"I know. I appreciate what you're doing. It was a lapse in judgment. Not your fault."

"Bottom line is, you might not be so lucky next time. We have intel that suggests someone else has taken the helm in Eastwood's place. Despite his absence, you remain a target."

Hearing that sent a shiver down her spine.

"Do you understand the severity of this?" Ted asked, point blank.

She nodded.

"Given the situation, the problem will not go away unless..."

"Unless?" she prompted.

"They succeed," Andrew said, inferring to a fatal end to things.

She figured they meant for the comment to set her straight. "I'm aware."

Certain they'd gotten through to her, Andrew decided to leave it at that.

Seeing them systematically scanning their surroundings, she said, "So, after school, is it okay to go to the graveyard?"

Not having an issue, Andrew replied, "Roger that, Miss."

"Thanks."

Andrew looked at the time on his phone. "You'd better get walking. You're going to be late."

Happy to see Shane's Jeep already there, Abi caught up to Laney who was waiting at the elevator. As she approached, her friend pressed the button. The two girls rode it to the top with her shadows on board.

When the doors parted, they found their friends gathered around the courtyard. Jade and Owen gazed into each other's eyes and talked. Ming, Ben, Mei, and Adrian laughed joyfully while Alan and Allie showed, once again, that they were two peas in a pod.

Abi spotted Shane alone, sitting on the steps, scrolling through his phone. She smiled just as he raised his head and found her. Grinning from ear to ear, the handsome QB got up and moved in her direction.

"Hey, good morning. How are you?" He casually kissed her, resting his hands on her arms and allowing them to fall to grasp her hands.

"I'm good. More importantly, how are you?" She ran her hand along the wound. "Is your arm okay?"

"It's fine. Just feels a bit sore. No pain or anything. Thankfully, it wasn't deep enough to cause anything major."

Mandy, Shiri, and Shiresse walked past them. Abi overheard their conversation.

"Did you hear that?" she asked Shane.

Starting to walk along to class, he said, "No, what?"

"What is Wish Recovery?"

Shane had heard of it. "It's a rehab center for troubled teens."

"So, she sent her there?"

"Who?"

"Emile's Mom. I saw them leaving the hospital on Friday."

He shook his head. "The woman is so out of touch when it comes to her daughter. Doesn't she know Em won't like being amongst average people? If anything, that right there will send her over the edge again."

Abi tried to understand. "So this isn't a good thing?"

"The problem here is nobody cares if she gets better. Not her Mom and certainly not her Father - especially after what happened this summer."

She waited for him to elaborate.

"Forget I said that. You didn't hear wind of it from me."

Confused, believing whatever it was seemed bad, she said, "Alright..."

"She has no siblings. That leaves her without anyone to turn to."

"Then, how do we help her?"

He stopped and turned to Abi. "It's nice of you to want to do that, but the girl is stubborn. She would never make herself vulnerable and let someone in. Not even me."

"Then, it's hopeless?"

"Maybe, by some miracle, the people at the facility will get through to her. Or maybe she'll befriend someone there. Who knows. I just don't want to get involved. It could set her back. Promise me you won't either."

"Okay," she replied. "I won't."

Opening the main door for Abi, she walked inside the foyer with her shadows on their tail. The two men matched the pace of the students moving along to class.

While climbing the stairs, Shane said, "By the way, Coach called a closed practice today. Sorry, but you won't be able to watch."

"That's okay. The guys can drive me where I need to go."

Hesitating, knowing she wouldn't be visiting the hospital anymore, he waited for her to clarify her plans.

"I might swing by the cemetery to visit my Mom," she said.

Relieved, he caressed her back. "Okay. That is a good idea."

"I think so, too."

Walking into math, Marco Cafaro entered at the same time. "Hey, El Capitano? How are ya feeling? Heard some crazy rumor that you got shot?"

Shane smacked the guy's chest with the back of his hand. "Keep that quiet, man."

"Whoa! Whoa! Okay!" Marco put his hands up defensively. "You're good, though, right?"

"I'm good. It's nothing."

Marco looked relieved. "Good to hear. We gotta big week comin' up."

"Don't worry. I'll be ready."

"Countin' on it."

Witnessing the banter between the two, Marco seemed like a completely different guy. Shocked by his transformation, Abi sat at her desk and whispered to Shane, "What happened to him?"

"What do you mean?"

"Well...he's... Normal."

He snickered. "All he needed was to feel like a valued part of the team. He earned that this weekend with five touchdowns. It made him worthy of respect."

"Incredible," she mumbled, hoping never to see the sleazy guy from last week ever again.

84

The Announcement

Partially present during their intense math class followed by a lab in science, Abi found it hard to slip into the school routine. Walking hand in hand with Shane down the hall toward the art studio, an announcement echoed through the corridors.

Excuse the interruption, teachers and students. Can I have Abi Acardi come to the office, please? That's Abi Acardi to the office. Thank you.

Shane looked at her. "What's that about?"

Scared to know, she shrugged her shoulders. "Not sure."

"Want me to come with you?"

"No, I'll be fine. Besides, you need to get to the gym."

He paused a second. "Come on. It'll only take a minute." Pulling out his phone, he texted Adrian to tell their Coach he'd be a few minutes late.

His friend replied that he would.

Moving through the halls, now quieter as the classes resumed, they descended the stairs and moved across the foyer. When he opened the door for Abi, she saw someone waiting for her.

"What are you doing here?" she asked her Father snappily.

Taking her aside, giving Shane the eye, he said sternly, "Don't talk to me like that," before saying, "I've been calling and texting. You never returned any of my messages."

"They weren't worth returning."

With two big men shadowing her and Shane waiting in the wings, Dr. Acardi felt outnumbered. "I want you to come home. We need to discuss this alone."

"There's nothing to say." About to walk away, she added, "I'm late for class."

Her Father raised his voice. "Abi!"

"What!" she shouted, startling the women behind the desks. "What do you want from me?"

"I want to explain."

"There's nothing more to say, Dad. You cheated on Mom while she was on her deathbed. Can't think of anything worse than that."

"But..."

"But, nothing... We're done here." Abi turned and walked out the door with the guys following her.

"Shane?" The man said in a desperate plea.

The football player stopped. "Yes, Sir."

"She trusts you. Can you talk to her?"

Not knowing what more to say, he silently agreed before leaving.

Partway up the stairs, Shane shouted, "Abs! Wait up."

She paced back and forth as he approached. Standing firm, arms crossed, she asked, "What did he say?"

"He wanted me to talk to you."

"And say what?"

"To me, the guy is in the wrong, but he has a point..."

"So, you're taking his side then?"

"No," he huffed. He stood tall before her, hoping to keep the peace. "All I'm saying is he just wants to talk, Abs. Don't you want to hear him out?"

"Never." Continuing down the hall and across the bridge to the art building, Abi could feel that Shane wanted to say something as he walked alongside her. "What?"

"The guy lost someone, too."

"Yeah? It didn't take him long to replace her with another woman."

Knowing she needed to calm down, Shane stopped her. "Abi?"

She faced him disapprovingly.

"Please don't be mad."

Frustrated, hearing his sincerity, she stated, "I'm sorry. I'm not mad." She ran her hand across her forehead. "It's just…"

"I get it. You don't have to explain."

She fell into his arms.

"It's gonna be okay."

Abi acknowledged him with an uncertain smile.

"I'll see you at lunch, then?"

She nodded. "I'll see you there."

Watching him walk away, he waved to her before disappearing around the corner. No matter how much she wanted to avoid her Father, she knew he wouldn't rest until this issue between them got resolved one way or another.

"Things will never be the same," she muttered. "When Mom died, our family did too."

85

A Day to Remember

About to walk into the studio, Abi stopped. Stepping away from the door, she leaned against the wall to hopelessly stare at the ceiling. Suddenly, it was hard to breathe. Her body vibrated inside uncontrollably. Feeling her feet falling through the floor, sparking this weird out-of-body experience, it felt like her soul was leaving its vessel and hovering above it.

Concerned, Andrew approached. "Are you okay, Miss?"

His caring tone caused a flood of emotions to surface. "No…" she said, exhaling at the same time. Colliding with him, her arms wrapped around his waist as the tears fell.

The guy turned to Ted with his arms raised and hovered mid-air above the girl. Out of his element, placed in an awkward position, knowing the protocol for such things, it pulled at his heartstrings to look down and see her crying. Compelled to comfort her, he slowly lowered his guard and gingerly wrapped his arms around her shoulders.

"There, there, Miss. Everything will be okay," he stated, not knowing what else to do.

"I want to leave," she whimpered.

Ted nudged Andrew. "We should take her to the office and have her sign out."

Andrew nodded and remained close. Escorting her with one hand lightly on her back and the other tucked behind his, he remained mindful of the girl struggling to deal with her current circumstances. Guiding her toward the main building, the men waited in the wings for Abi to get the yellow slip.

In the meantime, Andrew texted Burton and kept him in the loop.

When she returned, walking stoically, unsure which direction to go, the guys led her outside, where Matt had pulled up to the curb in the VIP lane. Opening the door, Andrew got Abi settled and found a seat opposite her while Ted took point in the front.

Sitting there, she realized this was the first day she wouldn't be going to see her Mother at the hospital. "Take me to Forest Lawn Memorial," she said solemnly, almost forgetting her manners. "Please..."

Matt responded, "Right away, Miss."

Upon leaving school, Abi stared out the window, remembering the last time she left at midday. It was when she found out her Mom was terminal and returned home to find her Dad with the nurses discussing her Mother's care.

Knowing Shane would be worried when she didn't show up at lunch, she took out her phone and typed, *Sorry, Shane. I needed some time alone. Please don't be mad. I left school. Go to practice, and I will see you afterward.* While waiting for his reply, she figured he'd be in the middle of a workout, so she put her phone away.

The sun dipped in and out from behind the clouds while driving along the highway. It caused flashbacks from the day of the funeral. Her heart broke as the same pain resurfaced. She wondered how she got here – how her life crumbled apart so quickly. It seemed her Mom was the glue that kept them together. Without her, there was no hope. Everything had changed overnight, and she could do nothing about it.

When they exited off the freeway onto Forest Lawn Drive, Abi got Matt to stop so she could pick up some flowers.

Handing Ted money, she asked, "Do you mind?"

He took it from her. "Sure. No problem."

"The white ones are pretty," she mumbled.

Rolling down his window, he pointed to the ones in the bucket to the right. "Hello, Sir," he addressed the man under the umbrella. "We'll take a bouquet of white roses."

The man brought them over in exchange for the money.

Ted handed them back to Andrew, who passed them along to her.

"Thank you," she said.

Signaling to merge into the flow of traffic, soon, Matt drove through the gates of the memorial gardens. Slowly winding their way to Ascension Road, passing the chapel, Abi got out quickly when Matt stopped the vehicle. Andrew went after her.

Seeing him, she turned and held up a hand. "No, I need to go alone. Please, I beg you..." she instructed with droplets streaming down her face.

The big man stopped in his tracks.

"Just watch me from there."

Andrew backed off peacefully as Abi continued to her Mother's grave. Approaching, she found the caretakers had covered the soil with a lush green piece of sod. Sitting beside it, she ran her hand over the blades, knowing her Mother was resting below.

"So, I'm sure you're not happy with me," she stated bluntly. The makings of the past few days muddled her thoughts. "Thank you for keeping me safe in Vegas. Otherwise, I think the guy might have, umm..." She paused and muttered under her breath. "...possibly succeeded." Recalling what Eastwood said, knowing he confessed to killing her Mom, she sat quietly. Having stared into the eyes of a demon, she knew the Oligarch was evil and hoped he had succumbed to his injuries. "Even if he did die," she said aloud, "It wouldn't matter. The guys say someone else has taken over the helm. It's like a life sentence. I don't know when I can stop looking over my shoulder." Distraught, she shifted on the grass. "I'm sorry... I know I should've never gone. I just needed...well..." Pausing, she sighed as the tears fell across her cheeks. There was no point in trying to justify it. Knowing the reason why she left, reliving that horrific moment in her Dad's office, she said,

"How could he do that to you? To me? To our family?" She wished she could hear her Mom's voice tell her everything would be okay – but there was nothing but the wind whistling through the trees and birds flying by in the distance. Heart pounding, she rested her head in her hands. "I don't know what to say to him – what to do about this? How can I go home and be under the same roof, knowing that woman could come around at any moment? I am not okay with this." Thinking more about it, wondering how she'd feel if the circumstances were different, she said, "I mean, if it happened down the road, I'd understand. But the day after, we buried you. Two days after you passed? No. Now, that's unforgivable."

The sound of an exotic engine growling stole away the peacefulness in the gardens. While the matte black McLaren drove up, she watched Burton park behind the guys. When he got out, he looked over the roof of his vehicle and offered a steady hand to greet her from afar.

She, in turn, did the same. Watching him close the car door, he spoke to the guys before walking towards her with more flowers.

"Hey, Abs," he said, placing the bouquet alongside hers.

"Hi."

A moment of silence only seemed fitting.

"Little early in the day to be leaving school."

"So, you're gonna get on my case now, too?" she snapped.

He quickly reevaluated his approach. "No. I was worried since this is out of character for you. Thought it was bad, so here I am."

She immediately felt remorse. "I'm sorry."

"It's okay." He waited to see if she would willingly divulge what set her off, aside from the obvious. Or if he'd have to drag it out of her. "Want to tell me what happened?"

"My Dad came to the school this morning. It wasn't good." Abi peered down at her feet and fidgeted with a long blade of grass. "He wanted to talk. I refused and walked away."

"Don't get angry at what I'm about to say."

She shot him a look.

"You will have to talk to him eventually. That said, I know you need a little space to process everything. It's understandable."

"I told him there is nothing to say."

"Abs..."

"What!" she barked again. "He's in the wrong, and nothing you say will convince me otherwise."

Burton paused and thought about what she said. "I don't disagree."

"Good. You'd better not. You're the only family I have left."

He reached over and rested his hand upon hers. "I'm not going any-where." Deciding to leave the subject lie for a while, he said, "I came here hoping you'd come for a drive with me."

"Where?'

"Bel Air house."

Curious, she questioned, "Why?"

He mysteriously revealed, "Well, I may or may not have a surprise waiting for you there. It's a little early, but I'm sure if we go now, it will be fine."

Her interest piqued.

"Up for it?" he mildly challenged.

"Perhaps?"

He got up off the grass and offered her his hand. When she grabbed hold, he effortlessly pulled Abi to her feet. The two stood in silence briefly.

"Bye, Mom. I'll be back soon."

Escorted down the hillside, Burton told the guys to follow them before opening the passenger side door. Andrew brought Abi's back-pack from the truck and handed it to her once she got seated.

"Thank you," she said.

"No problem, Miss," he replied, closing the dihedral door.

Burton got behind the wheel. "Ready?" he said, starting the ignition.

The engine growled.

"Yes, I'm good." Wanting an update on things, she asked, "Anything more on Eastwood's condition?"

"All we know is he made it through surgery by some miracle. They have him listed in critical but stable condition."

On the fence, she felt torn to hear that. "If you find out more, please let me know."

"Sure will."

Looking at the time on her phone, Abi got a message from Shane. Reading it, she sighed.

"What's wrong?" Burton asked on their way out the main gates.

"Shane's concerned that I left. Just found out that our math teacher is making him take the quiz we missed last week during study hall. He's reviewing a few concepts quickly but feels unprepared."

"No offense, but how is that your problem?"

"I'm tutoring him. He wants to get good grades. Kinda has to in order to keep his scholarship."

"So, then, it means he's gotta work harder and smarter."

"Yes, but I've put a wrench in our studies after last week. Being away at the All-American event didn't help matters either."

"University won't be any easier. If anything, it'll be harder, especially with the demands of football."

"I've told him that, but I feel like I haven't kept up my end of the bargain."

"I realize you feel some responsibility here, but that's on him. Not you."

She glared slightly in his direction.

Bouncing his sights between her and the road as they merged south on the 405, he stated, "You can't tell me what I'm saying isn't true."

"I just want him to do well. That's all."

"I get that."

Texting Shane, she typed, *do your best and go from there. Answer what you know first, then come back to the other questions. Remember your strategies.* While awaiting his reply, she said, "Guess that means I need to write it tomorrow, too."

"Don't worry. I won't keep you too long," Burton said.

"Speaking of which, you're not even going to give me a hint?"

"No, sorry. It'll ruin the surprise."

The corner of her mouth turned upward slightly. "Why are you so nice to me?"

Unable to believe she asked that question, he replied, "Don't you know the answer by now?"

She tilted her head. "Because you care."

He reached for her hand and gently squeezed it. "You're all I've got now. I have no other family. You're it."

"Well, you're in luck because it seems I'm in the same vote."

He shook his head. "No, you're not."

As much as she hated to hear that, she knew he was right. "I get it. I'll speak to him at some point. Just not now."

Moving across Sunset Boulevard, they turned into the gates of Bel Air. Managing the twists and turns easily, the guys followed suit as they approached his mansion on the hill. When they made the sharp corner and moved up the driveway, Burton waited for the garage to open. Abi noticed a convertible Bentley and two cargo vans near the entrance.

"Whose cars are those?"

"You'll see," he smiled.

Inching their way inside, parking the car on the turn table, he waited for it to swing around. Once stopped, Burton got out and helped Abi. Offering his hand, she stood as he took her backpack from her and slid it onto his shoulder.

Inside the house, they ascended to the first floor in the elevator. When the doors parted, Burton prompted her to exit.

Never having been on that level, she asked, "Which way?"

"Left," he said.

When they rounded the corner, Abi could hear a lot of commotion. "What's going on?"

Suddenly, a pretty blonde woman appeared past the sitting area in the hallway. A bit flustered, she approached them.

Burton offered an outstretched hand. "Rachel! Thank you for coming. Appreciate it."

"Of course, Mr. Baxter." Her attention shifted to Abi.

"Rachel, I'd like you to meet my long-time friend, Abi Acardi. Abi, this is celebrity stylist Rachel Z."

"So nice to meet you."

"Nice to meet you, too." Still confused about what was happening, Abi timidly waited to know more.

"Apologize. We're a bit early. Is that okay?" Burton hoped it wouldn't be a problem.

"That's fine. I believe everything is in order." Rachel walked away.

Burton held out his hand to Abi. "Walk with me," he said.

She obliged happily.

The two followed the woman into the largest guest room at the end of the hall.

Only a few feet inside the door, Abi was speechless. In shock, she quickly covered her mouth with one hand, overwhelmed by what she found.

To the left, racks of beautiful dresses lined the wall, with a few showcased elegantly on mannequins, their fabric flowing gracefully to the floor. To the right was an array of pretty shoes, neatly arranged, while a table of exquisite jewelry sparkled under the lights.

Seeing her reaction, he inched closer to her ear and whispered, "Surprise."

Abi swiftly left the room, embarrassed to cry in front of the ladies.

Burton followed and caught up.

With lips trembling, she turned to him and attempted to speak, the words catching in her throat, choking her with an overwhelming tide of emotion. Clutching her sleeve, she crumpled it in one hand, trying to dab her tears only to smear them. Each breath was a shaky gasp, her chest heaving as she fought for control.

He wrapped his arms around her as she clung to him. "I know you wanted to do this with your Mother, but I think she'd be okay if I helped you. I'm sure she's lovingly watching."

Slowly exhaling, she looked to the ceiling. A long, shuddering sigh escaped her lips as she blotted her face, trying to regain some semblance of composure. With every deep breath, she calmed herself enough to run her trembling hands through her disheveled hair.

Burton let go and gave her some space.

"I can't believe you did this for me." Another sob broke free, making her crumble and bury her face in the crease of his neck.

"Why wouldn't I?" he asked.

"Because of...."

"Shane?"

"Yes."

"I don't have a problem with him if he treats you right. I will always call him out on it if and when he steps out of line."

She didn't know what to say.

Avoiding the QB subject, he tried to gauge her reaction. "So, good surprise? Bad surprise?"

"No. Good surprise." Still trembling, she limply shook her hands out on either side of her. Mustering a timid smile, she said, "Oh, I'm nervous now."

"Don't be. I want you to enjoy this experience."

Abi took another deep breath and exhaled. "Okay..."

He led her back towards the room.

There wasn't a dry eye amongst the women when they walked in.

"I'm sorry about that," Abi apologized anxiously.

Rachel smiled. "That's perfectly fine."

Burton tried to ease her into it. "I'll wait out there. If you find a dress you like, come out and show me."

Abi turned to him and said, "I will."

"Don't worry. We will take good care of her," Rachel said.

On his way out, Burton watched an awestruck Abi shyly fawn over the pretty dresses as the famous stylist showed her the various features of each one. Rounding the corner, he sat on the sectional and opened his laptop to catch up on work.

While Abi walked about, Rachel kept analyzing the girl's movements.

"Feel free to look at everything and tell me if something catches your eye. I took the liberty of picking five of my personal favorites. They are on the mannequins. We created a change room for you in the closet with mirrors and a pedestal. And, once you decide on the final gown, we can make the necessary alterations."

Abi filed through the dresses. Rachel noticed she gravitated most to the powder blue ones. Some were short, flirty, sleek, and sparkly, and others were ball gowns made of silk taffeta.

Opting to try on one boasting a tight-fitting waist, spaghetti straps, and a full skirt with an appropriate side slit, Abi ducked into the closet to try it on. Rachel came in to help.

Turning toward the mirror, the woman zipped her up under the arm.

She stood back and smiled. "What do you think of this one? It's beautiful. Isn't it?"

Speechless, Abi daintily ran her hands over her torso, feeling the texture of the fabric. It fit her like a glove.

"I also have two others with different bodice and neckline variations." She walked out and took one from the rack with a ruched gathering onto one shoulder and brought it to her. "Jessica Serfaty wore this one on the Oscar Red Carpet. Interesting fact – she just got engaged to a billionaire." She left the dress hanging on a hook and went to sift through the gowns again, looking for another one she had in mind before returning. "Oooh! And this one was worn by Elsa Hosk in Cannes. It's strapless," she said while airing the skirt.

"They are both so pretty, but..." Abi gazed at herself in the mirror, "This is the one, I think." She hastily turned to the woman. "I'm so sorry. You put so much work into bringing so many. They are all beautiful. I hate to choose the first one I try on."

"My dear, seeing the look on your face when you saw your reflection is all I needed. You look stunning." She went to the shoes and pulled out a pair of Stuart Weitzman silver sandals. Slipping Abi's feet into them, she fastened the straps.

Abi beamed.

"How are those?"

She shifted to her left, exposing her leg through the skirt's side slit to see them in the mirror. "They're perfect."

"Would you like to show him?"

Barely able to contain herself, Abi nodded and answered, "Yes." Nervous energy flowed through her body. She wondered what Burton would think while walking out of the room. The pretty gown rustled while she moved down the hallway towards him.

He glanced up from his screen as his attention gravitated to her. Lost for words, he put down his computer and stood up from the sofa. All he could do was smile.

The moment she saw his face, both hands raised to cover her mouth as emotions surfaced.

Rachel accompanied her and fixed the skirt, wafting some air underneath to make her more picturesque.

Arms crossed in front of him - there was a brightness to his expression. "You look..."

On pins and needles, she waited to hear what he'd say.

"Beyond gorgeous," he said, realizing somehow she'd transformed from a girl to a young woman in minutes. "Shane will love it."

Abi tearfully agreed as Rachel's assistant blotted her face to keep the droplets from staining the silk.

"But there is one thing missing," Burton said out of the blue.

Abi glanced up at him. "What do you mean?"

When he turned around, Martin appeared with a red box in hand. Passing it along to him, he approached. "I think this will complement it. Rachel, tell me if I'm right."

Recognizing the signature packaging, the woman raised her folded hands to her lips in anticipation.

Not knowing what was happening, Abi watched Burton open it to reveal a diamond necklace, bracelet, and earrings. Brilliantly sparkling, her face reflected the same splendor.

Speechless, she didn't know what to say. "Burton? It's, umm. It's beautiful. But..."

Afraid to know, he asked, "You don't like it?"

"No, I love it." Hesitant, she pointed to the brand name inscribed on the inside. "The name says Cartier."

"Yes," he grinned from ear to ear.

"Isn't it expensive?"

Rachel intervened. "These pieces are a timeless addition to any woman's wardrobe. We consider them precious heirlooms since most get passed down through the generations."

"So, you approve?" Burton asked the stylist.

"Absolutely. The Essential Lines Collection is simple yet refined. It is stately and exudes luxury - a classic choice."

Burton handed Martin the box. Taking the necklace, he held it out in front of him as Abi turned and gathered her hair to the side, lifting it slightly for him to slip it around her neck. When he fastened the clasp, he did the same with the bracelet before reaching for the earrings.

"Sorry, I believe you will have to handle these."

One by one, she put them on.

Rachel stepped forward and twisted Abi's hair. Holding her hand out, blindly given a clip by her assistant, she created a symbolic updo to elongate her face.

A woman wheeled over the three-pane mirror. Opening it fully, Abi stared at her reflection. She felt like a princess.

Standing behind her, sharing the moment, Burton whispered, "So, is this the one?"

Grateful, she nodded and said, "Yes, it is."

He stood beside her. "I'm certain your Mom would love it too."

All the ladies there, including Rachel, tried suppressing their emotions as each applauded.

Intent on leaving them alone, Rachel announced, "Okay, ladies. Let's start bagging the gowns for transport, please."

Now, just the two of them, Abi glanced over her shoulder. "How did you do all of this?"

He chuckled, "I just made a few calls."

She reached and clung to him tightly.

His arms found a home across her shoulders.

"Thank you for everything."

"You're so welcome. I wanted to make this memorable."

"Well, you did." She casually kissed him on the cheek.

Afraid to insight any feelings, Burton had no choice but to draw a line and look away. "I'm glad," he said, backing off slightly.

Her heart gravitated to him and struggled to break from the moment. "I'm, umm, just going to go and get changed."

"Alright. Hurry back, I have another surprise for you."

She nodded excitedly. "Really?"

He smiled. "Yep."

Moving along, Rachel helped Abi carefully slip out of the gown after the seamstress checked the fit.

The short little woman said with a smile. "We don't have to alter it in any way. I think it fits her very well."

With that said, everyone left, allowing her to finish getting dressed. Abi got into her uniform. When she emerged, the stylist said, "I'll have it steamed and delivered here on Saturday," before handing her a blue silk neck and bow tie. "These are for Mr. Baxter. He can decide which one works best with his suit. That way, what he wears matches."

Not getting into specifics about Shane being her date, not Burton, she kindly replied, "Thank you. This has been amazing." Abi offered open arms. "Can I?"

Rachel hesitated but hugged the girl, knowing she wasn't like her other clients. "I am so happy you love it," she said.

"I do."

"My husband met Mr. Baxter at a Sotheby's Art Auction. They catch a Lakers game once in a while. You're a lucky girl."

Abi didn't know how much the woman knew about her and Burton's situation, so she stayed tight-lipped. "Yes, I am very grateful for our friendship."

"I hope I'm not overstepping my bounds, but a word of advice – woman to woman."

"Okay."

"That man is in love with you. I could see it a mile away. Don't wait because, eventually, he will belong to someone else."

Taken off guard, Abi timidly said, "I'll keep that in mind."

She smiled. "I hope so."

On her way out of the room, Abi found him still seated on the sectional, his attention glued to his laptop and phone. When he saw her, he quickly ended his call.

"All done?" he asked.

"Yes."

"Was it everything you imagined?"

"Do you mean the dress or the experience?"

He stood up and tucked his laptop under his arm. "Both."

"Absolutely. A dream come true."

"Good. Mission accomplished."

Still wearing the jewelry, she asked, "What should I do with these?" her hand resting on the necklace.

"I can take them if you like and put them away for safekeeping."

Abi stopped. "Yes, that is a good idea." She turned around and lifted her hair, expecting Burton to unfasten the clip.

Setting his laptop on the side table, he removed the necklace and the bracelet.

One by one, she placed the earrings in the palm of his hand.

Martin appeared with the red box.

Handing him the jewelry, the man secured each piece and left them.

Walking towards the staircase, about to head to the main level, Burton stopped and said, "I want to show you one last thing."

Moving through a sitting room into his bedroom, he bypassed the king-sized bed. When they entered the massive Carrera marble bathroom, beyond it was a fully equipped spa with glam chairs for hair, makeup, and mani-pedis.

"What do you think?" he asked, reading her reaction.

"This is incredible."

He laughed. "It hasn't even been used yet. I believe there's plastic wrap still on some of the chairs."

"I see that."

"So, I thought I'd hire a glam squad so you could get ready here on Saturday. That's if you want to. No pressure."

"But you've already done so much for me." She went quiet.

When she said that, he didn't know what she was thinking.

"If you want to invite your friends for pictures, you can. The upper gardens would make a great backdrop."

Knowing the night was about Shane and her, she felt awkward about accepting his offer. As he stood tall with broad shoulders and a confident exterior, she could feel, deep down, that he wanted that night to be everything she'd always dreamed of.

"Okay," she said. "Glam squad, yes." Pausing, she added, "As for the pictures? I'll have to see."

"I hate that our friendship puts stress on your relationship with him. It's not my intention."

She tilted her head sympathetically. "I know. It's not your fault. It's just…"

"No need to explain."

Abi felt her phone vibrating in her pocket. Glancing at the screen, she saw it was Shane. "Sorry, I've gotta take this."

"Sure, no problem. I'm going to head upstairs. Meet me there when you're done."

"I will."

When he left the room, Abi said, "Hello."

"Hi. Thought I'd call and let you know I'm leaving here now. Where are you? At Laney's?"

"Umm, actually…"

He sighed and knew right away. "You're with him?"

"I went to the graveyard to visit Mom. He found out I was there and dropped by."

"How convenient."

There was silence on the line.

"I've had a memorable afternoon, Shane. Please, I don't want to fight."

He backtracked and changed his approach. "I don't either. But you know he and I don't see eye to eye."

"I realize, but I'm here because he arranged a surprise."

"What's that."

"Remember at the observatory when I told you about how I always dreamed of shopping for a dress with my Mom?"

"I remember."

"Given my life now, I had to let go of that dream. Initially, I was going to borrow a dress from Laney since I didn't have the money to buy one and certainly wasn't going to ask my Dad. But, today, Burton introduced me to this woman named Rachel Z. She brought a selection of dresses for me to choose from, and I picked a really pretty one, just for you."

"As much as I love to hear that, I could have bought you a dress, Abs."

"I know, but I would've never asked." By the combative sound in his voice, she figured she should end this subject of conversation. "Look, I'm sorry. It was just nice to enjoy a moment of happiness for once, especially after the weekend we'd had."

He hated himself for what he said. "I'm sorry. It's fine. Don't apologize. I'm the one who should be doing that, not you."

Abi inhaled delicately and nervously bit her nail.

"I can hardly wait to see you in the dress."

"Please don't be mad," she said.

He sighed. "Abs, I'm not mad. I want to be the guy you come to for things like this. The one you confide in. It's hard that someone else in your life has that job, and I don't."

"It's not my intention."

With genuine sincerity, he replied, "I know."

"I often feel torn between you two. It's so hard..." Saying it caused her to sob.

He knew she was upset. "I'll do my best to get along with the guy. You're under enough stress. You don't need this on top of every-thing else."

She tried to compose herself.

"So, where are you? Can I pick you up?"

"Sure. I'm at his place on Chalon Road."

Recalling that she'd pointed where Black Lyon had taken her that Friday night, he said, "Wait? The mansion across the canyon?"

"That's the one. Text me when you're close. I'll come outside."

"I'll see you shortly, then."

Abi smiled. "See you soon. Love you."

"Love you too."

Ending the call, she left Burton's stately room and walked up the staircase. There, she found him discussing business with Martin. Hold-ing back, she listened.

"You must decide whether to accept or cancel the appearances scheduled over Christmas in Japan. Red Dragon's team needs to know in a day or two. We can't delay it any longer," his right-hand man said while referring to his iPad.

"I'm still thinking about it."

"This is a big opportunity to introduce Nightfall to that corner of the world. Crypto is a driving force there. We need to capture that market."

"Fine. Go ahead. Confirm with them. I'll make it work."

"That's wise, Sir," he said. "Next, we've finalized the monthly fee schedule for vault members. I've emailed it to you. On top of that, the Clubs in Miami and Ibiza should be up and running after the holidays. In Chicago, we've narrowed it down to three properties. I'll send you the proposals for each. See which one fits the brand best. Once you decide, we will get our design team moving quickly."

"Good."

"Today, we have been contacted by twelve more talk shows and received over two hundred interview requests."

"Axe the talk shows and send me the interview list. I'll review it."

"Very well, Sir."

A little frustrated, he asked, "What else?"

The older gentleman hesitated.

Burton picked up on it. "I know…"

"We must discuss the matter of Miss Abi's ransom, Sir."

This angered him. "They defaulted on that agreement after what happened in Vegas. As far as I can see, it's now null and void."

"It seems the new person at the helm doesn't think so, Master B."

"Leave that with me. I'll deal with it," Burton said sternly. "Anything else?"

Martin caught sight of Abi coming up the stairs. Giving him the eye, he said, "No. That's all for now," and left the room.

Burton watched as she walked over slowly. He could tell she'd been crying. Getting up from the sofa, he asked, quite concerned, "What did he say to you?"

"Nothing, I'm fine." She didn't want to set him off. "Shane is on his way to pick me up."

"I could have driven you."

"I know, but we need to instill some boundaries."

Confused, he said, "Boundaries? What do you mean?"

Abi looked to the sky in desperation. "He hates you! You hate him! And I'm stuck in the middle!"

"Hey, wait a minute. As you've just heard, I don't have time to hate the guy," he stated jokingly.

Not exactly liking his humorous approach, she stood there with arms crossed.

"So, what is it? He didn't like that I bought you a dress and hired a glam squad? This is such petty BS, Abs. I am doing these things to show you I care. In a roundabout way, it's for him, too." He walked up to her. "You're my best friend. I love you whether he likes it or not."

"And I appreciate that, but when it comes to you guys, I'm Switzerland, remember?"

No matter what he thought of Shane Coppersmith, he figured he'd have to do what was in her best interest.

"I'll make more of an effort. Just don't tell him when I do something nice for you. Then, he won't get jealous. Problem solved."

"So, you're blaming me? Basically, you're saying I should lie to my boyfriend? Great advice, Burton."

"That's not what I meant."

Getting a notification from Shane, she saw he was almost there. Dropping a pin on her location, she said, "Can you please tell the man at the gate to let him in?"

"Sure." Burton picked up the nearest handset and put it to his ear. Pressing a button, he said, "Hi, Max. Can you let Mr. Coppersmith through when he arrives?" With a pause, he added, "Great. Thanks." Saddened to see the happiness and excitement from that afternoon had faded, he offered open arms.

She hesitantly fell into them.

"Everything is going to be okay. I promise."

Abi nodded.

When Max notified Burton of the visitor's arrival, Burton said, "Come on. I'll walk you out."

Shane saw the two of them descending the stairs through the glass walls. His blood boiled.

Opening the front door for her to leave, Burton followed and watched Shane get out of the Jeep and greet her with a kiss.

"Hey, Abs." Realizing she wasn't overly excited to see him, he tried to save face. "Ready to go?"

"Yeah." She turned to Burton. "Thank you for everything. Have a good night."

"You're welcome." He waved to her and said, "You too."

While they drove away, Burton stood in the doorway, his hands buried in his pockets, unhappy with how the day ended.

Driving down Chalon Road, Abi asked glumly, "Can you just take me to Laney's? I'm pretty tired."

Shane turned to her. "Sure. No problem."

He kept his eyes on the road, hoping she'd say something. Stopping at the Bel Air gates intersection, waiting to turn left on Sunset, he sat back in his seat and rested his head.

"What's happening to us?" he asked. There was such sorrow to his tone.

She looked forward. Intent on easing his mind, she said, "I just wish you would trust me and not be concerned about Burton. I'm with you and he's with Sara – end of story."

Proceeding through the intersection, he thought about what she said. "It's not that I don't trust you. It's him I don't trust."

"Jealousy is not an attractive trait, Shane."

Abruptly making a right at the next street, he pulled over. "Abi, I'm not jealous. I love you, and I'm fighting to keep you in my life."

She calmly zeroed in on him. "He knew how much that experience meant to me. With my Mother no longer here to share it, he helped me make the best of it. I needed that today after visiting the graveyard for the first time. I had a wonderful afternoon until…"

"I ruined it…" He finished her sentence.

She pulled the neckties Rachel gave her from her bag. "These are for you. They match my dress." A few tears fell.

When she covered her face with her hands, he felt horrible. "Abs, I'm sorry."

"I need this feud between you to end," she whimpered.

He reached over slowly and wrapped his arm around her.

"Why can't we just go back to the way things were? You were confident about us. And happy. So was I."

"Abs, since we met, my life has changed immensely. I never knew I could feel this way about someone. Now, I'm just afraid to lose you."

"Then don't. Don't lose me by putting a wedge between us." She thought of his feelings, too. "Look, I placed boundaries on Burton."

"You did?"

"He's agreed to step back. Besides, he's focused on Sara."

Shane reevaluated it all. "Okay," he said. "Clean slate?"

"No. I want to continue exactly where we left off last week. I felt so much closer to you, then. I need that now."

"I can do that."

Desperate to kiss her, he sweetly cupped her cheek with his hand. Caressing one side with his thumb, he gently pressed his lips to hers and tried to be the strong guy she wanted by her side.

A vehicle behind them honked its horn.

Reluctantly parting, he put the truck in gear and held her hand. "Are we good?"

Wanting to keep the peace, she said, "We're good."

Shane waved the vehicle onward and made a U-turn before continuing down the road. Moving toward Sunset Plaza Drive, maneuvering the hillside's winding curves, Abi texted Laney to let her know she was almost there. Homes on either side, with manicured hedges and ornate trees, soon they made it to the end of Rising Glen Road. Laney had opened the gate for them to drive through.

Shane parked near the front door and switched off the ignition. About to get out, he said, "I'll walk you inside."

Mentally exhausted, she said, "No, it's okay. It's been a long day. Can we talk later tonight?"

"Sure. Whatever you'd like," he replied, not knowing what to make of it.

"Sorry. I just need a minute to breathe."

"I understand."

"This has nothing to do with us. It's a grief thing."

He rubbed her hand. "I'm always here."

"I know," she smiled, "Thank you." Opening the door, she got out on her own. "I'll call you before I go to bed. I promise."

"Sounds good."

She waved to him and shut the door. Watching as he drove away, Abi found Laney standing there waiting.

"What's going on between you two? Did you have a fight?"

"Well, maybe. I'd rather not talk about it."

"Okay…" Laney could tell whatever happened was still fresh. "Are you hungry, then? Michelle made chicken tacos. Interested?"

"Yes, thank you. That would be great."

86

Sealed with a Kiss

Ready for bed, now with a full stomach, Abi reviewed some homework and looked at her phone. Walking to the glass wall, she peered at the canyon painted crimson as the sun descended in the western sky. Reflecting on her dinner conversation with Laney, she realized that Shane and Burton cared for her in distinct ways. As the girl pointed out, she was entitled to have male friends and knew Shane shouldn't feel threatened by Burton as long as she was committed to their relationship. Turning around, she went and sat on her bed.

"Laney's right. I shouldn't have to choose," she whispered while dimming the lights to FaceTime her boyfriend. As it rang on his end, she waited. About to end the call when he didn't answer, believing he might not want to talk, she suddenly saw him pop up on the screen.

Bare-chested and wrapped in a white towel, he said, "Sorry, Abs. I just got out of the shower. Give me one second?"

"Sure. Take your time."

Able to see the phone tossed on the bed, she heard him wrestle with a sweatshirt and shorts over damp skin. Soon after, he jumped onto the covers and said, "Hey. Sorry about that."

"That's okay." She watched him run his hand through his wet hair. "I'm about to do the same. I plan to turn in early tonight."

"I'm glad you called."

Abi wanted to keep the lines of communication open. "I'm sorry I've been all over the map recently."

"Don't apologize. I know you're going through a lot."

"Yeah. That's an understatement."

"If anything, this is my fault. I added to your stress and ruined your day." He paused. "Look, I've been thinking. With everything we've been through, maybe we should spend some time together – just you and me. You know, go on a date. Reconnect and have some fun. Maybe you could come here tomorrow. I'll order dinner from Drago. I'm sure Jacob would like to see you."

"I'd love that."

"Remember, I leave Thursday morning. We are back late Friday night. Our game on Saturday is at two o'clock."

"I remember."

"Will you be okay while I'm gone?"

"I'll probably chill out and stay in my room every day after school to rest up and regroup for the weekend."

"Speaking of that..."

She watched him get off the bed and virtually move through his closet. Flipping the camera around, he pointed at the dark navy suit hanging up and the necktie she gave him paired with a white shirt, brown shoes, and a matching leather belt.

"Does this work or..." He shifted to the opposite side of the closet. "Do you want me in a black one instead? More formal, with the bow tie."

Never having been to a homecoming dance before, she said, "I think either one is perfect. You'd know better than me."

"I know the guys are leaning toward the navy versus black."

"Then do that. I think it would look great with my dress."

"Decision made."

A silence fell upon them while he got comfortable on his bed again. "So, how is it living at Laney's?"

"Pretty nice. The house is beautiful."

"But?"

Abi exhaled. "It's not a long-term solution. I can't live here forever. I've got to figure out what I'm gonna do."

"Well, you are always welcome here."

"Thank you for that, but I'm kinda scared of your Dad."

He chuckled. "I can understand why."

"I just can't go home. The last thing I want is to see that woman there."

Witnessing her frustration, he said, "Well, we can always get our own place. My trust fund allows for that."

Never having considered it, knowing it was a big step, she muttered, "Umm... I'd have to think about it."

"No pressure. I just hate that you're living out of a suitcase."

"Lesser of two evils in my eyes," she replied. "I'll figure something out. Besides, you've got enough happening this week. You should focus on winning games."

"Abs, I'll never be too busy to think of you." He recalled the first time he saw her. "You know, on Orientation Day, I walked into the foyer believing senior year would be the same as all the others. Then I saw you, and everything changed."

She smiled and tilted her head.

"When we bumped into each other in the parking garage, I felt like it was fate in a way – especially when you talked football," he laughed. "And don't get me started on the whole stats analysis thing," he chuckled fondly. Gazing into her eyes on the screen, he added, "That sealed it for me."

She laughed. "What? That I could record stats?"

"No, that you cared enough about me to do that."

His voice sounded so grateful it made her heart leap. "Is that right?" she blushed.

"Yeah. I knew then we were perfect for each other."

"You're so sweet."

Unafraid to say it, he divulged, "There was this feeling I got." He placed his hand over his heart. "Right here. Since then, I've learned who you are as a person. And I love her."

Taken aback, she smiled and shyly shot him a look.

"What?" he asked, unsure what to make of it.

Overwhelmed with emotion, she said, "I wish I could kiss you right now."

"Really?" he grinned from ear to ear.

"Yes."

Shane could tell she was dead serious. It gave him an idea. "Well, on that happy note, I should let you get some sleep."

"I probably should." She kissed the screen. "Goodnight. Guess that will have to do for now."

"Suppose so," he replied happily. "Night, Abs. I Love you," he said, hoping she'd say it back.

"Love you too."

Relieved, he waved before ending their FaceTime call.

Staring at the black screen, Abi felt her heart aching. "You've got to appreciate who God brings into your life because it is for a reason." Immersed in what she thought to be someone else's dream, Abi flopped into the pillows, thinking of him. Looking through a few pictures they'd taken together, she could see what she felt for Shane was still very strong. Releasing a lighthearted sigh, she went into the bathroom, seemingly floating mid-air. Quickly showering, she soon got out and finished getting ready for bed.

While brushing her teeth, all the nice things Shane said resonated, making her tear up. He was everything she had always hoped for despite their struggles.

"Mom would've loved you," Abi said quietly, remembering her absence.

Suddenly, Laney hurried past the door, sliding her slippers along the hardwood before clicking down the marble slab staircase.

Abi wrapped herself in a robe, assuming Shawn had arrived based on her friend's urgency. Wanting to check on her, she walked down the hall, leaned over the railing, and listened. "Lane?" she shouted, her voice echoing through the massive home. "Is everything okay?"

"Umm, yes!" she yelled from inside the perfect pantry. "Just have a sugar craving!"

"What would Michelle say!" Abi replied humorously on her way downstairs.

"Don't you dare!" the girl yelled, knowing Michelle would outright disapprove.

Just as Abi stepped foot on the main level, the doorbell sounded.

"Can you get that? It's probably Shawn!"

Abi walked over to the large set of doors. Swinging it open, she froze.

"Shane? What are you doing here?"

Interrupting her, he scooped her up as his heart beat out of his chest. "I wanted to kiss you, too." With arms slipping to her waist, Shane flexed his muscles and effortlessly lifted her off the floor. She instinctively wrapped her legs around him as his embrace tightened. Longing for her, his kisses, soft and gentle at first, slowly grew with intensity. Immersed in each other, the rest of the world faded and soon ceased to exist. Parting briefly to catch their breath, Shane knew Abi was his person - the one heaven sent for him to love.

With her body trembling, he looked at her and grinned. It left her speechless.

Amidst the rush of emotions, Laney appeared. "Holy moly, that was smokin' hot!" she giggled while snacking on popcorn. "Get a room!"

Snuggling into Shane's neck, embarrassed to know her friend witnessed everything, she felt her feet touch the floor as they joyfully reveled in the aftermath.

Since the show ended, Laney went about her business.

Alone, Shane rested his forehead against hers. "I hate when we argue."

"Me too," she whispered.

Kissing her sweetly, she leaned back.

"I can't believe you drove all the way here just for this."

"How could I not?" he smirked mischievously. Knowing it was late, he said, "So, I guess I should go so you can get some sleep."

Stepping away, still holding her hand, not wanting to leave, he felt her pull him back before she placed her hands on his cheeks and kissed him innocently. Standing there in awe, falling for Abi all over again, he hugged her and sealed it with a kiss before burying his face into the hollow of her neck. "Sweet dreams, Abs."

"You too," she whispered.

"I'll pick you up at eight, okay?"

"I'll be ready."

Kissing her one last time, letting go at the very last second, he waved before getting in his Jeep and pulling away.

Laney appeared atop the stairs after Abi closed and locked the door. Pressing the gate button on her phone app, she asked, "Why didn't he stay?"

Joining her, Abi replied, "It's not that I didn't want him to. We just aren't there yet."

The blondie was surprised. "Well, nothing like a slow burn to keep the romance alive."

"Yes, I suppose so," she said, reveling in the aftermath of the loving moment.

Putting two and two together, Laney exclaimed, "Oh... Wait, I get it now. You two haven't, you know..."

Uncomfortable with the topic, she said sharply, "No."

"How on earth are you dating Shane Coppersmith and not wanting to just....umm, yeah, all the time..." The girl looked away as if creepily visualizing it.

Abi ducked into her room to avoid the awkward conversation at all costs. Leaving her friend in the hall, she said, "Goodnight, Laney!" while slowly closing the door, hoping she'd get the hint. Watching the girl accept defeat, Abi shut it entirely.

Now alone, she got under the covers and set her alarm. Replaying Shane's romantic gesture sent an overwhelming rush of emotions. Texting him a pink heart, he, in turn, sent the cutest GIF of a big teddy bear daydreaming under a tree with hearts fluttering above his head.

It made her wish he'd stayed.

87

She said...

Dreaming of Shane half the night and Burton invading the other, Abi woke up stressed. Forcing herself out of bed, she quickly walked into the bathroom to prepare for the day. Still reeling from her romantic moment with Shane last night, she unknowingly struck a comparison to her experience with Burton in Tahoe. Guilt ravaged her heart. She couldn't help but continuously wince.

"Shane deserves better," she said, disappointed in herself.

Wishing her Mom was there to sit on the bed and share her words of wisdom, the void left behind expanded and became more visible. Aware she was close and always listening, Abi said, "What do I do, Mom?"

Laney's comment echoed through her mind. Conflicted, she whispered, "How do I date Shane Coppersmith and not...?" Blushing, she chuckled and said, "With great difficulty." Knowing she wanted to move to the next level in their relationship, she hoped things would flow naturally if and when the time came. Not wanting to stress over it, the thought was scary. It was a big step. With that, Burton came to mind. She knew the makings of this decision would ultimately affect him. The last thing she wanted was to hurt his feelings, especially after what he did for her yesterday. She still couldn't believe he arranged for the dress fitting. It was like a fairytale dream. The magnitude of that could never be measured. It was one of the sweetest and most considerate things anyone had ever done for her. Counting herself fortunate to have him in her life, she didn't know how to repay him for his kindness above all things. Torn, she exhaled just as a knock came to the door. Abi opened it.

"Morning, girlfriend. How did you sleep?"

Annoyed by how refreshed Laney looked, Abi said, "Not as good as you, apparently."

The pretty blonde was confused.

Clarifying, Abi said, "I had a rough night."

"I can see that. Why? Were you dreaming of two handsome men?"

Stunned, Abi happened to smirk.

The girl pointed at her. "See, I knew it. What did I just say?" Analyzing Abi's reaction, she added, "Can I offer a little advice?"

"Sure."

"Go with the flow. Focus on today, not two or three years down the road. You're seventeen and dating the captain of the football team. Hell, he's on track to play in the NFL. Embrace these treasured days. They go by fast."

Almost convinced, she replied, "Perhaps you're right."

"Besides, Burton is with SWAT girl and is too old for you right now. Pretty sure it's not even legal, you know."

Abi couldn't believe she used Burton's exact words to describe their situation. "Yeah, I get it."

"Good. See, when it comes to matters of the heart, I'm usually bang on," she boasted with enormous pride. "Ready to head out soon?"

"Shane is going to pick me up. Hope that's alright?"

"Sure, no problem. I'm in the mood for a race to school," she said while they descended the stairs.

Hearing them, Michelle quickly stuffed the straws in their protein smoothies and finished brewing their Americanos.

Abi received a text. "He just pulled up."

Laney pressed the gate button and watched on the cameras as Shane drove into the courtyard. "Invite him in. It's okay," she said.

"I told him I'd be out in a second. Maybe you want to come with us this morning?"

"And miss the chance to challenge Coppersmith? I don't think so." Laney realized Abi assumed she was serious. "I'm just joking. I need my vehicle after school today. Some of us don't have security to drive us around everywhere."

"I wouldn't either if it weren't for..."

"Burton," she mentioned dreamily.

"To tell you the truth, I miss my Mini Cooper. Guess my Dad has probably sold it by now."

"Maybe not?"

Abi tilted her head.

"Okay... Maybe he did."

"Here you go, ladies. Two smoothies and coffees to go."

"Thank you, Michelle! You're the best!" Laney praised.

"Yes, thank you so much, Michelle. It was a great way to begin the day yesterday, too. Appreciate it."

"You're very welcome." The woman replied brightly. "Have a good day, girls."

They waved on the way out.

When Laney opened the BMW convertible's garage door, Abi dipped under it and walked out. There, she found Shane leaning against the truck and checking his phone. Staring at him, she thought he looked sharp in his navy khakis, uniform-collared shirt, and grey jacket.

"Hey," he said in a sexy tone. "Let me help you." Taking the coffee cup from her, freeing up one hand, he opened the passenger side, allowing her to settle in easily.

The scent of his cologne caught Abi's attention. The spicy fragrance had citrus undertones and a deep masculine base of amber, and cedarwood.

Reaching across to place the coffee in the holder, his face mere inches from hers, he said, "Morning." Confidently flashing a sexy expression, he kissed her lovingly.

Breathless as he backed away and closed her door, she counted herself lucky to be with him despite their recent challenges. Trying to stay grounded, Abi watched as he got behind the wheel. At the same time, Laney backed out and stopped beside them. Her window rolled down.

"Ready, Shane?" The pretty blonde gripped the wheel.

Understanding what she meant, he prompted with a wave of his hand. "After you."

The second the gate slid open, the BMW drove off, leaving them in her dust.

"Now, normally, I would go after her, but the guys are parked right outside, and I don't exactly want that to get back to *you know who*, so..."

"Probably a good call," Abi giggled, waving to Andrew, Matt, and Ted on their way past. Exchanging the smoothie for the coffee, she savored the espresso and closed her eyes momentarily.

Shane reached over to hold her hand. "How did you sleep?"

"Not the best. Just going through the motions."

"I know every day is tough. But I'm here."

Feeling his sincerity, she smiled. "Thank you. I appreciate that more than you know."

While following Laney, they turned onto Sunset Boulevard. Shane anticipated an opening in the left lane and quickly snuck in. Passing her by, he waved.

The girl wasn't happy.

"This happens every other morning," he said.

"What does."

"The race to school. Lane's always on time and has a mean competitive streak. Kinda reminds me of someone else I know." He squeezed her hand and shot her a sexy smirk.

Suddenly, the Bimmer passed them and zigzagged three car lengths ahead.

"Umm, Shane Coppersmith, did you just get duped by Laney Bass?"

His eyes caught the black SUV behind them. "Apparently so," he chuckled and refrained from trying to keep up with her.

As expected, the girl beat them to school by a mile. Passing the security gatehouse and not seeing Gerald there, Abi knew she needed to find him – and today. She only wanted to understand why he left and if he was safe. Opting not to bother Shane with it, she planned to go hunting for Gerald while he was at football practice. Planning to enlist the guys to help, she figured she'd be safe with them tagging along.

About to reverse into his parking spot, Shane saw Laney bolt.

Gathering their things, the two left the Jeep and started walking as the blonde turned and yelled from the elevator, "I'll see you up there! Shawn is waiting for me!"

Abi acknowledged her as Andrew and the team approached.

"Morning, Miss," the big guy greeted, with a bottled protein shake in his hand.

"Morning, guys," she said.

Ted nodded. So did Matt.

On the move, with twenty minutes to spare, Abi looked out at the gatehouse as the man inside watched them like a hawk. Waiting for the elevator, they got in when the doors parted. Everyone seemed more tired than usual.

Arriving in the courtyard, they found most of their friends hanging around the artisan steps, enjoying the sun's warmth despite the wind being a bit cool.

"Morning, you guys," Mei said with her arms hooked around Adrian. Ben and Ming looked on.

Noticing Abi was quiet, Mei asked, "We missed you yesterday. Everything okay?"

"Yes and no," Abi divulged. "My Dad showed up here, and we didn't see eye to eye, so I took a break from everything and went to the graveyard to visit my Mom."

Upon hearing that, the girl looked slightly panicked, not knowing what to say.

To save her, Abi added, "Don't worry. I'm doing better now."

Able to breathe, Ming said, "Oh, that's good. I'm happy to hear that."

Abi, deciding never to mention it again, spotted Jade and Owen walking by. Not having talked to her best friend since yesterday, she missed hanging out with her. Sadly, dating Owen Karp meant Jade was running in a different circle of friends.

Amidst it all, Shane saw a familiar face emerge from the main office. "Hey, man!"

Turning around, Abi found a sharply dressed Reggie Wilson approaching.

"Hey," Reggie greeted, reaching for a manly dap and pat on the back. "Good to see you." Zeroing in on the girl beside him, he offered open arms. "I'm so sorry to hear about your Mom. My deepest condolences."

"Thank you. Appreciate that."

Since she looked uncomfortable, Shane purposefully changed the subject for Abi's sake. "So, what are you doin' here? Taking a break from the corporate world?" he asked him.

"Yeah, you could say that." Reggie immediately caught sight of Jade in Owen Karp's arms. He pretended like it didn't bother him. "Came to settle my tuition."

The QB thought he heard him wrong. "Tuition? What do you mean?"

Unable to move his eyes away from Jade, he replied blindly, "As of Monday, I'm back. I hope to speak to Coach this afternoon. We have a Championship to win."

"That's awesome, man!"

"Yeah. Just have a few more things to finalize this week before starting my new life."

Abi glanced at her boyfriend.

"New life? What do you mean?" Shane hoped he'd clarify.

"I emancipated. It was the only way. Otherwise, I wouldn't have the freedom to do anything."

"How did your Dad take the news?"

Reggie smirked. "Don't know. He should find out within the hour. I'm sure shit will hit the fan then."

Jade saw him and froze.

"You were at Nightfall on Saturday." Trying to fish for information, Abi knew he was using Burton's vault. "What were you doing in Vegas?"

His attention gravitated elsewhere. Not hearing a word she said, Reg asked, "What's the 411 on those two? Has she said anything to you, Abi?"

It was clear things between them weren't over. "I believe she's biding her time. She still loves you. But she's hurt and feels rejected."

His thoughts were noticeably smoldering as he glanced at his watch.

"Reg?" Shane said, trying to break the guy from his daze.

"Hold that thought, man. I'll be right back."

They watched Reggie confidently walk across the courtyard towards the girl. The volume of the crowd around them suddenly increased, and it wasn't hard to figure out why.

He stopped a few feet away to avoid invading her space too soon. "Morning," he said calmly.

"Hi," she replied, looking annoyed.

"Can we talk?"

A little hesitant, feeling Owen's arm wrap around her waist, she said, "There's nothing to say."

"Just a moment of your time. That's all..." Knowing she would love his gentlemanly demeanor, he added, "Please..." in the sincerest tone.

Unable to disconnect from his intense stare, she told Owen, "I'll be right back."

Leery of what was happening, the junior QB replied, "Sure."

Having no choice but to watch the two move further away, Owen scanned the courtyard as every set of eyes did the same.

Stopping a fair distance from the crowd, Jade crossed her arms defensively. She could see the love still burning in Reggie's eyes. Hurt by what happened between them, she snapped, "What are you doing here?"

He didn't know where to start.

"Hurry, please. I need to get back to…"

"Owen Karp." There was a hint of dislike in his voice.

Mad, she replied loudly, "Yeah, well, at least he cares about me!"

Ready to step in to protect her, Owen stormed over. Standing firm behind the girl, he asked, "Is this guy bothering you?"

Reg could tell he wanted a fight.

The team quickly gathered to wait in the wings in case they needed to break it up.

Tension building, Jade sighed. "It's okay. I'm fine. Please, go and wait over there."

He gave Reg the eye before backing off.

When he was far enough away, she stated, "Make it fast. I need to get to class."

"Now you're with him?"

"What did you expect, Reg? For me to sit around and watch you marry into royalty while my heart broke into a million pieces?" Her eyes welled.

"Jade…" He reached for her.

Not wanting any contact, she said, "No," and immediately took a big step back. "You moved on. So I did, too." A few tears fell across her cheeks, making her quickly look away. She didn't want him to see the depth of her pain.

"I haven't moved on."

Confused, she said, "What?"

"I came here today to get you back."

Stunned, she quickly accused, "So, you think I'm just gonna forget all about this and run back to you with open arms? May I remind you, you gave up on us, remember?"

"I know, and I'm sorry. I hate myself for that."

"You should." Her tone softened.

"Look, if you tell me it's over and want me to leave, I will honor that and never bother you again. But I need to know one thing. Do you still have love for me in your heart?"

"Why does it matter what I feel? You're engaged."

More than ready to address that, he answered, "Not anymore."

Suddenly, their conversation took a turn.

"I don't understand."

His sights moved to the ground beneath his feet. "Where do I start? There's a lot I need to tell you. So much has happened."

She waited for him to elaborate.

Having difficulty building the courage to say what he wanted to convey, Reggie looked away and slipped his hands in his pockets. "I left my family, Jade."

"What? Why?"

"I left them - for you."

Jade realized the gravity of that and tilted her head frustratingly. "Oh, Reg. What have you done?"

"There's more. I came to tell you that as of Monday, I'm returning to school to finish the year and hopefully graduate with a championship win."

"So, you're returning to play football?"

He swiftly replied, "Not entirely."

"Just spit it out, please!"

Confident, he zeroed in on her. "I severed ties with my father. Moved out. Got my own place. Gave up my position in the family business and started day trading. Leveraging the money from that, I invested well. During the recent bullish run, I made enough to sustain myself for a while. So, long story short – as of yesterday, I'm free to make my own decisions."

She didn't look interested.

Inching closer, he reached for her hands. "I hear there is a homecoming dance this Saturday."

"Owen already asked me to go with him. You're too late."

Without skipping a beat, he said, "Not if you say yes," and promptly got on one knee and pulled a small black leather box from his inside pocket.

Her heart dropped. "What are you doing?"

Through the gasps blanketing the crowd around them, Reg presented it to her, revealing the most beautiful three-carat oval stone with an ornate diamond-encrusted band.

The chimes sounded and echoed through the buildings. Nobody moved a muscle as Reggie continued.

"Jade. Even though we started dating weeks ago, I have been in love with you for two years. Admiring you from afar, afraid to speak to you, I waited, hoping you'd be mine one day. Since our first date, life just seemed that much brighter. It was like living in black and white, and you brought an array of colors. While I was gone, I had a lot of time to think. I imagined my life in the future, and you were there - no one else. I need you by my side from now until the day I die. So, Jade Webber? Will you do me the greatest honor of becoming my wife?"

Hands trembling, tears streaming down her cheeks, Jade felt mixed emotions. As she gasped for air, her heart beat uncontrollably. "This is crazy."

"I don't care. I love you—I always have and will. I'd marry you today if you'd let me."

All their friends held their breath as the girl looked deeply into his eyes. They could hear a pin drop while awaiting her answer.

Covering her mouth, afraid for the words to escape, she nodded and whimpered, "Yes."

A joyful smile broke Reggie's stressful expression as he took the ring from the box and slipped it onto the third finger of her left hand. Rising off his knee, he wrapped his arms around her waist and swung her around. Lovingly kissing her with every ounce of his being, her feet slowly landed on the ground.

The courtyard erupted with whistles, applause, and enthusiastic banter.

"She said yes!" Reggie shouted with their hands held high in the air.

Witnessing the special moment, embraced in Shane's arms, Abi patted the tears from her face before clapping and cheering along with everyone around them. "I can't believe they're getting married," she sobbed. "That was just beautiful." Embarrassed, she noticed she wasn't the only one crying. Every girl seemed enamored by the scene unfolding. Recalling what Shane said during his homecoming proposal - that it would be the first of many milestones in their future - she smiled fondly at the thought of him asking her one day. Sadly, at the same time, she witnessed Owen quickly leave the courtyard before anyone could say anything to him. It was unfortunate that he got caught in the crossfire.

Their close-knit group rushed over and gathered to hug and congratulate the newly engaged couple. The girls fawned over the ring while the guys offered gentlemanly handshakes to commemorate Reggie's big moment.

Amidst it all, Jade looked for Owen. But he was nowhere to be seen. Feeling bad, she knew she'd have to find him and explain.

The last to greet their friends, Abi hugged Jade as the two girls cried. "We are so excited for you both."

Shane's hand resting on the small of her back reminded her he was there.

"Thank you," her friend replied, still looking in disbelief at the ring on her finger.

Leaving Jade free for Shane, Abi switched to Reg.

Still crying, Reg knew how happy Abi was for them. The pretty girl could barely speak.

"What is the meaning of this?" the headmaster grumpily shouted as students dispersed. "Everyone! Proceed to class! Now!"

Reggie turned to Jade. "Can we get out of here? There is so much I still need to say."

Without hesitation, she agreed. "Yes. Let's go."

As the two walked away happily, Shane and Abi waved.

For some reason, Abi felt slightly jealous since they were embarking on this journey to adulthood faster than she was. Daydreaming about being married one day, with a house and children, a part of her wanted to speed up time. But with Shane by her side, she knew they had a long road ahead before they could even contemplate such a monumental decision.

Moving with the flow of students into the lobby and up the stairs, Shane said, "Penny for your thoughts," while walking down the hall, listening to the announcements.

About to round the corner and enter the class, she said, "I just hope someday that will be us."

Without hesitation, he smiled. "I guarantee it."

88

Where is Gerald?

When Abi got to Study Hall, she prepared to write the math unit test. Told to sit apart from Shane, she answered the questions under the watchful eye of Professor Walker and caught the handsome QB looking at her intensely from time to time. She wondered what he was thinking.

When the chimes sounded, she handed it in.

"Thank you, Miss Acardi," the man said.

She nodded quietly.

"I was sorry to learn about your Mother's passing. My deepest sympathies to you."

"Thank you, Sir."

"Should you need some leniency during this time, let me know. Deadlines can be flexible in light of your circumstances."

"Appreciate that, Sir. But I'm doing okay."

"I'm glad to hear it."

Abi mustered a smile and walked to Shane waiting by the staircase.

"So, how'd you do?"

"Pretty good. One question made me stop and think."

He had a hunch which one it was. "Number nine?"

"Yes," she pointed and laughed.

"I didn't know how to answer that, so I wrote down the equation and went for process marks - if nothing else," he laughed.

Meeting up alongside Adrian, Mei, Ben, and Ming, they got in the elevator to descend to the parking garage.

"Closed practice, again, Cap?" Ben questioned.

Shane checked his phone to confirm. "Yeah, that's the word on the street."

When the doors parted, they exited one by one.

"So, I'm heading out with the guys then?" Abi assumed.

"Yeah, sorry. Coach wants us to focus. We have another big week ahead. The season officially begins on Thursday. Three games in three days," he explained. "The media might get crazy. We'll have to see."

"It's fine. Don't worry."

"Can we meet up later?"

"Absolutely," she said with a smile.

Matt pulled up as Andrew and Ted emerged from taking the stairwell.

Hand in hand, Shane walked to the Jeep with Abi by his side. Tossing his backpack in the front, he turned and pulled her in close. "I'll call you when we finish for the day. Are you still up to pizza at my place tonight?"

"For sure. I'm looking forward to it." She nudged him gently. "We haven't had time alone in a while."

Leaning in, he kissed her sweetly, knowing those words would fuel him through the grueling two-hour workout ahead.

With the guys watching, Shane backed away. "Think we can ditch your shadows?"

"I'll see what I can do," she said.

He stole one last embrace. "I gotta go. I'll see you later."

"Okay. Good luck."

"Thanks."

As he left, Abi waved while Andrew walked up beside her.

"What's the plan, Miss?"

Fully knowing how to spend the next few hours, she said, "I need to find someone. Can you help me?"

"Certainly."

"But, first, I need to make sure Burton is free." She dialed his number. Hearing it ring, she heard him hastily pick up.

"Hey, Abs? What's going on? Everything okay?"

She could feel he was going from zero to sixty. "Calm down. I'm fine."

"No, really. What's wrong?"

"I need your help."

"Where are you?" There was an urgency in his voice.

She smiled at Andrew and Ted. "With your guys at school."

Without hesitation, he stated, "What do you need?"

"The school's gatehouse security guard disappeared. I need to know why."

"Alright. I'm listening."

"His name is Gerald Thomas. I'm scared for his safety. The men who took his place look suspicious." She got into the back seat of the SUV as Ted closed the door.

Andrew got in on her left. He noticed the stranger in the gatehouse watching all the student departures.

"This might not be related to Eastwood but a part of something bigger," she divulged. "It's like they are staking out the place."

All business, Burton instructed, "Put Andrew on."

Abi handed the device to the burly guy.

"Yes, Sir," Andrew said, focused in. "I agree. It is suspicious." He paused while listening to his boss on the other end. Answering his question, Andrew replied, "We've noticed a few things out of the norm. I included them in last week's entries." Silent, he said nothing more and just ended the call.

When he handed her phone back, she asked, "What did he say?"

"We are heading to the Bel Air house to pick him up."

Matt nodded and shifted the truck into gear. On their way out of the garage, Andrew and Ted had eyes on the heavily tattooed man inside the gatehouse. Dressed in the uniform with gold chains hanging around his neck, Ted said, "I'd bet my life someone hired that guy to do a job."

"What kind of job?" Abi naively questioned.

"It could be a kidnapping for ransom scenario, or he could be gathering intel on a student to threaten or blackmail family members into adhering to demands. Hard to know for sure. Don't worry. Once this escalates, it gets dealt with quickly."

"By who?"

"Can't say," Ted replied before glimpsing back at her with a smirk.

She knew he was purposefully withholding information. "Are the students here in danger?"

"We'll know soon."

Andrew changed the subject. "Do you have a line on the man you are looking for?"

"I have an address." She showed him what she found on 411.

He copied his name down and texted it to his coworker.

Receiving the message, Ted immediately took out his laptop and started the search.

The drive to Burton's house was quiet. With two guys immersed in their devices, Matt battled stop-and-go traffic with his head on a swivel.

Upon arrival, they passed through security at the bottom of the driveway and climbed the hillside. Burton was at the entrance, talking with Martin when the vehicle stopped.

Rolling down his window to speak to his boss, Ted said, "Hello, Sir. What's the plan?"

"I'm going to drive. You guys follow."

"Will do, Sir."

"Send me what you got thus far."

Abi inched forward and shouted to Burton, over Ted's shoulder, "What about me! Can I drive with you?" Seeing Matt's reaction, she did a little damage control. "No offense. I just need a change of scenery."

Burton smiled. "You can come with me. On the way, you can fill me in more on what's been happening."

Opening the door for her, Burton offered his hand to help Abi out of the SUV.

A safe distance away, the guys turned the truck around to wait for them.

Inside the glossy showroom, the G-Wagen's lights flickered and beeped on approach. Getting her door as he normally did, he waited until Abi settled before closing it and getting in beside her.

"Where are we off to?" He read what Ted sent.

She pointed to the address on her phone.

Starting the engine, Burton used the voice command to enter it in the GPS, then exited the garage. Inserting an earpiece, he said aloud, "Yes, they are aware of what we're about to do."

Abi tried to figure out who he was talking to and what was happening while he listened to someone on the line.

"Got it," he said, "Yep. Good. Bye."

When he ended the call, she asked, "What's going on?"

"I let the bureau know what we're doing just as a precaution," he said, descending the driveway with the guys behind them.

"Why?"

"They've been watching the staff exchanges at Gilderson for the past ten days. I didn't want to overstep, so we cleared it with them first. They will be providing backup if we need it."

"Is that really necessary? I don't want to spook Gerald."

Heading south on Bellagio, he looked at her with a serious expression. "That's assuming we will find him alive. Nobody knew anything about a guy named Gerald. It's like they wiped his name from the record."

She went silent and rested her elbow on the window ledge to hold up her chin.

He noticed and reached for her. "Hey, I'm sure that won't be the case, but if it is, I need you to prepare for the worst. But we will hope for the best."

Abi nodded reluctantly.

Slowly moving across Sunset, Burton merged south on the 405. Following the GPS instructions, he adhered to the Santa Monica Boulevard sign before leaving the highway. At the next intersection, he made a right.

"We've gotta backtrack a bit. It should be just around the block."

Burton made two right-hand turns. On Beloit, he kept checking the GPS and looking for a building on the corner. Finding a three-story apartment complex, he realized the address seemed tucked behind it. They pulled over onto the sidewalk. Matt did the same.

It was a sketchy neighborhood, even in the daytime. Adjacent was an old, run-down rooming house. The stucco had yellowed and cracked in places - the windows dusty and slightly warped.

Turning off the engine, he said, "Wait here. Lock the doors. Do not get out under any circumstances."

Scared, she said, "But I want to come with you."

"No, just wait. We will check it out first, then I'll return to get you."

She nodded in agreement. Seeing him join Andrew and Ted, Abi felt better knowing Matt remained in the vehicle, too. Doing what he said, she locked the doors and watched them enter the rickety building and disappear.

On pins and needles, fidgeting in her seat, Abi scanned their surroundings. Located next to the off-ramp, it was such a busy spot. With the building's roof shingles heaving on the place, the constant hum of traffic, and an eerie construction site right next door, her heart sank. The conditions the poor man lived in were far from ideal.

Glancing in her side mirror, she quietly repeated, "Please be okay."

Suddenly, Burton and Andrew surfaced, but nobody else. She held her breath as he walked toward her. Unlocking the door, he opened it.

"Did you find him?"

Burton pointed down the street. There, standing with Andrew, was Gerald.

Relieved, she said, "Can I...?"

"Sure."

When Abi got out, the elderly man's face lit up. "Miss Abi? What are you doing? You shouldn't be here?"

"I haven't seen you recently and was worried, so I got a little help and came to check on you."

"Thank you, but I don't work there anymore. I quit."

"Why? I thought you were happy at Gilderson. Did something happen?"

Burton stood behind her while Andrew and Ted kept scanning the perimeter. They could tell the man was apprehensive.

Cars passed by, and traffic off the freeway was bumper to bumper.

"Are you okay?" she asked. "Please tell us."

"The past week has been tough." He hesitated before divulging, "I shouldn't say anything, but..." Immediately, he looked fearfully up and down the street.

This behavior worried Burton. "Who are you looking for, Sir?" he asked.

It sparked the guys to go on high alert.

"I am not at Gilderson because these men told me not to return or..."

"Or what? Sir?" Ted prompted, getting a bad feeling in the process.

"Or there would be consequences."

Ted interjected. "Elaborate on these consequences..."

"That they'd hurt Miss Abi."

Not wasting a second, Andrew stepped away and called it in. They knew who was responsible for this.

Taken off guard by their reaction, Gerald apologized. "I'm sorry. You should go. Thank you for checking on me. That was kind of you, my dear."

Burton's sights bounced between Andrew and Ted. They all knew this guy's life would be in danger the moment they left.

"Abi, get in the truck," Burton instructed urgently.

"Why? What's wrong?"

"Don't ask questions."

Abi did as he said.

When she got in the fancy SUV, Gerald got visibly upset. Resting his hand along his forehead, he said to Burton, "They won't hurt her, will they?"

Andrew stepped up. "Not if we can help it."

"I need you to gather your things, Sir." Ted guided the man to the door of the building. "You're coming with us."

"Am I under arrest?"

"No," Burton said. "You're going to work for me."

Gerald was bewildered. "I beg your pardon. I don't understand?"

"I need a security guard at my gate. You are a veteran, correct?" Burton read his file off his phone. "US Navy retired, 1985? San Fran Coast Guard, District 11? Retired 2005?"

"Yes, Sir."

"Good. That's all I need to know. Pack your things. I will guarantee your safety and will provide room and board. But you've gotta move."

His face brightened. "Then, I accept."

"Perfect."

Abi watched Gerald hurry along inside. Ted went with him while Andrew and Burton spoke beside the truck. Shaking hands, they parted ways when Gerald emerged with three army-green military seabags. Matt raised the hatch and placed everything inside before the elderly man found a seat in the SUV.

"What's going on? Where are you taking him?" Abi asked when Burton got in beside her.

"He's going to work for me. He's a Navy Vet and retired Coast Guard. Did you know that?"

"No," she said, a bit confused. "Wait? You offered him a job?"

"I need someone else at the gatehouse. If he wants a change of scenery now and then, I'll transfer him to the Malibu property or one of my other establishments for short stints. Whatever he wants."

She reached over and wrapped her arms around Burton's neck. "Thank you," she said happily.

Surprised by this, he looked away when she hugged him tightly, trying not to read too much into it.

"He has no criminal record and a stellar military service CV. We couldn't risk leaving him behind. But we need to find out who threatened him."

Unmarked cars arrived on the scene. Burton subtly raised a hand to acknowledge their presence. "We have people onsite now. They will keep an eye on the place. See who comes and goes."

His phone rang. "Yeah?" Listening in, he said to Ted on the other line, "On the way home, they said to take a detour," he paused. "Right. Got it."

Worried, she said, "I should have tried to find him sooner."

Burton checked his mirrors, signaled, and got them moving. "No, your timing was perfect. Since nobody suspicious was looking for him, I assume the tags lost interest. If you came here last week on your own, God only knows what could have transpired."

Merging onto the freeway, Matt shadowed his boss' every move until Abi noticed them veer left a few car lengths ahead when they exited right onto Hwy 10 West.

"Where are they going?"

"It's protocol. We need to split up to make sure nobody followed us." He looked up through the sunroof.

Abi saw two helicopters high in the air - one above them and the other seemingly tracking the guys.

"They are surveilling everyone within a one-mile radius - running plates and gathering intel like driver descriptions, make and model of cars. If there is anyone of interest, the highway patrol will pull them over. If it's clean, we go home."

"If it's not, then what? Do you have a plan B?"

"Always. Leave that to me."

Despite all the secrecy, Abi felt safe. Highly protective and very intelligent, she never had to worry when Burton was around.

He received another call. Tapping his Bluetooth earbud, he said, "Yeah?" Listening to someone on the other end, he said, "Good. Text Andrew and give him a heads-up. Thanks." He turned to her. "We got the green light. All good."

It was then Abi understood the seriousness of this. Even though Eastwood was fighting for his life in the hospital, the crime family was still operational, regardless. To them, it was business as usual.

"So that you know, there are a few things I haven't told you that happened in Vegas."

"What's that."

"First, Eastwood mentioned Emile Raven supplied information to him about Reggie's party."

Burton changed lanes. "That's the mean girl from the coffee shop?"

"Yes. She tried to end her life on Sunday, the day after the explosion. From what Eastwood said, she was angry with Shane and me and told him we would be there. Even with security everywhere, how was someone able to plant a bomb under Shane's Jeep? Wouldn't that look suspicious?"

"No. The bomb from the party was about the size of a cell phone. It was very easy to plant. Anyone could have done it."

"Oh..."

His mind was reeling. "As for this Emile girl. Why did she do that? There had to be a reason."

"From what Eastwood said, when she found out about the explosion, she assumed Shane died because of what she did."

"Where is she now?"

Abi pulled out her phone. "Her friends mentioned this luxury rehab center in Calabasas. Wishing Well Rehab? I assume she's there."

"Text me the place. I'll look into it."

She did as he asked, trusting him. "One more thing..."

Eyes on the road, he waited for her to elaborate.

"Eastwood also said he killed my Mother."

Burton took his foot off the gas and glanced her way. "What..."

Abi looked down and fidgeted with the edge of her skirt. "He said she had one foot out the door anyway. He just helped her along."

There was silence after she said that.

Suddenly, the sound of her phone cut through it. She saw it was Shane.

Burton noticed his picture on the screen. He could see her struggling with what she'd just shared with him.

Not answering in time, she called him back. "Hi, sorry. Just missed you."

"That's okay. We just finished here. Are you at Laney's?"

Abi hesitated. "Umm, not exactly."

89

Moving

Afraid to confirm his gut feeling, Shane stayed quiet, then got up the courage and asked, "Where are you? Please don't tell me you're with him..."

Abi didn't know what to say.

Her silence spoke volumes. Getting the hint, Shane wasn't happy, and she could tell.

"Listen," she said, "I asked the guys to help me find Gerald. We got him. He's okay."

"As much as I am glad to hear that, why did Burton get involved?"

"Because I asked him to."

Shane knew she was in the vehicle with him. He could hear the rumble.

"I can meet you at Laney's in fifteen minutes. Then we can go for dinner."

Angry and needing time to think, he replied, "You know what, Abs? I think I'm good. I'm just going to head home. Don't worry about it."

"Shane, no..." she said before pleading, "Please don't do this. I was looking forward to tonight."

"Sorry, I gotta go."

Before she could say another word, he ended the call. Distraught, she slowly lowered the phone from her ear.

"Did he hang up on you?" Burton assumed as much.

She nodded. "I just can't do anything right."

"This has nothing to do with you. It's him. He's insecure." Needing to fix this, Burton pulled out his phone and scrolled through his contact list.

"What are you doing?"

Furious, he said, "Calling him."

"No, please don't. You'll make it worse."

He was appalled by the guy's behavior. "Shane has no right to treat you like that."

She rested her hand on his forearm. "Please, just let it go. I'll deal with it later."

About to give in, he said, "No, sorry, Abs. I can't," and dialed the number anyway.

"Burton!"

"Trust me." He listened as Shane's phone rang. As expected, the guy didn't answer. It went to voice mail. After the beep, he said, "I don't like how you treated Abi just now. She did a noble thing and saved a man's life today, and you fixated on the fact she was with me? Damn! Get over it! If you don't, you're gonna lose her!"

Watching him end the call abruptly, Abi felt sick.

"That will light a fire under him. He'll call you."

She wasn't certain of that. "I think he'll probably be more mad that you interfered."

"Well, we'll soon see." Burton paused and briefly made eye contact with her. "About Eastwood and your Mom..."

She turned to him.

"I will have them take security camera footage from Laney's house. If we have audio of him saying that, we can put him behind bars for a long time."

Unable to speak, she silently acknowledged with a nod and continued looking out the window.

He left her be.

Returning to the Bel Air mansion, Burton pulled into the garage as the door closed behind them. "Since you no longer have dinner plans, maybe you want to join Sara and me?"

"No, I couldn't impose. It's your time with her. You don't need me hanging around."

Before getting out of the truck, he wanted to clarify his position. "Abs, you will always be my priority, above all else." The look on her face made his heart ache. "Besides, I have something to run by you."

"What is it?"

He exited the vehicle and grabbed her bag from the back seat before leading her inside to the elevator. Pressing the button, he said, "I want to ask you something, but I think I should show you first."

"Show me what?"

"You'll see." He smiled as the doors parted.

Stepping inside, they soon arrived on the first floor and walked toward the sectional sofa. Burton set her backpack there and continued down the hallway to the room Rachel Z used for the dress fitting.

Before going in, he moved aside and said, "Open it."

"Why?" she asked curiously.

He prompted again. "Trust me."

Scared to know what was behind the door, Abi slowly walked in and looked around. The place had changed significantly. Dressed in white with hints of the softest greys and calming slate blue tones, she couldn't believe the transformation. The seating area now had a plush sofa, chairs, and fluffy cushions. She also noticed a television mounted on the wall and beautiful raw silk draperies. Adjacent to that was a white desk, custom fabric ergonomic chair, and desktop computer.

"This is beautiful."

"I'm glad you think so because it's yours if you want it."

Confused, she said, "I don't understand."

He stood tall with his arms across his chest. "When you were here on Monday, I could sense how displaced you felt. As much as I would like you to forgive your Dad eventually..."

She tilted her head disapprovingly.

"Here me out," he said, holding up his hand.

She decided to let him explain. "Fine."

He repeated, "As much as I would like you to forgive him, I know it's too soon. So, if you need a home base, you can move in here."

Waiting to hear her thoughts, she noticeably seemed torn.

"This way, you have security and a place to call your own. I decorated it in the same color scheme as your room, hoping you'd feel more comfortable."

"Burton, it's lovely, but..."

He had a hunch why she was hesitant. "Despite what Shane thinks or feels, you need stability, and right now, your father is not providing that. Look, whatever you wish to do, it's your decision. I will never walk into this room. It will be your domain. You can come and go as you please. Obviously, based on my lifestyle, having people over would be difficult, which I'm certain you understand, but otherwise, no pressure. I just wanted to give you the option."

She scanned the pretty room and snuck a peek into the color-coordinated bathroom, with a soaker tub, makeup desk, chair, and large walk-in closet. "Can I think about it?" she said.

"Of course."

Inching closer, she wrapped her arms around his waist and hugged him as he gingerly did the same.

"So," he said, "Getting back to the subject of dinner?"

"Don't worry about me. I'll figure something out."

He ignored her comment. "We can go out to a restaurant instead? Anton wouldn't mind the night off, I'm sure. I know of this quaint place with the most amazing pasta dishes."

"What about Sara?"

"She will be with us. Maybe Martin, too. We will make a night of it."

"If you're sure, I'm not imposing. I don't want to take you away from her."

"You're not. It's fine."

"Okay."

He led the way out of the room.

"Any chance I can go to Laney's and change first?"

Not giving it a second thought, he grabbed her backpack off the sofa. "Sure. Come on. I'll drive you."

"Alright." Contemplating his offer on their way out the door, Burton grabbed his keys for the McLaren.

"Umm, can we take the truck?"

Without hesitation, he exchanged the car fob for the SUV.

"I think we will need space to move my stuff."

Not surprised she'd made the decision so quickly, he asked, "Are you sure? You don't need to give me an answer right this second."

They walked out to the garage.

"I know. I just feel good about it. But it isn't forever. I'll stay until I figure out what to do next."

"Absolutely." He opened the passenger door of the G-Wagen. "Whatever you want to do."

He set her bag on the floor beside her when she got in.

Calling Laney, she heard her pick up. "Hey, it's me. I wanted to make sure you were home. I'm just heading there now."

On the other end, the girl joyfully replied, "Yes, I am."

Abi watched as Burton got in.

"Please don't be mad, Lane, but Burton asked me to move in with him, so I'm coming to get my things."

"Wait, Abs? What do you mean moving in?"

"He had a room decorated for me. It's so nice. I couldn't say no." Abi looked at him and smiled. "This way, I can have a home base until this whole Dad thing gets resolved." When she said it out loud, she second-guessed herself. "Well, if it ever does..."

"Wait? Abi? Are you sure this is a good idea? I can't see Shane supporting this arrangement."

"Well, he and I didn't see eye to eye on a few things today." Overly frustrated, she sighed. "I'm under a lot of stress, and Burton is offering me the stability I need right now."

"What's wrong with you just staying here? I thought we were having fun?"

Hearing her say that, Abi felt bad. "Please don't take offense."

"No, I'm not. But..." She whined a little. "It was so nice to have someone else around. This house is so big. Sometimes, I feel I might get swallowed up in it."

Burton listened in. He figured the girl might sway Abi to change her mind.

"Hey, I'll make you a deal."

"Alright, what?" Laney replied, wondering what she would suggest.

"I will stay with you at least once a week."

She jumped at that. "Or twice if I need you?"

"Fine," Abi agreed.

"Deal!" The girl stopped. "But what about Shane? He'll be furious about this. I know him. This could end things between you."

"It's not his decision. It's mine. I need to do what's best for me."

"Okay, don't say I didn't warn you."

Afraid her friend was right, Abi panicked a little. The fact that Shane hadn't called her after Burton left the message could prove Laney right.

"Well, I'm home. Drop by whenever you'd like."

"Alright, we'll be there shortly," Abi said as they turned onto Sunset.

"We?" the girl asked.

"Yes, Burton is driving me over."

Worried by Abi's sudden change of direction, Laney assumed the influential DJ was instigating things. "I'll see you soon."

When she ended their conversation, Burton answered a call of his own.

"Yeah?" he said to the person on the line. "Are you sure?"

Abi sensed a bit of urgency.

"Alright. Thanks for letting me know." Moving in traffic at a snail's pace, Burton said, "Eastwood disappeared from the Vegas hospital. Don't know how that could've happened with the police guarding his room around the clock. In his condition, it wouldn't have been easy to move the guy. Somebody must have seen something. They believe he got help from the inside."

Hearing this, Abi knew her life was still in danger.

He took her hand. "Given this new development, staying with me is the right decision."

She silently agreed as they turned onto Laney's street.

90

Awkward

Burton drove up the hillside, maneuvering the many twists and turns before arriving at Laney's mansion. The security guard at the main gate waved them through. There, they found her friend sitting and waiting on the front step. She stood up when he turned the SUV around and backed it up.

Abi got out. "Hi," she said, closing the passenger side door.

"Hey," she replied, zeroing in on Burton as he exited the vehicle to make a phone call.

He knew she was mad by the way she glared at him. Not following Abi inside, Burton knew better than to enter the house alone with two minors.

All the way up the staircase, Laney didn't say a word. Helping to gather Abi's things and pack what little she had, she brought everything down when it was time to go.

One by one, the girls left the suitcases and tote bags on the front step. Burton loaded it in the back.

Moments later, having to say goodbye, Abi hugged her friend.

Laney glanced over her shoulder and shot the famous DJ an evil eye while he paced the courtyard on another call.

Grateful for her generosity, Abi said, "Thank you for taking me in. For a minute, I knew what it was like to have a sister."

"Awww... Yeah, I thought that, too." She grabbed hold of Abi and said, "Remember? You promised one day a week, right?"

"Yes," Abi replied. "I remember. Just let me get settled. I'm still processing, well, you know..."

"Of course, I understand. You tell me when you're up to it."

Burton watched their interaction.

Giving her one last hug, Laney whispered in her ear, "I hope you know what you're doing?"

"Well, if it doesn't work out..."

"You can always move back here," she smiled, willing to rescue her again.

"Thanks for all the support." Abi teared up. "You've been so kind to me."

Totally loving the compliment, the blonde-haired bombshell flipped her hair. "You should be! I'm the best, aren't I?"

They giggled as Abi descended the stairs and waved.

"Tell Michelle I'll miss seeing her in the morning. The smoothies and Americanos have been great."

"I will. Bye, Abs. See you tomorrow."

"Yes. I'll text you later."

"Okay. Sounds good."

When Abi got in the vehicle, Burton ended his call. "Everything okay?" he asked her while putting on his seat belt and throwing the truck in gear.

"Yes. All good," Abi said. "Any more news on Eastwood? I saw you on the phone."

"No, but it looks like they might move on Gilderson. There's enough evidence to proceed. It's been escalated."

"Gilderson?"

"You were right to question what was happening there."

"Just got a bad feeling, that's all."

"Your gut instinct was spot on. Trust it, and it'll never steer you wrong."

She couldn't help but feel what he said had another meaning.

They stopped at the red light at the end of Sunset Plaza. After taking inventory of her life, she felt confident in her decision and hoped to establish a new normal sooner rather than later.

Able to read her like a book, he said, "So, you're sure you're okay with moving in?"

She looked straight ahead as he turned right. "When I'm with you, I feel secure. There's no fear. You saved me from Eastwood and assigned me security detail when I didn't even know I needed it. And don't get me started on the whole explosion aftermath and extraction. To this day, you have always had my best interest at heart. That said, Shane did technically take a bullet for me, but around you, there is just this added feeling of protection. Perhaps I'm just accustomed to that. And, now, with Eastwood's disappearance, you're right. The timing couldn't be more perfect."

Reaching out, he rested his hand on her arm. "For the record, I will protect you with my life. Always have. Always will."

Abi nodded, trusting what he said wholeheartedly.

"For me, you're my only family now, so we need to look out for each other."

Abi silently acknowledged that.

"And, yes. Korolev being M.I.A definitely changes things."

"What do we do?"

Focused on the road and their surroundings, he said, "Pay more attention. Don't become complacent."

Their conversation dwindled. Burton stayed quiet to give her some time to think.

Once they reached his place, he parked in the garage and noticed the guys had returned. Hoping to enlist them to help move Abi's things to her room, he said, "Come on. Let's get both you and Gerald settled in, shall we?"

Grabbing a few tote bags and a suitcase, Burton walked into the house with the heavy load. Arms full, Abi followed. There, they found

Gerald speaking with Martin. While placing the luggage in the elevator, they noticed his right-hand man fitting the new employee with a uniform.

Exiting the security room, Gerald saw them. "Hello, Sir."

Burton shook his hand. "Welcome. I see you've met Martin. He is in charge. If you need anything, feel free to speak with him."

"Will do, Sir." The man was in awe of the large home.

"Show him to his room and the staff quarters," Burton told Martin. "Afterwards, give him a tour of the grounds and introduce him to Max. He can share our daily routine."

"Very good, Master B."

The two men disappeared down the hall to their right as Burton got the rest of Abi's things from the garage. She helped.

"Thank you for doing this for him. He's a very kind man."

Burton smiled. "It is hard to find loyalty in this day and age, let alone kindness. We lucked out. He's skilled and willing to work." Closing the hatch of the SUV, he said, "Now, let's finish up here. I'm hungry."

They walked inside and loaded the elevator to the brim before Burton pressed the button. Needing to catch it when it opened on the next level, the two bounded up the airy floating staircase enclosed in glass.

Just when they reached the top, the doors parted. Burton quickly locked it in place.

Unloading what she could, Abi maneuvered the long hallway to her room while Burton rolled the suitcases with the remaining tote bags hanging on one arm. He left the baggage just inside the door. Not entering the space, he said, "I'll let you do your thing. If you need me, just text." Receiving a notification, he looked at his phone. "I'll check on you shortly."

"Alright."

When he left, Abi wondered who caught his attention. Walking to the window, she spotted a grey Audi Q4. Sara got out. In seconds, Burton went out to greet the pretty girl with a hug. Casually kissing her, Abi's heart sank.

"She's a year older than him and has a picture-perfect body and stunning good looks. On top of that, she has a badass job, too. Huh. No wonder he's attracted to her," she mumbled, suddenly feeling like a little kid in comparison. As the two talked, Abi felt an unwillingness to share him. He'd always been there for her when she needed him. The thought then crossed her mind. *What would happen if and when he committed to someone?*

"This is ridiculous," she whispered, "You're just friends. He has every right to have a girlfriend." At that point, she knew how Burton felt having to see her with Shane. "No wonder he's acted the way he did." Going about her business, moving away from the window, she opened her suitcase and started hanging her clothes in the closet. Organizing the space, she remembered she'd forgotten her backpack in the truck and decided to go and grab it. Abi rushed down the hall. About to descend the stairs, she stopped. Burton and Sara were on their way up, hand in hand.

"Oh. I didn't know you had company," the girl said. "Hi, Abi."

"Hey, Sara."

Burton explained, "Abs is having trouble with her Dad, so she's moved in for a bit until things settle down."

She flashed a surprised look. "That's nice of you."

Abi could tell she disapproved.

"If you don't mind, I'm just going to go and change," she said, kissing his lips before departing.

Staring into her eyes, he held her hand until having to let go.

Once she disappeared into his room, Abi muttered, "Well, that moved fast."

"What do you mean?"

Arms crossed, she stated, "It's only been ten days since Tahoe? You seem pretty close."

"Aren't you the one who encouraged me to work things out with her?"

She looked away. "I know..."

"If I'm not mistaken, I might say you're a little jealous."

"No, I'm not."

Suspicious, he mumbled, "Hmm."

Without warning, Sara resurfaced. Abi assumed she'd heard their conversation.

"I left my backpack in the truck, so...." Abi pointed to the garage level. "I'm just gonna grab it."

Being the gentleman that he is, Burton offered, "I'll get it for you."

"No, it's okay."

While she darted down the stairs, Burton's sights bounced between her and his girlfriend. Expecting friction between the two women in his life, he asked, "Instead of eating in tonight, I thought we'd go out."

Sara's face lit up. "Sure. I'd love that."

Abi popped back inside and climbed the stairs.

"So, Abs, have you decided if you want to join us for dinner?"

Caught between a rock and a hard place, Abi shuttered when the girl shot her another look. Not wanting to be the third wheel, Abi said, "Umm, no. You and Sara go ahead. Like I said, I don't want to intrude."

"It's your first night here. Please join us," he prompted.

Curious about Sara's intentions, mainly because of the vibe she was giving off, Abi decided to accept the invitation. "You know what? On second thought, sure. Why not." If anything, she figured she'd see if the woman was genuine and above board.

Happy she had a change of heart, he said, "Perfect. We'll meet back here in, say, twenty minutes?"

"Okay. I'll be ready."

Fawning over Burton, clinging to him, Sara asked, "Where are we going?"

"I know of this quaint Italian place. I've eaten there before. It's really good."

"What should I wear? Is it upscale because I didn't bring anything suitable with me?"

"It's business casual. I'm sure whatever you choose, you'll look beautiful."

While the two disappeared into his room, Abi glanced back and couldn't figure out why she was so bothered by them being together. "Just chill, Abs," she said, shaking her head.

Quickly walking into her closet, she tried to decide what to wear. Pulling pieces from her suitcases, for whatever reason, she felt the urge to compete. Assuming Sara would be wearing something casual, Abi opted for timeless. Selecting a LBD with a royal blue Ralph Lauren cardi and her neutral flats with the matching Chloe bag, she laid everything out on the bed.

"It's feminine but mature," she said. "I think this will work." Slightly wrinkled, she wondered where the laundry room was. "Maybe I'll throw it in the dryer quick. It'll be fine."

Taking the dress with her, she didn't see anyone around. Unable to text Burton, having left her phone in her room, she lightly knocked on his door. Since it was open a crack, she peeked inside. Finding them kissing, she quickly backed away, hoping they hadn't spotted her. Almost scott-free, she heard Burton's voice.

"Abs? Wait!" Parting from Sara, he ran out after her. "Is everything okay?"

Embarrassed, Abi swiftly shuffled away.

"Abi, stop."

Unable to look him in the eye, dress in hand, her heart beating a mile a minute, she didn't know what to say. "I'm so sorry. I didn't mean to interrupt..."

"It's fine. Don't worry about it. What do you need?"

"Umm, where's the laundry room?"

He looked to his left and opened a door a few feet away. "Here."

"Thanks..."

"Sure thing." He could tell she was upset and swiftly guided Abi into the room. "Give it to me..." he put out his hand to silently ask for the dress. "Need it to go in for a steam?"

"Ah, yeah. Please."

Checking to ensure Sara hadn't followed them, he closed the door. "Hey, is everything alright?"

Watching the dress tumbling, she replied, "Yes, why wouldn't it be?"

"Because you're upset." Uncertain of the reason, having a hunch, he asked, "Is it because of Sara?"

"No. Why would you say that?"

"Maybe because you've been off since she got here."

"Sorry, I'm just having a bad day."

"Is it Shane?"

Realizing he was her way out of the uncomfortable conversation, she replied, "Yeah, mostly."

Deciding to leave it alone, he added, "I'm sure things will work out. You just have to give him a little time."

As of now, she figured things might be over.

"Look, I'll leave you to it. Are you okay here?"

"Yes. All good. You go ahead."

He stared into her eyes, trying to read her mind. "Okay. We'll see you shortly."

"Yep." When he left, she didn't want to join them anymore. Closing the door, she leaned against the wall. "What are you doing?" she whispered, mortified by her actions. "This isn't going to work. What were you thinking?" Unwilling to witness his love affair day in and day out, Abi slowly slid her body toward the floor while waiting for the machine's cycle to finish. "You are with Shane. Or at least you were until you screwed it up today." She buried her face in her hands. Hating that he was angry at her, she racked her brain on how to fix it before wondering how she could ever face Sara and Burton now. "Crap... You just had to walk in on them? So stupid. Stupid. Stupid..." she muttered repeatedly, hitting her hand to her forehead.

The buzzer sounded. Removing the dress, Abi returned to her room. Ready to make an excuse for why she should stay home, she recalled how many times Burton confronted Shane. "He always wants to make sure the guy is above board and treating me right." While hanging the dress up, she also felt protective of him and believed she should return the favor. It wasn't like he hadn't seen her kiss Shane. "What if I was wrong and she's only after him for his money? Or fame? Or both?" Ripping the dress from the hanger, she bravely said, "You need to find out what her deal is."

Confidence brewing while slipping into the LBD, Abi fixed her face and hair. Devising a plan as the minutes passed, she looked in the mirror and said, "Okay. Time to do some recon of my own."

With a bounce in her step, she left her room. Hearing Burton and Sara talking, she rounded the corner to find the woman standing beside him in a casual navy tube dress and a cream blazer with sleeves rolled to her elbows. Paired with cute white sneakers and her hair down, Abi smiled. The girl looked nice, but she knew she looked better.

"Ready to go, Abs?" he said as Sara looked on, clinging to him.

By how she looked at her, Abi could tell she was impressed by her style. "I'm ready."

"I invited Martin, but he says he's busy, so it's just the three of us."

The disappointment on the woman's face was evident.

Unable to turn back now, Abi knew she'd have to sit through the next three hours and pretend to enjoy herself. Capable of rising to the challenge, she had an idea.

"It's okay, Burton. You guys go ahead. I don't want to impose. I'll stay back and order something in. Besides, I have a lot of unpacking to do."

"Don't be silly. I don't want to leave you home alone."

Sara hated him showering her with attention.

Abi assumed she'd gotten under her skin. "Well, if you're sure?"

"Yes, of course. Please," Burton waited for his girlfriend to agree. "Right, Sara?"

Shadily, she replied, "Yes, umm, we'd love to have you," trying to seem believable.

Certain his new girlfriend was up to no good, Abi was now on a mission. "Thank you. I appreciate that."

Burton smiled and said, "Great. Let's go."

Walking out to the guys waiting in the SUV, Abi got in first and slid to the opposite side. Sara got in the middle, followed by Burton.

Staring at his phone, he blindly said, "You're going to love this place, Abs. The food is amazing."

She rubbed her palms together. "Oh, now I'm excited."

The drive along Sunset to the 405 North was a quiet one. Not much was said between them.

Burton returned a few emails while Sara just stared straight ahead.

Willing to spark a conversation to look good in his eyes, Abi asked, "So, Sara? How was your day today?" Just as the girl was about to answer, Abi noticed Burton glance at the two of them. Seemingly glad to hear his friend make an effort, he continued his work.

"I'm not really at liberty to say. Top secret, you know." When she smirked, it caused the conversation to drop there.

Assuming Sara knew what she was doing, Abi asked, "So, did Burton tell you what he and I did this afternoon?"

"No, he didn't." She turned to him curiously.

"He never ceases to amaze me," she gushed.

Noticeably bothered, she replied, "Is that right?"

"He helped me find Gilderson's missing security guard and then offered him a job. I knew something was going on there. Just had this gut feeling."

Sara swiveled around. "She was with you?"

"Yes. Like she said, she's the one who stumbled upon it." He stopped, knowing he couldn't say anything more.

"And you offered the Navy Vet a job?"

"Yes, he did," Abi interjected. "Gerald is the nicest man."

"From what I hear, he was in the wrong place at the wrong time?" she said.

"I suppose so," Abi agreed wholeheartedly.

The driver turned right at the intersection.

Suddenly recognizing where they were, Abi started to panic. *Oh, no. No. No. This can't be,* she thought to herself.

Arriving in front of Il Segrato, their driver slowed to a stop.

Abi scoured the parking lot for Shane's Jeep. Relieved not to see it anywhere, she sighed. *Oh, thank God.*

"Here we are," Burton said. Getting out, he offered his hand to Sara. As she stood alongside him, Abi slid over next, making Burton do the same for her.

Notably more possessive of her man, the girl suddenly clung to his arm before Abi could.

While they approached the restaurant, being the gentleman that he is, Burton reached for the door, allowing both ladies to walk inside.

Drago looked across the restaurant and saw Abi. Immediately recognizing her, he looked around, expecting to see Shane. "Bene, ciao, signorina, Abi. Come stai?" the chef greeted.

She fluently replied, ready to show off her skills, "Sto bene, Drago. Sono così felice di rivederti." Abi could see Burton was impressed.

"Incontrerai il signor Coppersmith questa sera?"

Realizing it was rude to speak another language amongst those who didn't understand, she changed to English. "Umm, no, Drago. I am not meeting Shane."

"One moment, Miss." Drago's attention moved to Burton. "Hello, Mr. Baxter. I have your table ready."

Burton shook the man's hand. "Good to see you, Drago. Thank you."

The chef realized Abi was dining with them. "Oh, Miss Abi, you are with the Baxter party of three?"

"Yes."

"Molto bene. Proprio in questo modo." He said, translating into English, "Sorry, umm, right this way."

About to ascend the stairs to the upper level overlooking the tables below, Abi stopped in her tracks. There, standing mere feet from her, was Shane and his little stepbrother, Jacob.

"Abi? What are you doing here?" he said, surprised to see her.

"I joined Burton and Sara for dinner."

His sights floated past her burly friend to the pretty blonde beside him. Realizing the two weren't alone, he said, "That's nice of them."

She quickly clarified, "I didn't know we were coming here, so..."

Burton piped up. "Drago? Sara and I will seat ourselves at my usual spot. Can you find Mr. Coppersmith a table for three, please?"

The man obliged. "Yes, I sure can."

Abi stared at Shane. "You don't have to stay if you don't want to." Hoping he'd accept the invitation, she awaited his answer.

"Yeah, I guess we could eat here versus grabbing takeout."

"Good, umm," she managed a smile. "I'm glad."

Drago led them to a spot by the window, conveniently within full view of Burton on the second floor.

Shane pulled back her chair for her before Jacob plopped down and pulled his gaming device from his pocket. Slipping his headphones from his neck, over his ears, he shut off from them instantly. Wishing the boy would limit his screen time, Shane allowed it just this once to give them time to talk privately.

"Burton and Sara knew I would be alone tonight, so they invited me to join them." When Abi said that, she wondered how to tell him she'd moved in with Burton for the time being.

Drago returned with menus. "Here we go. I will leave you to decide on your orders."

"Umm, it's okay. I know what we're getting." He turned to Abi. "Do you know what you'd like?"

"Yes, just a Margherita pizza for me." Pausing, she asked, "Can you throw a dash of fresh arugula on that?"

The chef jotted down her special request. "I certainly can, signorina." Looking at Shane, he asked, "And for you? The usual? One Coppersmith special and one pasta pomodoro?"

"That would be great. Maybe three iced teas, too. Thank you, Sir."

"Very good. Coming right up."

When the man left them, Shane stared at the napkin on the table. The silence between them was deafening.

"Arugula, huh?"

"Yeah, umm, it's my new thing."

Returning with their iced teas, Drago set each in front of them, reading into their awkwardness. Tapping Jacob on the shoulder, he asked, "Mr. Jacob, would you like to watch us make the pizzas?"

The young boy's face lit up. Immediately putting away his device, he said, "Yeah, that would be awesome."

Leaving his equipment behind, Abi knew what the chef had done. She looked up at Burton holding hands with Sara. Just then, he happened to get a glimpse at them.

"Look, I'm sorry for canceling our plans tonight," Shane said.

"I understand."

The talented QB shook his head. "I shouldn't get angry about you and him." Shane saw the couple staring into each other's eyes, deep in conversation. "So, those two are really together?"

"Yes. I told you that."

"I know," he confirmed.

Wanting to come clean, she said, "Before we go any further, there is something I need to tell you."

"What is it?"

"I moved out of Laney's house today."

"Oh, so you decided to go home?" he assumed.

Mumbling, she said, "Not exactly."

"I don't understand."

"Burton offered to let me stay with him until I figure out this whole Dad thing."

"Wait..." He flashed a blank expression and turned away. "You moved in with the guy? You're joking, right?"

"No."

Under his breath, he leaned closer to her and whispered, "Abs. You don't know what he's mixed up in."

"It's not like that."

"The hell it's not. Abi, you're not safe there. If you needed a place to go, I told you, you could've stayed with me."

Fidgeting, she said, "But you abandoned me today. What was I supposed to do?"

The jab cut deep and didn't help matters.

"Besides," she said, "I couldn't move in with you anyway."

"Why not?" he questioned. "Don't you trust me?"

She looked him in the eye. "Honestly, I don't trust myself."

"Why?"

"Shane, if you and I were under the same roof, it would be..." She selected her words carefully. "...hard to keep our distance."

He reached out to her. Holding her hand, he quietly asked, "Is that such a bad thing?"

"No... But it makes it complicated."

"I promise nothing would happen unless you wanted it to."

"I know."

Frustrated by the thought of her living with the celebrity, he looked at the guy lovingly talking with Sara. "I'm glad to see he's with someone, at least."

"Yes, it's still new. Apparently, they're getting closer by the day."

Shane nodded.

"I did this because today we learned Eastwood escaped police custody at the hospital in Vegas."

"Are you sure?"

"Yes, they don't know what happened yet. So, for safety reasons, I accepted his offer."

It made more sense now. "Why didn't you lead with that?"

She laughed. "I'm not exactly thinking clearly at the moment."

Shane recalled the message Burton had left earlier. "What's this about him helping you save Gerald?"

"When we found him, he told us why he no longer works at Gilderson."

"And?"

"And that he was threatened and told there would be consequences if he returned."

"Threatened by who?" Shane sat up straight in his chair. "What were the consequences?"

"He didn't know who, but they told him they'd hurt me."

"You specifically?" Shane questioned.

"Yes, that's what he said."

"Then it must be a Korolev connection."

"I guess we will find out tomorrow. Don't tell anyone, but this whole Gerald situation sparked an investigation."

"That's concerning."

"In the meantime, Burton removed him from his scary living conditions. Concerned that someone could be watching and he'd be in danger if we left him behind, Burton took him in."

"Took him in?"

"He hired Gerald to work the gatehouse at his place and gave him a room in his staff quarters."

"Really?" Shane suddenly felt like he'd misjudged the guy again. "Well, that was generous."

"Yes, it was." Abi further revealed, "He discovered that he was a US Navy veteran and used to work for the Coast Guard."

"Wow."

Jacob returned to their table, carefully carrying his bowl of pasta. Setting it in front of him with Shane's help, he unrolled his cutlery from the napkin and dug in without saying a word.

"That looks great, little bro," Shane complimented.

The boy's eyes rolled. "I've been waiting for this all day."

They laughed at his reaction while Drago arrived carrying their pizzas.

"Here we go. One Margherita with a dash of arugula and one Coppersmith special."

"Oooh. Thank you!" Abi said excitedly.

Throughout dinner, the conversation flowed. Shane and Abi surpassed the troubles that plagued them that day. Quickly getting back on track, it seemed like nothing had happened.

Burton heard the joyful sounds coming from their table below. Thankful to see things seemed better, he relaxed and focused on his time with Sara.

91

Three's a Crowd

Having had their fill, Shane asked Drago for the check when he seated another couple next to them.

"No need," the chef said happily. "Mr. Baxter already settled the bills."

Not thrilled, he looked up at Burton, who had his eye on them. When he offered a single nod, Shane lifted his fingers off the table to acknowledge it.

Burton mimicked the same gesture.

"That was thoughtful," Abi said, knowing it bothered him. "Perhaps he is just trying to make amends?"

"Maybe."

About to leave, with Jacob immersed in his device, Shane and Abi saw Sara and Burton weren't far behind them.

Clinging to the guy again, Sara seemed to be acting more and more possessive.

In a competitive mood, Abi held onto Shane. Outside the courtyard, the five of them gathered around.

Face to face with the famous DJ, Shane had no choice. "Thank you for dinner," he said, "That wasn't necessary."

"It's fine. Don't worry about it."

The tension between the guys was evident.

"Are you driving with us, Abs, or with Shane?" Burton inquired, not sure what her plan was.

Abi looked up at the tall football player.

"You can drive with us if you want," he offered.

She nodded. "I'd like that."

With it settled, Burton said, "So, I guess we'll see you at home then?"

"Yeah, see you there."

As they walked away arm in arm, Shane turned to Jacob. "Ready to head out, little dude?"

Aloof, the young boy did not look his way.

Seeing this, Shane took the game from his hands.

"Hey! What are you doin'?" his stepbrother complained.

"Pay attention so you don't get hit by a car."

Listening to him, the boy spotted the Jeep and bolted towards it wildly.

They followed as Shane gently put his arm around Abi's shoulders.

She, in turn, wrapped hers around his waist.

Clicking the fob for Jacob to jump in, he handed him his device and closed the door, with him now safe in the back seat.

About to get in the front, Shane pulled Abi gently to the back of the vehicle. Not sure what was happening, she looked into his eyes.

Embracing her, the intimacy of his hug healed their wounds.

"Hey, umm, I'm sorry about what happened today. I screwed up - again."

"Don't say that."

He shook his head, disappointed in himself, knowing his relationship with Emile had damaged him. "I should trust you. I know I should. But it's hard. It's not your fault. It's mine."

Abi brought him in closer. "I understand."

He leaned in at her level and picked her off the ground. "The last thing you need is me complicating your life further."

As he set her feet back down, his comment scared her. "Wait? What are you saying? Are you breaking up with me?"

Shocked by that, he said, "No. Never."

"You had me worried for a second."

"Told you I wasn't good with words."

Wishing the world would stop so they could catch their breath, they felt a profound blend of relief, warmth, and rekindled affection.

He leaned back slightly and looked into her eyes. "I can't stand the thought of you being with anyone else."

"But, there is no one else."

"I see that now," he said.

Abi raised on her tiptoes. "Are we good?"

"I believe so."

Resting her hands along his cheeks, the guy was like putty in her hands. "So, we can put this whole jealousy thing behind us from now on?"

Under her spell, he answered, "I'll try."

About to kiss him, she whispered, "Good."

The side door opened.

"Hey, are you guys coming or what?" Jacob asked, noticeably disgusted by their locked lips.

"Yeah, we're coming." Kissing her a little longer, Shane said, "Maybe I should drop him off first. That way, we get some time by ourselves."

"I'd like that."

Opening the passenger door for her, Shane closed it when she got settled. Rounding the vehicle, slipping in behind the wheel, he started the engine and pulled out of the busy parking lot. Winding their way along Mulholland Drive, it didn't take long to get to Beverly Park. Easily passing through security, Shane moved closer and closer to home. When they arrived, he inched toward the wrought iron gates and waited for them to open. Slowly crossing the bridge, they stopped near the front door.

Shane turned around to Jacob, who remained immersed in his game. "Hey, dude? We're here. You go ahead inside and see Nanny. I'm just going to drive Abi home."

Almost paying attention, he got out robotically and said, "Yeah, sure."

Shane watched as he disappeared inside and closed the door. "I'm gonna have to fix that kid. He worries me. At least my parents had me in sports. I don't think he plays anything. Now it's almost too late for him to start from a competitive standpoint."

"Well, he can still play recreationally."

"But it's not the same." He held her hand tightly. "Guess we should get you home."

He reversed and put the Jeep in gear. Driving out of the gated community, Shane zigzagged toward Sunset Boulevard before heading north on Bellagio. Coming up on the fully illuminated mansion on the hillside, Shane stopped and waited at the gate.

"Can I help you?" Max said.

"Hey, I'm just dropping Abi off."

She waved to the guy.

Without emotion, he instructed, "Go ahead."

When the barrier opened, Shane accelerated to climb the steep incline and parked in front of the main doors.

Most of the rooms in the house were dark. Abi noticed Sara's SUV was still there.

"Do you want to come in? Maybe see my room?"

"I don't know. It feels weird you being here."

"Please?" she asked.

"Fine. Just for a few minutes. But I'm not making small talk with the guy."

When they got out, Shane locked the Jeep. Opening the tall door, they went inside. Leading Shane up the staircase, they could hear Sara and Burton playfully interacting on the upper level. Notified by Max that Abi was home, Burton peered over the upper balcony.

"You got back safe and sound?" he said, surprised to see Coppersmith with her.

"Yeah. I'm just going to show Shane my new room."

The guy was noticeably bothered by that but nodded and reminded himself Abi needed her freedom to come and go as she pleased. Sadly, that included a particular football player in the mix.

Not saying another word to him, they walked together to the end of the hall and opened the door. Closing it behind her, Shane looked around the large space.

"Are you kidding me? This is all yours?"

"I think it's the secondary primary suite."

The football player sat on the expansive sectional sofa. Abi joined him as the plush cushions engulfed them in comfort. With a playful grin, he lifted his arm, inviting her to snuggle closer. She willingly obliged, believing Burton and Sara were doing the same not far away.

"Maybe we should have stayed at my place?" he said.

"With all the cameras?"

"Good point," he laughed. "But, I'm sure he has the same?"

"Maybe in the main areas. But not here."

Hearing that sparked memories of their passionate night a while back. He turned and focused on Abi's nervous stare while tenderly tracing his fingertips across her forehead, sending shivers of anticipation surfacing everywhere. Lovingly moving strands of hair aside, his eyes filled with intention as he lifted her legs across his.

Abi's heart raced when he leaned in and closed the gap between them.

The simplest of movements amplified their gentle kisses. In the soft glow, every touch and caress held meaning and purpose.

Shane could feel her apprehension. Her body was rigid and tense. Realizing it was a new experience for her, he immediately backed off. Desperate to read her thoughts, it seemed she was waiting, hoping he'd return.

Resting her hand upon his chest, she felt his heart rhythmically thumping as he caught his breath. Unable to wait any longer, she gently grabbed his shirt and pulled him close.

He grazed his cheek alongside hers, buying time, battling with what he wanted to do but knew he shouldn't. Lips brushing together, he kissed her slowly as they fell back to stretch across the sofa. Bodies aligned in perfect harmony - they fit like pieces of a puzzle.

Snuggled against him, she could feel his strength as he brought her closer. Nestled in, she released a contented sigh. The sound of it escaped as their legs entangled and fingers interlocked in a silent promise of devotion. With every breath, they were in sync.

Lying there, he quietly said, "You are the only one I need by my side."

She offered the sweetest smile.

A knock came on the door, breaking their moment and causing them to recoil.

Parting, Abi reluctantly got up and whispered, "Hold that thought." Out of breath, she straightened her posture, fixed her hair, and exhaled before swinging open the door.

"Can I talk to you for a second?" Burton asked before leaving her to follow him down the hall.

"I'll be right back," she told Shane.

Speedily catching up, she whispered, "What the hell was that?"

"I just sent Sara home," he blurted.

Confused, Abi replied, "So? What does that have to do with me?"

"I figured I should set a good example."

"Really? That didn't apply last week, now did it?"

He knew what she was referring to. "That's different. You weren't here then."

Abi rested her hands on her hips. "You're not the boss of me."

"No, I'm not." Sliding his hands in his pockets, he said firmly, "Now, it's time for you to do the same and send Shane home."

By the look on his face, she knew he was serious.

Silence lingering, she waited, then said, "Fine."

"Good." In seconds, he walked into his bedroom and disappeared.

Ticked off, Abi returned to Shane and closed the door.

"Everything okay?" he asked. "What did he want?"

She started pacing, pondering Burton's angle on this.

"What's wrong?"

"He sent Sara home. Apparently, he wants to set an example for me while I'm staying here."

Shane grinned and got up off the sofa. Hugging Abi, he said, "That's not such a bad idea."

"What? You're siding with him?"

"No, but I just think we might have gotten a bit carried away otherwise." He nudged his nose against hers and smiled mischievously. "Not that I'm complaining, but I don't want you to feel uncomfortable or forced."

"I wasn't."

Kissing her, he said, "I should go."

As much as she wanted him to stay, she knew they should call it a night. Hand in hand, they headed down the hall to the staircase and out the front door. Walking to his Jeep, she went with him to the driver's side.

"Sorry about him."

"It's fine. Don't worry about it. I'll see you tomorrow." Offering one last kiss, he said, "Goodnight, Abs."

"Goodnight."

He got in and started the engine. Rolling down the window, he added, "Sweet dreams."

"You too."

While Shane drove away, Abi saw the light go on in Burton's room. He was standing above her, watching everything unfold. The second Shane was gone, he turned and left.

Angry, she stormed into the house and straight up the stairs. Bursting through his double doors, she yelled, "Burton!"

He calmly exited his closet. Dressed in pajama bottoms, he slipped a white t-shirt over his head.

"Why did you want me to stay here? I want the truth."

The famous DJ looked at her. "You said it yourself. I've been saving you my entire life, mostly from pain and hardships, but above all, harm. I didn't come all this way to give up now."

"What does that even mean?"

Resting his arms across his chest, muscles bulging, he said, "Tonight, going to Il Segrato wasn't a coincidence."

She mimicked his combative stance. "I figured as much."

"I owe you one for pushing me to pursue things with Sara. After what happened today, I wanted to fix things between you and him. So, I orchestrated dinner. It wasn't hard. We've been tracking Shane's movements this whole time. I knew his usual routine."

"What?"

Without remorse, he said, "I check on all your friends."

"Why?"

"In light of my unexpected reveal in Vegas and with a few of them knowing my secret, I had to. It's an insurance policy."

"What do you mean insurance policy? Were you looking for dirt on them? Something to blackmail them with?"

"Perhaps. But hopefully, I don't have to use any of it." He paused, realizing how bad that sounded. "Abs, I have my trusted circle. Those individuals have earned their spot. Then, there's the one person I trust above all others."

"Martin?"

"No," he paused. "You."

Hearing that, Abi didn't know what to say. Her tone softened. "Burton..."

"Tonight, I wanted to stop you from making a mistake."

"But that's not your decision."

"No, it's not. To me, it was a test."

"A test? For whom?"

"Him and Sara. Given the situation, I wanted to know what they would do and how they would respond."

Abi believed Burton was off his rocker. "We aren't a science experiment."

"I'm aware. But it proves their loyalty and willingness to continue the relationship despite that major disruption. Correct?"

She thought about what he said and how Shane reacted. It was sweet. "How did Sara take the news?"

"Initially, she was disappointed but wholeheartedly understood." He said proudly, "We made plans to go out tomorrow night."

Since Shane and the team were leaving Thursday morning, she hoped to see him, too.

"Are you okay?" he asked, with her deep in thought. "Don't be mad."

She simmered down. "I'm not."

"Good." Knowing it was safe to get close, he approached her with open arms. "So? Truce?"

Hugging him, she said, "I suppose."

Parting ways, he added, "It's a school night for you, and I have to be up by five for a workout on the roof. So, I'm gonna say goodnight."

"Okay," Abi nodded and walked toward the door. Before leaving, she turned. "Burton?"

"Yeah?"

"Thank you." She squinted one eye. "I think..."

"You're welcome."

"Goodnight." Abi started walking away.

"Night, Abs."

Heading to the opposite side of the house, she went to her room. Showered and freshened, she got ready for bed and slipped on a night-gown. Realizing how much had happened that day, she was exhausted just thinking about it.

Covered up, with her alarm set, Abi found a message from Laney asking how she was doing. Texting her back, she apologized for not calling and told her she was fine. Refraining from sharing more details, Abi suggested they talk tomorrow.

Seconds after pressing send, Laney sent a thumbs up and replied, *See you in the morning.*

Trying to calm her mind, Abi put down the phone. Arm resting above the fluffy covers, her gaze drifted to the sofa sectional, where less than an hour ago, she and Shane lay tangled in a moment of bliss. The memory stirred her heart with tenderness and a pang of longing, making her blush. She remembered how his eyes sparkled when he looked at her, the kind of look that made her feel truly seen. It was a moment of pure connection where the rest of the world fell away, leaving just the two of them wrapped in the warmth of each other's presence.

"Maybe Burton was right," she whispered. "It is too soon."

92

No School

Barely hearing her alarm as the sound floated around the large room, Abi woke a little disoriented. Realizing where she was, she turned it off, sat up, and leaned against the tufted headboard. All at once, her phone sparked with a flurry of texts.

She rubbed her eyes and tried to focus. "What's going on?"

Perusing the notifications and seeing her friends in a panic, she found a security alert from the school. In reading it, she knew what had happened despite everyone else speculating.

Her phone rang. Seeing Shane's face on the screen, she answered it. "Hello?"

"Hey. Morning. Did you see the alert?"

"Yes, I did."

"You were right. Something major must be going down if the headmaster canceled classes until further notice."

"There's reason to believe the men at the gatehouse are casing the place. Maybe plotting something," she divulged.

"If that's true, it's a big deal. You'd think the school would vet them better based on the families who attend there."

"Yes, obviously not."

Wanting to make the most of a free day, he said, "So? What do you want to do?"

"I don't know. Too early to make that decision," she laughed.

"Looks like I'm free until three o'clock. Pretty sure practice is still a go, regardless. Haven't heard otherwise."

"Okay." Abi checked her other messages. Reading one from Ming, she said, "Ben and Ming invited everyone down to Manhattan Beach. Up to going there?"

"Sure. What time?"

"She says any time after eleven." Texting Ming in the group chat, she noticed Jade replied also. "Looks like Reg and Jade will be there."

"I see that. It should be fun."

Abi could hear him rustling around.

"Well, I'm gonna get ready. I'll pick you up in an hour. Does that work?"

She flung the covers off and sat on the edge of the bed. "I'll be ready," she said.

"Maybe you can ditch the shadows today."

Knowing that wasn't a good idea, she replied, "Yeah, probably not."

He understood. "Fine. I'll see you soon, then?"

"Sounds good."

Ending their call, Abi got moving. While getting dressed, she realized what day it was. "It's already been a week," she whispered. Happy to skip over her uniform, she dressed casually and tried to keep the negative thoughts from bombarding her mind. After brushing her hair, she put on a little makeup and headed to the kitchen on the upper floor, where she noticed a flurry of activity around the house. A few people were coming and going.

Finding Martin speaking with Anton in the kitchen, she approached.

"Morning, Miss Abi. How was your first night?" the older gentleman asked.

"It was okay, I suppose. Just felt a little out of sorts."

"Understandably."

"Martin, what's all the commotion?"

With his iPad in hand, he said, "Master B has a remote interview today at two o'clock with EDM.com. Our people are prepping for that."

"Wait? He's not going to show his face on camera? Is he?"

"No, deary. He will stay covered to keep up appearances." Checking his phone, he said, "I'm sorry. They need me downstairs. Excuse me a moment."

"Sure," she said while sitting across from Anton.

"What can I get you, Miss?" he asked joyfully. "I'm just finishing Master B's eggs, broccoli, avocado, and bacon."

"Just a small portion of that would be great, thank you."

While she waited, Burton appeared from around the corner. Saying goodbye to a huge guy Abi assumed was his trainer, the man descended the main staircase as Burton looked over and found her sitting along the island.

"Hey. Good morning." He looked at the time. "Aren't you going to be late for school?"

"No school today." Abi noticed his suspicious look. It was like he had a parental instinct. She pulled up the school's notification.

He read it. "Guess they decided to proceed with the op. Make sure you are nowhere near there today."

Abi smiled. "Will do. A group of us is heading to Ben's place for a few hours."

"Who is Ben?" he questioned nosily.

"One of the new football players. He's dating Ming."

"Right... I have no idea who those people are."

She laughed. "I didn't expect you to."

"So, you're going with Shane or the guys?"

"Both."

He nodded. "Good call."

"Everything will be fine. It's a house along The Strand. Do you know of it?"

"I do." He didn't want to frighten her. "Just keep a close eye on your surroundings today."

"I will."

Aware of what day it was, he decided not to make mention. "So, how'd you sleep – being the first night and all?"

"I had a lot on my mind. Took me a bit to drift off."

"Yeah, me too."

Anton handed him his plate.

About to pass it to Abi, she held up her hand. "No, go ahead. He is prepping mine."

Sliding it in front of him, he took a bite of his eggs.

Anton presented Abi with her plate.

"Thank you," she said.

"No problem, Miss."

The awkward silence between her and Burton made it hard to say what he needed to.

Out of the blue, with eyes focused on his food, he said, "I'm sorry for interrupting the two of you last night... I promised when you moved it that you'd, umm, have privacy."

She smiled. "It's fine. I understand. I was thinking about what you said."

Still not looking her in the eye, he asked, "And?"

"And you were right," she confirmed. "It's too soon."

Facing forward, Burton offered a subtle sigh of relief. "That's good to hear."

While Anton cleaned the kitchen, Abi could see him listening intently to their conversation since he'd run the cloth over the same spot at least ten times.

"Look, I know you are protective of me, but I'm not that little girl from Boston anymore."

Holding his breath, he knew very well she wasn't. "I know. I just..."

"I get it. And it's not like I'm not grateful for everything you've done."

He nodded. "I understand."

"So, we're good?"

Sitting stoically, he answered, "Yes."

She finished the last few bites on her plate. "You invest in Sara. I invest in Shane?"

The famous DJ answered, "Agreed."

Abi looked at the time. "I've gotta go. He'll be here shortly." She got up from her chair to take her plate to the sink.

Anton intervened. "Don't worry, Miss. I'll take that."

"Thank you for breakfast," she said.

Pretending he hadn't heard their intimate discussion, he replied, "Enjoy your day."

"You too." About to leave, Abi walked up behind Burton and wrapped her arms around his broad shoulders. Resting her head on his back, she felt him place one hand on her arm. "I'll see you later. Good luck with the interview."

"Yeah. Thanks. You're gonna miss all the craziness."

"You'll do fine. I believe in you."

He smiled. "Appreciate that."

Letting go, he turned to her and raised a steady hand.

"Bye," she said.

"See ya."

Once Abi left the kitchen and descended the steps, Burton finished his breakfast as Martin reappeared from the lower level.

"Everything alright, Sir?" he asked, his spidy senses tingling.

Before he could answer, Anton interrupted. "He and Miss Abi had a heart-to-heart talk."

Burton shot the chef an evil eye.

Martin got antsy. "Despite what you may have discussed, please do not let this interfere with business today."

He nodded robotically.

Handing him a piece of paper, the gentleman added, "Here is the list of questions we've prepared. They are fairly straightforward."

Perusing the list, Burton said, "Okay."

His right-hand man knew his boss was quite unhappy. "Please cheer up, Sir. This is a big day. The launch of Nightfall Inc worldwide has become somewhat, well, legendary. Prelaunch memberships for the vault have skyrocketed, and the app is averaging thousands of tickets a minute."

"That's awesome."

Not getting the response he wanted, the wise elder said, "If I may, Sir. Have you told her about Miami and Chicago yet?"

Burton turned to him. "No."

"I advise you not to leave that too late." Martin was sure the young man was only half listening to what he'd said. "Master B?"

Taking a deep breath, Burton got up from the chair. "I'm good, Martin. Let's get this done, shall we?"

They watched him walk downstairs and disappear.

"Keep this on the down-low, Chap," Martin said to Anton. "I need you to send me a detailed transcript of their conversation."

Willing to do that, he agreed. "I'll send it right now."

"We need to keep that boy focused and his heart intact."

93

Manhattan Beach

Having packed her crossover bag, Abi received a text from Shane telling her he was minutes away. While wandering down the hall to the main staircase, she inched through the frenzy of strangers coming and going and wished she could stay and support Burton through this, but she couldn't. Seeing Shane at the gate, she went outside to wait for him to pull up.

The football player rolled down his window upon seeing Gerald.

"Mr. Coppersmith. Good to see you."

"You as well. Abi said you were working here now."

He nodded graciously. "Yes. So grateful. Such a nice young man."

Not fully agreeing with the guy, he replied, "So I hear."

The gate opened. "Miss Abi is waiting for you, I'm sure."

"Yes, she's expecting me." Slowly moving past, he said, "I'll talk to you later, Sir."

"Absolutely."

When he got to the house, he found Abi sitting on the steps.

Without hesitation, she got in before he could open her door for her. "Hello," she said, eyes glued to the windows, almost in search of someone.

About to kiss her, she moved back. "No, not here. Cameras."

Understanding, he said, "Okay, then," before putting the truck in gear and leaving.

Both waved to Gerald on the way by.

Abi could see her shadows were already close behind.

"Can you find the address of Ben's place? Ming said in the chat this morning that there is a parking lot about a five-minute walk from the house. We need to go there."

Finding it on Google Maps, she magnified the location and pointed to the screen. "You're right. It's just south of there." Her voice was low-toned and less lively.

Reaching for her hand, he gently squeezed it and asked, "Did he say something to you?"

Unwilling to discuss her interactions with Burton, she decided to skirt around the topic. "No, everything is fine."

Not convinced, he questioned, "Are you sure?"

"Yep. All good."

Getting the feeling he shouldn't press his luck, he changed the subject. "Kinda weird having a Wednesday off."

"In all honesty, I needed it."

When she said that, Shane knew something was troubling her. "Well, how about we make the most of the walk along the beach before joining the others today?"

Her face brightened. "Yeah. I'd like that."

Approaching the gates of Bel Air, Shane stopped at the intersection and waited for the light to turn. With her hand in his, he leaned over, hoping she'd meet him halfway.

She obliged and gently rested her opposite hand on his cheek as her soft, glossy lips touched his and made for a better start to their day.

"Remember the last time we drove out this way?"

"I do," Abi fondly recalled. "Little did I know we would make a connection that afternoon."

"I was nervous when I saw you walkin' across the parking lot."

"You were not," she challenged.

"No, it's true. I was."

Mimicking his actions, she said in a tough voice, "Hey! New England?"

Embarrassed, he replied, "I can't believe I called you that."

"Well, it was cute at first."

"Then, you melted when I called you Abs."

She bashfully tilted her head to the side and rested it on his shoulder. "A lot has happened since then," she said, going quiet.

"About that. Have you talked to the one who shall not be named?"

Knowing he was referring Father Father, she said, "No. Not since Monday. And it's not like he's tried to contact me." She sat up in her seat. "Besides, I don't care either way."

Shane spotted the guys in the rearview mirror. "So, will they be with us the entire afternoon?"

She checked their proximity. "I'll make sure they keep their distance. Given what's happening at Gilderson, I feel safer with them there. No offense."

"None taken." He fished for more info. "Has Burton heard anything more on that?"

"No, he didn't say."

It compelled him to ask, "So, is he a cop? Or from a three-letter agency? He never really confirmed either way."

"Between you and me, I assume the latter."

"Interesting."

"You can't breathe a word of that. Please, I don't want to put him in danger."

"I won't. I get it."

Following the GPS instructions, they found the oceanside parking lot. Thankfully, there were lots of spots available. Seeing a few black SUVs at the far end, with drivers congregating together, Abi figured they were close.

Shane parked facing the water. Across from them was a long pier. Getting out, about to lock up, he said, "Where do you want to start? I've got the blanket in the back, too."

"Definitely take the blanket."

He grabbed it from the tailgate and tucked it under his arm. "Ready?"

"Yes," she said, gazing out at the ocean.

Moving along the path, he looked at her, knowing something was off.

Andrew and Ted tried to keep a buffer between them.

The small waves rolled in with the winds as the sun sparkled on the water.

Taken by the salty air, she stopped and breathed deeply, hoping to recharge her spirit. "This is a good spot," she said.

Spreading out the blanket, Abi sat on it first, then Shane joined her.

"I'm worried about you," he said, noticeably concerned.

"Why?"

"Did I do something wrong? Move too fast last night? Did I make you feel..."

Before he could finish his sentence, she raised her hand to cover his mouth. "No, you didn't do any of those things."

Lowering her hand, he asked, "Then what?"

"It's not you. I'm just feeling down. It's been a week since Mom passed."

"Oh, Abs. I'm sorry." He felt like a terrible boyfriend. "I should've paid more attention."

"Don't feel bad. It's fine." She answered, "I'm just going through the motions."

"With all the drama and the media attention, I've gotten caught up in that instead of being here for you."

"I know you've got a lot on your plate."

"All that aside, if it affects you, it affects me. It's written in the boyfriend agreement," he said humorously, hoping to bring a smile to her face.

She bumped his shoulder with hers. "Boyfriend agreement, huh?"

"Strict rules, you know."

A little less burdened, she gazed at the clouds drifting past.

His demeanor changed. "Seriously, though. I want you to feel comfortable sharing your struggles with me – anything, really."

"I will. I'm still processing. It's hard to believe. Sometimes it feels like a bad dream." Determined to move forward, she said, "Come on. Let's go and find our friends. We still have a ways to walk."

Shane got up and helped her to her feet. Folding the blanket, they dropped it off at the Jeep before walking down The Strand to Ben's beach house along 18th Street.

Taking the path between the rows of houses, they followed the sound of laughter from the elevated patio where their friends had gathered.

Addressing Andrew and Ted, Abi asked, "Can you guys watch from here?"

The big guy nodded and gave her a thumbs-up. Parting ways, they took their positions at opposite sides of the house.

Ming looked over the balcony and saw them below. "Hey! Shane and Abi are here!" she announced as all of their friends turned and waved.

"Sorry, we're late!" Abi said, looking up at her.

"No problem! You're here now. That's the important thing." She pointed to her left. "Come around to the front door! I'll meet you there!"

They followed her instructions and climbed the steps to the custom entryway, where they found Ming waiting.

"Welcome, you guys."

Abi hugged the girl. "Thank you for inviting us."

Realizing his girlfriend was courageously putting on a brave face, Shane kept a close eye on her.

"Hey, Cap," Ben said, offering a friendly handshake. "Glad you guys could make it."

"Thanks for the invite, man. Appreciate it. Nice place." He watched Abi mingling.

Ben nervously replied, "Yeah, it's small. But the location is great."

Adrian joined them. "So, what do you think happened at school this morning?"

"Not sure," Shane said, keeping tight-lipped.

Ben chimed in. "Everyone is saying this has never happened before?"

With his sights on Abi, Shane said, "I've been there three years. Never experienced anything like this."

"There must have been an extensive breach for them to shut us out. Makes you wonder who the target was?" Adrian questioned.

Wanting to add his two cents, Ben increased the speculation. "Well, my bet is on that guy, Reggie. Rumor has it he just majorly screwed ovFather Father or something? Maybe this is about him?"

"Reg is my best friend." The QB quickly defended. "He didn't screw over his Dad. It's a long story. But he's not in the wrong."

"Yeah, I agree with Cap," Adrian said, voicing his opinion.

"Sorry, guys." Ben apologized embarassingly. "I didn't know." Seeing they weren't happy to hear his take on things, Ben tried to save face. "Help yourself to beverages at the bar. The food is just inside the kitchen on your right."

Preoccupied by Abi sitting with the girls on the patio, Shane made eye contact.

When he looked her way, she subtly waved to let him know she was alright.

"Can I get you something to eat? Maybe something to drink?" Ming asked her, wanting to be the ultimate hostess.

"Just a water would be good for now," she said. "I had a late breakfast."

Laney walked up the stairs looking fabulous in a burnt orange maxi dress and closed-toe Stuart Weitzman wedges.

"Well, hello, everyone! The party can start! We're here!"

She stood out against Shawn's dark, all-navy designer joggers with a matching long sleeve as he escorted her, his hand resting on her back.

Immediately making her way to Abi, she hugged her friend. "How was the first night?"

"Oooh, first night for what?" Allie asked nosily.

"You haven't told them yet?" Laney blurted, causing a hum amongst their friends. "She moved in with Burton."

Upon hearing this, it piqued Shane's interest.

Needing to correct Laney, Abi tried to recover. "It's not like that. I'm still not talking to my Dad. I just needed a place to stay and he graciously offered."

Her friend felt notably slighted. "You still could have stayed with me, you know."

Abi could tell the girl was upset. "I know. I didn't want to impose. He's like family."

Laney found the bar and loudly expressed, "So you say."

Scared, knowing the pretty blonde knew his true identity, Abi hoped she wouldn't reveal the truth about him.

"I believe you." Allie saw the worry on Abi's face. "If you two grew up together, he's probably the closest thing to a brother, right?"

"Yes, that's right."

"Then, you're lucky to have him."

Abi agreed. "Yes, I am. For sure."

"So enough about this. What do you think happened at school?" Allie put it out there to hear everybody's thoughts.

Uncomfortable, Abi knew the answer but needed to stay quiet. "Does it matter? We got a day off. How great is that?"

Laney cheered! "Woohoo!"

The girls watched her stumble over to the guys and hug them.

"How much has she had?" Allie whispered. "It's barely noon."

Able to tell she was harboring something, Abi walked over and stood beside Shane to get a closer look at her eyes.

"Hey, Lane? Want to go inside and check out the snacks with me?" Abi suggested, hoping to get food in the girl's stomach.

"Sure, Abs." Walking with Abi's arm around her, she whispered, "So, where did you sleep last night?"

"My room, why?" she questioned, handing Laney a plate before getting one for herself.

"Just wondering."

Concerned about her behavior, she said, "Laney, I'm sorry I left your place so quickly. I hope I didn't hurt your feelings. That wasn't my intention."

"It's all good. I get it. Why wouldn't you want to move in with your famous friend?"

Hearing that knocked the wind from her. "Please, keep your voice down. You promised."

"Oh, yes. Our little pact..." she giggled.

Not sure how to handle this, Abi panicked. "How much have you had to drink today?"

Laney casually raised her glass. "This is my fourth! Or is it fifth? Maybe eighth? I don't remember."

About to take the glass from her, the girl yanked it back, spilling it everywhere.

"What are you doing?" she said accusingly.

"Perhaps you should switch to water or have a coffee."

The girl turned mean on a dime. "No! You're gonna ruin all the fun!"

Attempting to keep her calm, Abi said, "You're right. I'm sorry..."

Shawn rushed over.

"She thinks she's better than me, Babe!"

Abi could see how difficult it was for Shawn to deal with her. He whispered to AbiFather father came back with a new woman. His girlfriend, partner, whatever he calls her, is furious. So is her Mom. He broke their arrangement and brought the new girl to the house. It's good that you weren't there last night. It wasn't good."

Suddenly, everything escalated. "Don't tell her that!" Laney shouted, walking out onto the patio. "Abi thinks she's above us now!"

Witnessing what was happening, Shane came to her defense. "Shawn, you should take her home."

About to lead his girlfriend down the steps, Laney slapped his hands away. "No! I'm not leaving!" Staring at Abi, she said, "Let's play a game! We should play truth or dare! Who's first!" She pointed at the new girl and zeroed in sharply. "Truth? Is it true that your friend Burton is DJ Black Lyon?"

Shocked by the outburst, Shane went into damage control mode. "That's not true. The guy is a student at UCLA - a science nerd, not a DJ."

Laney rebutted, "That's not what Eastwood said!"

Their friends were stunned.

Allie looked at Abi. "What did Eastwood say?" she asked, incredibly intrigued.

With perfect timing, Jade and Reggie arrived. Finding their friends at odds, they stood there, assuming Abi was perhaps at the center of it, given all eyes were on her.

"What's going on?" Jade could see there was friction.

"You're just in time! Abi hasn't answered!" Laney exclaimed.

Able to tell her friend had been drinking by the slur in her words, Jade joined the girls. "What did I miss?"

"Haven't you heard? Her friend, Burton, is DJ Black Lyon!" the unstable blonde divulged.

Eyebrows raised, Jade knew how to handle this. "No, Laney, I think you're mistaken. I've seen the guy on campus at UCLA. He's a student. Computer science. Apparently, he's some kind of genius."

"That's what I said." Shane backed up her statement, hoping to ward off suspicion.

Ready to leave, Shawn checked his phone. "My driver is close by. Help me get her out of here, guys." Taking hold of her hand and guiding her along with his arm circling her waist, the team gathered around them in a circle.

"Wait? What are you doing?" she questioned unsteadily.

"I'm taking you home, Lane."

"No, I don't want to go there, Babe! That's where she is – that girl!" She turned to Abi and said, "Now I know how you felt about the woman your Dad is dating. Is she half his age, too?"

Not wanting to get into it, she answered truthfully, "Yes. She is."

"See, Shawn! Her Dad did the same thing! That's why I can't go home."

"It's okay, Lane. You can stay with me. We need to grab a few things from your place first, okay?"

She calmed down somewhat. "Yeah, I should pack a bag."

"Exactly."

Reading the look on Shawn's face, Abi knew he was stressed and embarrassed but understood why Laney was struggling. Thankfully, the girl agreed to leave without much fuss.

The group kept their distance just in case they set her off.

When Shawn's driver pulled away, everyone relaxed again.

Suddenly circling back, rehashing what Laney sparked, Allie asked, "So, is it true?"

"Is what true?" Abi questioned, hoping to avoid answering.

"About Burton? Is he Dark Demon?"

The girls gathered around, wanting to hear what she'd say.

"No, he's not. Burton is a Computer Science genius pursuing his PHD." Having reiterated his cover, she scanned each face, hoping they'd show some sign that they believed her.

Jade joined them, holding a plate of food. "Well, that was drama I didn't expect today."

By saying that, Abi could see Jade changed the course of their conversation. "Apparently, her Dad returned and brought a much younger woman home. From what I gather, her Mother found out and his partner."

"But if her parents live separate lives, who cares?"

Realizing Jade knew the dynamics of Laney's family, her comment ignited a heated debate amongst the girls.

Not wanting to get involved, needing to escape any further Burton speculation, Abi said, "I'm just going to grab something to eat."

Shane watched her disappear inside as he sat around with the guys. "So, Reg? How are things going, man?"

"Truthfully? My life is over. Despite Laney's display, I could use a drink, too. Is there any hard liquor here?"

Ben said, "Behind the bar. Pick your poison."

"Whisky on the rocks?" Reg requested.

When Ben returned, Reggie slung the drink back in record time. Handing him the empty glass, the player refilled it for him again.

"What's the update?" Shane asked.

"My Father didn't take to kindly to the court documents from my lawyer. Since then, he's vowed to make my life a living hell by suing me for lost revenue since the engagement got called off."

The QB wasn't surprised. "How much does he want?"

"Five hundred million."

"Holy shit!" Shane said as Jade returned outside.

By the look on the QB's face, Jade could see the news was out. "He told you, didn't he?"

"Tell you what?" Abi didn't know what she'd missed.

Jade turned to her as she took a drink of water. "His Dad is suing Reg for five hundred million."

"Dollars?" Abi said, almost choking.

"Yep." Reg stood tall and inhaled deeply. Each friend's reaction made the situation feel more and more hopeless. Not about to surrender, he said, "Don't worry. I'll figure something out. There's gotta be a way to beat him."

Jade joined Abi. "I don't know what we're gonna do... Reg is so stressed. His lawyers are doing everything they can to find some sort of recourse. The man was technically pimping out his son so he can make more money. Isn't that against the law?"

"I would say so." Abi felt sick for them. "I hope no judge in the world would side with his Father based on that."

Without missing a beat, Jade said, "Unless his Dad pays him off first."

"He can do that?"

"It happens all the time."

Allie waved Jade over.

"I'll be right back, Abs. Give me a second."

Having had enough drama for one day, Abi looked around as the guys moved on to talk to Alan, Ben, and Adrian. Left alone, she wandered inside to explore the pretty house decorated in warm honey hardwood, custom cabinetry, ivory walls, and clean lines.

Minutes later, the guys went to replenish their plates and fill them with munchies.

Shane followed. Not seeing Abi on the patio, he expected to find her sitting in the living room after the girls moved inside. But she wasn't there. Slightly panicked, he set his plate down and scoured the main floor before urgently calling out the front door to Andrew and Ted.

"Hey, guys? Is she with you?"

The men swiftly converged on the home, creating a cause for alarm amongst their friends.

"Shane? What's happening?" Reggie asked, ready to help.

"I can't find Abs."

"She couldn't have gone far." Reg started searching the main floor with security as Shane bounded up the stairs. His friend was close behind.

Ducking in and out of the bedrooms and bathrooms on the second level, Shane reached the primary suite near the back of the house. Flinging open the door, he spotted someone.

"Abi?" It took a second to calm down. Returning to the staircase, he shouted to Andrew and Ted, "It's okay. I found her."

Reggie took a breath. "Okay, good," he said, telling Jade all was well. The guys called off the search.

"Give me a minute," Shane asked before returning to the room.

Andrew nodded.

Taking a breath, he came up behind his girlfriend. Seeing her earbuds in her ears, he knew she couldn't hear him. Walking around to the far side, hoping not to scare her, she saw him out of the corner of her eye and jumped.

"Sorry..." he said with hands raised defensively.

"It's fine," she laughed. "Wasn't expecting to see you there."

"You gave us a fright."

"Why?" she asked, straightening her posture.

"You disappeared. I didn't know where you were."

Abi shoved over and gave him room to sit. "I should have told you I was coming up here."

He sat beside her.

"I just needed to escape the crowd. It's been a crazy day, and I wanted some quiet time."

"I get it," he said. "The Laney thing was unfortunate."

"I can't believe she spilled Burton's secret." She looked down at her feet. "But in the state she was in, I'm not surprised."

"Because of that, they'll probably think she made it up."

"I hope so."

"Be prepared, though. The truth always surfaces eventually."

"As long as it doesn't come from me," she replied quickly.

"For sure," he paused. "Then there's Reg. What parent sues his son for damages because he didn't want to marry the girl forced upon him?" Swinging back and forth, Shane rested his head on the cushions. "This is a really calming spot."

"Isn't it? I think so, too," she whispered, her mind still reeling. "How did life get so damn complicated? What happened to just worrying about good grades? Homework? Sports?" Soon, her thoughts stole her away again.

"What are you thinking about?" He got more comfortable.

Spilling the first thing that came to mind, she asked, "I've been thinking about what happened in Vegas."

"Which part?"

"What made you come into the house when Eastwood had me at gunpoint? What were you thinking?"

"That's just it. I wasn't. I just needed to act and do everything in my power to save you."

"Even though you could have failed?"

Without hesitation, he answered, "Yes."

"It could have ended badly."

"But it didn't," he reassured, assuming she might be dealing with some post-traumatic stress.

"There's this fear I have. It causes me to constantly look over my shoulder, almost as if I'm waiting for the ball to drop - ever since I saw him outside the hospital. That day, he looked straight at me. It was like he was the devil himself – just evil." She shimmied around. "Every sound, every bit of movement out of the corner of my eye, I think it's him. Nobody notices my fear."

"Why didn't you say something?"

"And what? Look weak? This damsel in distress who constantly needs saving?"

"This isn't a joke, Abs. It's not like you're dealing with a bully or a mean girl. These people are dangerous. There's a difference."

She silently agreed and said, "I'm thankful the guys are there when you aren't. They're a blessing in disguise. My safety net."

"Despite being around all the time and invading our privacy, I'm glad they're there too."

Abi was happy to hear him say that.

Shane looked at the time on his phone. "We should probably get moving. I've gotta get to practice."

"Alright." On the verge of tears, hating that he'd be away for two days, she said, "I'm going to miss you when you're gone." The second she said it, her eyes glistened.

Hugging her, he said, "I'll miss you too. But we can talk on the phone as often as you like. I'll send you the links so you can watch the games. I'll even give you secret signals from the field. How's that?"

She sobbed. "Really?"

"Absolutely. And at night, we can FaceTime. I can watch you fall asleep."

Blotting her cheeks, she said, "I'm sorry for unloading on you."

"Honestly, I'm thankful you did."

She laughed. "Why?"

"Because it means you are letting me in. Usually, that is reserved for him, not me."

"Hey..."

"I'm just stating the obvious."

"He has a name, you know."

He chuckled. "Oh, I'm well aware. I just don't like it."

She tilted her head disappointingly. "I thought we were past this. I want you guys to get along. Can't you do that for me?"

"I'm trying," he replied humorously. Hearing their friends talking below them, he said, "Sounds like the party is breaking up."

"I'm good to leave whenever you are." About to stand, she cuddled against him. "But maybe we should wait five more minutes?"

Sliding closer, he kissed her cheek and held her tight. "Sure," he said.

Soaking up the last of their quiet time, they sadly left their perfect spot.

On the way downstairs, he said, "So, what will you do while I'm on the field tonight?"

"I am going to hang out in my room. Maybe I'll watch a movie after finishing the math and science work. We've got a lot to review later this evening. Up for it?"

"It's a date."

94

Homebound

Saying their goodbyes, everyone thanked Ben and Ming for hosting before their group crossed the charming beachfront avenue and descended the weathered concrete steps to the beachside path. The scent of saltwater mingled with the air, and a gentle breeze rustled the palm trees overhead as they walked toward the parking lot.

Andrew and Ted were close by.

Abi noticed them scanning their surroundings, their eyes sharp and attentive, ready for any sign of trouble.

Shane, too, moved with purpose, his presence reassuring.

Mingling amidst the group, she felt more secure, not so exposed. Thankful to be part of a tight-knit circle and no longer alone, she clung to Shane's arm while they strolled.

Finally arriving at the Jeep, their friends waved and offered cheerful farewells, then loaded into chauffeur-driven SUVs or exotic cars.

Shane opened the passenger side for Abi.

Before closing it, Andrew walked up. "Where are we headed, Miss?"

"The Wasserman Center. Then, can you guys drive me home after that?"

"Certainly." He could tell her voice was solemn.

"Thank you."

"Sure thing." He closed her door and went to join Ted and Matt.

Shane got in his seat. "Ready?" he asked.

"Yep."

He started the truck and put it in gear. Holding her hand, they pulled away with everyone else.

Abi barely spoke for much of the trip.

Hoping to sway her thoughts in a more positive direction, Shane asked, "Any words of wisdom for me today?"

Her mind went blank, and she panicked a little. "I, umm..."

Giving her hand a few gentle squeezes, he said, "Abs, I need you to tell me the truth."

She turned to him.

"Is there something you don't want to tell me? Or can't? If so, I need to know."

"I promise. It's nothing. I'm just feeling down and don't know how to fix it."

Realizing she was grieving, he brought her hand to his chest. "Whatever you need, please, lean on me. I can take it."

She smiled through her tears.

"Everything is going to be alright. You have to take one day at a time. Agreed?"

"Agreed." She leaned over and rested her head upon his shoulder.

Letting go of her hand, he slipped his arm around her and pulled her close while listening to Forester on Spotify.

When they arrived at the Wasserman garage, Shane parked the Jeep on the upper level as the guys pulled up behind them and waited.

"I'll text you when I finish here," he said.

"Okay."

"Maybe you want to study at my place tonight?"

"Sure. I'd like that."

Not wanting to leave, he hugged her tightly. Cheek to cheek, pulling back a little, Shane kissed her lips once, then twice. Seeing she expected more, he looked into her eyes before melting her to pieces. Amidst the blissful moment, he whispered, "I can hardly wait to see you tonight."

What he said sparked butterflies in her chest. "Me too. I love you."

Without hesitation, he replied, "I love you more."

Letting go, he got out and walked around to her side.

The men were waiting a few feet away.

Shane escorted Abi to their SUV and opened the door. Kissing her goodbye, he waited as she settled in before closing it. Resting his hand on the window, he saw hers on the other side. As they drove away, he waved before grabbing his gear and joining Ben and Adrian, standing nearby.

As the truck moved through the dark garage, they soon hit the light again.

Abi stayed quiet.

Matt turned on some music, knowing she'd appreciate it.

Hearing the soft Simple Minds tune again, reminding her of her Mother, she turned and tearfully smiled. "Thank you for that."

"Absolutely, Miss."

95

The Moment

Pulling up to the gatehouse, Abi spotted Gerald on duty and felt relieved. She shuddered, wondering what might have happened if they hadn't found him.

Andrew rolled down his window. "Hey, Gerald. How is your first day going?"

"Pretty good, thank you for asking," Gerald replied warmly.

"Glad to have you aboard," Andrew said.

"I appreciate that."

As the gate opened, Matt saluted Gerald before driving through.

He, in turn, returned the gesture.

Hearing their conversation, Abi was happy the guys showed such respect for him. Given his courageous history, he deserved that.

Noticing a handful of cars still there, Abi figured the interview wasn't over.

Stopped at the front door, Ted swiftly got out and helped Abi. Offering his hand, she took hold and set her feet on the ground.

"Thank you, gentleman. Appreciate your help today."

Silently acknowledging, Ted walked her into the house. "Have a good afternoon, Miss."

"Yes, you too."

"Let us know if you need us."

"I will."

When she entered the foyer, Burton was climbing the stairs from the lower level. Still dressed in his black hood, his face hidden underneath, he didn't see her while passing by in quite a hurry.

Martin noticed but didn't say anything.

She immediately knew something was wrong. Watching his right-hand man follow him into his bedroom, Abi reached the top of the stairs and waited.

About to close the door behind them, she heard him say, "Master B? Miss Abi has returned."

Assuming he wanted to speak to her, Abi stepped inside the entryway as Burton shouted from his bathroom, "Don't say anything! I'll tell her myself!" When he emerged and found her there, he stopped dead in his tracks.

"Tell me what?" she asked.

Moving his sights from Abi to Martin, he requested, "Can you leave us, please?"

"Very well, Sir."

She got worried as the man shut the door.

"What is it? Did something happen?"

Promptly offering her a seat on the chair, she did as he asked.

Watching Burton pace, her anxiety heightened.

His arms crossed over his chest. "In every country around the world, there are crime families that run things in the shadows. Some you see, others you don't."

Confused, she replied, "Okay..."

"Anyone doing business in these territories controlled by these people always receives a calling card when they expect a cut of whatever money is changing hands. They do this and promise a peace agreement in return. For those who don't adhere to the rules, issues arise, and it becomes almost impossible for that business to survive. They make sure of it." He took a deep breath. "This afternoon, we were contacted by a family in Miami and another from Chicago shortly after. Threats accompanied them."

She stared straight ahead. "Threats?"

"Until now, those who wanted access to my vault system have paid for it. The Tracante and Falcone families are demanding exclusive rights to settle their cut because I'm operating my clubs in the areas they own. They've threatened action should I not comply," he paused. "The Oligarchs and I have had an understanding. They've invested heavily in my services and have gotten wind of this. Now, they want it for themselves and plan to block others from gaining access."

Staring blankly, she assessed what he said. "In essence, this has started a war?"

"So it seems." Pacing again, he added, "To resolve it, I'm flying to Miami tomorrow and Chicago on Friday." He looked out the window, deep in thought.

"What is to stop them from simply taking what they want."

"Nothing. If they've set their sights on my technology they will take it peacefully or by force. The agency wants me to leverage this negotiation and gather whatever intel I can."

Abi lowered her head, realizing the seriousness of the situation. "They've given you no other option?"

"No."

"What can I do?" She listened intently for further instructions.

"I'm sending you to a safe house while I'm away. You must stay out of sight."

"But..."

"No, buts. This is not up for debate. I'll have my guys, Martin and Sara, with me and others waiting in the shadows. I just need you safe, that's all."

"Then what?"

"Hopefully, we'll reach an agreement and resolve this issue. Once everybody gets what they want, the danger will pass, for now. That said, I will never give up what's rightfully mine. I will fight to keep it."

The sheer certainty in his voice frightened her.

He gazed out the window. "I'm sure these families have done their due diligence."

"What do you mean?"

"They know who I care about. Who I'm deeply connected to." His expression softened when he approached her. "Please tell me you'll do as I ask and not deviate from it until you hear from me?"

Without hesitation, Abi nodded. "I will."

Rubbing his palms together, he said, "Tomorrow, we leave for Van Nuys early in the morning. I'm boarding the plane, and you'll take a helicopter to the safehouse. I'm sending Anton, Rosa, and the guys with you."

Confident, she stood up, her voice steady but her heart racing. "I'll go pack a bag."

"And please don't share this information with your friends. I don't want anyone on the wire to get wind of it. That could compromise things."

"I won't."

Just as she turned to leave, he stopped her. "Abi?"

She paused and faced him. "Yes?"

Filled with regret, he said, "This is my life. I'm sorry you got dragged in. It's my fault."

Crushed to see the look on his face, she walked back and slowly hugged him.

He, too, clung tightly.

"We will figure this out," she said, her voice trembling with a mix of determination and fear. Knowing Burton was about to be placed in harm's way, she reassured him, "You're going to be alright. You are smarter than they are. I believe in you."

He did not reply.

While standing there, his cheek against hers, Abi could tell her words offered little solace. Spying his golden lion pin just below eye level, she ran her fingertips over it, recalling the brave man who scooped her up in his arms amidst the darkness and brought her to safety. Leaning back, hoping to lift his spirits, she asked, "I bet you have a whole closet of these?"

He looked down at the hoodie and managed a weak smile. "Wanna see?"

Excited, she peered up at him and nodded, hoping her interest would cast a thin veil over her worry.

Leading the way into his large walk-in closet, Abi followed him to the very end, where he reached under the shelf and pressed a hidden button. Instantly, a secret door popped open, and the lights flickered on. Inside was a room filled with hoodies on one side and a mural anchored by his Black Lyon and Dark Demon logos on the other.

He pointed to the wall. "This is an aerial photograph of the first rave I ever hosted. There were easily a thousand people there. I couldn't believe it. One minute, I was a lonely guy living in the land of ice and snow, studying and making music, and the next, all my dreams came true."

Loving the sentiment, amazed by what he described, Abi felt the tension between them building.

Burton slipped his hoodie off and hung it neatly in line with the others. His movements were slow, and his mind weighted.

"Back then, all I wanted was to be seen. Funny, now all I do is hide my face under a hood."

"But you're not hiding from me anymore," she replied, stepping closer.

His eyes filled with gratitude. Nervous, not knowing what tomorrow would hold, he hesitated, then gently took her by the arms. "Abs, I need you to listen closely."

Her heart skipped a beat at the urgency in his voice, her breath catching in her throat.

"There is always an element of risk in my job. If something happens to me, I want you to know..."

"Nothing is going to happen," she quickly interrupted. "You'll go and come back. Everything will be fine." The thought of it was horrifying.

"Abi..." His voice was a plea sealed with the weight of unspoken fears.

Overwhelmed by emotion, she turned away, embarrassed for him to see her cry.

"I want you to know you are more than I could ever ask for. You've cared for me, accepted me, and, most of all, never gave up on me."

Her tears flowed.

"Like I've hinted many times before, I've had feelings for you for as long as I can remember. Over the past few weeks, that has only intensified, whether it's wrong or not." Resting his hand upon her shoulder, trying to offer comfort, he gave her space but could feel her body trembling. It made him second-guess his decision to tell her the truth. Letting his hand slip from her, about to take a step back, she whisked around desperately.

"Tell me you'll be okay..." she pleaded, "...because I can't go through life without you. I've lost so much. I can't lose you, too."

Quickly embracing her, lips close to her ear, he whispered, "I will do my best. That's all I can promise."

As they parted slightly, her sights locked on his. Abi raised her hand to cover his heart and felt it beating violently. Inching upward, it soon cupped his cheek, causing him to lean into her touch.

For him, it was a reminder that she remained his only weakness.

Time slowed each second, stretching into eternity. Her hand fell to his shoulder, then covered his heart again. Lips hovering inches apart, her breath was soft and warm, mingling with his own in the small space separating them.

Scanning the contours of her face, Burton memorized every line and shadow as if etching it into memory as his fingertips gently traced her hairline.

Heat radiating from his body, his gaze intense, Abi's chest fluttered, every beat echoing with the anticipation of what was about to happen. Spying his hand reaching to meet hers, feeling its gentle but firm presence caused waves of tingles to course through her. Able to see a battle raging within him, she saw his brows furrow as he drew a deep, unsteady breath. Suddenly, his thumb unexpectedly brushed across her face, signaling a silent apology embedded in the tender caress.

"I'm sorry," he whispered, his voice barely audible. Searching her soul, knowing what he wanted to do, Burton held back and looked away. "We can't... umm..." His voice trailed off, conflicted. He knew what he needed to be for her, and right now, that was a protector, nothing more.

Abi resigned to the rejection and lightly kissed him on the cheek, leaving her lips to linger. When she leaned back, she tried to read his thoughts as a voice spread through the house.

"Burton? Burton!" Sara shouted, sharp and urgent.

Shoulders tensed, he released Abi from their embrace. Walking out of the secret room, holding her hand, he closed the door and said, "Wait here. I'll take her upstairs so you can leave. I can't risk her seeing us together. Please understand."

Knowing the turmoil it could cause, she nodded.

About to leave the closet, he composed himself, turned, and looked back.

She knew he didn't want to go.

Listening and waiting for a few minutes, she assumed the two had gone to the upper level as their conversation moved further away. Cautiously peeking into the hallway, once the coast was clear, it didn't take long to exit and swiftly return to her room. Ever so gently, she closed the door and turned to lean against it as she gazed up at the ceiling.

"What are you doing?" she questioned, inevitably drawn in by the feelings from Tahoe resurfacing.

Amidst it all, her phone rang. About to accept the call, she found Shane's picture on her screen. Hating herself beyond measure, she answered, "Hello?"

"Hey. I'm done for the day. Still feel like hanging out tonight?"

A little dazed, she replied, "Umm, sure... What did you have in mind?"

"Well, we could go to grab food, then come back to my house and watch a movie or we could just drive up the coast and grab something on the fly?"

Not wanting to be seen in the public eye, she asked lightheartedly, "And when does homework factor into that?"

"Well, there's no school with the breach, so..." He hoped she'd let it slide.

"But they are still assigning work. You can't fall behind."

He conceded. "Okay, okay!" he laughed. "We'll get food and return to my place to study. Agreed?"

"Yes."

"Fine. I'll swing by to pick you up shortly."

She smiled. "I'll be waiting."

The Night Out

Slipping the phone in her pocket, Abi took a deep breath. Confused, her emotions swirling all over the place, she tried to focus and forget what had transpired but couldn't. Forced to change clothes and freshen up, Abi found herself analyzing every second of her interaction with Burton as guilt swallowed her whole.

After receiving Shane's text warning that he was two minutes away, Abi reached for her door handle. Not knowing how to face Sara, let alone Burton, she sighed. "Just go and act like nothing happened."

When she left her room, she heard Sara's voice carry through the house. Their serious discussion reverberated off the walls, and it seemed heated. She assumed he'd told her the same news.

The woman spotted her emerging from the lower level and immediately clammed up. It was like she needed to refrain from spilling top-secret information.

Noticeably catching Burton's attention on the way into the kitchen, Abi couldn't help but stare while slinging her crossbody bag and backpack on one shoulder.

Seeing this, Sara asked, "Hey, Abi. Where are you off to?"

"Shane is picking me up. We need to review math and science. The classes are virtual tomorrow. I plan to get him up to speed before he leaves for two days."

"Got your phone?" Burton inquired, his eyes locked on her sharply.

"Of course." She could tell he didn't want her to go.

"Keep a low profile."

"I will," she said as her device chimed. "He's here. Umm, I've gotta run. I'll see you two later."

Happy the girl was departing, Sara waved. "Bye. Have fun," she said while Burton looked on.

Bounding down the stairs and out the front doors, she realized the guys had left for the day and assumed they might be flying solo tonight. Joining Shane in the Jeep, she jumped in. "Hello," she said.

He leaned his elbow on the center console and bridged the gap between them. "Hey, you." His sights drifted from her eyes to her lips.

Meeting him halfway, she soaked up each gentle kiss.

Parting, he asked, "Ready to go?"

About to answer, she noticed two unnamed guards load into an SUV.

I guess I spoke too soon, she thought.

Shane saw them also. "Damn. I figured we'd be on our own. Sadly, not."

"So close," she chuckled, secretly thankful someone was coming with her.

When Shane turned the Jeep around, Abi saw Burton standing by the window, his hands buried in his pockets.

Waving to him, he did the same.

"So," Shane said, "I was thinking we could grab sushi or pasta. What are your thoughts?"

"Sushi would be nice. Haven't had that since Vegas."

"Decision made." Feeling like the few hours apart didn't help her mood, he grasped hold of her hand and gave it a few gentle squeezes.

When he did that, she hated herself even more. It made her roll her eyes in disgust. *How could you betray him?* She thought.

While driving toward Sunset Boulevard, Abi's phone rang. "It's my Dad," she said.

Debating on answering it, Shane intervened. "Maybe just hear him out."

Not ready to do that, she declined the call. "There's nothing to say."

"What if he's had a change of heart?"

"I highly doubt it."

The phone rang again. "It's him," she revealed.

"Just answer it, or he'll keep calling."

Reluctantly, she did as he suggested, knowing he was probably right. "Hello?"

"Abi?"

"What do you want, Dad?"

"I'm calling to check-in. I haven't heard from you. How are you doing?"

"How am I? You're kidding, right?" The anger and confusion that surfaced the past half hour exploded. "Let me see. My Mom died. Who I thought my Dad was isn't, and now I have no family and no home."

"Well, you still have a home, but you are too stubborn to return to it," he exclaimed sternly. "And no matter how you feel about me, I'm still your Father, and we're family."

"Whatever helps you sleep at night. Oh, wait! That's probably your new girlfriend's job."

The air between them went dead.

"I don't want to fight anymore," he said wearingly.

"So, you left Jenna?"

"No."

"Well, then, we have nothing further to say."

"I want you to come home."

Abi huffed. "Not going to happen."

"Then you've given me no choice."

She didn't know what he'd say next.

"I'm going to sell the house. It's too big if it's just me here," he said with little remorse.

That feeling of hopelessness returned. "Fine. I'll grab the rest of my things and Mom's, too. 'Cause I'm sure you'll toss everything she owns anyway."

"Abi, please..."

"I think we're done here." She ended the call and leaned her head against the window.

Shane reached over. "Abs?"

"What?" she snapped. So many thoughts rolled through her mind. Quickly backtracking, she said, "I'm sorry. I hate this..."

"I know."

"Things just keep getting worse and worse."

"When are you going to pick up your stuff? I don't want you going there by yourself."

"I don't know. You are away Thursday and Friday. Burton is, too. We've got homecoming on Saturday..."

"Where is he going?"

"Who? Burton?" she asked.

"Yeah."

"He is heading to Miami and Chicago."

"So, you'll be alone for two days?" A look of concern flashed across his face.

She had to come clean. "No secrets, right?" she stated as they turned onto Mulholland Drive.

He took his foot off the gas. "Oh, no. What is it?"

"I need to stay in an undisclosed location for a couple of days, just as a precaution. Burton's had threats."

"Against you?"

"In a roundabout way." To defuse him, she revealed, "Look, I'll be fine. The guys will be with me twenty-four-seven. So, will Rosa and Anton."

"Who the hell is Anton?"

"That's Burton's chef. Rosa is his housekeeper."

Thinking through what she said, he asked, "Did he say why he received the threats?"

"Yes, but I can't say and won't..." She turned to him. "You just have to trust me."

"Trust?"

"Yes."

"I trust you. But not him?" Shane pulled into the Beverly Glen Plaza.

"Maybe you want to grab your things tonight? We can do it. There can't be much left to pack since you moved out."

"My Mom has a whole closet of stuff. And I'm not leaving it behind."

He tried to think of a solution. "My grandfather used to say that many hands make light work."

"What do you mean?"

"What if we gather our friends together to help? That way, we'll finish in a short amount of time."

Abi contemplated what he said and the consequences that could follow. "If he leaves the house tonight to go and see her, we'll go."

"Okay, then. Let's gather the troops over sushi."

97

Roll with the Punches

Hidden at a table in the far corner of the restaurant with their orders placed, the two created a group chat and asked their friends for help. Each responded quickly, wondering what the mission was. Explaining that Abi needed to move her things out of her house, everyone confirmed they were in.

With their sushi and sushimi delivered to the table, Abi read through the messages and realized Burton was the only person she hadn't attached to the blast. Dipping a roll into wasabi-tainted soya sauce, she debated whether to include him in what was happening, knowing he had a lot going on. Afraid to add to his troubles, she understood how upset he'd be if she didn't inform him.

"Should I include Burton and Sara?"

Shane was swift to mention – "All of our friends have replied. That's ten plus us. Twelve in total. I think that's more than enough, don't you?"

"I guess so. But the thing is, Burton and my Dad have a connection. If he returns to the house unexpectedly while we're there, maybe he can talk some sense into the man if he's angry."

"And I can't?"

"I didn't say that. But, three against one isn't a bad thing." She could tell he didn't like the idea.

Shane asked, "Besides, there are no guarantees this will happen tonight. We don't know if he will leave the house and go to…"

"Her place?" she finished his sentence. "I'm certain he will. He's been with her every night for weeks." Abi checked the security cameras at the house. His car was still in the driveway. "I'm sorry this ruined our night out."

"You didn't ruin it. Sometimes, life just happens. Gotta learn to roll with the punches," he said, reminded of what she had divulged earlier. "Have to say, I don't like the idea of him hiding you for two days. Reminds me of when he took you to Tahoe."

On that topic, she dropped one more bomb. "I probably won't have cell privileges again."

"Privileges? Abs? Listen to yourself?"

"You know what I mean. We don't want anyone tracking my whereabouts, remember?"

"I don't like this – any of it. I told you the guy was involved in something illegal. Now, here we are."

"First of all, how can it be illegal?"

"Who knows?' he said suspiciously.

"Besides, I'm only focused on what comes after the two days. It's Homecoming." She directed all her attention to him and said, "Look at me."

Shane turned.

"Promise you'll just focus on the games. You need three wins this week. Can you do that?"

"The team is ready. I'm confident we can."

"And you won't worry about me."

He stopped. "I will try not to worry about you when I'm on the field, but I can't make any promises when I'm off it."

She smiled. "I'm good with that. Don't panic if you can't get a hold of me."

Shane shook his head. "Do you know the hell you put me through when this happened last time?"

"Yes, I realize, but I've given you a heads-up."

Abi watched the man place their bill on the table between them. When she went to grab it, Shane gently snatched it from her and waved the waiter over. "No way. That's for me. You check to see if your Dad's car is still at home."

Abi pulled up the cameras. "It's gone," she said.

"Really?" he replied while punching in his pin on the mobile POS.

Quickly rewinding the feed, she watched her Father leave with a duffle bag in hand. "Yeah. It looks like he's gone for the night. He packed a bag."

Finished paying the bill, he said, "Well, let's get a move on."

Leaving the plaza, Abi sent a blast out to their friends. In an instant, everyone on the list said they were racing toward Stradella from every corner of Bel Air and beyond.

Nervous about going to the house, Abi was quiet the entire way.

When they arrived, she got out and left the gate open for their friends. In the process, she noticed one of her unnamed shadows making a phone call. That is when she knew the guy had called his boss.

Ignoring them on her way inside, she propped open the door and bounded up the stairs. Grabbing empty suitcases from her mother's closet, she removed her clothes in piles and packed the special things she'd brought in keepsake boxes.

Shane cleared out the rest of Abi's things and gathered a few bins she'd stored there.

One by one, their friends arrived.

Jade and Reggie were first, followed by Alan and Allie. Ben, Ming, Adrian, and Mei weren't far behind. Sadly, Shawn arrived solo.

Rolling suitcases down the hall, the guys carried them to Shane's vehicle and, when the Jeep was full, started packing Abi's security SUV.

Within twenty minutes, she did a sweep of the place. "I think that's it," she said before walking out the door. Locking up, she turned and found Burton standing there.

"Abs, what are you doing?" he questioned.

"My Dad is selling the house. I told him I would pack up my things."

Figuring there was more to the story than what she was willing to divulge, he said, "This is not the way to do it."

"Then, how?"

"Respectfully? Maturely? Not sneakily."

Shane stepped forward. "Nobody invited you."

"Yeah, if you had, Abi would not have destroyed any chance of reconciliation down the road."

She stood firm beside Shane. "I will never forgive him for this."

"Abs, no matter what he did, he's your only family."

As her friends looked on, Abi broke down. Tears streaming across her face, she said, "I told you. He's no longer that to me."

"In the end, I guess that's your decision. But is it the right one?" Burton said with much conviction. Getting into the G-Wagen, he said before closing his door, "I'll see you at home."

Watching him leave the courtyard, she somehow knew he was right.

Their friends gathered around.

"Thank you for your help, everyone. I really appreciate it."

"No problem, girl," Jade replied. "If it's any consolation, I would have left too."

Allie chimed in. "Yes, stand your ground."

Mei and Ming hugged her. "Remember, you can always forgive," Mei said, "But you will never forget," Ming added, finishing her sister's sentence.

"You're right," she nodded.

When everyone left, they got in the Jeep. Abi knew she had to return to Burton's and face the music. Driving out of the gate, she turned and closed it one last time. What few memories she had there were now a piece of the past.

98

Be Strong

Abi's nerves tightened as they drove along Bellagio Road's winding curves, the thick trees casting creepy shadows on either side. By the time they reached the house, a sense of dread loomed.

The gate was left open, making her even more anxious. Pulling alongside the front doors, Burton was waiting. His frown hinted at what was to come.

When Abi got out, Shane started unloading everything and leaving it inside the foyer to move to her room afterward.

Enlisting the men to help, Burton joined in to get it done faster.

Too tired to argue, she let it happen.

Knowing Shane had things to do to prepare for his road trip, she said, "You go ahead home. I'm sure you have a mile-long list to prepare for tomorrow."

"It's fine. I can stay and help you organize everything."

She could tell Burton wasn't happy. "You know what, I'm exhausted. It's been a long day."

About to walk inside the house with her, Burton held out his hand and stopped him. "Sorry, man. No company tonight."

"You're joking, right?" Shane said angrily.

Burton silently kept his cool, stood his ground, and stared him down.

Turning to him in defiance, Abi said, "What the hell, B?"

He shot her a stern eye. "You and I need to talk."

About to respond with an enormous amount of pent up attitude, he stopped her.

"Now," he said firmly.

Shane puffed his chest and intervened. "She's not going anywhere without me."

Realizing something was wrong, she held him back. "Just wait, Shane. Give me a second."

Burton walked into the house and did not say another word. With perfect timing, two of his men appeared and guarded the door.

Shane watched them closely through the glass as Abi followed him.

Ushered into the office, he closed the door and stood before her with his arms crossed. "I thought I told you to keep a low profile? That meant not bringing undue attention to yourself."

She stayed quiet.

"Abs, what were you thinking? Your home has been under surveillance for weeks, and for good reason. There wasn't a security presence there beforehand. You could've gotten hurt or worse."

"But I wasn't." She didn't know what more to say. "I'm sorry. I screwed up."

"This may have compromised this house, my staff, and your friends. You should have consulted me first before making that decision."

Lowering her head, she fired back, "Why were you there then if it was dangerous?"

"To ensure your safety." In that instant, she looked like the little girl from next door. Calming down, he said, "Look, I'm sorry for getting angry. We have received threats from every angle, and my priority is you."

"Maybe I don't want to be your priority anymore." The second those words launched from her mouth, she regretted it.

Taken off guard, he stood there a moment. Ignoring her statement, he instructed, "Send Shane home." Before walking away, he added, "Given what's happened, perhaps you moving in wasn't a good idea after all."

When she heard that, her heart sank. Knowing she acted on emotion and did not use common sense, she returned outside, somewhat shell-shocked, and found Shane sitting in his Jeep.

Seeing her emerge, he quickly got out. "What was all of that about? What did he say to you?"

"It's complicated."

"Abs, I want you to come home with me. I can't leave you here. Not after this."

She slowly shook her head. "No, I need to stay. I'm sorry. I can't explain. You need to trust me."

Shane desperately questioned, "Is he holding something over your head? I hate that he controls you like this. Why do you always do what he says?"

"Because he's keeping me safe."

"How?" Shane got frustrated. "How is he doing that? All I see is a guy demanding things of you, and for whatever reason, you go along with it." He reached for her and said, "Please, I'm begging you. Please come with me. Abi, please..."

Staring at his hands, she knew what she had to do.

Wrapping her arms around his waist, he sighed, thankful she'd agreed to go with him. Expelling a sigh of relief, he opened the passenger door for her, but she suddenly pulled back.

Stepping away, Abi said tearfully, "Good luck this week. Make sure you don't lose your focus. Remember, we need three wins." Kissing him tenderly on the lips, she said, "I love you."

In shock, he shook his head repeatedly. "No, Abs... No, come with me."

"I'm sorry. I can't." She stayed super calm. "I know you don't understand. Just trust what we have." Her thumbs caressing his hands, she added, "I need you to play the best football of your life. Do not let this interfere with that. You hear me?"

He stared at her in disbelief.

"Shane?"

He looked away.

"Will you do that for me?"

Taking a deep breath, he tried to control the anger brewing in his heart.

She could feel it. Hugging him tightly, she didn't want to let go. "I will see you on Saturday at the game. After that, we will dance the night away."

He stood there, stoic.

"I'll see you in a couple of days," she whispered before kissing him again, hoping it would offer reassurance. "I love you so much."

Unhappy with her decision, he walked away and got in his truck. Starting the engine, she pressed her hand against the window before he left.

Watching as he drove away, she waited until he was out of sight before she buckled over and cried as the men looked on. Taking a minute to compose herself, she passed them by as one held the door open for her. About to move her things, she noticed all of her suitcases and boxes had already disappeared. Assuming they'd taken them to her room, she walked up the stairs and down the hall. Closing the door, she found everything placed neatly along one wall.

Hearing a knock, Abi knew who it was and opened it.

"Can I come in?" Burton asked.

"It's your house."

Silently following her, he sat beside Abi on the sofa. Leaning forward, he rubbed his palms together. "I didn't mean what I said before. I don't regret asking you to stay here. I'm mad at myself for not giving you more guidance."

She did not respond.

"For years, I've kept a certain level of secrecy. Guess I just expected you to do the same. I'm sorry. I take the safety of my staff and mine very seriously for obvious reasons. Especially now."

"I understand."

Without warning, he said, "Martin thinks we should vacate the house."

"What do you mean?"

"Over the next two days, we are moving everything out. He has a line on a new place in the hills."

Abi panicked. "Is this because of me? Because of what I did?"

"No. I should have been more careful from the beginning. It's my fault." He looked around. "Don't worry about your things. My people will make sure nothing is left behind."

She didn't know what to say.

"Pack a bag. We are heading out tonight."

"What? Now?"

"Yes, you are going to the alternate location while I head to Miami."

She knew then that it wasn't safe to stay there. Afraid someone could hurt Shane or her friends, she was thankful they all had security at their homes.

"We leave in a half hour." He got up from the sofa and walked out.

Abi quickly gathered her toiletries, backpack, textbooks, laptop, and charging cords. Taking a few pieces of her Mother's clothing from a suitcase, she stuffed them in the bag with the rest at the last minute. Looking about the pretty room, she snapped a picture of it, saddened by all the work he'd done, only to now leave it behind.

Arms full, she met Martin, Anton, Rosa, and the nameless security team in the foyer as Sara surfaced from Burton's room with him, wheeling out their suitcases. She looked at Abi and was noticeably annoyed.

Andrew, Matt, and Ted pulled up and parked their SUV in line with the others.

Martin surfaced and addressed Burton. "We are good to go, Sir."

"Good," he said before walking out the door.

Sara held back and whispered to Abi, "Out of sight and out of mind for two days. Understand? Don't do anything stupid."

Right then, Abi saw her true colors. She knew the lighthearted girl from Vegas never existed.

Burton overheard his girlfriend's words and intervened, "Abi understands. She doesn't need reminding. That's not your job."

Sara shot him a glare so intense, it felt like daggers. She didn't like that he came to Abi's defense.

Martin systematically split everyone up into three SUVs and secured the house. "Anton, Rosa, and Abi. Go with Andrew, Ted, and Matt," he pointed as Burton and Sara prepared to get in the one parked ahead of them.

Before leaving, Burton looked back and walked over to her. "Remember, turn off your phone and leave it in this." Handing her the special envelope, she took it from him, turned the device off, and slipped it inside. "Handing her a set of cards, he said, "Here's a new set of SIMs. The guys will help you with them. When you get to the house, do not access any of your accounts on the internet. Nothing traceable. You can surf the web from their computers. Just don't leave your mark anywhere. And don't worry about Gerald. I transferred him and Max to the Malibu house." His sights on her lingered. "When we get to the airport, we're going separate ways. Listen to what the guys tell you. If you don't know, ask," he said.

"I will."

About to walk away, she feared that could be the last time she saw him. "Burton..."

He looked at her. "Yeah?" Finding tears rolling down her face, he returned and hugged her tightly. His hand held her head against his chest. "Don't worry. I'll be fine. I need you to be strong. For me?"

She nodded. "Be safe."

"I will." Not caring what Sara would say, he kissed Abi's forehead before letting go of her and walking back to the SUV, raising a steady hand before disappearing inside.

Witnessing what had happened, Anton got out. "Miss Abi, we've gotta go. Come on, Sweetie. Get in."

Seated behind Andrew, unable to control her sobs, Matt looked across at her. "Don't worry, Miss. He'll be alright."

The bright neon lights suddenly went dark when they pulled away from the mansion across the canyon. It was eerie. In the distance, she noticed the lights on the pergola at the Stradella house. For some reason, she felt like she was leaving and never coming back.

99

Darkness Falls

They arrived at Van Nuys, surrounded by darkness. Watching Burton's SUV pull up beside the plane, she saw him, Martin, Sara, and his security team climb the stairs before their vehicle veered left to a helicopter waiting.

Stopped a safe distance away, the guys loaded their bags quickly as everyone got strategically seated in the luxury chopper based on weight. Noticing a familiar face, Abi settled down. Mac, the pilot who flew them to the yacht, sat at the controls and started the engine before getting clearance from the tower.

While they waited, she watched Burton's jet taxi away. Trying to keep her emotions in check as he left the ground and soared into the sky, Abi kept her eye on them until she could no longer see its lights.

Focusing on herself, she looked to her right. She could see Rosa's hands shaking in fear. Reaching over, she held the woman's hand and smiled.

Rosa grasped Abi's forearm.

"We will be okay," she said.

The woman nodded nervously.

With everyone buckled in, the engine roared as the blades spun above their heads.

Terrified, unable to see anything, Burton's words echoed through her mind. "You need to be strong," she repeated silently. When they lifted off, she remained calm. Minutes later, they were hovering above the city lights, unsure of their destination.

Mac seemed to follow the coastline, but Abi couldn't initially distinguish their direction. Eyes on the brightness to her left and darkness to the right, she determined they were heading south. Keeping her bearings, she sat quietly. Nobody else said a word either. Hearing Rosa praying, she did the same, hoping Burton would be okay and they'd arrive safely while the helicopter drifted in the crosswinds.

Only in the air for twenty minutes, she suddenly felt them descending.

By the light of a half moon, hidden inside the confines of a lush estate by the ocean, she figured they couldn't have left the state of California.

As the blades slowed to a stop, Andrew, Matt, and Ted got everyone out and divided up the baggage. Led to the large, cliffside home, Ted punched in a code to open the main door. Walking inside, he turned on the lights while they gathered in the foyer to await further instructions.

"Upstairs, there are nine bedrooms," Andrew said. "Select rooms adjacent to one another. Do not spread out."

Anton looked at Rosa and Abi. "Come on, Ladies. Let's settle in."

Following him, they climbed the spiral staircase to the second floor. The spa scent of the house was alluring, but it seemed a bit stuffy, like the windows hadn't been open recently. Finding a beautiful room with an ocean view, Abi walked in as Anton and Rosa took rooms across the hall.

Sitting on the bed, trapped and alone, her thoughts quickly gravitated to Shane as she took the padded envelope from her bag, wishing she could call him. Rolling over, knowing she couldn't, she cuddled with a pillow. Scared for Burton, hoping he would do what he had to and return home sooner rather than later, she recalled everything he'd said and wondered if he shared his feelings for a reason.

Does he know something I don't? She thought, preparing herself to receive bad news eventually. Her heart ached at the thought, so much so that she clutched her chest and sobbed. Thinking about the times they'd spent together and how attached she'd gotten, overwhelmed, she covered up with the blanket and decided to sleep, hoping the pain and uncertainty would dissipate.

100

Change of Plans

The time away at the oceanside estate was difficult, but the beautiful surroundings made it bearable. Each morning, the screeching of seagulls woke Abi early as the sunrise cascaded through the sheers. The water views transferred a sense of calm. Thankful to be hidden inside the fifteen-foot stone walls surrounding the property, it offered another layer of protection while Andrew, Ted, and Matt rotated shifts around the clock.

By Friday afternoon, Abi was counting down the hours. Confined indoors, unable to explore the grounds, she spent most of the time working on assignments and catching up on lessons offline. Staying busy kept her mind from wandering negatively. Thinking of Shane, she'd focused on creating a study guide in math and science to help him stay on top of his studies until classes resumed.

Desperate to see footage from his last game, not having access to the links he had sent her, she searched the house and located the study. It had three desks, each with a computer. She fired one up but hesitated before logging into the Gilderson website, mindful of what Burton had said. Sara's words then haunted her.

"Don't do anything stupid," she whispered.

Immediately turning it off, she walked out, deciding to explore the contemporary, Spanish-styled home instead. Floating through the gaming room to the wine cellar and cigar bar, where French doors led to the cliffside pool and outdoor living areas, she roamed the long subterranean corridors before seeing a brightly lit room at the end of one hall.

When passing through the threshold, her eyes drew upward whimsically to the blue skies visible through the cathedral glass roof. Slowly returning to Earth, her gaze scanned the tall potted trees living in harmony with the walls of books at every turn. Walking about the space, she found cozy reading nooks in various corners, each unique in its own way. As her fingertips brushed the spines on the shelves, a voice suddenly cut through the silence.

"Miss Abi?"

Startled, she turned, afraid to hear what Andrew would say. "Yes."

"Anton wanted me to tell you lunch is ready."

"Thank you," she said. Relieved to receive good news and not bad, she followed him, hoping to return to the library later to find the perfect book to escape into.

When she returned to the kitchen, Abi grabbed a plate and sat on the patio in full view of Andrew. Staring out at the ocean, she watched the waves roaring toward the shore and could hardly wait to return to the city but knew a mix of emotions would follow. Her heart felt torn while thoughts of Burton and Shane swirled, creating an internal tug of war.

With his easygoing nature and infectious spontaneity, Shane brought out her carefree and adventurous side, producing lighthearted moments despite the rollercoaster ride of Burton Lancaster drama. Trying to think fondly and block out the negative, she remembered how they first met and the highs and lows they'd shared. The good outweighed the bad. Cherishing their trips to the beach, their quiet times together, and his incredibly thoughtful Homecoming proposal at the Observatory, Abi looked at pictures from that night and felt so lucky to have met a knight in shining armor who was handsome, strong, and protective - a warrior on and off the field. Wearing his heart on his sleeve, she felt the closest to him in the aftermath of her Mother's passing. Having dropped everything to be there for her, his love grew deeper by the day.

On the other hand, Burton was her constant. With him, everything felt familiar. Drawing out her maturity, he knew her better than she knew herself. Portraying an air of mystery and power sparked an attraction. His intense focus and quiet strength also inspired it. She recalled how often he had saved her from harm. His protective instinct never failed. They had history – this lifetime of secrets and a strong bond that remained intact the entire time they were apart. Having said he'd had feelings for her before, it seemed different this time, like if he didn't tell her, he might not have another opportunity. A stroke of fear hit her, making Abi shake her head to rid it of the negative thoughts.

At a crossroads, she knew Shane was the sun, warm and radiant, making her feel vibrant and full of life, while Burton was the moon, calm and constant, living in the shadows but illuminating the darkest corners of her heart. Each offered her something the other couldn't. Unable to decide which version of herself she wanted to embrace, the decision weighed heavily on her, knowing that whichever path she chose, a part of her would always long for the other.

Needing a distraction, she finished her lunch, got up, and headed toward the library. Along the way, she ran into Andrew again, making the rounds.

"Hello, Miss. Is everything okay? Are you hanging in?" he asked.

"Yes, I'm trying. Almost there, right?"

"I expect Master B to arrive early this evening. Around six o'clock, I'm told."

Surprised to hear that, Abi asked, "Wait? He's coming here? Aren't we going home tonight?"

"Sorry, Miss. Change of plans."

"Thank you for the update."

"Sure thing."

Concerned, Abi shuttered at the thought of Shane not knowing where she was if she didn't return tomorrow. Hoping for the best, trying to give off positive thoughts to the universe, she was glad Andrew had heard from them and even more so that Burton would be there soon. It meant he was okay, and everything went well. At ease, she continued on her way and walked into the library. Perusing the vast array of books, she found a romantic adventure novel about the Whitsunday Islands of Australia. Intrigued by the cover, with hues of crystal blue waters and white sand, she started reading the opening chapter. Hooked, she took it with her and went to find a place to read and pass the time peacefully.

Outside the living room doors, she sat on a comfy sofa under a heated portico and marveled at the ocean view while the water jets trickled into the pool.

The hours passed, minute by minute.

Immersed in the story, she barely looked up as the sun slowly descended along the western horizon.

"Excuse me, Miss?" Ted said, making the rounds. "We are closing up the house for the night. Can you kindly move indoors?"

"Sure. No problem. What time is it?" she asked.

"It's seven-thirty."

"Thank you."

Realizing Burton hadn't arrived yet, she went inside as her stomach growled. Moving through the kitchen, she found Anton tidying up.

"There you are, Miss Abi. You missed dinner. Would you like me to warm it for you?"

She offered a grateful smile. "Yes, I'm sorry. Do you mind? I got lost in a book." She held it up, her pointer finger bookmarking her last page.

Anton placed her warmed seafood pasta on the placemat in front of her as she sat along the kitchen island. Eating while reading, she finished and rinsed out her pasta bowl before placing it in the dishwasher. In search of a new reading nook, she looked for a spot with a view of the front door. Finding a chair with a floor lamp next to the fireplace with stacked lava cannon balls amidst the flames, she cuddled with a Hermes blanket.

As night fell upon the estate, Abi glanced up from the pages. Spying a clock on the wall, she noticed it was almost eleven as Matt walked by.

"Any news on Master B?" she asked.

He didn't know how to answer her.

The look on his face sparked concern. "Is he okay?" she questioned. "What's going on?"

"I'm sorry, Miss. Martin went dark three hours ago."

"Dark? What does that mean?" Abi sat straight in the chair.

He stopped and radioed Andrew.

"Please just tell me."

Matt held up his finger. "Andrew is coming - one second."

Afraid to know the details, she waited on pins and needles.

When the guy arrived, he sat down across from her.

"Matt said Martin went dark."

"We've lost communication with them," he revealed.

A bit angry, she stated, "And you didn't think to tell me this because?"

"I was instructed not to."

"By who?"

"That's not important. We are waiting for comms to resurface."

"When will that be?"

"I don't know, Miss."

Abi closed her book, stood, and began to pace the floor.

"Please try and stay positive. If I hear anything, I'll let you know."

"You promise?"

"Yes."

When he walked away, Abi sat on the sofa and brought her knees to her chest. Clutching the blanket, she watched the fire dance between the spheres.

In the worst frame of mind, she thought, *That's it. He's not coming back.*

With barely any tears left to cry, her stomach hurt. Fearful of what the next day would bring, exhausted beyond measure, eyes heavy, she rested her head on the pillow and drifted off, dreaming of Burton and Shane.

Waking periodically, disoriented, she scanned the room aimlessly. The house seemed quieter each time, and every little sound magnified tenfold. The only movement she found was the flicker of the fire dancing on the walls.

By two o'clock, there was still no Burton.

Closing her eyes again, she knew he was gone. The ache in her heart knew it, too. He hadn't made it back like Andrew said he would. A tear streamed down her cheek. More followed as she closed her eyes.

Amidst her grief, suddenly, she felt the couch cushion dip. Not having heard anybody enter the room, her heart raced. Terrified, she envisioned Eastwood sitting before her as a fingertip gently traced her brow. Feeling it's unwanted touch, she flinched. Opening her eyes, she found someone watching her.

"Burton..." she whispered.

"Hey, Abs," he said quietly. "What are you still doing up? It's almost three in the morning."

Realizing she wasn't dreaming, she exhaled before reaching out and clinging to his neck so tightly he thought he'd break. "You're here? Are you okay?"

He slipped his arms around her as she nuzzled her face into the hollow of his neck.

"I'm fine. I stopped to do three sets in Vegas at the Club."

Gaining clarity, she looked at his face. Seeing a white bandage along his hairline, she said, "You're hurt..."

"It's nothing."

Hugging him again, she said, "I was so worried. Tell me what happened."

He sighed. "How about we leave that until morning? I'm pretty tired," he mumbled, barely able to string a sentence together.

Abi noticed Martin and the security team flooding the foyer. "Find an open room upstairs. Get some sleep," he instructed casually, spotting the two of them in the process. "We leave tomorrow at eleven hundred hours."

Believing someone would probably occupy her room shortly, she curled up in the same spot, too tired to move.

Upon seeing this, Burton got comfortable at the other end. Taking a blanket from the back of the sofa, he fluffed a few pillows after removing his shoes and hoodie. When he stretched out, his feet touched hers.

"Night, Abs," he whispered.

"Good night."

101

Good Talk

The heavenly aroma of bacon filled the air as Abi stirred. Believing she imagined his return, she quickly looked to the opposite end of the couch. He wasn't there. Finding the blanket folded neatly, she sat up and peered about the room.

The first person she saw was Anton in the kitchen, trying to prepare breakfast quietly. Seeing the panic on her face, he silently raised his knife and pointed outside.

Following his line of sight, Burton stood beyond the pool, admiring the view. The early morning light illuminating his back, she walked outside, thankful to see him.

About to take a sip of his coffee as the updrafts swirled around, he turned to find her. A smile spread across his face.

"Good morning," he said. "Sleep well?"

"Somewhat." Desperate to hug him and make sure he wasn't a figment of her imagination, she refrained. Instead, she asked, "So, did everything go according to plan?"

He raised his hand to the bandage on his forehead. "Not exactly, but we accomplished what we set out to do."

She nodded nervously. "That's good."

Smiling, he couldn't elaborate further.

"I'm glad you're safe," she whispered.

"Me too."

Martin appeared. Not wanting to interrupt, he had no choice. Clearing his throat, he addressed, "Excuse me, Master B?"

Burton turned to him. "What is it, Martin?"

"A word, Sir."

Reluctantly ending things, he said, "Sorry, Abs. Give me a minute."

"Sure. I'm just going to go to my room and freshen up."

"I'll see you shortly then."

As she walked away, the man showed Burton his iPad. Their conversation seemed to take on a serious tone.

Moving through the home and ascending the stairs, she peered into her room, expecting to find a security guard sleeping in the bed. But there was nobody there. Cautiously searching the bathroom, finding it empty, she walked back and locked the door so she could shower and get changed.

While the water warmed, she looked out the window and found the two men still talking. A few others had joined. In an instant, Abi realized someone was missing. Sara wasn't here. Or was she, and she just hadn't seen her yet?

Breaking from her thoughts, needing to return to Burton, she quickly washed her troubles away. Moments later, wrapped in a towel, hair wet and face feeling fresh, she took her Mother's hoodie from her bag with a pair of black tights. Cozy, she looked in the mirror and realized it was Saturday.

"It's Homecoming," she said, thinking of Shane. Not knowing what happened with the team the past few days, she hoped he led them to victory.

A knock came to her door.

Quickly going to open it, she found Burton standing there.

"Is everything okay?" she asked, hoping he'd share what he could.

"Reports are surfacing that Eastwood may have succumbed to his injuries. They are still awaiting confirmation."

"What does this mean? Is it over?"

Needing to be honest, he walked over and sat on the bed.

Abi did the same.

"His existence or lack thereof doesn't make a difference since someone else has taken the helm in his absence. There is always another waiting to step up and take their place. So, now we need to find out who. This person may not have the same vendetta Korolev had against me. Then again, they may continue where the others left off. Only time will tell."

The sense of relief was short-lived.

Wanting to change the subject, he said, "So, it's your big day today."

Abi returned to reality. "Yes. But we aren't going home. How do I get ready? Where will Rachel deliver my dress? How will Shane pick me up?"

He smiled from ear to ear. "Leave all of that to me."

Homecoming festivities aside, so many questions floated around her head. "Can I ask you something?"

"Sure. Shoot."

Given his full attention, she asked, "Who is Martin, really?"

Burton's sights dropped to the floor as his hand slid across his mouth while pondering how to answer that. "Let's just say he's more than a butler and my assistant. He's, umm, an *asset* to me," he winked. "Understand?"

She smiled, knowing his explanation was cryptic. "Right."

"Good talk," he said, lightly tapping his hand on her knee. "Come on. Let's go and have some breakfast. We need to get you to a football game."

About to walk out the door, she said, "One more thing."

He turned and waited to hear what she would say.

"While you were away, I had a lot of time to think."

"That's dangerous," he replied humorously, curious where the conversation was heading.

"At the Forum concert, you had pictures of us from Tahoe," she recalled, "...and that song, did it all have meaning? I need to know."

He walked back to her. "Truth?" he asked.

"Always."

"Abs, it should not come as a surprise that you inspired that music. I created it while we were at the lake house. It seemed only fitting to add the pictures to set the mood for the track. Never thought you'd see it, though."

"I loved it."

"I'm happy to hear that. I often incorporate pieces of my life into my music. It captures the audience and makes them feel connected." He could tell another question was about to roll off her tongue. "Anything else?"

"I can't help but notice Sara isn't here."

He stood straight and ran his hand through his hair. "No, she's not."

Abi waited for him to say more.

He fell silent, then said, "Can we leave it at that?"

Knowing it wasn't her business, she said, "Sure."

About to leave, he approached the door. "I'll let you finish up. Meet you downstairs shortly?"

"I won't be long."

When Burton walked out, she couldn't decide what to feel. Emotions running amuck, she knew today was supposed to be about her and Shane but couldn't stop thinking about what he just said.

Quickly packing and scouring the room to make certain she hadn't forgotten anything, Abi grabbed the unfinished novel from her bedside table and tucked it in her bag, believing nobody would miss it given the vast selection left behind.

About to walk out of the room, she sighed. "Time to head home."

102

The New House

It wasn't long before everyone loaded into three SUVs. Sitting beside Burton, his elbow resting along the window, holding up his head, she wondered what he was thinking. Was he dwelling on the aftermath of his trip? Perhaps what happened between him and Sara? Or was he thinking of her?

His left hand rested on the armrest between them. Abi's heart pounded, contemplating what to do.

Reaching out, she tapped it gently, startling him. "Hey?" she whispered, leaving it on top of his. "Are you okay?"

"Umm, yeah..." he hesitated as if breaking from a daydream. "I'm good. You?" he said, grasping hold, intertwining their fingers.

"Yes." His touch made her heart flutter.

Barely able to produce a smile, he looked down at their hands lovingly connected and suddenly let go to pull his laptop from his satchel. "Do you have your phone?" he asked.

She slipped the padded envelope from her bag and handed it to him with the fob.

Unlocking the device, Burton connected it to his computer and focused on the black screen while typing in lines of code. Fidgeting, he replaced the SIM card with another before typing some more.

Abi saw her home screen light up.

Detaching it from the cord, he handed it back. "You can use it now. Might want to check for messages from Shane. I'm sure he is worried about you."

"Thank you," she replied, sure that wasn't the case. "As for Shane, I don't expect to hear from him."

"Why's that?"

"He left that day in anger because we argued." Using her fob, she waved the phone over the top of it, and the device unlocked. Scrolling through her texts, she found nothing from him.

Letting the device fall to her lap, she turned and looked out the window.

Burton saw this. "What? No messages?"

"Umm, no. Nothing..." she sighed. "He's probably still mad."

"About what?"

"At the house, he begged me to leave with him and not stay..." she turned to Burton. "...with you."

Her friend stared straight ahead.

"He doesn't like the hold you have on me."

He smirked. "If he only knew the truth, he'd understand."

Abi raised the device and started typing.

"What are you going to say?" he asked.

"Simply that I am on my way home. That all is well."

"And..."

"And hope and pray he's still not angry with me."

Silence between them, Burton said, "And if there is?"

"Then, I guess it's over."

Staring at her, he saw the thought of that cast a sense of rejection.

"Don't worry," he said. "If he's smart, which I think he is, he will respond."

About to send her message, Abi's finger hovered a moment. She felt sick. Pressing send, she watched for a read receipt to register as her heart beat violently.

Time seemed to stand still, making her shift her gaze.

"He will answer. I promise. He would be stupid not to."

Suddenly, she looked at the screen. Seeing a read receipt, she covered her mouth with her hand. "Oh, my…"

"Did he text back?"

"Not yet. But he read it." Sitting on pins and needles, she suddenly saw his thinking bubbles activate. "He's typing."

"I told you."

Receiving a response, she read what he said.

Are you alright? Where are you?

She typed, *I'm fine. We are on our way back to the city.* Reading it, she thought she'd remove the WE part so he wouldn't get the wrong idea. *I'm on my way back to the city,* she retyped. At the last second, she added, *I miss you.*

There was a long pause before his thinking bubbles went active again. Suddenly, his text popped up.

I missed you, too.

Abi sighed with relief.

The sound caused Burton to glimpse her way briefly.

Thankful Shane wasn't angry with her, she replied, *I'm so glad.*

Another awkward pause seemed to fall upon their conversation. Intent on keeping it going, she asked, *How is the team doing? Did you win?* She hoped he'd say yes.

Waiting, seeing he'd read the message, Abi read his reply.

Yes, both games thus far. One more to go.

She smiled. *That's great. I'll be there to watch.*

I'll look for you.

Good luck. You know what to do. Sending a pink heart, she thought he'd sign off. Waiting for a reply as the bubbles cycled, she found his long message.

Yes, but I'm not focused on the game right now. My sights have moved beyond our win this afternoon. All I want is to dance with you tonight in that pretty dress.

Abi gasped and couldn't help but smile tearfully.

Burton witnessed her reaction.

Typing, she said, *I want that too. I'll see you soon.* Ending with another pink heart, Shane sent a blue one in return.

Putting her phone down, Abi watched as they pulled up to a security checkpoint outside the confines of the airport.

"All good?" Burton asked.

She turned to him. "It seems so."

"Happy to hear it."

Martin dealt with the particulars from his seat in the vehicle ahead of them.

When the gate opened, all three SUVs passed through and rounded the corner. To their right, his black jet was waiting for their arrival.

Not wasting any time, the men got everyone on board in an orderly manner. Burton helped Abi with her bags and got her settled in the seat beside him.

Within minutes, they lifted off.

Soaring high into the sky, making a long right turn, they headed north along the coast.

Not knowing their location, she asked him, "Where were we?"

"Newport. South of LA."

Afraid to ask what they were returning to, she said, "And now? Where are we headed?"

He turned to her and smiled. "Your new home."

"And where's that?"

Smirking mischievously, he answered, "You'll see."

Feeling the plane descending, Abi said, "That didn't take long."

"Twelve minutes, door to door. Otherwise, it would have been an hour and a half in traffic. We need to get you to that game."

"But it doesn't start until two o'clock."

"Yes, that's just enough time to show you the house before leaving for the stadium."

Abi got excited. She didn't know what to expect.

Feeling the landing gear deploy, soon, they were on the ground again.

As the plane taxied to the hangar, Burton said, "Safe and sound."

When the plane stopped, he grabbed her things and his. Carrying them, he let her exit first. Carefully descending the steps, Abi looked up. Stunned, she saw Sara standing there, waiting for them. Her heart dropped as Burton led her to the middle SUV and placed her bags inside before turning to greet Sara.

"Hi," she smiled, wrapping her arms around his neck. Kissing him, the girl shot Abi a look.

It made her blood boil. She had a bad feeling about her. *I just need to prove it*, she thought.

Burton walked back over. "We'll see you at the house, Abs."

"Fine..."

He could tell she was upset. Reaching out, he grasped her arm and gave it a gentle squeeze before opening her door for her to have a seat. "I'm sorry," he whispered.

"For what?"

His sights gravitated to the girl waiting for him. "I'll explain later." Closing the door, he walked back to Sara.

Abi watched as she got into the SUV, and he followed.

Rosa and Anton got into the vehicle behind them.

Suddenly, Martin opened the door opposite her. "I guess it's just you and me, Miss."

"Yes. I see that."

The older gentleman asked, "I wanted to review your agenda today, if I may?"

"Agenda?"

Half listening, she heard him speak of the game and the spa services arranged for her, but Abi could only fixate on one thing. Why had Burton apologized for Sara, and what did he intend to explain later?

"Miss? Are you listening?" Martin asked.

Breaking from her thoughts, she turned to him. "Sorry. You were saying?"

"...And I took it upon myself to invite your friends for photos at the new house."

"And where might that be?"

He smiled brightly. "Ahh, that, my dear, must remain a secret. Master B wanted it to be a surprise."

"He did, did he?" Wondering if she could get anything out of the man, Abi knew she had to outsmart him. "Martin?"

"Yes, Miss?"

"Can I ask you something?"

"Certainly." He turned and rested his hands on top of his lap.

"Does he love her?"

"Who, Miss?"

"Sara?" she said bluntly.

The man paused and looked down. "I believe their relationship is of convenience."

Abi turned to him. "Convenience?"

"This is something the two of you need to discuss, Miss. It's not my place."

Considering what he said, Abi nodded and replied, "Okay."

When they merged off the highway and diverted south, the caravan drove through a residential area with average-sized homes before reaching Mulholland Drive. With the scenery looking much more familiar, they headed east and slowed before turning right.

Abi recognized the gatehouse. "Martin?" she said. "This is Shane's gated community?"

"Yes, Miss."

"Why are we here?"

He fell silent as they passed through security. Rounding the bend, Abi kept looking at Martin as he prepared to witness her reaction.

When they slowed again, the line of trucks waited as a large black gate opened on their right. Proceeding beyond it, Abi couldn't believe her eyes. There, before them, was an enormous stone chateau.

"What is this?" she asked.

"This is your new home, Miss Abi. Master B wanted you to be close to Mr. Coppersmith."

"Wait? I don't understand."

"It is much safer here."

The SUVs stopped in unison between the flowing fountain and the magnificent structure. Ahead of them, Abi saw Burton and Sara emerge. He immediately looked back to see Abi's reaction.

Ted opened her door.

She got out with a look of amazement on her face.

Burton smiled and walked over, leaving Sara behind. "So?" he said, looking up at the huge home. "Do you like it?"

"It is very different from your modern homes."

His face brightened. "I thought I'd go for something more homey."

"It's beautiful."

"Come on, let's go inside."

Abi's sights moved upward to the soaring cathedral ceiling and dual spiral staircase when they walked through the black iron doors. Contemporary in style with a more classic undertone, she was in awe. It was bright and airy with hues of grey and white.

Burton suddenly turned and looked out the door, prompting her to see what had captured his attention.

"Abs?" a voice said.

She was so surprised. "Shane? What are you doing here?"

"Burton sent me a text and told me to drop by. Does this mean we're neighbors now?" Towering above her, he looked at the guy standing alongside Sara.

"I guess so," she answered.

Wanting to give them a minute, Burton nodded before walking away.

"I'm sorry, I can't stay. But I wanted to see you before I head out."

"I'm glad you did." She looked up at him as he smiled.

Feeling an awkwardness, they didn't know what to say.

Shane suddenly broke the silence. "So, you're good?"

"Yes."

He nodded and reached out for her.

As his arms wrapped around her shoulders and pulled her in tightly, she clung to his waist and rested her head on his chest. "I'm sorry," she whispered. "For everything."

"Me too."

"Are we okay?" She was afraid to look into his eyes but gained the courage.

His sights fixed on hers. "Yes, absolutely." Kissing her lips gently, both felt their spirits lifted.

"Alright. I have to head out. I'll see you there?"

Abi walked him outside and waved as he left.

Martin reappeared. "Shall I show you to your room, Miss?"

"I'd like that."

Gingerly ascending the ornate staircase, they passed through the arches at the top. Abi followed him down the long hall to the fifth door on their left.

He stepped aside. "Here we are."

Abi walked into the spacious all-white room with accents of powder blue. To one side, she found her dress on a mannequin with a card hanging around its neck. Slipping it out of the envelope, it read, *Enjoy the Ball, Cinderella. Love Rachel Z.*

Overwhelmed by emotion, she walked to the king-sized bed dressed in beautiful linens and silks before spying the Juliet balcony adjacent to her desk, complete with monogrammed stationary and a tufted ergonomic chair. Running her fingers over the embossed *AA* letters, she cried.

"So, do you like your new room?" A voice asked.

She turned to find Burton leaning on the doorway.

Martin quickly bowed out to leave the two alone.

Requesting permission to enter, she nodded.

"Why are you crying?" he asked, quickly grabbing a tissue for her from the bathroom. Blotting her cheeks, he said, "You should be happy."

"I am. This is amazing."

He walked over to another door and opened it, prompting her to walk in.

There, she found her closet with all her things and her Mother's, hanging neatly with her school uniform pressed and freshened.

"How did you do all of this in two days?"

"When money is no object, things get done fast," he chuckled. "How are you doing? Did you and Shane make amends?"

"Yes," she sobbed.

Wanting to lighten her mood, he opened his arms and said, "Come here." Embracing her, he held her as she tried to catch her breath.

Soon, her body calmed down. "I don't know why I've been so emotional lately. I seem to cry at the drop of a hat."

"You've been through a lot the past while. It's understandable." He kissed her forehead. "You should probably get ready to go. The stadium is a forty-minute drive."

"Are you coming to watch?"

He paused. "Probably not."

Abi's phone started lighting up with texts.

"I'll leave you to it. Make sure you're downstairs in fifteen minutes if you want to be on time. After the game, the guys will bring you back here. Martin scheduled the glam squad for five o'clock."

In amazement, she said sincerely, "Thank you."

"Absolutely, Abs," he smiled before walking out the door.

Quickly checking her messages, she found countless texts from the girls, each revealing a link to a news headline confirming the death of a young Oligarch.

103

The Game

That afternoon, under a cloudy sky, Abi gathered with her friends to watch the game inside Rose Bowl Stadium. Gilderson had the ball on their own thirty-yard line, facing a fourth-and-long situation. The tense battle had brought them to the last quarter, tied at twenty-one.

With pompoms in hand, Abi and the girls huddled together in the stands, dressed in navy, white, and grey school colors. As her shadows stood on guard, she felt safe and protected.

All eyes were on Shane. Media stationed along the sidelines and in news boxes called the live play-by-play.

Taking the final snap and dropping back, he quickly scanned the field for someone open as the Bulls' defense blitzed, putting pressure on him to step up in the pocket. Just as all seemed lost, Shane found his favorite target, wide receiver Alan, barreling down the field. With pinpoint accuracy, the QB launched a deep pass towards the end zone before getting taken down.

From field level, Shane watched his friend, covered tightly by two defenders, suddenly leap in the air with arms fully extended. In a moment frozen in time, the ball seemed to hang in mid-air as Abi held her breath. Miraculously, Alan made the catch and cradled the ball to his chest as he crashed to the ground a foot inside the end zone!

The stadium erupted as the Gilderson team emptied the sidelines to celebrate the win. Watching Shane drop to a knee and bow his head, pointing to the sky, she wondered if he'd seen his sister that day. She figured by his display, he probably did.

Mobbed by his teammates, fireworks popping off in the distance, they clinched the third win in the thrilling final play of the game.

Amidst the crowds, Shane scanned the stands.

Abi knew he was in search of her. "Shane!" she shouted on her way down the steps.

Hearing her call his name, he followed the sound of her voice and found her running towards him. Carefully threading through the chaos, she launched into his arms as he passionately embraced her. Surrounded by loud, deafening cheers and celebratory mayhem, they shared a pure, unbridled moment. With every kiss, he could feel her dedication and unwavering support.

While hugging him, Abi suddenly caught a group of people high in the stands. They were the only spectators still seated. Surprised to find Burton and Sara sitting alongside Martin, with several security guards flanking him, she watched them get up and leave. Refocused on Shane, she smiled as all the girls celebrated with their beaus, each ready for the night of partying to begin.

104

Tranquility

Riding high after their thrilling victory, Abi and Shane returned to the house in his Jeep, exhilaration still buzzing in their veins. Andrew, Ted, and Matt followed in the shadows.

Stopping outside the sprawling mansion, Shane turned to Abi. His smile was infectious. "Guess I will see you at six-thirty?"

"I'll be ready," she said with a grin. "Just a reminder, Martin invited everyone for pictures here before we leave for the dance."

"Okay, sounds good."

Abi hopped out and waved goodbye. Going inside, she bounded up the spiral staircase to her new room. Excitement building, she knew the day was finally here. Admiring the elegant dress, she could hardly wait to put it on.

"Well, Mom. This is it..." she whispered. Her voice filled with emotion.

A knock on her door made her jump. Clutching her heart, she said, "Come in."

"Hey, Abs. Sorry, didn't mean to scare you."

"That's okay," she said as he approached. I saw you at the game."

"Yeah, I couldn't focus on work, so I thought I'd see what all the Coppersmith hype was about," he snickered. "The guy definitely has skills."

"He did an amazing job today." She looked past him. "Where's Sara?"

Burton looked away. "She went home…"

Not wanting to interfere, she said, "Oh. I guess it's been a long three days for her."

"Yeah, you could say that."

Abi could tell something more had happened.

Burton said, intently changing the subject, "Martin asked me to tell you the women are ready in the spa downstairs."

"Alright," Abi paused. "And where might that be?"

Extending his elbow to her, he said, "Come on. I'll show you."

Abi took hold and walked with him to the main level.

While moving through the arched hallways, he asked, "So… Excited about tonight?"

She rubbed her hand across her tummy as butterflies fluttered. "Yes, but I don't know what to expect, so I'm a bit nervous."

"Don't be. Just go and have fun."

"I'll try."

Passing by the gym with glass walls to one side, Burton stopped and opened a door on the left. "Here we are."

The spa, bathed in soft lighting with calming music playing in the background, was a sanctuary of relaxation. Burton smiled at her pleasant reaction as she looked around. "This is where I leave you. Enjoy. I'll see you soon."

"Okay."

Asked to sit in the plush chair by a petite woman, Abi reclined in it and closed her eyes. Washing her hair and prepping her face, she extended her hands on either side for four other women to work on her fingers and toes simultaneously as the stress of the last few days thankfully melted away.

105

The Unwelcomed Visitor

After two hours of pampering, Abi was thrilled with her new look. Her hair, styled in a chic updo, framed her face perfectly. Her nails were polished, and her makeup was flawless, highlighting her natural beauty. She felt like a movie star getting ready for the Oscars. While staring at her reflection, excitement bubbled up inside her, and she couldn't stop smiling, even though her cheeks started to hurt. Ready for the night to begin, Abi felt like she was on top of the world.

"Thank you so much, ladies. I love it," she said tearfully, trying her best not to ruin her makeup.

"You are very welcome, Miss. Enjoy your evening," the tiny woman said as the others looked on happily.

Anxiously clutching her hands under her chin, she said, "Guess it's time I get dressed. It's almost six o'clock."

Hoping to find her way back, she soon located the foyer and climbed the stairs. Inside her room, she ducked into the closet with her dress and changed before slipping on the pretty shoes. When she turned to face the mirror one last time, she didn't recognize the girl staring back at her.

"So much has happened for you to get here," she grinned. "And you survived." Feeling courageous and strong, almost able to conquer anything, she drifted down the hall as the baby blue taffeta gown rustled with every step.

When she reached the top of the staircase, she stopped. Below, in the foyer, she found Burton waiting. Next to him was Martin, holding the red box in his hands. As she gracefully descended the steps, Burton's eyes lit up at the sight of her. Watching her slide her hand along the railing elegantly, her radiant smile captivated him.

"Wow, Abs. You look beautiful."

Trying to control her emotions, she clenched her fist to distract herself. "Thank you," she said, unable to fully look her best friend in the eye.

Martin opened the red box while her heart fluttered with excitement.

"Can you help me with the necklace?" she asked, her voice barely a whisper.

Burton obliged. "Certainly. I'd love to." His tone was smooth and reassuring.

Upon fastening it around her neck with a steady hand, he smelt the aromatic Dolce scent the esthetician misted her with. The alluring fragrance lingered in the air, drawing him in. Entranced, he reminded himself to keep his distance.

His touch, gently clasping the bracelet around her wrist, sent shivers up her arm before she put on the earrings.

Admiring more than the jewelry, Burton took hold of her hand and spun Abi around. Her laughter echoed through the air as a playful breeze blew through the doorway, catching the hem of her skirt and lifting it just enough to reveal her dainty shoes. Seemingly immersed in a scene from a classic Hollywood movie, he thought the pretty girl and the flirtatious flutter of fabric captured the timeless charm.

A flood of gratitude washed over her. "So, do you think I'm ready for Homecoming?"

"Yes," he said, "I believe so."

Looking into his eyes, she stopped. "Burton…"

"Yeah."

"Thank you for making my dreams come true."

Arms outstretched, she hugged him, mindful of her dress.

"You're welcome," he said, soaking it all in. "Shane is a lucky guy."

They spotted security gathering around as her friends arrived through the open gate. Guiding traffic in, guards were everywhere. Amongst them was Gerald, who looked on happily at the teen's celebration.

"You should go and greet them," Burton said.

Abi nodded.

Shawn and Laney were the first inside the new home.

"Hi, my friend," the girl, dressed in Versace, said sheepishly.

Wondering whether she'd address what happened, Abi said, "Hello."

Embarrassed by her behavior, Laney apologized. "Look, I hate myself for what I did the other day. Please forgive me."

Understanding the stress she'd been under, Abi's face brightened. "Don't worry about it. All is forgiven and forgotten."

"Thank you," she replied, clutching her arms around her.

Happy with that out of the way, Abi said, "Welcome! Come in. Grab some punch."

Shawn looked on, thankful the two girls had made up.

Adrian, Mei, Ming, and Ben joined them as the volume of banter in the foyer increased.

Watching from a distance, Burton gave Abi space.

Everyone gathered around, overly excited for the evening to begin. The girls talked about fashion while the guys discussed football.

Soon, Alan and Allie ascended the front steps with Jade and Reggie behind them. Impeccably dressed, name-dropping who they were wearing, the energy in the house was magical.

With her guests present and accounted for, Martin started corralling the couples for pictures in the back garden as Abi caught sight of a handsome man ascending the steps with a corsage in hand. Dressed in a designer navy suit, perfectly tailored to accentuate his athletic frame, Shane cut a striking figure against the sunset sky.

The second their eyes met, his smile broadened as he saw her in the radiant powder blue gown and sparkling diamond jewelry.

The way he stared sent warmth flowing through Abi's heart.

In awe, he stopped - his voice filled with genuine admiration. "Wow... You look stunning."

"Thank you," she said, "You look very handsome too."

The tall quarterback opened the container and removed the beautiful white orchid. Slipping it onto Abi's wrist, he took her hand and kissed it.

Her stomach fluttered.

Martin interrupted them politely. "Can you follow me, my dear? We are ready for you."

"Okay," she said while Shane offered his arm to escort her outside.

Led to the beautiful gardens by the pool, they gathered with their friends as each couple posed for the photographer.

When it was their turn, the man got Shane to stand behind her with his arms around her waist as the two smiled joyfully. About to take another from a different angle, Abi spotted a security guard bolt at lightning speed into the house. Then another.

Shouting back and forth, a few surrounded them, listening intently to instructions from their earpieces.

An uneasiness crept in. "What is going on?" Abi muttered, letting go of Shane.

"I'm not sure," he said, moving closer, surveying the grounds, eyes peeled.

"Everyone gather in the poolhouse," a guard suggested. The men extended their arms outward and guided them to the safe location.

When Martin urgently left, Abi's body trembled. Hearing shouts from inside the home, a stroke of terror ripped through her. Defying the guards' advice, she lifted her dress off the ground, threaded through the men, and ran across the grass.

Shane immediately ran after her, yelling, "Abs! No! Wait!"

Almost out of breath, she climbed the steps and walked through the French doors with Shane tight to her left. Approaching the foyer, they discovered a tense standoff. Martin and Burton were near the entrance.

Andrew was with them. Over a dozen men had surrounded a black SUV in the driveway. Some had guns drawn.

Seeing this, Shane bravely stood between her and the altercation.

"What's happening?" she asked a man in passing.

"Unknown guest," he said, arms straight with his gun pointed to the floor, ready to burst into action. "I need you to get back."

Abi didn't move.

"Now, Miss!" he shouted.

Ted heard them and swiftly changed positions. "Get down!" Pointing to a hiding spot behind a chair, he looked at Shane. "You, too!"

They both stayed by Abi's side.

Sights glued to the black SUV, not knowing what would happen, Shane and Abi saw their friends rush in, each wondering what all the fuss was about.

Witnessing the tense situation, Laney said, "What the hell's going on?"

Burton's head snapped sharply in their direction upon hearing her. He raised his hand sternly. "Stop! Don't move!" Eye on Abi huddled with the football player, he shouted, "Shane! Get her out of here!"

Andrew handed Burton a weapon as he racked the slide on his gun.

"He's exiting the vehicle!" a guard shouted.

"Stay down!" Ted ordered before Shane could move Abi to safety. The guards behind them forcefully moved their friends around the corner out of harm's way.

Fixated on the back door of the ghostly truck, Burton signaled to Martin, unsure what to expect. Preparing for the worst, they stood their ground.

A man in a suit emerged, hands raised peacefully above his head. "Don't shoot!" he said, "I come in peace!"

The security team watched as he cautiously left the vehicle.

"I am looking for Burton Lancaster!" the man yelled.

Martin swiftly answered before Burton could. "Yes, that's me." He stepped toward him. "How can I help you?"

Tension filled the air as the stranger got closer. About to climb the steps to speak to him, the man quickly lowered one hand and slipped it into his inside jacket pocket.

"He's reaching!" a security guard shouted.

Instantly, Abi watched the guys tackle him. Shane covered her with his body as she screamed, "No!"

Holding his arms, having wrestled him to the ground, Matt frisked the unwelcome visitor for a weapon but only found an envelope. Handing it to Martin as he hovered above them, he opened it. Reading the legal documents enclosed, he turned to Burton.

"What is it?" his boss asked.

"It's a court order, Sir," Martin said, handing him the papers.

Perusing its contents, Burton scanned the foyer for Abi.

She emerged from their hiding spot with Shane still guarding her. "What's wrong?" she asked.

"It's a restraining order. It says I must stay away..."

"Stay away? From who?"

"You," he said concretely.

The guys got the man to his feet.

"Burton Lancaster, you've been served," he announced with great anger before straightening and dusting himself off. Stomping to his vehicle, he got in before the truck drove away.

"What does he mean by served?" Abi questioned. "Who sent it?"

"Your Father," Burton replied gravely.

And, just like that, every stitch of joy she had vanished.

Shane intermittently gripped her hand to offer silent support.

Her famous friend approached.

Tears welled in Abi's eyes. "Why would he do this?"

Before he could answer, Martin stepped in as the guards began securing the area and closing the gate. "We need to regroup, Sir."

Burton nodded.

With her mind racing, Shane ushered Abi along while the men gathered everyone in the living room.

Tapping the QB on the shoulder, Burton asked, "Do you mind if I talk to her alone for a minute?" Met with combativeness, he added, "Please?"

Hesitant, Shane turned to Abi. Getting the okay from her, the big QB backed off.

Led to the study at the front of the home, she could see the painful expression on Burton's face.

Addressing her, he said, "If you want me to fight this, I will."

"What happens if we don't?"

"You will have to return home, and if anyone sees me near you, your father can have me put in jail." Burton's eyes softened as he looked at her.

"I don't want to go home, and I am not parting from you. How can he do this? On what grounds?"

"If I were to wager a guess, I'd say he believes I have too much influence on you."

"But that's not the case."

"We know that. But he doesn't."

Given the circumstances, Abi pondered her options. Looking up at him, she didn't need to think twice. "I want to fight it."

He nodded. "I'll get my legal team on it." Knowing what the judge would require, he said, "You'll need a legal guardian until you turn eighteen in December."

"But who can I get to do that? I don't know anyone else."

Martin stepped into the room.

Both of them looked his way.

"It would be a great honor to help you, Miss."

Abi smiled at the grey-haired gentleman. "Thank you, Martin."

"It is my pleasure," he said, lowering his head slightly.

She flashed a relieved expression, "I guess that's settled."

The three of them emerged from the study.

Shane was waiting in the wings. "Everything okay?" he asked as she got closer.

"Everything's fine."

Their friends gathered around as a luxury coach parked near the front steps.

"Your transportation has arrived," Martin announced.

Each couple happily walked out arm and arm.

About to leave with them, Abi turned and found Burton standing in the foyer, his hands buried deep in his pockets. Turning to Shane, she said, "You go ahead. I'll be there in a second."

Respecting her request, he did as she asked.

When he'd gone, Abi said, "So, I'll see you later?"

"I'll be here."

She slowly approached and reached for him.

Obliging, he wrapped his arms around her. "Have fun," he said. "Enjoy this right of passage. It's the beginning of a year filled with change."

"I will," she nodded joyfully, causing her to gasp.

Letting go of him, she turned to leave. Hearing her heels click against the marble floor and the fabric of her skirt rustling, she seemed to float through the door as Burton followed and watched Shane present his hand to help her board the vehicle.

Martin came up behind his famous boss. "How are you holding up, Sir?"

Despite his hard exterior and lack of emotion, he struggled for words while staring straight ahead.

"I know it's difficult to see her in the arms of another, my boy." Showing empathy, Martin rested a hand on Burton's shoulder and offered some familiar wisdom as the coach bus drove away. "Eventually, an opportunity will present itself," he reminded. "The timing isn't right yet. Like I've said before. One must be patient."

His trusted advisor left him to his thoughts.

Alone, Burton raised his sights to the ceiling and swiveled around. "Be patient, the guy says. That's so much easier said than done."

Frustrated, he sighed, ran his hand through his hair, and mumbled, "The thing is... I don't know if my heart can wait much longer."

106

HOMECOMING

The luxury coach bus entered the immaculately landscaped grounds of the Four Seasons Westlake. Abi thought the hotel's grandeur was the perfect backdrop for this memorable night.

Valets in crisp uniforms opened and closed car doors while excited chatter filled the air as friends reunited, new couples made their grand debuts, and talk of the Gilderson Prep's football victories stood at the center of it all.

Students dressed in their finest attire flooded the ballroom for the much-anticipated end to the Homecoming celebrations. Transformed into a regal wonderland, exuding elegance and sophistication, tall, silver candelabras adorned each table, their flickering flames casting a warm, inviting glow against the rich velvet drapes in shades of navy and white framing the walls.

Soaking in every detail, Abi peered up at the crystal chandeliers hanging above, their light reflecting off the custom-tiled dancefloor embossed with the school's coveted crest. The beautiful floral arrangements, bursting with white roses, orchids, and lilies, artfully caught her eye. Their delicate fragrance wafted through the room.

Shane looked at her. "Is it everything you thought it would be?"

Unable to fathom how the backward girl from Boston landed in the world of palm trees and sunny beaches by some strange twist of fate, she replied, "It's so lovely. I can't believe I'm here." A smile appeared on her face from ear to ear.

Shane thought her eyes sparkled like the diamonds around her neck.

Suddenly, the lights dimmed, and music filled the room. A slow, romantic vibe helped launch the evening, bringing every couple together on the floor.

Shane offered his hand to Abi. "May I have this dance?"

Cordially accepting, her heart raced excitedly. "Yes, you may."

While they moved gracefully, his hand warm and steady on her back, they engaged in a quiet conversation punctuated by laughter and smiles. Lost in the melody, Abi danced in the arms of the boy who'd stood by her through so much. Thinking back to his perfect proposal, she knew he'd swept her off her feet.

When the first song ended, everyone took their seats.

For the next hour, throughout the dinner, the student's attention gravitated to the buffet tables, laden with a sumptuous array of food. Each tempted even the most disciplined guests, from hors d'oeuvres to fresh seafood and gourmet sliders to the crowning jewel of decadent pastries and sweets.

Amidst abundant conversation and laughter, Abi felt like she was living in a dream. Spotting Andrew, Ted, and Matt mingling nearby, she felt safe amongst the crowd.

Jade broke away from Reggie. "Have you seen Owen around?" she whispered to Abi, wondering if he'd shown up.

"No, I haven't."

Saddened, she replied, "I feel so bad. I've tried calling him, but he hasn't answered or even texted me back."

"He's probably still upset about how everything went down. Give him some time. I'm sure he's just processing."

"You're probably right. Doesn't make it any easier, though." Unable to do anything about it, Jade said, "Well, if you happen to see him, give me a heads-up."

"Don't worry. I will."

Once the evening was in full swing, Abi, Shane, and their friends watched the Headmaster appear on stage, ready to announce the Homecoming King and Queen, voted by the student body. The anticipation in the room was electric, with whispers and anxious glances exchanged among the crowd gathered.

The man's voice mistakably boomed through the speakers, causing a stunned reaction. He moved the microphone back from his mouth to recover from the disruption. "And now," he said, "The moment you've all been waiting for." The Headmaster paused again for effect. "The announcement of your Royal Court." With a simulated drum roll from the DJ, the man revealed, "Your honorary homecoming King is none other than..." Looking about the room, he suddenly zeroed in on one student. "Your football team captain, Shane Coppersmith!"

Cheers and applause erupted.

Abi felt her heart swell as his eyes met hers for an intimate moment that spoke volumes. Kissing her, he said, "You're next."

Releasing Shane from her embrace, beaming as their friends congratulated him with pats on the back and high-fives, he humbly made his way to the stage and ascended the steps to accept his crown.

Marco whistled loudly for the QB, with his pretty date linked to his arm.

Abi couldn't help but feel a blend of excitement and nervousness. While reading everyone's reaction to Shane taking a bow, she noticed Shiri, Shiresse, and Mandy glaring at her with attitude. There was no sign of Emile. It wasn't difficult to see the girls thought the honor of Queen, should go to their friend.

Jade slipped her hand into Abi's. "Are you ready?" she asked eagerly.

"Ready for what?" she repeated. "I'm certain it's not me. It can't be."

The Headmaster's voice commanded the room. The microphone echoed as he spoke. "Every King needs a Queen," the man said.

The atmosphere tensed again, and a hum spread amongst their classmates while everyone waited with bated breath.

"Please welcome your Homecoming Queen..." he paused.... "Miss Abi Acardi!"

Hearing her name knocked the air from her lungs while the room broke into shouts and cheers. Hit by a rush of emotions - shock, joy, and overwhelming gratitude - she turned and saw Matt and Ted applauding while Andrew recorded the moment, making her wonder if he was live-streaming it for his boss.

Her friends surrounded her, hugging her tightly and offering congratulations.

Shane applauded and looked her way with an affectionate smile.

"Go on," Jade urged, pushing her along.

Heart pounding, she gently lifted the hem of her dress, climbed the steps, and took Shane's hand, waiting partway up as his eyes locked to hers.

The Headmaster placed the delicate tiara on her head as the school cheered for their Homecoming Royals.

"Congratulations, Abi," the Headmaster said, shaking her hand, knowing the past month had been difficult for the girl.

"Thank you so much," she replied, trembling terribly.

Turning to face the crowd, lights blinding her, Shane's hand still nestled in hers, the moment became a beautiful blur.

When the soft strains of music began, Shane gently guided Abi to the dance floor. "Care to dance, my Queen?"

"I would love to."

Overflowing with emotion, they circled the dance floor beneath the twinkling lights. Despite their recent ups and downs, she couldn't help but believe in the enchanting magic of fairytale endings.

Grateful for her blessings, Abi thought of her Mother, wondering if she was happily looking down on her at that very moment. Feeling a warm, comforting presence, it was like her spirit was there, sharing her joy and excitement. Abi closed her eyes briefly, imagining her loving gaze, hoping she was proud of her. It gave a deep sense of peace.

Elated, she felt the gentle pressure of Shane's hand on her back, guiding her with ease amidst the soothing, slow tempo and muted whispers surrounding them.

Circling the ballroom, she noticed Andrew recording her on his phone once more. She wondered if the guy wanted to capture the moment for her or if he was again doing this on his boss's behalf. Knowing Burton was probably curious about how the night was going, the image of him standing alone in the house earlier tugged at her heart and filled her with guilt.

Conflicted, her thoughts returned to the person who'd helped make this night memorable. With kind eyes that always understood her without words, she gained a sense of clarity. Forever a source of steadfast strength and unwavering support, the accumulation of their late-night talks and shared silences, she knew he always did what was best for her. A strong feeling of love filled her heart.

Out of the blue, she recalled her Mother's words. Her voice was clear as day: *If you want to know where your heart is, look where your mind goes when it wanders.*

The strapping quarterback peered down at her. "Hey, you..." he said softly.

She looked up into his blue eyes.

"You seem a million miles away," he asked with a loving smile.

Lost in reverie, she brought her attention back to Shane. "I'm here. Sorry, my mind was just wandering."

Little did he know, her thoughts were with Burton.

TO BE CONTINUED.....

BLACK LYON and DARK DEMON are available now on Amazon.

Watch for BOOK THREE – RED DRAGON

Available Soon!

Visit EAStarkBooks.com for more on

THE ABI ACARDI SERIES

and other Young Adult and Women's Fiction.

Looking for more Young Adult Fiction Stories?

Check out SURVIVING VALOR arriving - Summer 2025!

A Sci-Fi Apocalyptic Romance that will leave you breathless.